PEANUTBUTTER & JEREMY's
BEST BOOK EVER!

by JAMES KOCHALKA

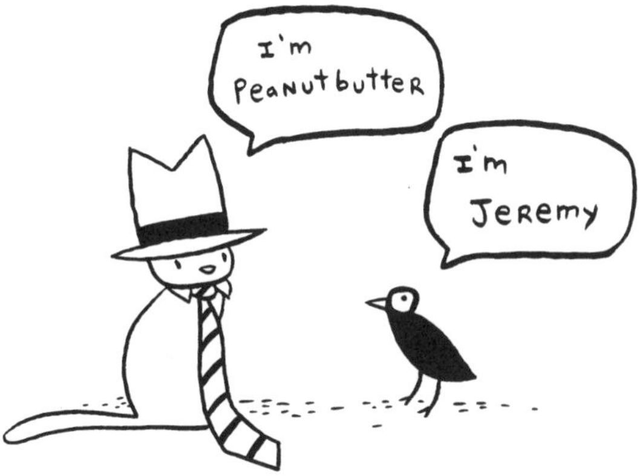
I'm Peanutbutter
I'm Jeremy

...and this is "Peanutbutter & Jeremy's BEST Book EVER!"
that's not saying much.

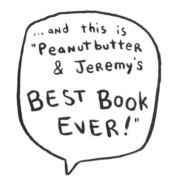

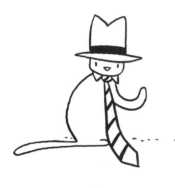

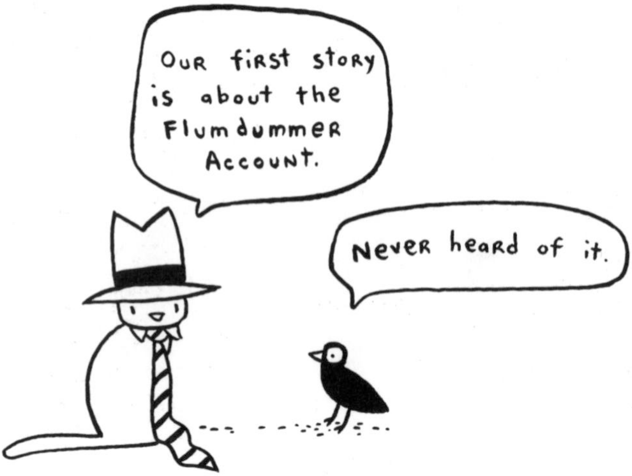
Our first story is about the Flumdummer Account.
Never heard of it.

THE FLUMDUMMER ACCOUNT

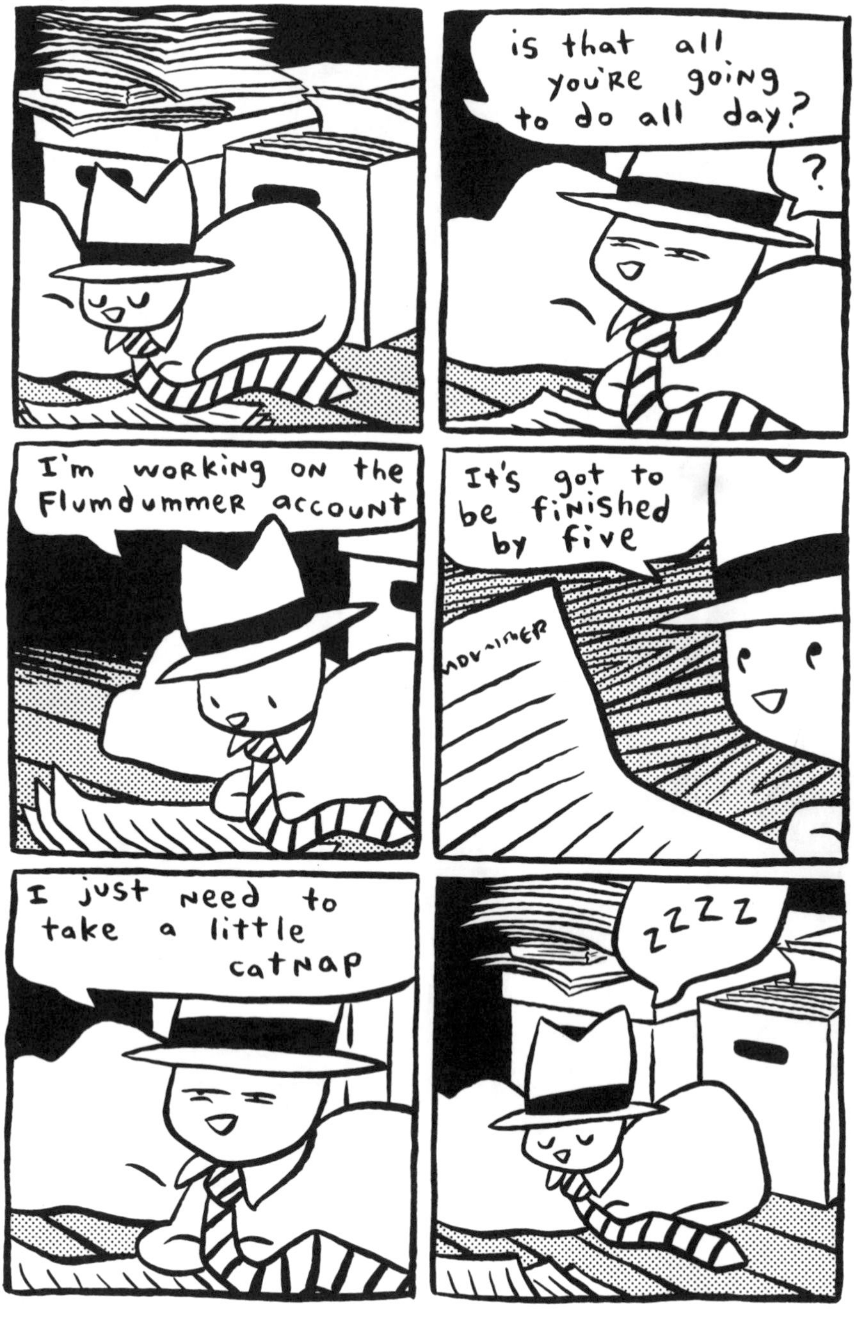

is that all you're going to do all day?
?
I'm working on the Flumdummer account
It's got to be finished by five
I just need to take a little catnap
zzzz

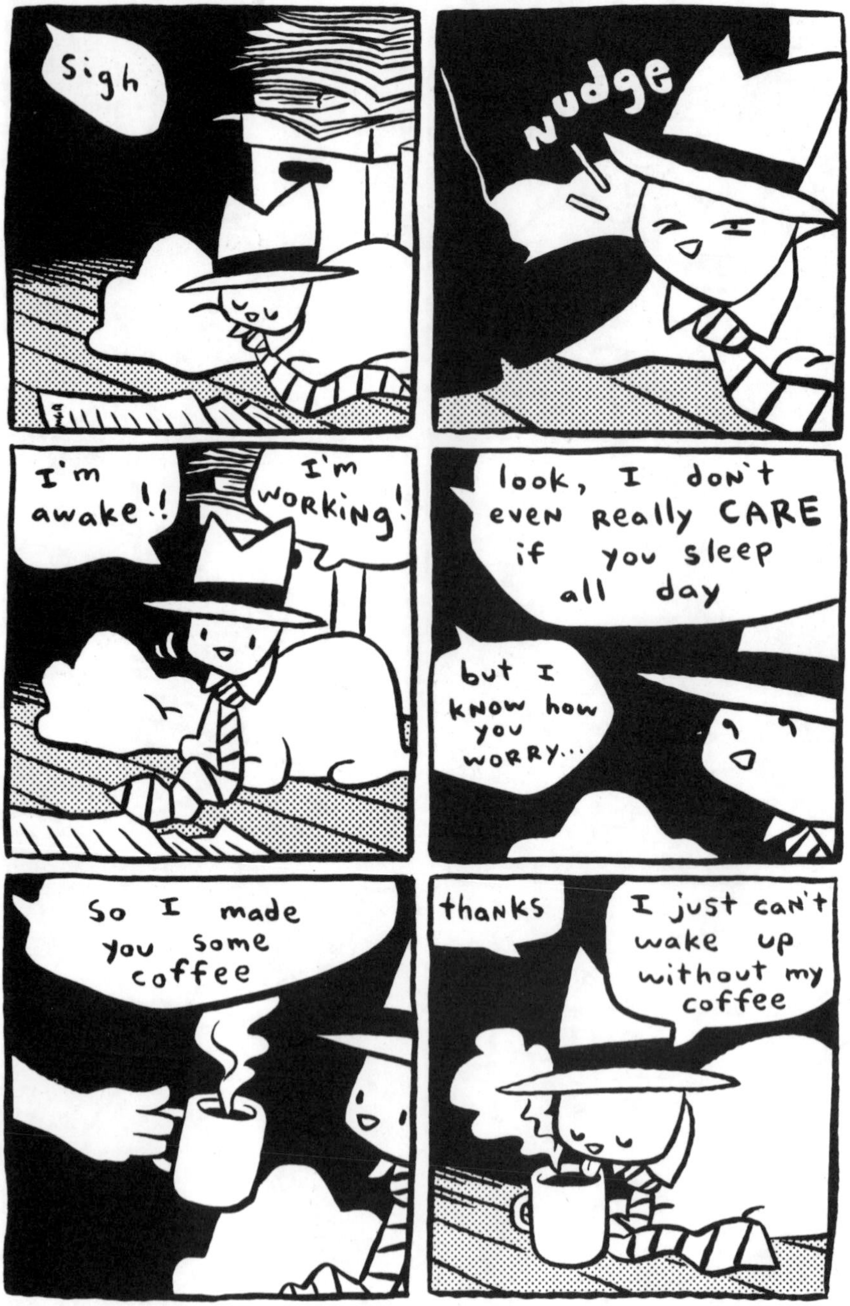
Sigh
nudge
I'm awake!!
I'm WORKING!
look, I don't even Really CARE if you sleep all day
but I KNOW how you WORRY...
So I made you some coffee
thanks
I just can't wake up without my coffee

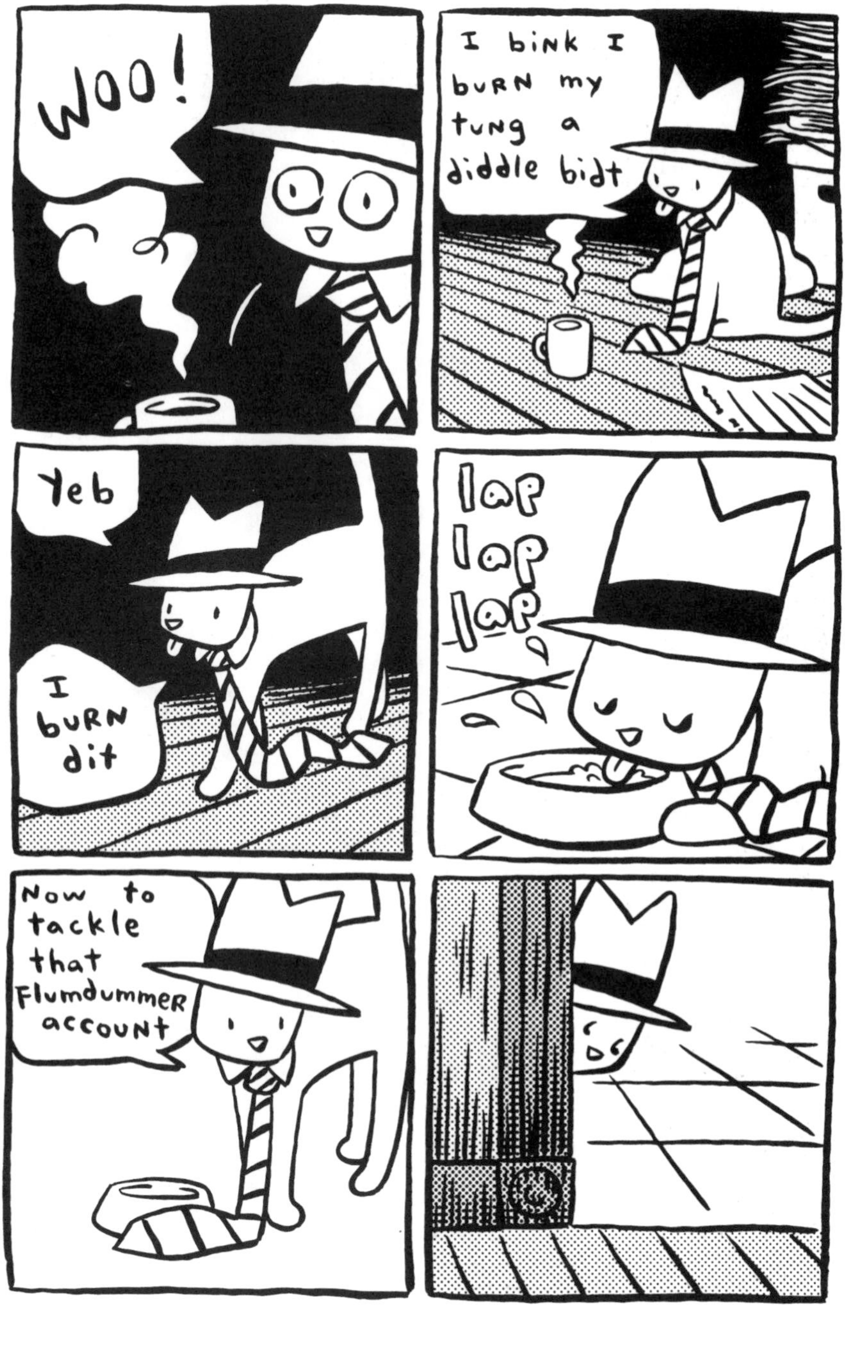
WOO!
I bink I burn my tung a diddle bidt
Yeb
I burn dit
lap lap lap
Now to tackle that Flumdummer account

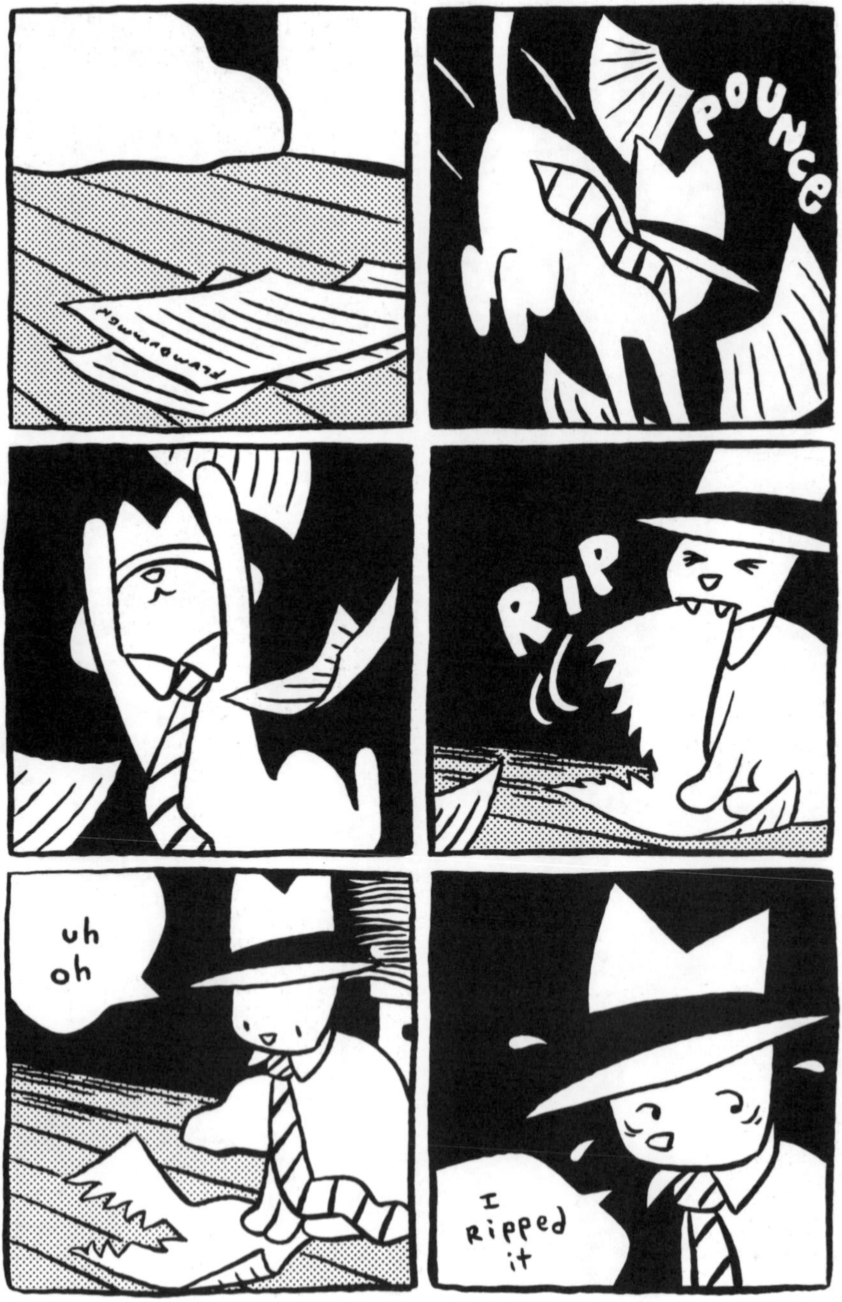
POUNCE
RIP
uh oh
I Ripped it

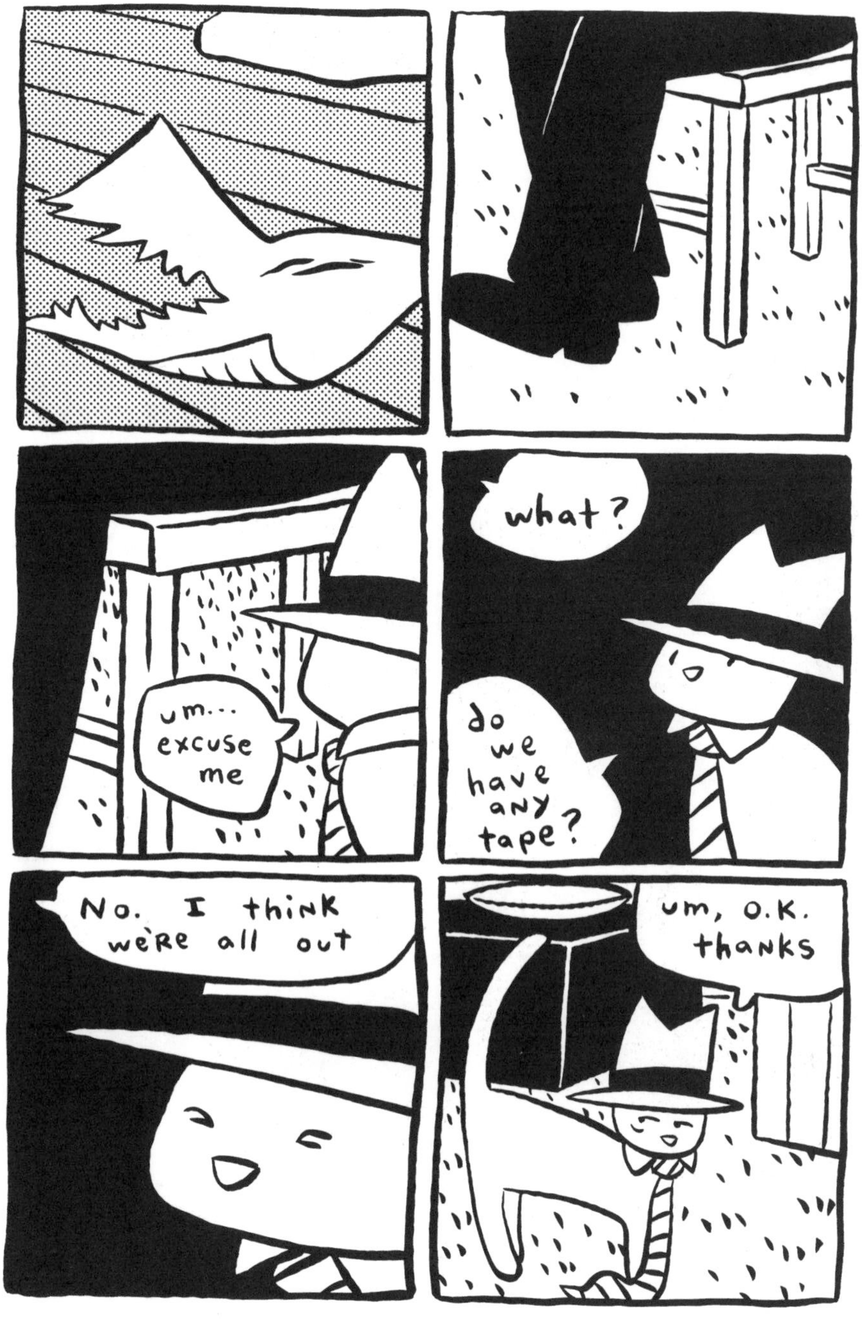
um... excuse me
what?
do we have any tape?
No. I think we're all out
um, O.K. thanks

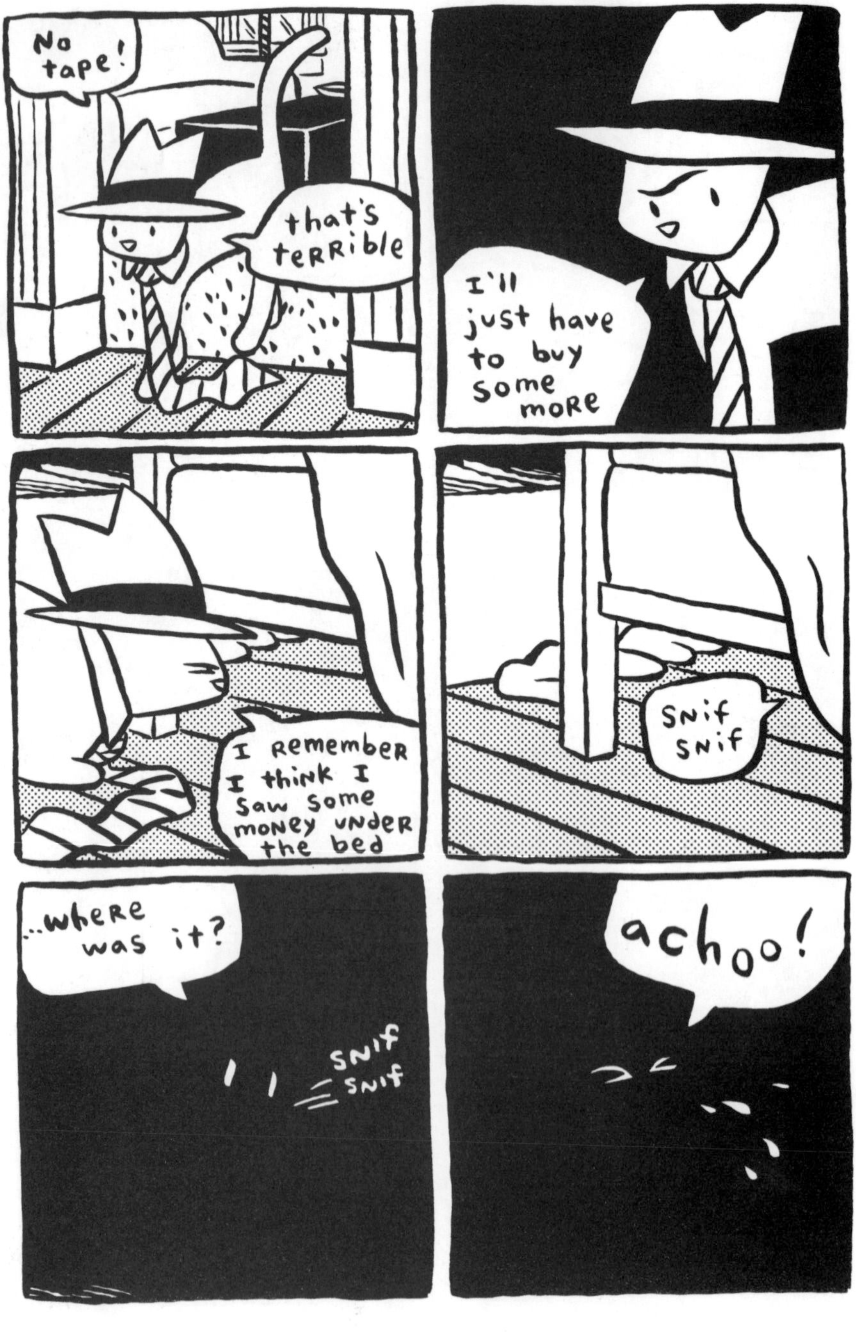
No tape!
that's terrible
I'll just have to buy some more
I remember I think I saw some money under the bed
snif snif
...where was it?
snif snif
achoo!

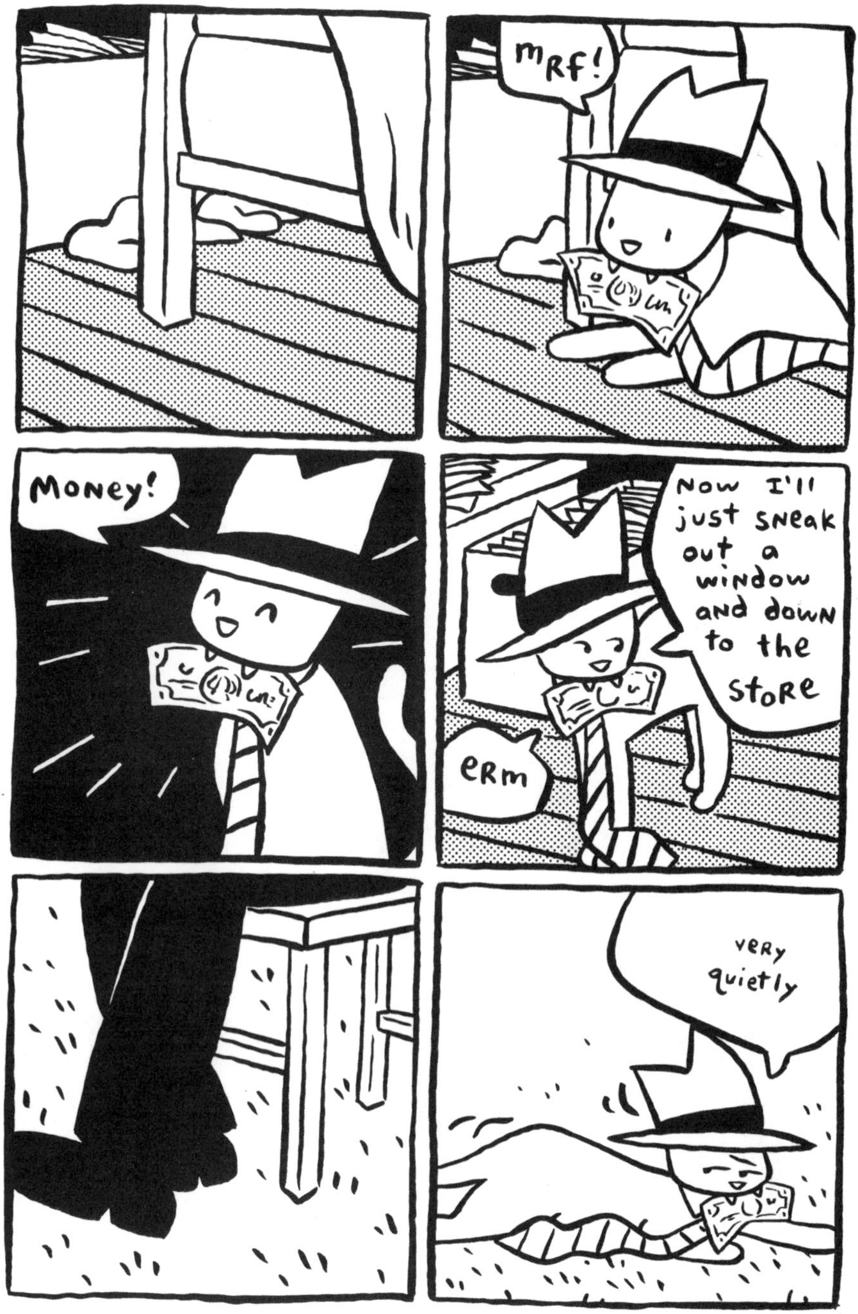
mRf!
Money!
Now I'll just sneak out a window and down to the store
eRm
very quietly

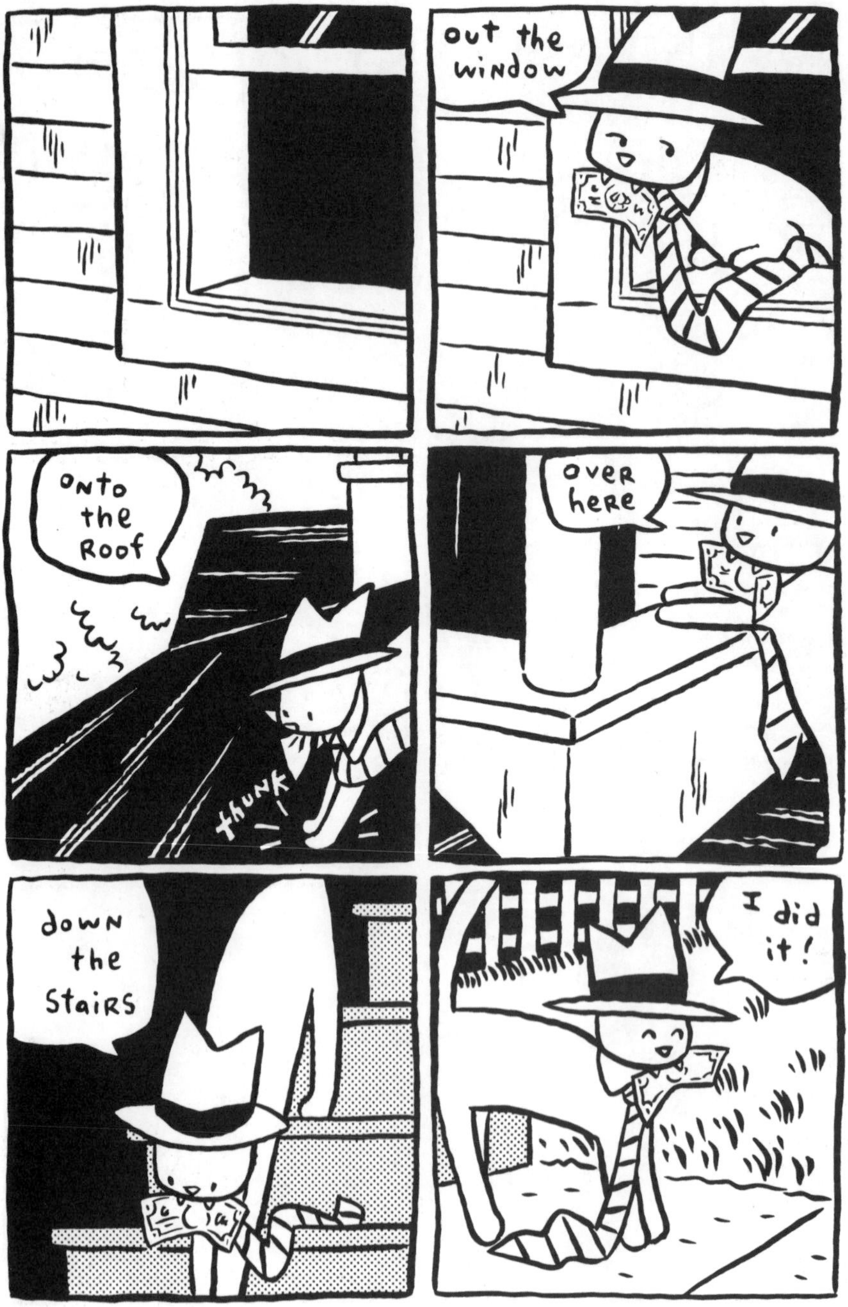
out the window
onto the Roof
thunk
over here
down the stairs
I did it!

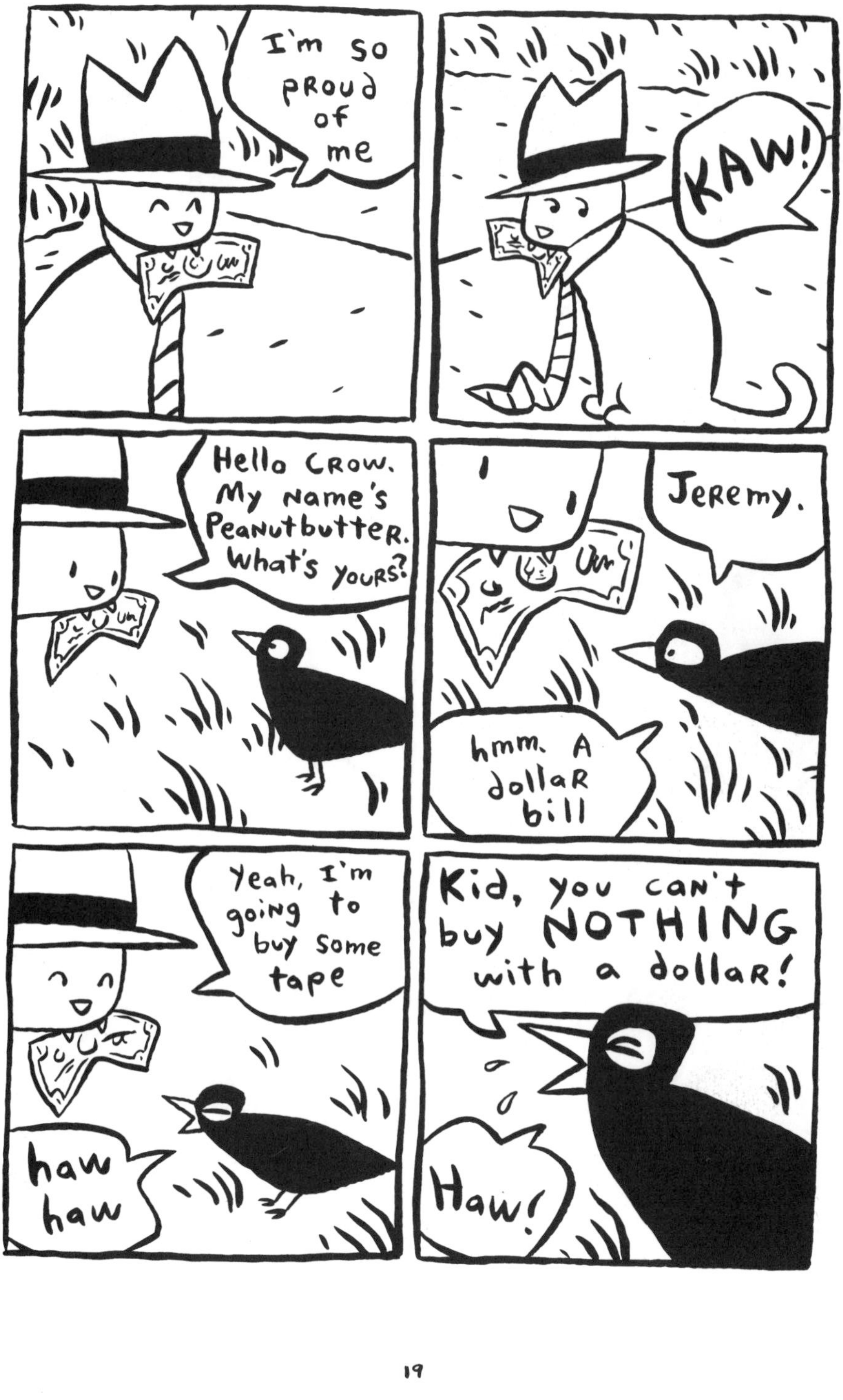
I'm so proud of me
KAW!
Hello crow. My name's Peanutbutter. What's yours?
Jeremy.
hmm. A dollar bill
Yeah, I'm going to buy some tape
haw haw
Kid, you can't buy NOTHING with a dollar!
Haw!

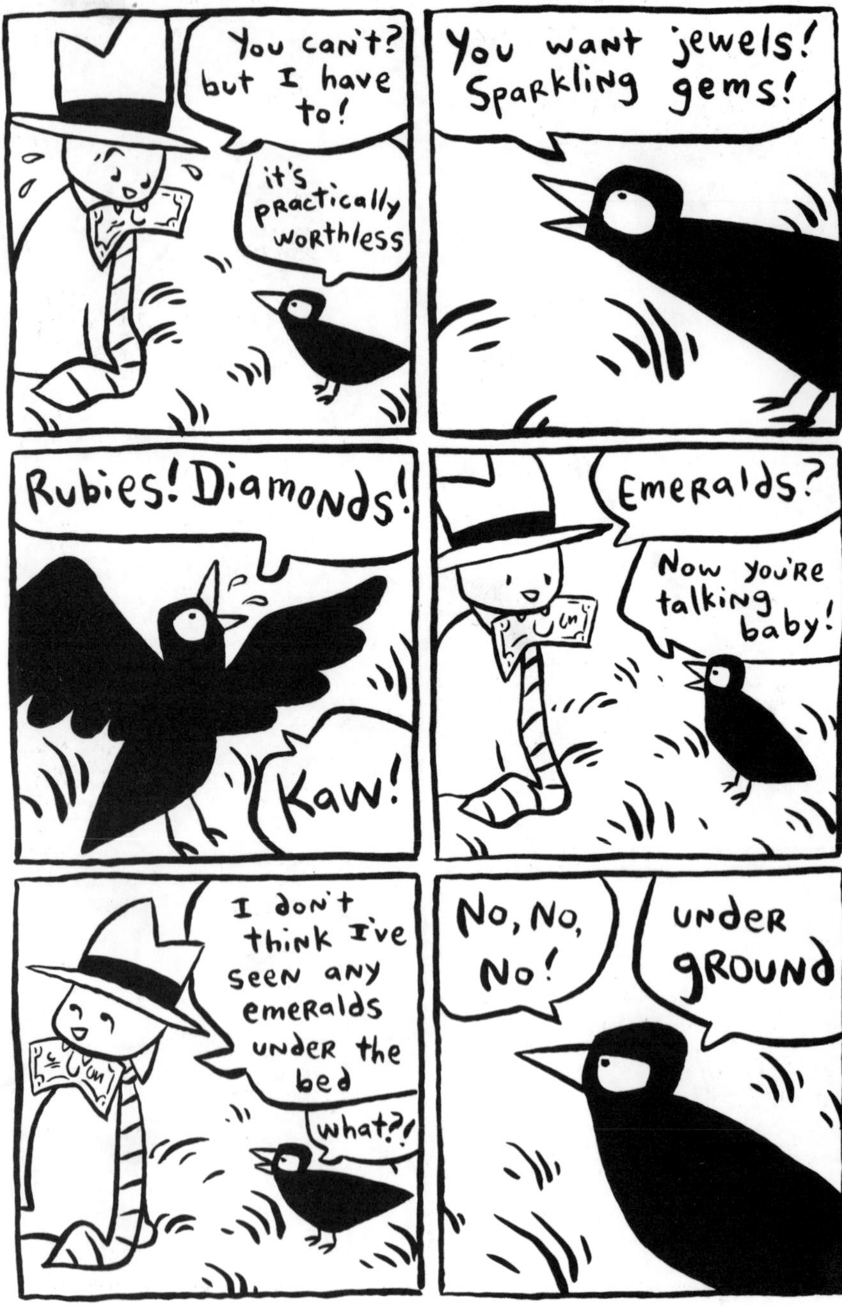
You can't? but I have to!
it's practically worthless
You want jewels! Sparkling gems!
Rubies! Diamonds!
Kaw!
Emeralds?
Now you're talking baby!
I don't think I've seen any emeralds under the bed
what?!
No, No, No!
under GROUND

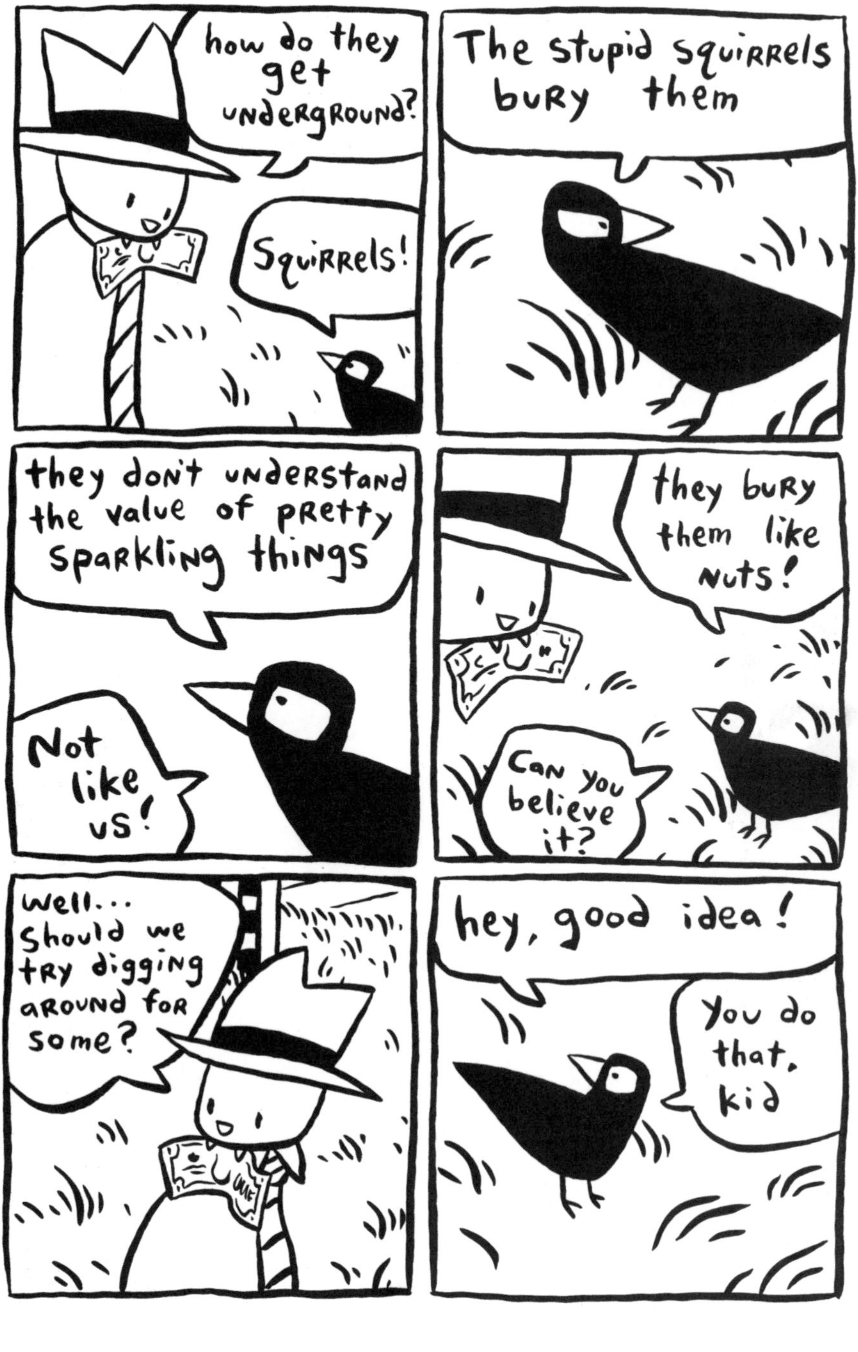
how do they get underground?
Squirrels!
The stupid squirrels bury them
they don't understand the value of pretty sparkling things
Not like us!
they bury them like nuts!
Can you believe it?
well... Should we try digging around for some?
hey, good idea!
You do that, kid

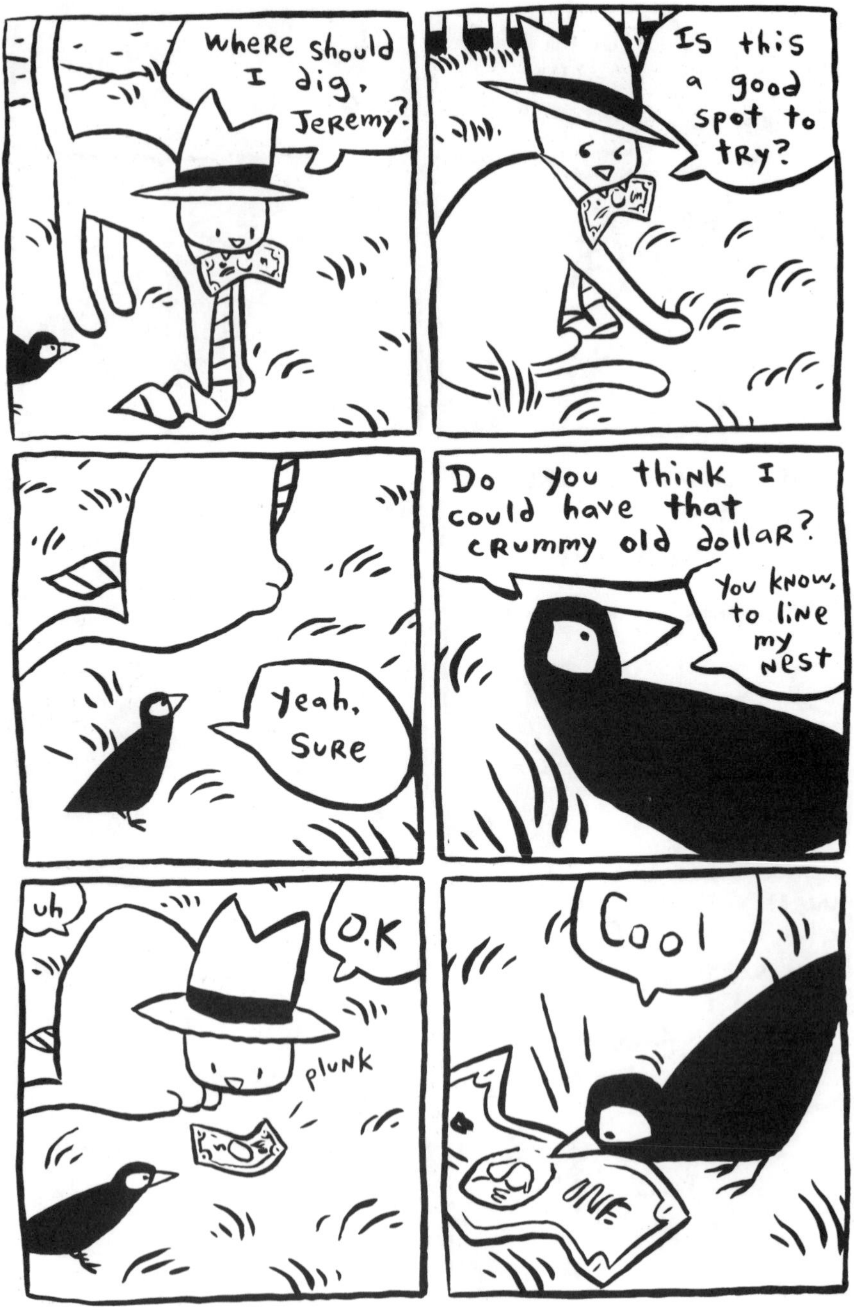
Where should I dig, Jeremy?
Is this a good spot to try?
Yeah, sure
Do you think I could have that crummy old dollar?
You know, to line my nest
uh
O.K
plunk
Cool
ONE

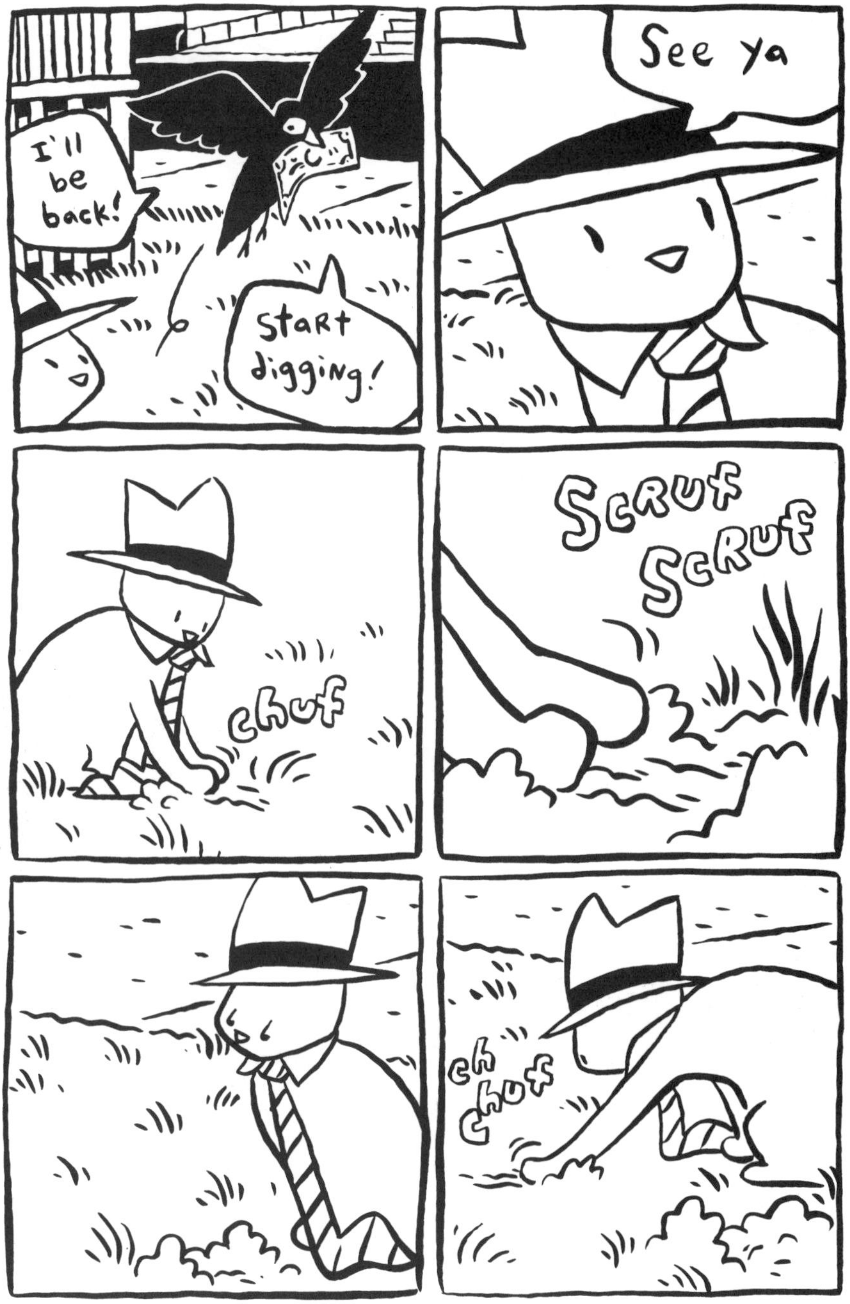
I'll be back!
Start digging!
See ya
chuf
SCRUF SCRUF
ch chuf

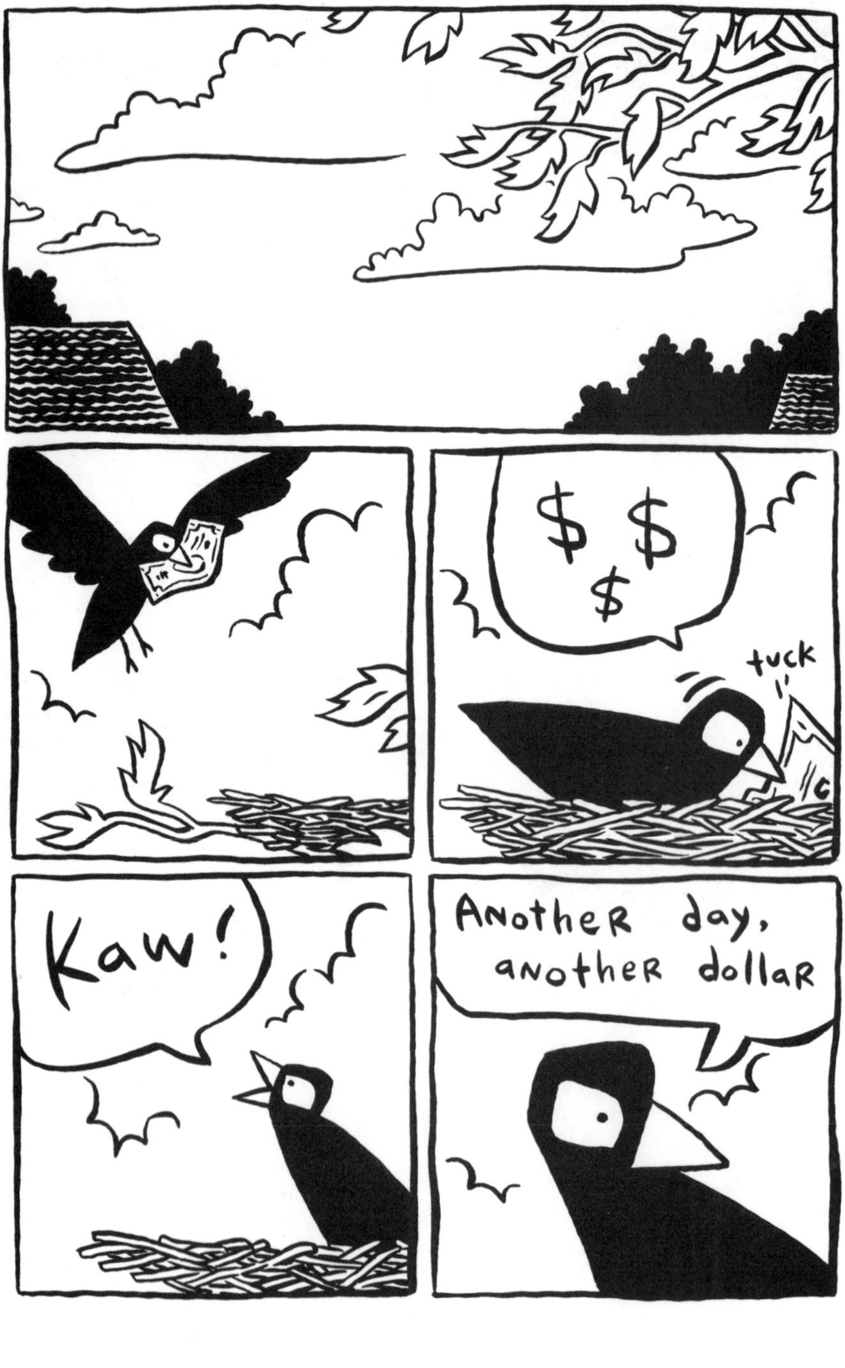
$ $ $
tuck
Kaw!
Another day, another dollar

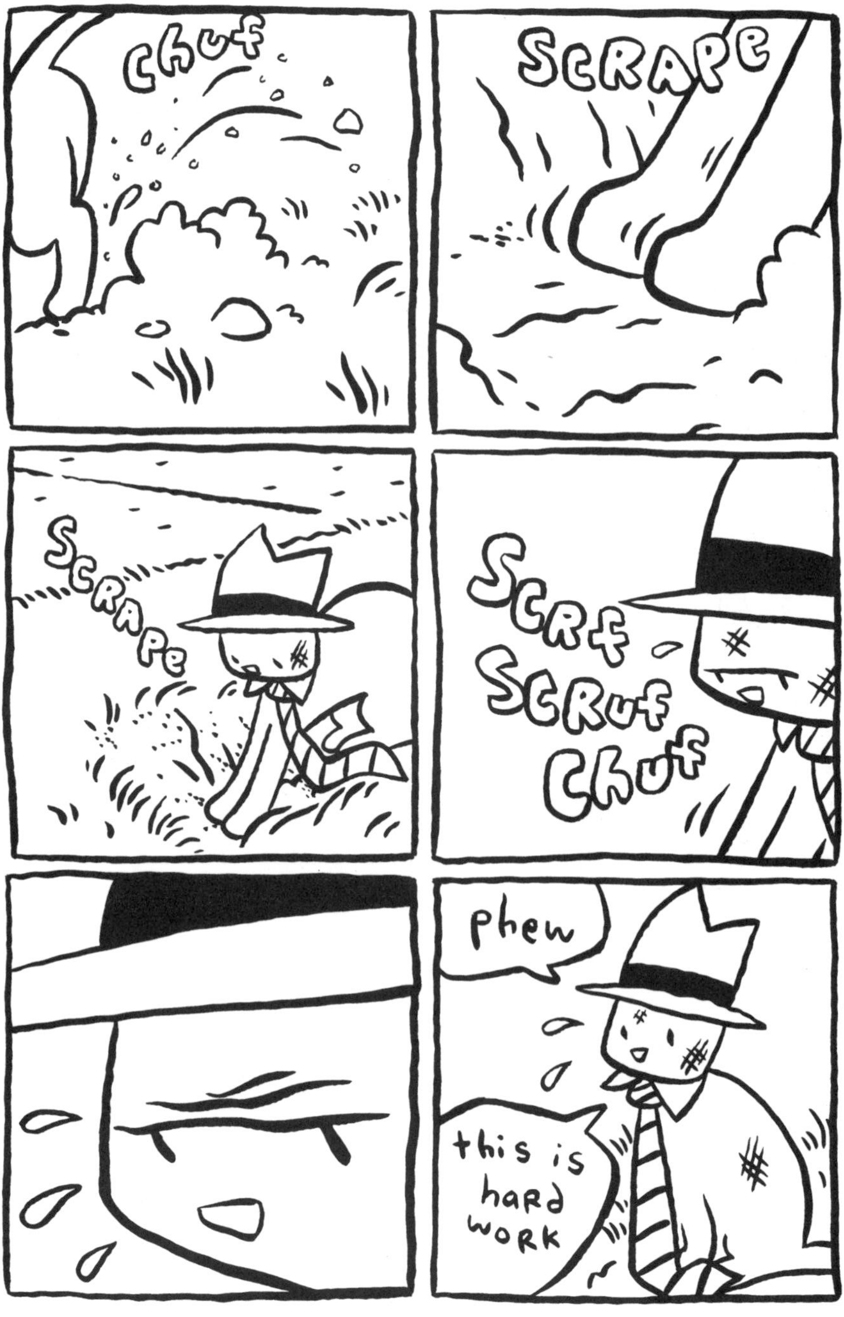
chuf
SCRAPE
SCRAPE
SCRf
SCRUf
Chuf
phew
this is hard work

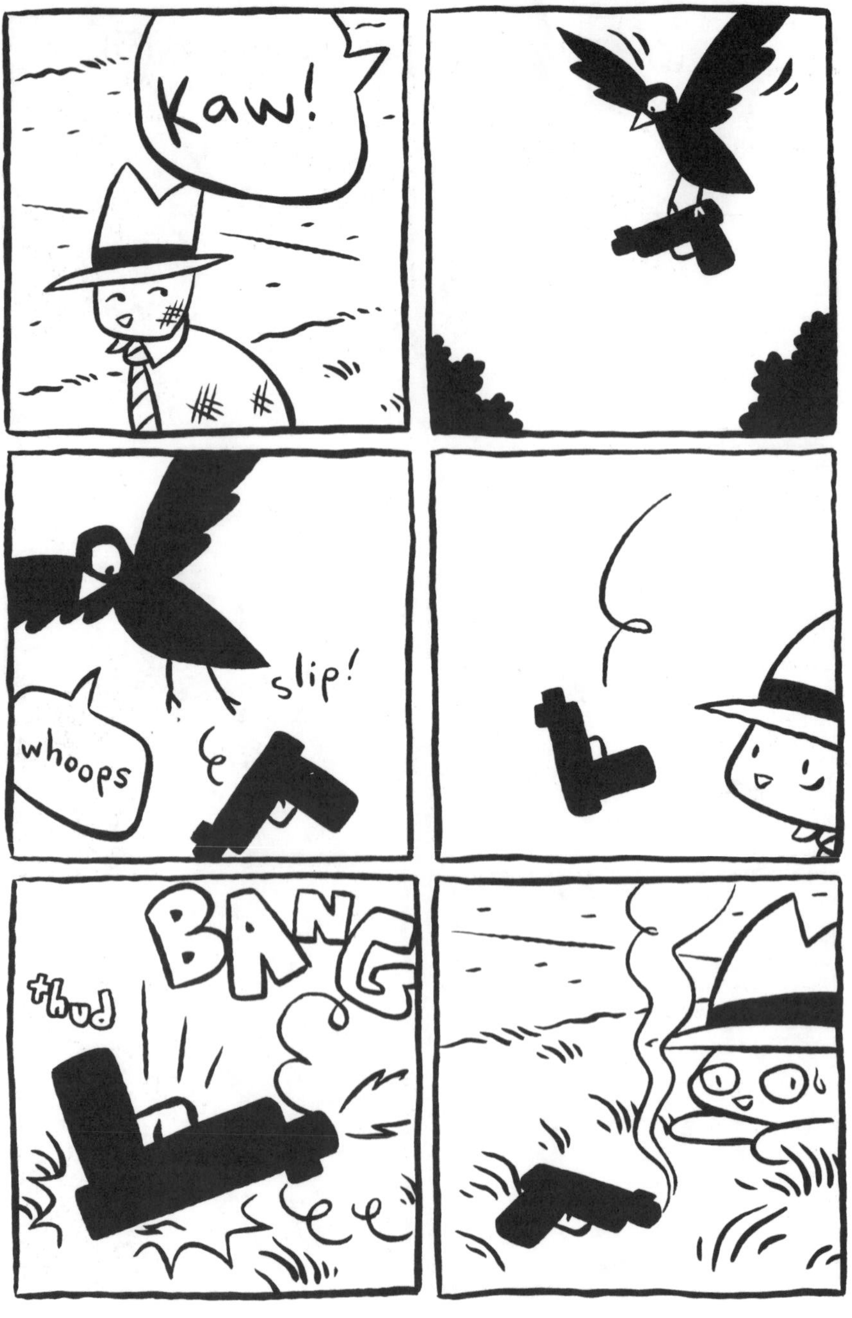
Kaw!
whoops
slip!
BANG
thud

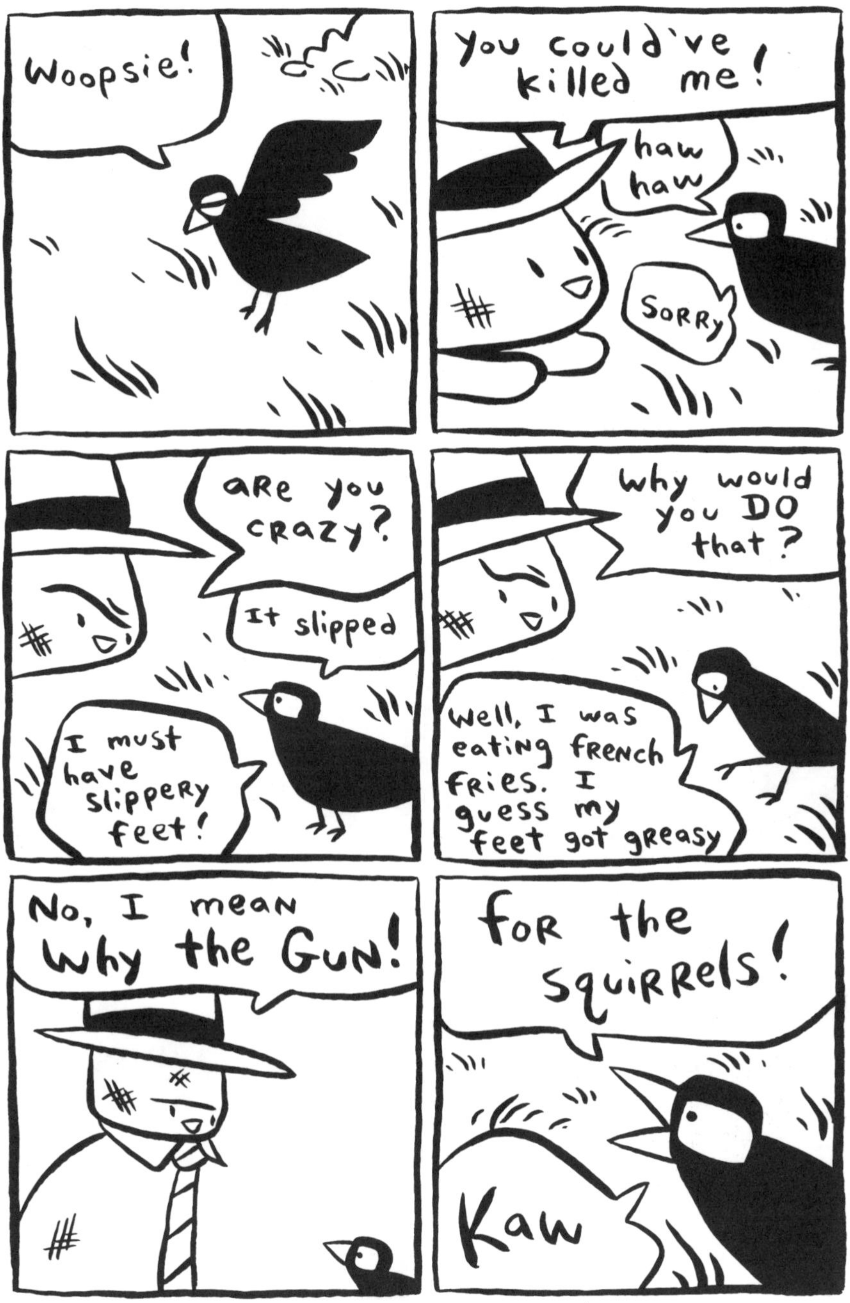
Woopsie!
You could've killed me!
haw haw
SORRY
are you crazy?
It slipped
I must have slippery feet!
why would you DO that?
Well, I was eating french fries. I guess my feet got greasy
No, I mean why the GUN!
for the squirrels!
Kaw

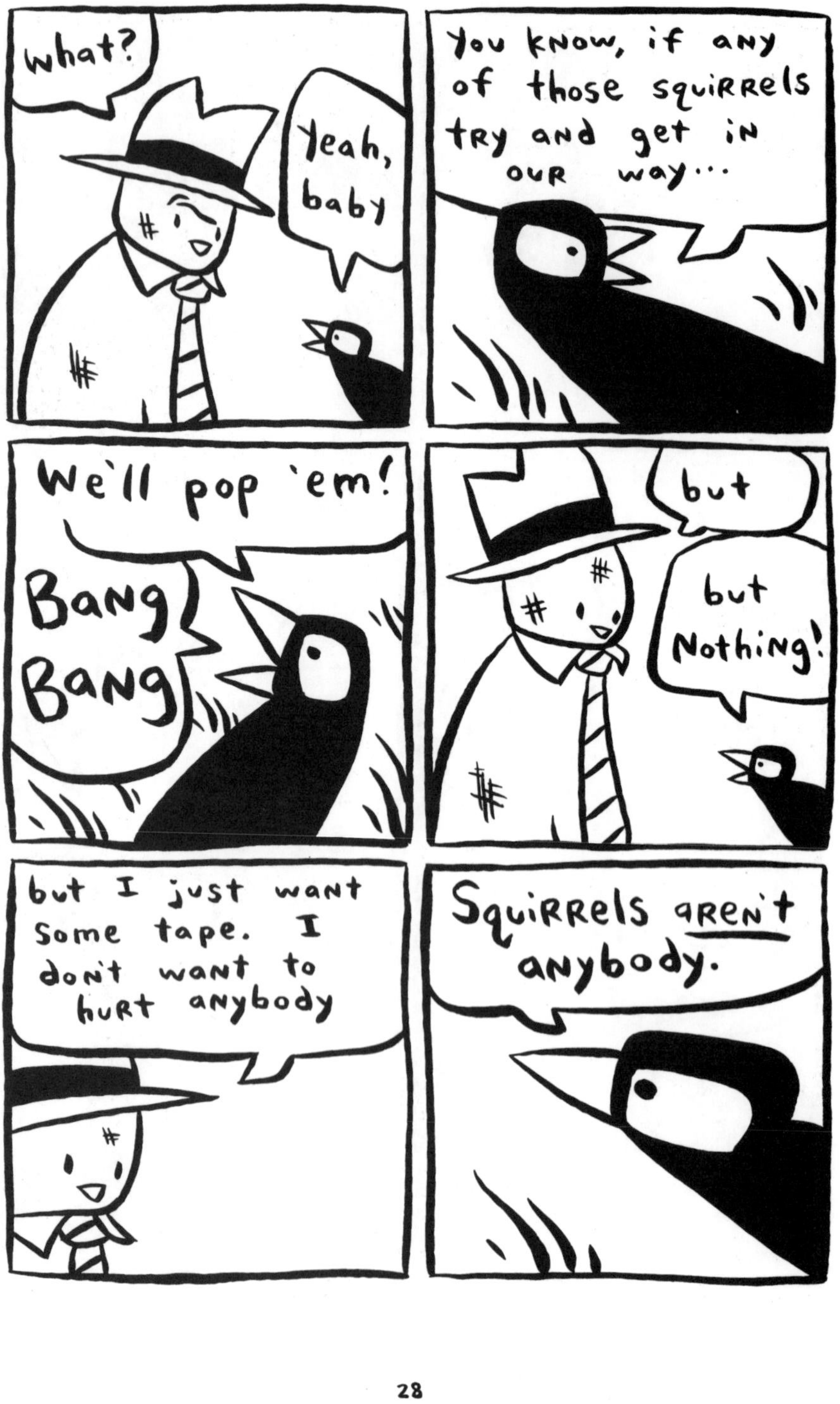
what?
Yeah, baby
You know, if any of those squirrels try and get in our way...
We'll pop 'em!
Bang Bang
but
but Nothing!
but I just want some tape. I don't want to hurt anybody
Squirrels aren't anybody.

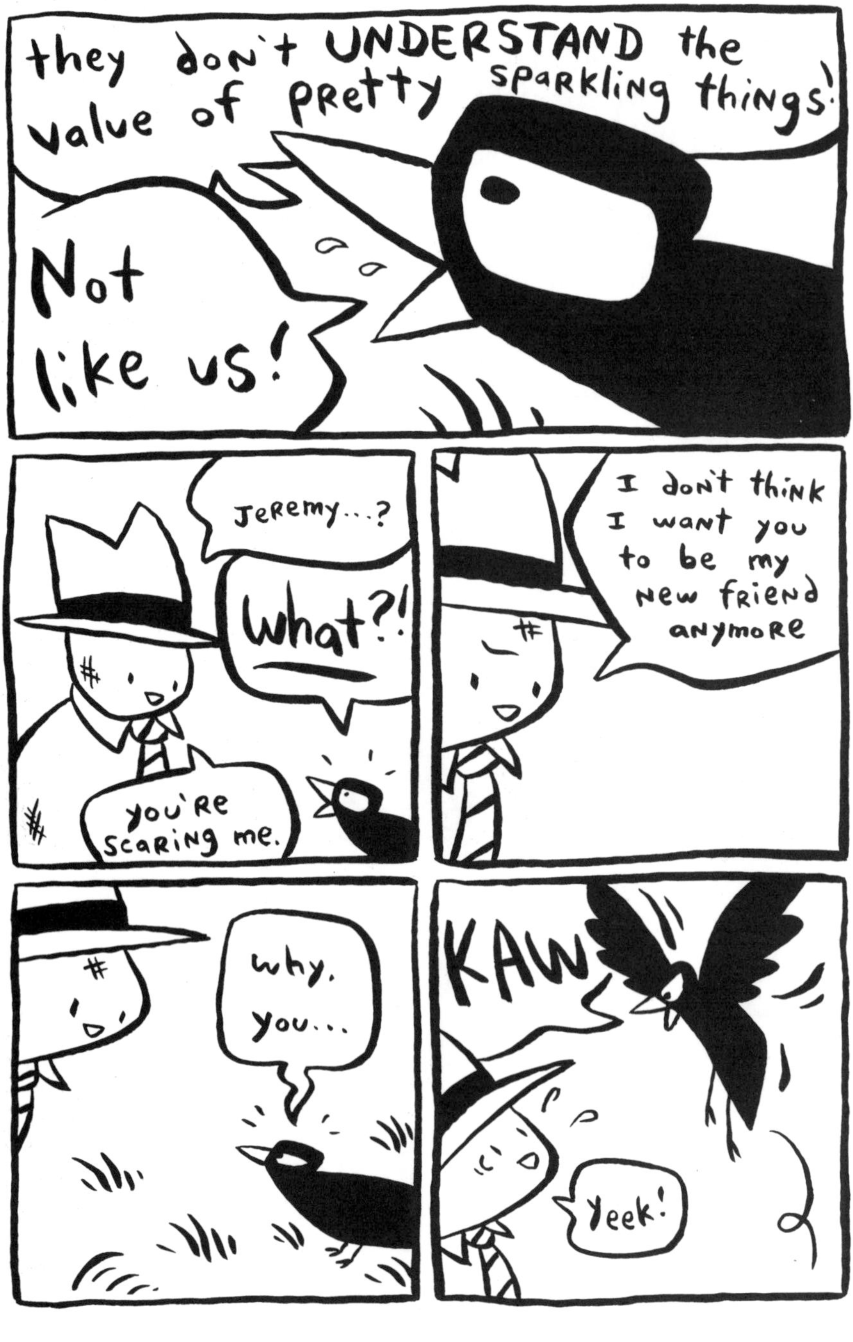
they don't UNDERSTAND the value of pretty sparkling things!
Not like us!
Jeremy...?
What?!
you're scaring me.
I don't think I want you to be my new friend anymore
why. you...
KAW
Yeek!

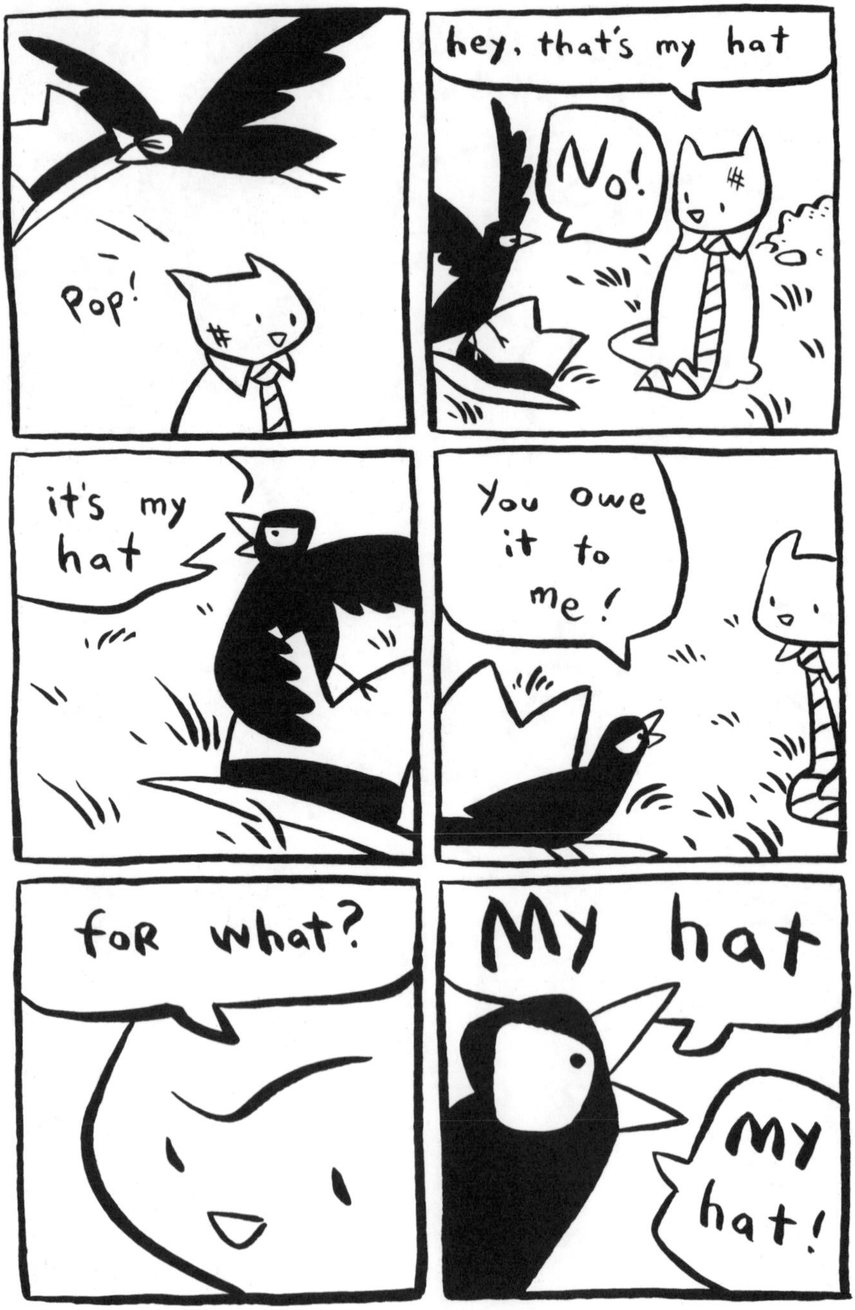

Pop!
hey, that's my hat
No!
it's my hat
You owe it to me!
for what?
My hat
my hat!

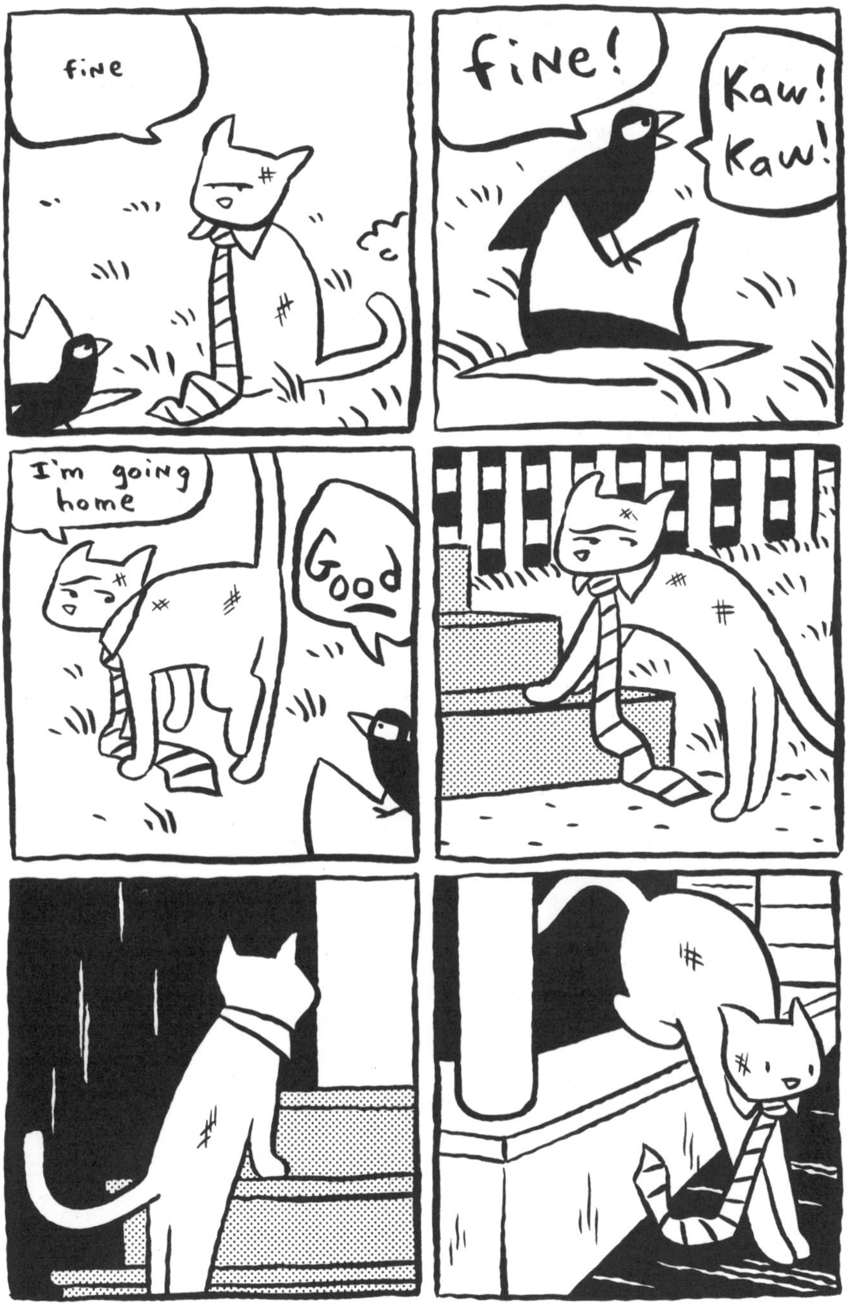
fine
fine!
Kaw! Kaw!
I'm going home
Good

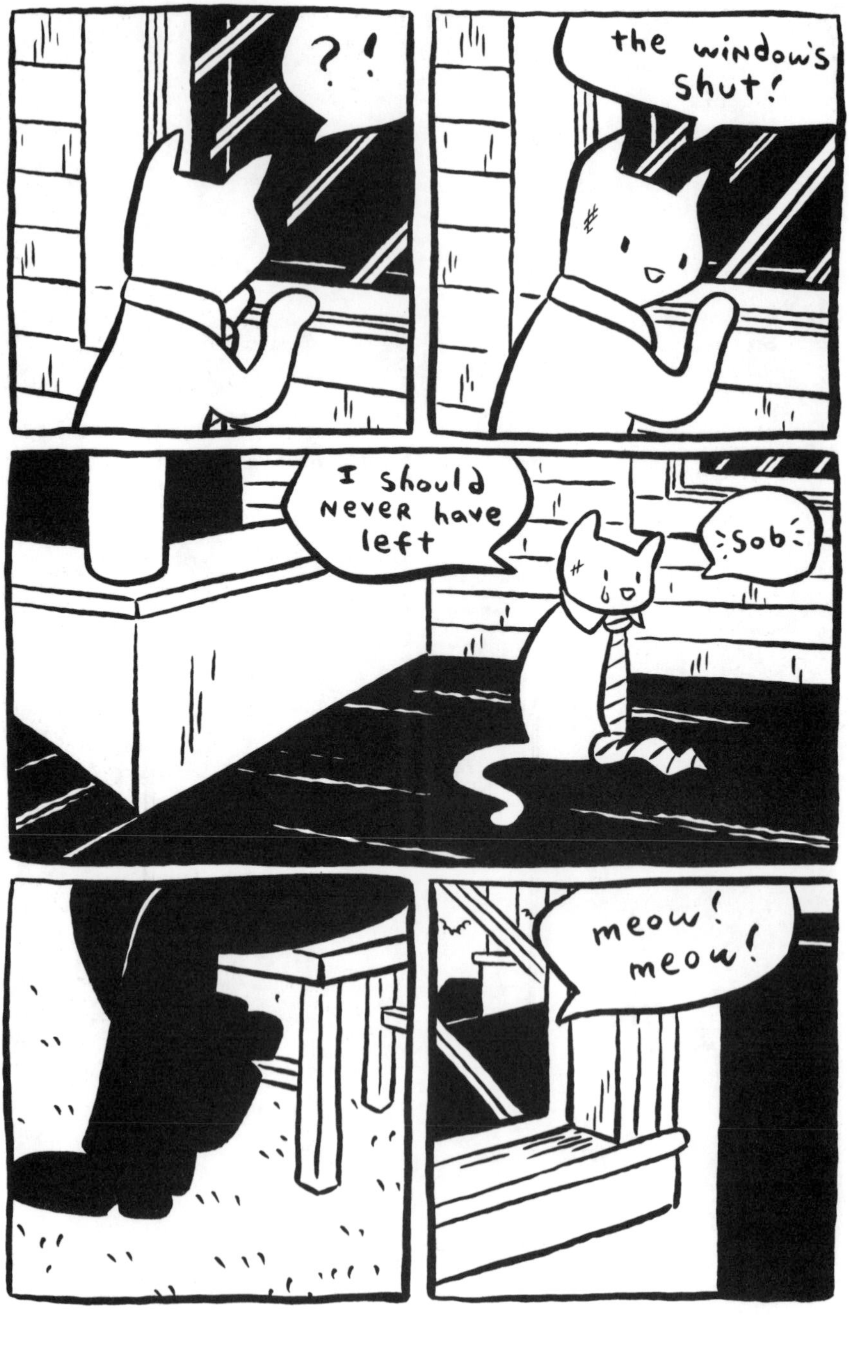
?!
the window's shut!
I should never have left
sob
meow! meow!

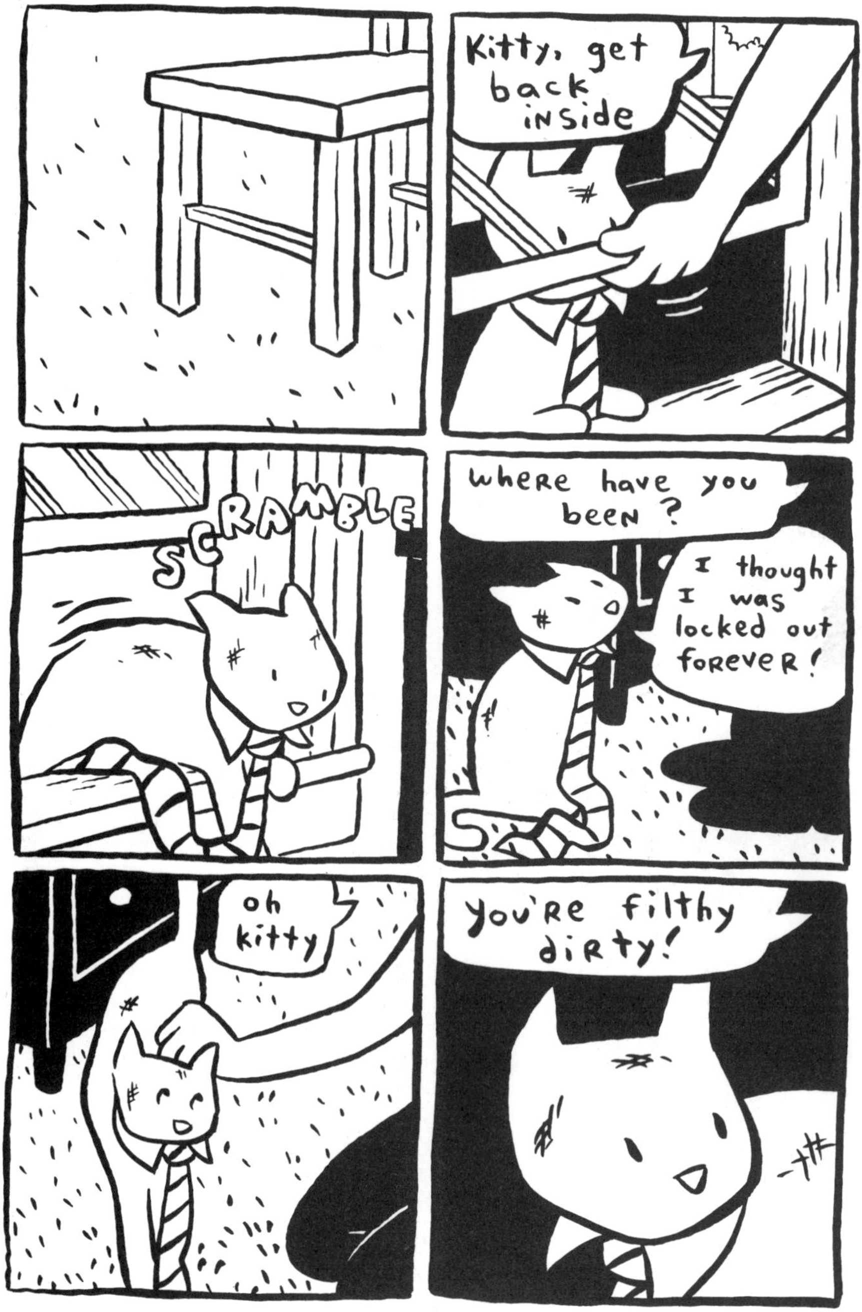
Kitty, get back inside
SCRAMBLE
where have you been?
I thought I was locked out forever!
oh kitty
you're filthy dirty!

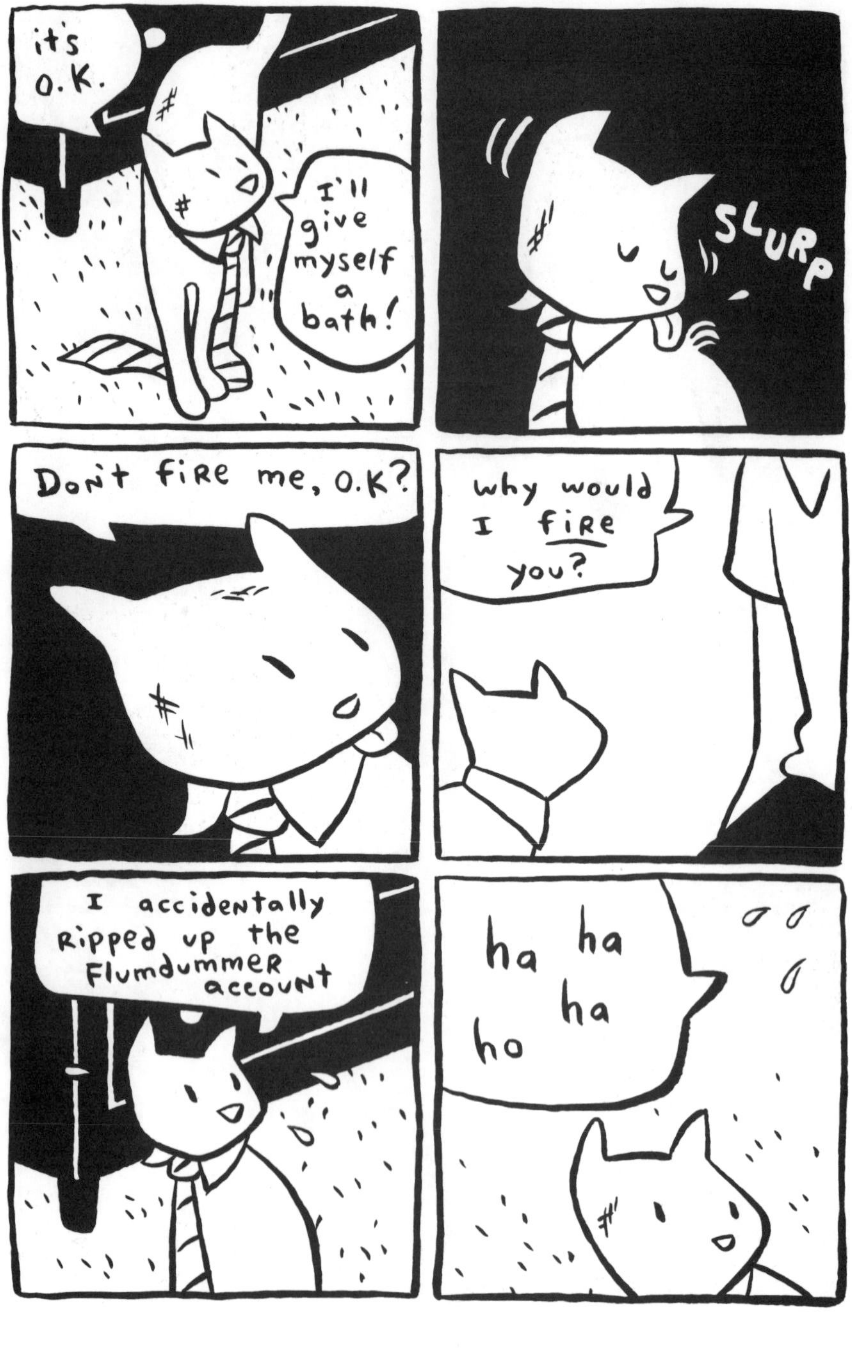
it's O.K.
I'll give myself a bath!
SLURP
Don't fire me, O.K?
why would I fire you?
I accidentally ripped up the Flumdummer account
ha ha ha ha ho

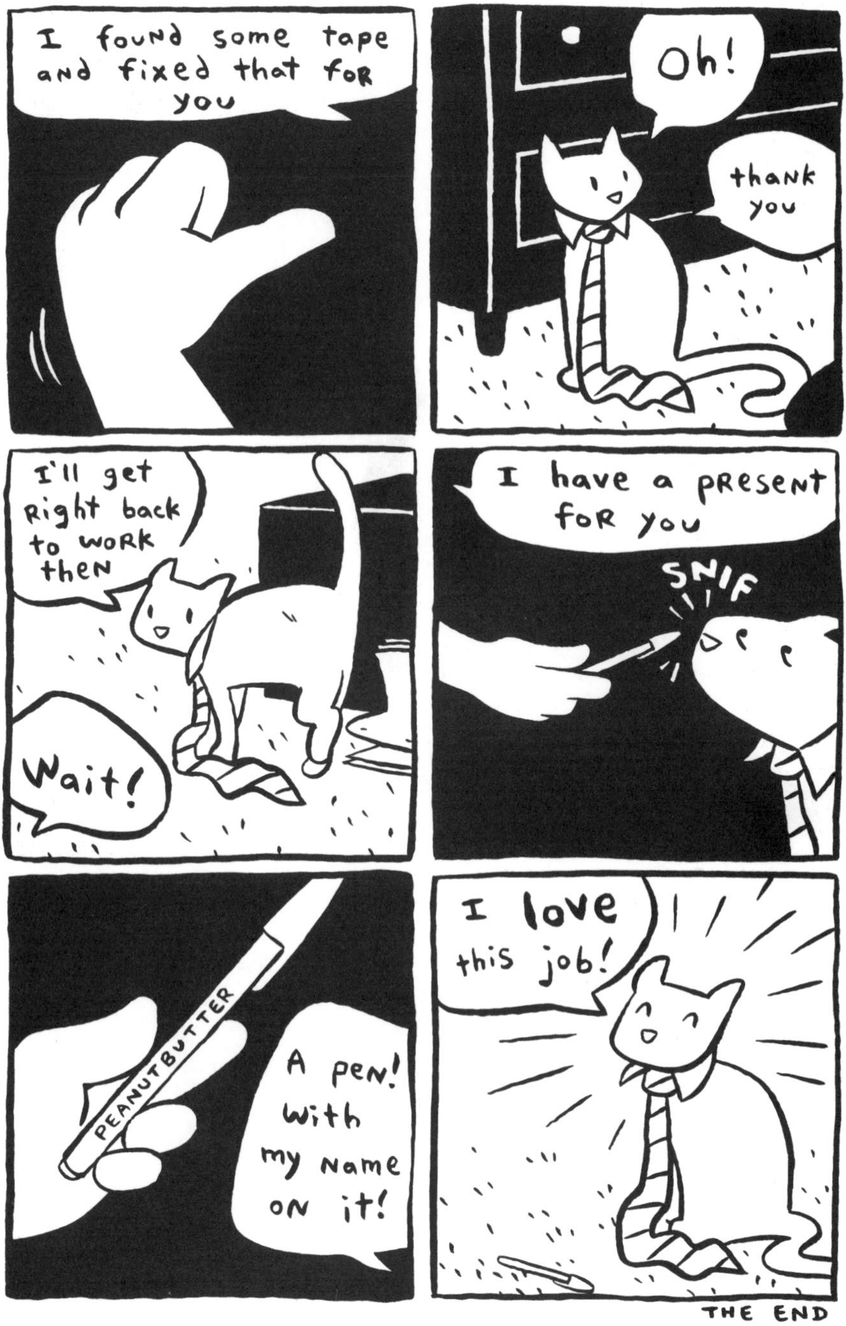
I found some tape and fixed that for you
Oh!
thank you
I'll get right back to work then
Wait!
I have a present for you
SNIF
PEANUTBUTTER
A pen! With my name on it!
I love this job!
THE END

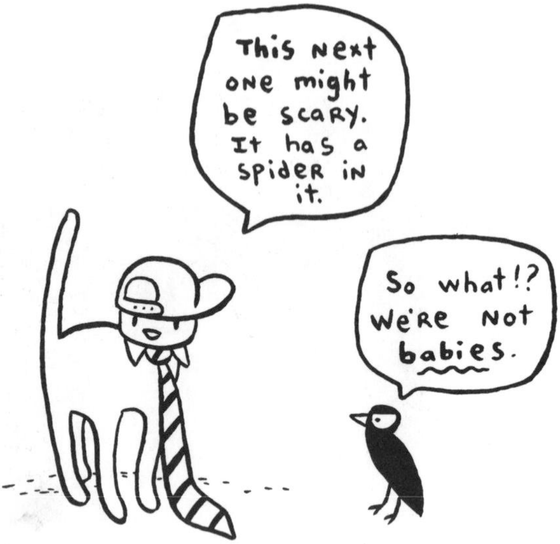
This next one might be scary. It has a spider in it.
So what!? We're not babies.

THE FLIBBLEDIBBLE FILE

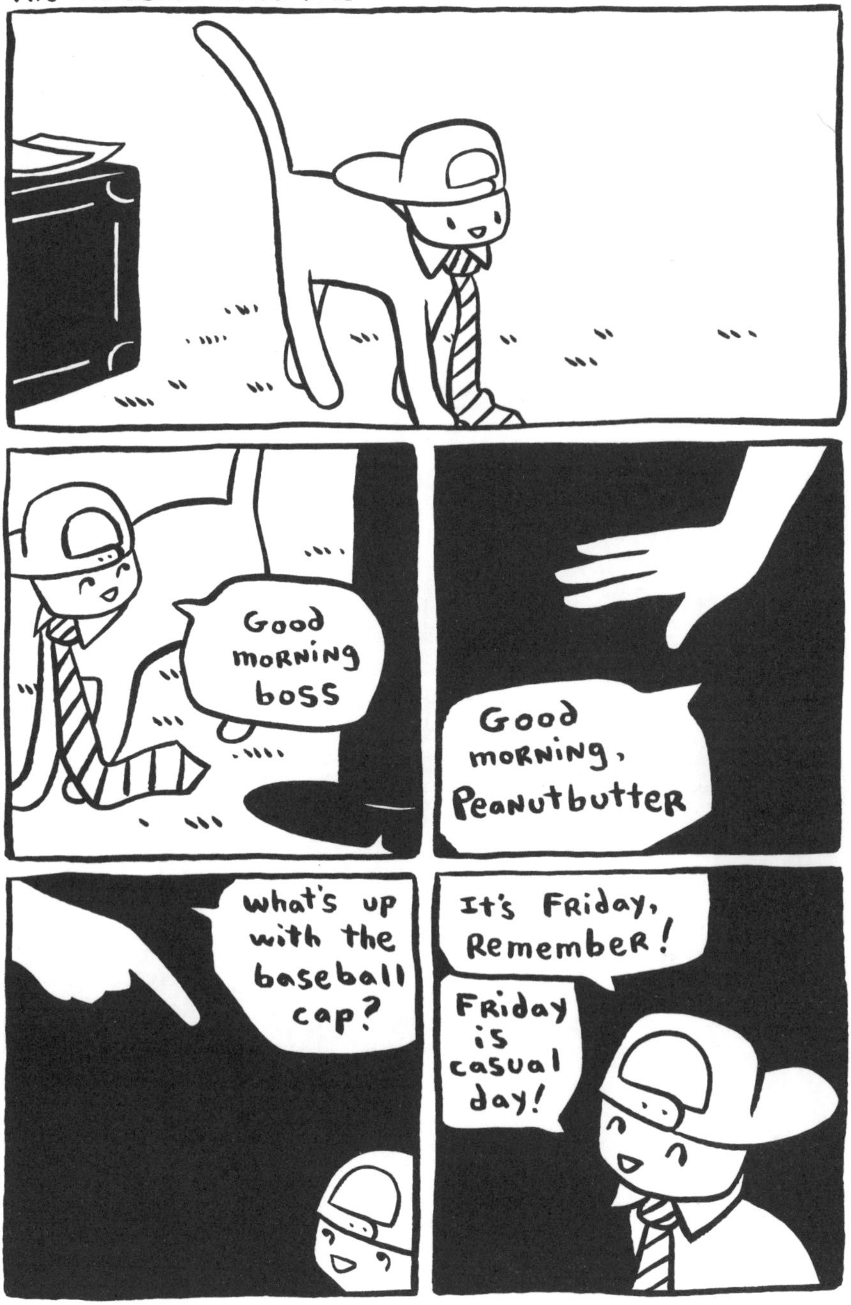
Good morning boss
Good morning, Peanutbutter
what's up with the baseball cap?
It's Friday, Remember!
Friday is casual day!

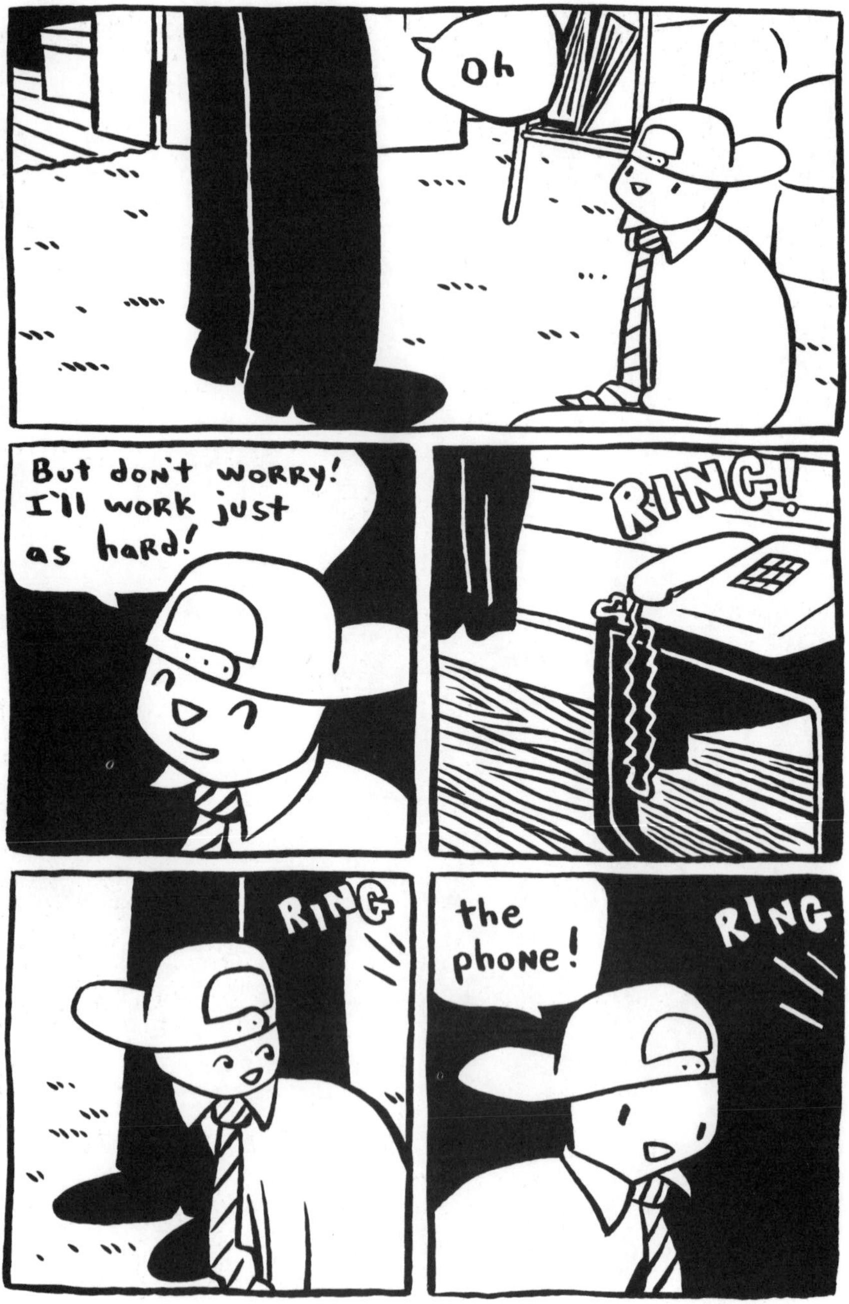
Oh
But don't worry! I'll work just as hard!
RING!
RING
the phone!
RING

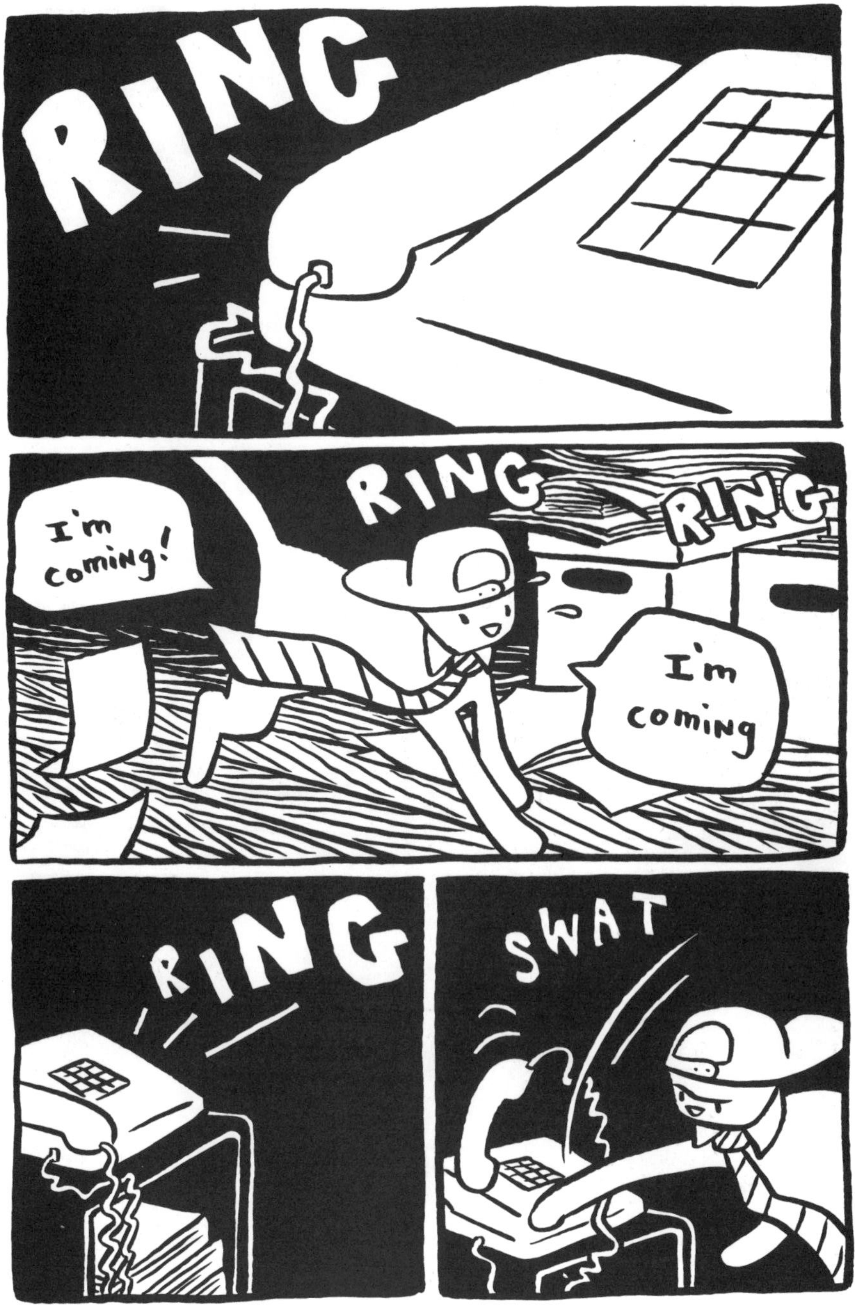
RING
RING
I'm coming!
RING
I'm coming
RING
SWAT

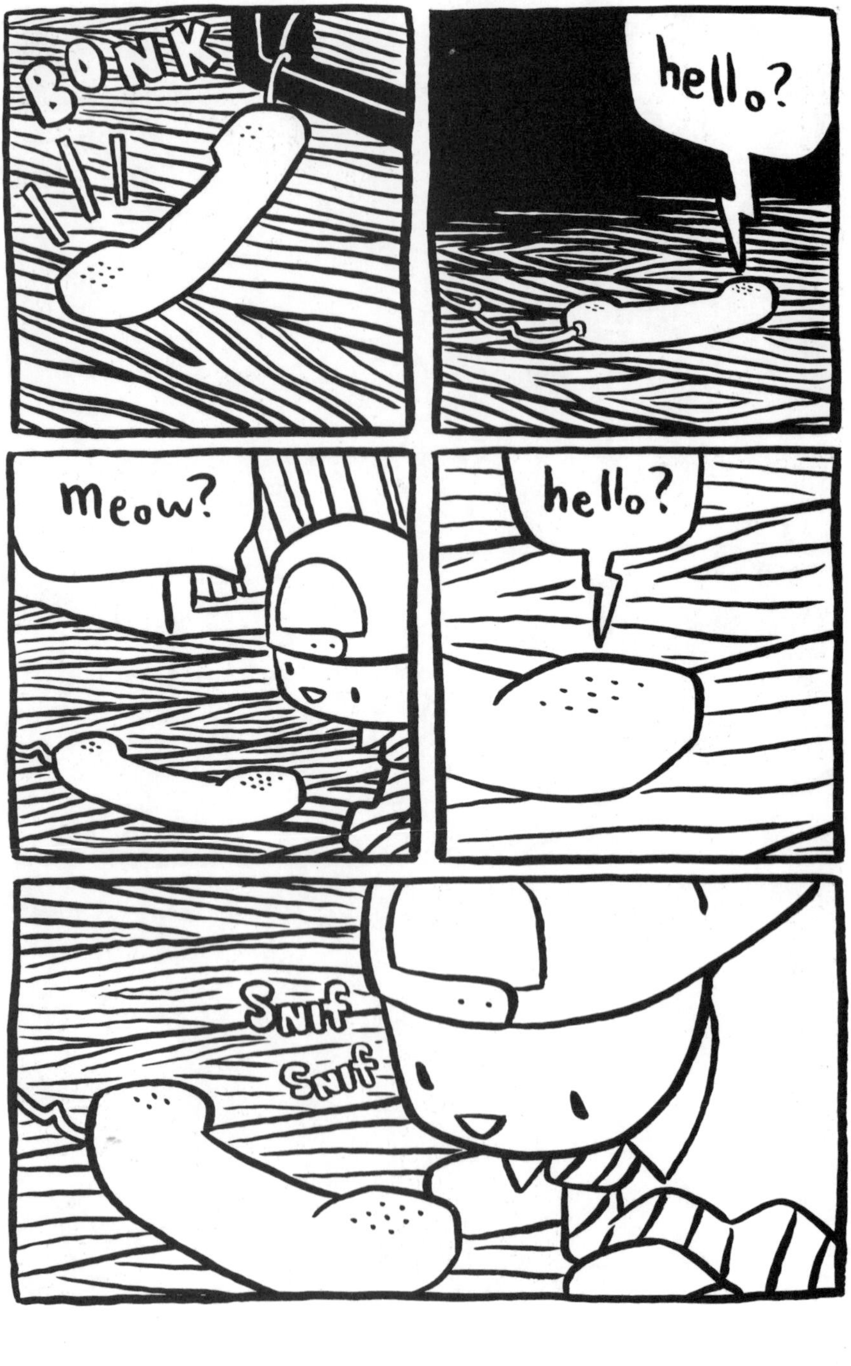
BONK
hello?
meow?
hello?
Snif
Snif

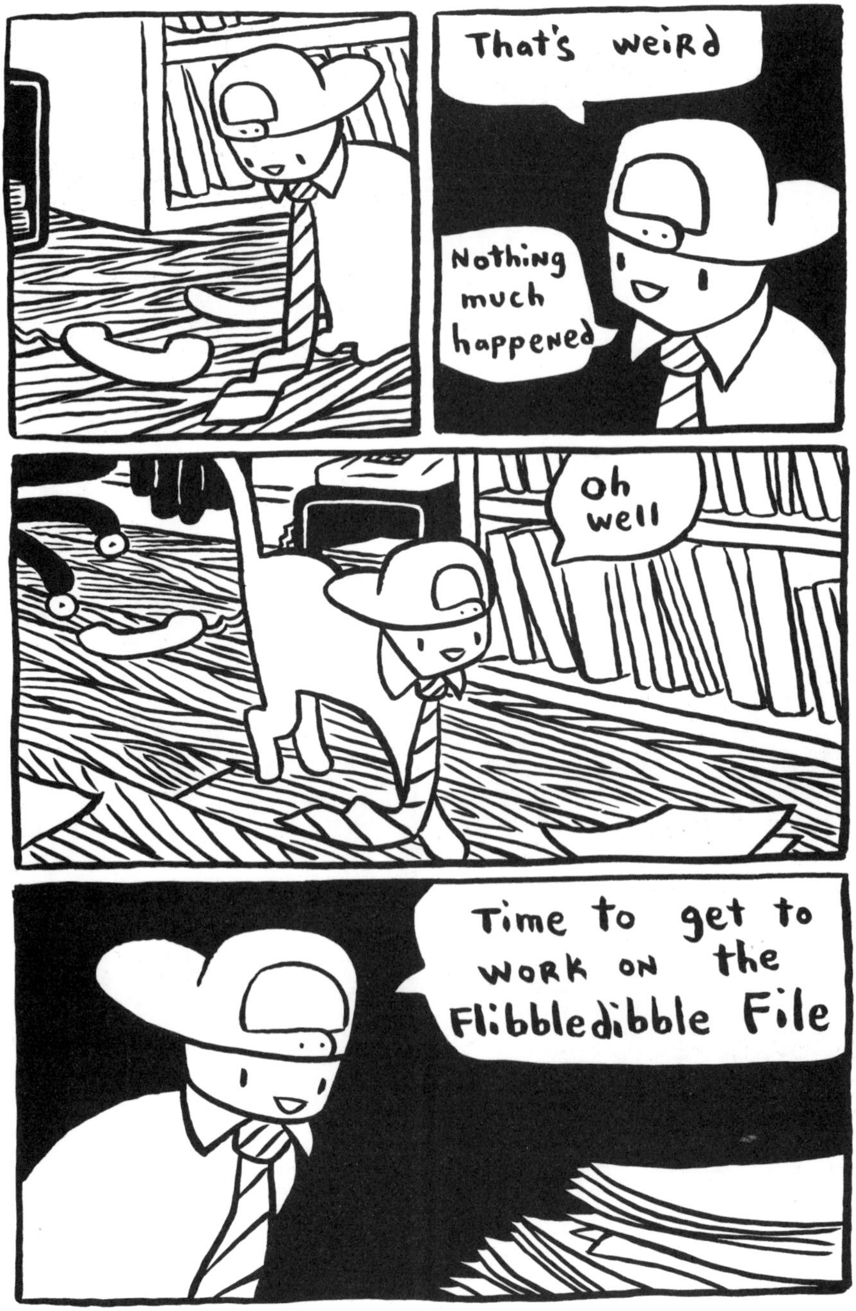
That's weird
Nothing much happened
Oh well
Time to get to work on the Flibbledibble File

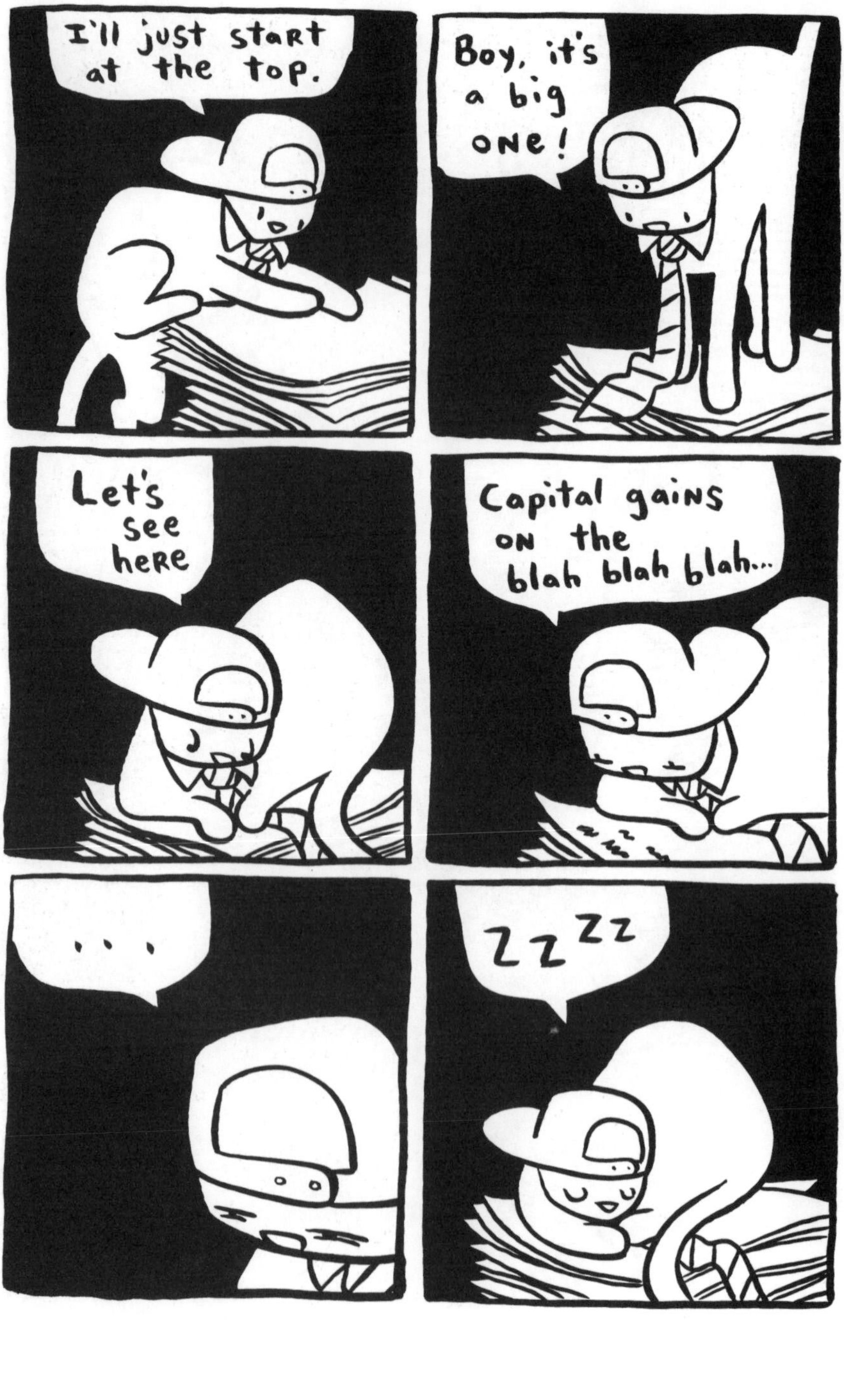
I'll just start at the top.
Boy, it's a big ONE!
Let's see here
Capital gains ON the blah blah blah...
. . .
ZZZZ

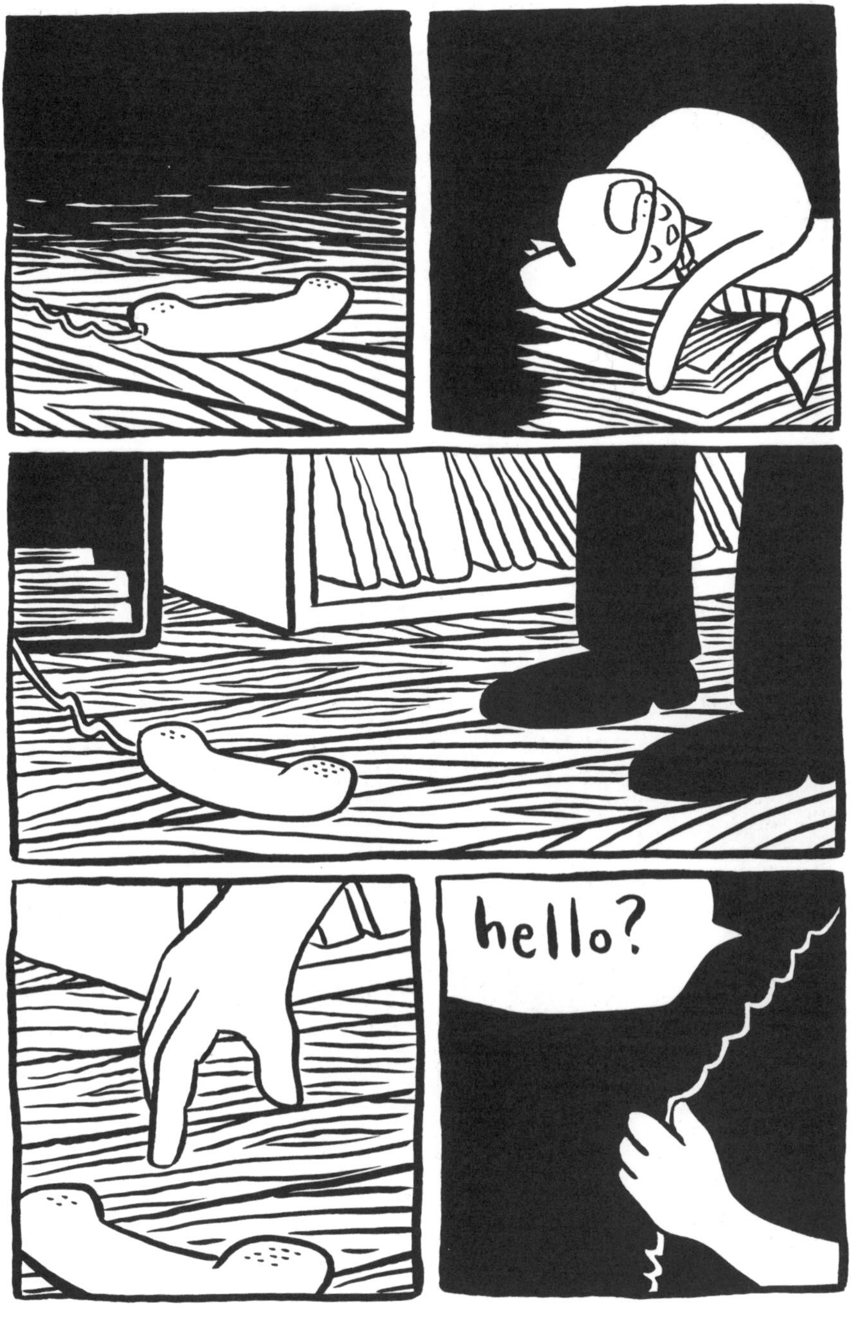
hello?

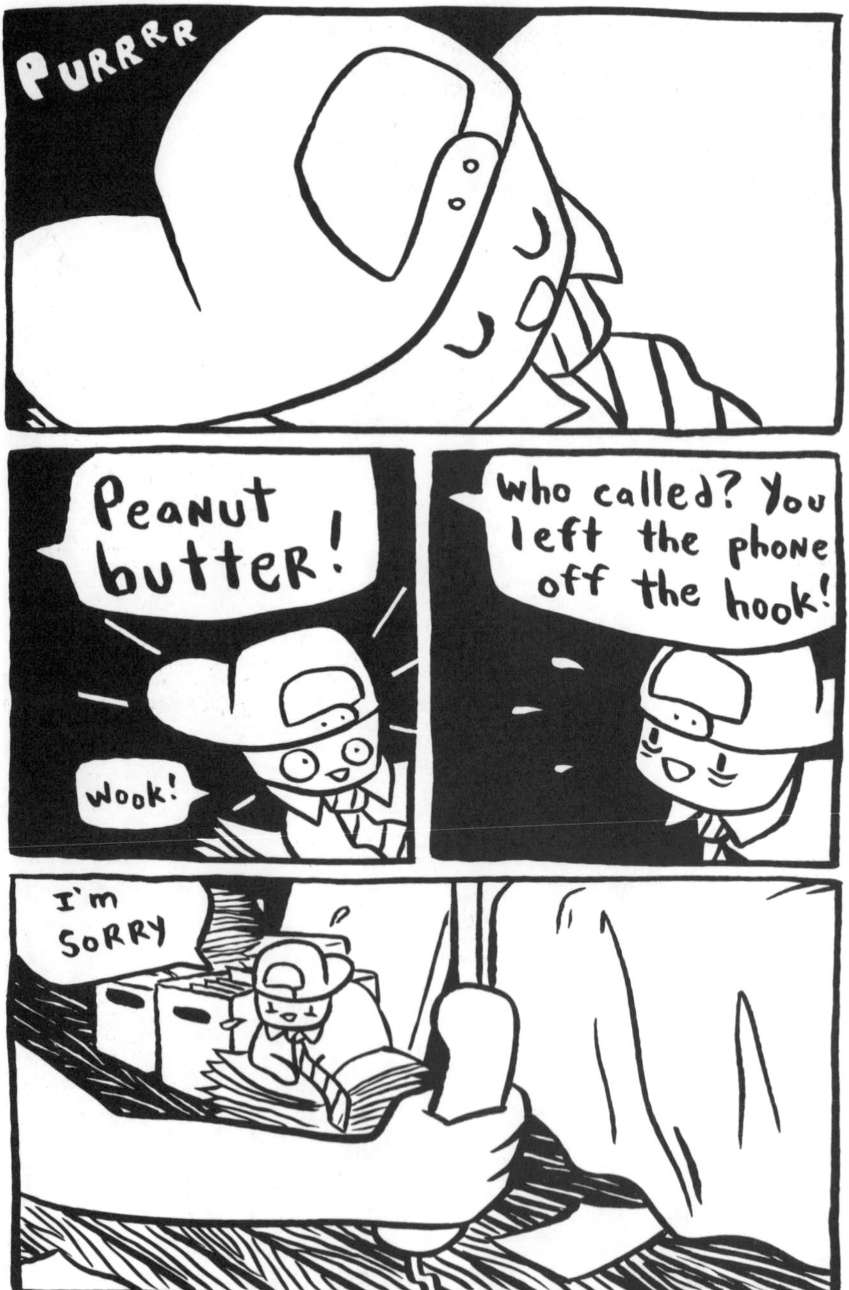
PURRRR
Peanut butter!
Wook!
Who called? You left the phone off the hook!
I'm SORRY

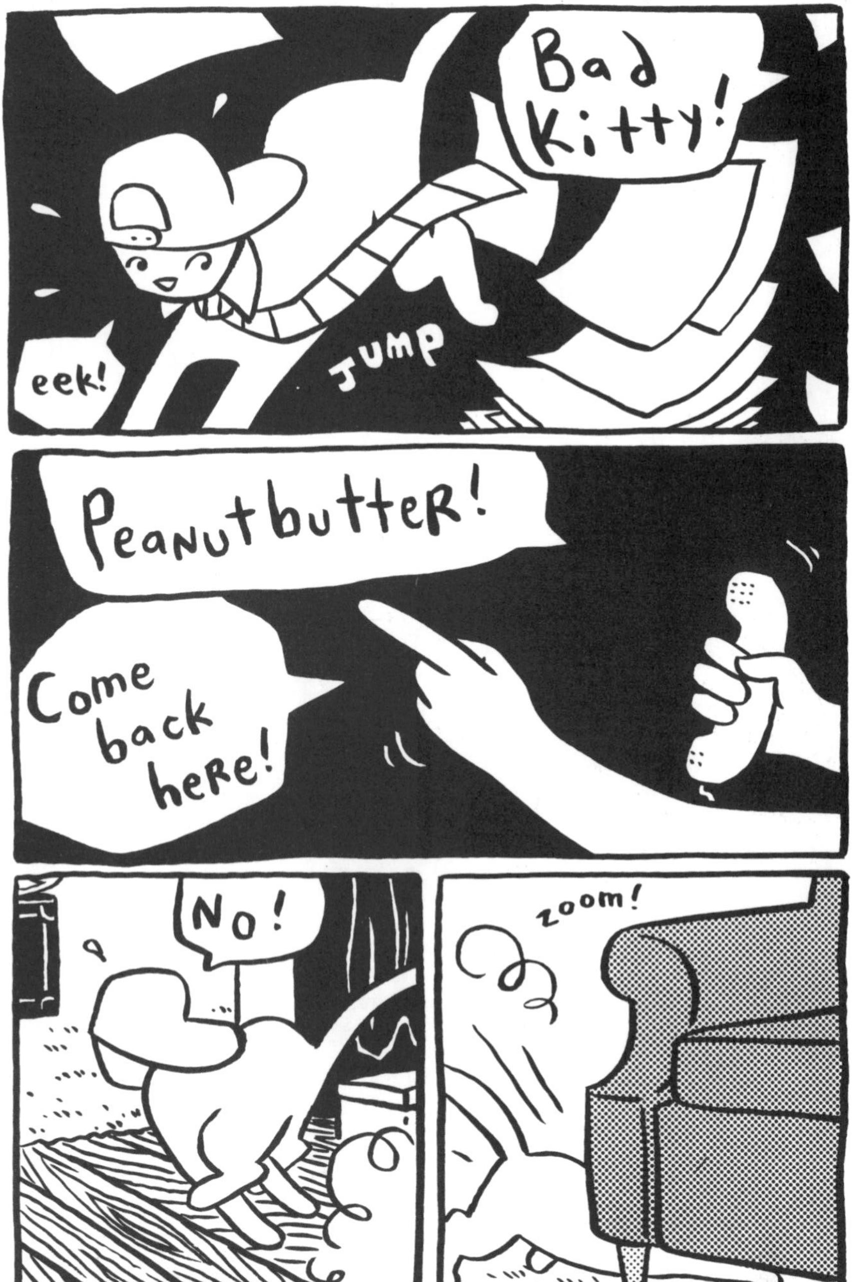
Bad Kitty!
eek!
JUMP
Peanutbutter!
Come back here!
No!
zoom!

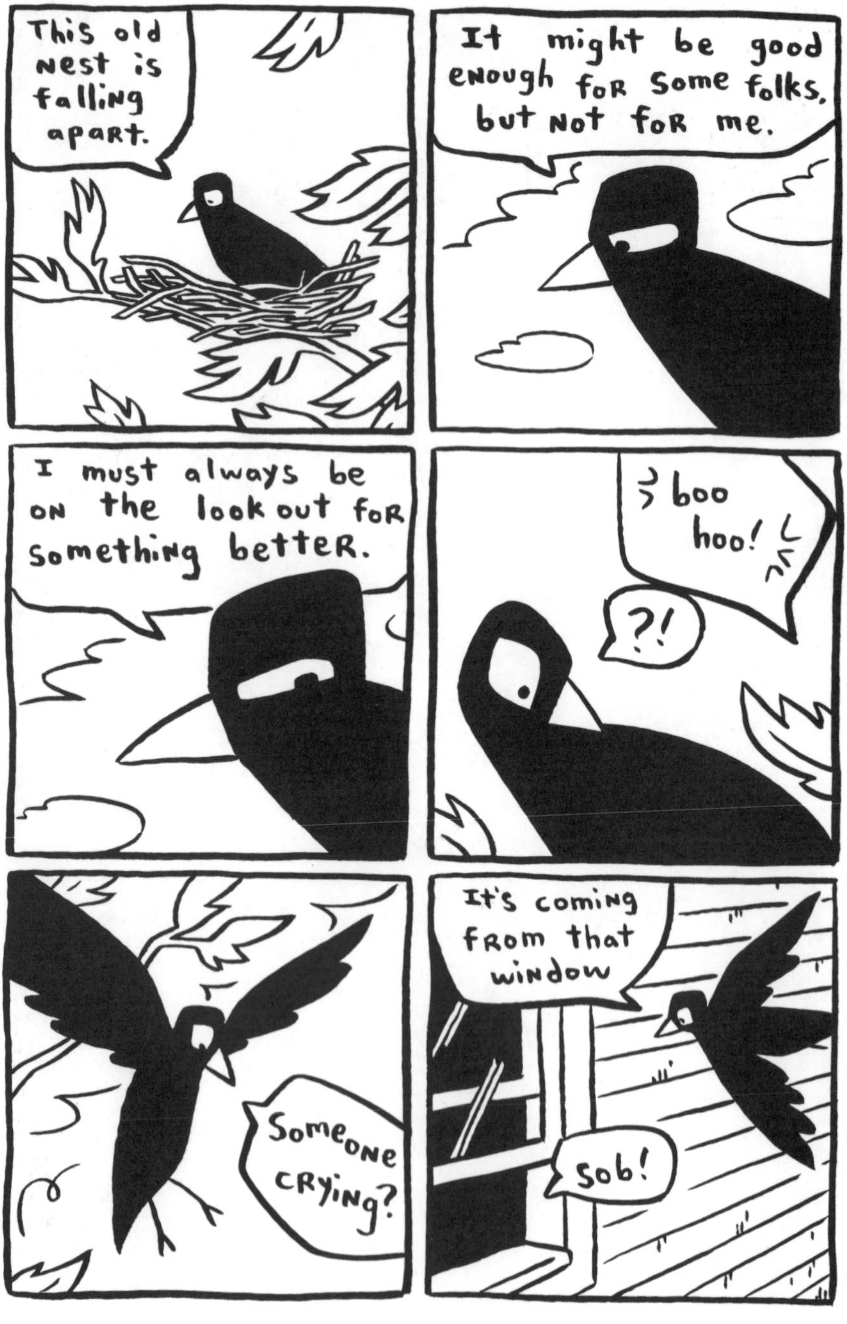
This old nest is falling apart.
It might be good enough for some folks, but not for me.
I must always be on the look out for something better.
boo hoo!
?!
Someone crying?
It's coming from that window
Sob!

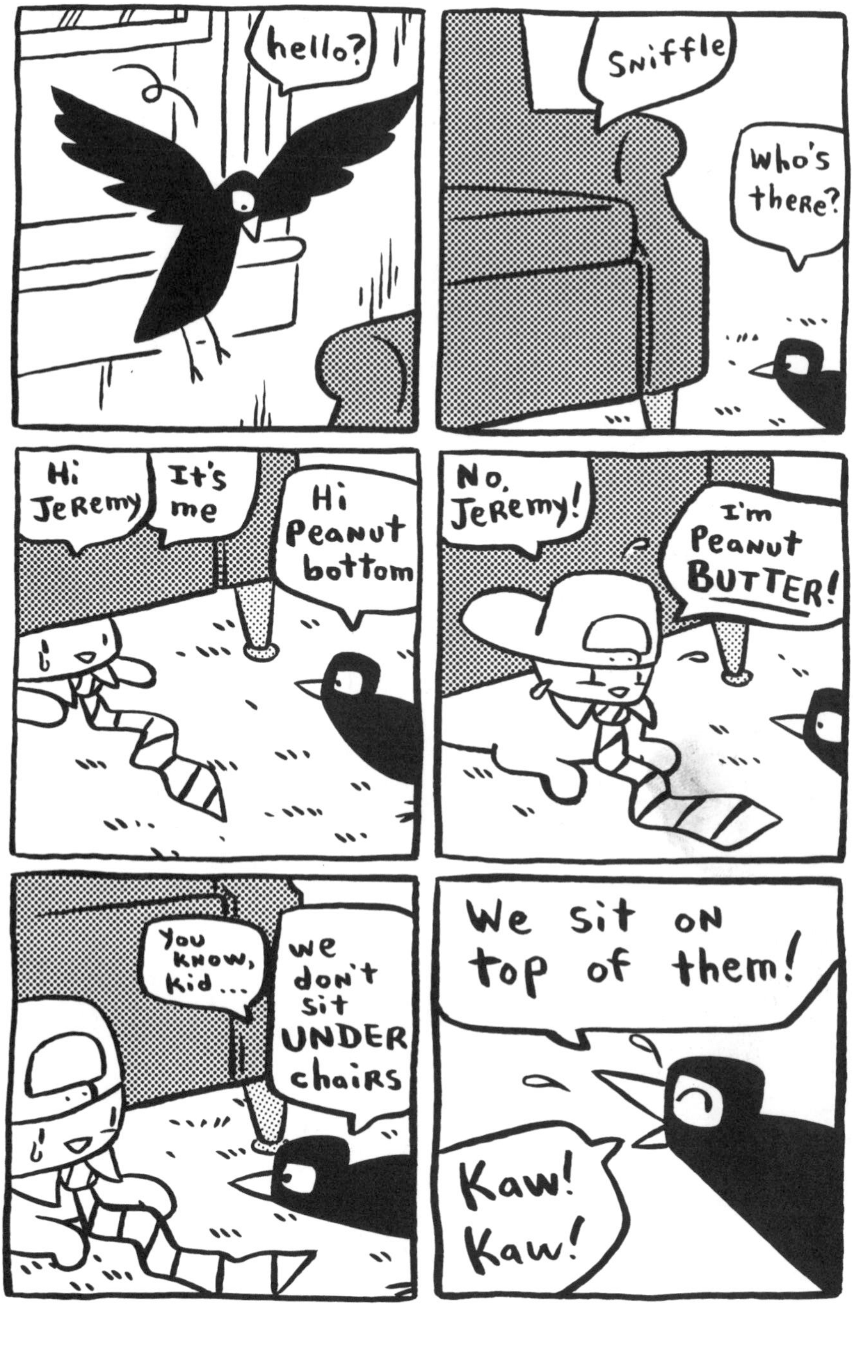
hello?
Sniffle
Who's there?
Hi Jeremy
It's me
Hi Peanut bottom
No, Jeremy!
I'm Peanut BUTTER!
You know, kid...
we don't sit UNDER chairs
We sit on top of them!
Kaw! Kaw!

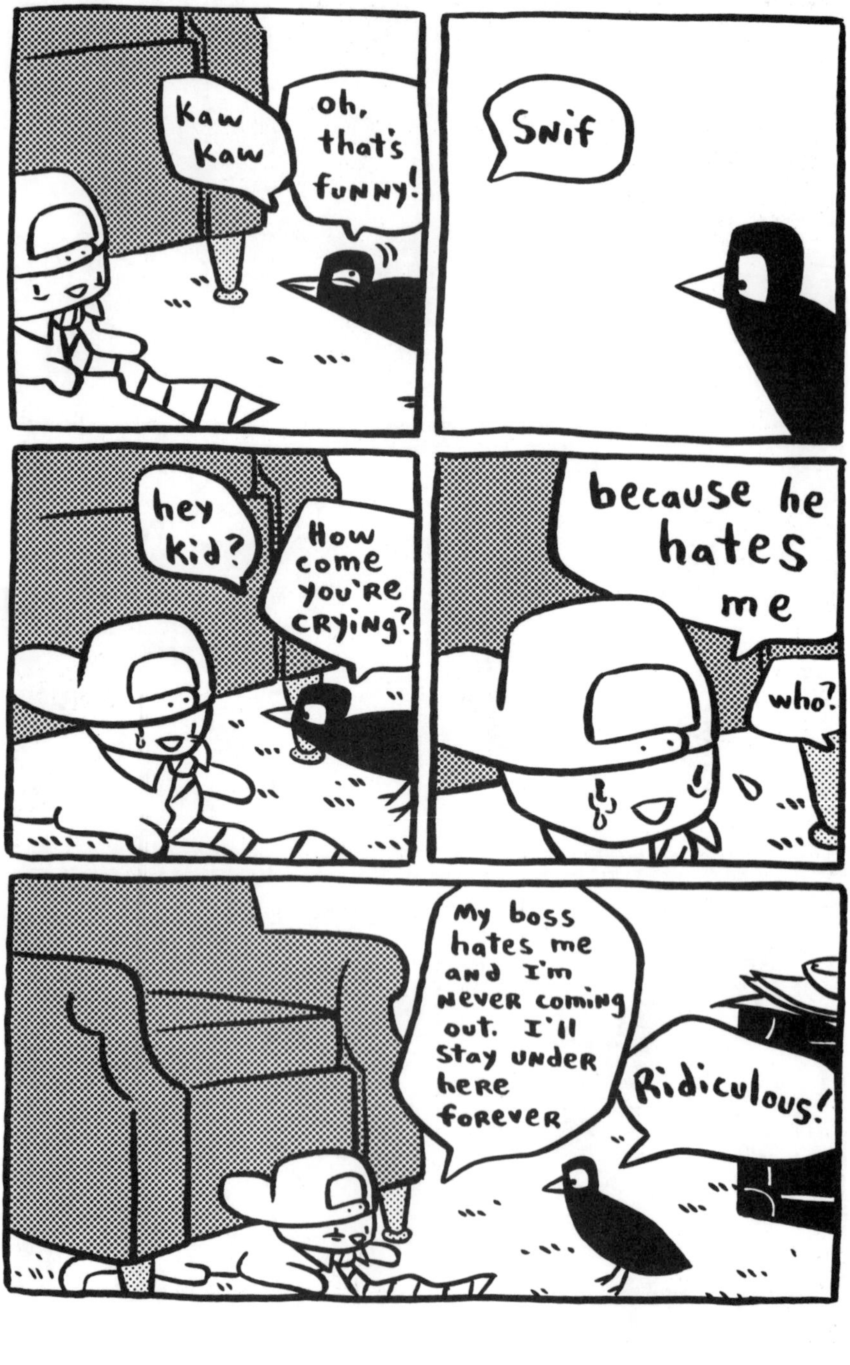
Kaw Kaw
oh, that's FUNNY!
Snif
hey Kid?
How come you're CRYING?
because he hates me
who?
My boss hates me and I'm never coming out. I'll stay under here forever
Ridiculous!

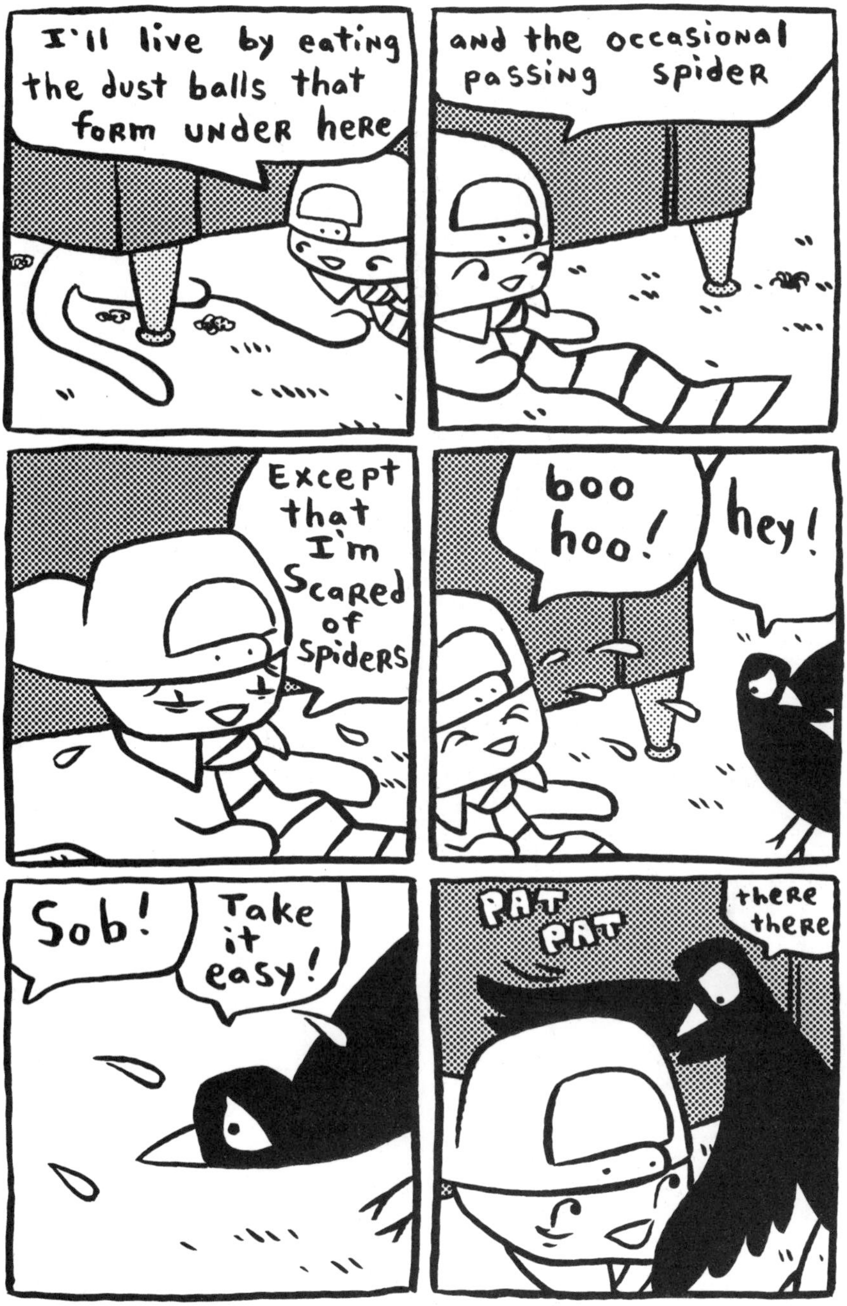
I'll live by eating the dust balls that form under here
and the occasional passing spider
Except that I'm Scared of spiders
boo hoo!
hey!
Sob!
Take it easy!
PAT PAT
there there

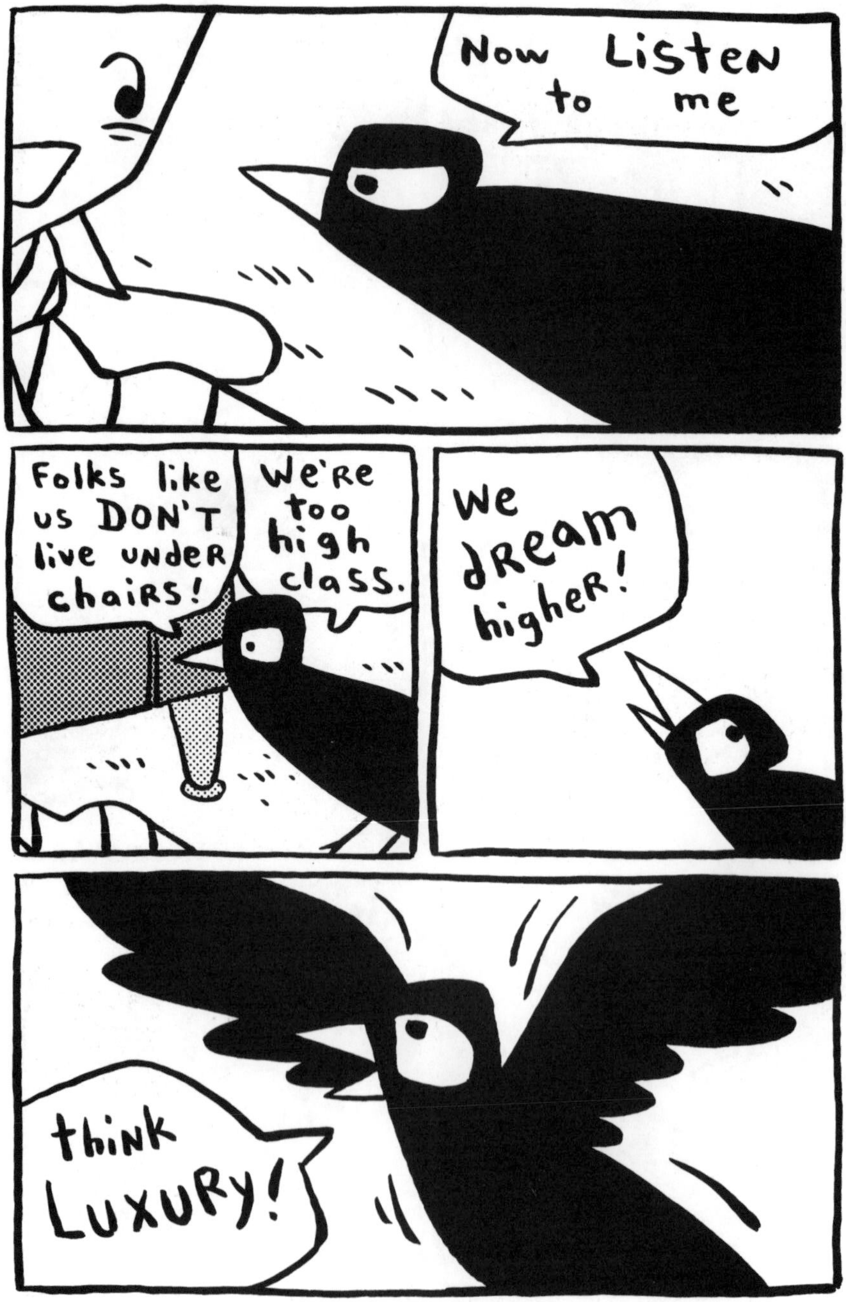
Now LISTEN to me
Folks like us DON'T live UNDER chairs!
We're too high class.
We dream higher!
think LUXURY!

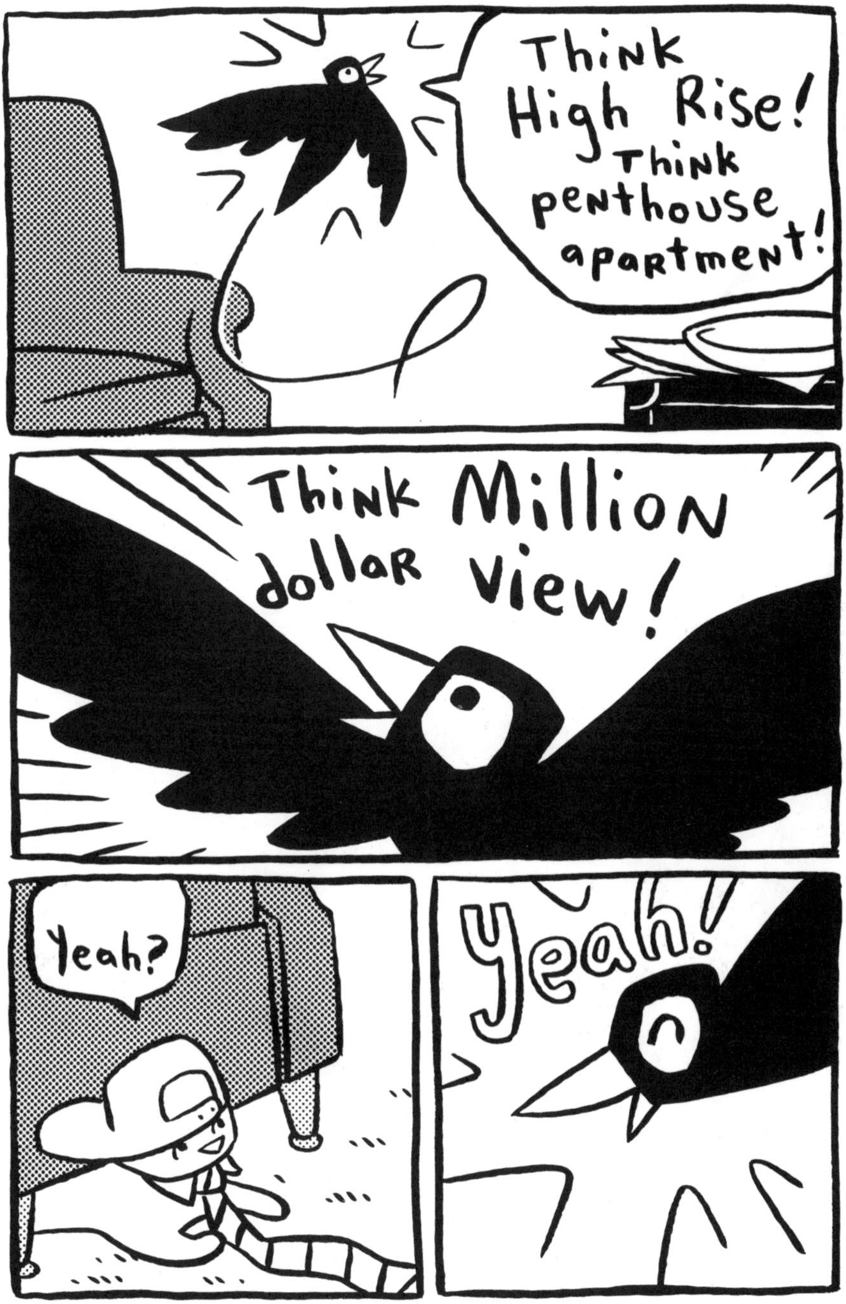
Think High Rise! Think penthouse apartment!
Think Million dollar view!
Yeah?
Yeah!

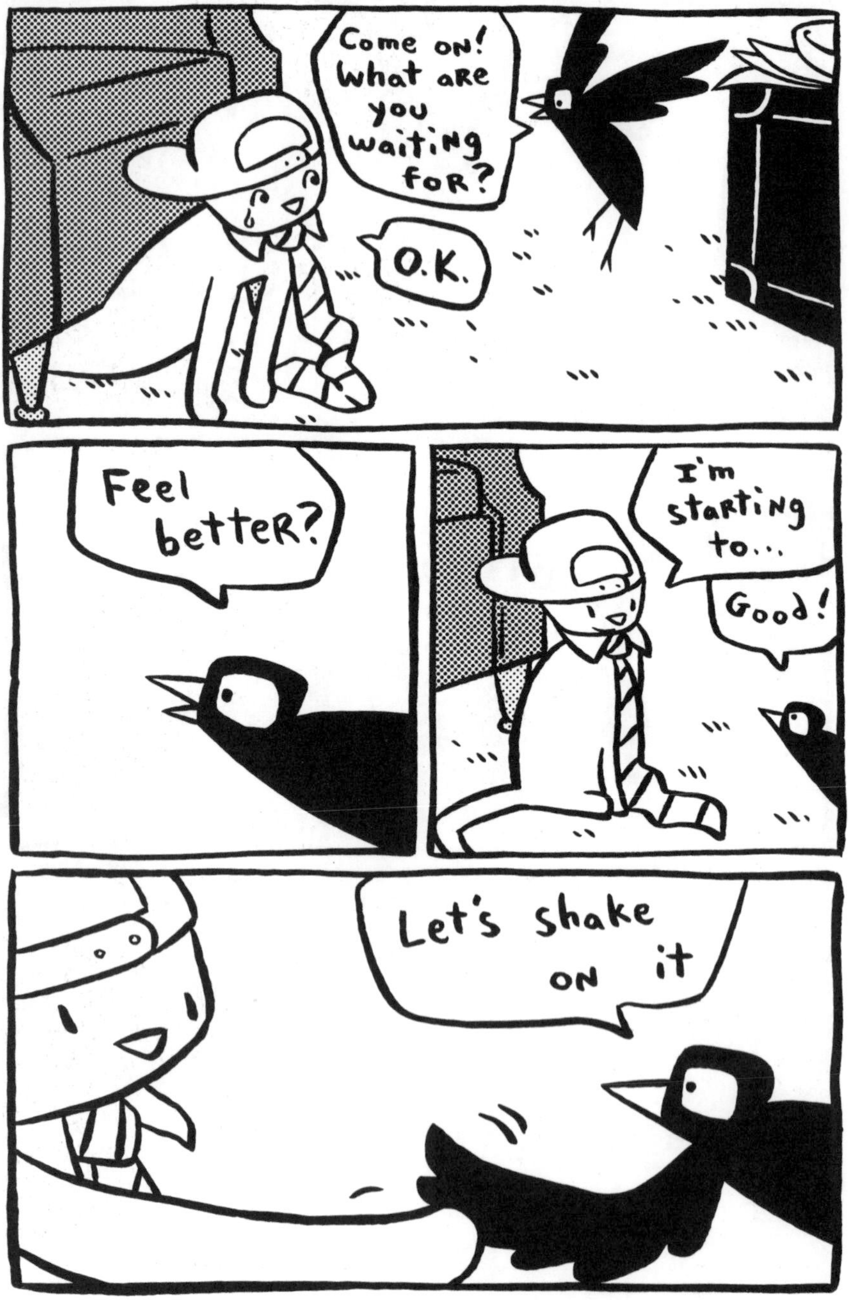
Come on! What are you waiting for?
O.K.
Feel better?
I'm starting to...
Good!
Let's shake on it

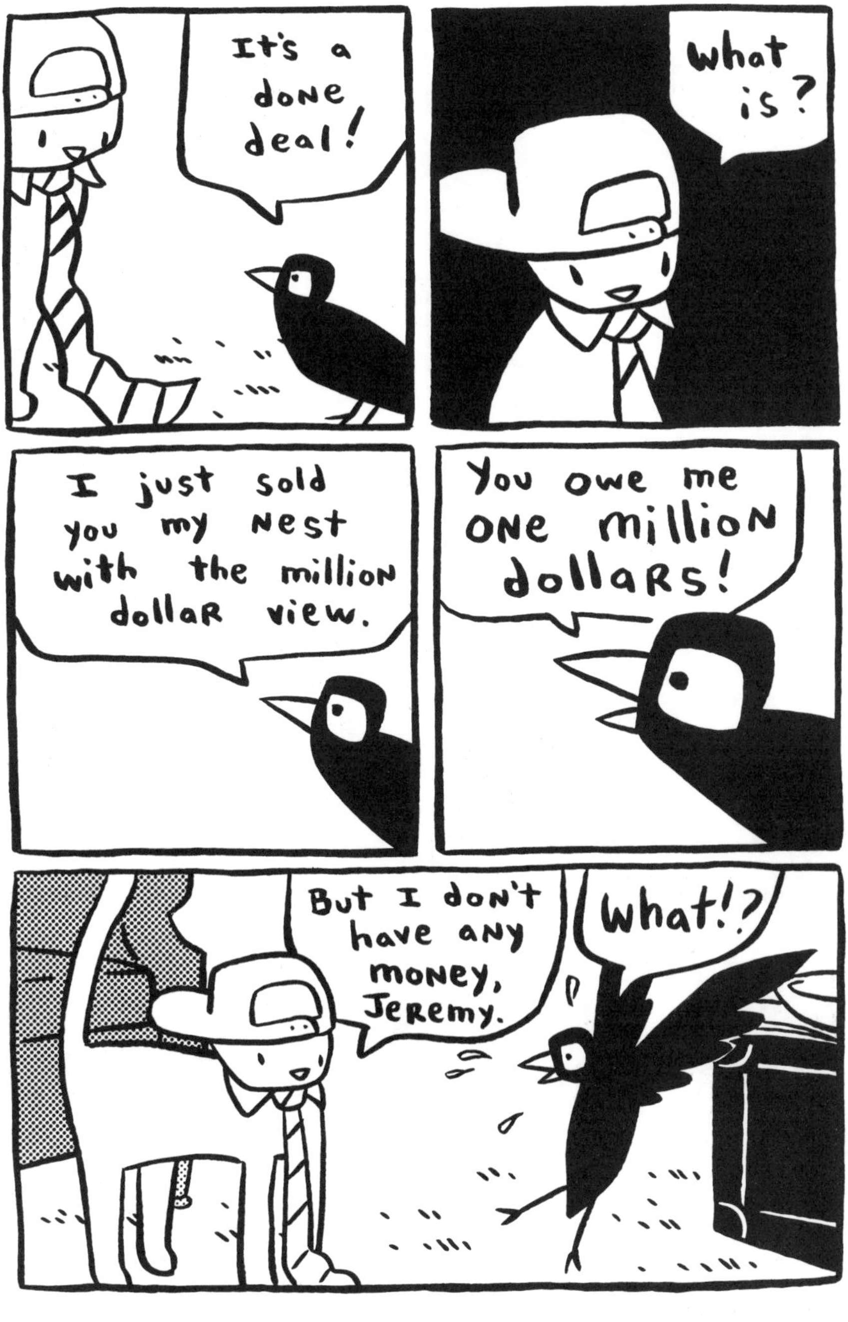
It's a done deal!
What is?
I just sold you my nest with the million dollar view.
You owe me one million dollars!
But I don't have any money, Jeremy.
What!?

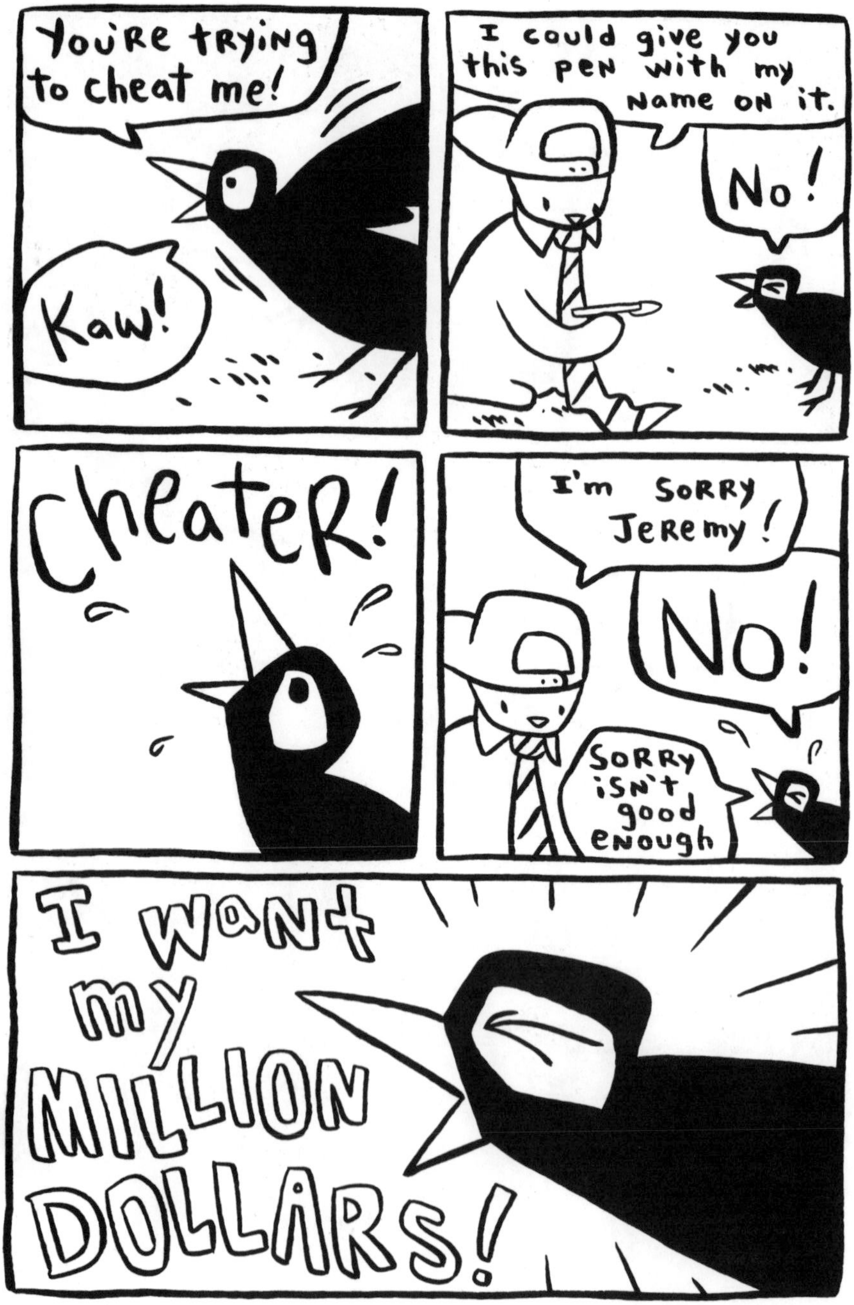
You're trying to cheat me!
Kaw!
I could give you this pen with my name on it.
No!
Cheater!
I'm sorry Jeremy!
No!
Sorry isn't good enough
I want my MILLION DOLLARS!

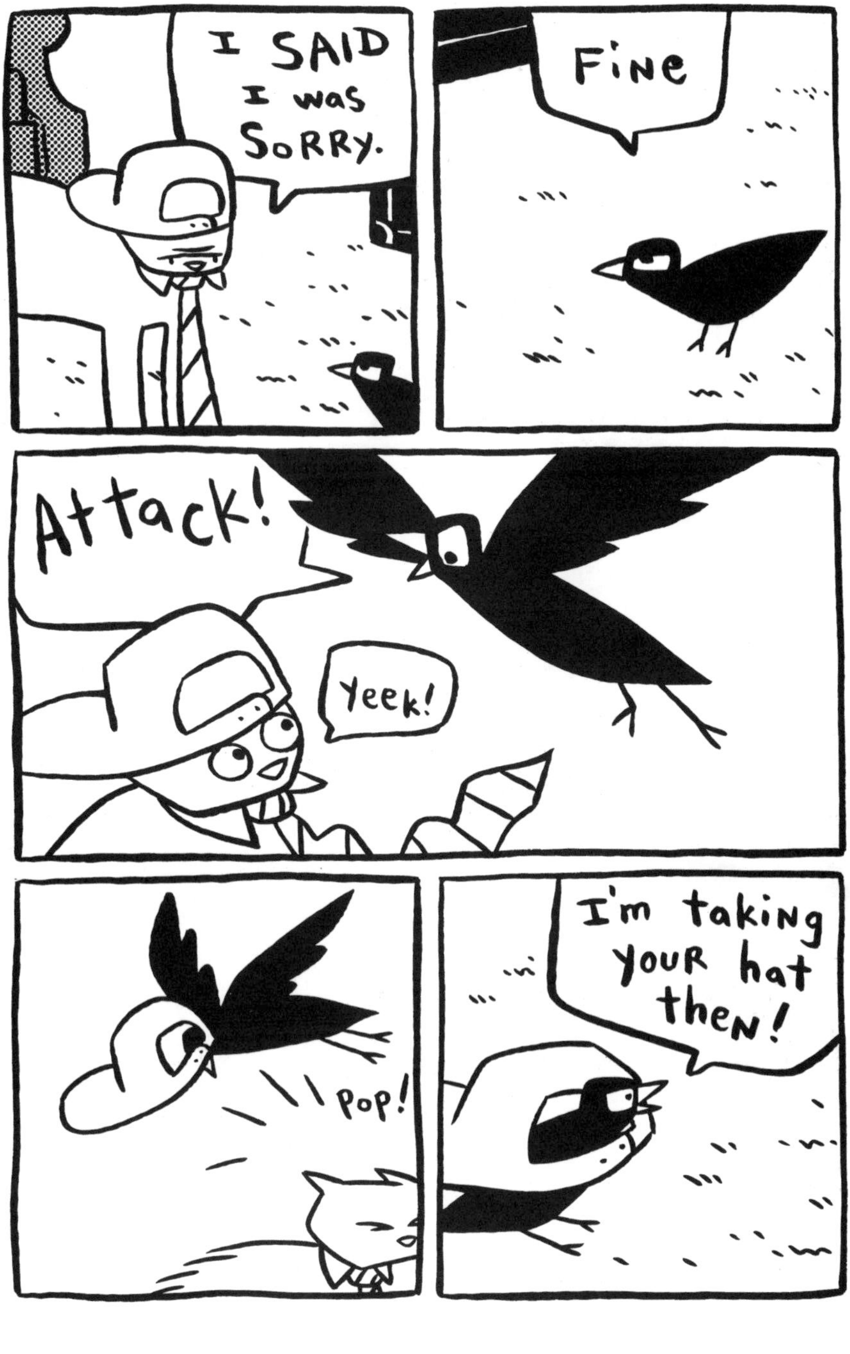
I SAID I was SoRRy.
Fine
Attack!
Yeek!
pop!
I'm taking your hat then!

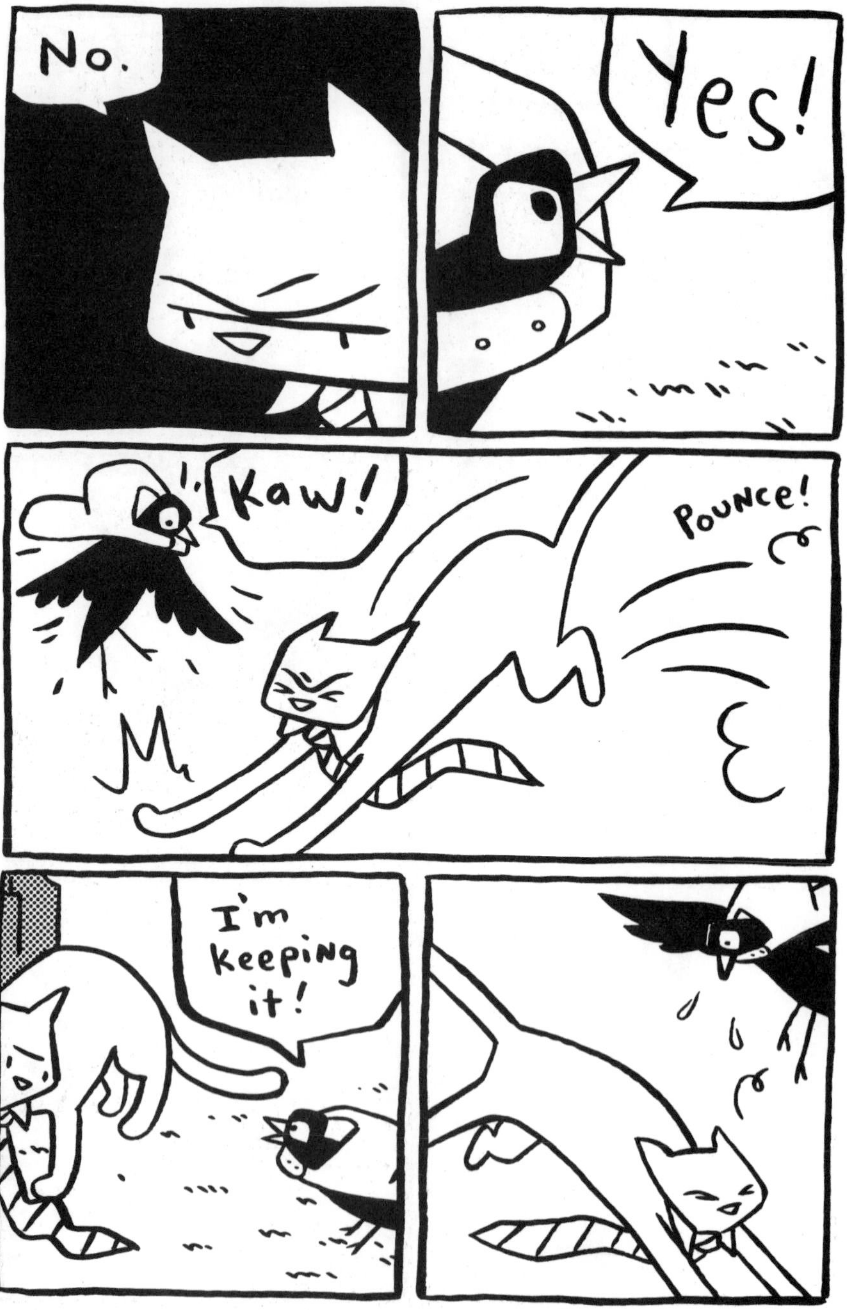
No.
Yes!
Kaw!
Pounce!
I'm keeping it!

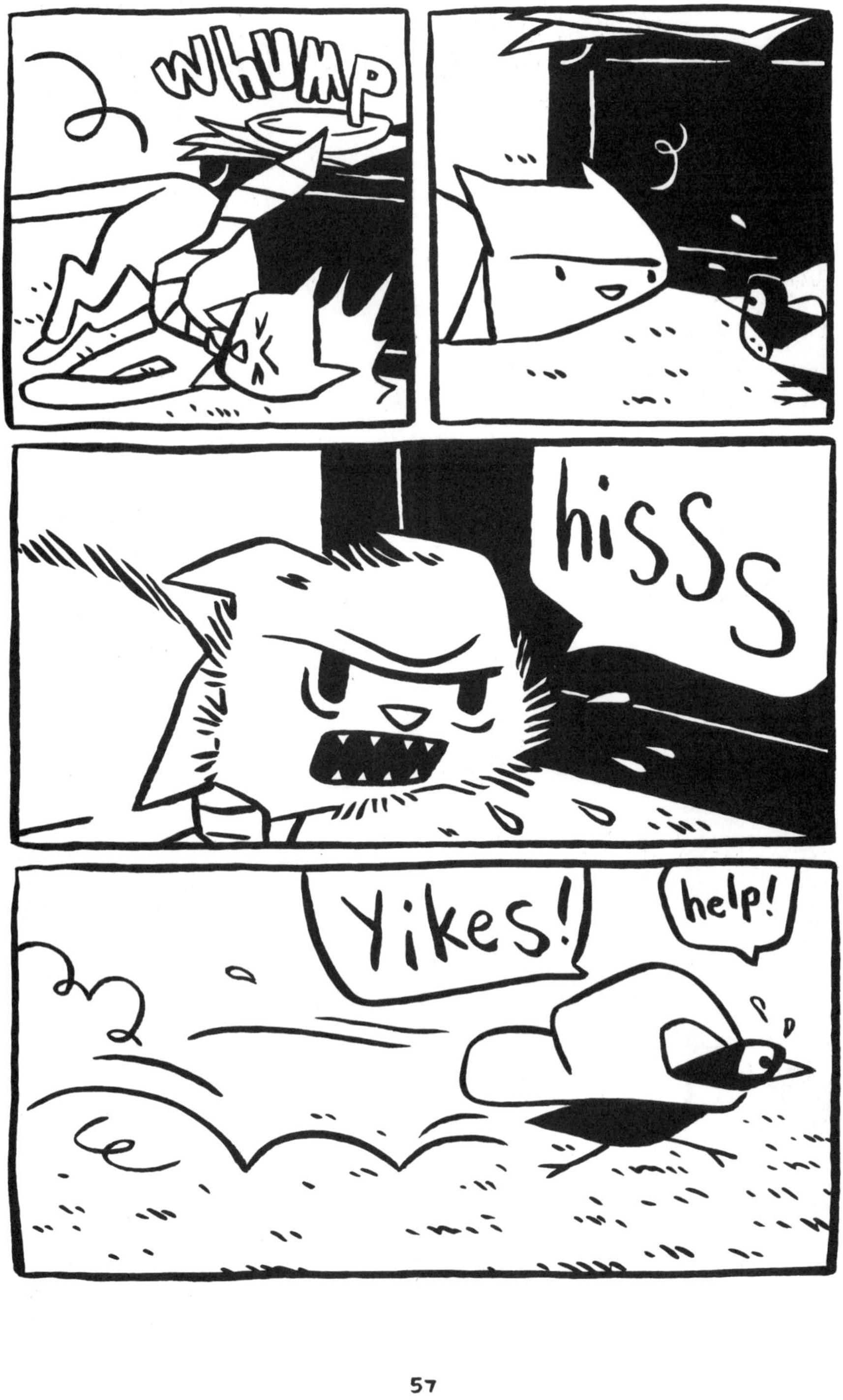
WHUMP
hisss
Yikes!
help!

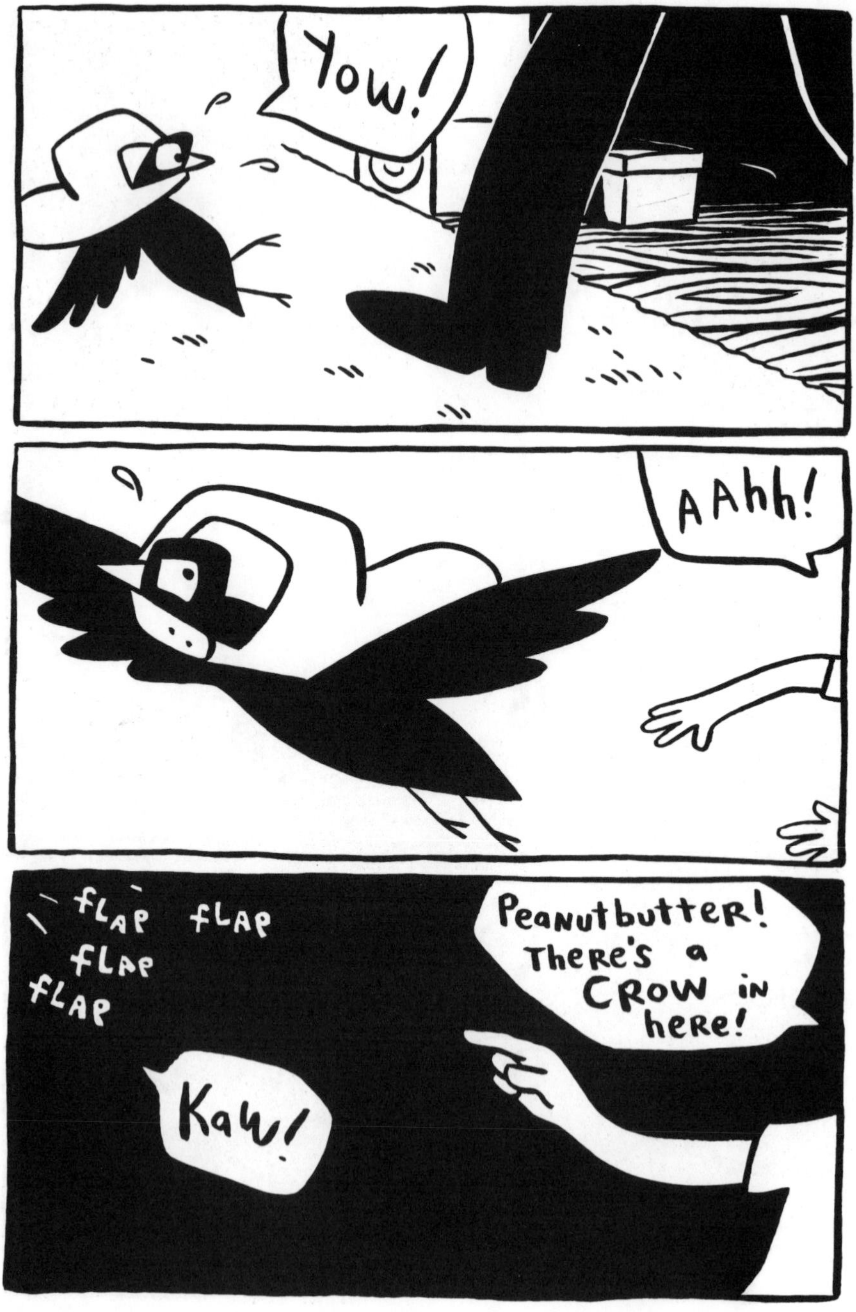
Yow!
AAhh!
flap flap
flap
flap
Peanutbutter! There's a CROW in here!
Kaw!

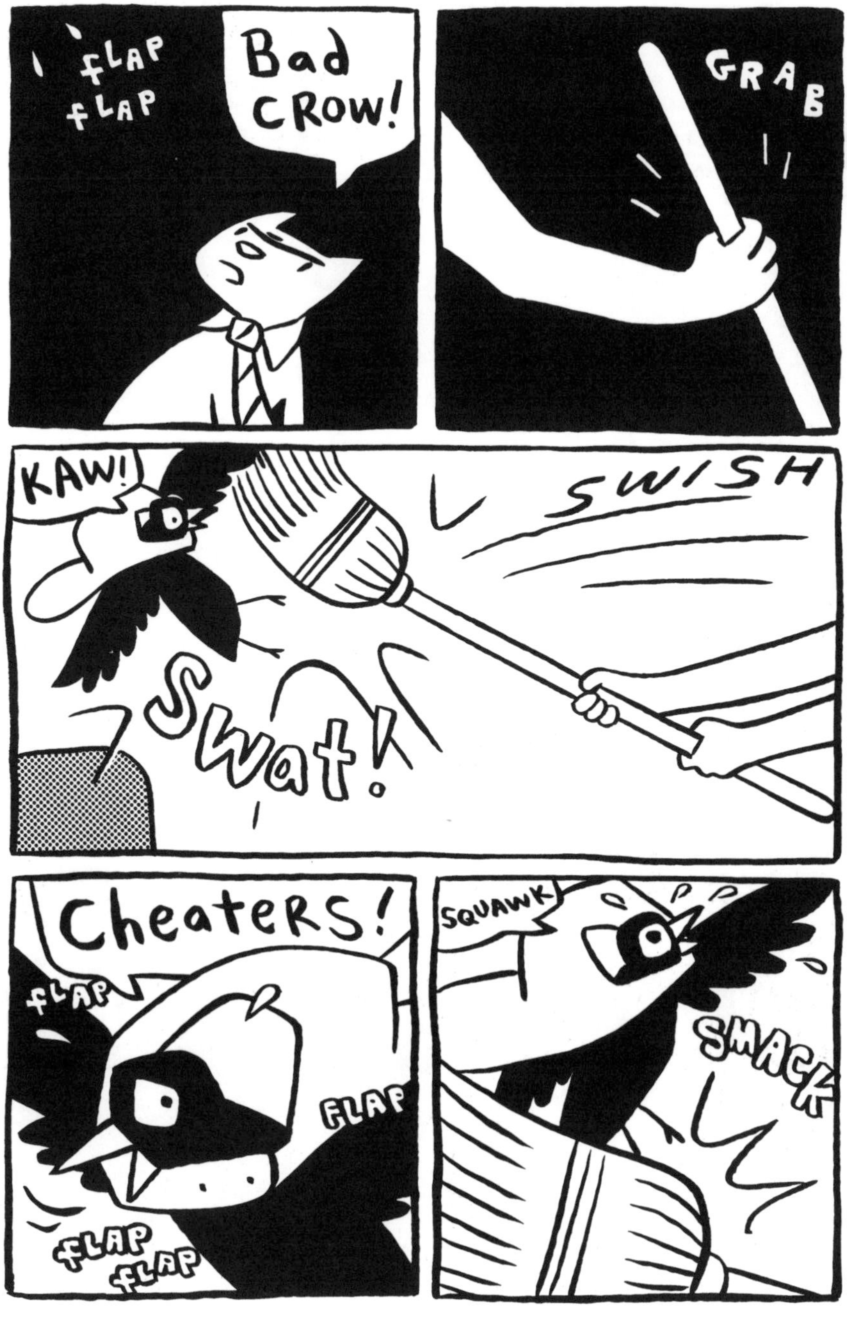
FLAP
FLAP
Bad CROW!
GRAB
KAW!
SWISH
Swat!
Cheaters!
FLAP
FLAP
FLAP
FLAP
SQUAWK
SMACK

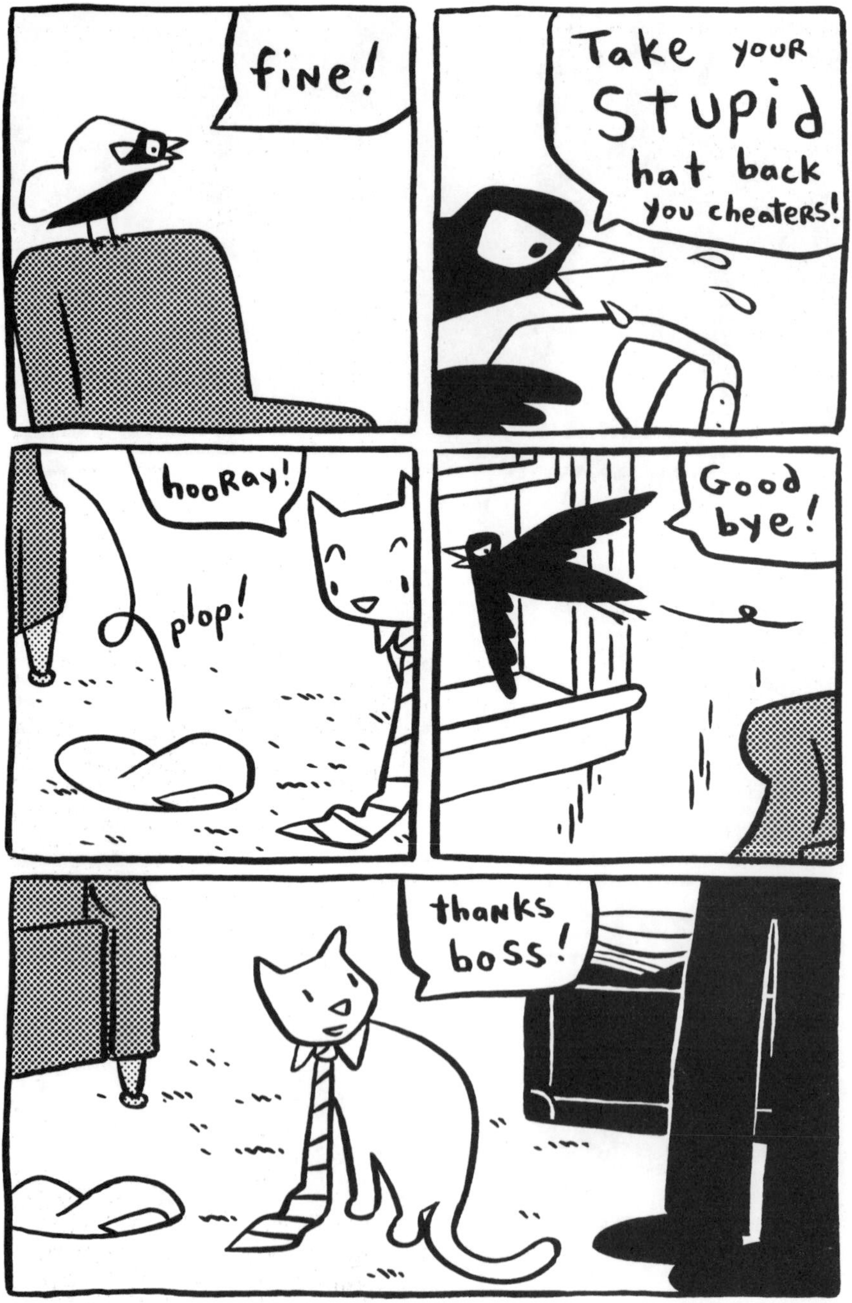
fine!
Take your STUPID hat back you cheaters!
hooray!
plop!
Good bye!
thanks boss!

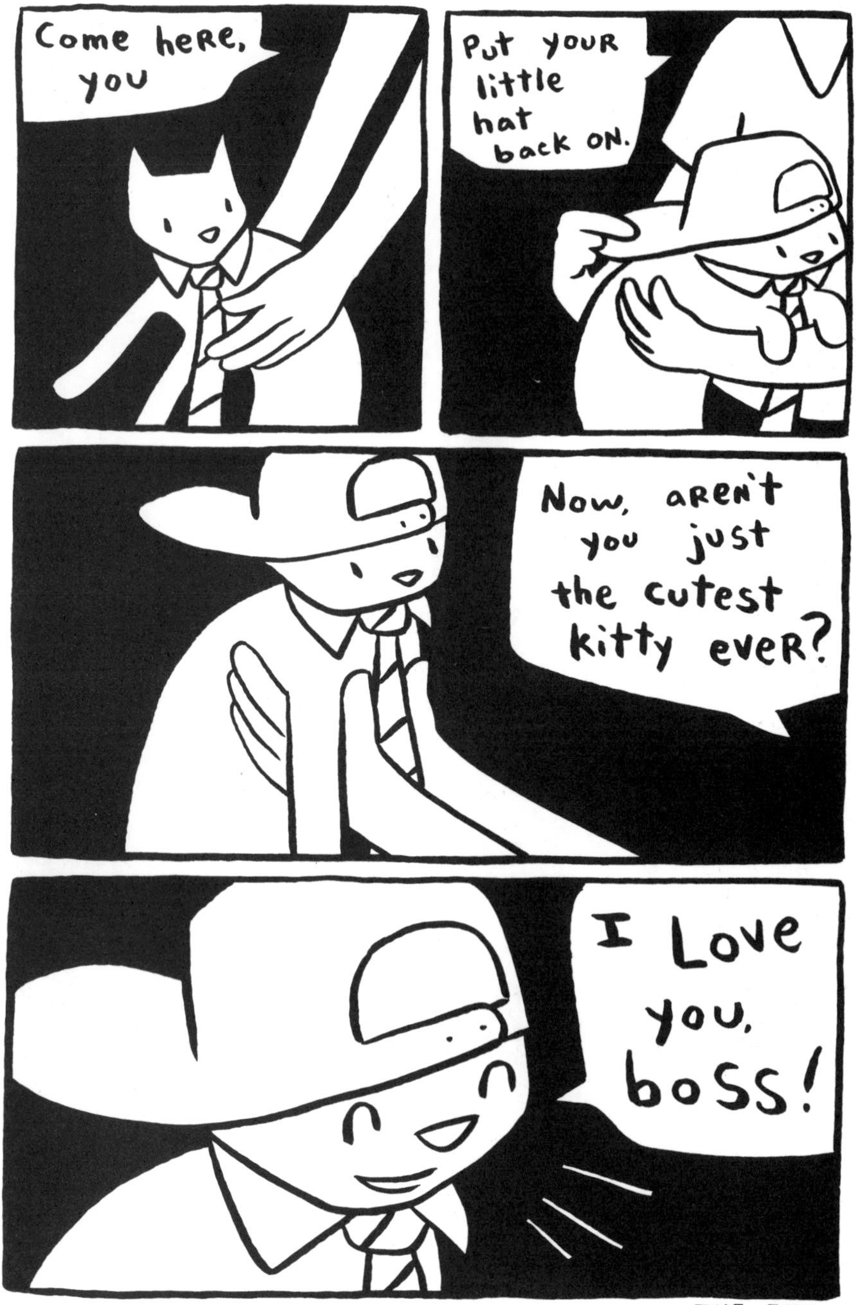
Come here, you
Put your little hat back on.
Now, aren't you just the cutest kitty ever?
I Love you, boss!

THE END

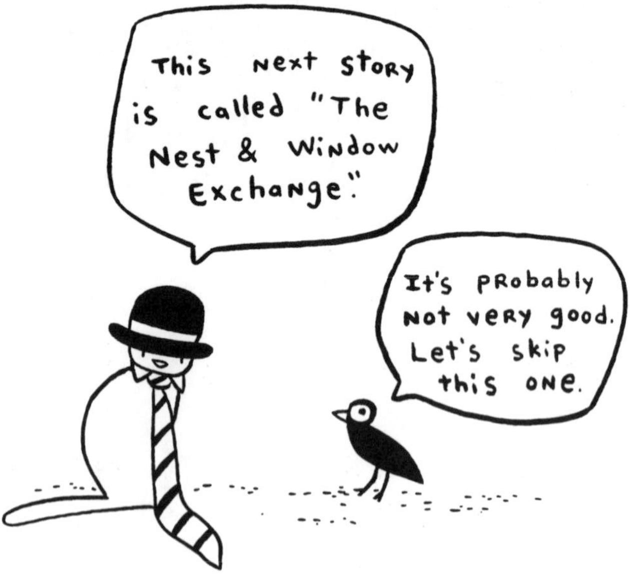
This next story is called "The Nest & Window Exchange."
It's probably not very good. Let's skip this one.

THE NEST & WINDOW EXCHANGE

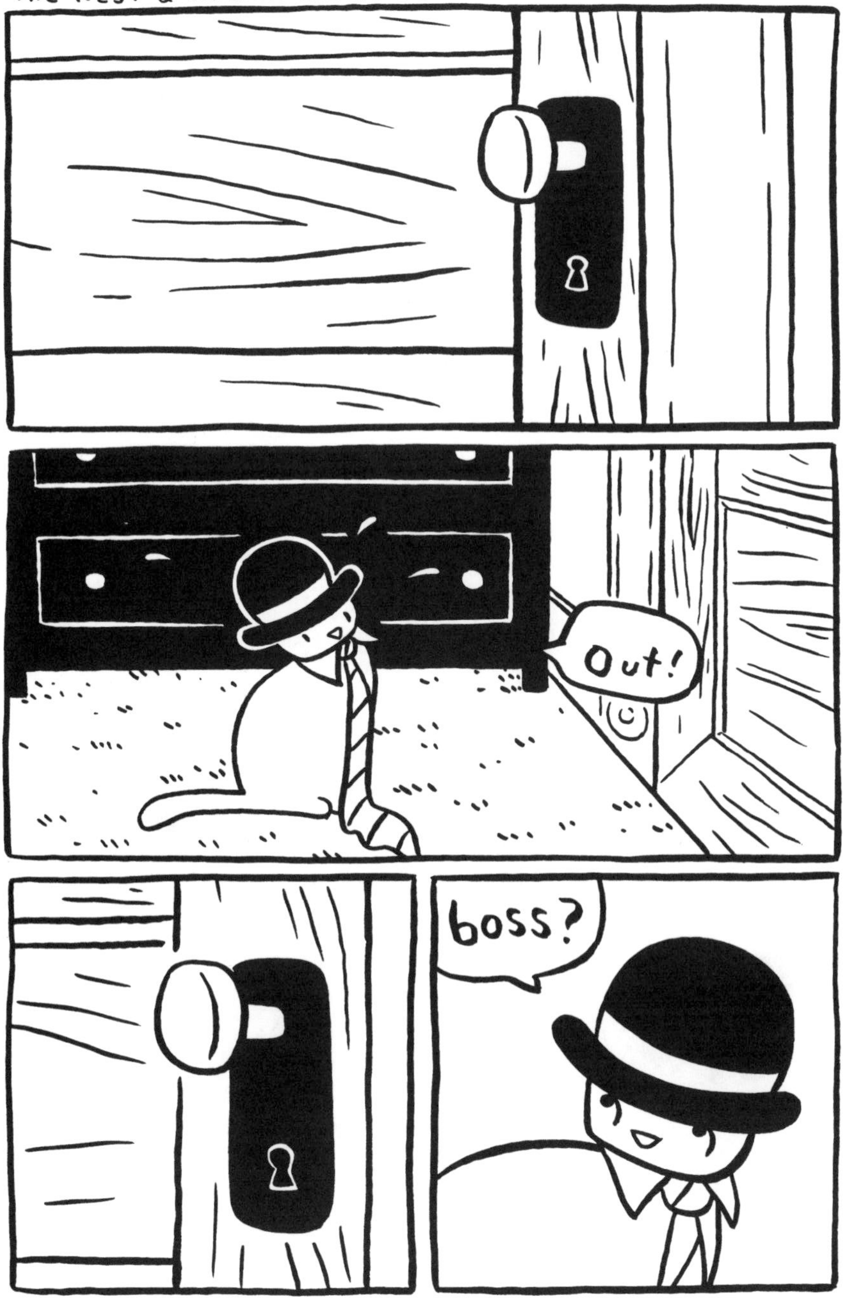
Out!
boss?

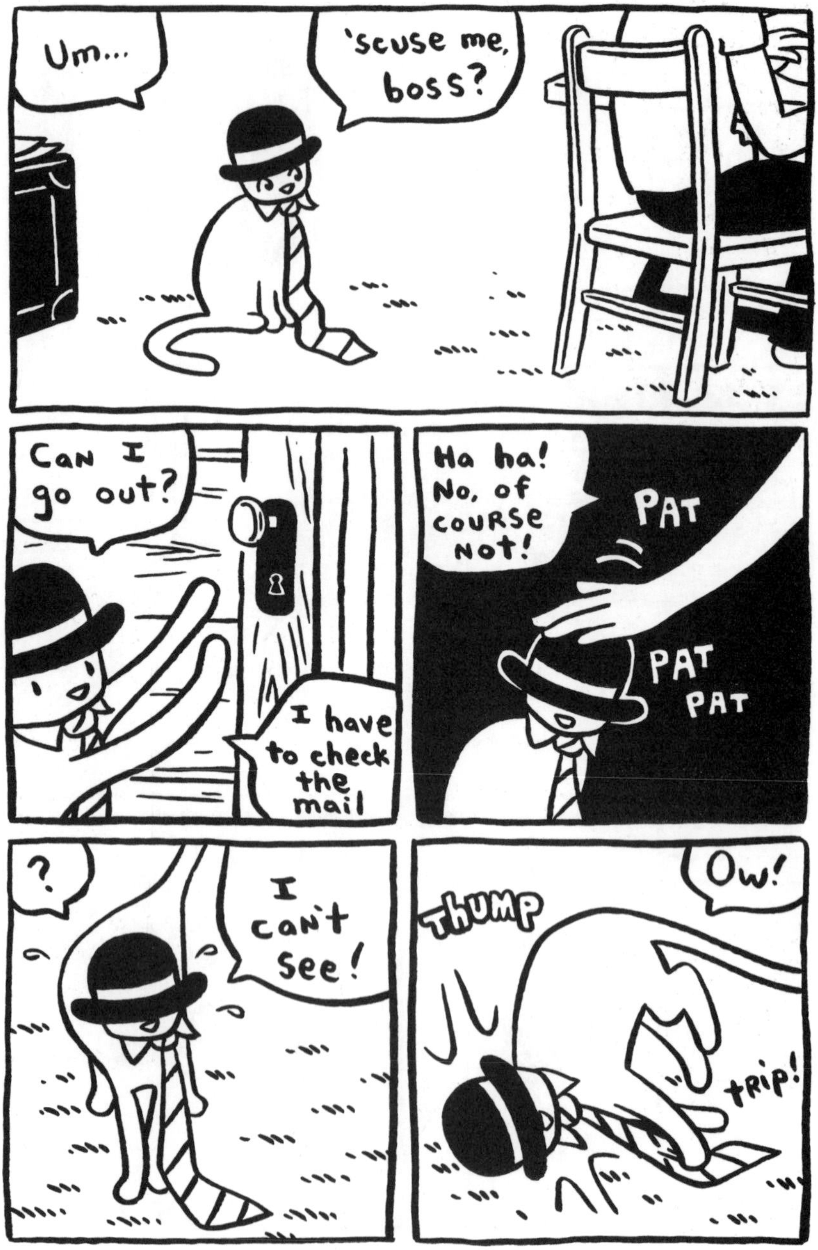
Um...
'scuse me, boss?
Can I go out?
I have to check the mail
Ha ha! No, of course not!
PAT
PAT
PAT
?
I can't see!
THUMP
Ow!
TRIP!

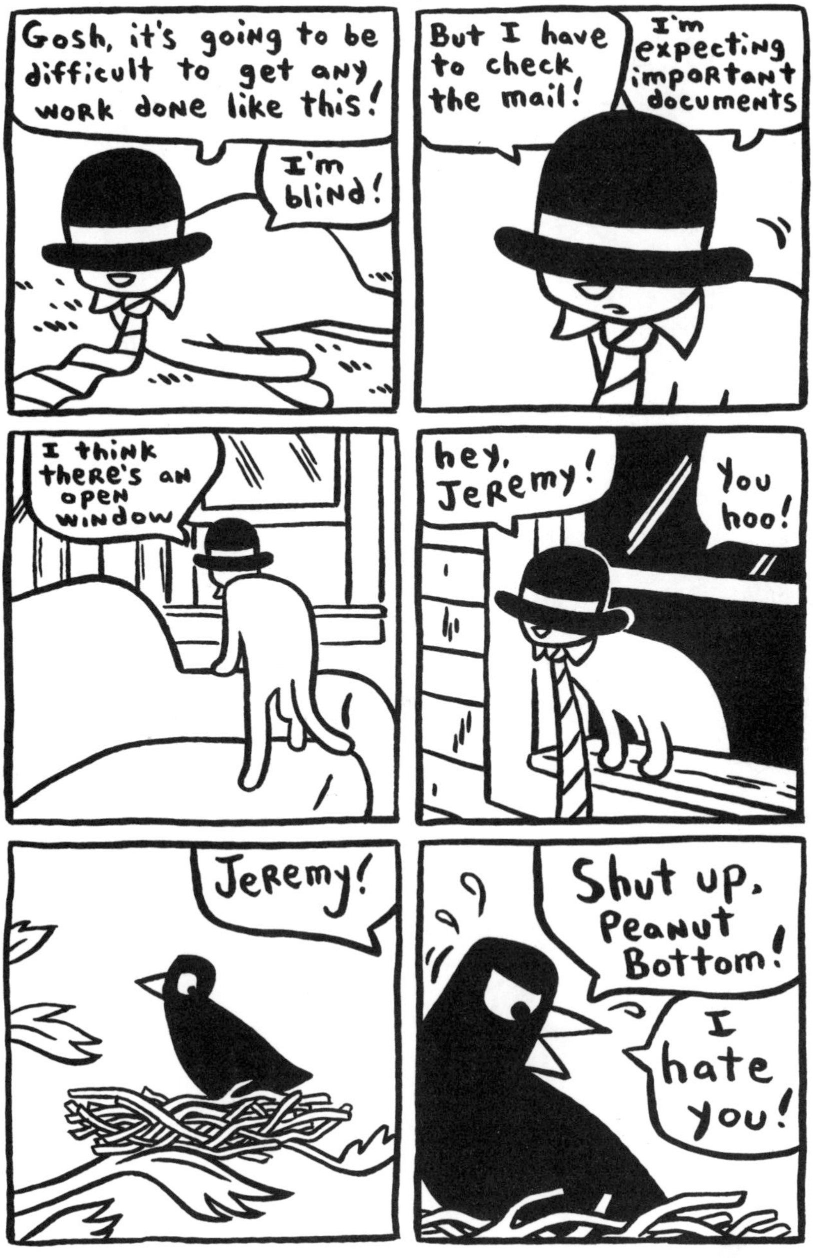
Gosh, it's going to be difficult to get any work done like this!
I'm blind!
But I have to check the mail!
I'm expecting important documents
I think there's an open window
hey, Jeremy!
You hoo!
Jeremy!
Shut up, Peanut Bottom!
I hate you!

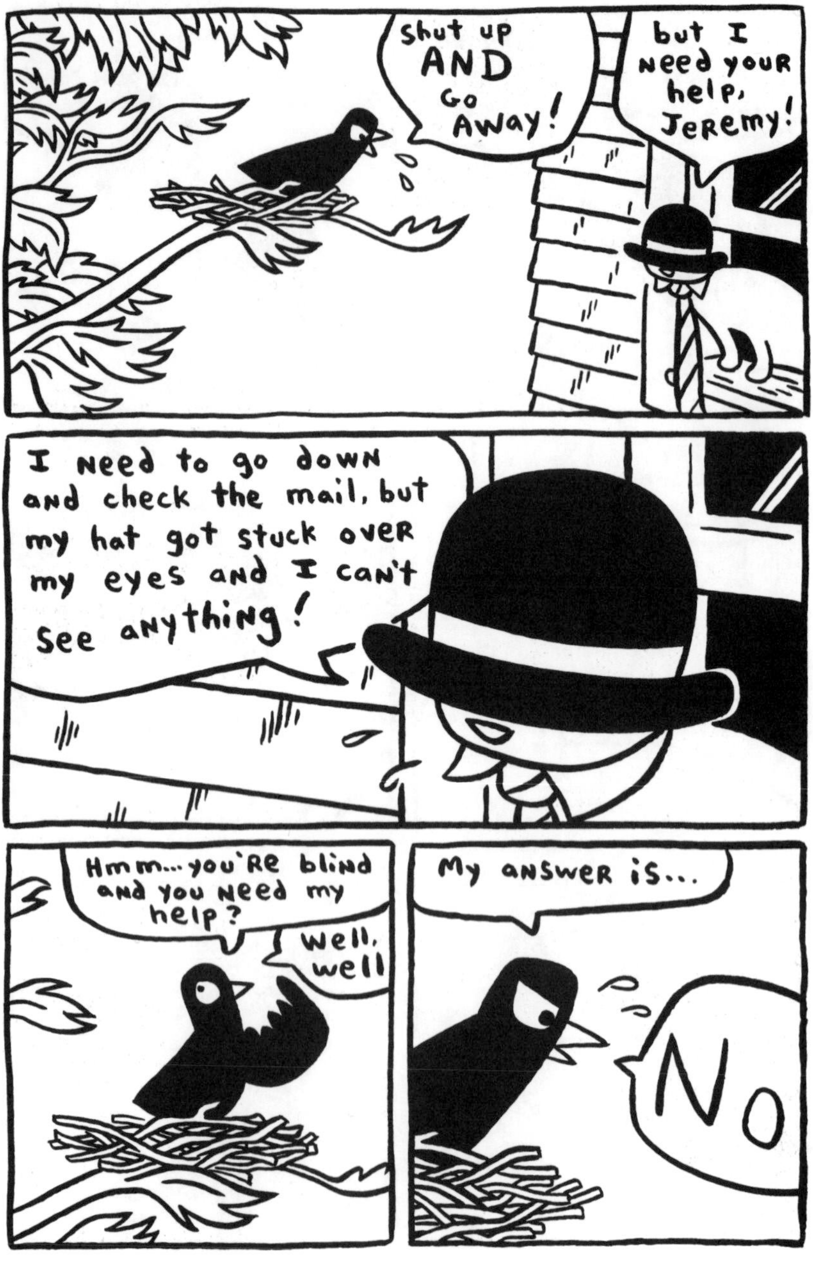
Shut up AND Go AWay!
but I need your help, Jeremy!
I need to go down and check the mail, but my hat got stuck over my eyes and I can't see anything!
Hmm... you're blind and you need my help?
well, well
My answer is...
No

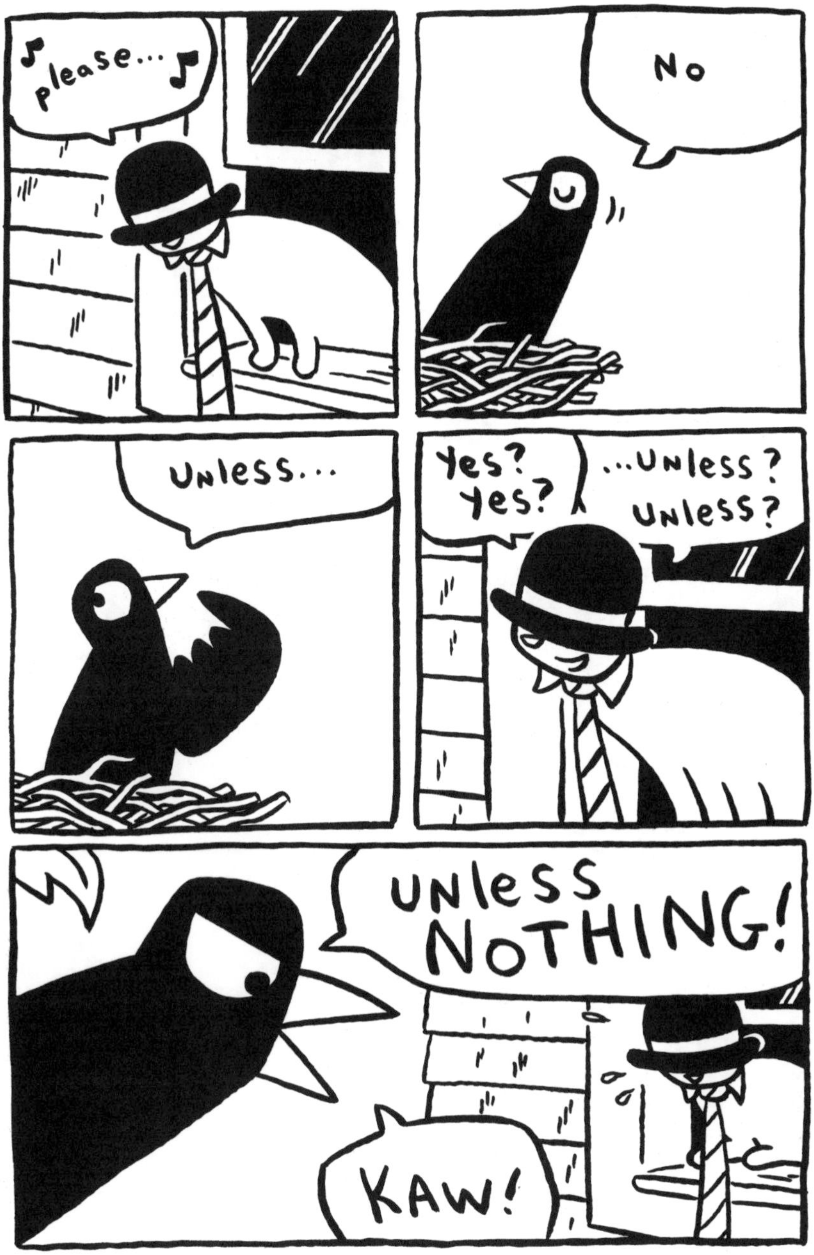
please...
No
Unless...
Yes? Yes?
...Unless? Unless?
UNLESS NOTHING!
KAW!

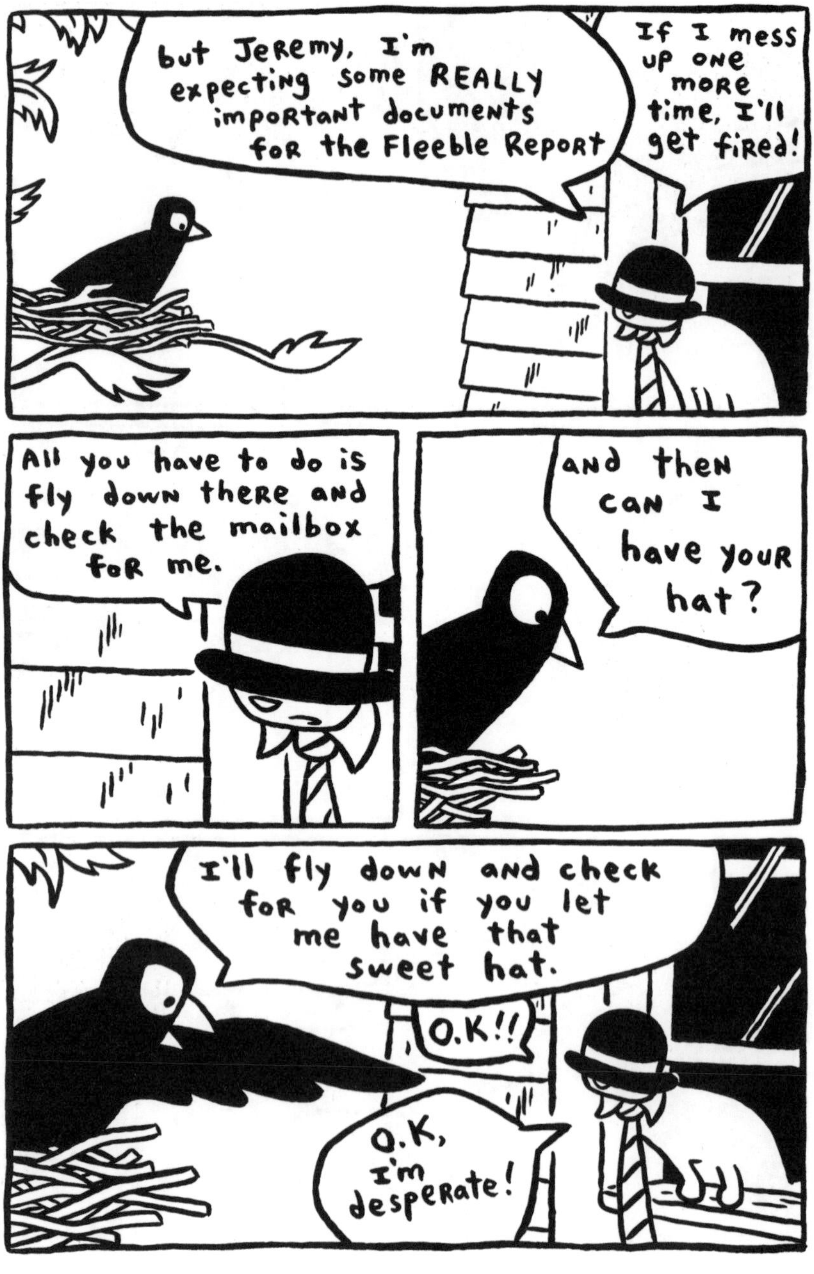
but Jeremy, I'm expecting some REALLY important documents for the Fleeble Report
If I mess up one more time, I'll get fired!
All you have to do is fly down there and check the mailbox for me.
and then can I have your hat?
I'll fly down and check for you if you let me have that sweet hat.
O.K!!
O.K, I'm desperate!

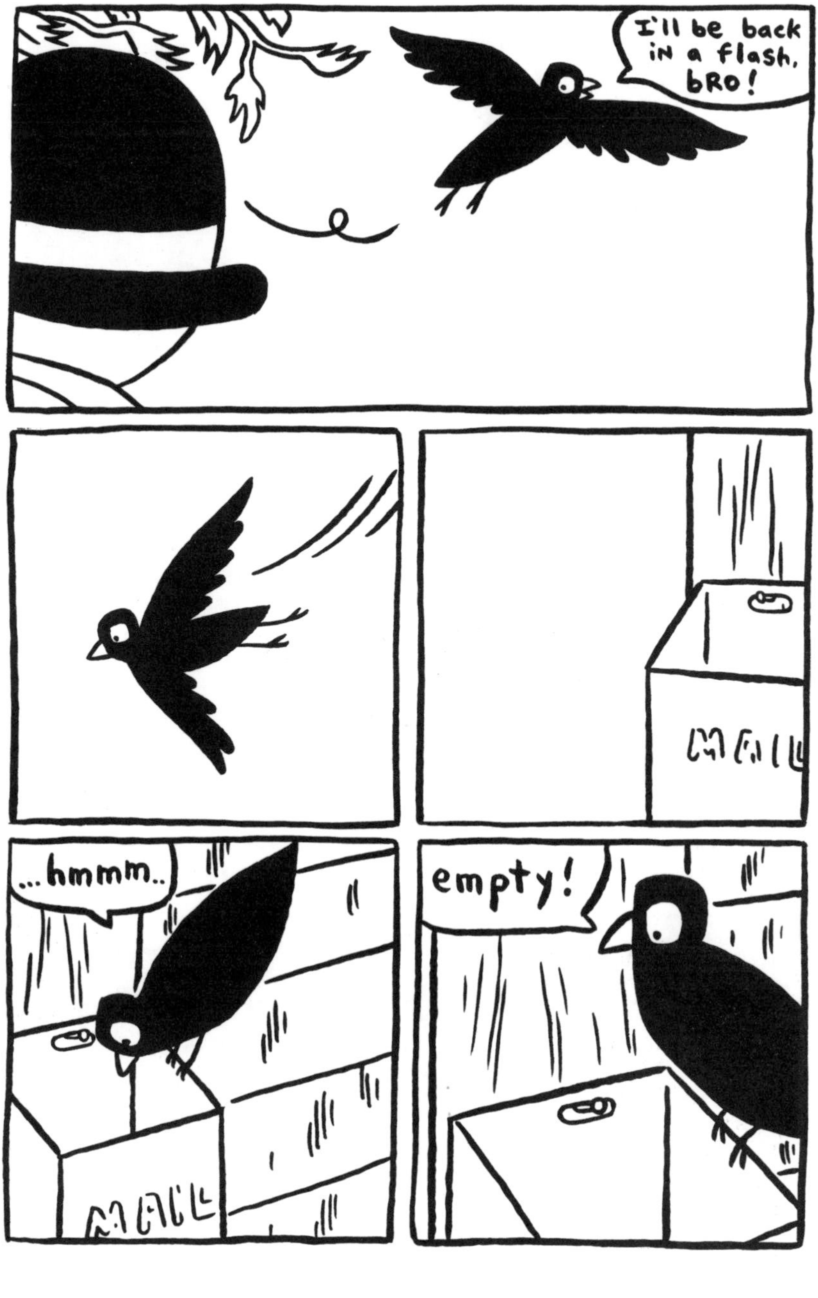
I'll be back in a flash, bRO!
MAIL
...hmmm..
MAIL
empty!

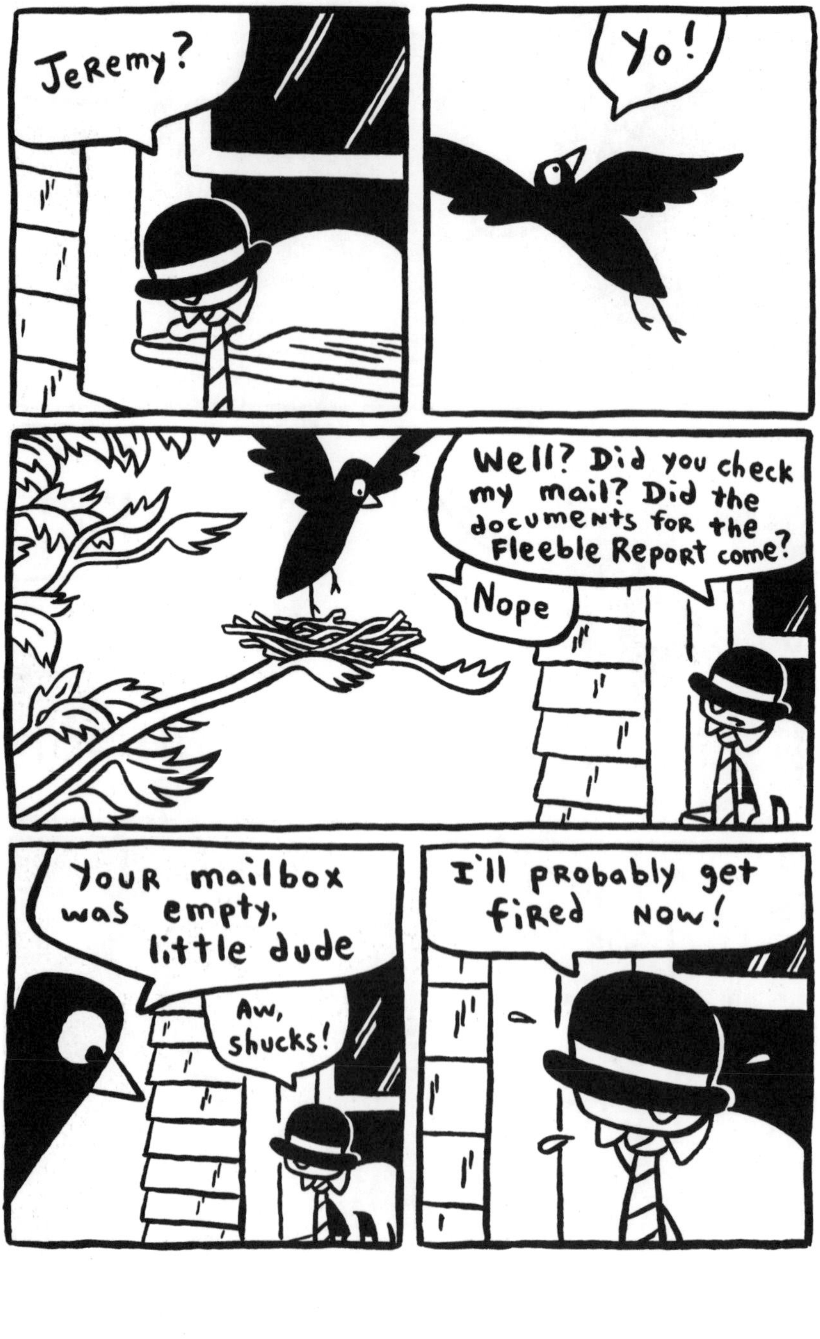
Jeremy?
Yo!
Well? Did you check my mail? Did the documents for the Fleeble Report come?
Nope
Your mailbox was empty, little dude
Aw, shucks!
I'll probably get fired now!

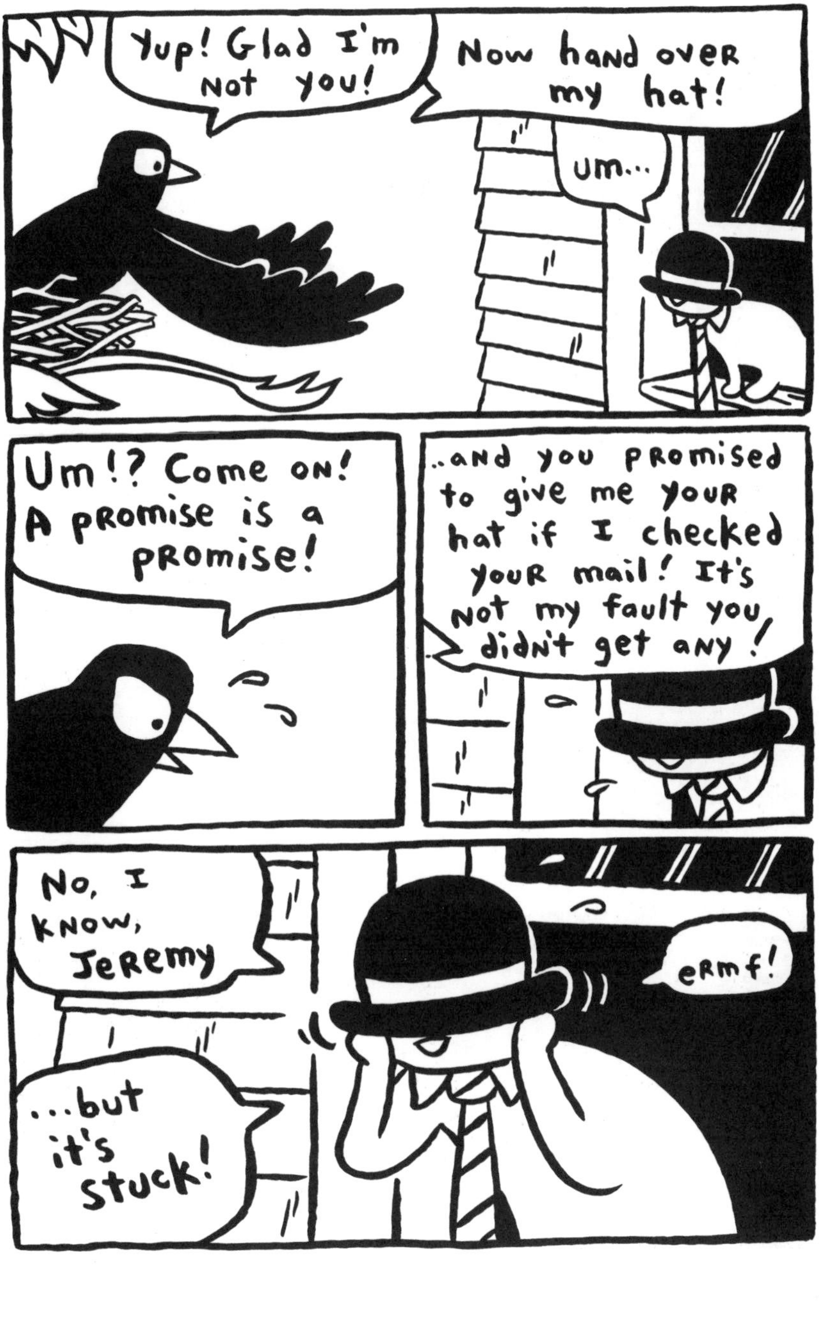
Yup! Glad I'm not you!
Now hand over my hat!
Um...
Um!? Come on! A promise is a promise!
..and you promised to give me your hat if I checked your mail! It's not my fault you didn't get any!
No, I know, Jeremy
...but it's stuck!
ermf!

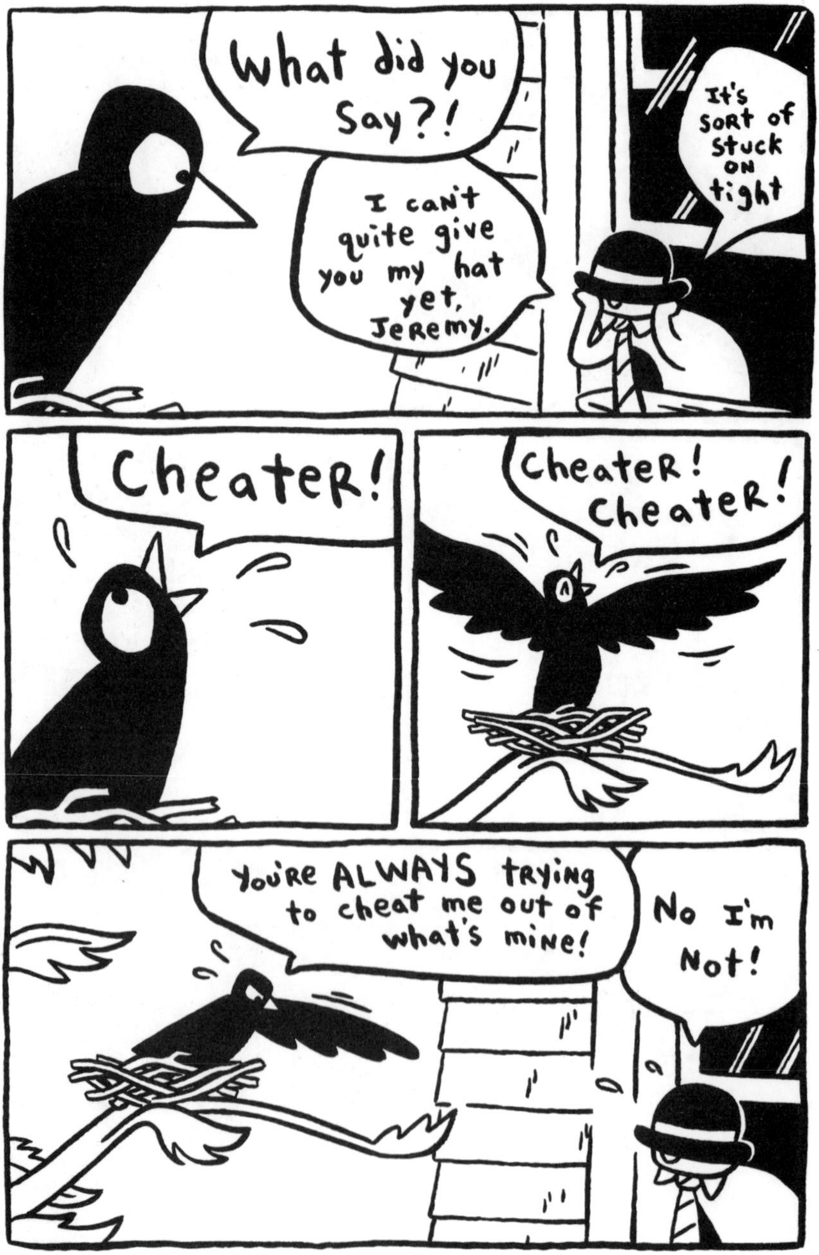
What did you say?!
I can't quite give you my hat yet, Jeremy.
It's sort of stuck on tight
Cheater!
Cheater! Cheater!
You're ALWAYS trying to cheat me out of what's mine!
No I'm Not!

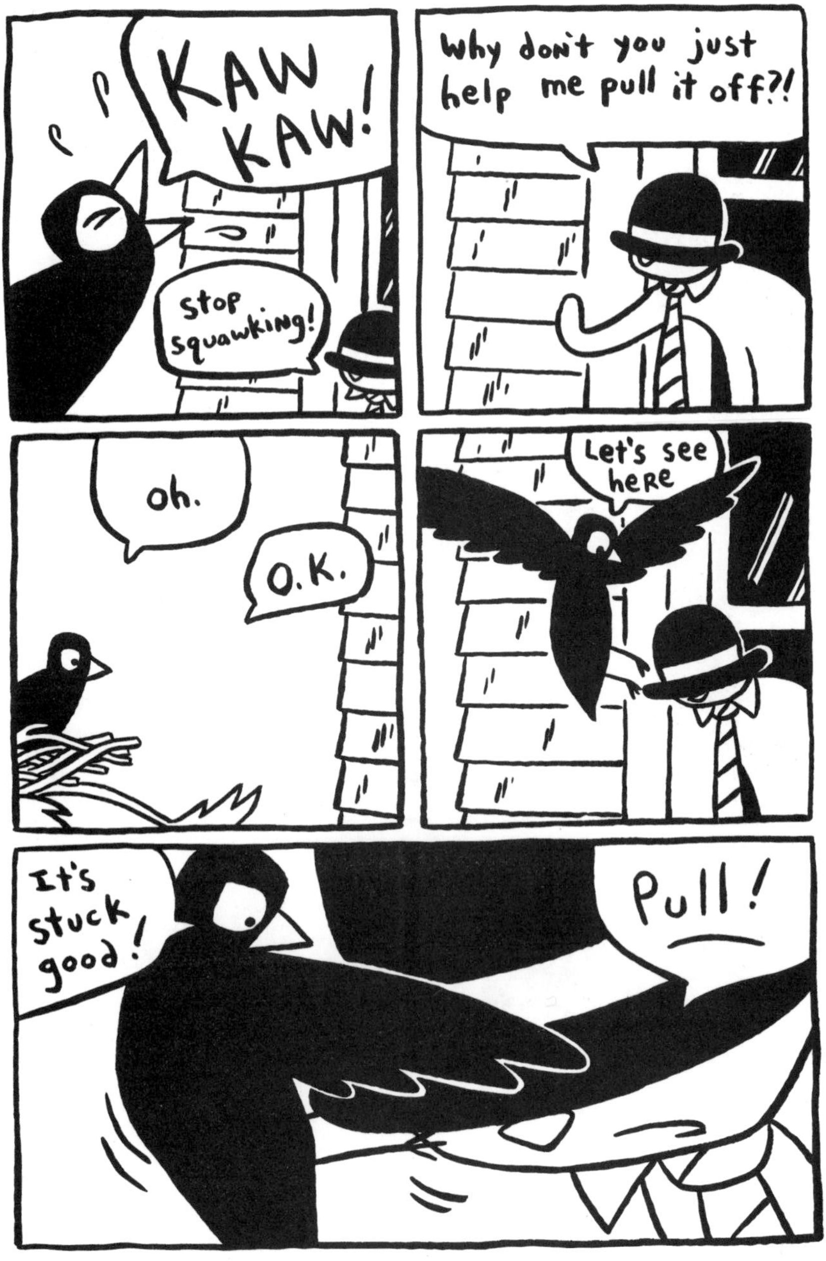
KAW KAW!
Stop squawking!
Why don't you just help me pull it off?!
oh.
O.K.
Let's see here
It's stuck good!
Pull!

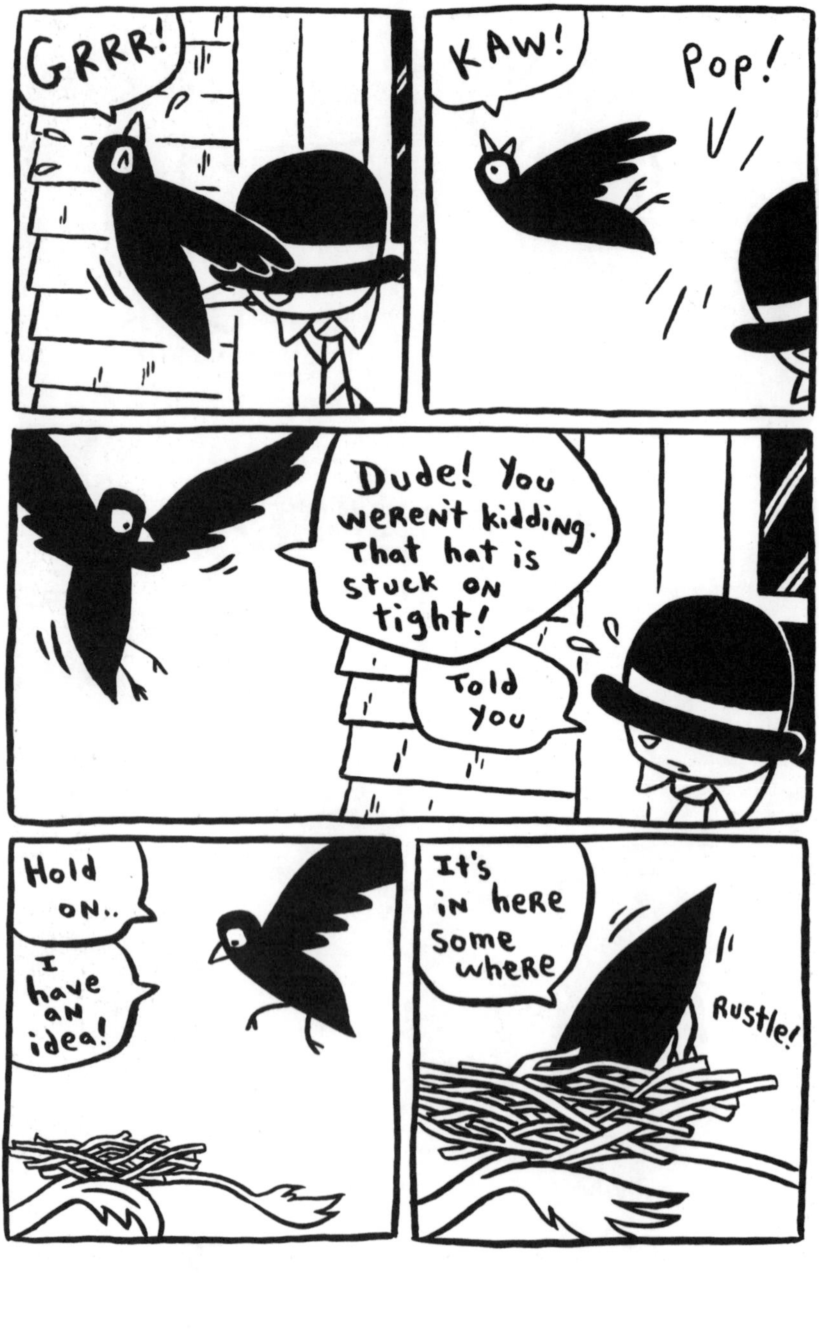
GRRR!
KAW!
Pop!
Dude! You werent kidding. That hat is stuck on tight!
Told you
Hold on..
I have an idea!
It's in here some where
Rustle!

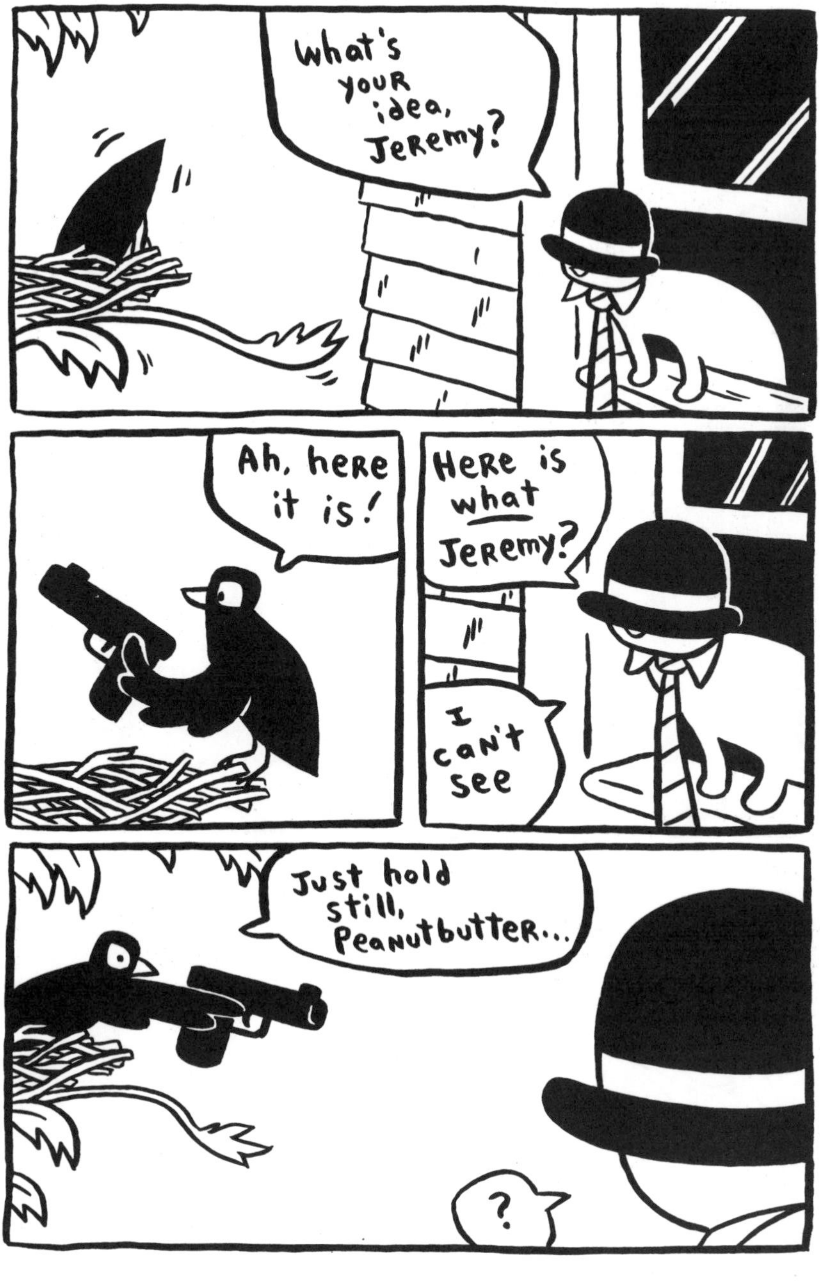
What's your idea, Jeremy?
Ah, here it is!
Here is what Jeremy?
I can't see
Just hold still, Peanutbutter...
?

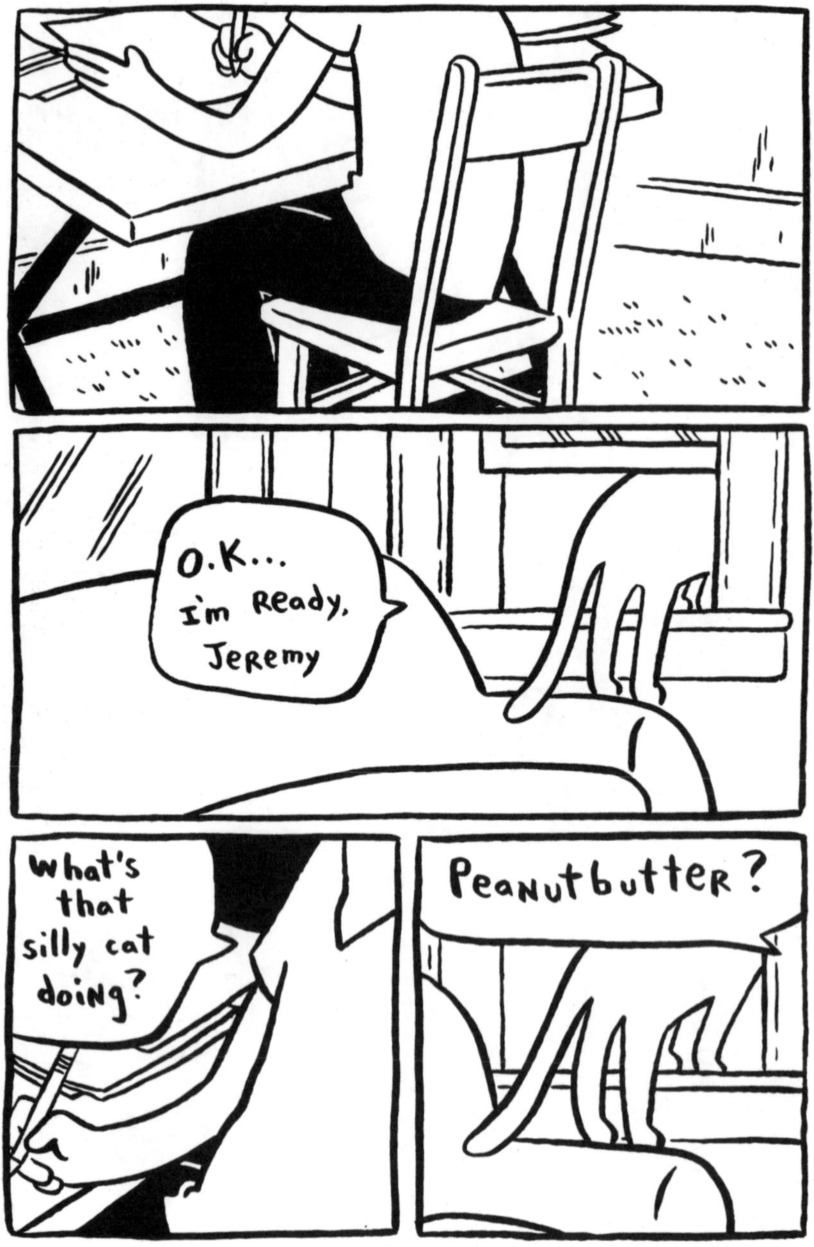
O.K...
I'm Ready, Jeremy
what's that silly cat doing?
Peanutbutter?

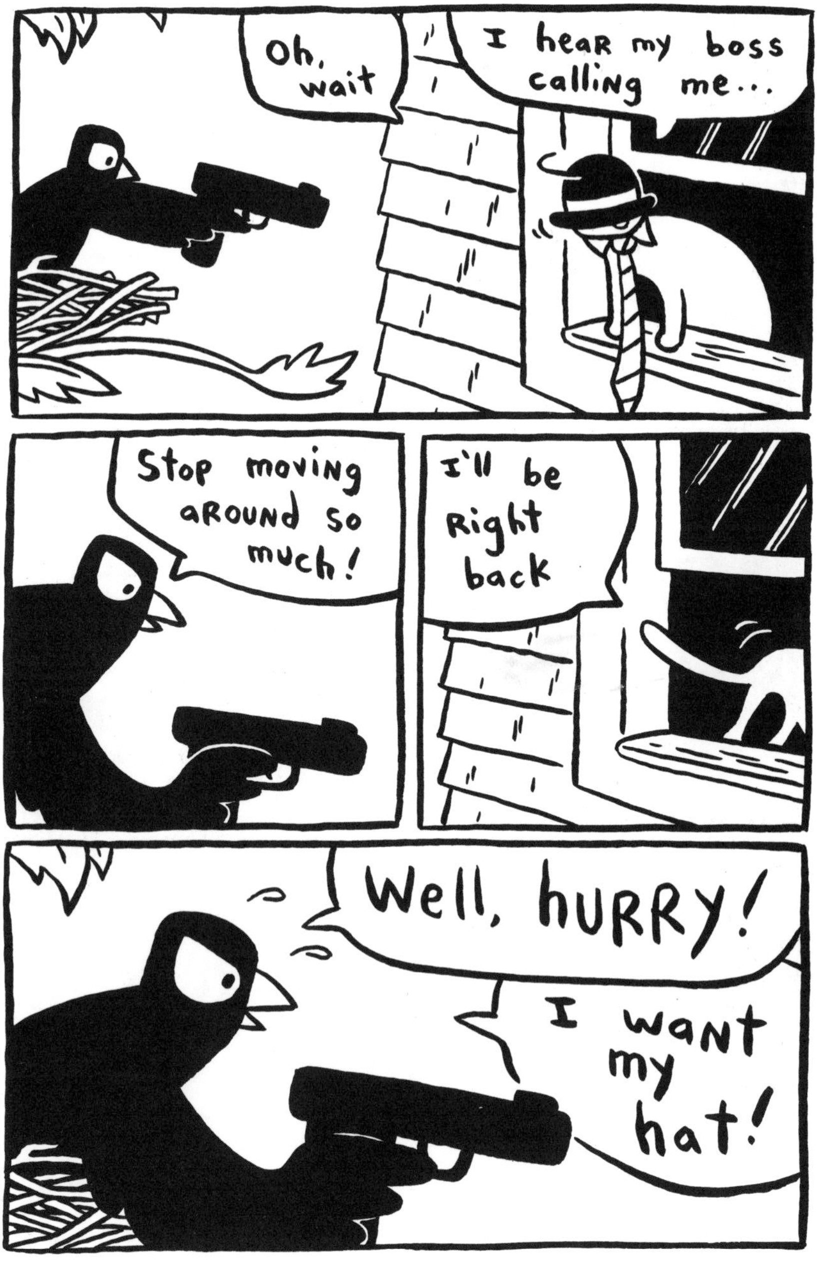
Oh, wait
I hear my boss calling me...
Stop moving around so much!
I'll be right back
Well, hurry!
I want my hat!

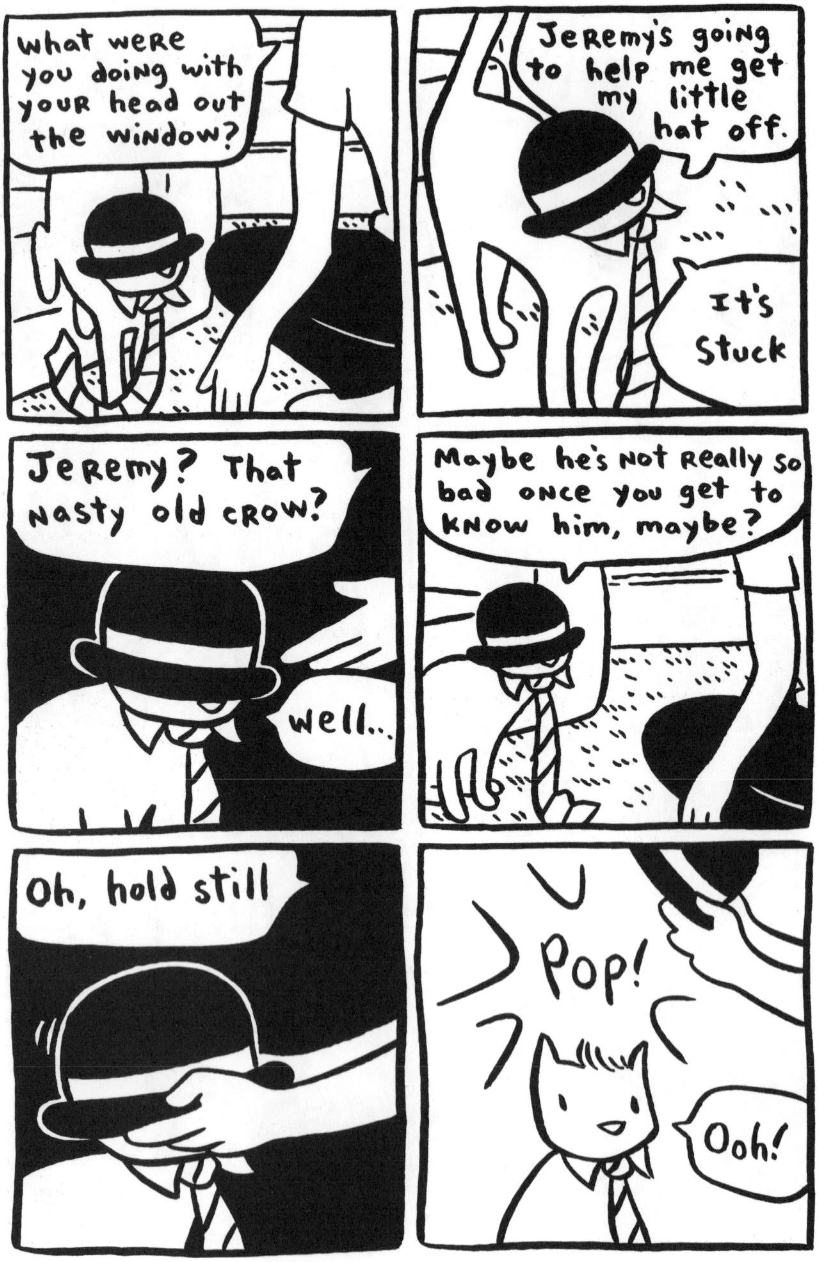
What were you doing with your head out the window?
Jeremy's going to help me get my little hat off.
It's stuck
Jeremy? That nasty old crow?
well...
Maybe he's not really so bad once you get to know him, maybe?
Oh, hold still
Pop!
Ooh!

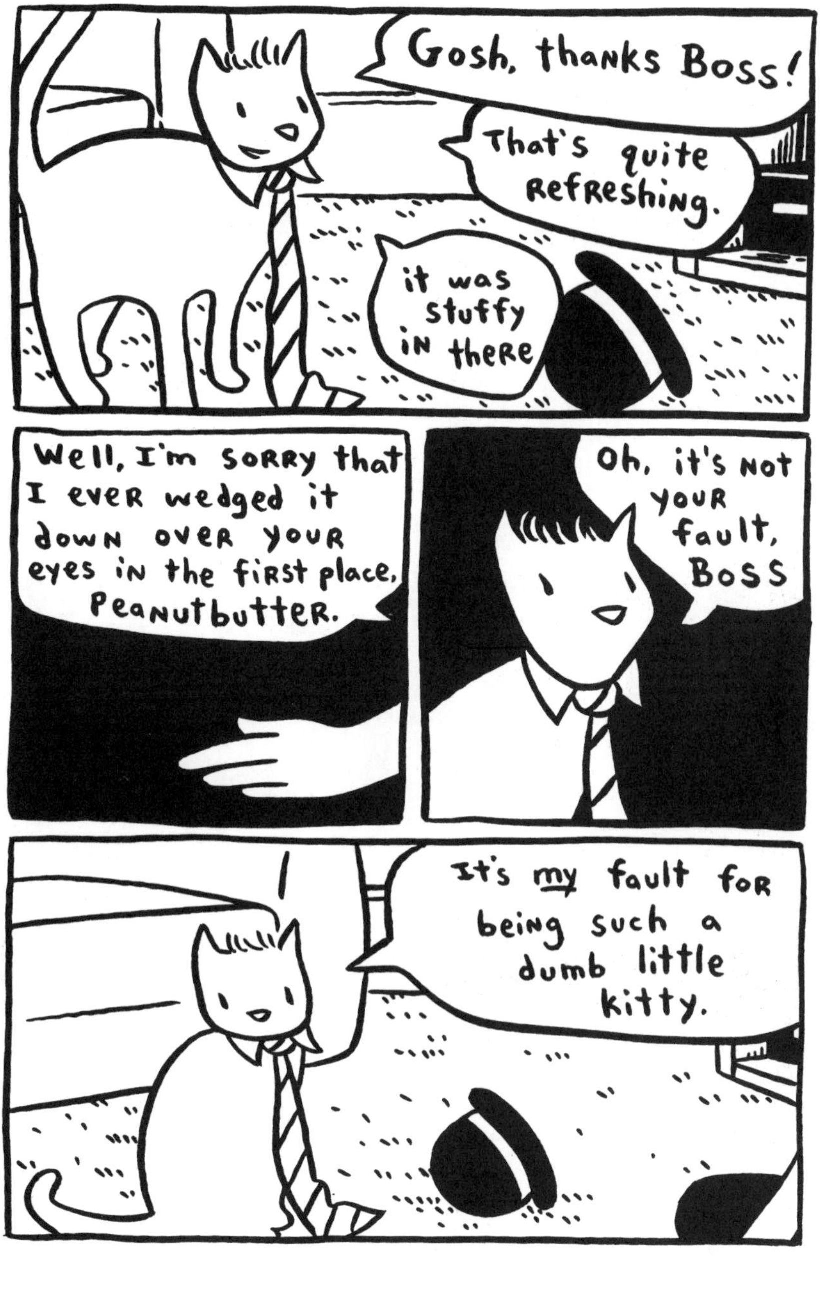
Gosh, thanks Boss!
That's quite refreshing.
it was stuffy in there
Well, I'm sorry that I ever wedged it down over your eyes in the first place, Peanutbutter.
Oh, it's not your fault, Boss
It's my fault for being such a dumb little kitty.

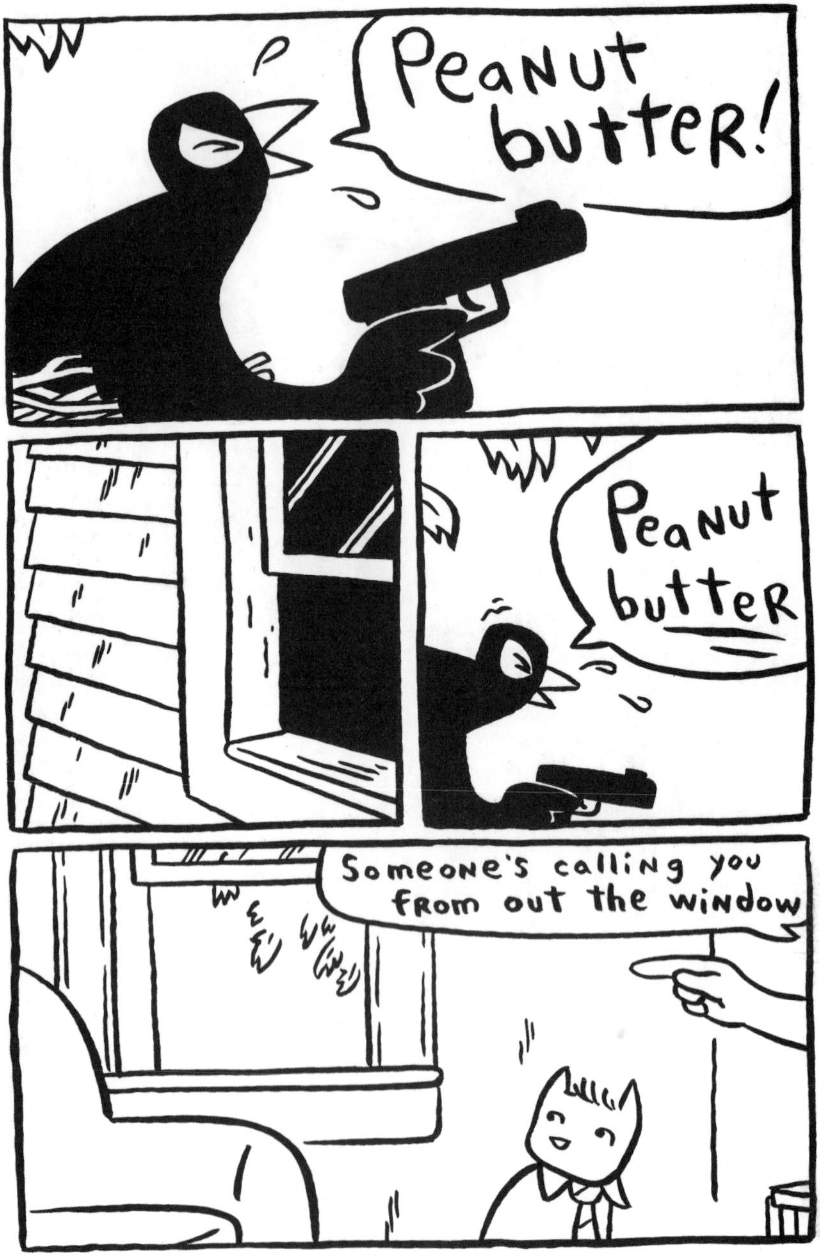
Peanut butter!
Peanut butter
Someone's calling you from out the window

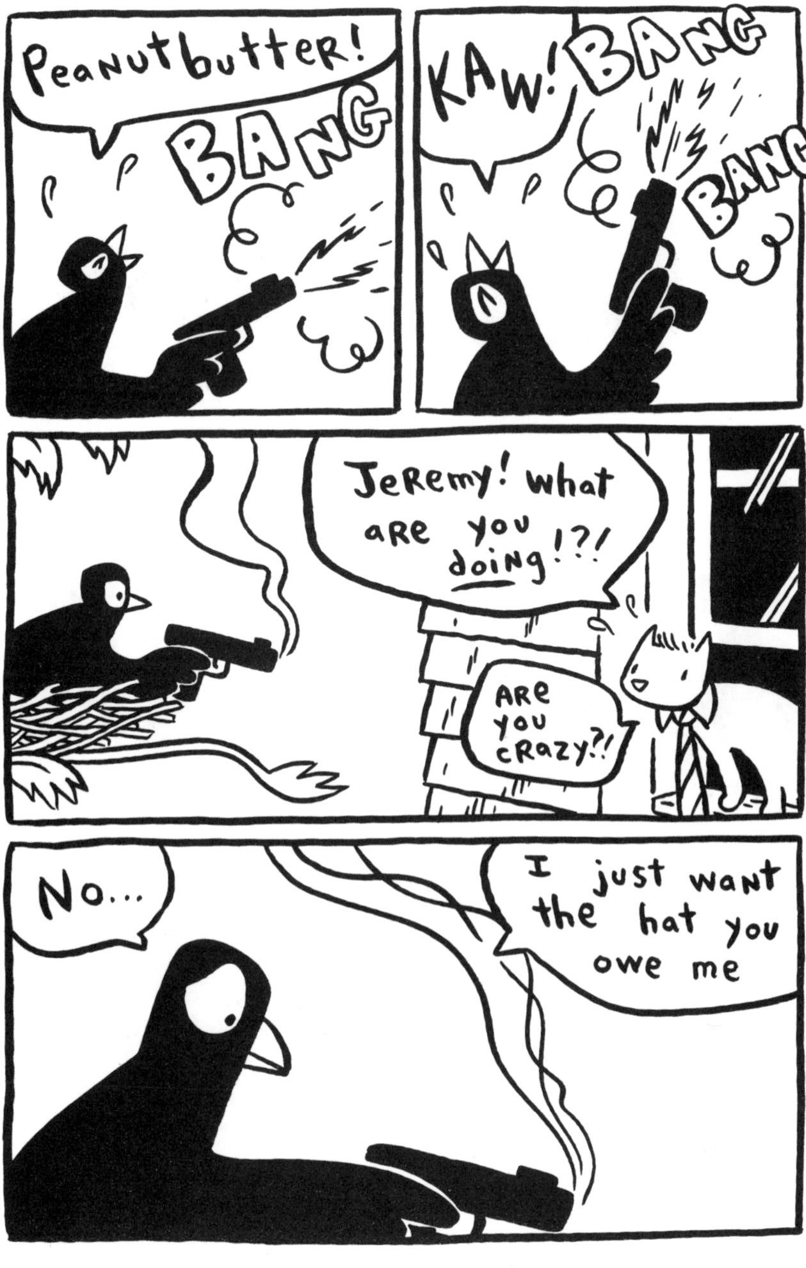
Peanutbutter!
BANG
KAW!
BANG
BANG
Jeremy! what are you doing!?!
ARE you cRazy?!
No...
I just want the hat you owe me

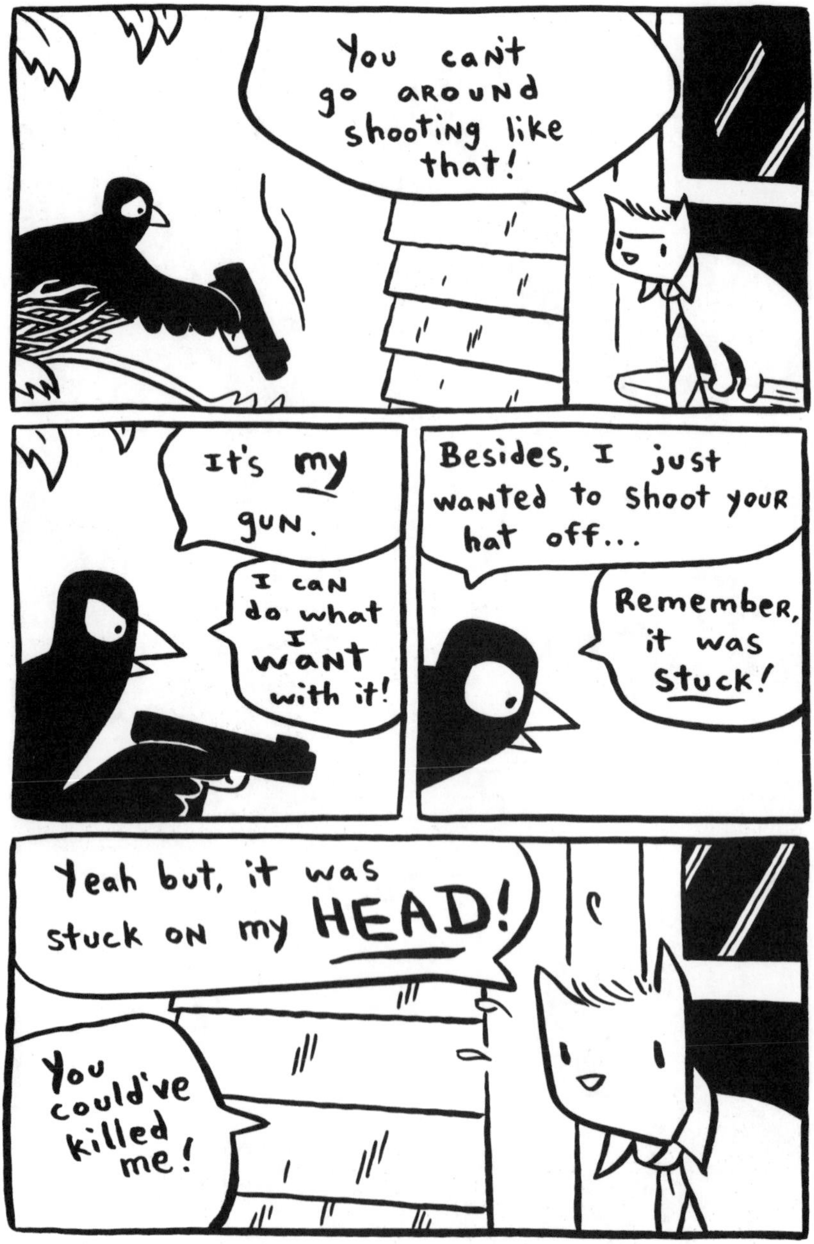
You can't go around shooting like that!
It's my gun.
I can do what I want with it!
Besides, I just wanted to shoot your hat off...
Remember, it was stuck!
Yeah but, it was stuck on my HEAD!
You could've killed me!

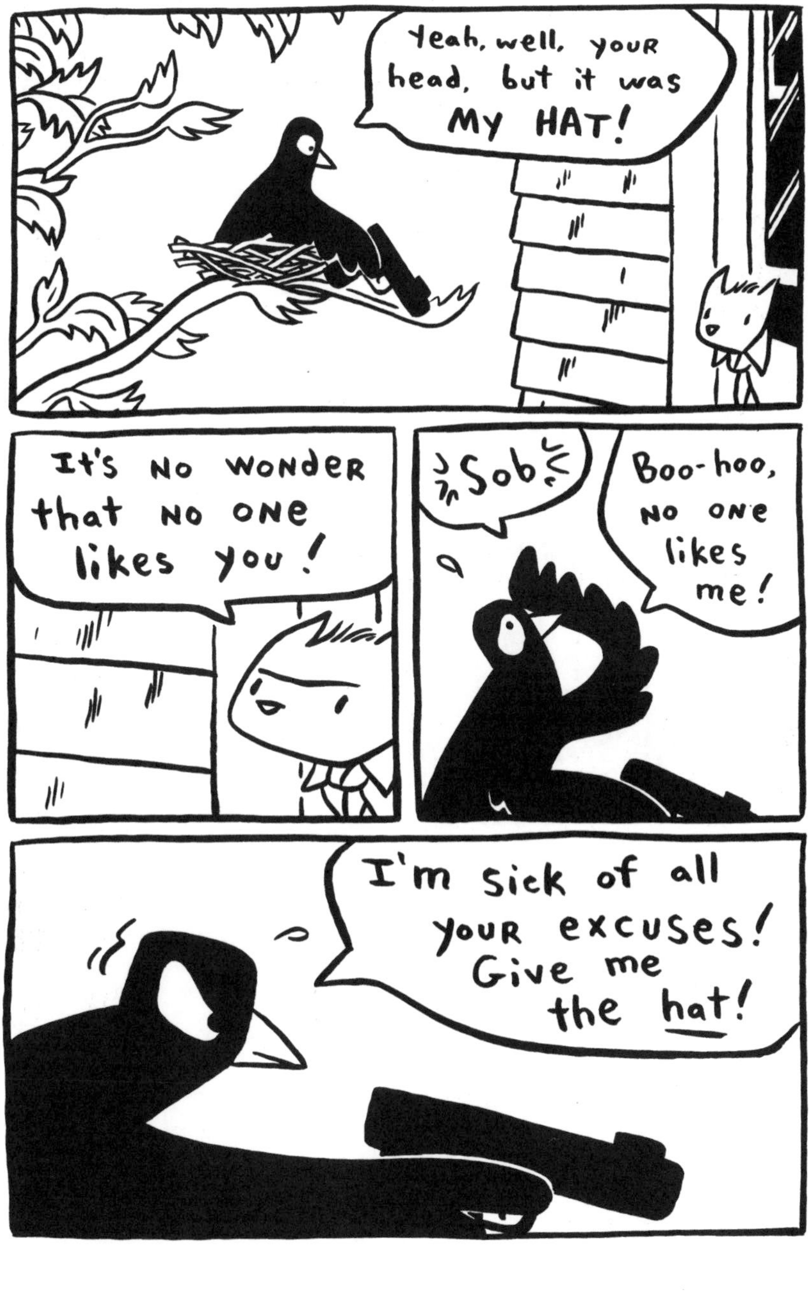
Yeah, well, your head, but it was MY HAT!
It's no wonder that no one likes you!
Sob
Boo-hoo, no one likes me!
I'm sick of all your excuses! Give me the hat!

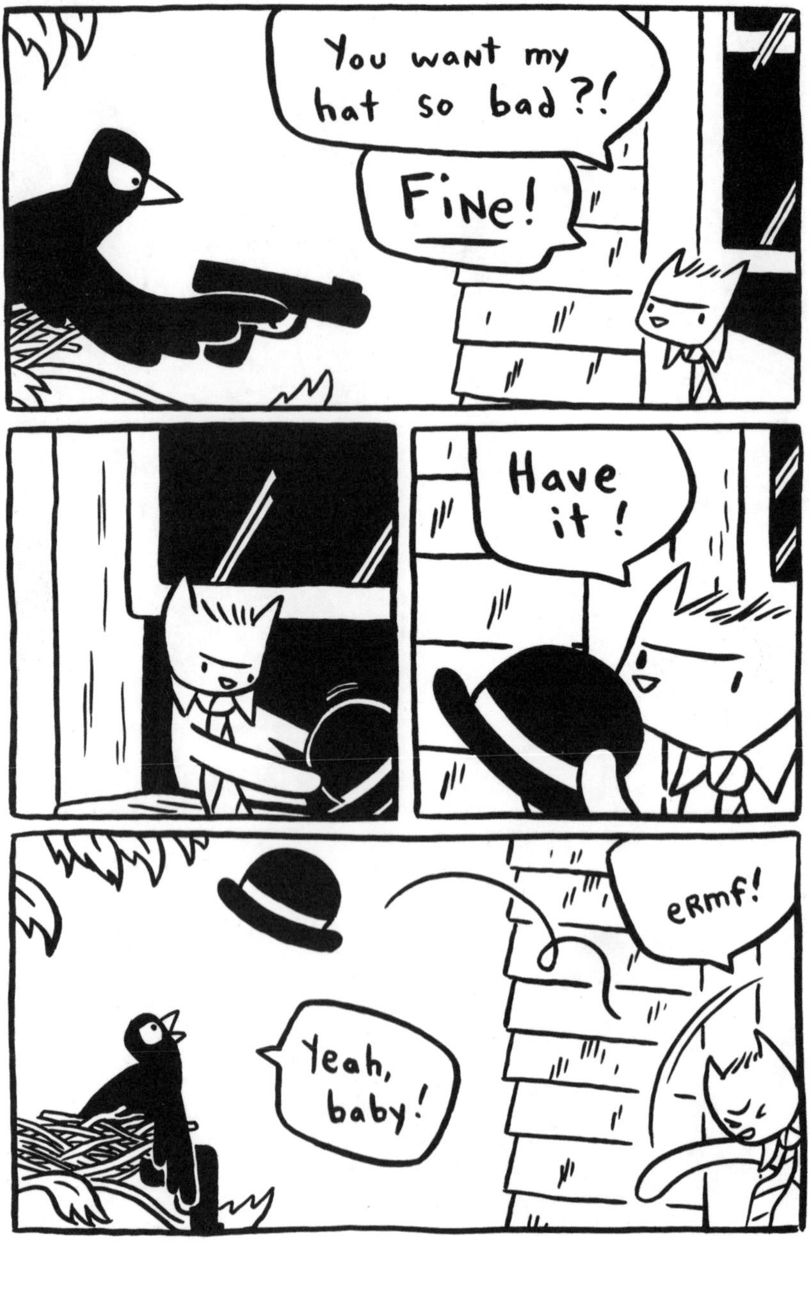
You want my hat so bad?!
Fine!
Have it!
ermf!
Yeah, baby!

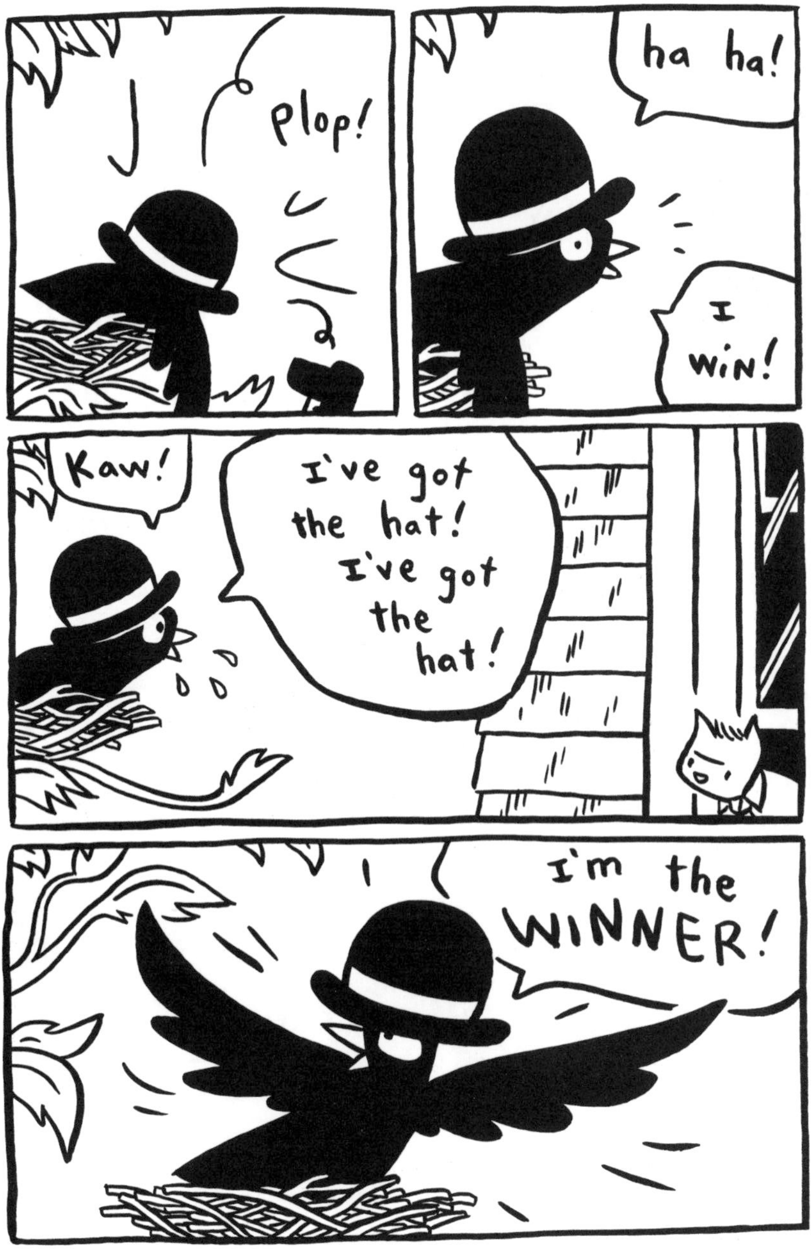
Plop!
ha ha!
I WIN!
Kaw!
I've got the hat! I've got the hat!
I'm the WINNER!

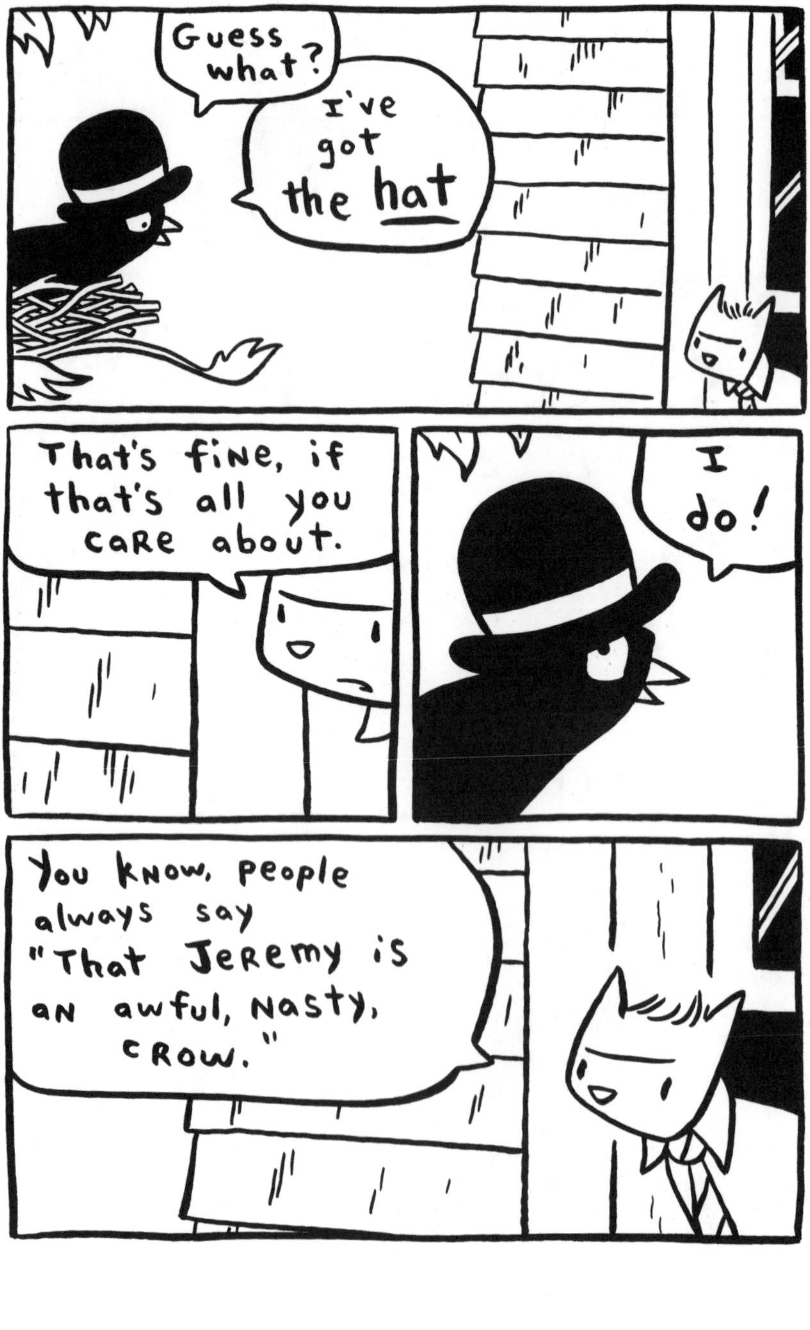
Guess what?
I've got the hat
That's fine, if that's all you care about.
I do!
You know, people always say "That Jeremy is an awful, nasty, crow."

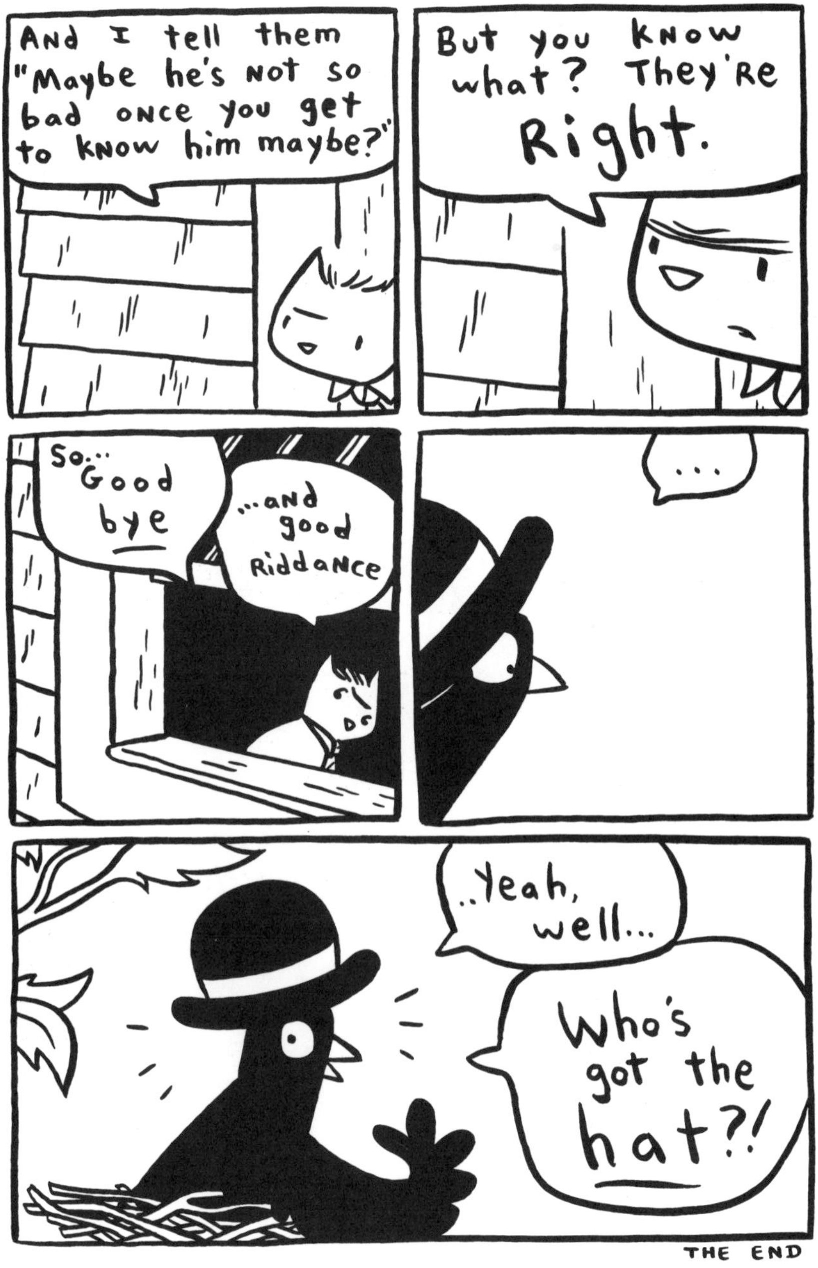

And I tell them "Maybe he's not so bad once you get to know him maybe?"
But you know what? They're Right.
So... Good bye
...and good Riddance
...
..Yeah, well...
Who's got the hat?!
THE END

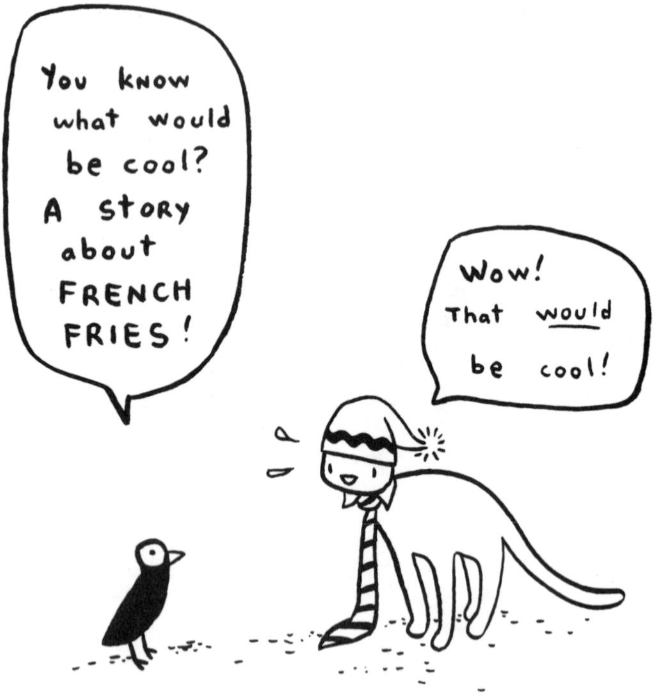
You know what would be cool? A story about FRENCH FRIES!
Wow! That would be cool!

THE FRENCH FRY STORY

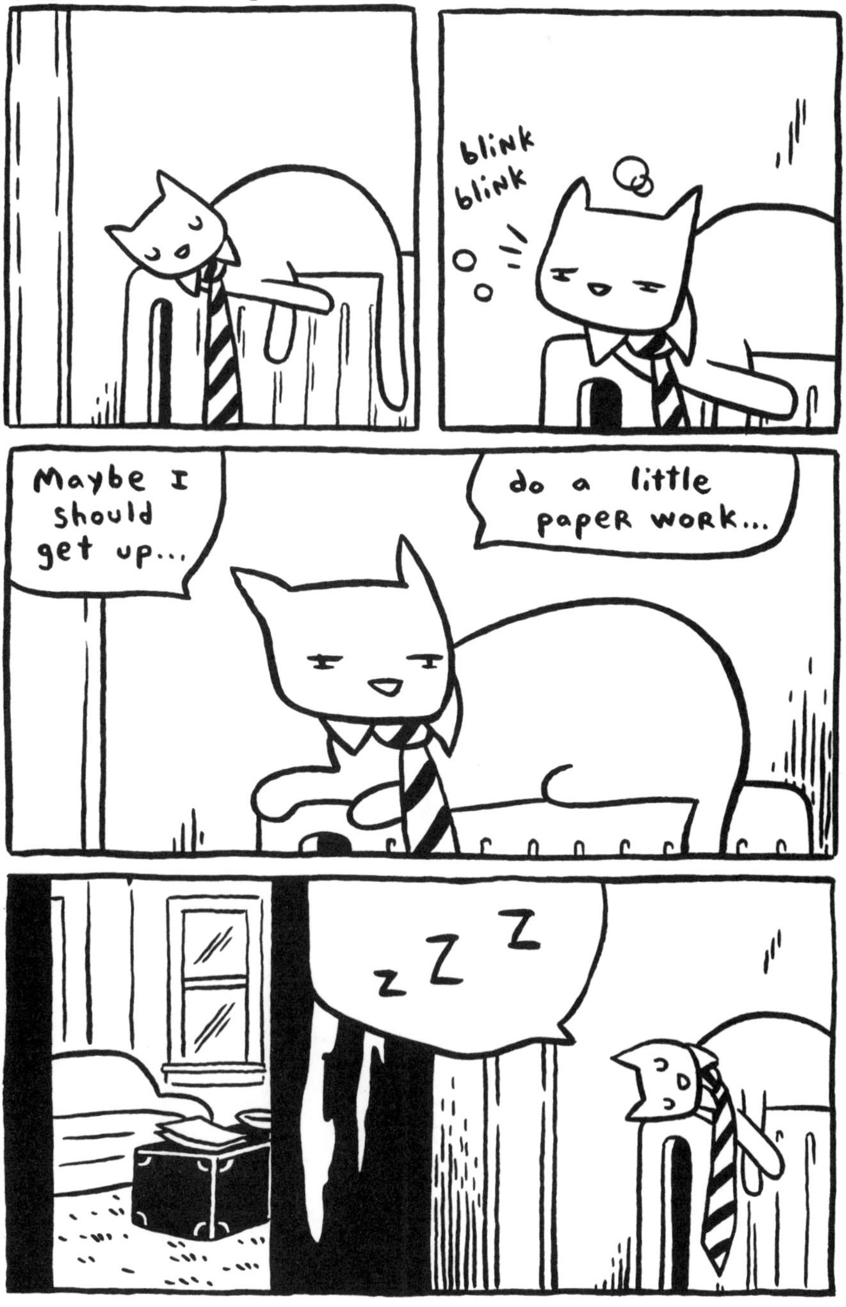
blink
blink
Maybe I should get up...
do a little paper work...
z Z Z

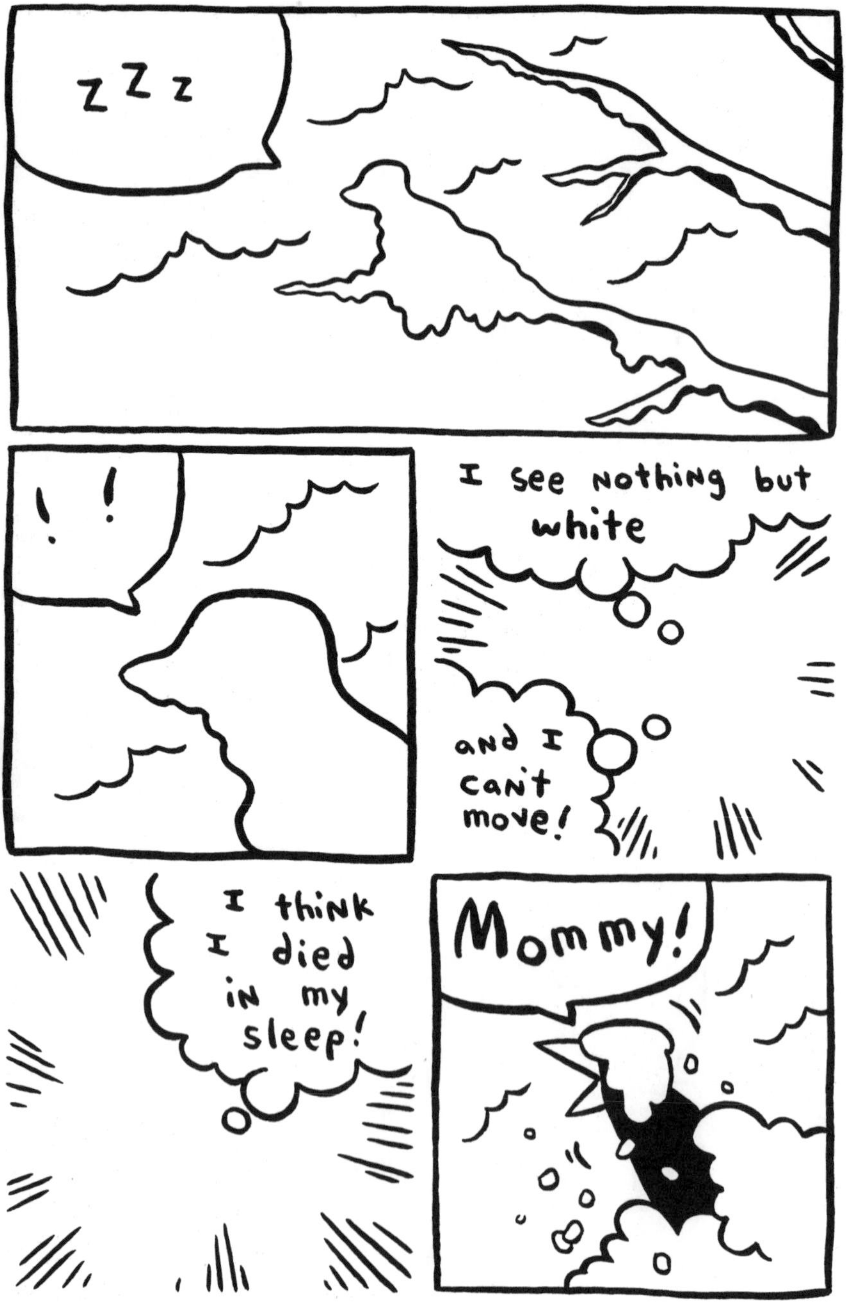
z Z z
! !
I see nothing but white
and I can't move!
I think I died in my sleep!
Mommy!

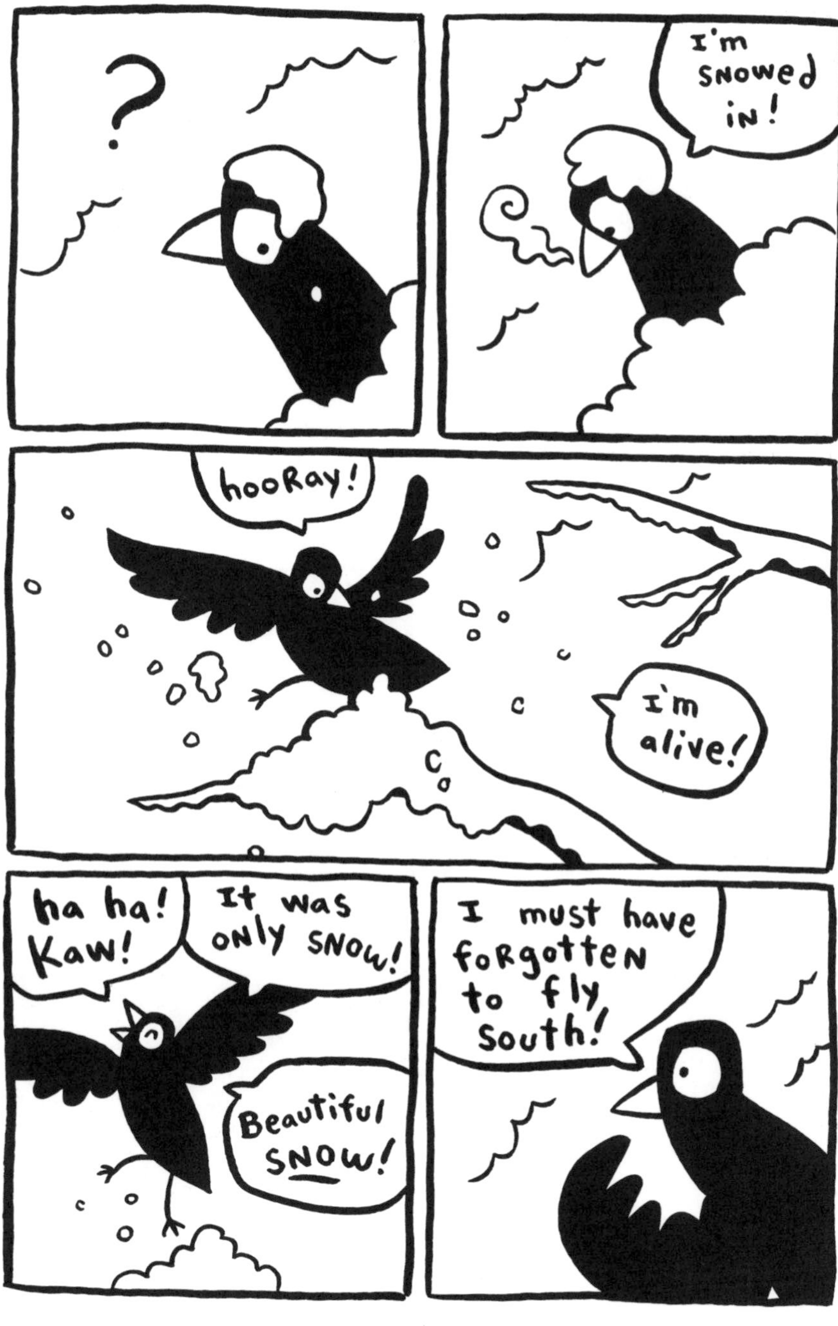
?
I'm SNOWED IN!
hooRay!
I'm alive!
ha ha! Kaw!
It was ONLY SNOW!
Beautiful SNOW!
I must have forgotten to fly South!

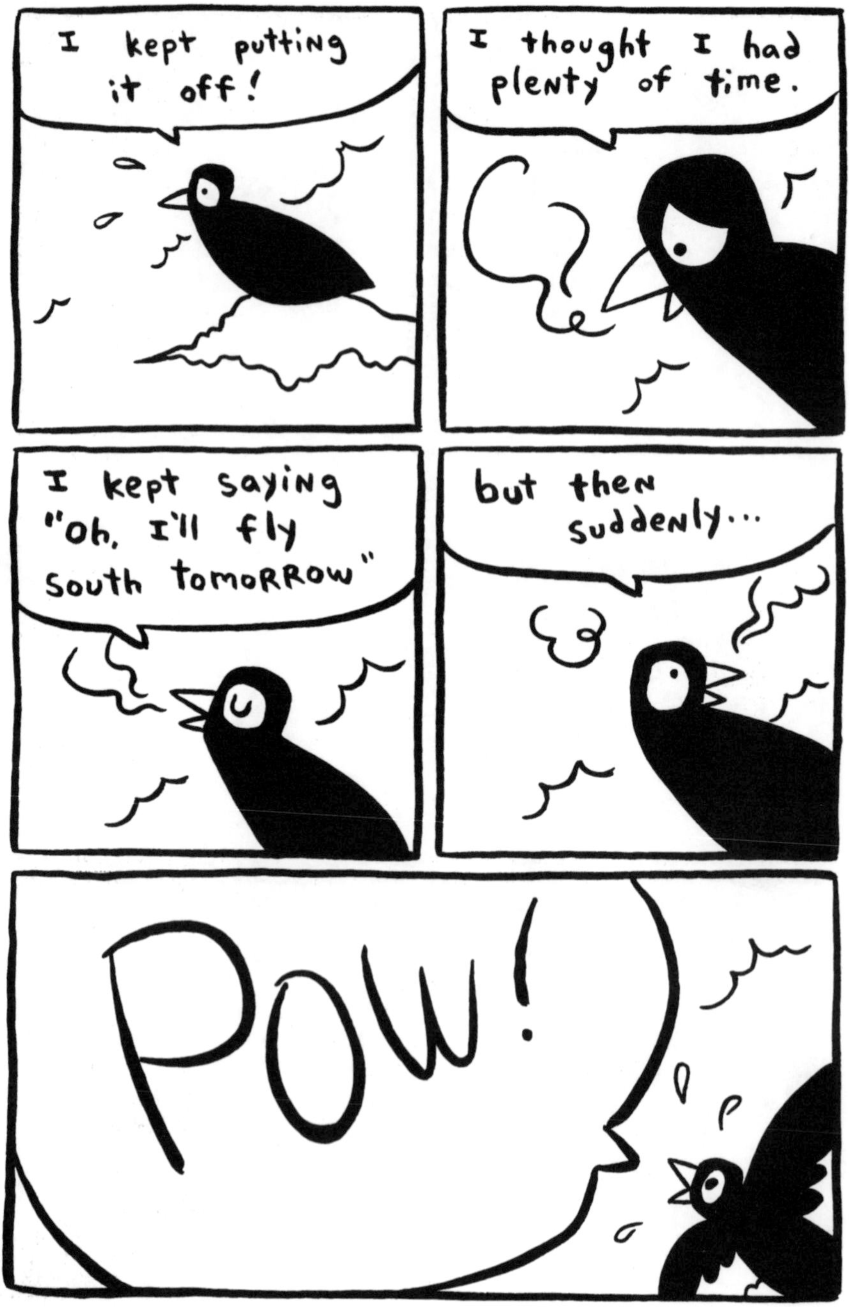
I kept putting it off!
I thought I had plenty of time.
I kept saying "Oh, I'll fly south tomorrow"
but then suddenly...
POW!

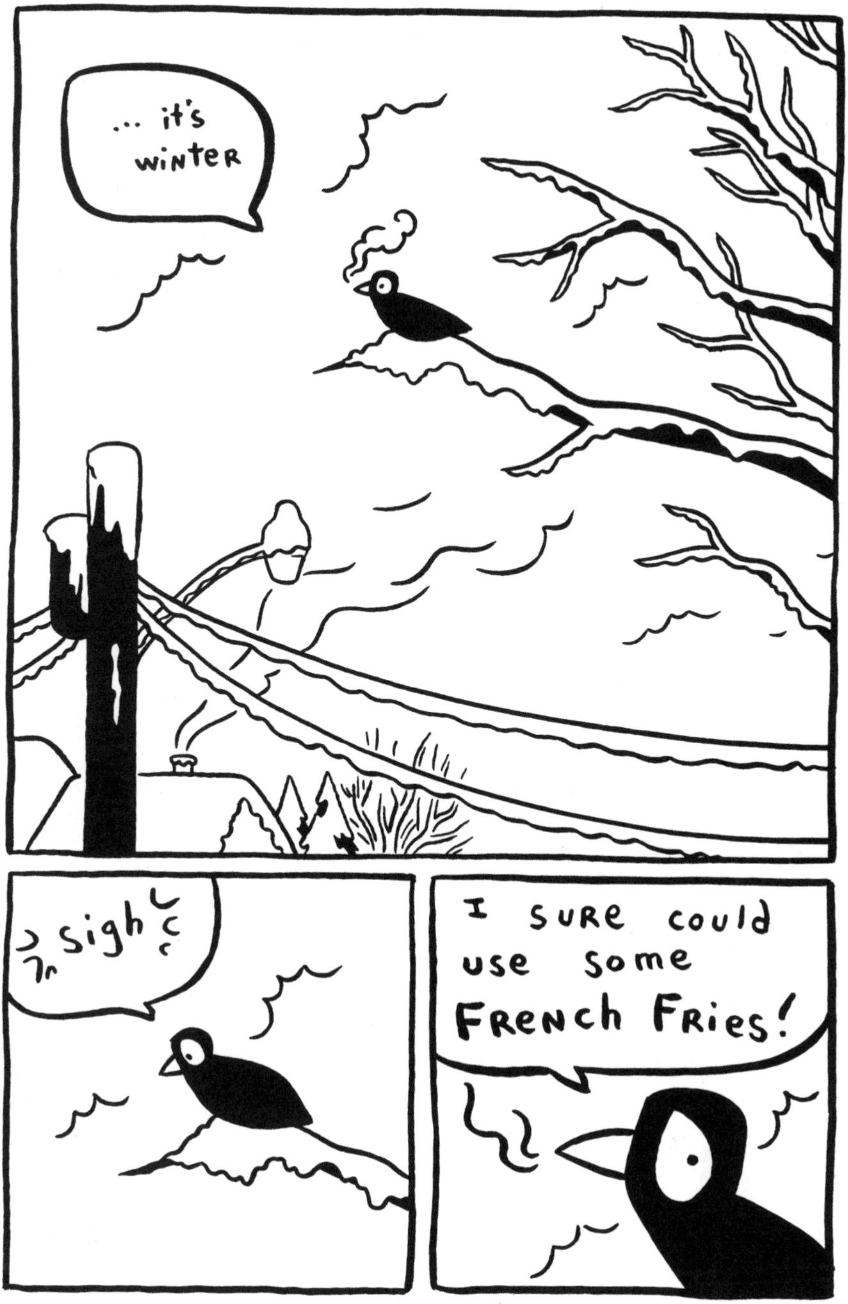
... it's winter
sigh
I sure could use some French Fries!

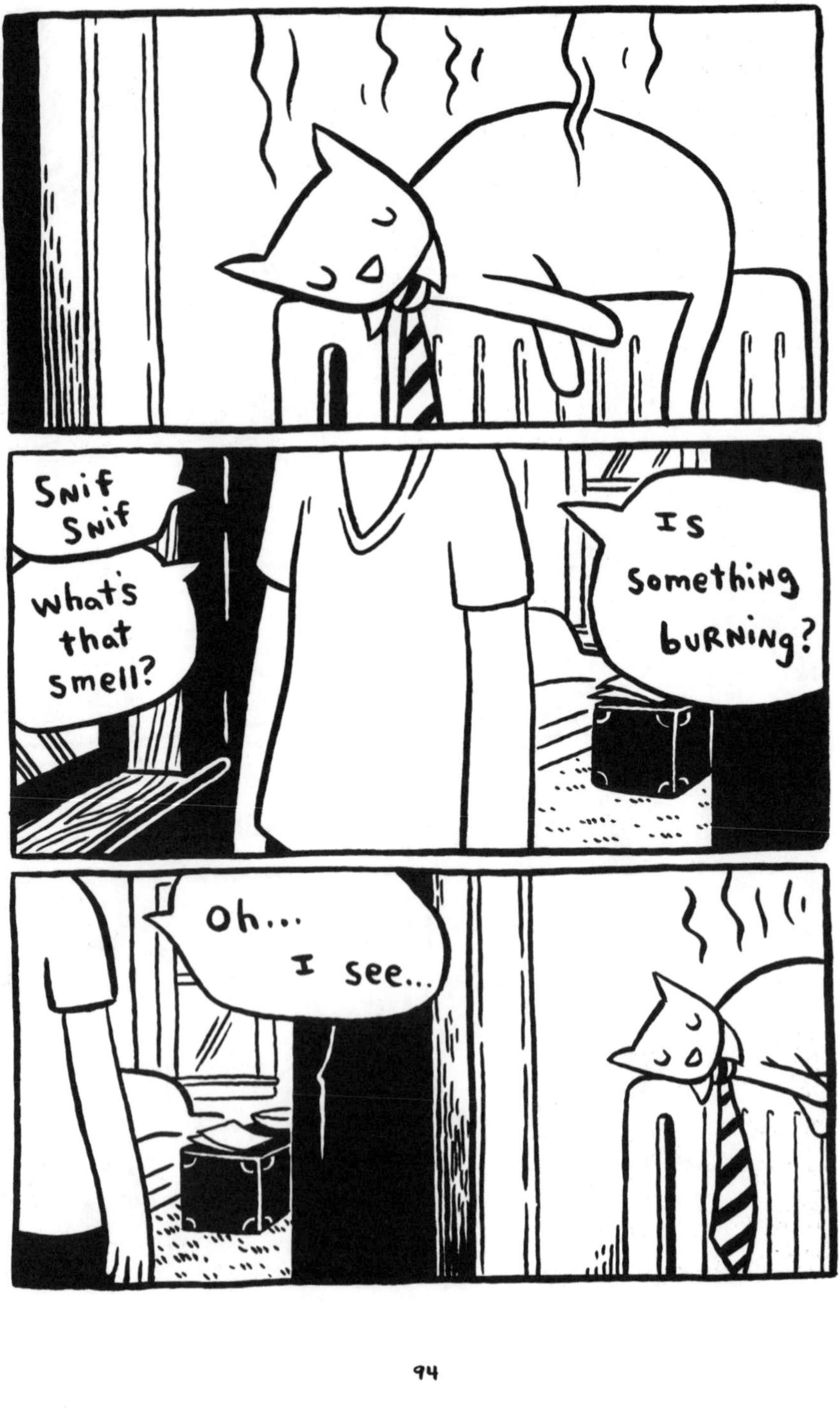
Snif Snif
what's that smell?
Is something burning?
Oh... I see...

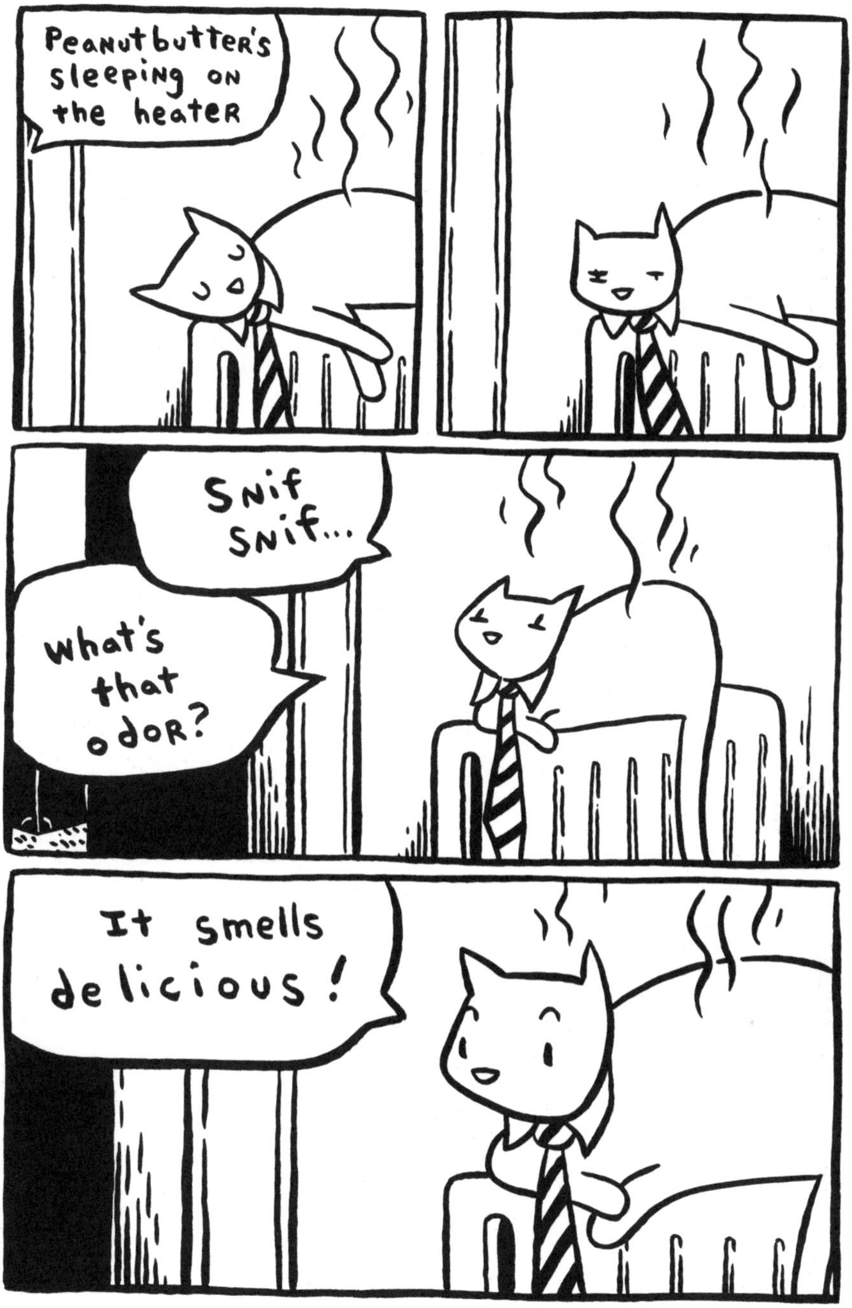
Peanutbutter's sleeping on the heater
Snif snif...
what's that odor?
It smells delicious!

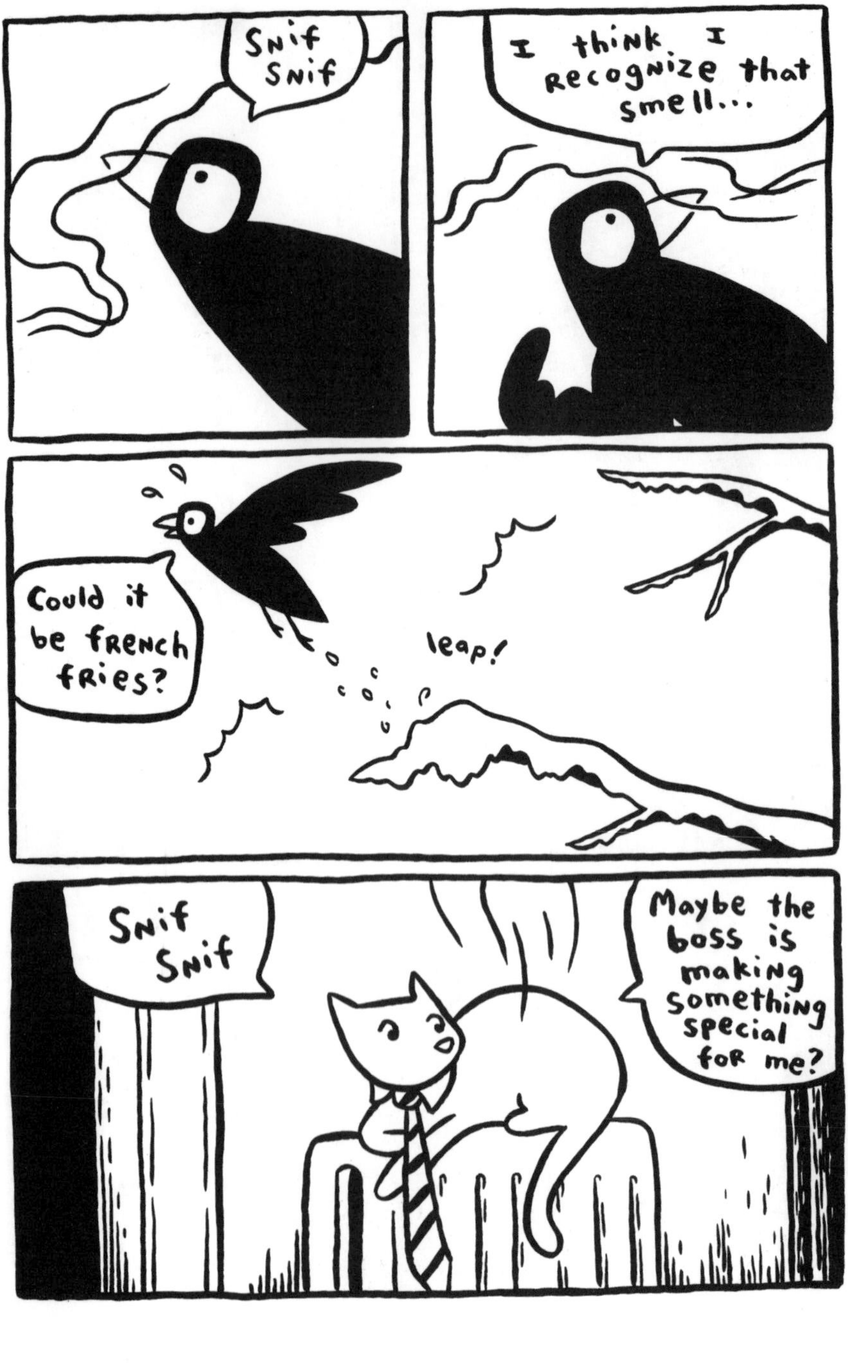
Snif Snif
I think I recognize that smell...
Could it be french fries?
leap!
Snif Snif
Maybe the boss is making something special for me?

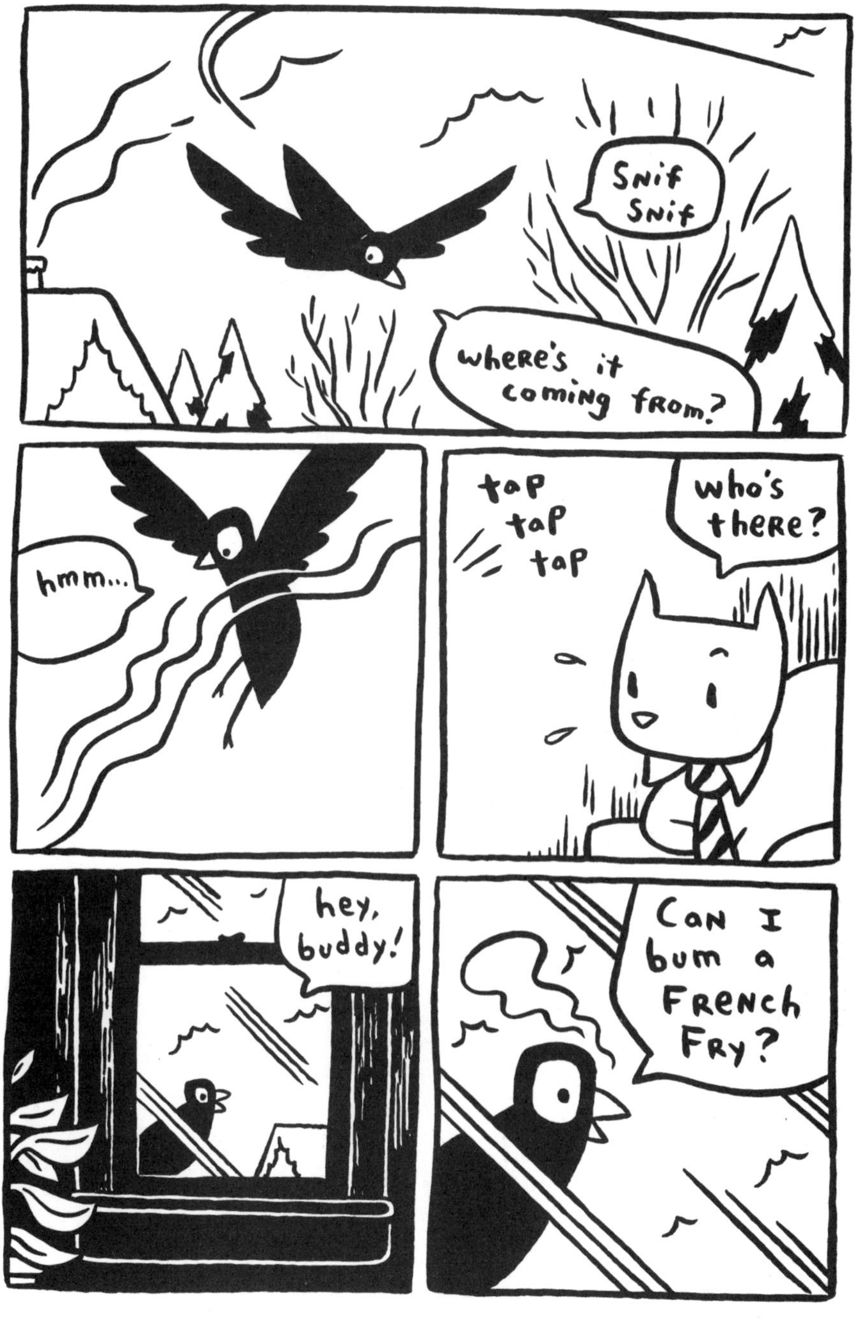

Snif Snif
where's it coming from?
hmm...
tap tap tap
who's there?
hey, buddy!
Can I bum a French Fry?

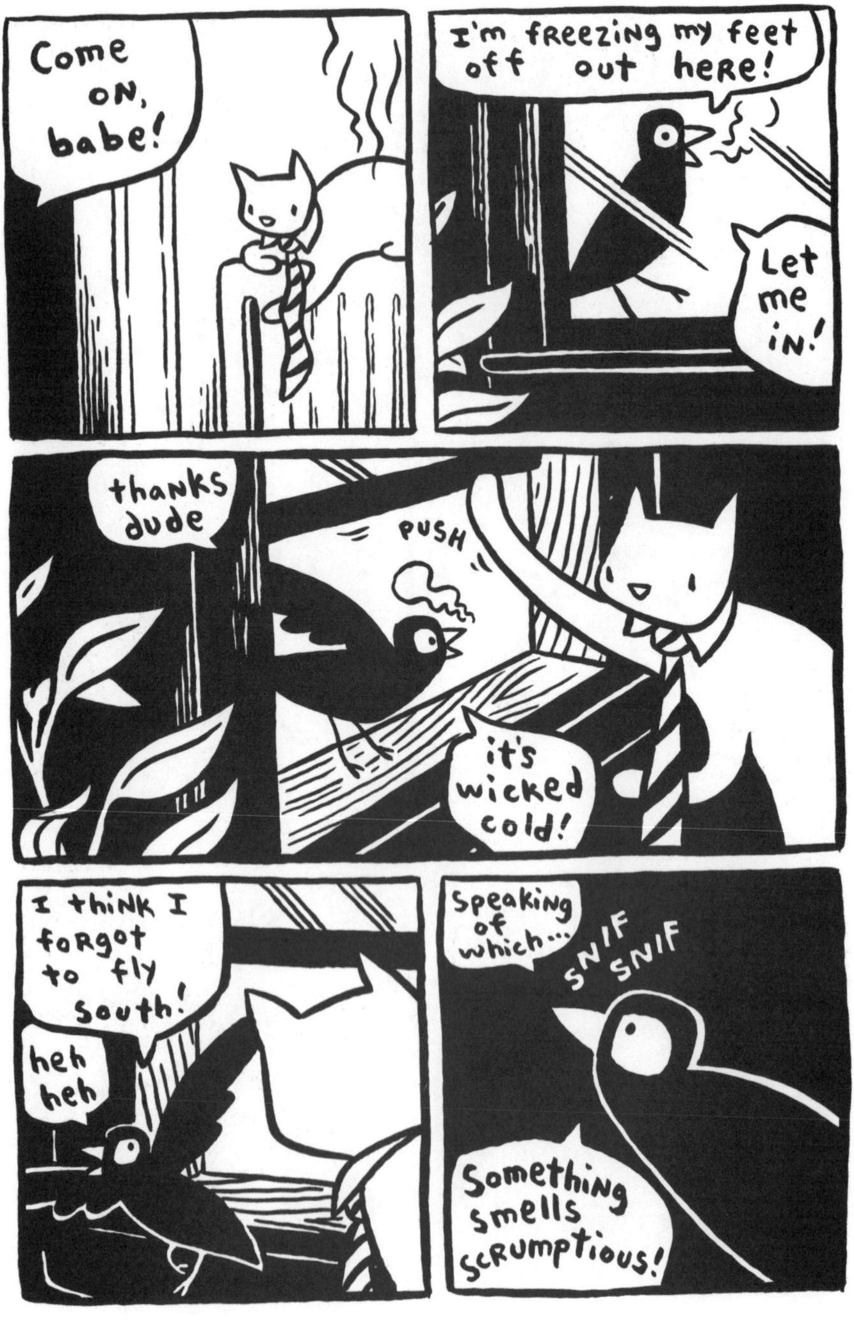
Come ON, babe!
I'm freezing my feet off out here!
Let me in!
thanks dude
PUSH
it's wicked cold!
I think I forgot to fly south!
heh heh
Speaking of which...
SNIF SNIF
Something smells scrumptious!

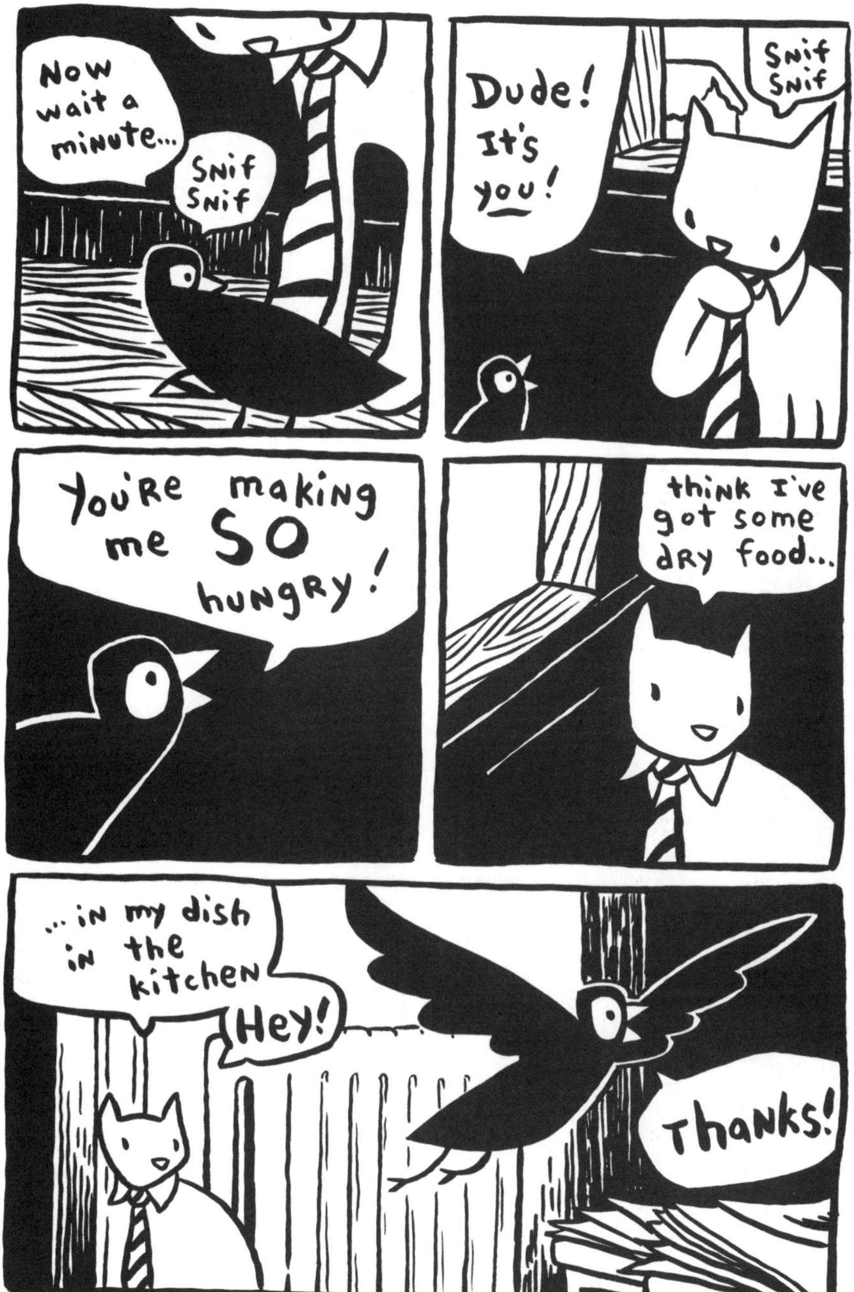
Now wait a minute...
Snif Snif
Dude! It's you!
Snif Snif
You're making me SO hungry!
think I've got some dry food...
...in my dish in the kitchen
Hey!
Thanks!

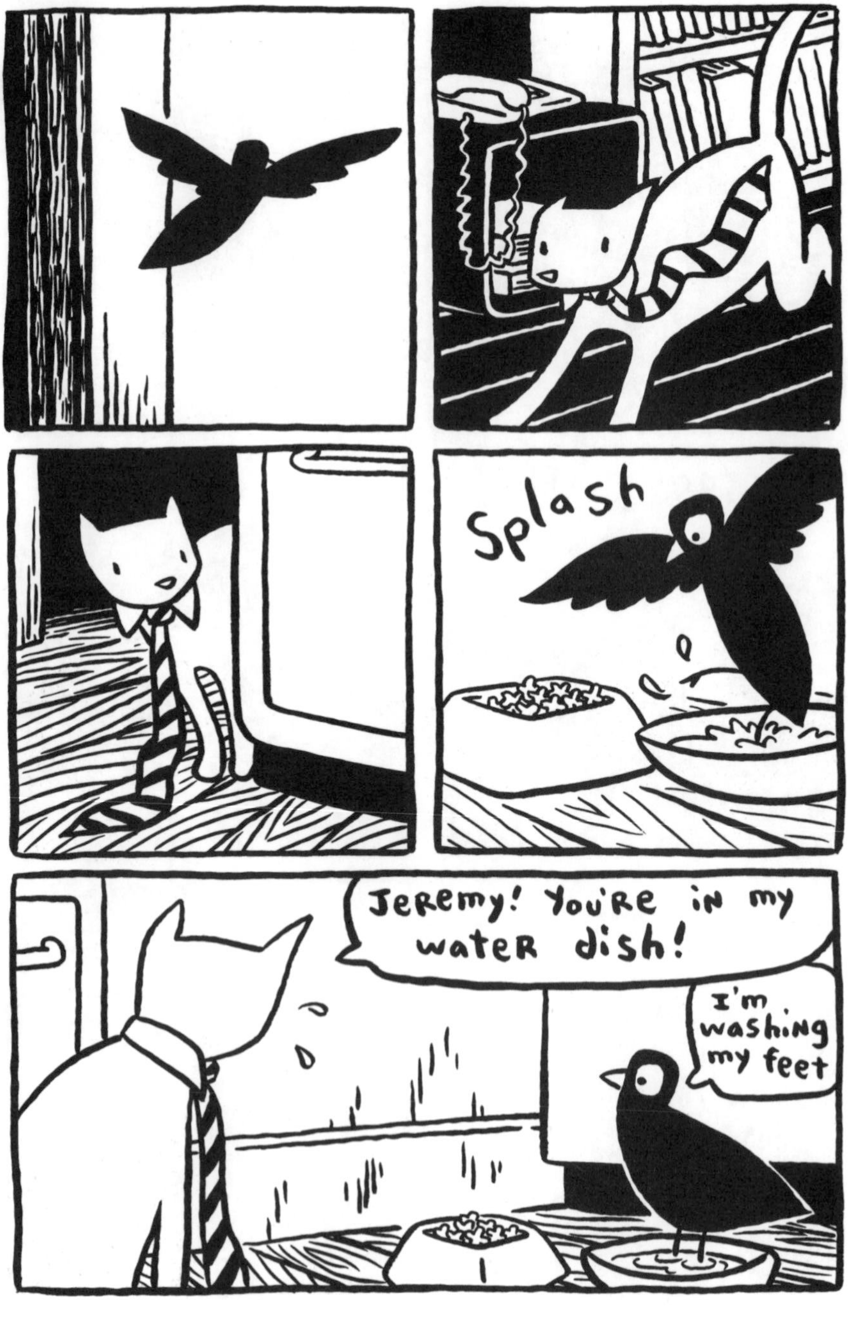
Splash
JEREMY! YOU'RE IN MY WATER DISH!
I'm washing my feet

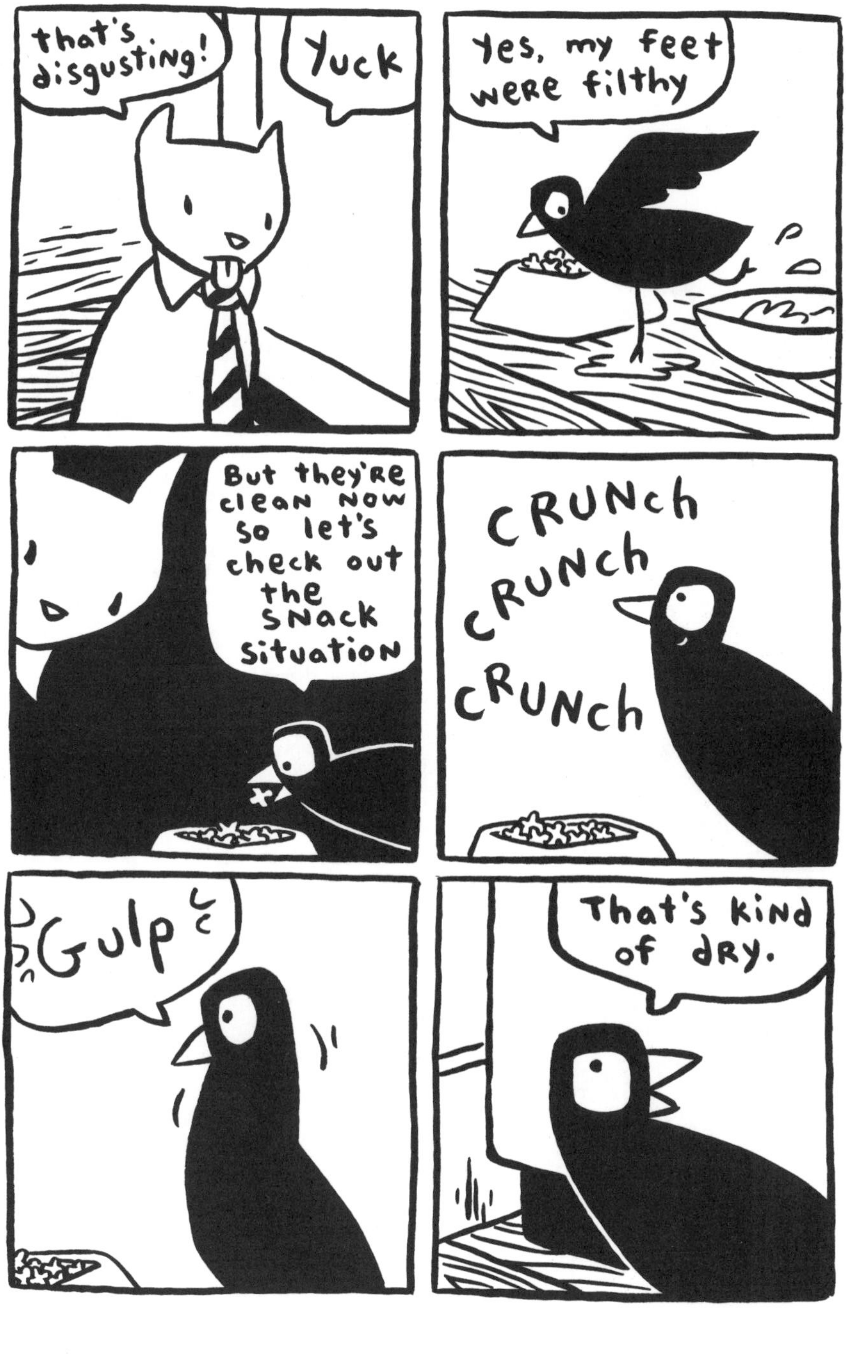
that's disgusting!
Yuck
Yes, my feet were filthy
But they're clean now so let's check out the snack situation
CRUNch
CRUNch
CRUNch
Gulp
That's kind of dry.

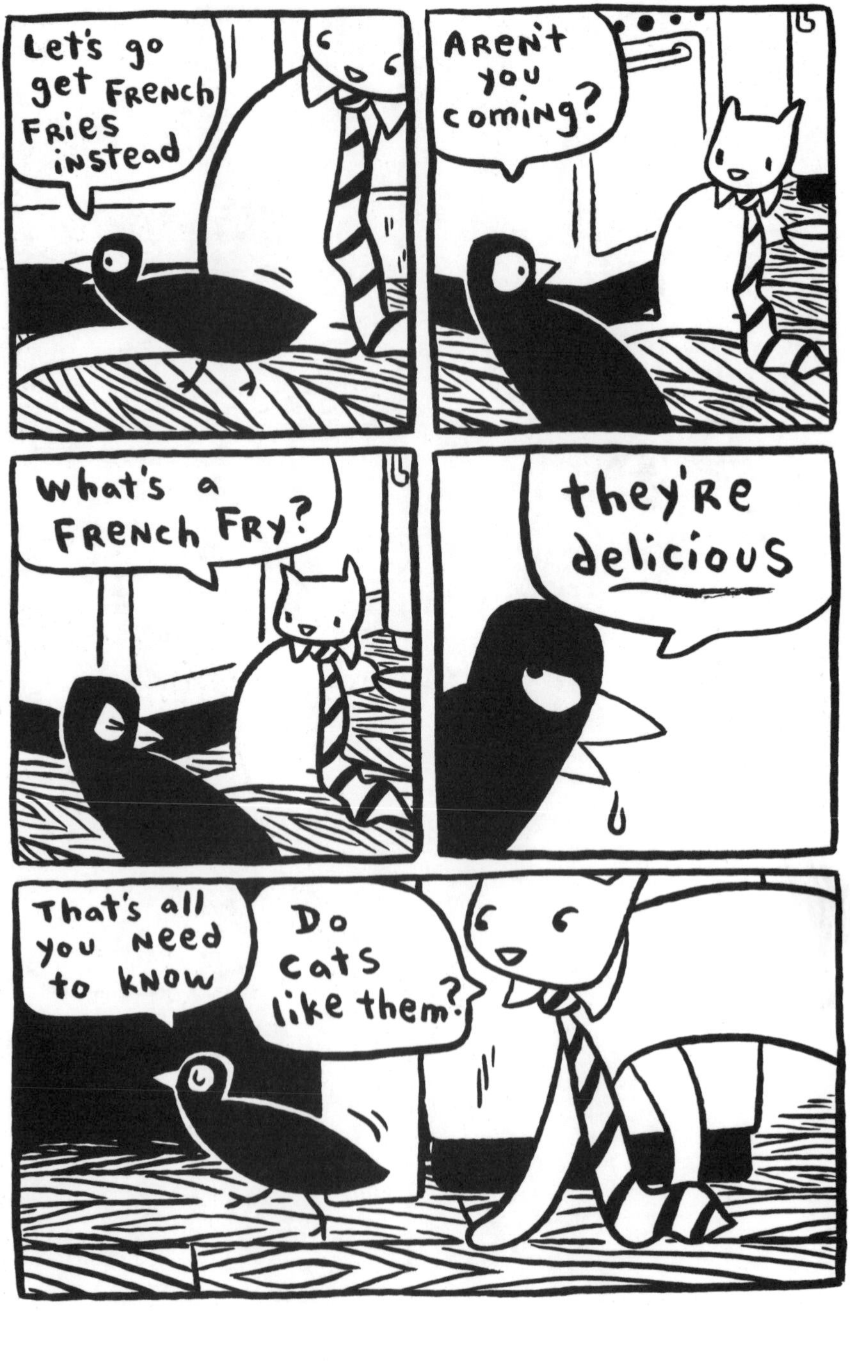
Let's go get FRENCH FRIES instead
AREN'T you coming?
What's a FRENCH FRY?
they'RE delicious
That's all you NEED to KNOW
Do cats like them?

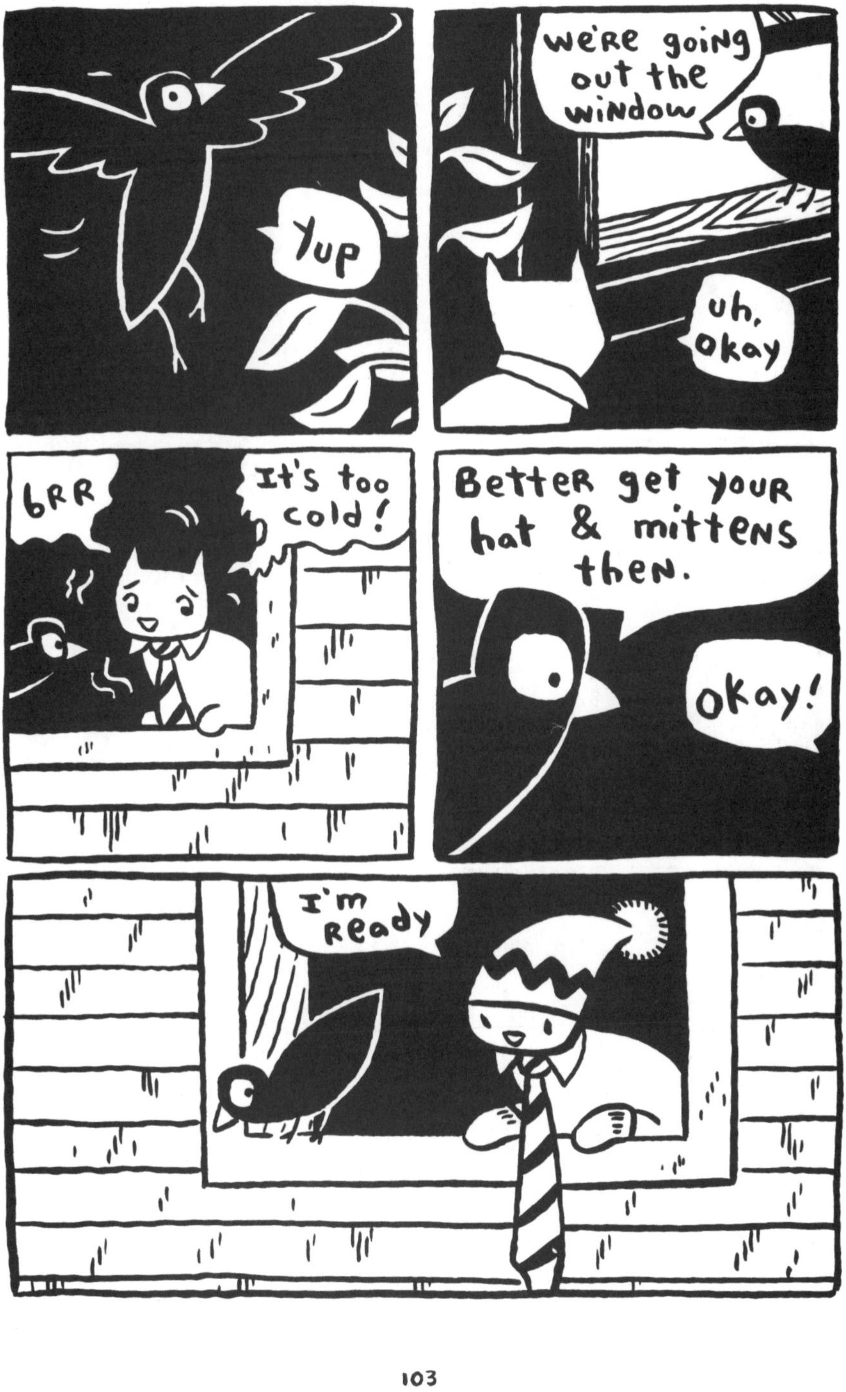
Yup
we're going out the window
uh, okay
bRR
It's too cold!
Better get your hat & mittens then.
Okay!
I'm Ready

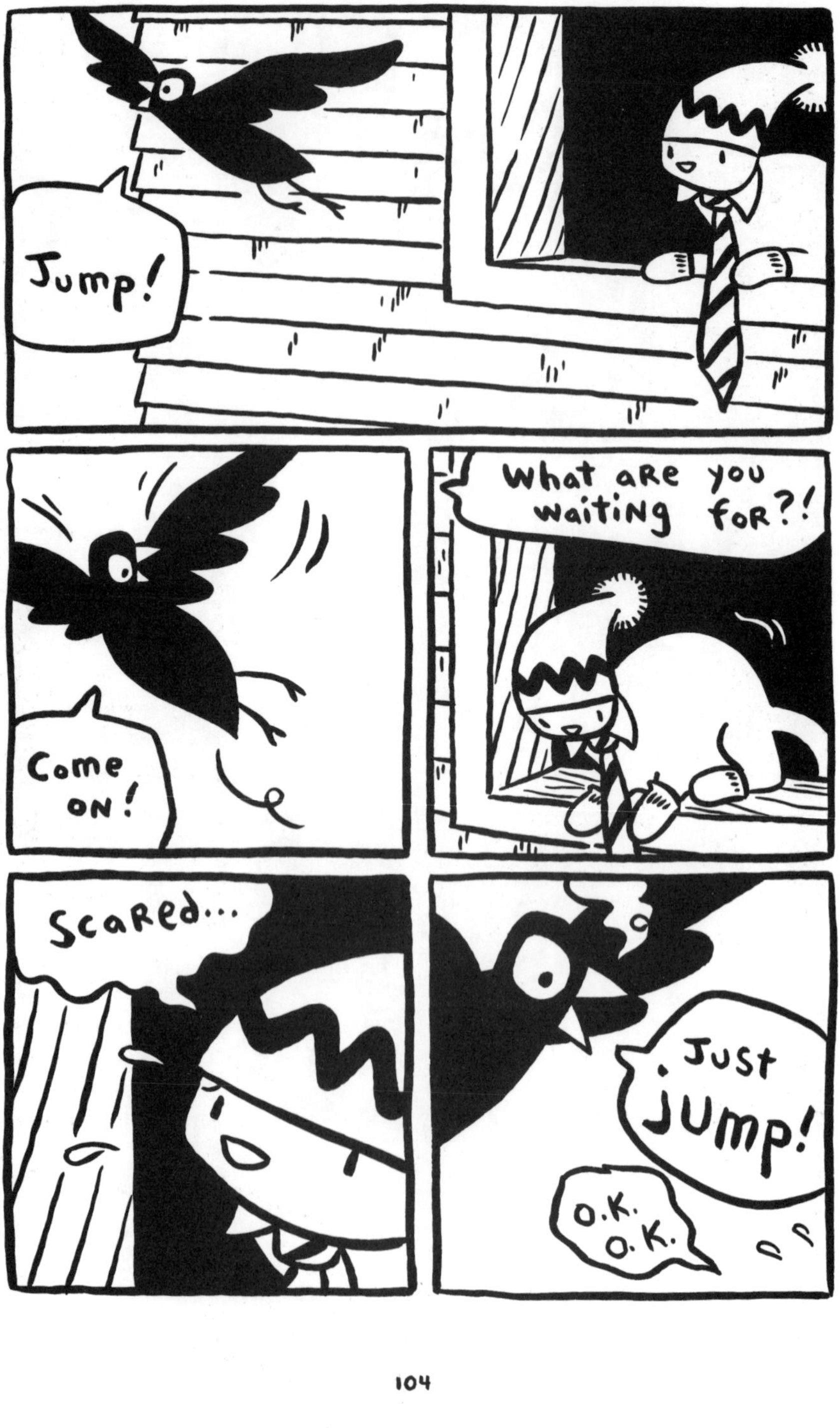
Jump!
Come on!
What are you waiting for?!
Scared...
Just JUMP!
O.K. O.K.

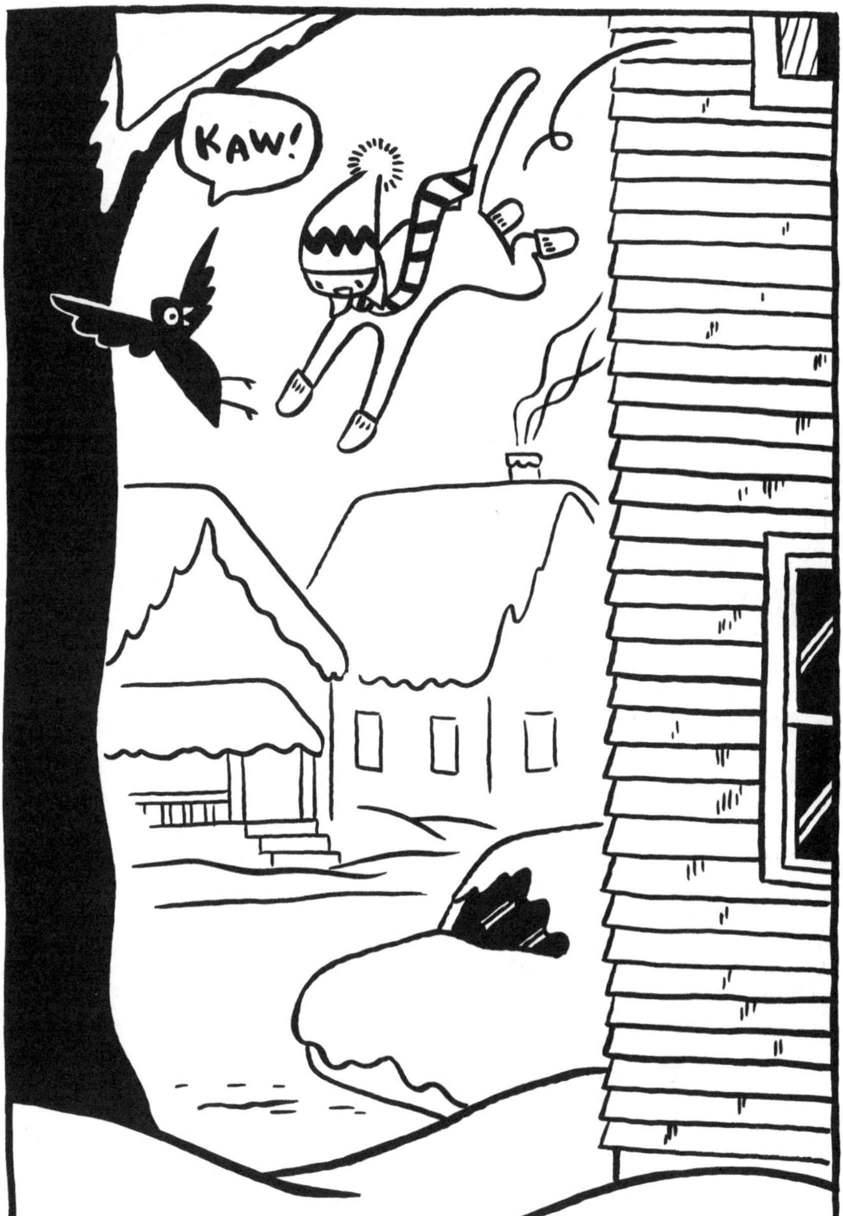
KAW!

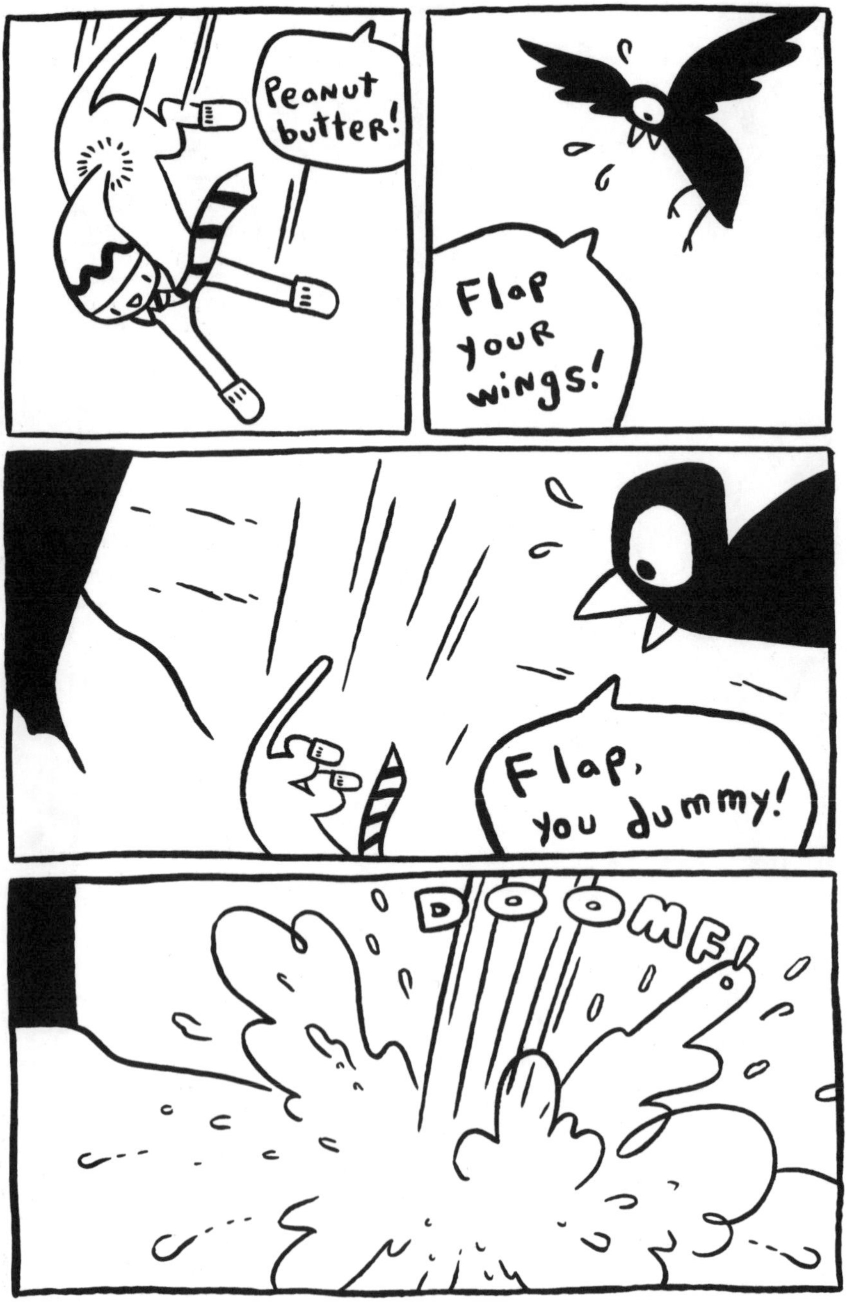

Peanut butter!
Flap your wings!
Flap, you dummy!
DOOMF!

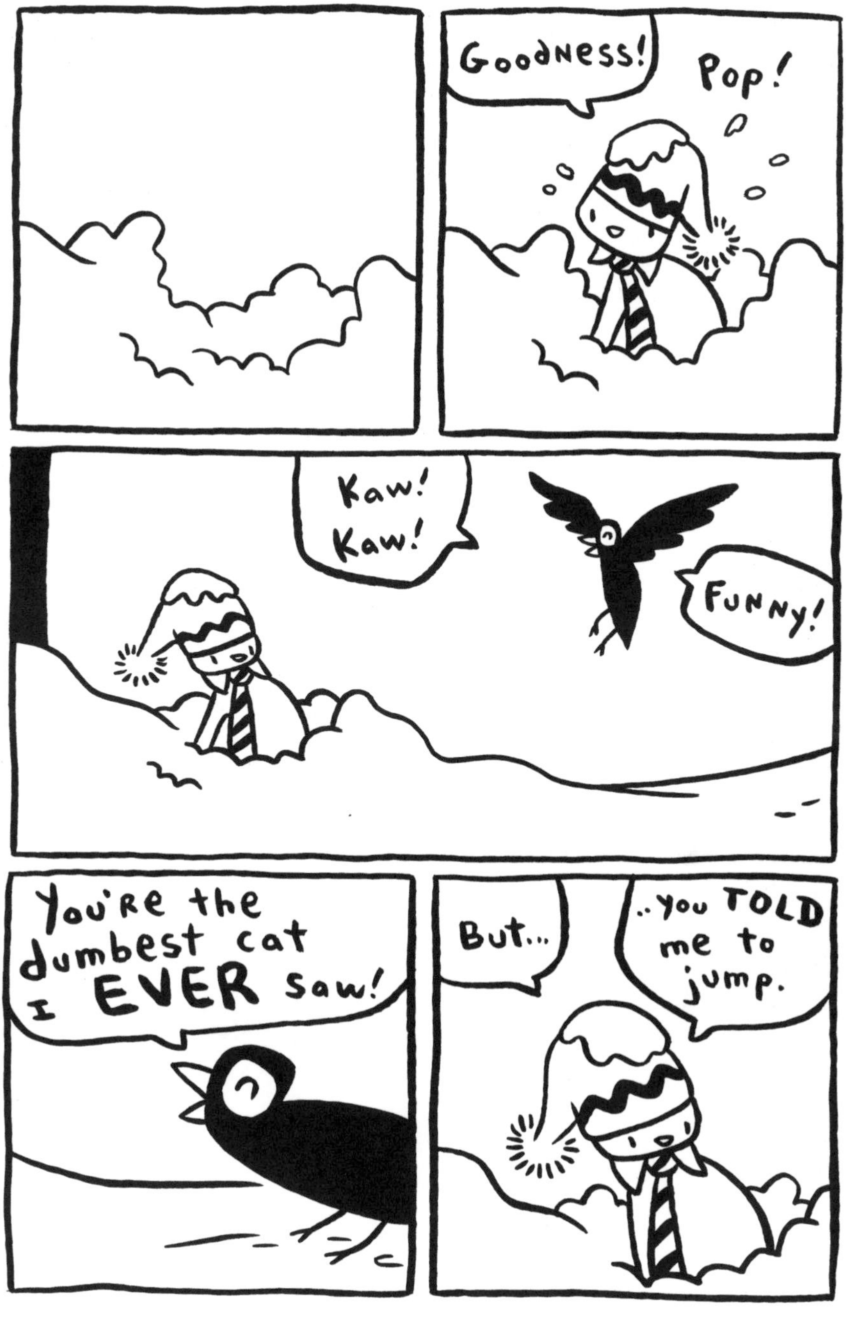
Goodness!
Pop!
Kaw! Kaw!
Funny!
You're the dumbest cat I EVER saw!
But...
..you TOLD me to jump.

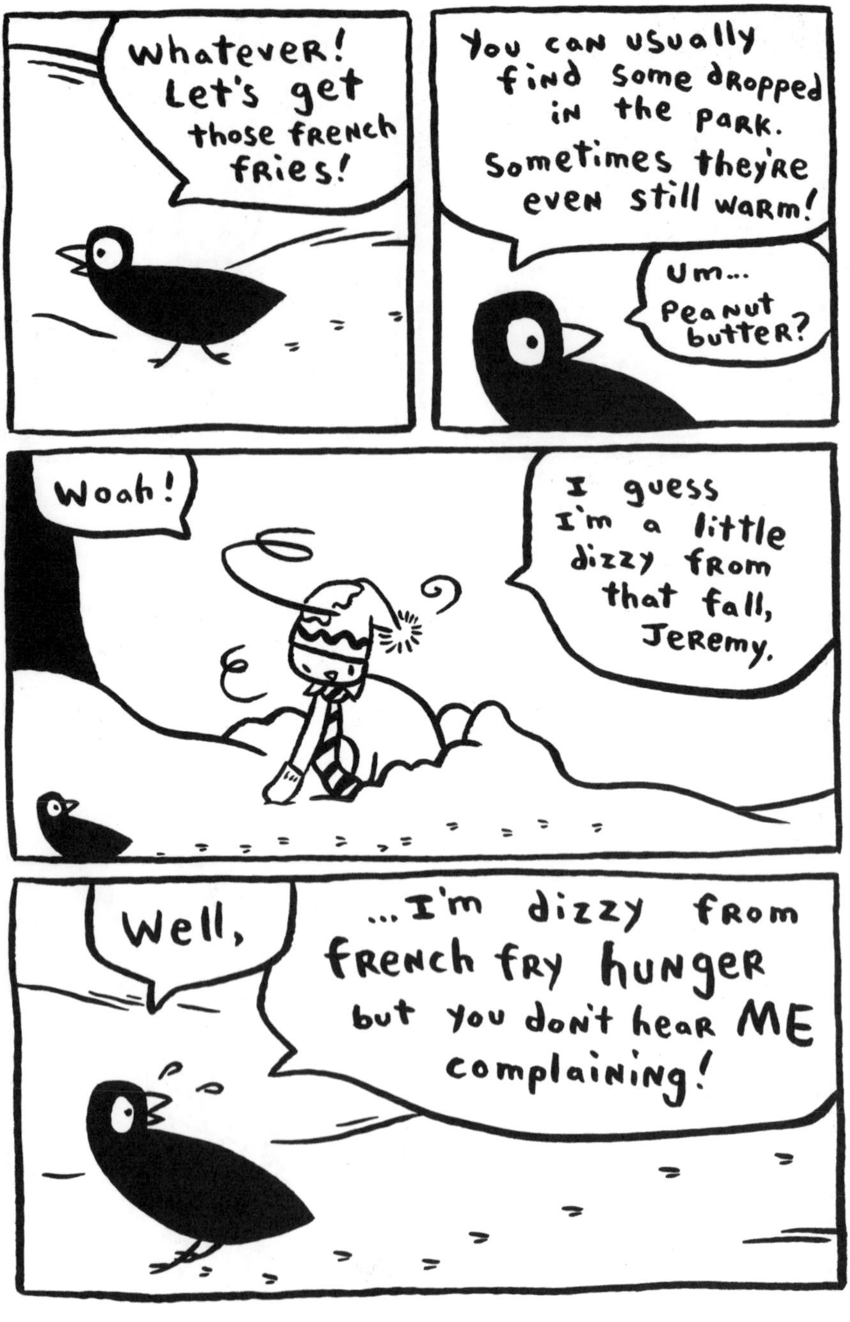
Whatever! Let's get those french fries!
You can usually find some dropped in the park. Sometimes they're even still warm!
Um... peanut butter?
Woah!
I guess I'm a little dizzy from that fall, Jeremy.
Well,
...I'm dizzy from french fry hunger but you don't hear ME complaining!

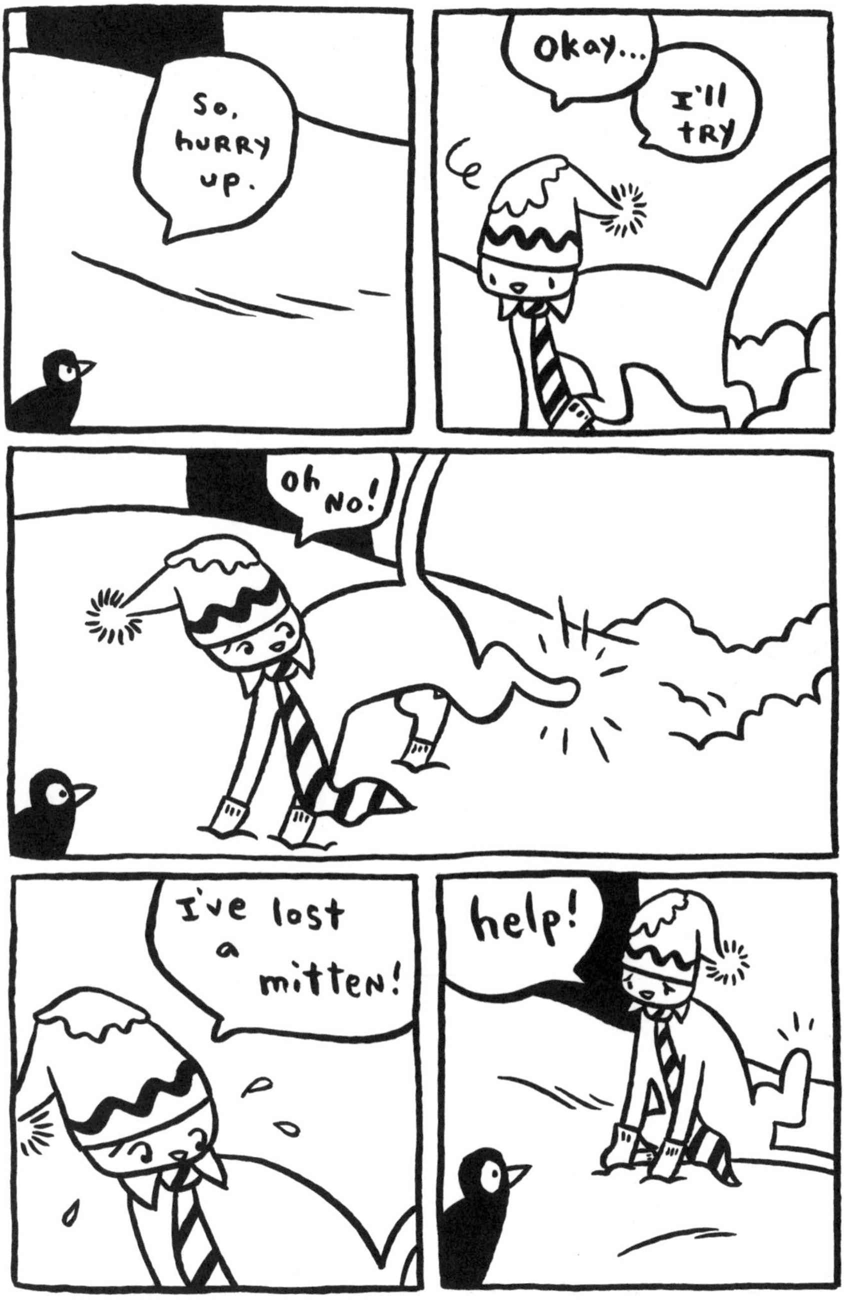
So, hurry up.
Okay...
I'll try
Oh no!
I've lost a mitten!
help!

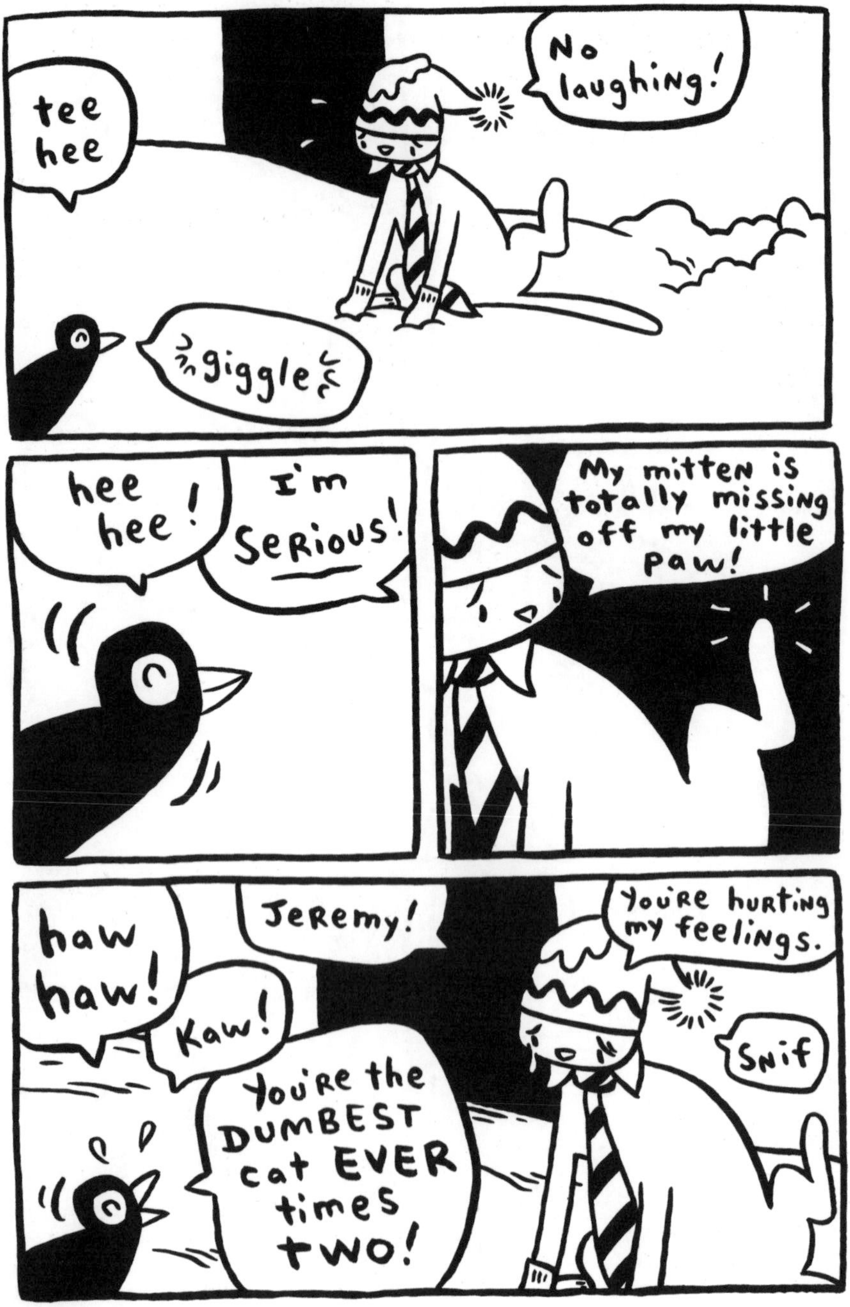
tee hee
No laughing!
giggle
hee hee!
I'm SERIOUS!
My mitten is totally missing off my little paw!
haw haw!
Jeremy!
You're hurting my feelings.
Kaw!
Snif
You're the DUMBEST cat EVER times TWO!

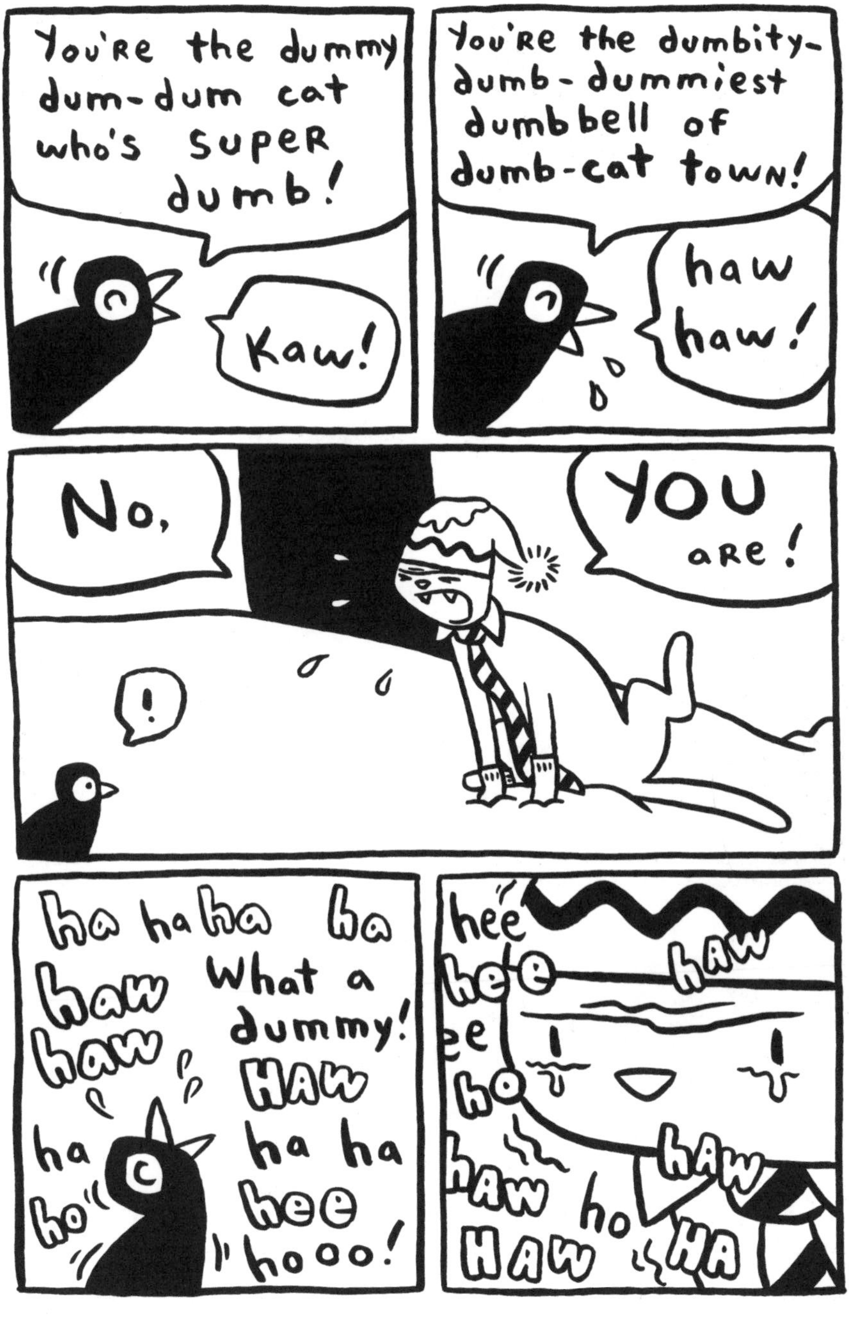
You're the dummy dum-dum cat who's super dumb!
Kaw!
You're the dumbity-dumb-dummiest dumbbell of dumb-cat town!
haw haw!
No,
YOU are!
!
ha ha ha ha ha haw haw
What a dummy!
HAW ha ha hee hooo!
ha ho
hee hee ee ho
HAW
HAW
HAW ho HAW
HA

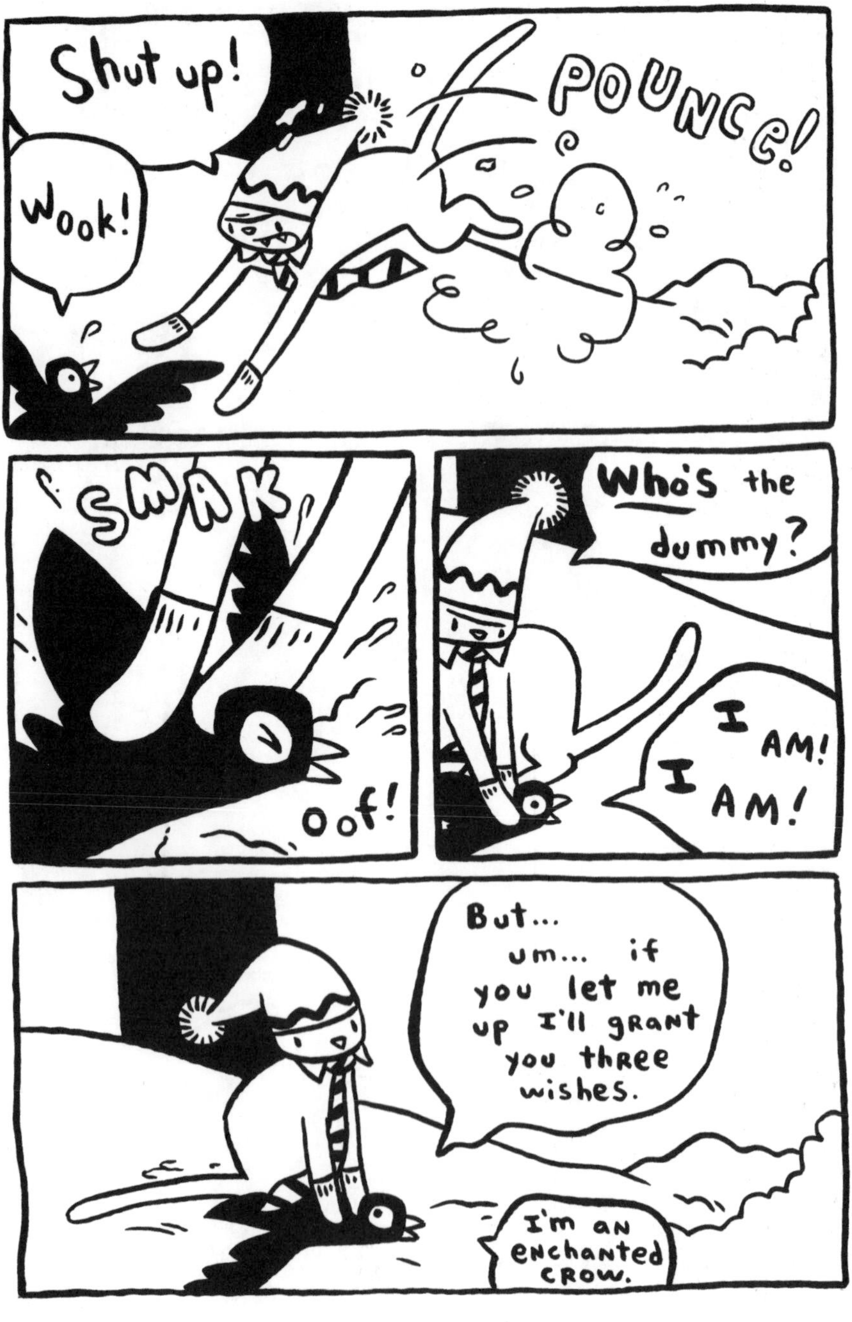
Shut up!
Wook!
POUNCE!
SMAK
Oof!
Who's the dummy?
I AM! I AM!
But... um... if you let me up I'll grant you three wishes.
I'm an enchanted crow.

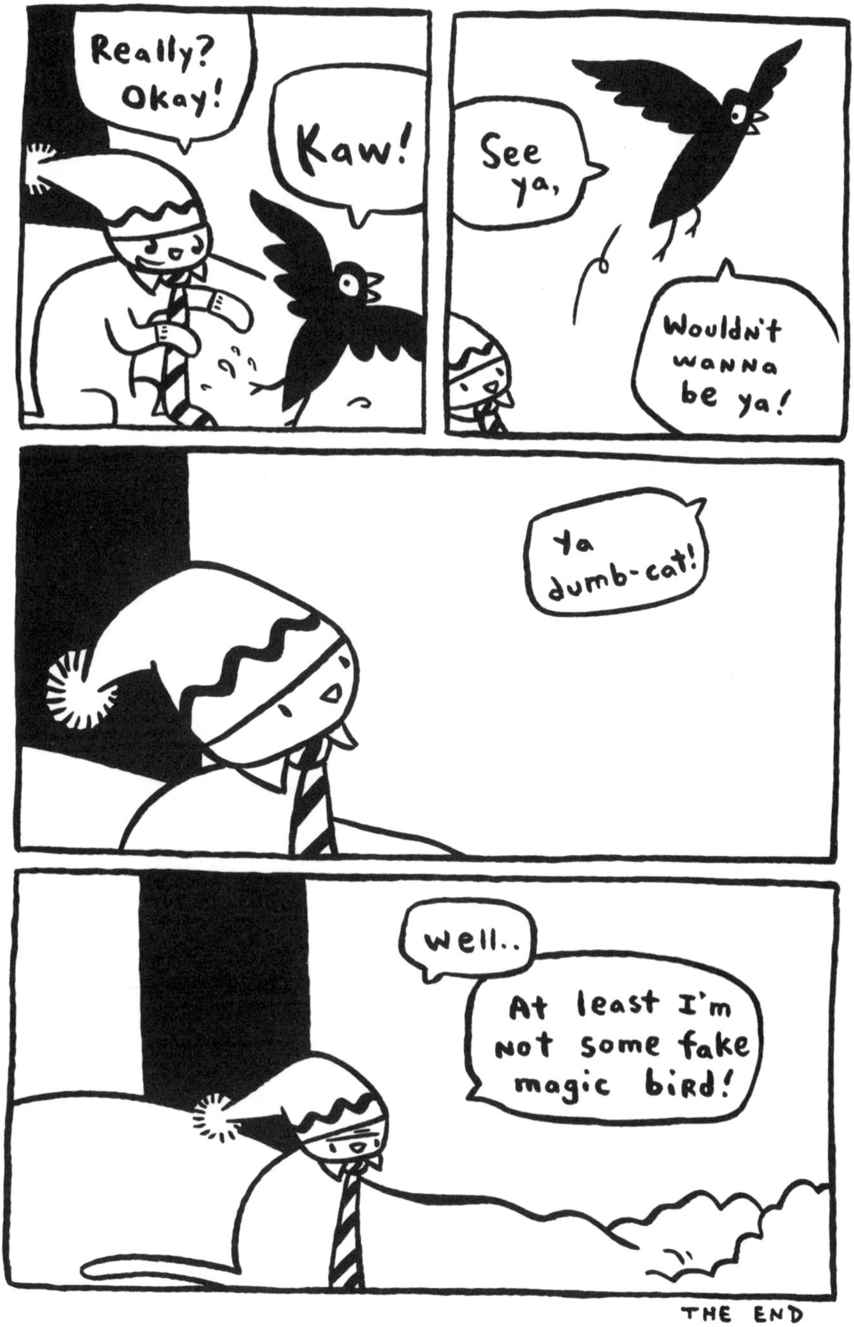
Really? Okay!
Kaw!
See ya,
Wouldn't wanna be ya!
Ya dumb-cat!
well..
At least I'm not some fake magic bird!

THE END

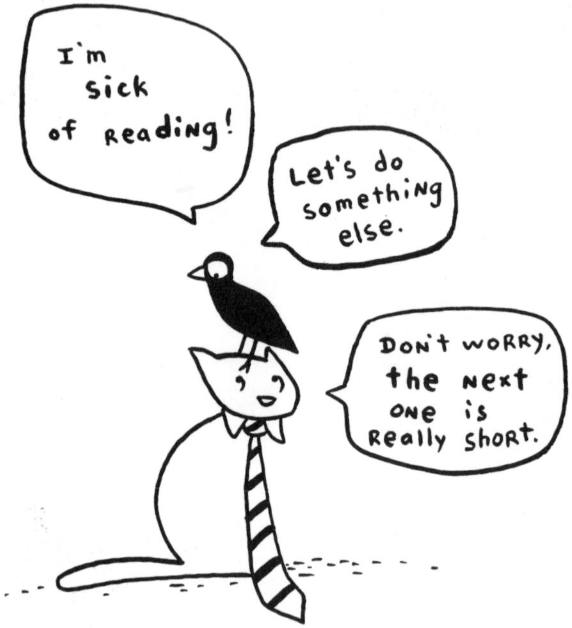
I'm sick of reading!
Let's do something else.
Don't worry, the next one is really short.

THE SNOWFLAKE BREAK

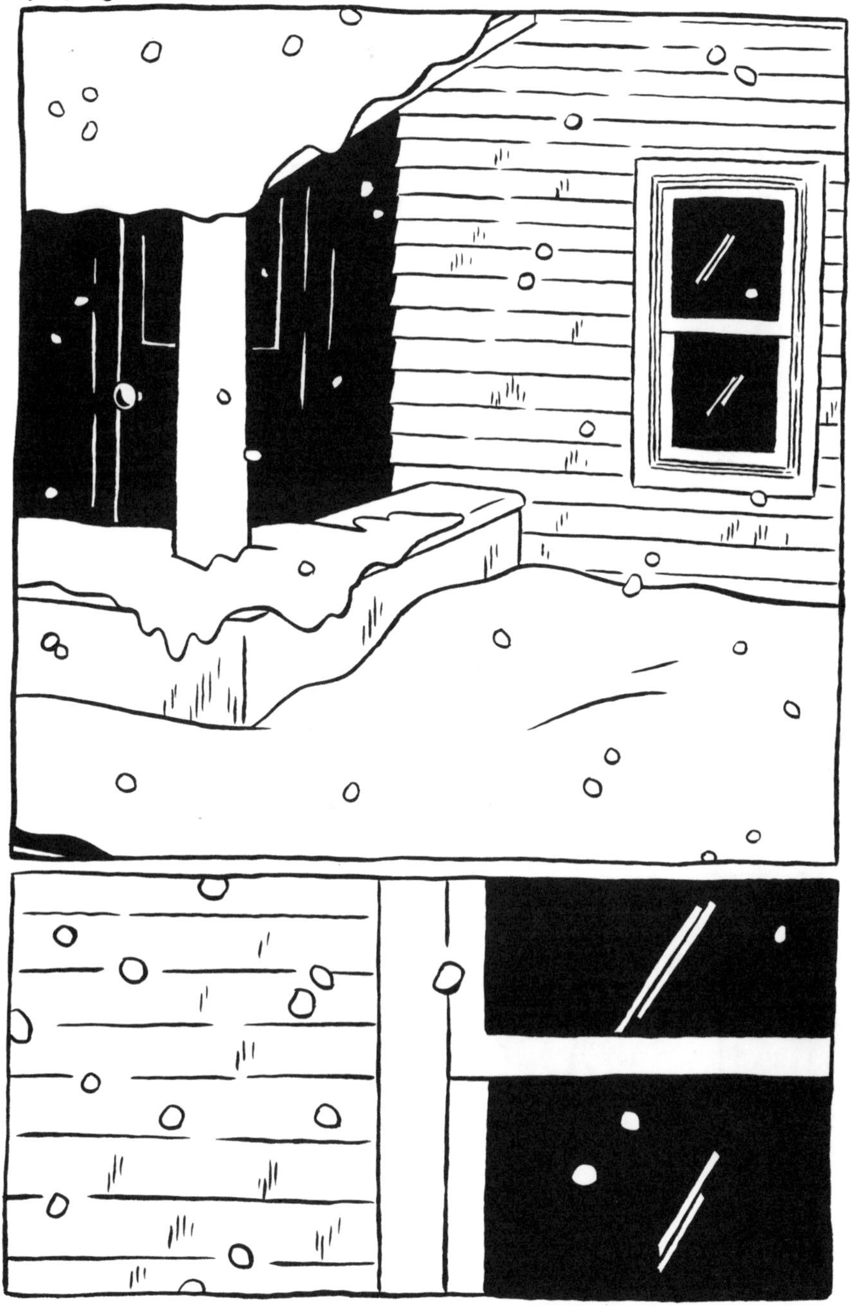

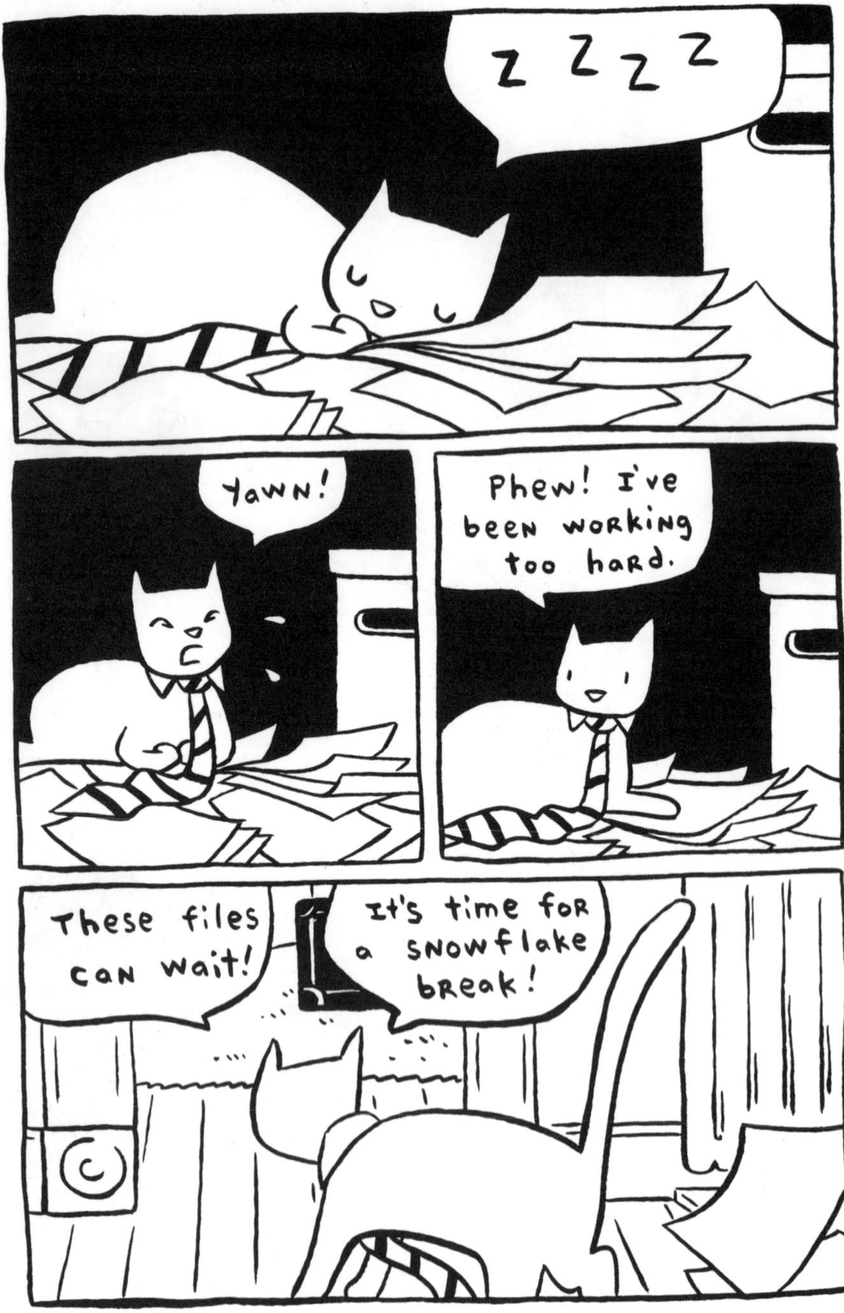
Z Z Z Z
Yawn!
Phew! I've been working too hard.
These files can wait!
It's time for a snowflake break!

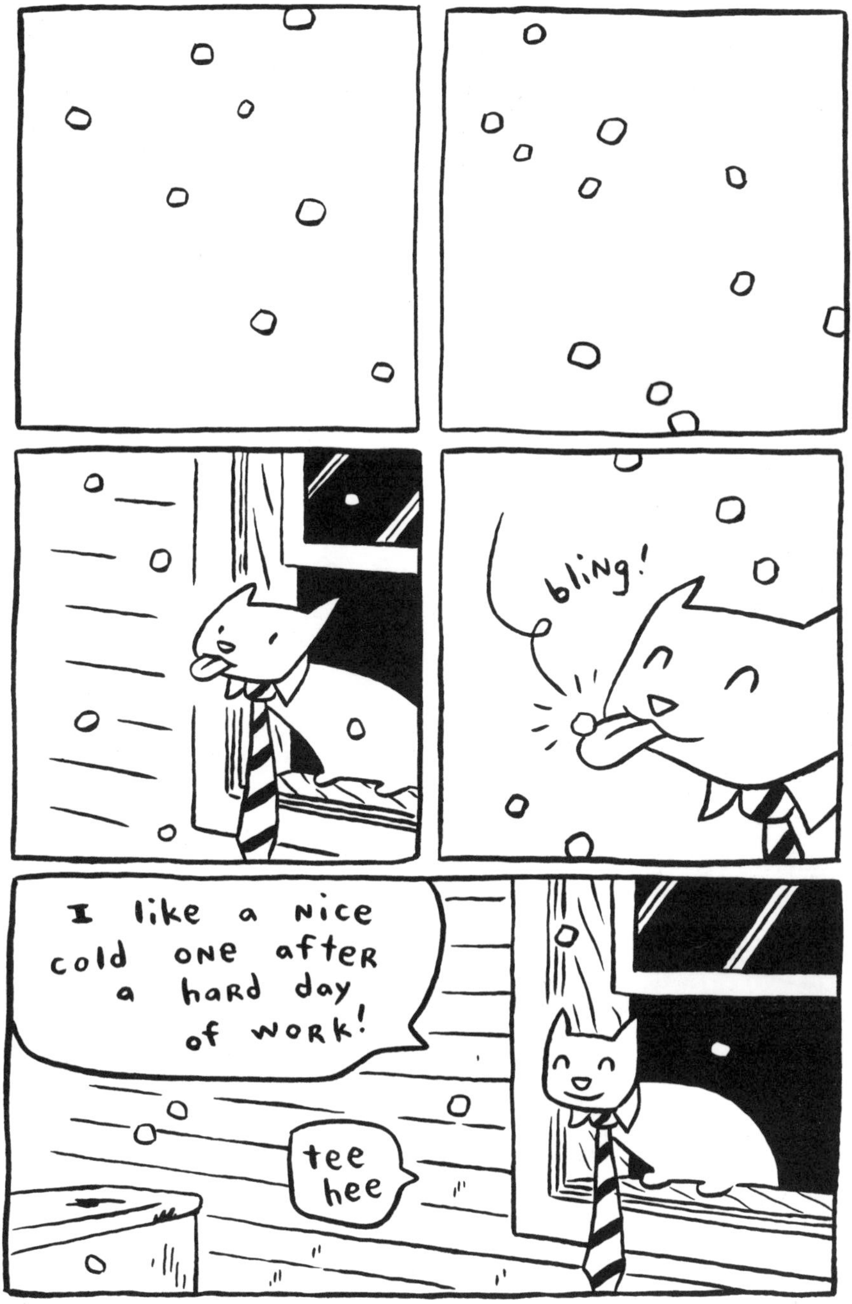
bling!
I like a nice cold one after a hard day of work!
tee hee

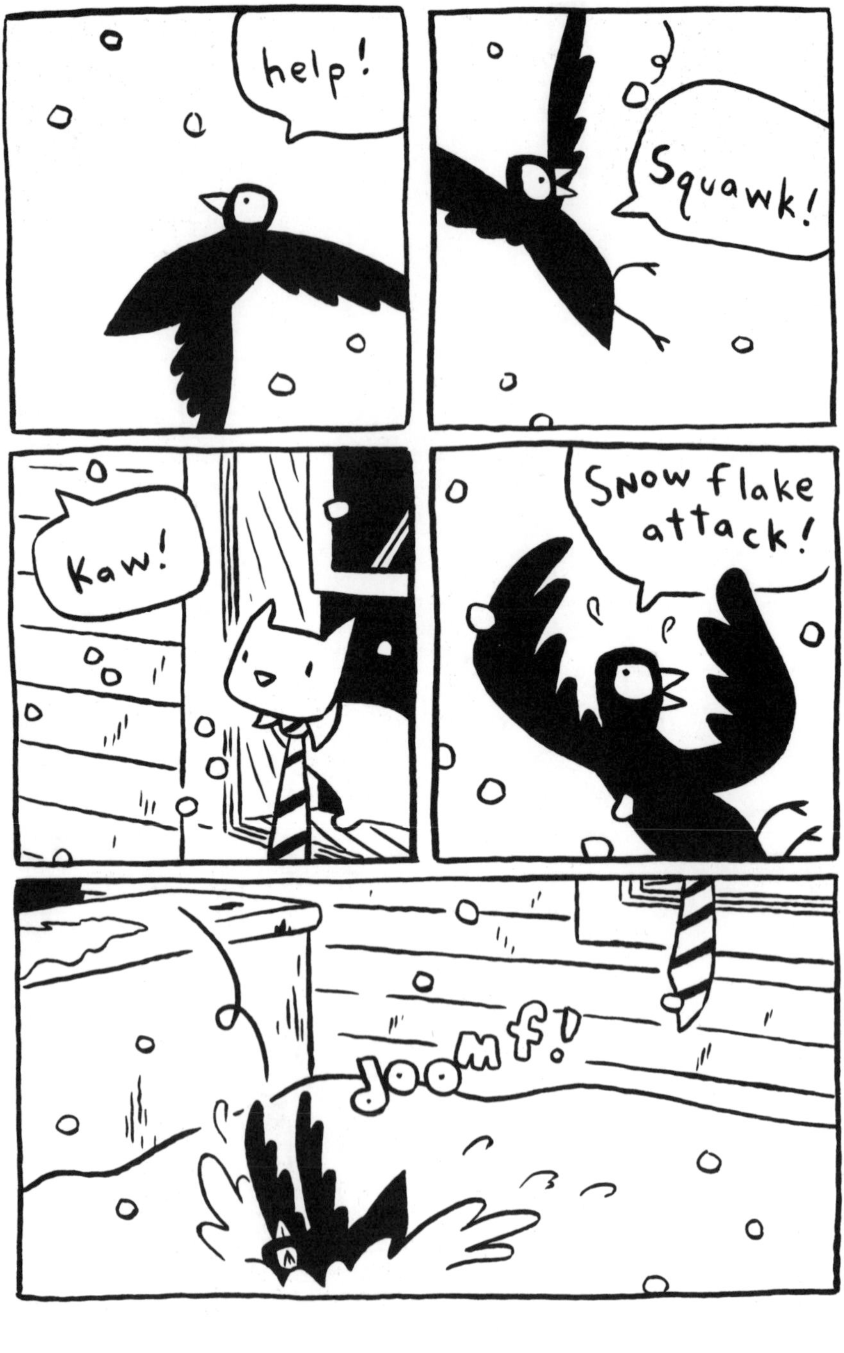
help!
Squawk!
Kaw!
Snow flake attack!
Joomf!

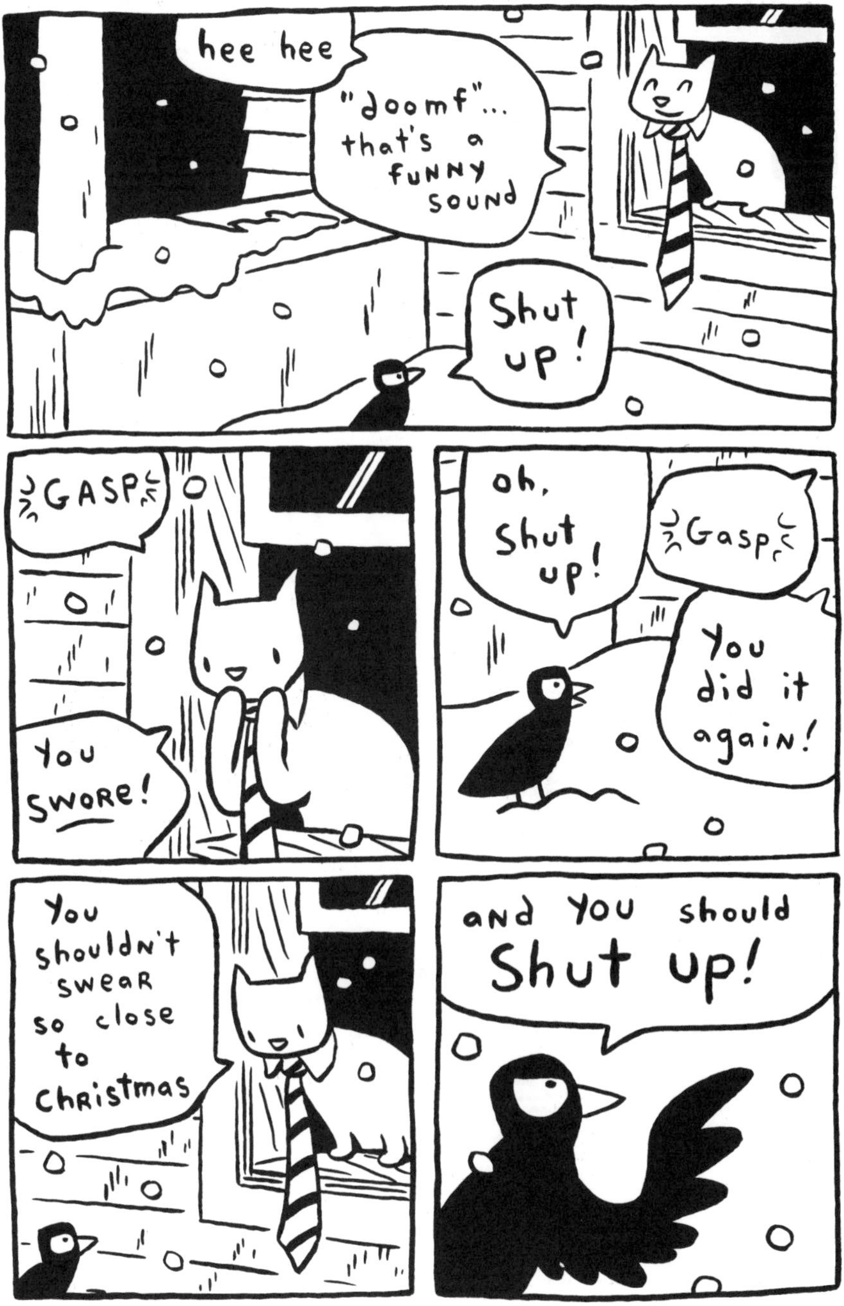
hee hee
"doomf"... that's a funny sound
Shut up!
GASP
You swore!
oh, Shut up!
Gasp
You did it again!
You shouldn't swear so close to Christmas
and you should Shut up!

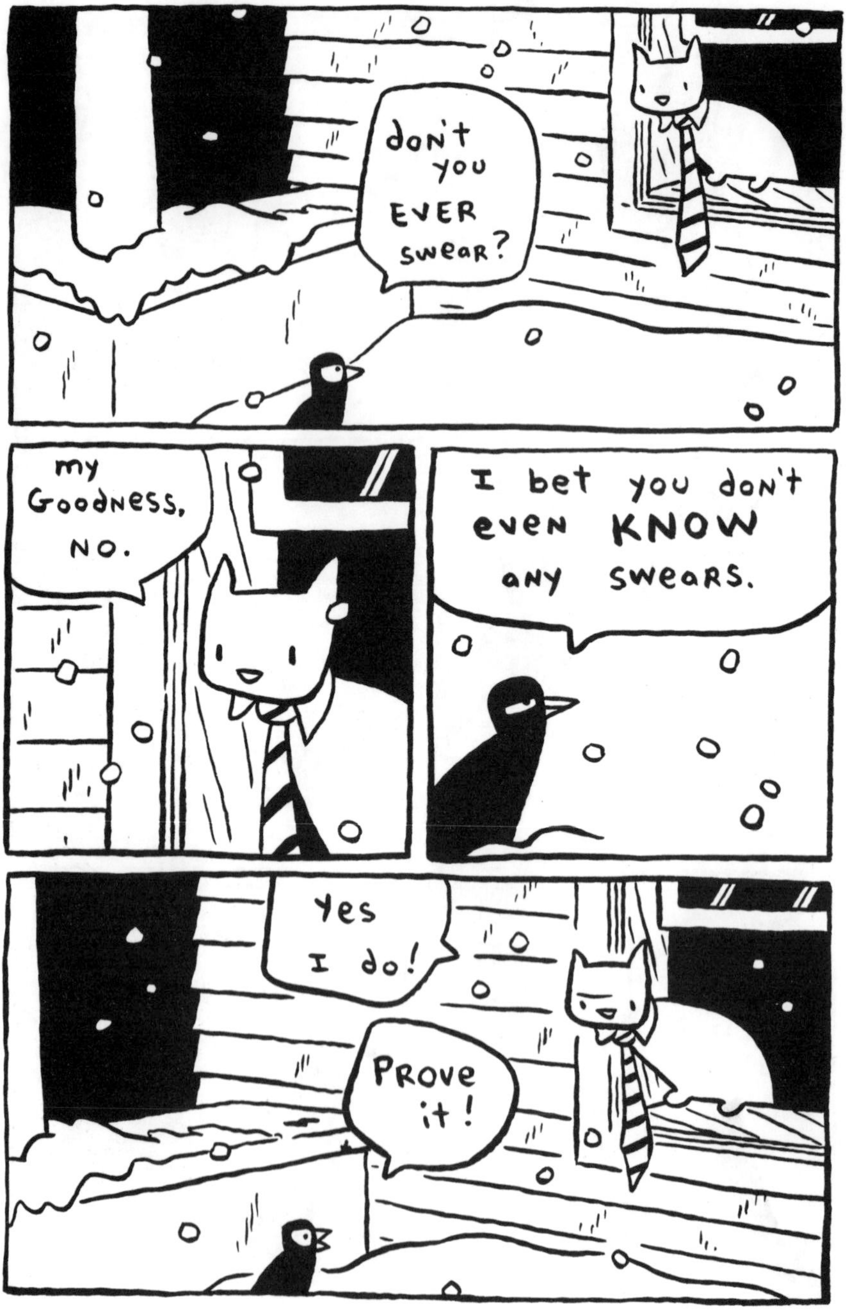
don't you EVER swear?
my Goodness, NO.
I bet you don't even KNOW any swears.
Yes I do!
Prove it!

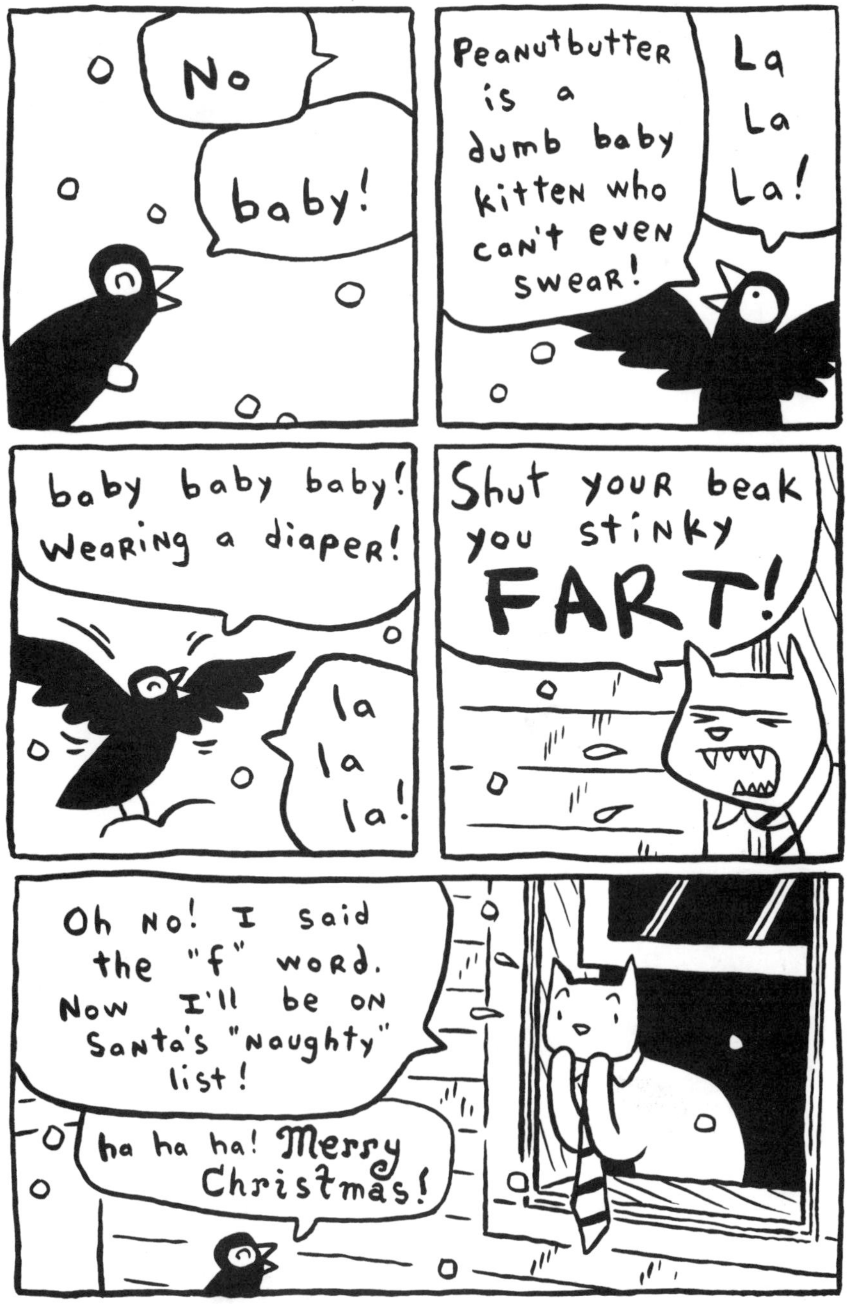
No
baby!
Peanutbutter is a dumb baby kitten who can't even swear!
La La La!
baby baby baby! Wearing a diaper!
la la la!
Shut your beak you stinky FART!
Oh no! I said the "f" word. Now I'll be on Santa's "naughty" list!
ha ha ha! Merry Christmas!

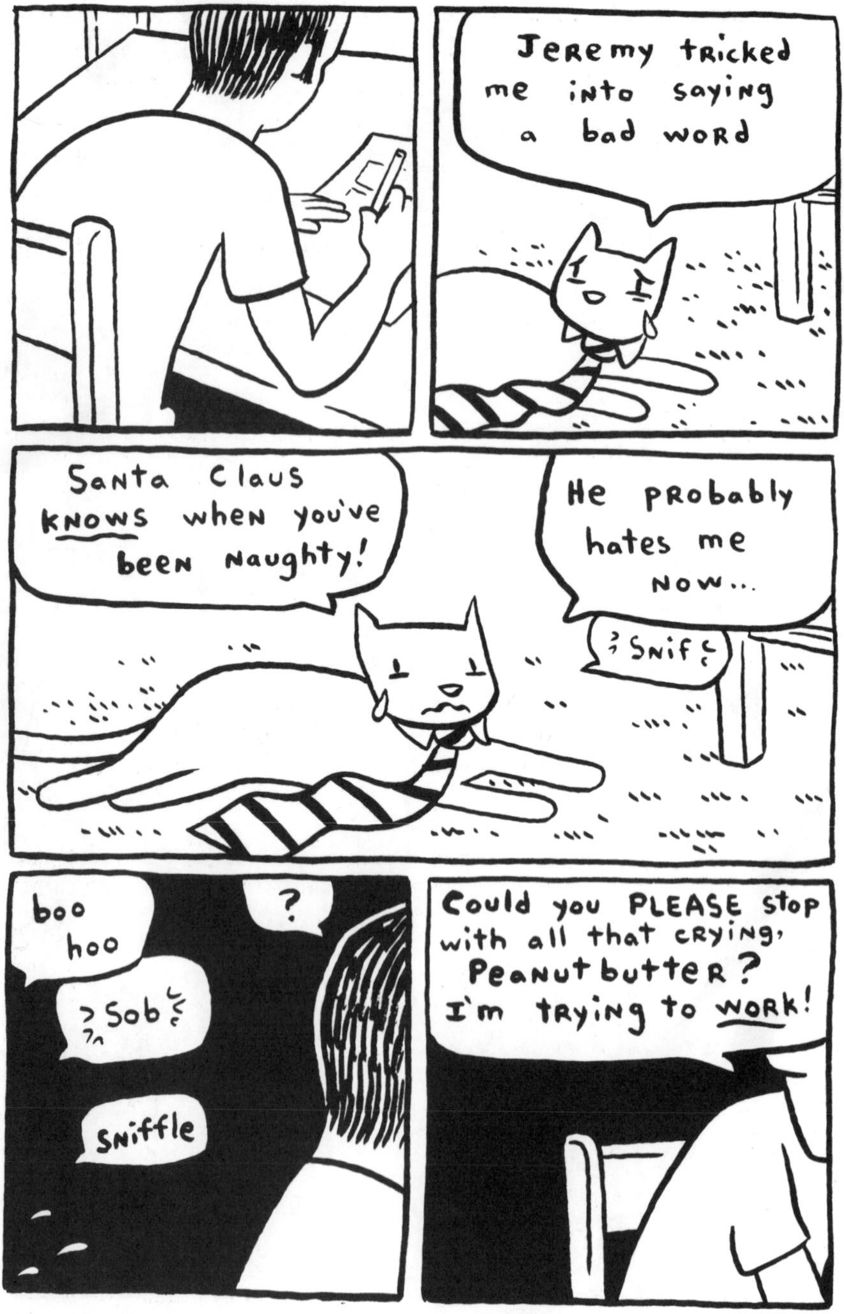
Jeremy tricked me into saying a bad word
Santa Claus KNOWS when you've been naughty!
He probably hates me now...
Snif
boo hoo
?
Sob
sniffle
Could you PLEASE stop with all that crying, Peanutbutter? I'm trying to WORK!

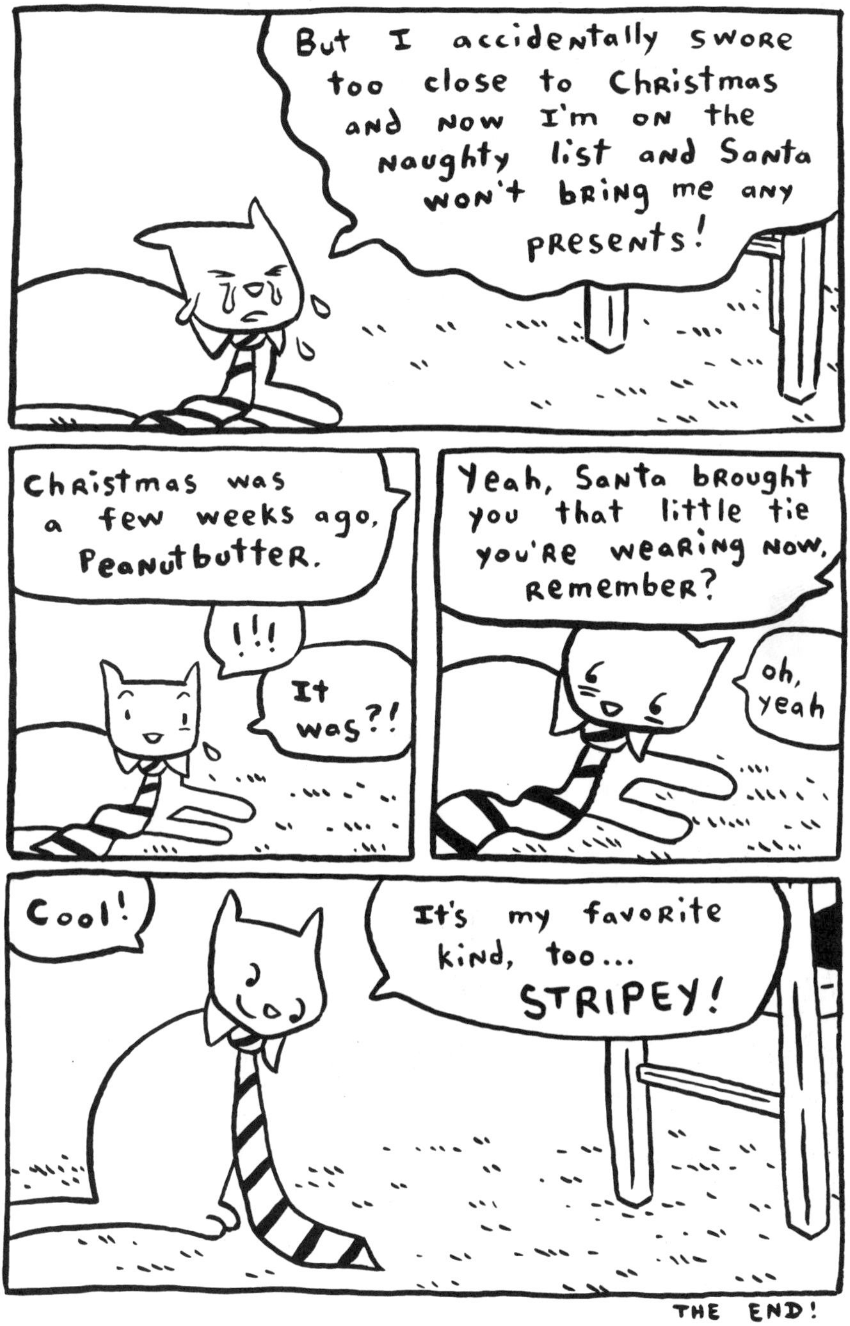
But I accidentally swore too close to Christmas and now I'm on the naughty list and Santa won't bring me any presents!
Christmas was a few weeks ago, Peanutbutter.
!!!
It was?!
Yeah, Santa brought you that little tie you're wearing now, remember?
oh, yeah
Cool!
It's my favorite kind, too... STRIPEY!

THE END!

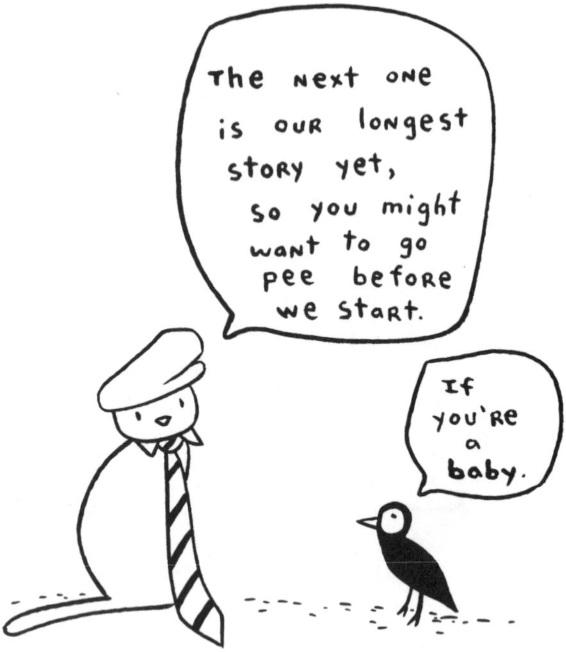
The next one is our longest story yet, so you might want to go pee before we start.
If you're a baby.

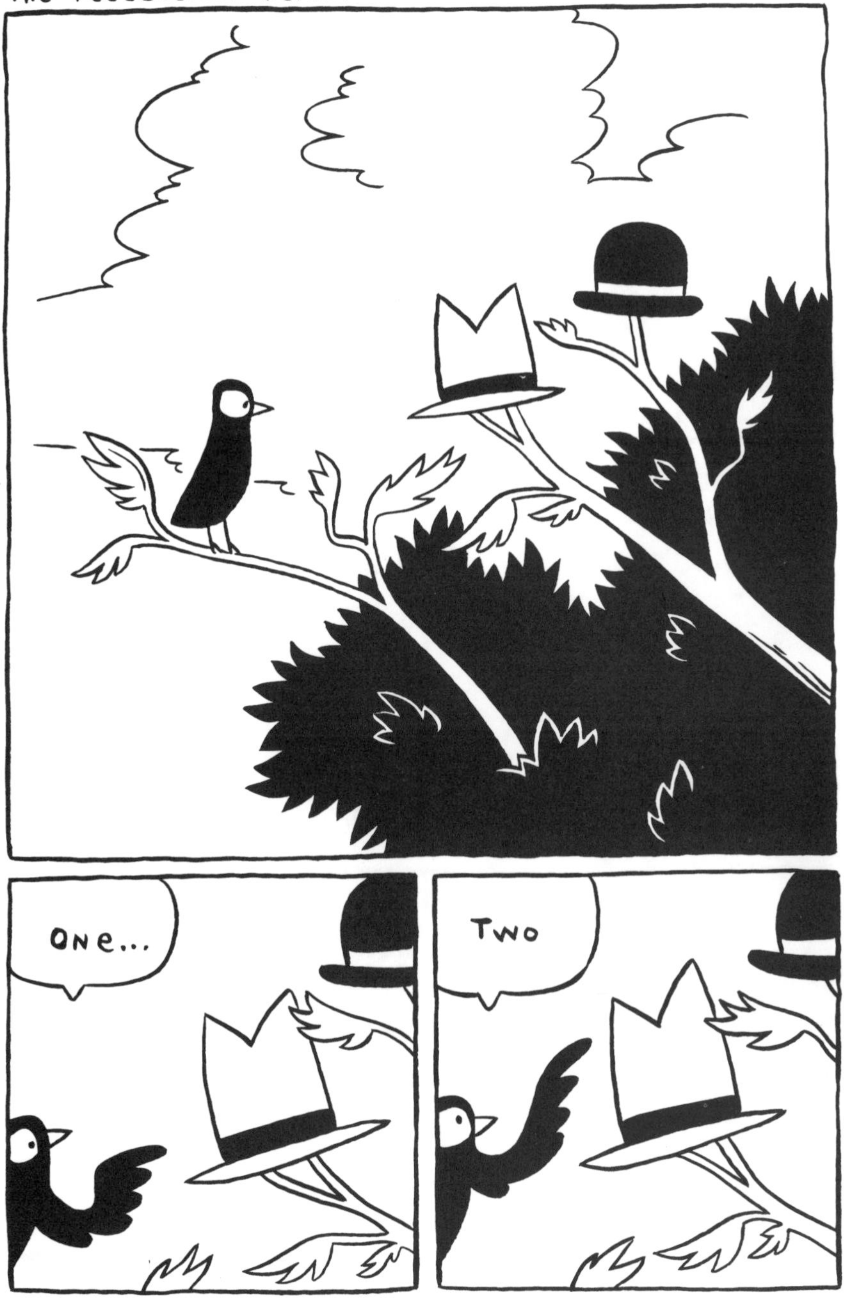
One...
TWO

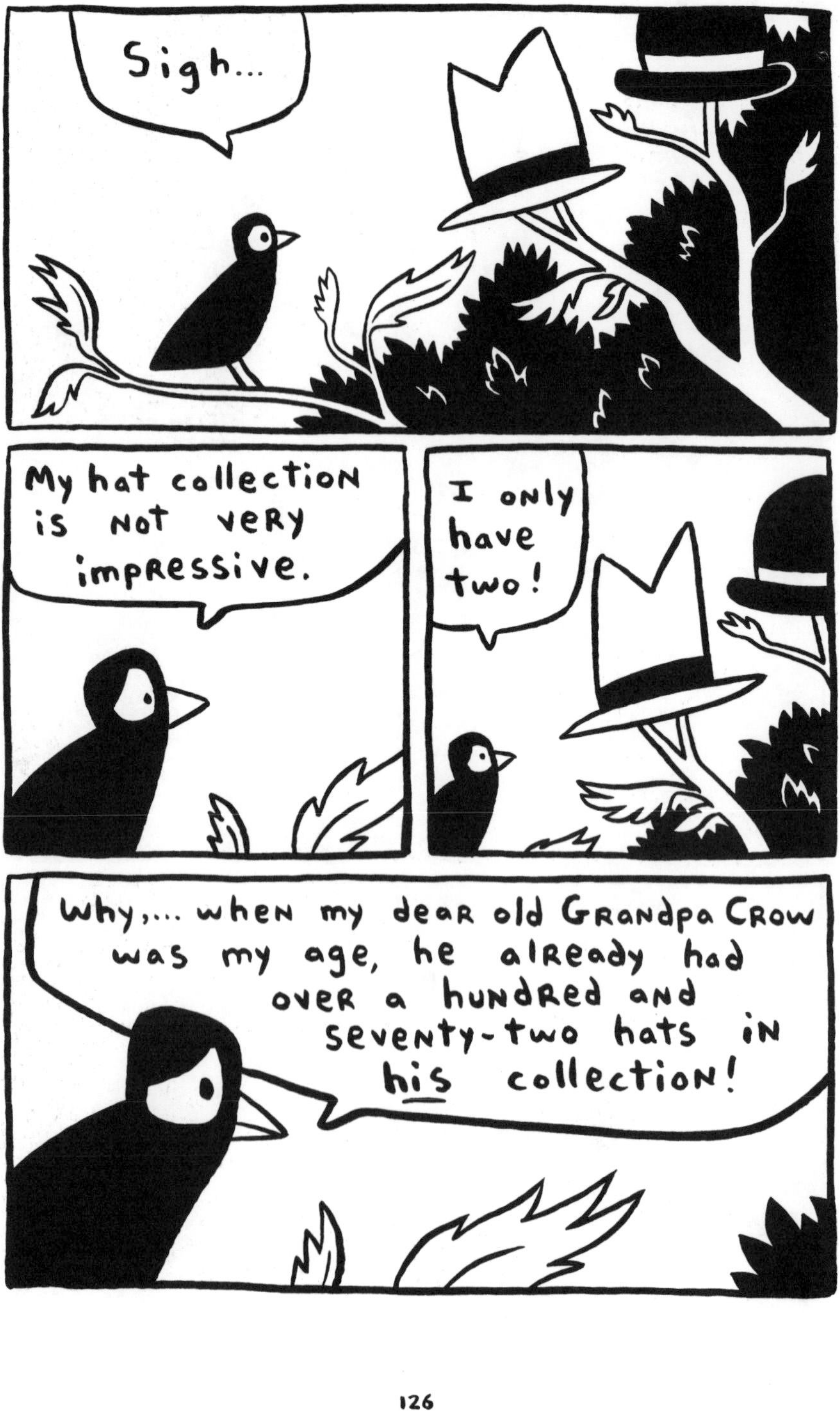
Sigh...
My hat collection is not very impressive.
I only have two!
Why,... when my dear old Grandpa Crow was my age, he already had over a hundred and seventy-two hats in his collection!

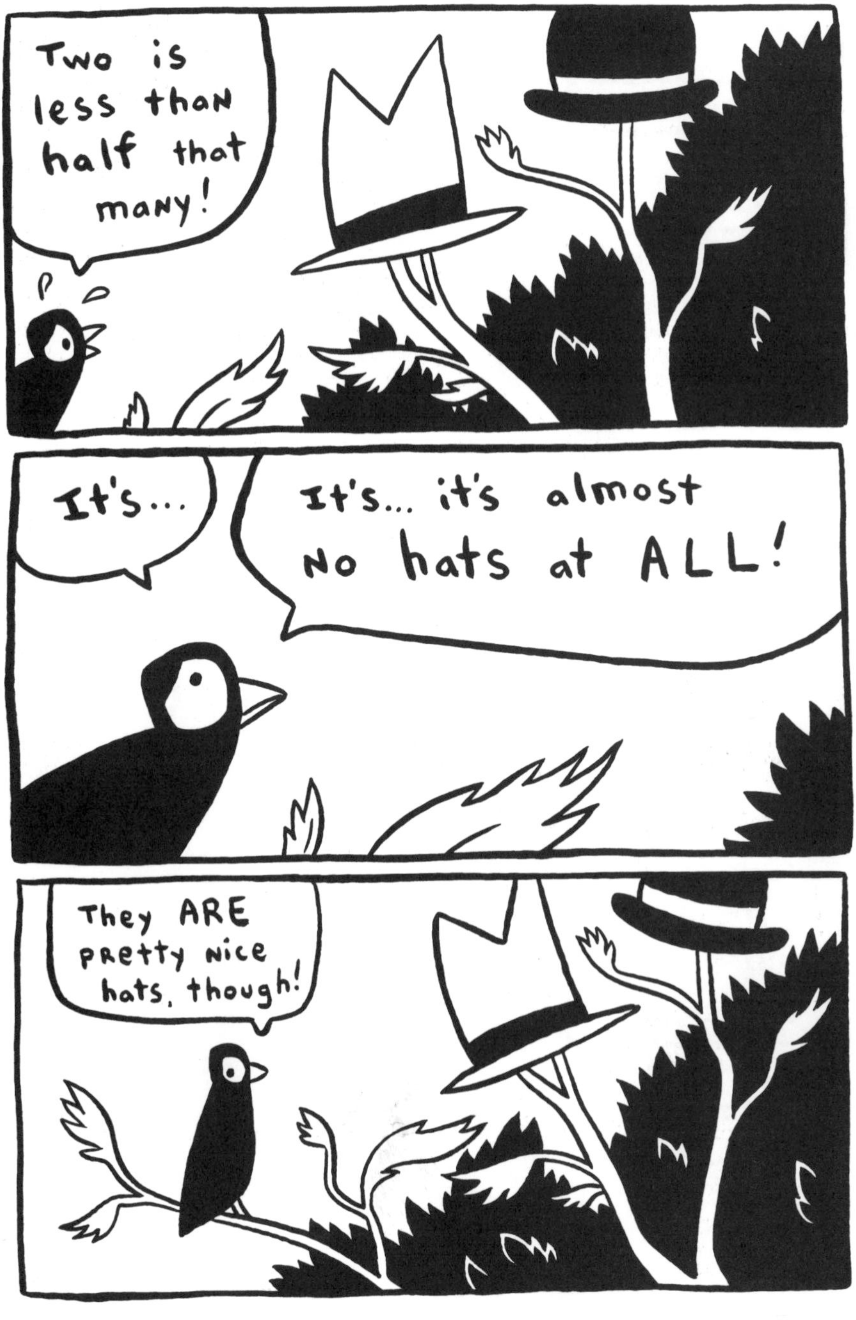
Two is less than half that many!
It's...
It's... it's almost no hats at ALL!
They ARE pretty nice hats, though!

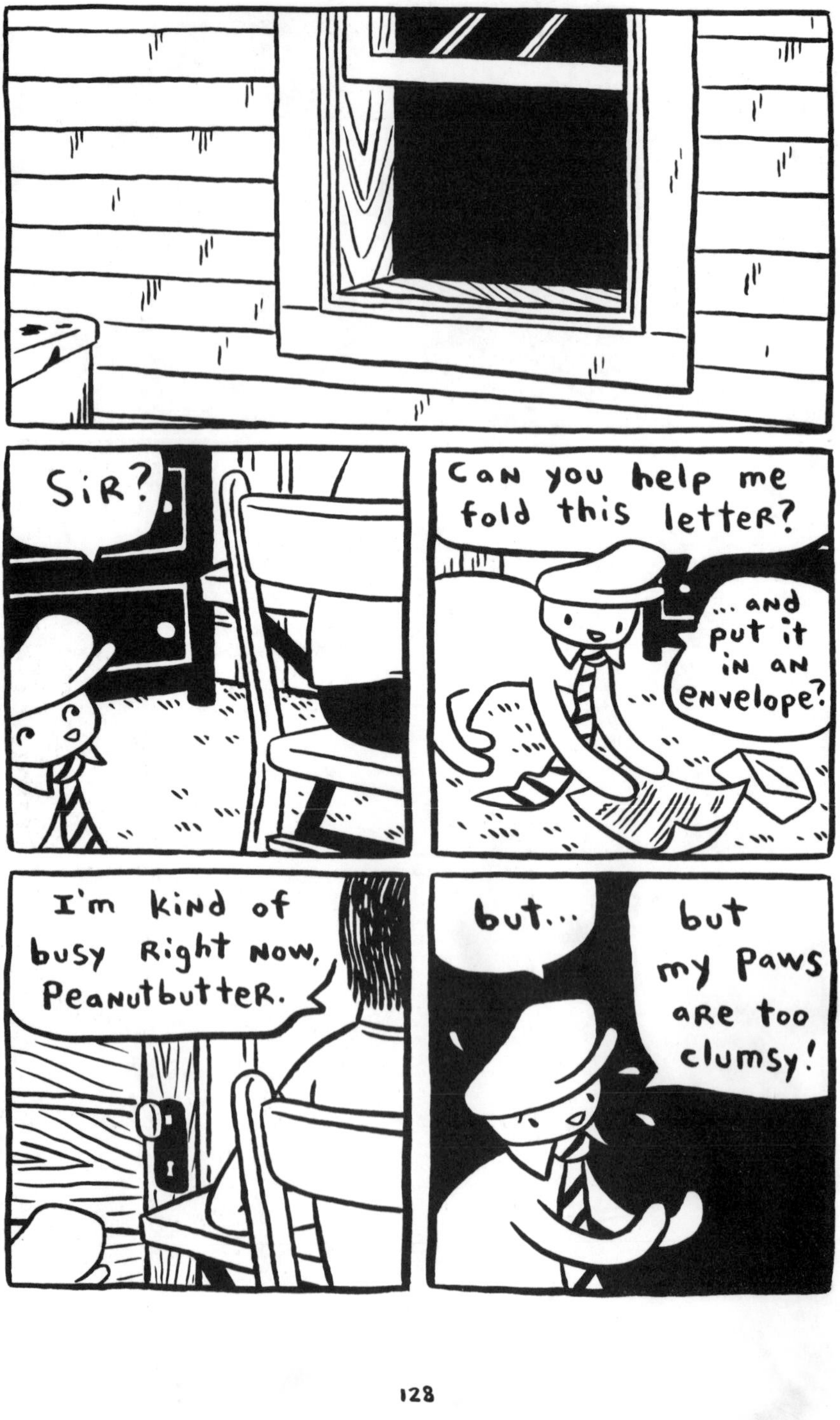
SiR?
Can you help me fold this letter?
... and put it in an envelope?
I'm kind of busy right now, Peanutbutter.
but...
but my paws are too clumsy!

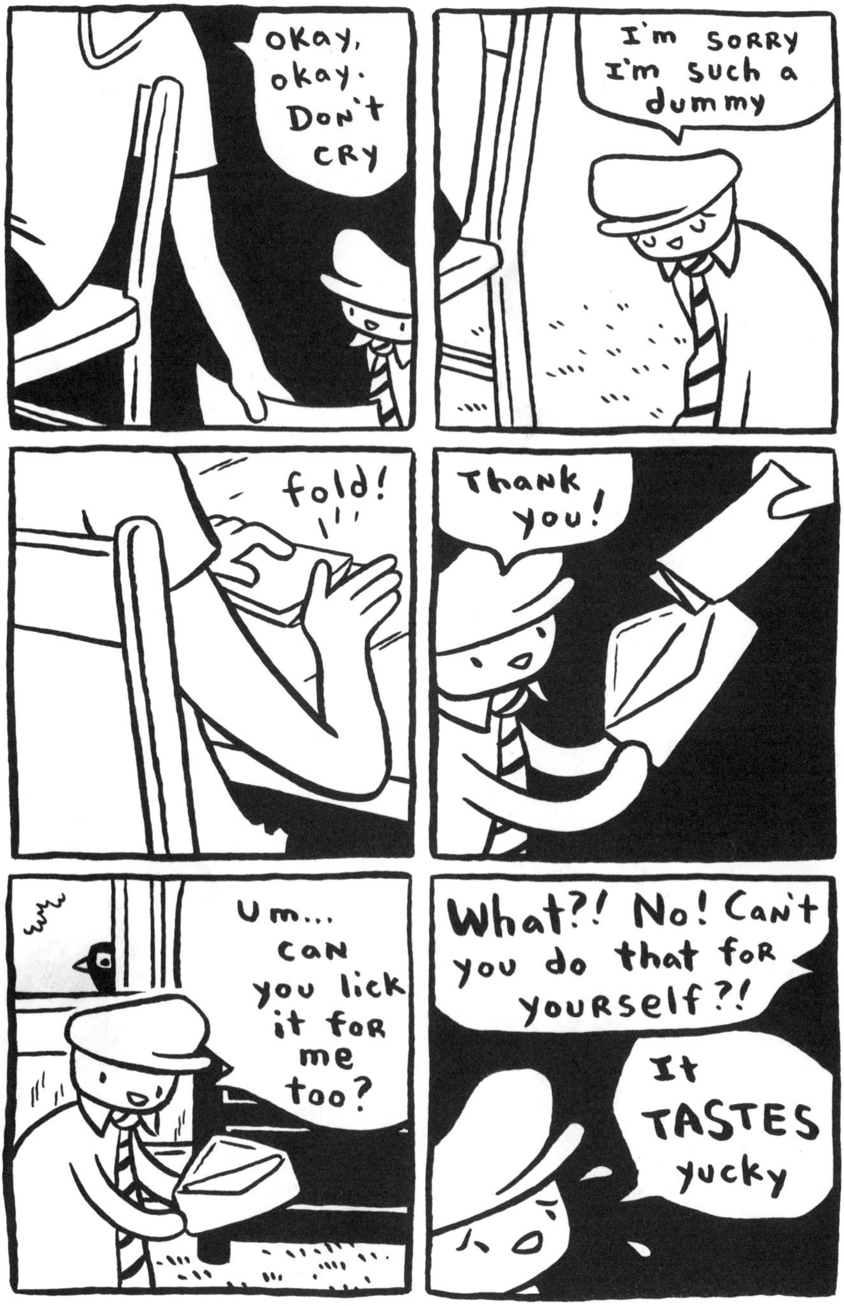
Okay, okay. Don't cry
I'm sorry I'm such a dummy
fold!
Thank you!
Um... can you lick it for me too?
What?! No! Can't you do that for yourself?!
It TASTES yucky

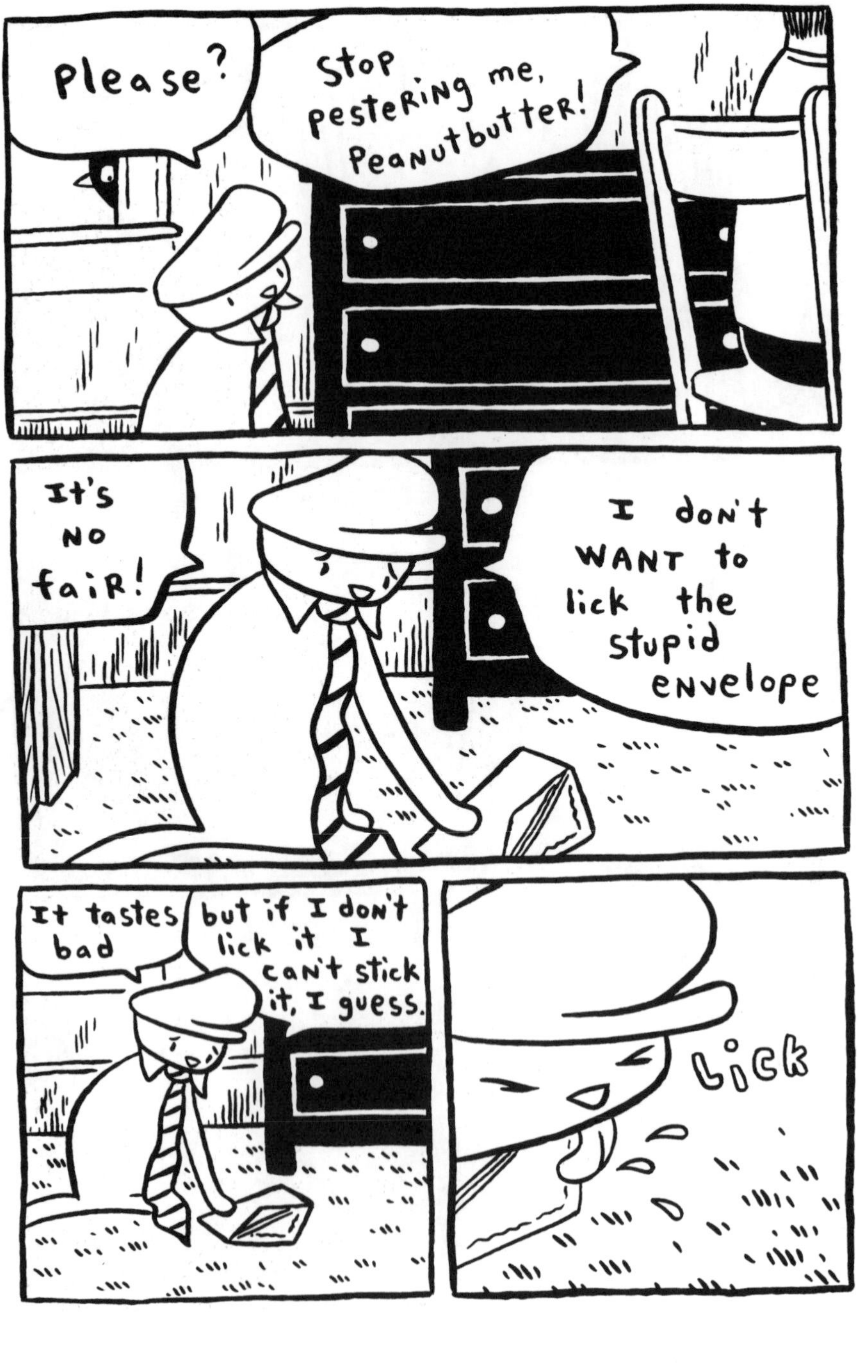
Please?
Stop pestering me, Peanutbutter!
It's no fair!
I don't WANT to lick the stupid envelope
It tastes bad
but if I don't lick it I can't stick it, I guess.
Lick

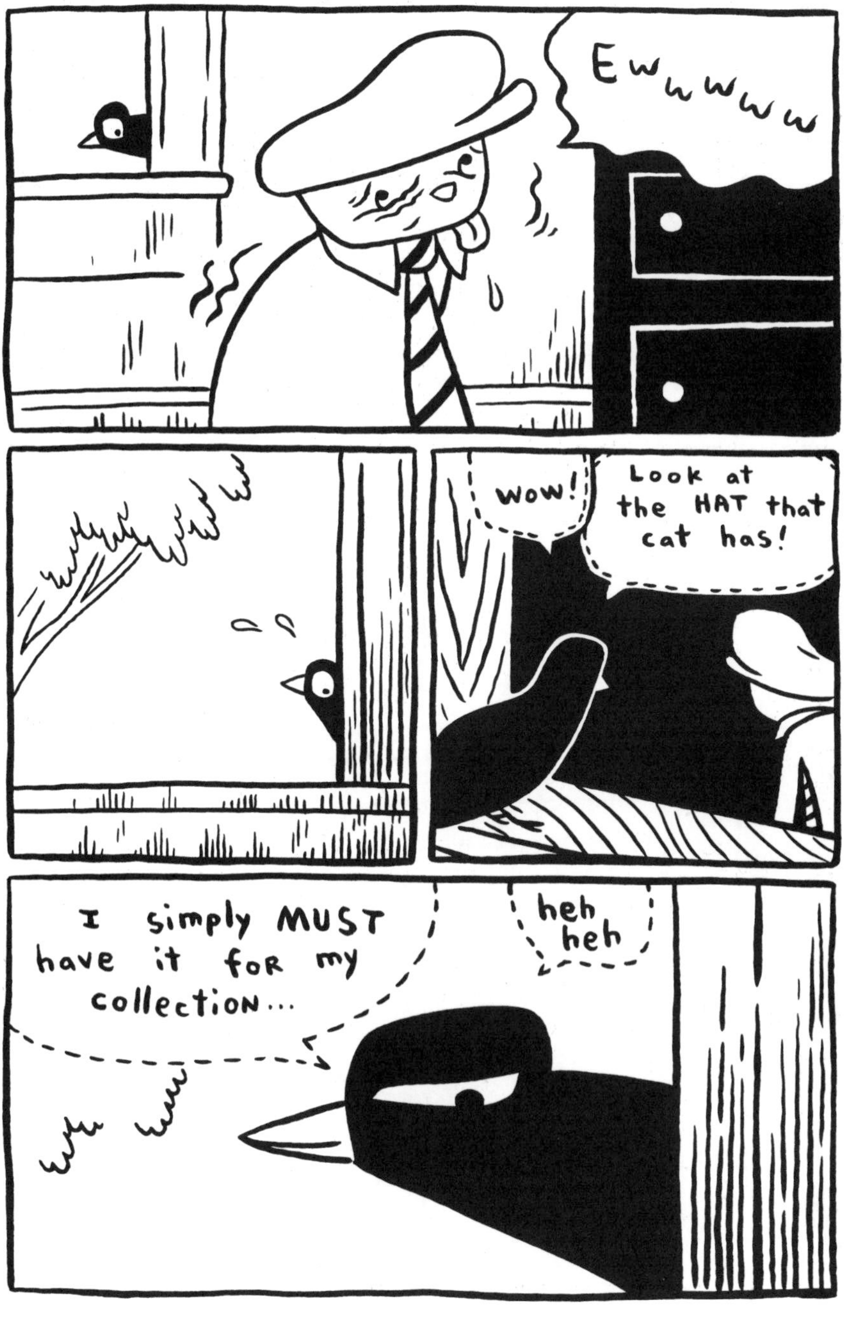
Ewwwwww
WOW!
Look at the HAT that cat has!
I simply MUST have it for my collection...
heh heh

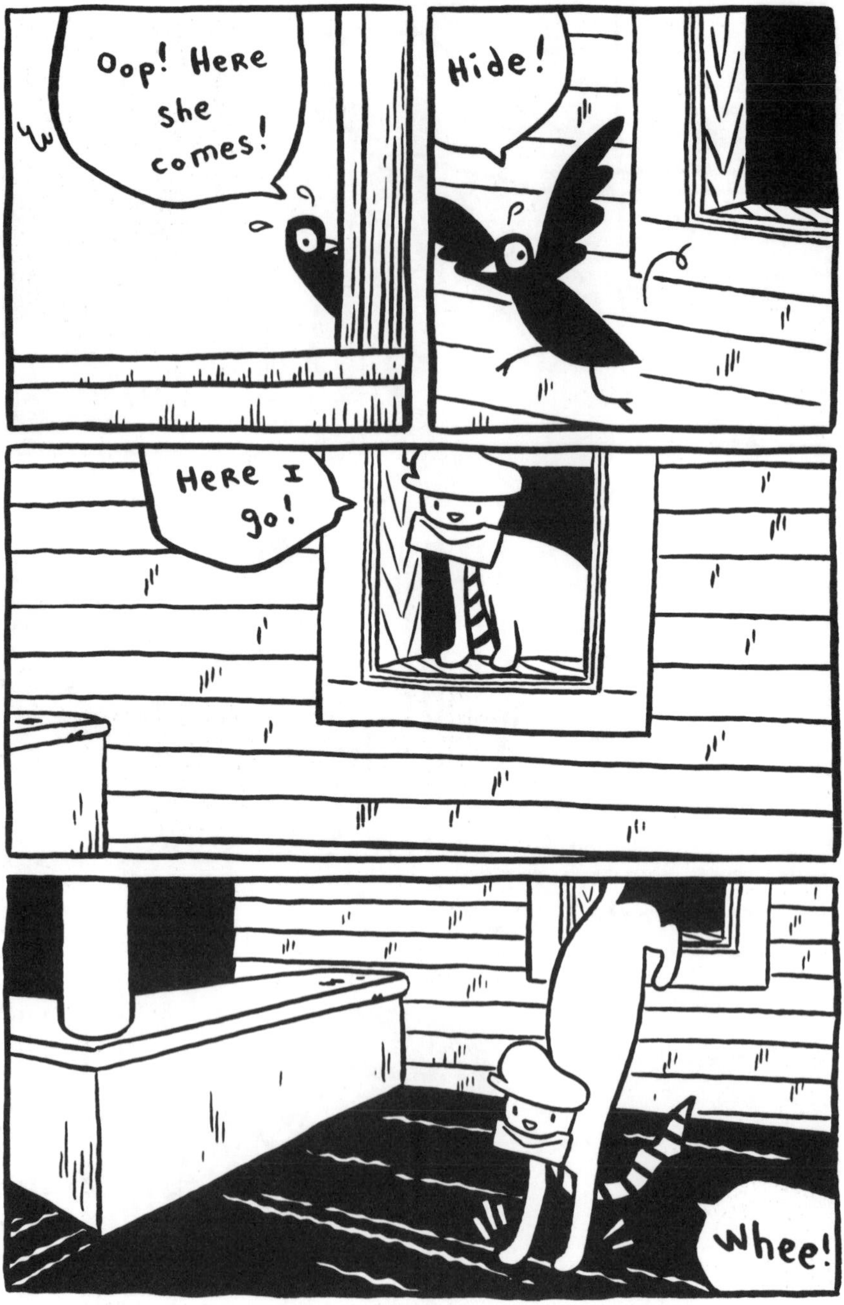
Oop! Here she comes!
Hide!
Here I go!
Whee!

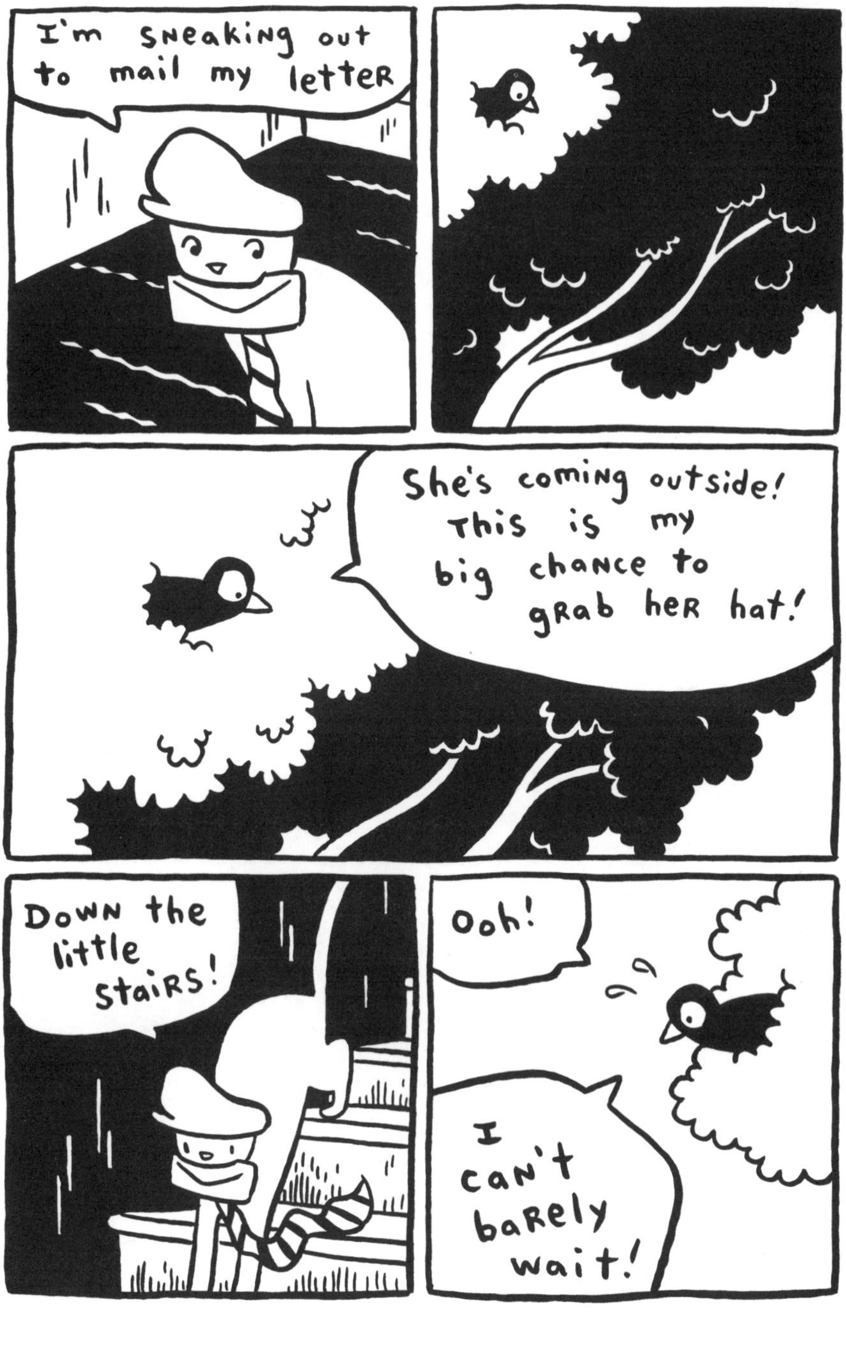
I'm sneaking out to mail my letter
She's coming outside! This is my big chance to grab her hat!
Down the little stairs!
Ooh!
I can't barely wait!

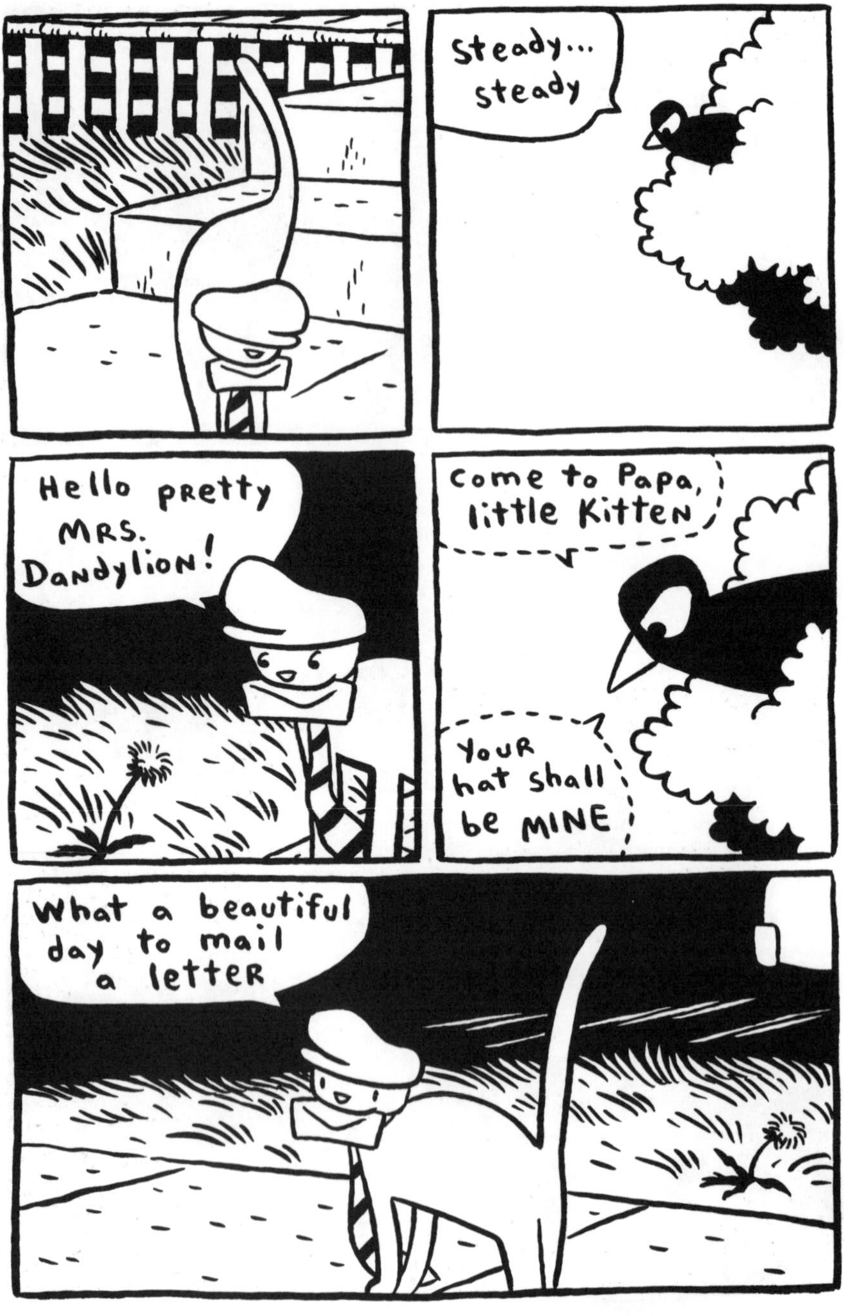
Steady... steady
Hello pretty MRS. Dandylion!
come to Papa, little Kitten
YOUR hat shall be MINE
What a beautiful day to mail a letter

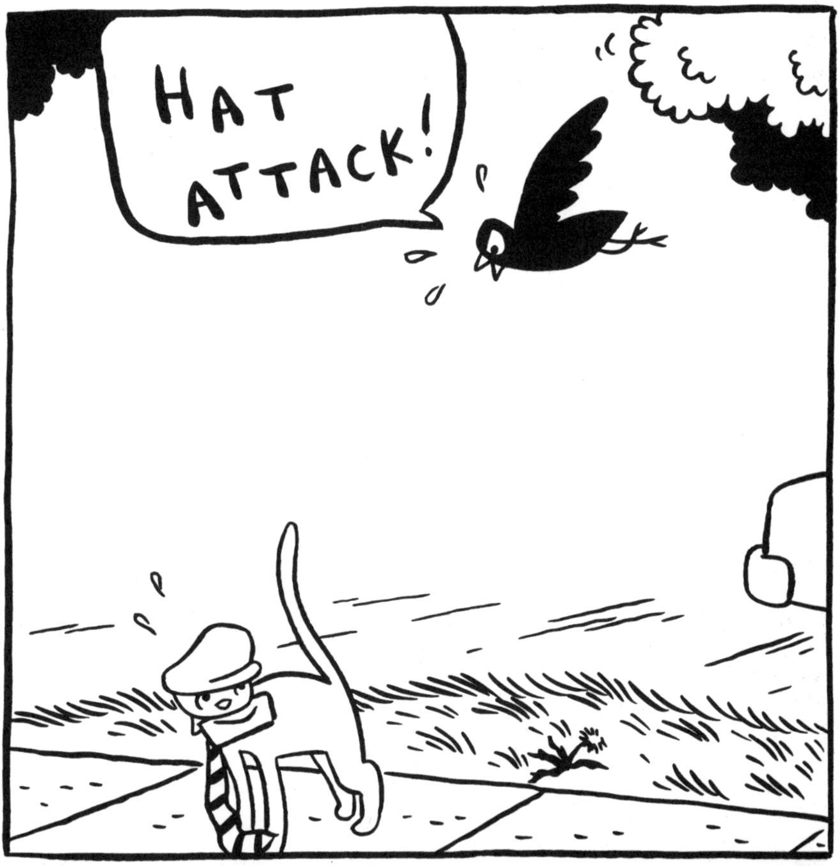
HAT ATTACK!

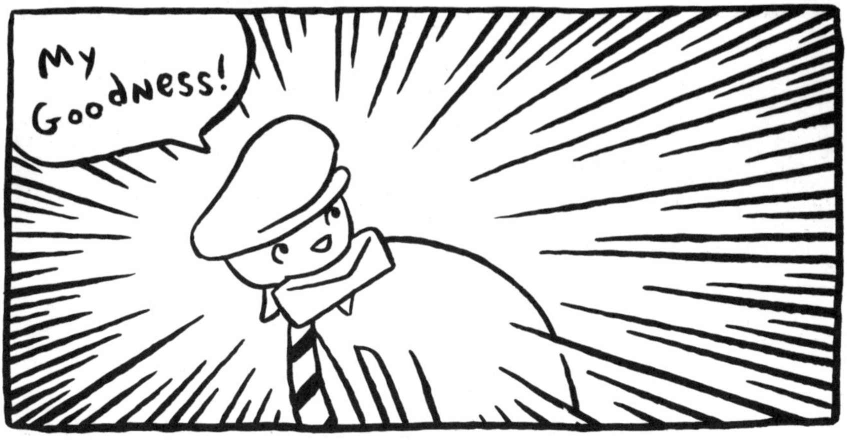
My Goodness!

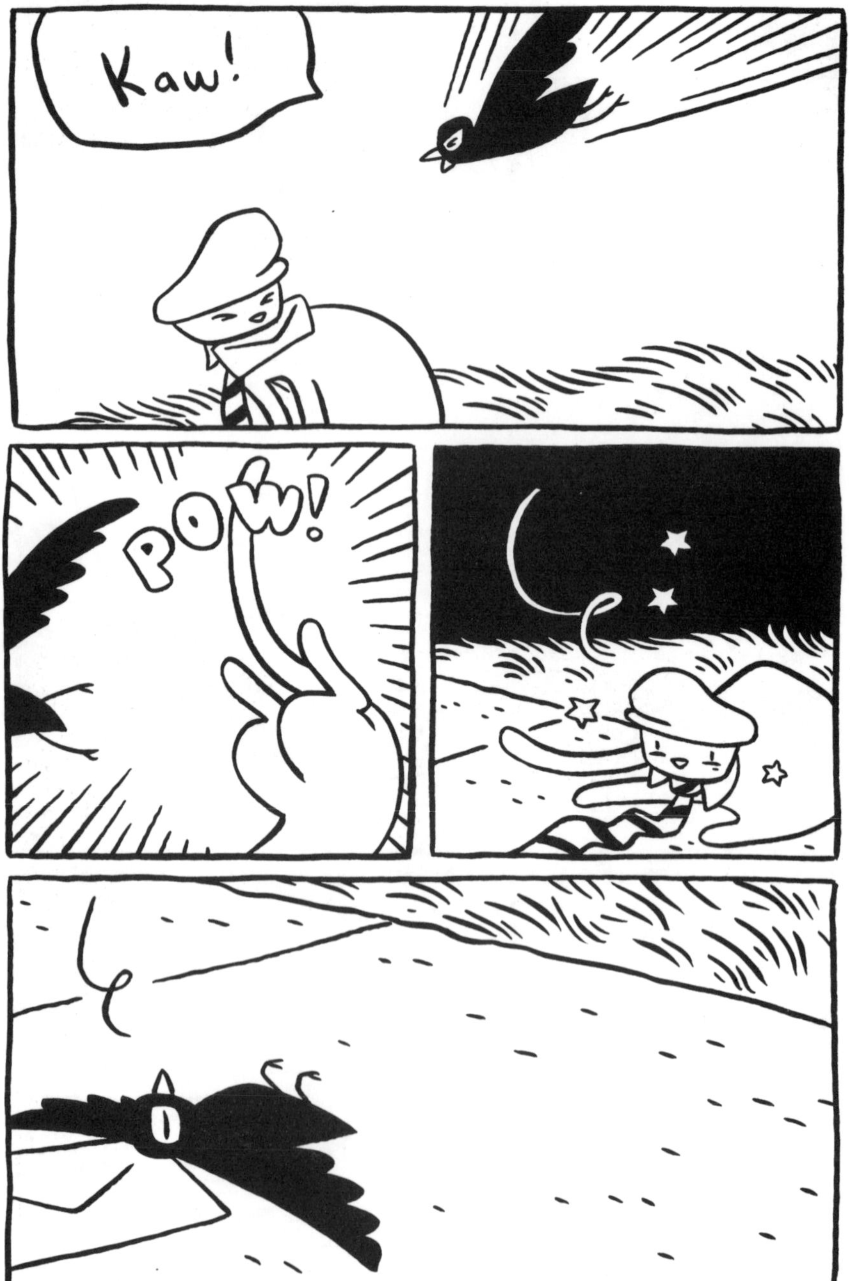
Kaw!
POW!

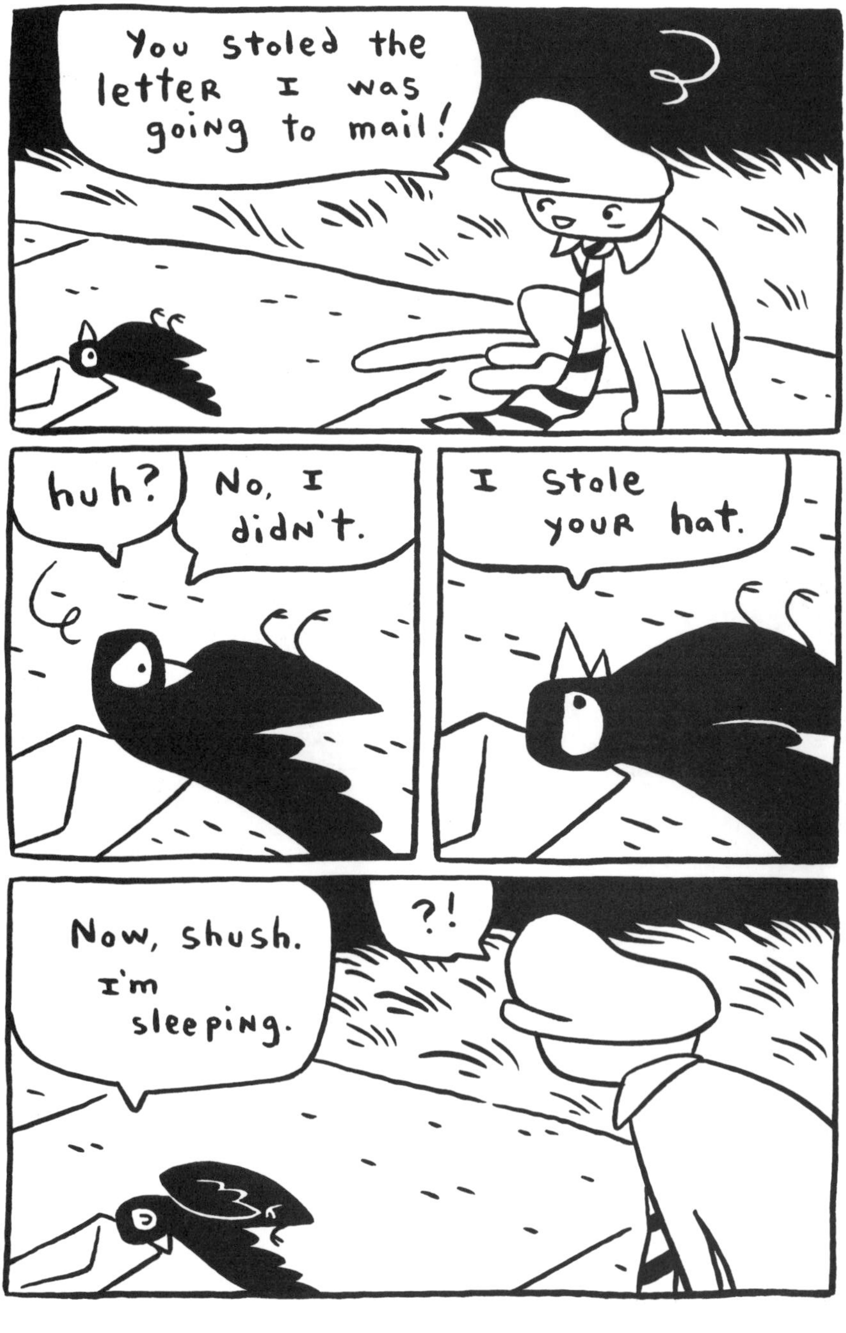
You stoled the letter I was going to mail!
huh?
No, I didn't.
I stole your hat.
Now, shush. I'm sleeping.
?!

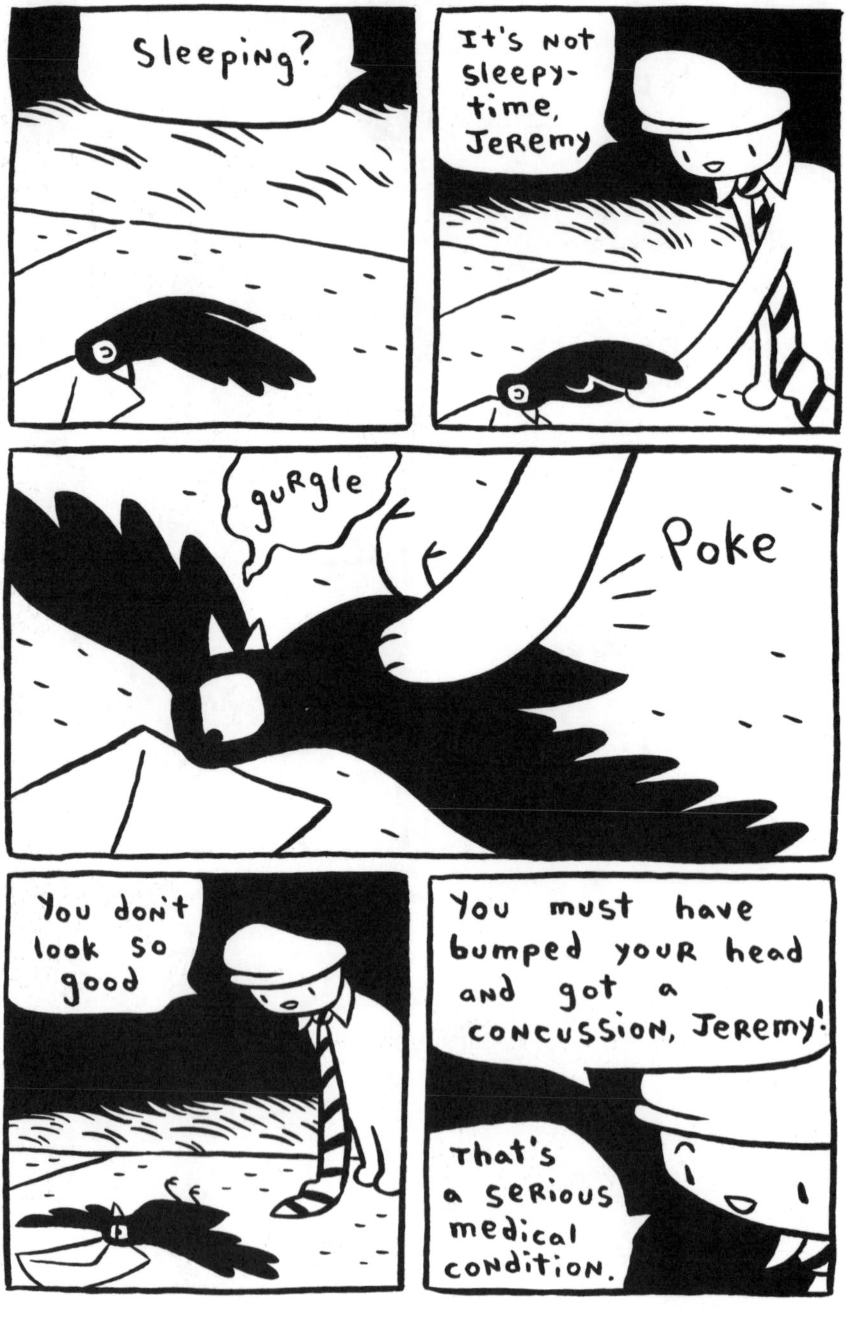
Sleeping?
It's not sleepy-time, Jeremy
gurgle
Poke
You don't look so good
You must have bumped your head and got a concussion, Jeremy!
That's a serious medical condition.

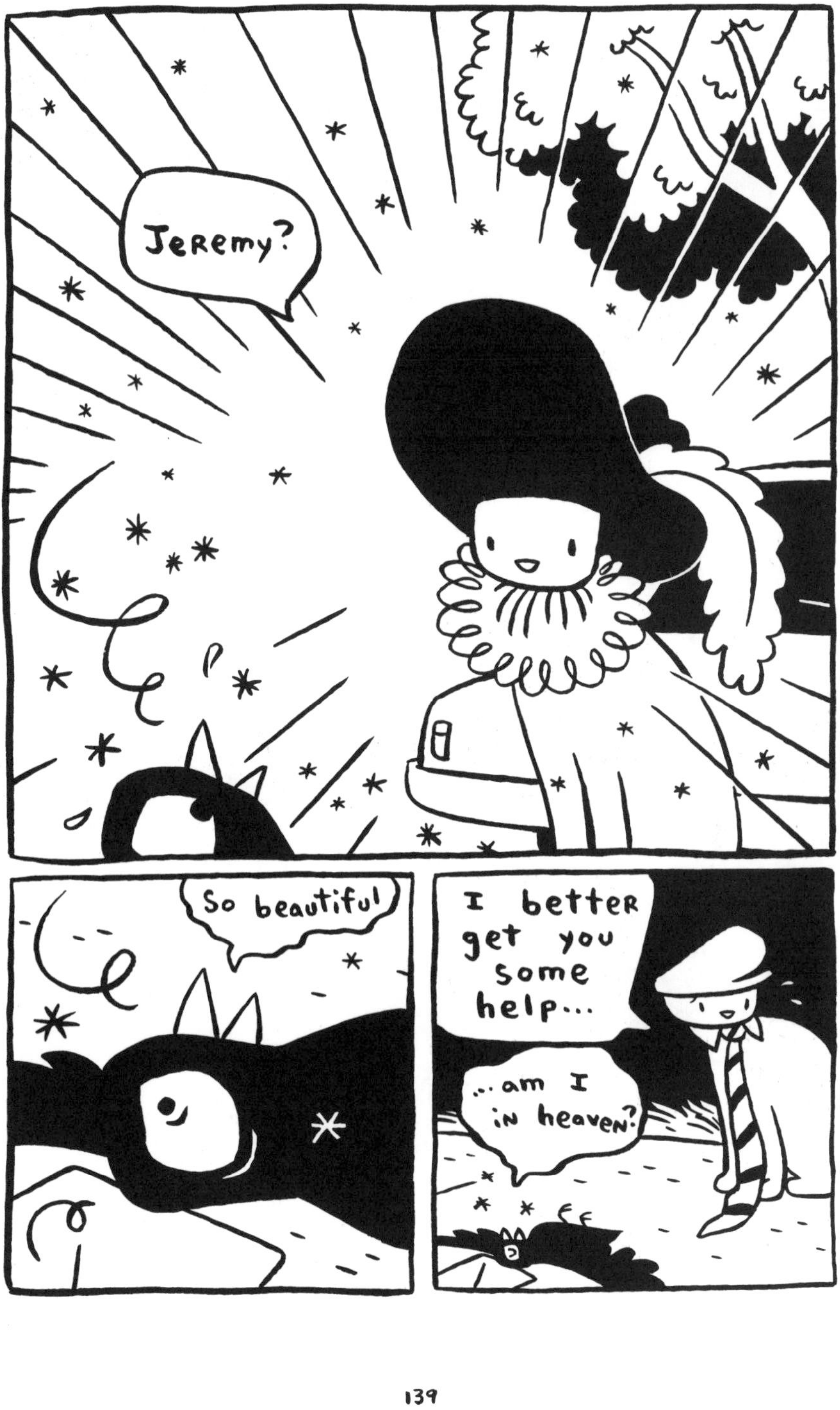
Jeremy?
So beautiful
I better get you some help...
...am I in heaven?

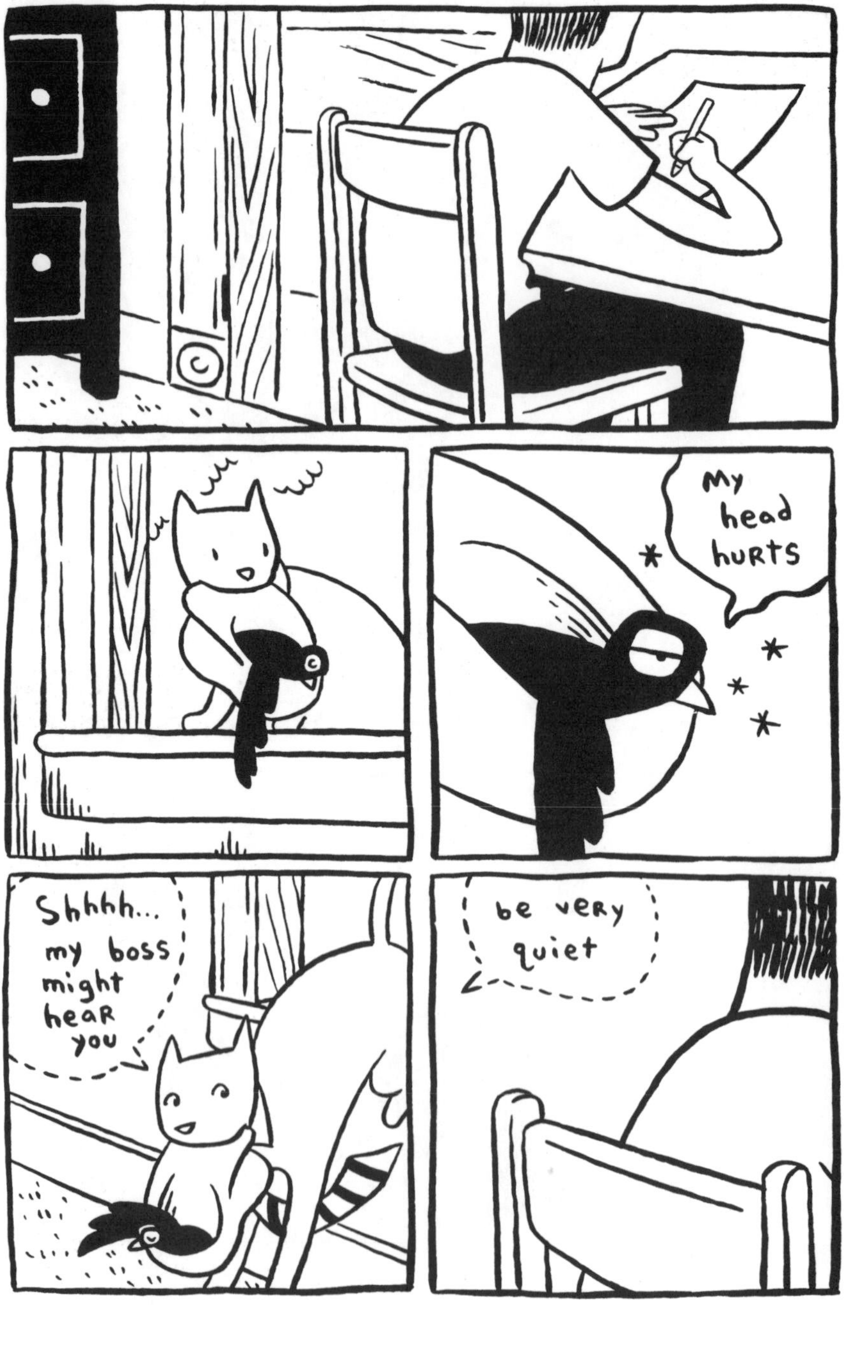
My head hurts
Shhhh... my boss might hear you
be very quiet

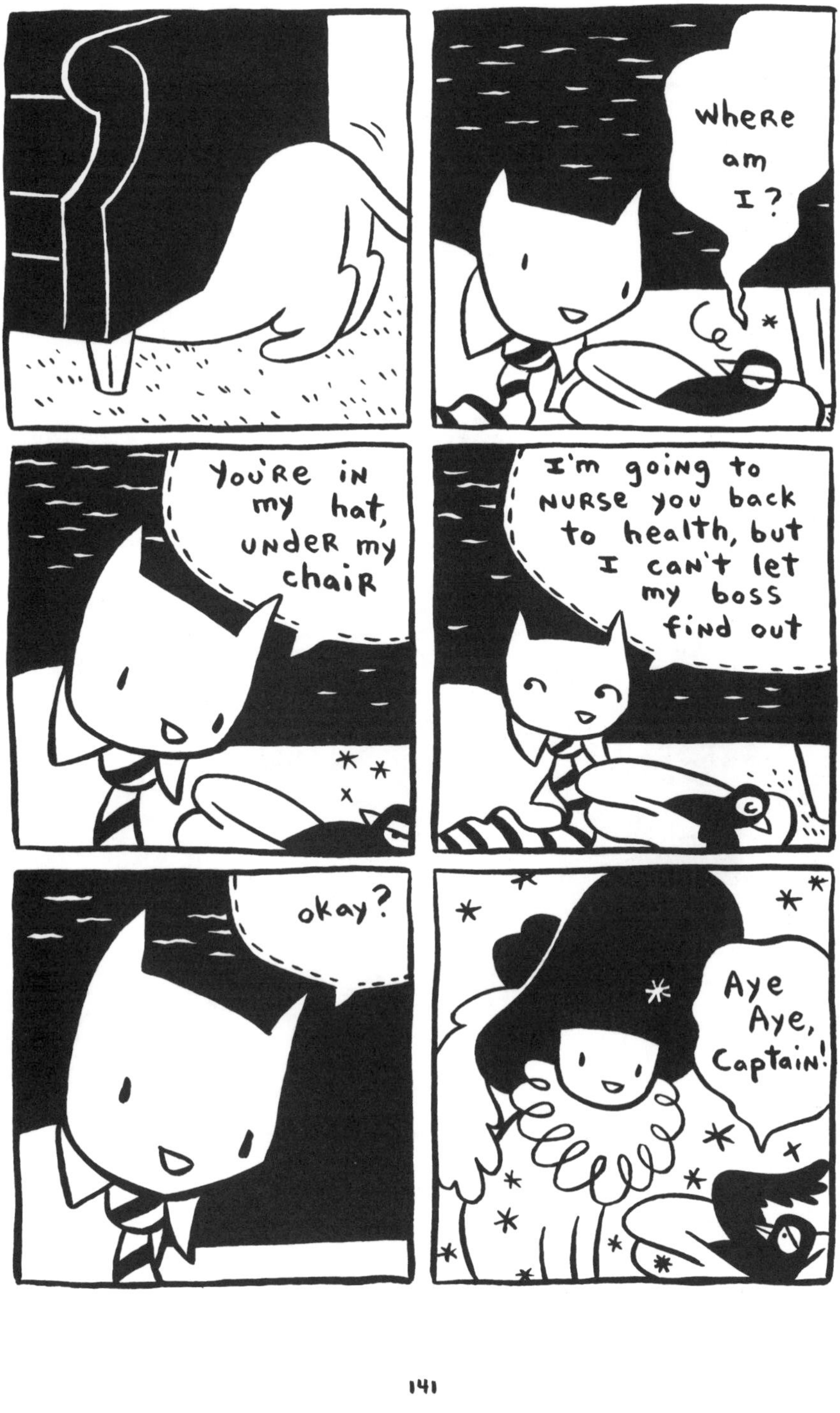
where am I?
You're in my hat, under my chair
I'm going to nurse you back to health, but I can't let my boss find out
okay?
Aye Aye, Captain!

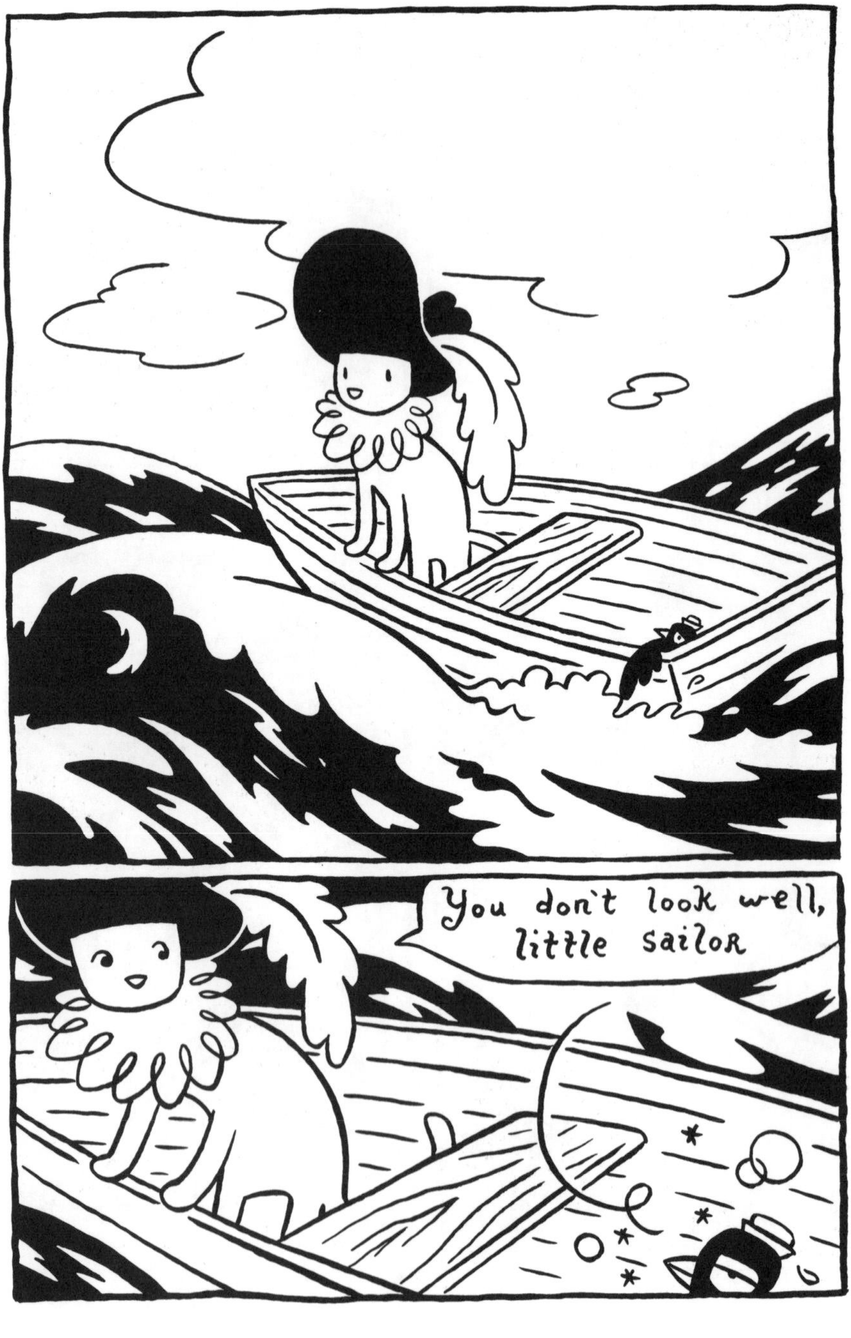
You don't look well, little sailor

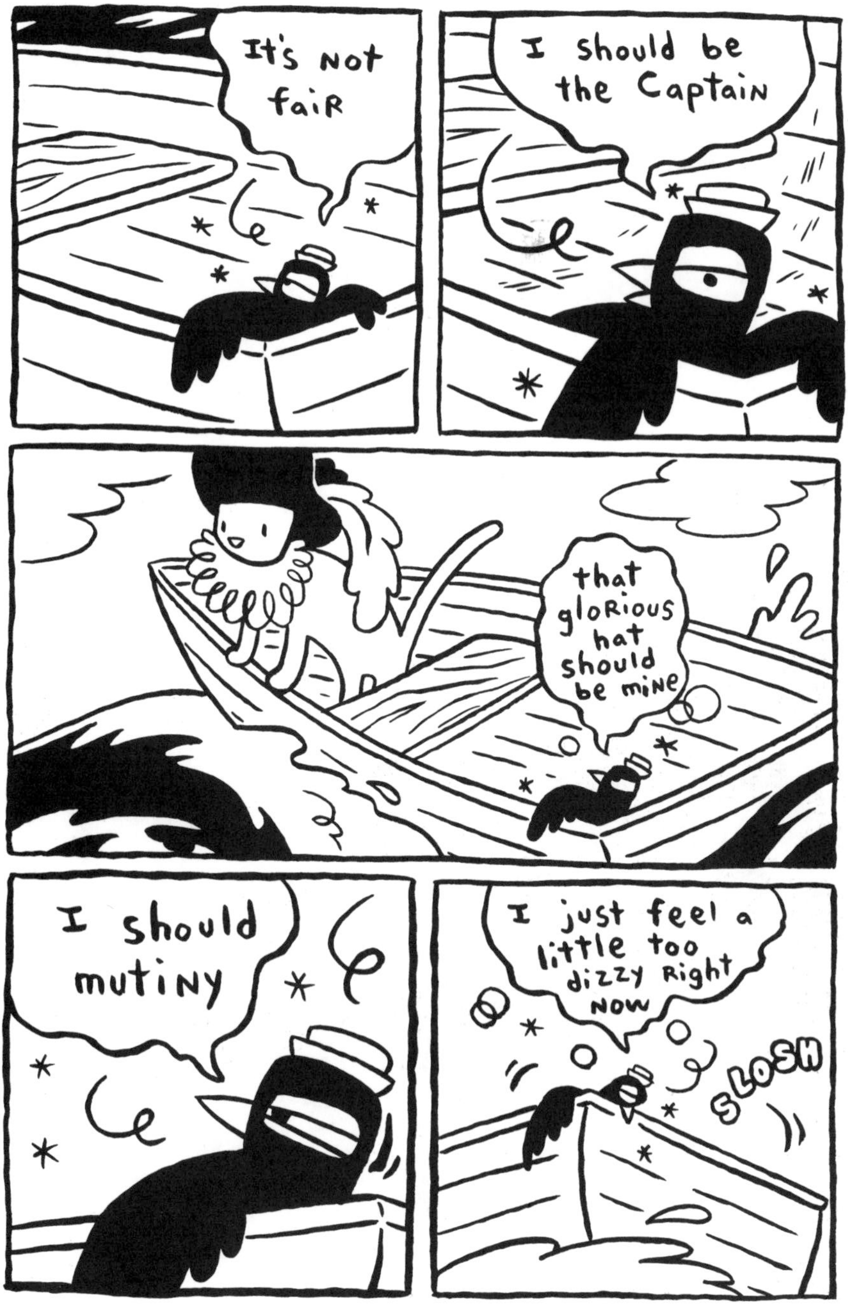
It's not fair
I should be the Captain
that glorious hat should be mine
I should mutiny
I just feel a little too dizzy right now
SLOSH

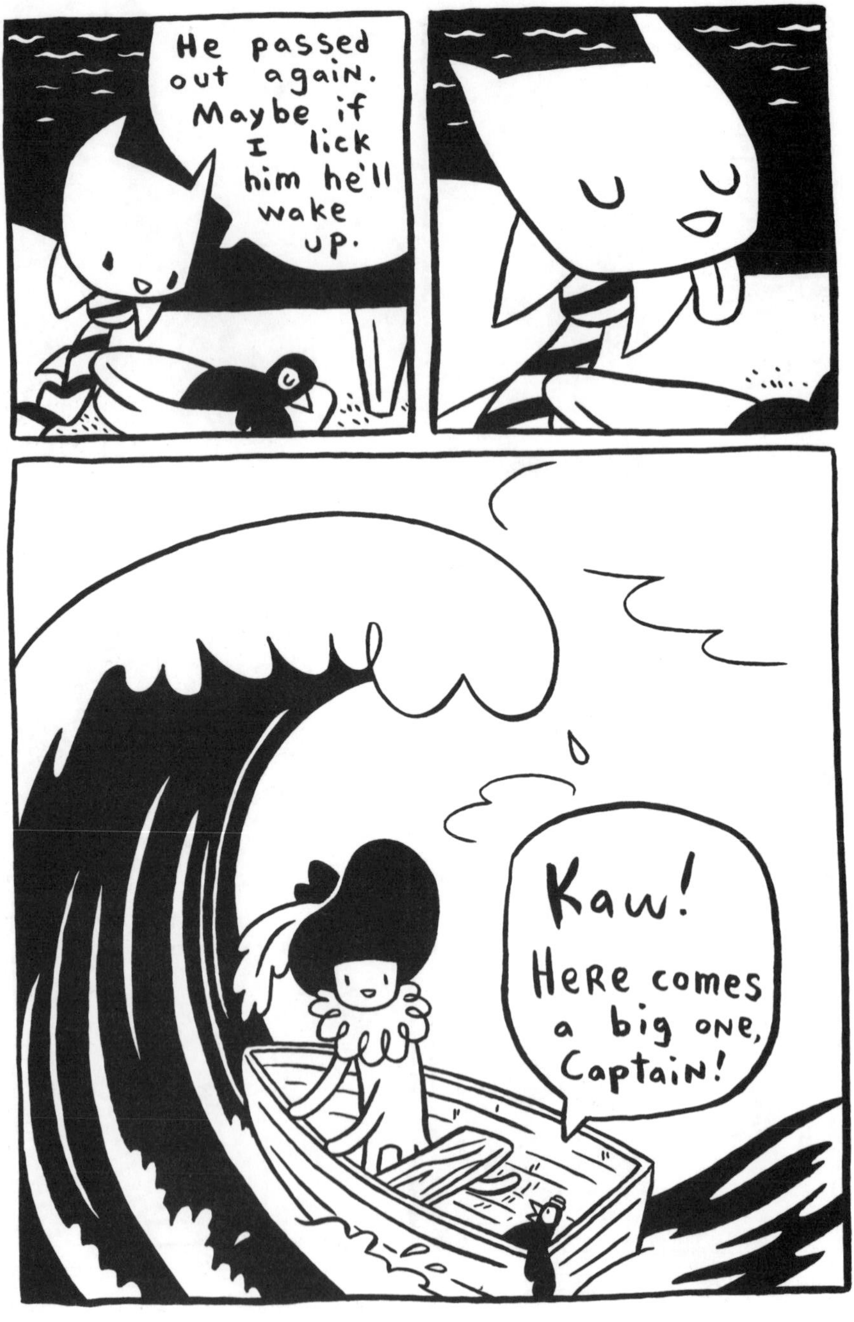
He passed out again. Maybe if I lick him he'll wake up.
Kaw!
Here comes a big one, Captain!

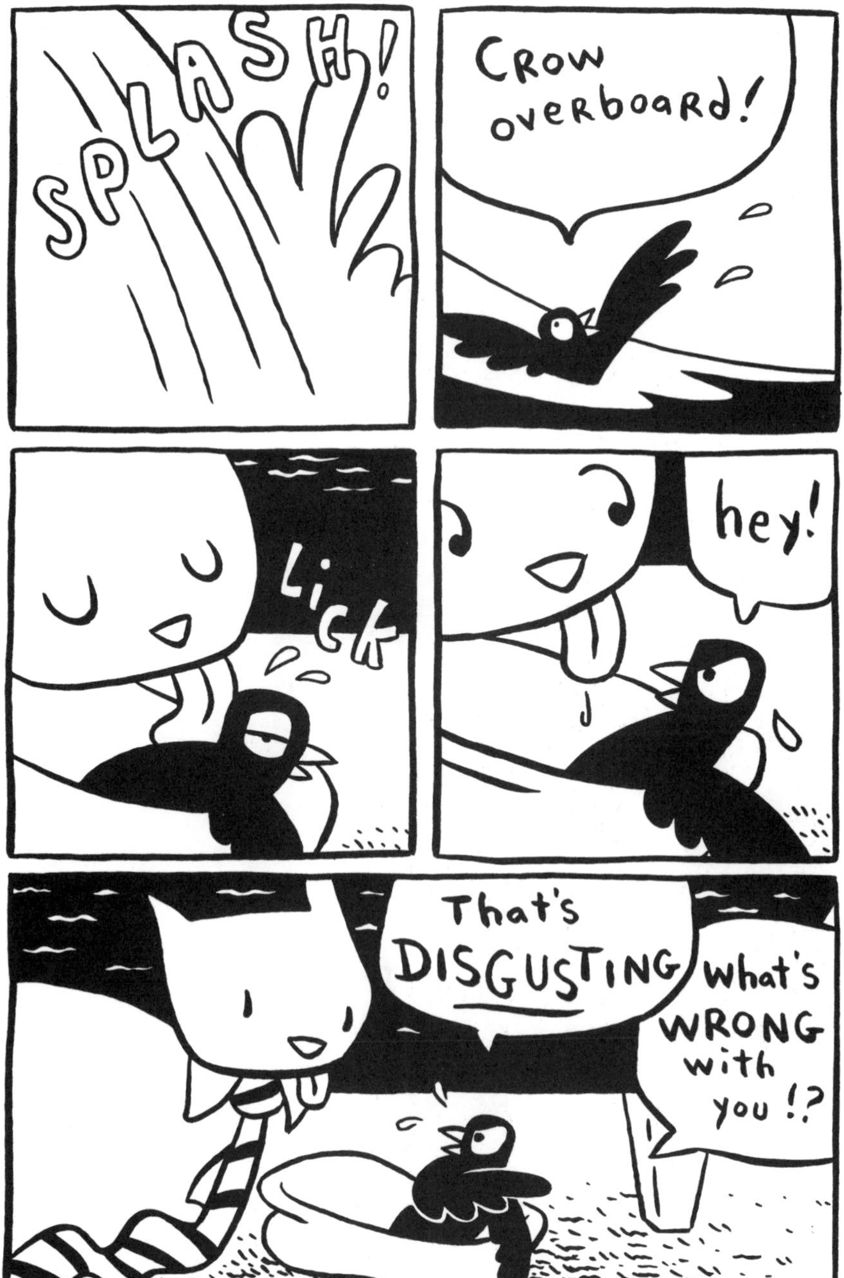
SPLASH!
Crow overboard!
Lick
hey!
That's DISGUSTING
What's WRONG with you !?

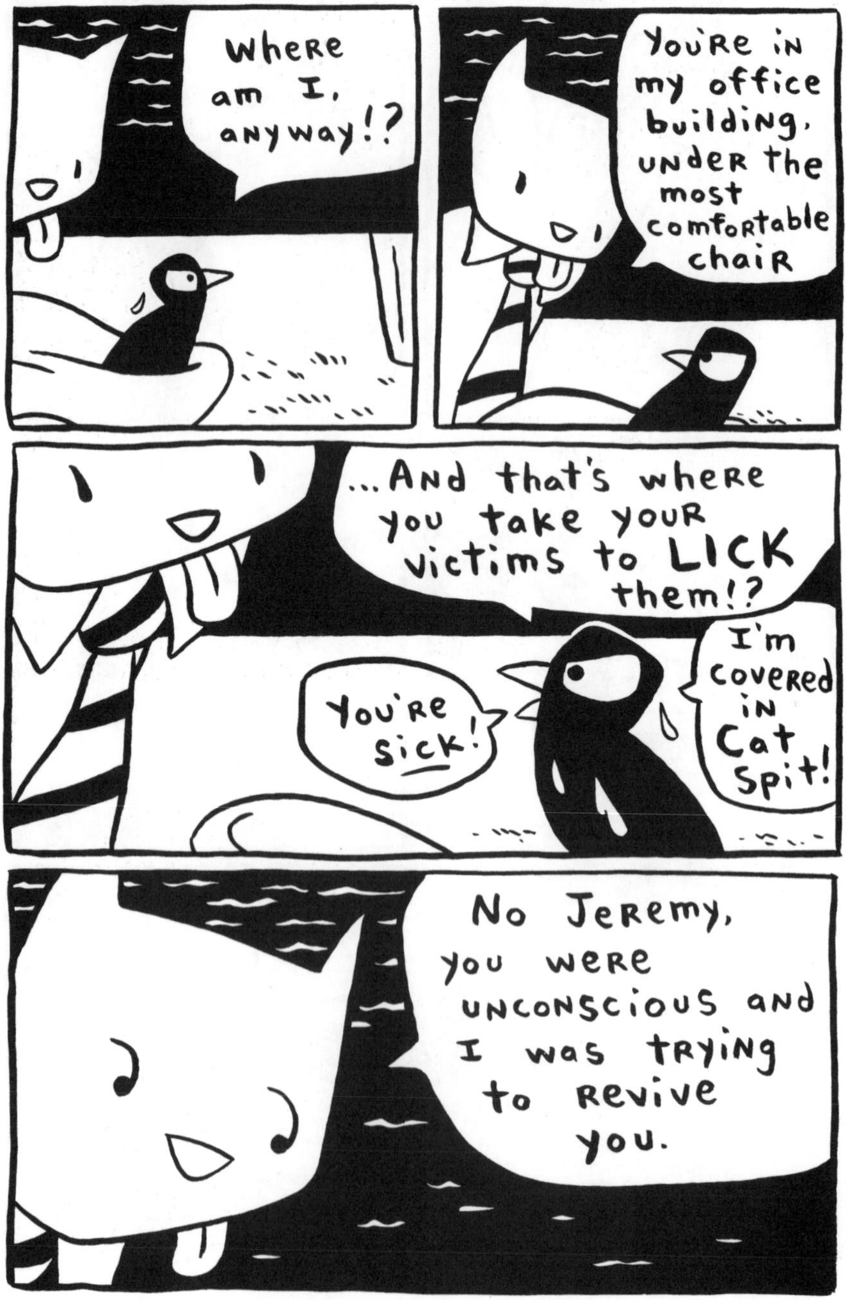
Where am I, anyway!?
You're in my office building, under the most comfortable chair
...And that's where you take your victims to LICK them!?
I'm covered in Cat Spit!
You're sick!
No Jeremy, you were unconscious and I was trying to revive you.

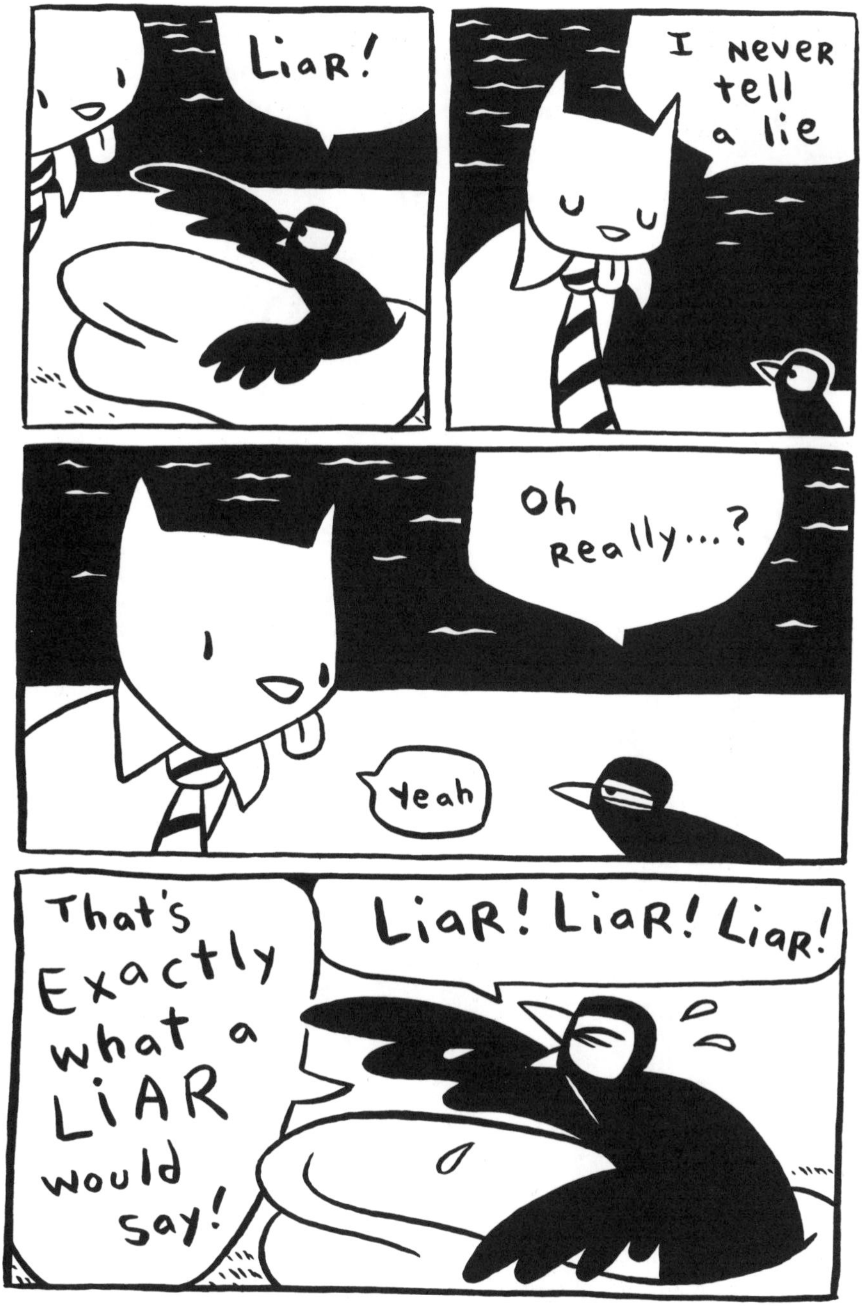
Liar!
I never tell a lie
Oh really...?
Yeah
That's Exactly what a LIAR would say!
Liar! Liar! Liar!

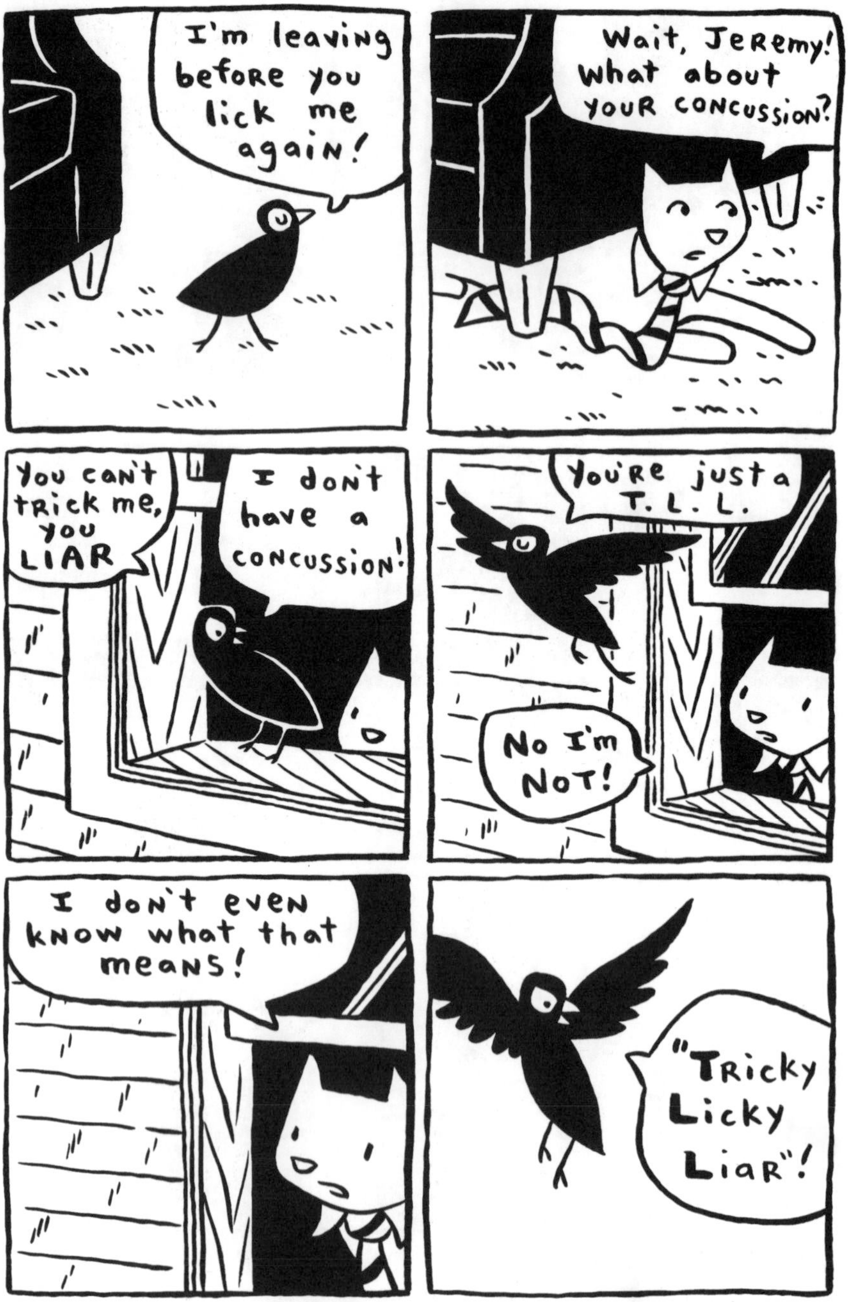
I'm leaving before you lick me again!
Wait, Jeremy! What about your concussion?
You can't trick me, you LIAR
I don't have a concussion!
You're just a T. L. L.
No I'm NOT!
I don't even know what that means!
"Tricky Licky Liar"!

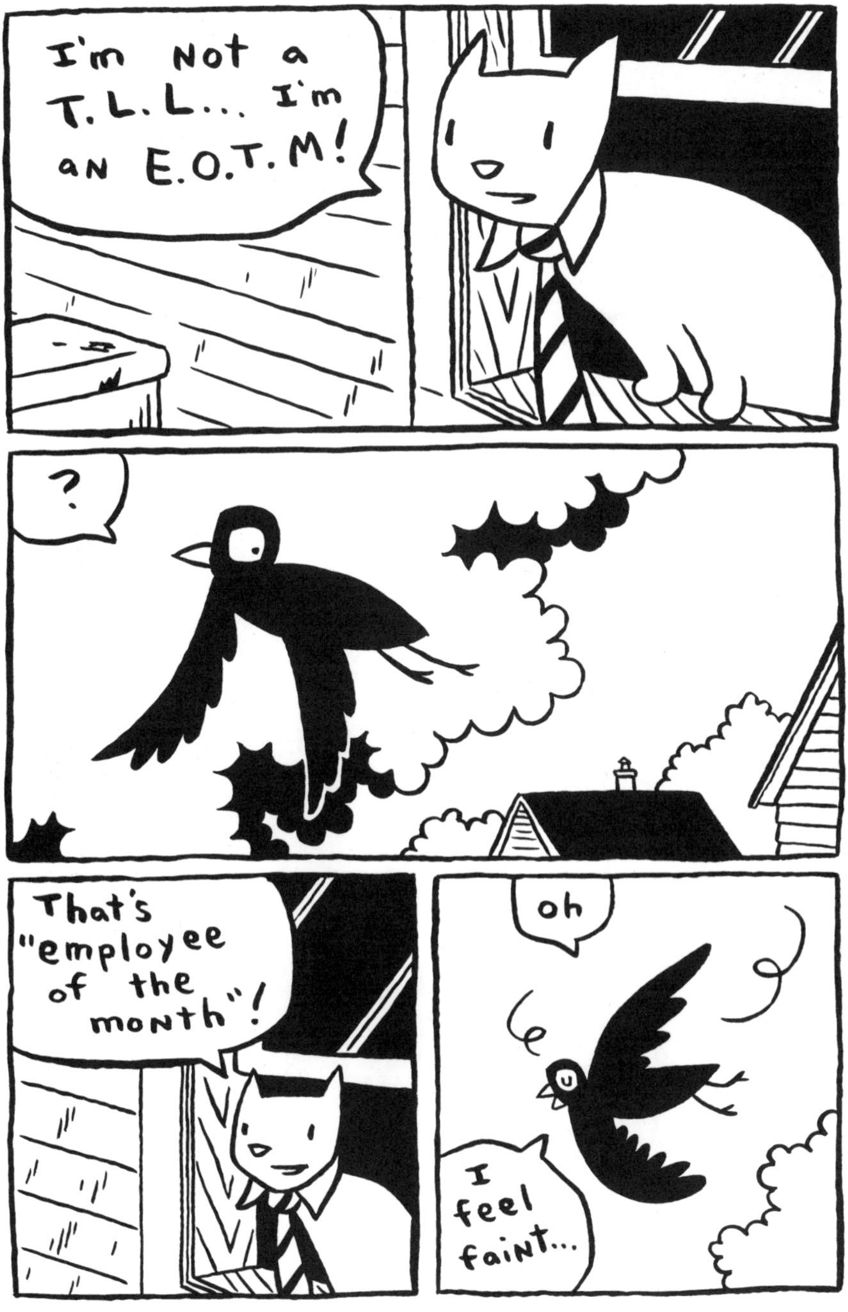
I'm Not a T.L.L... I'm an E.O.T.M!
?
That's "employee of the month"!
oh
I feel faint...

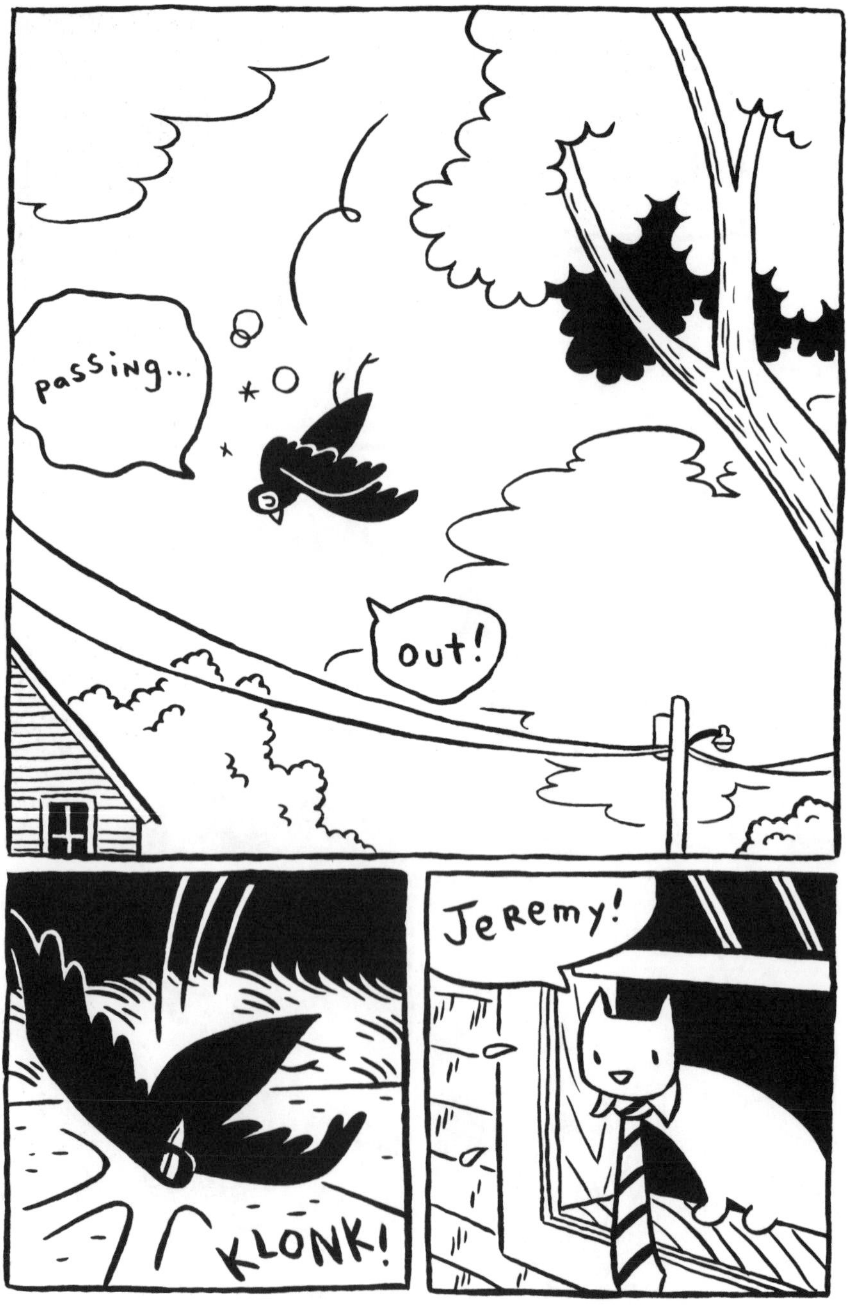
passing...
out!
KLONK!
Jeremy!

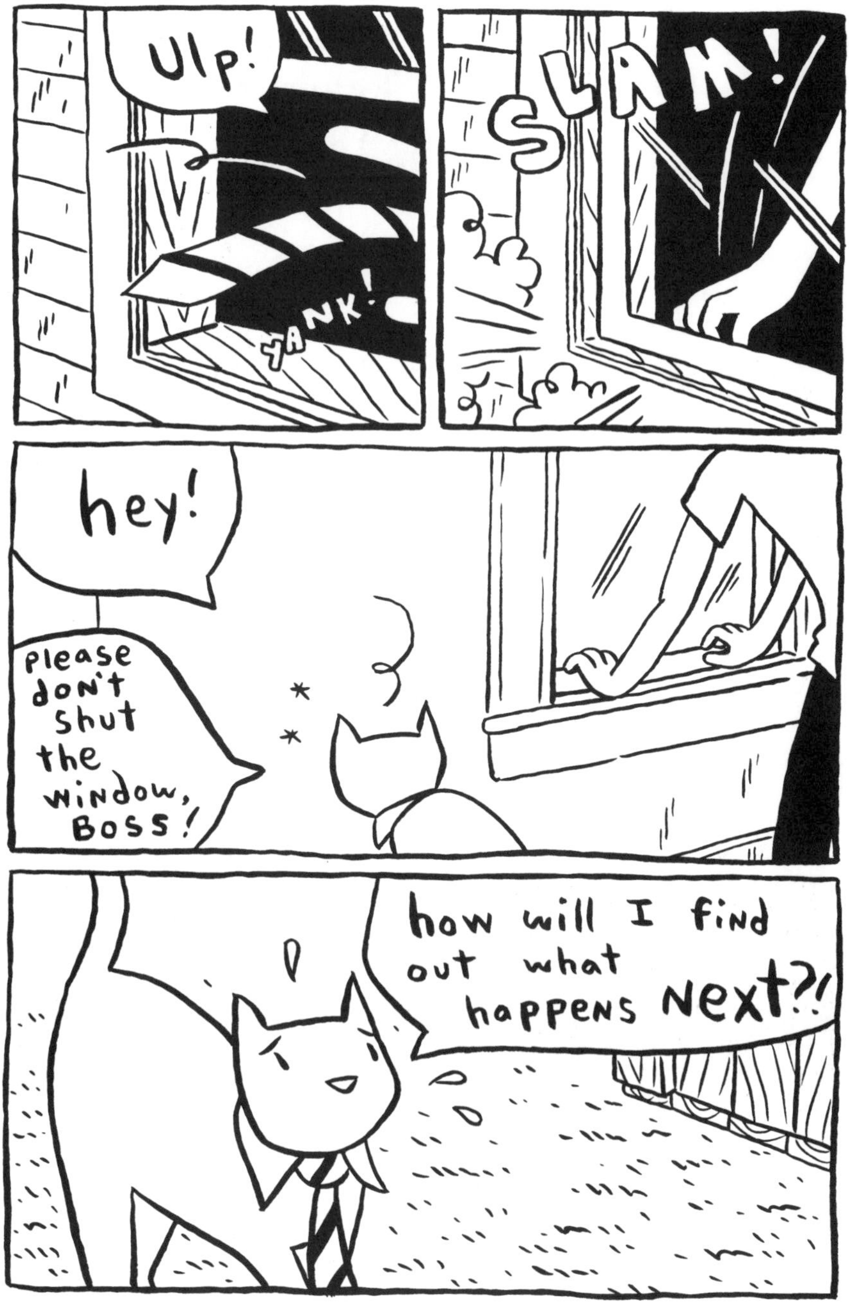
Ulp!
YANK!
SLAM!
hey!
please don't shut the window, BOSS!
how will I find out what happens NEXT?!

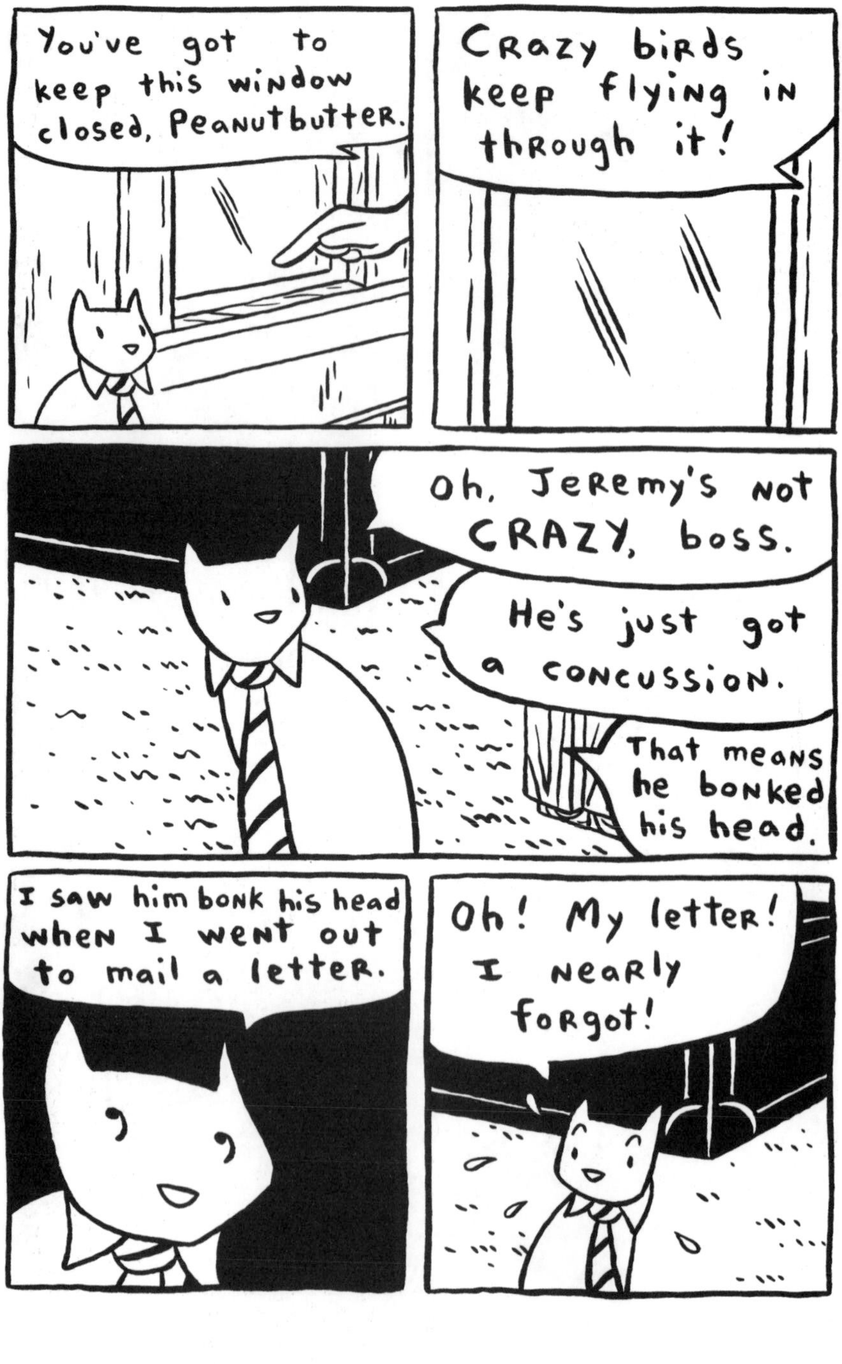
You've got to keep this window closed, Peanutbutter.
Crazy birds keep flying in through it!
Oh, Jeremy's not CRAZY, boss.
He's just got a concussion.
That means he bonked his head.
I saw him bonk his head when I went out to mail a letter.
Oh! My letter! I nearly forgot!

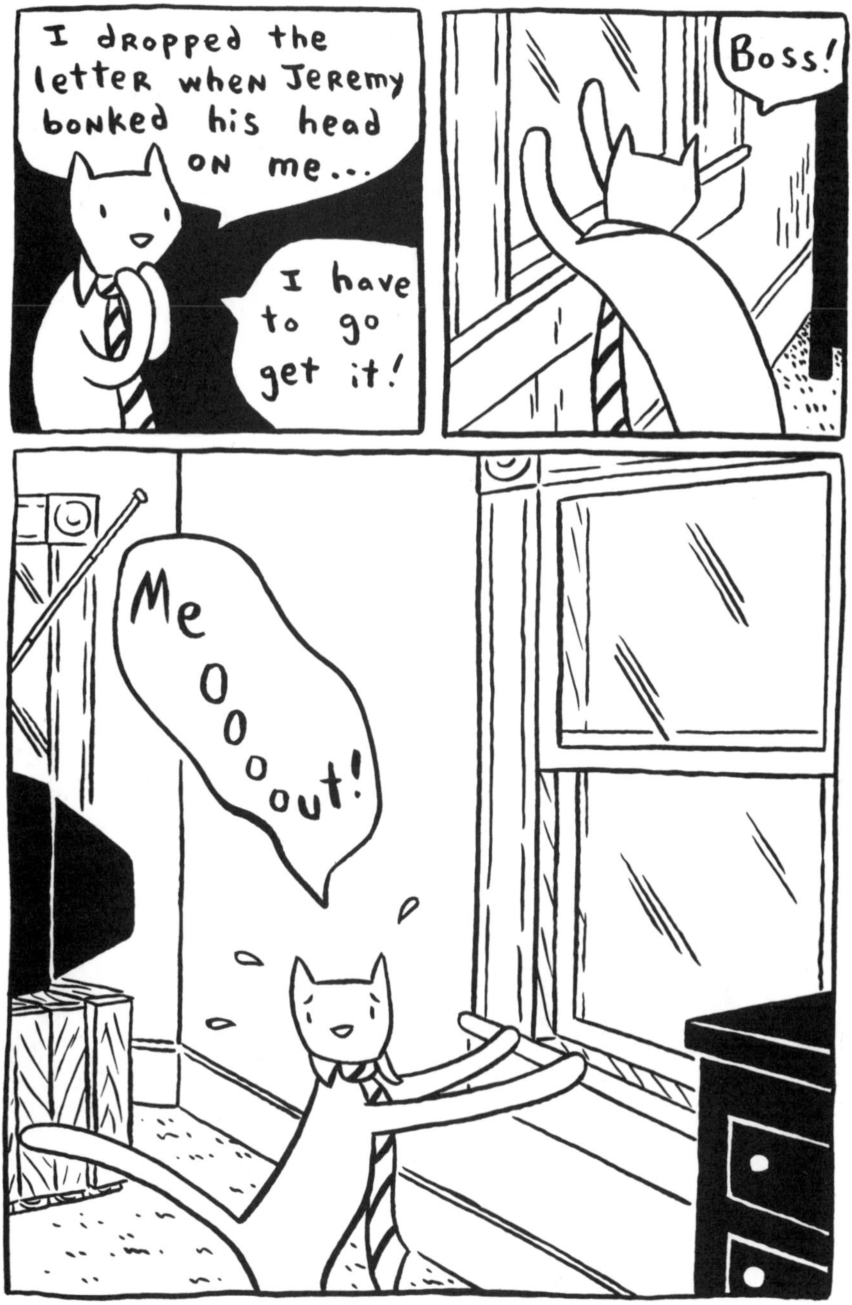
I dropped the letter when Jeremy bonked his head on me...
I have to go get it!
Boss!
Me OOOOout!

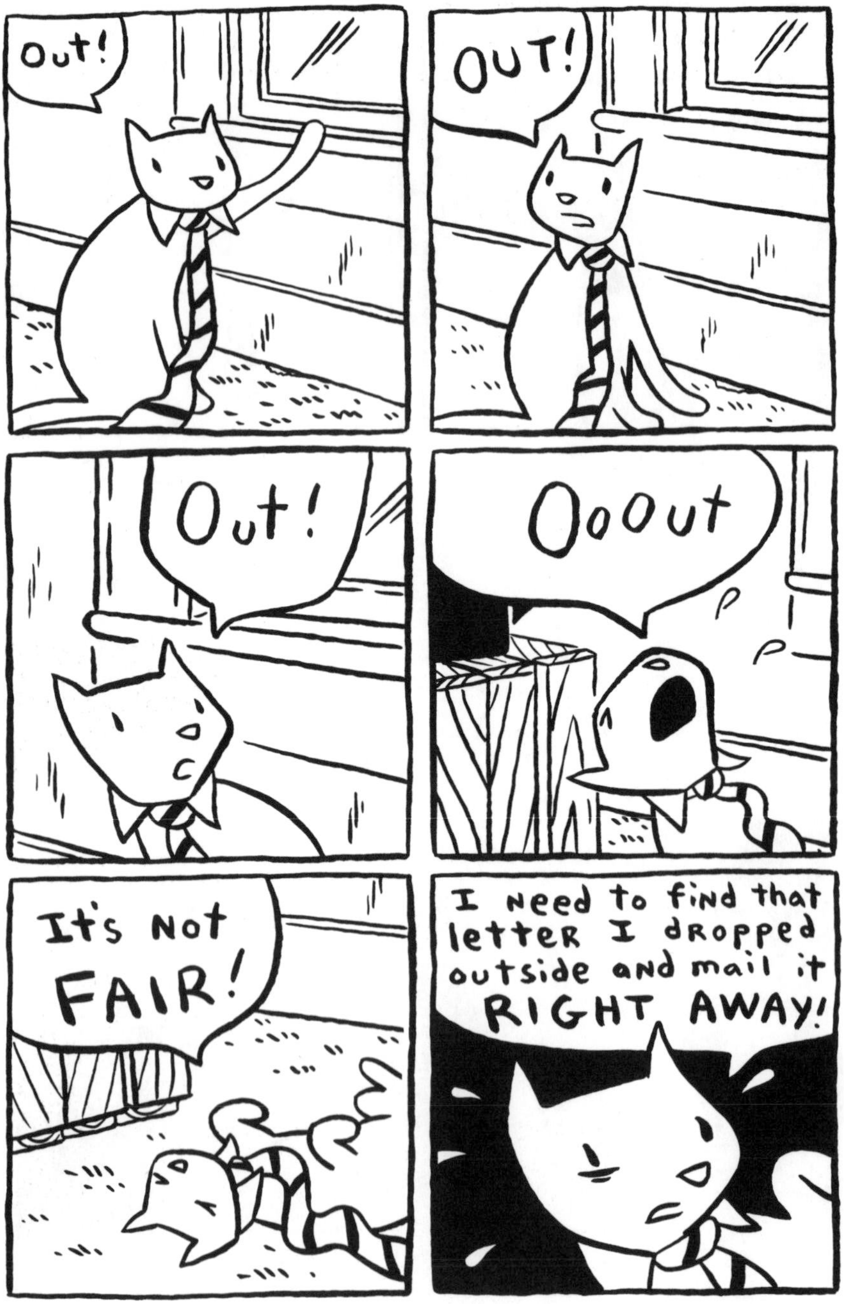
Out!
OUT!
Out!
OoOut
It's Not FAIR!
I need to find that letter I dropped outside and mail it RIGHT AWAY!

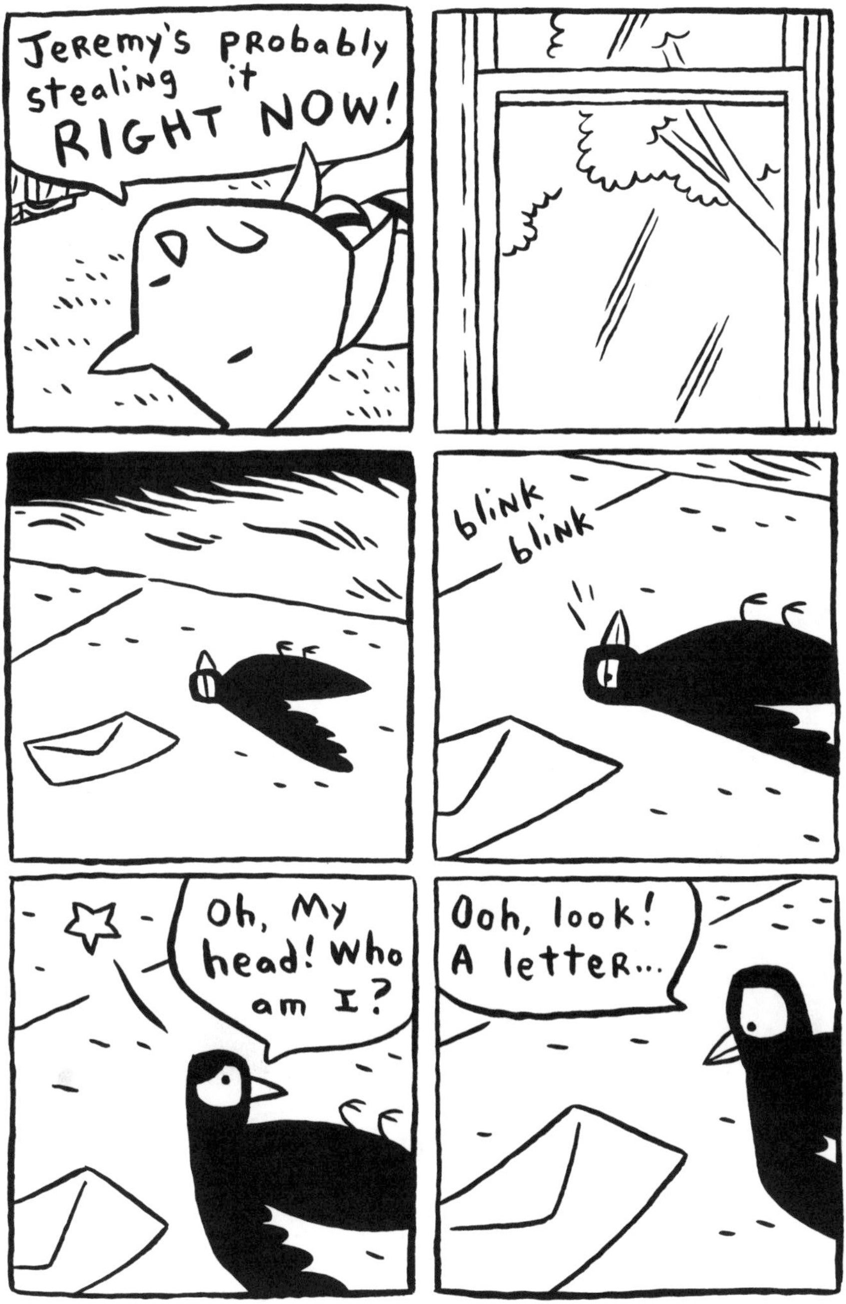
Jeremy's probably stealing it RIGHT NOW!
blink blink
Oh, my head! Who am I?
Ooh, look! A letter...

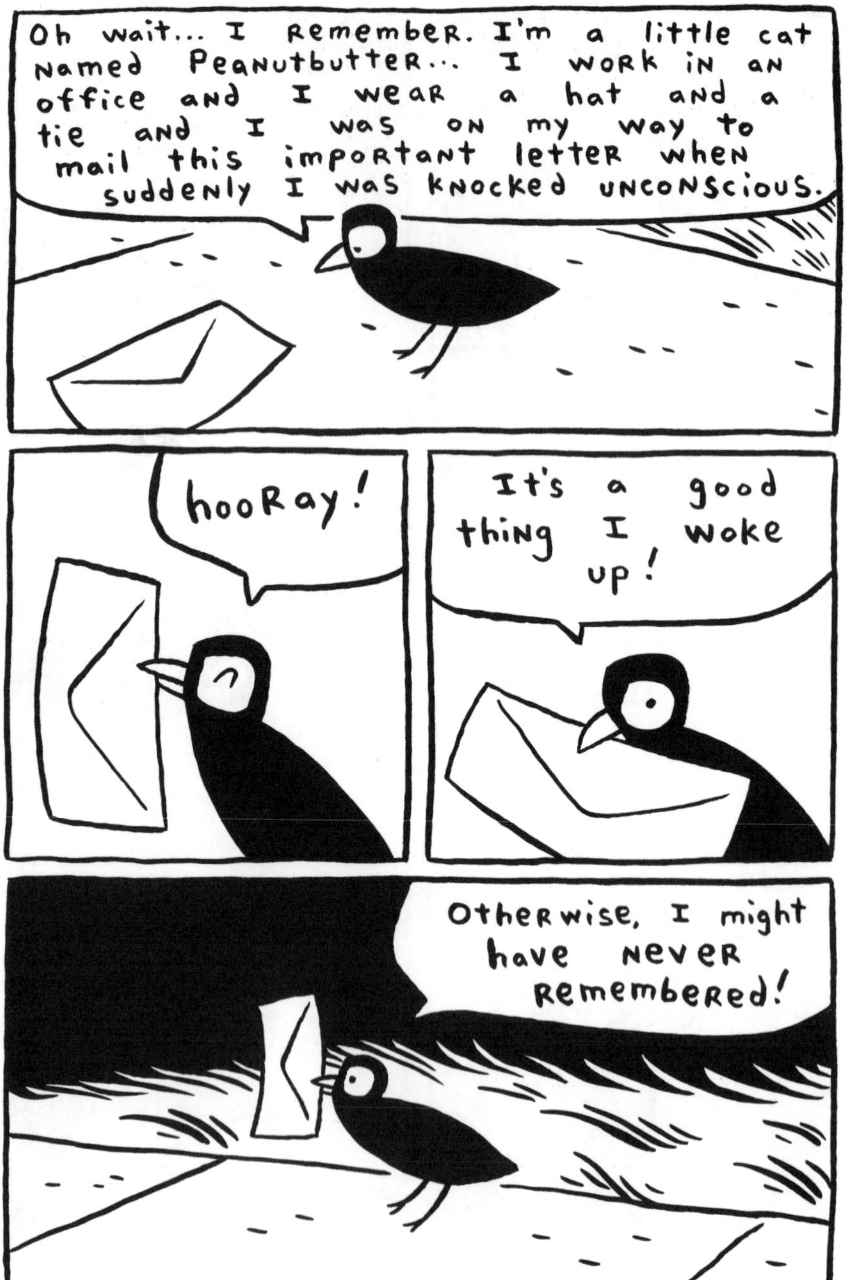
Oh wait... I remember. I'm a little cat named Peanutbutter... I work in an office and I wear a hat and a tie and I was on my way to mail this important letter when suddenly I was knocked unconscious.
hooray!
It's a good thing I woke up!
Otherwise, I might have never remembered!

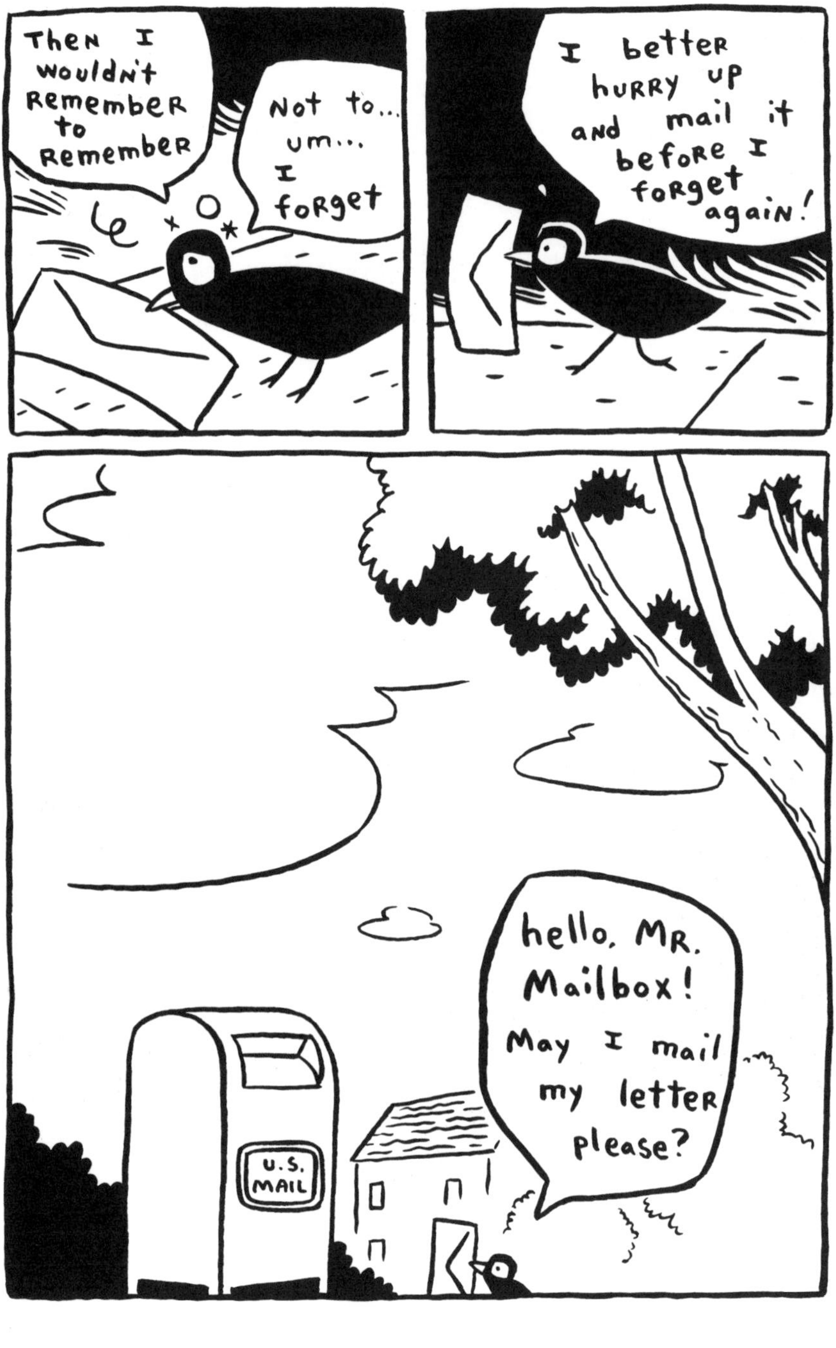
Then I wouldn't remember to remember
Not to... um... I forget
I better hurry up and mail it before I forget again!
U.S. MAIL
hello, Mr. Mailbox! May I mail my letter please?

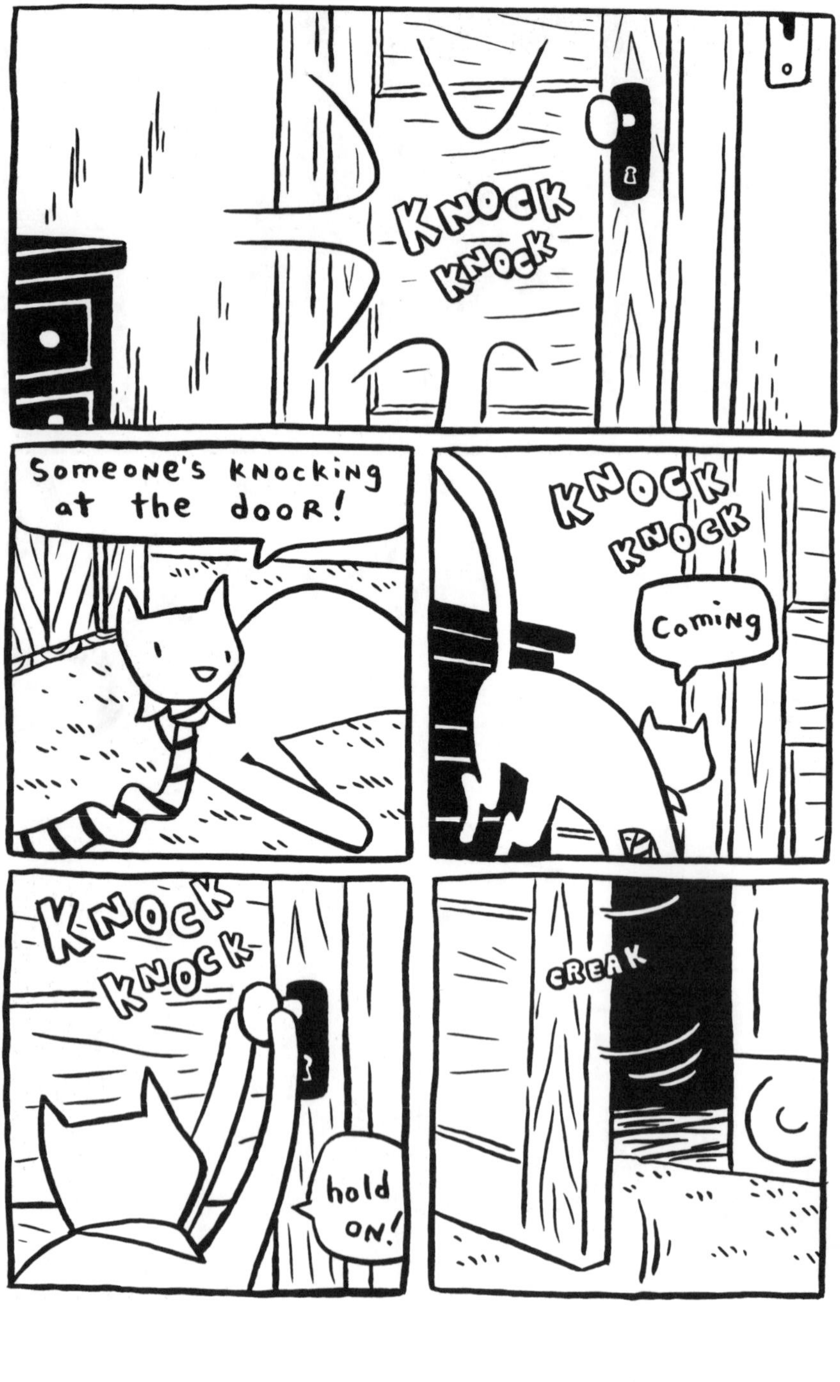
KNOCK
KNOCK
Someone's knocking at the door!
KNOCK
KNOCK
Coming
KNOCK
KNOCK
hold ON!
CREAK

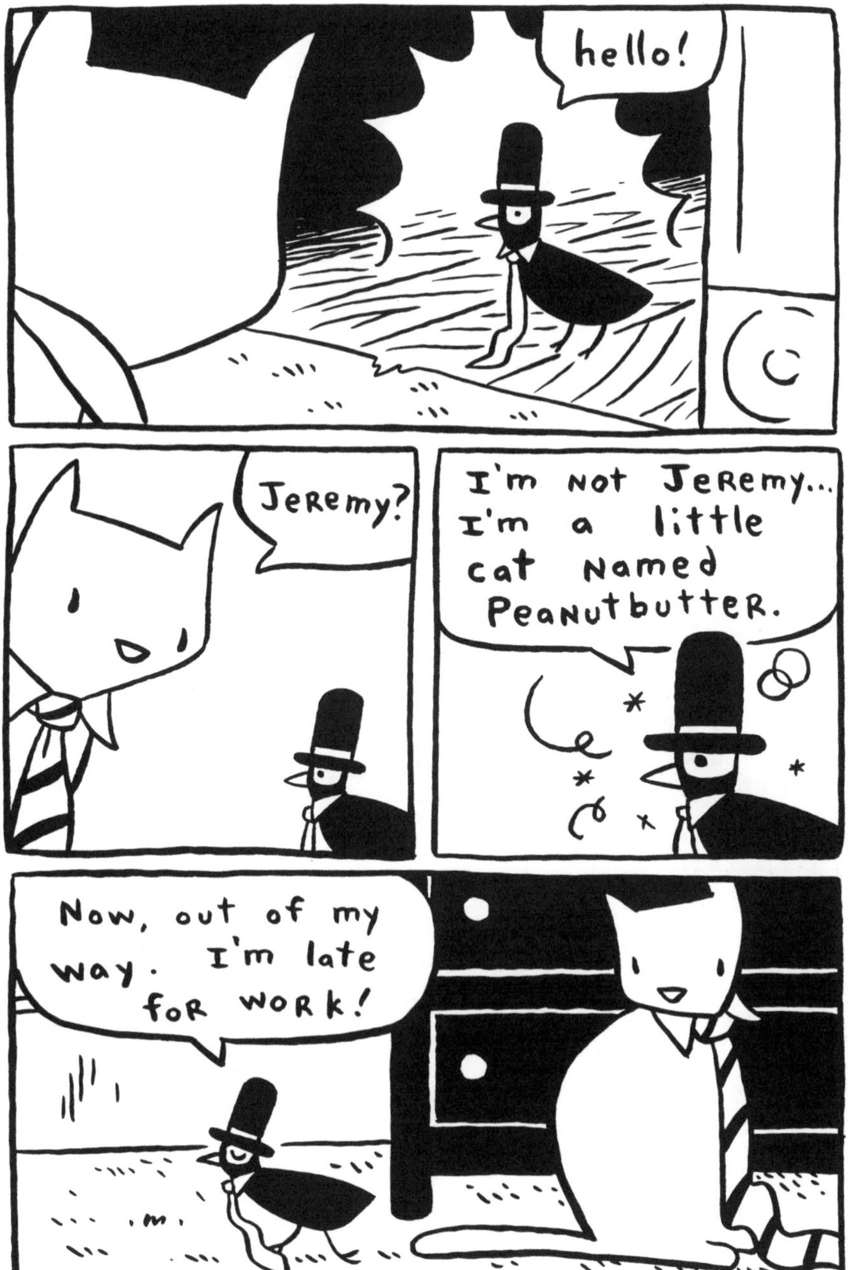
hello!
Jeremy?
I'm not Jeremy... I'm a little cat named Peanutbutter.
Now, out of my way. I'm late for work!

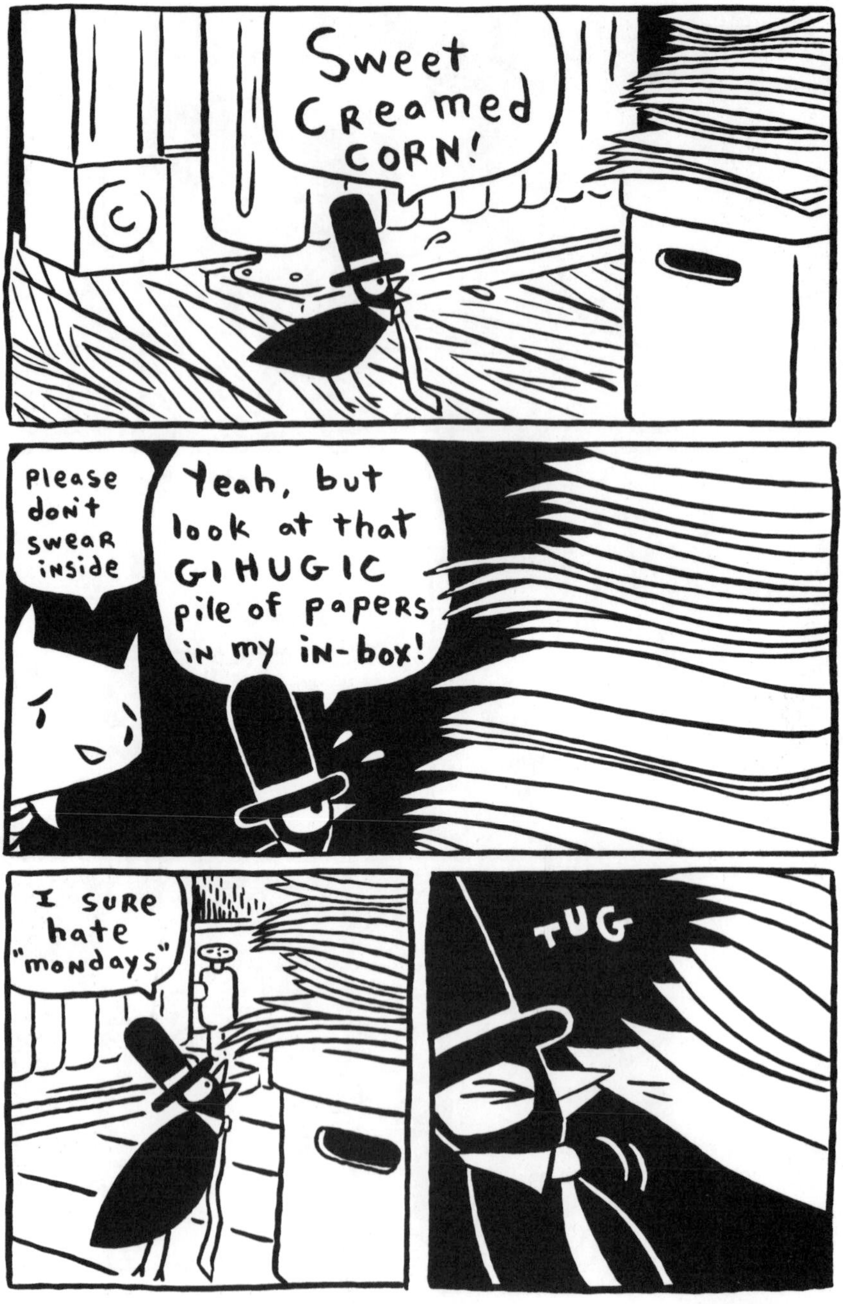
Sweet Creamed CORN!
Please don't swear inside
Yeah, but look at that GIHUGIC pile of papers in my in-box!
I sure hate "mondays"
TUG

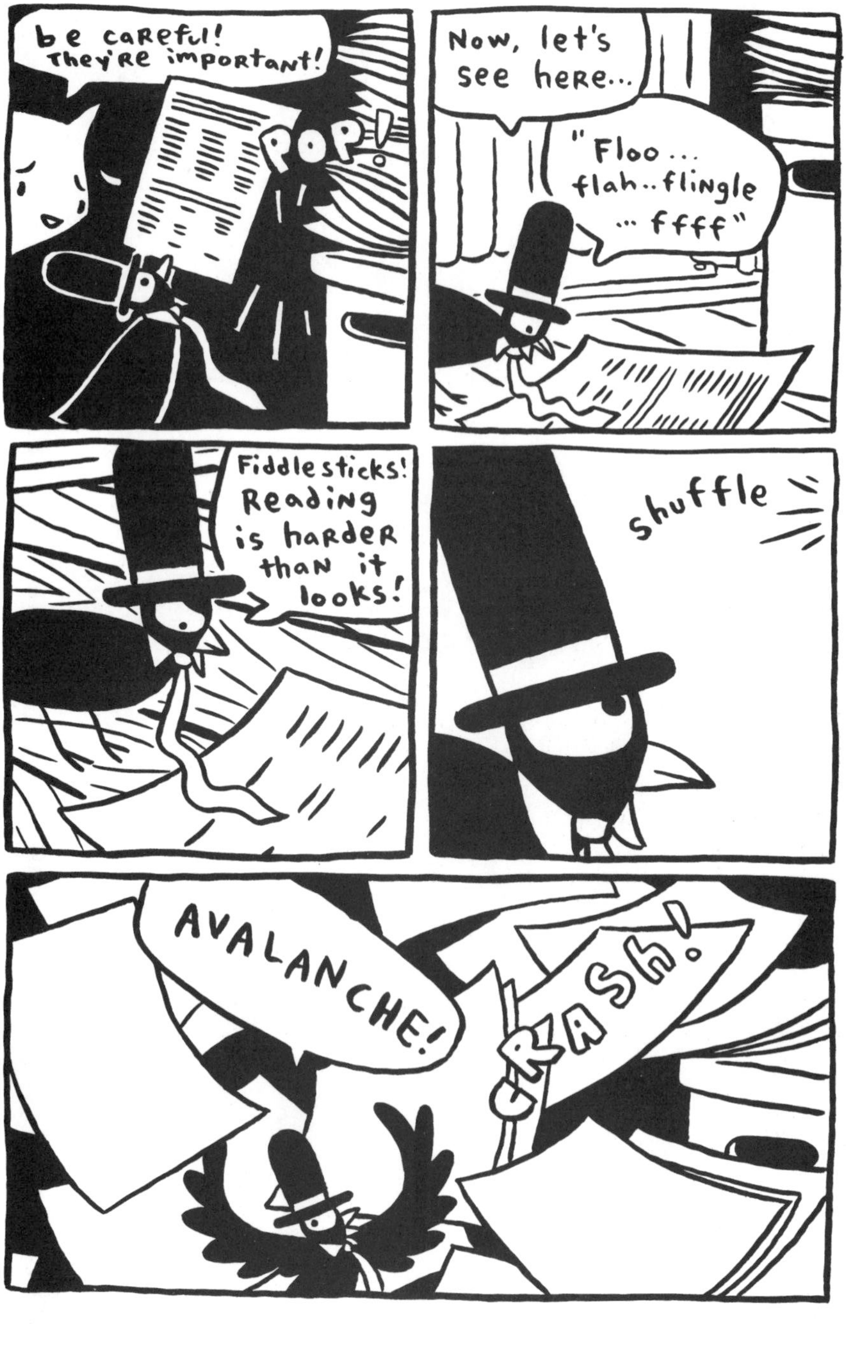
be careful! They're important!
POP!
Now, let's see here...
"Floo... flah.. flingle ... ffff"
Fiddlesticks! Reading is harder than it looks!
shuffle
AVALANCHE!
CRASH!

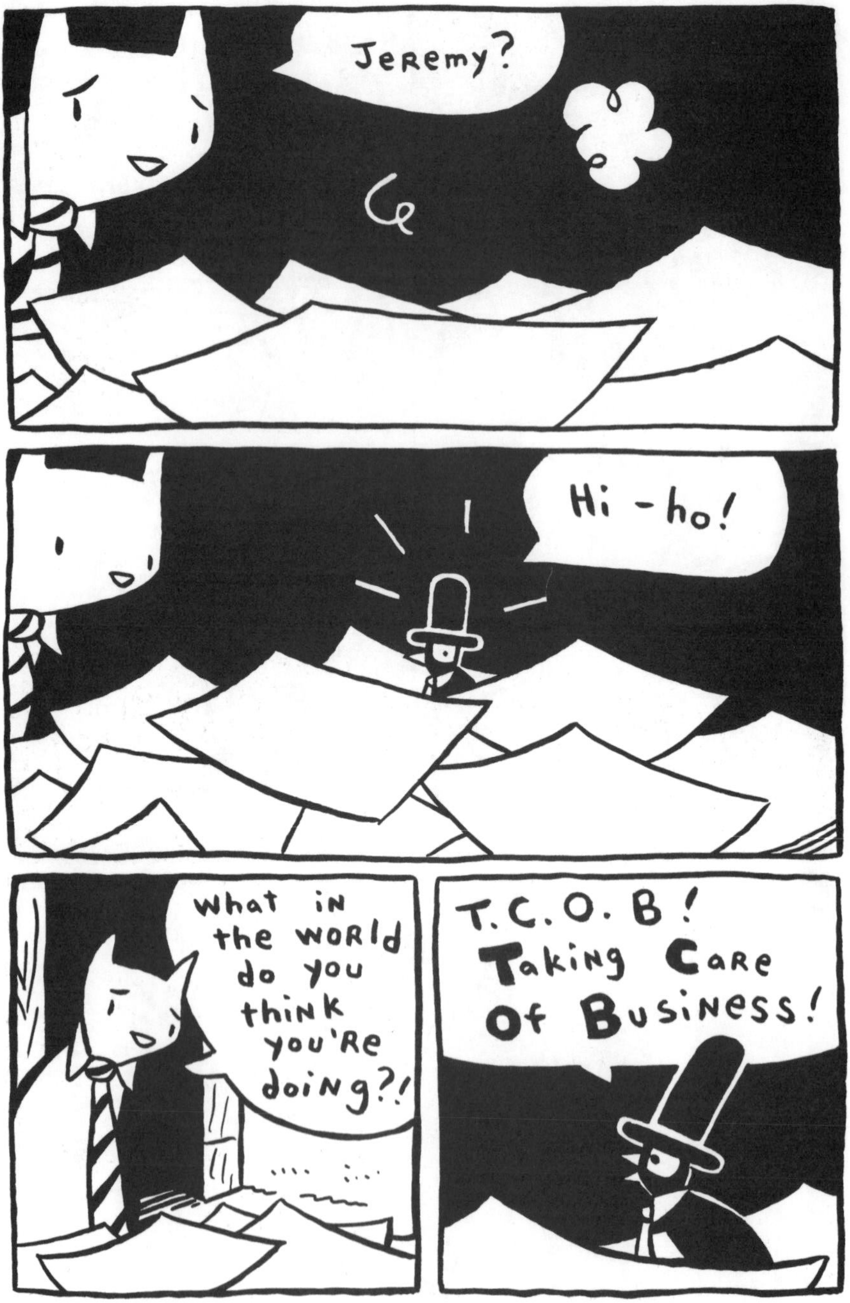

Jeremy?
Hi-ho!
What in the world do you think you're doing?!
T.C.O.B! Taking Care Of Business!

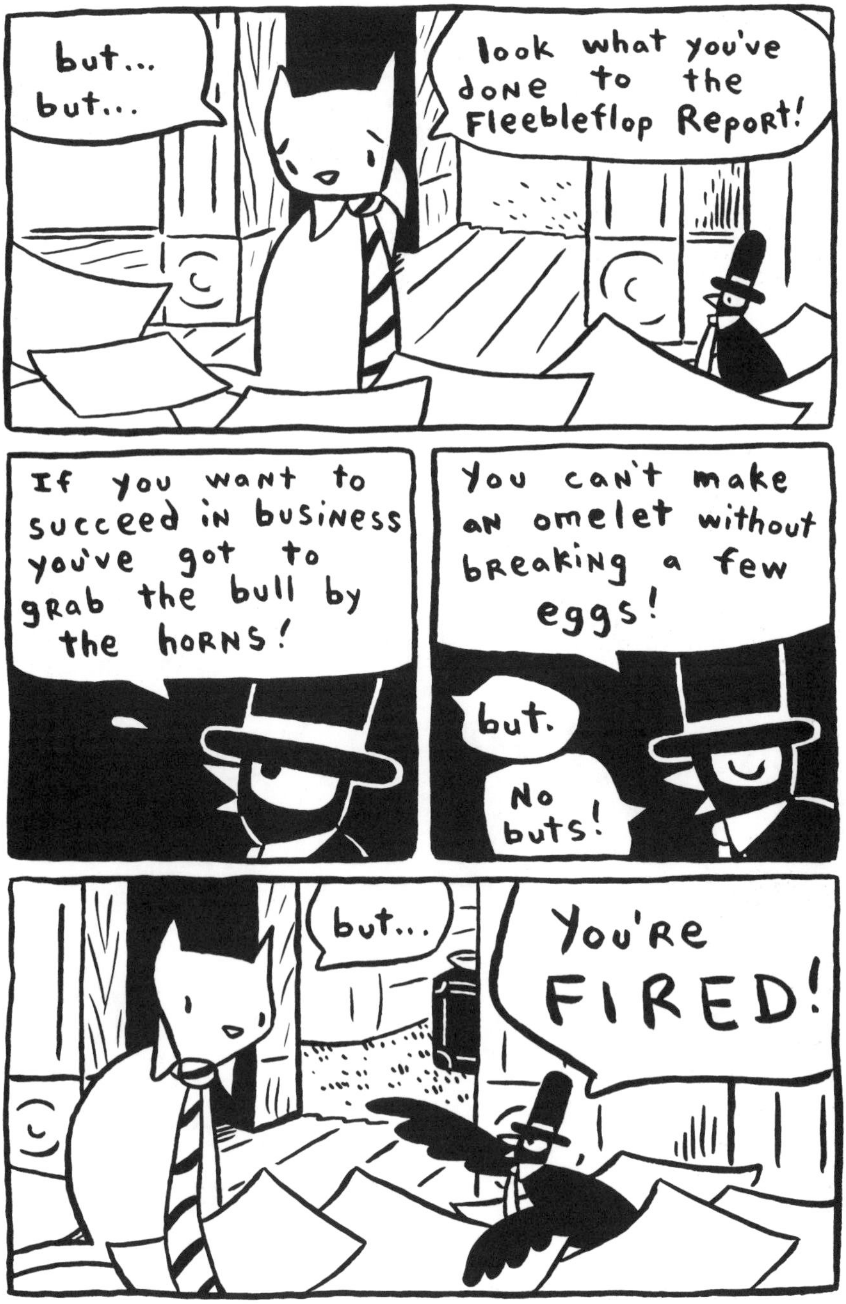
but... but...
look what you've done to the Fleebleflop Report!
If you want to succeed in business you've got to grab the bull by the horns!
You can't make an omelet without breaking a few eggs!
but.
No buts!
but...
You're FIRED!

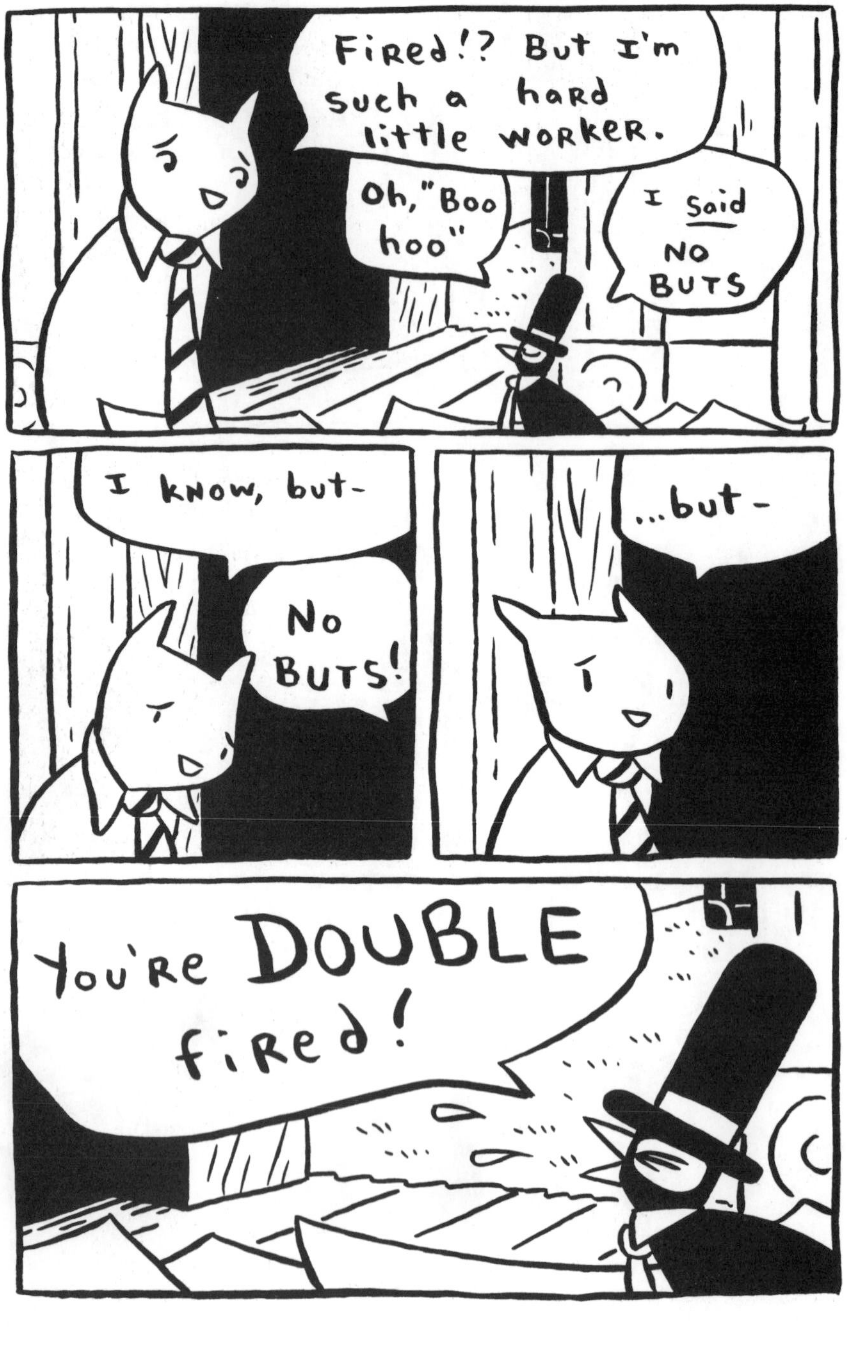
Fired!? But I'm such a hard little worker.
Oh, "Boo hoo"
I said NO BUTS
I know, but-
No BUTS!
...but-
You're DOUBLE fired!

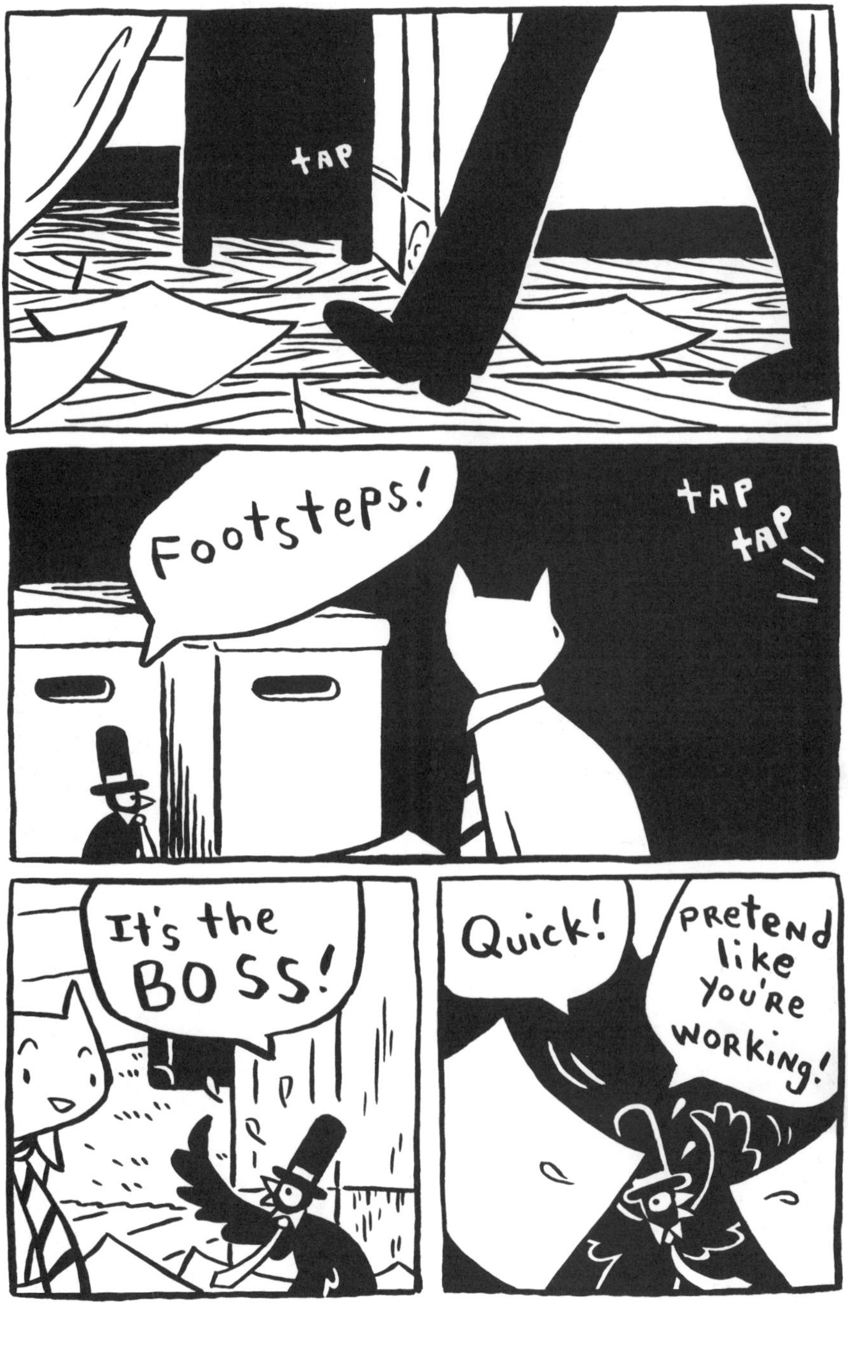
tap
Footsteps!
tap
tap
It's the BOSS!
Quick!
pretend like you're working!

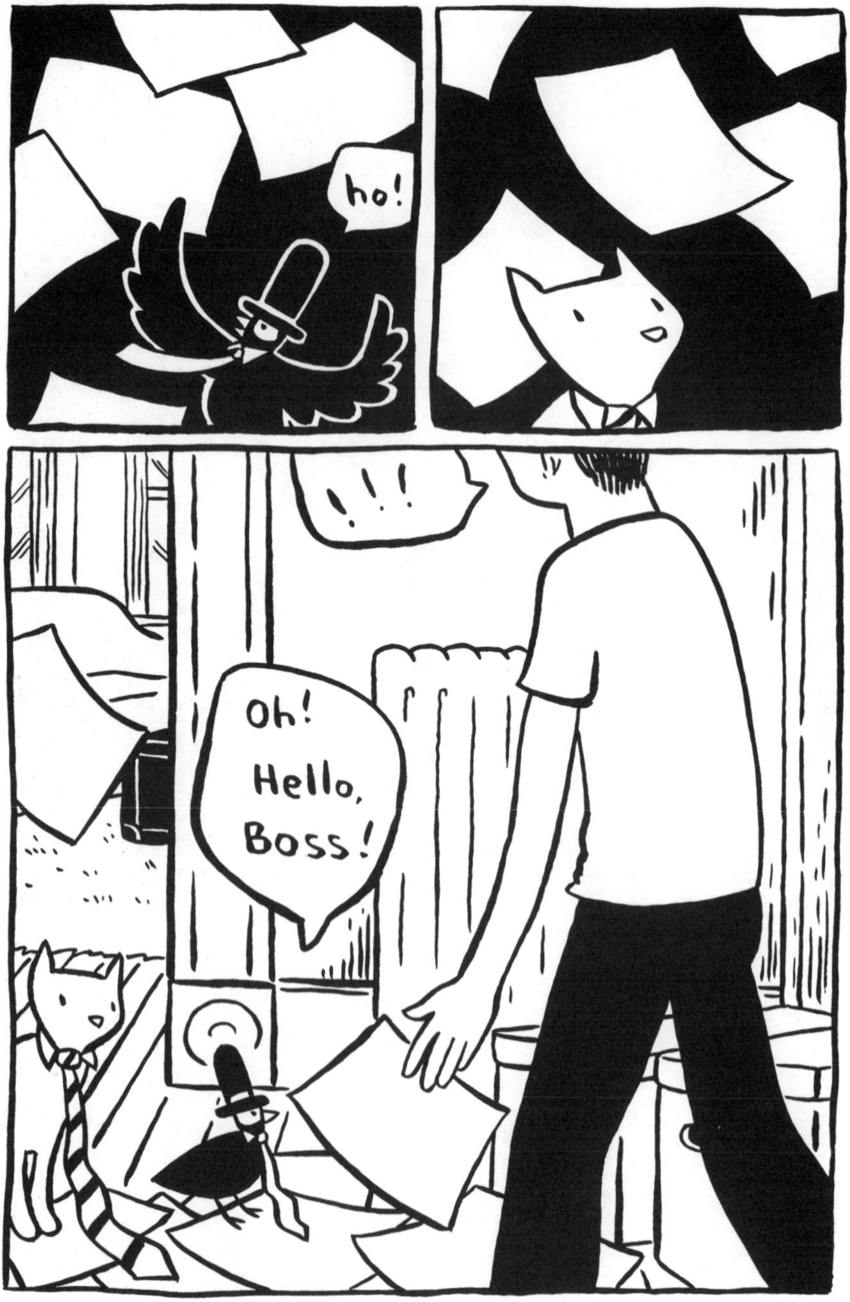
ho!
!!!
Oh!
Hello, Boss!

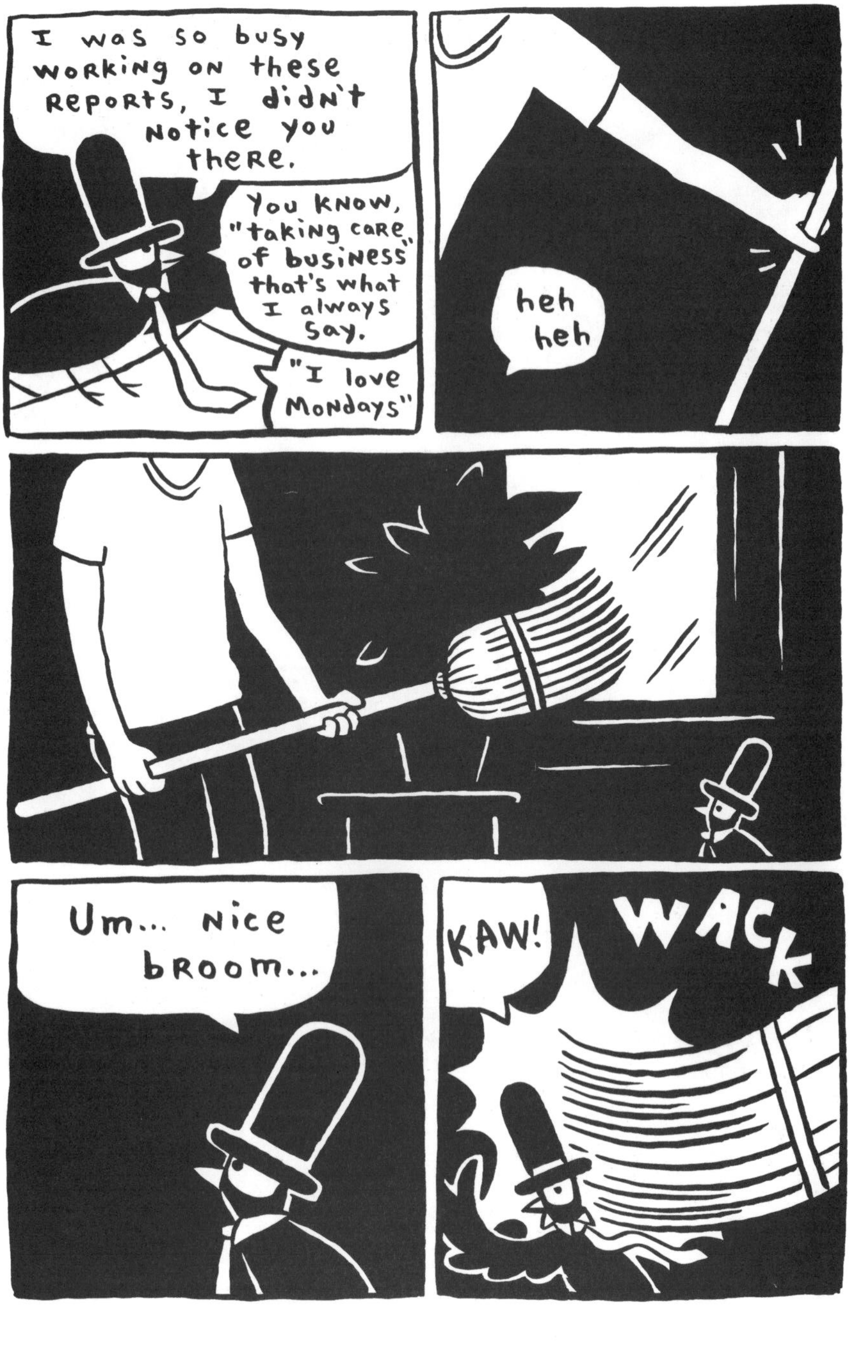
I was so busy working on these reports, I didn't notice you there.
You know, "taking care of business" that's what I always say.
"I love Mondays"
heh heh
Um... nice broom...
KAW!
WACK

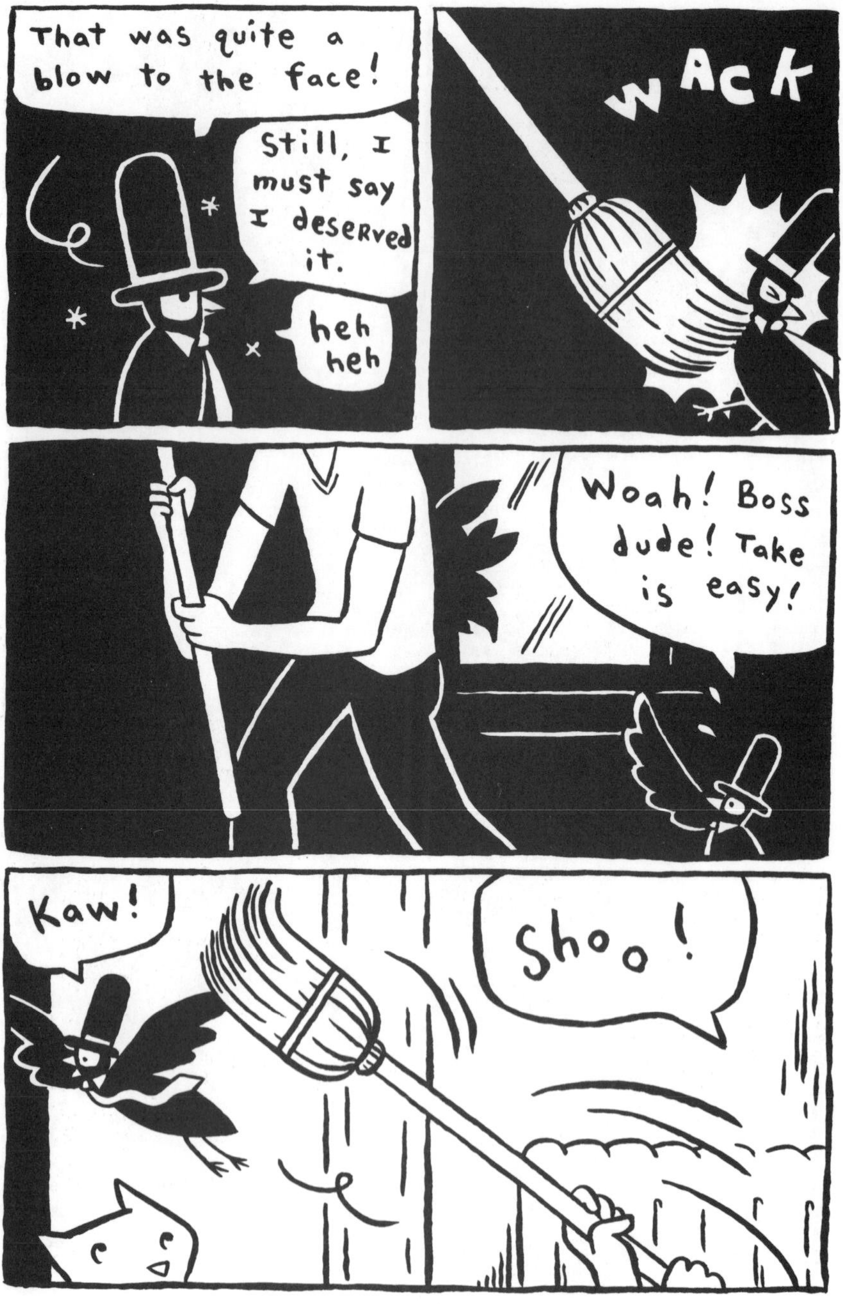
That was quite a blow to the face!
Still, I must say I deserved it.
heh heh
WACK
Woah! Boss dude! Take is easy!
Kaw!
Shoo!

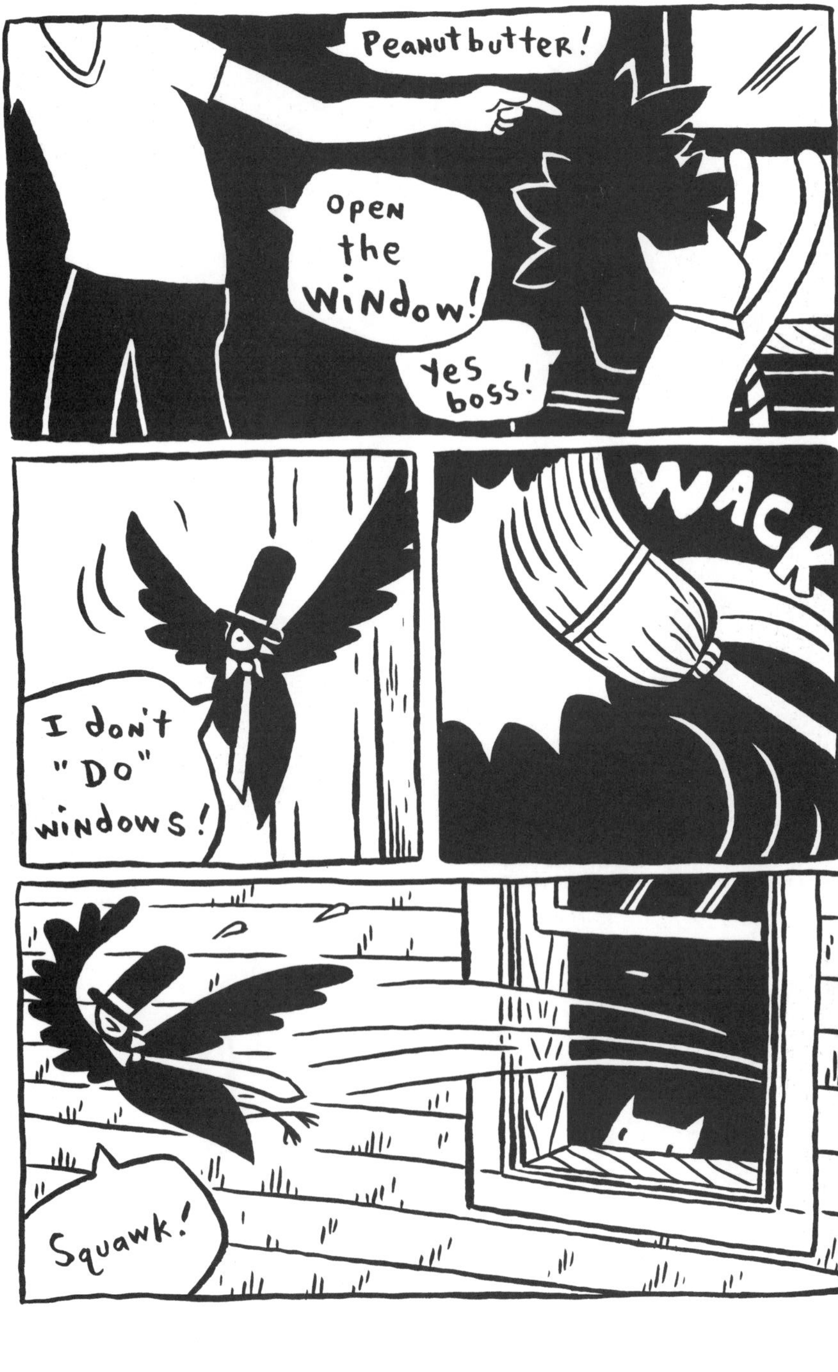

Peanutbutter!
Open the window!
Yes boss!
I don't "DO" windows!
WACK
Squawk!

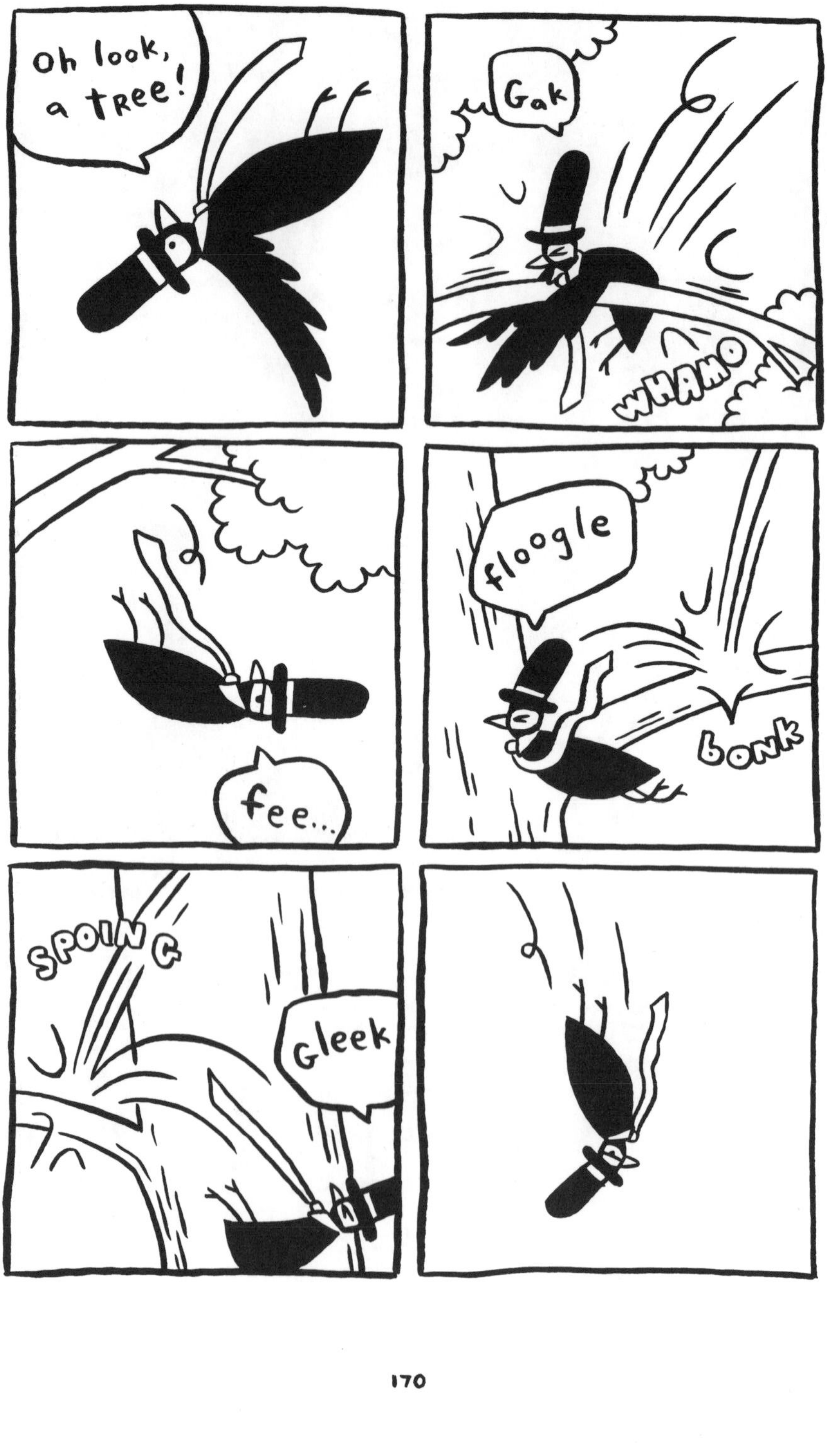
Oh look, a tree!
Gak
WHAMO
fee...
floogle
bonk
SPOING
Gleek

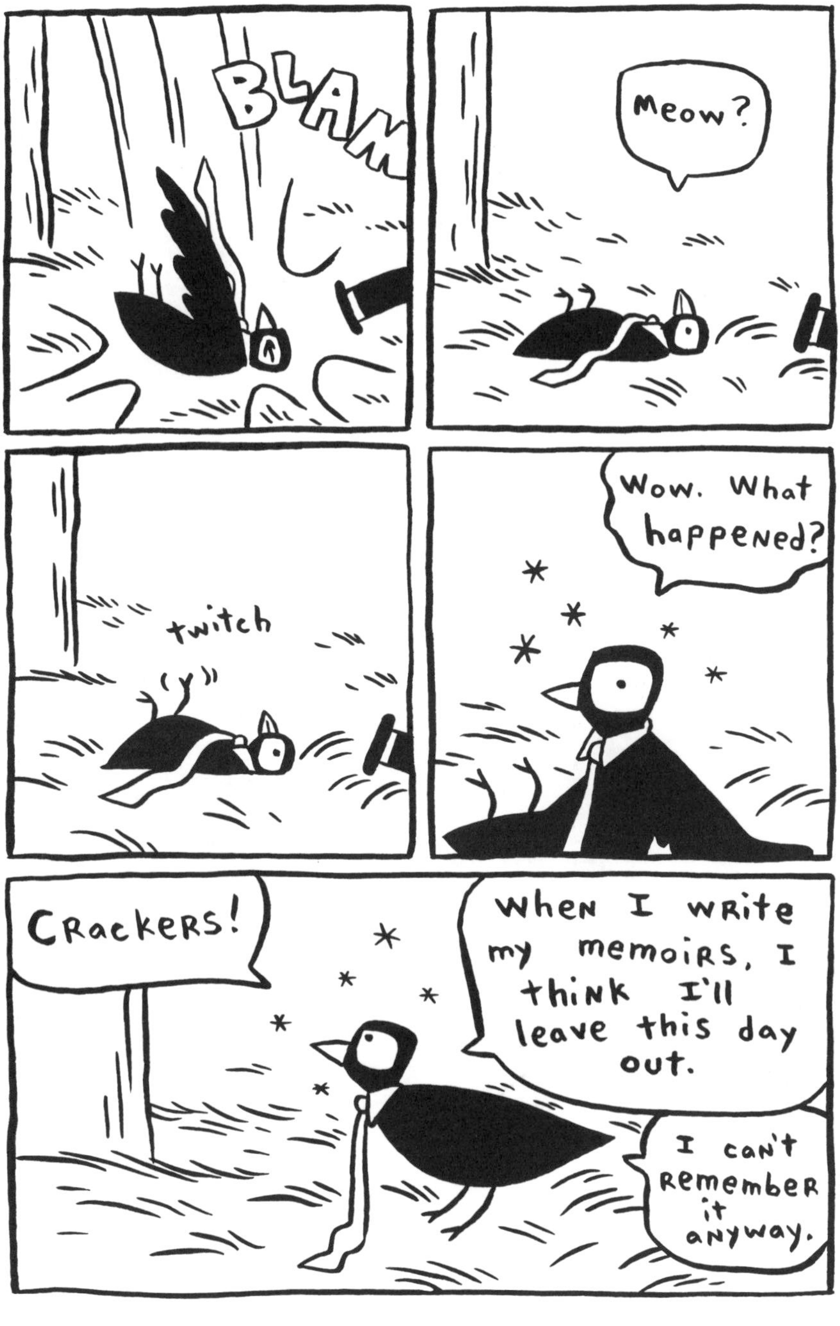
BLAM
Meow?
twitch
Wow. What happened?
Crackers!
When I write my memoirs, I think I'll leave this day out.
I can't remember it anyway.

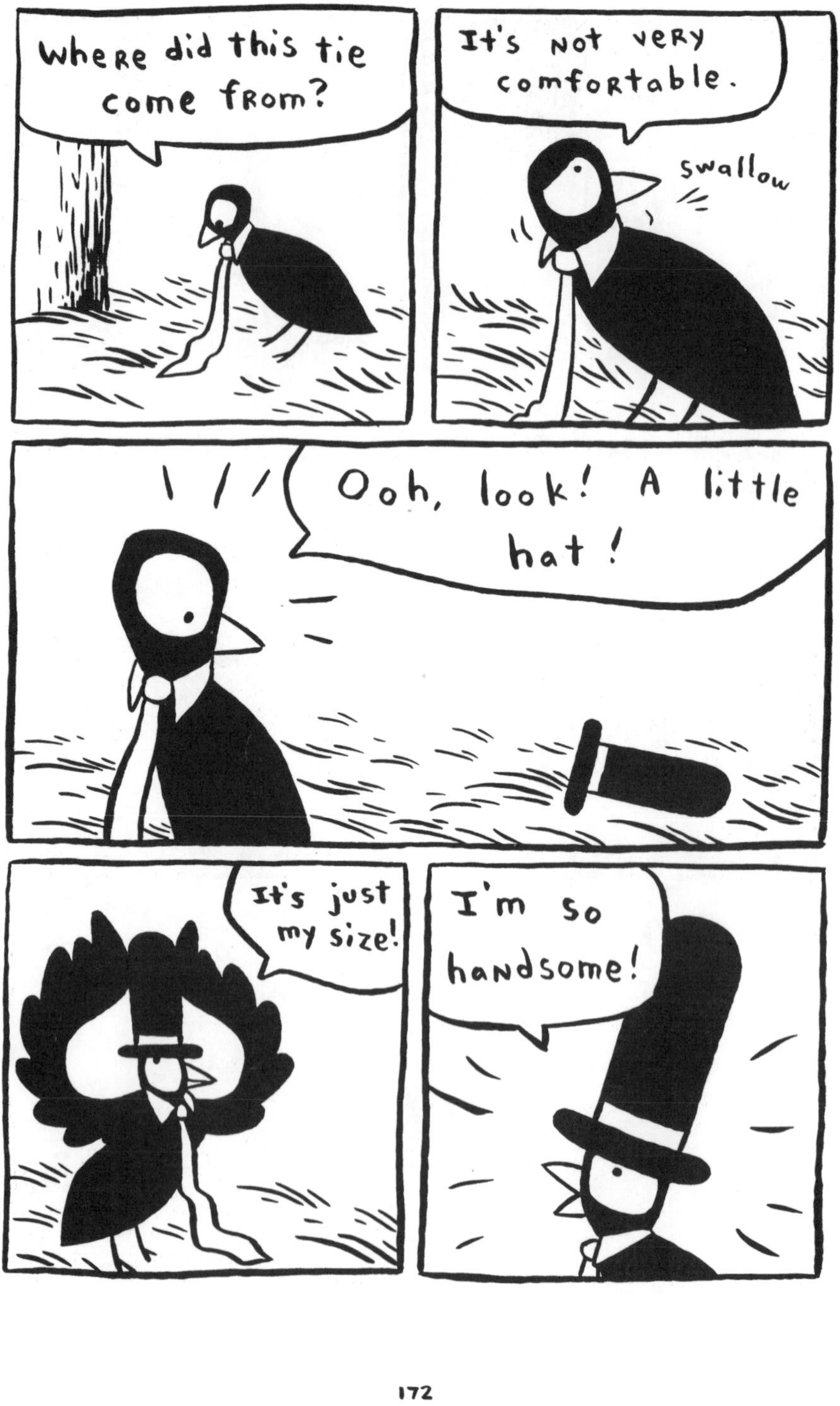
Where did this tie come from?
It's not very comfortable.
swallow
Ooh, look! A little hat!
It's just my size!
I'm so handsome!

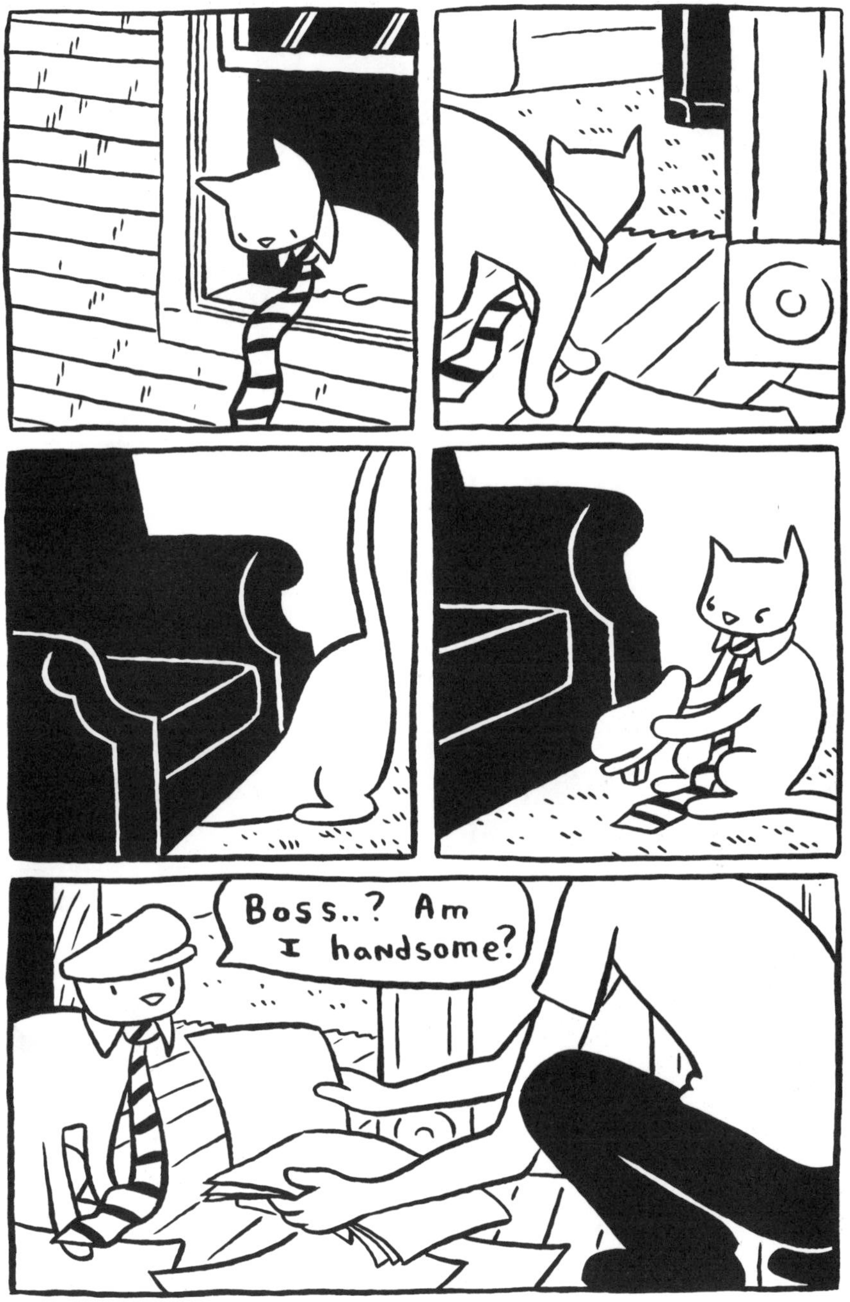
Boss..? Am I handsome?

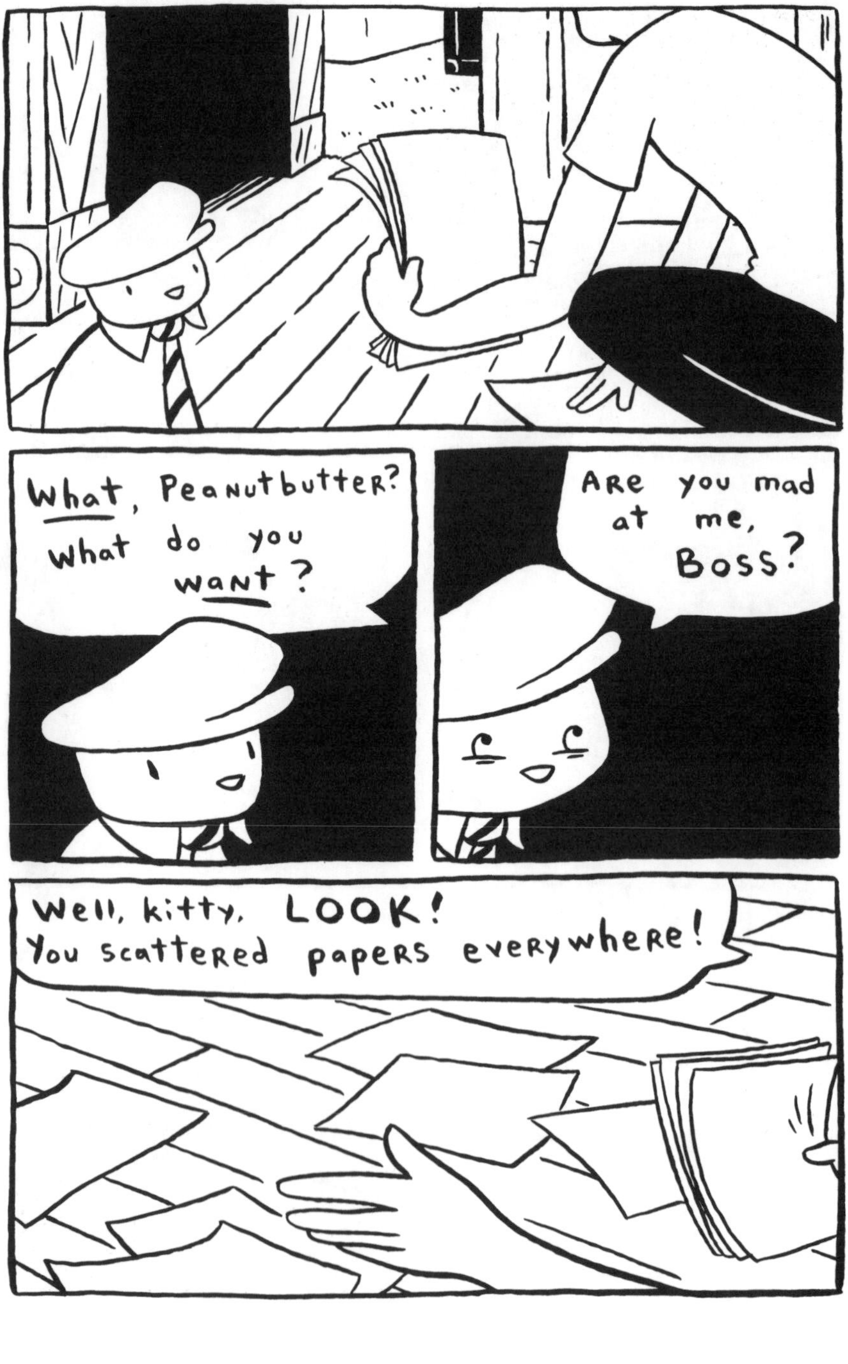
What, Peanutbutter? What do you want?
Are you mad at me, Boss?
Well, kitty, LOOK! You scattered papers everywhere!

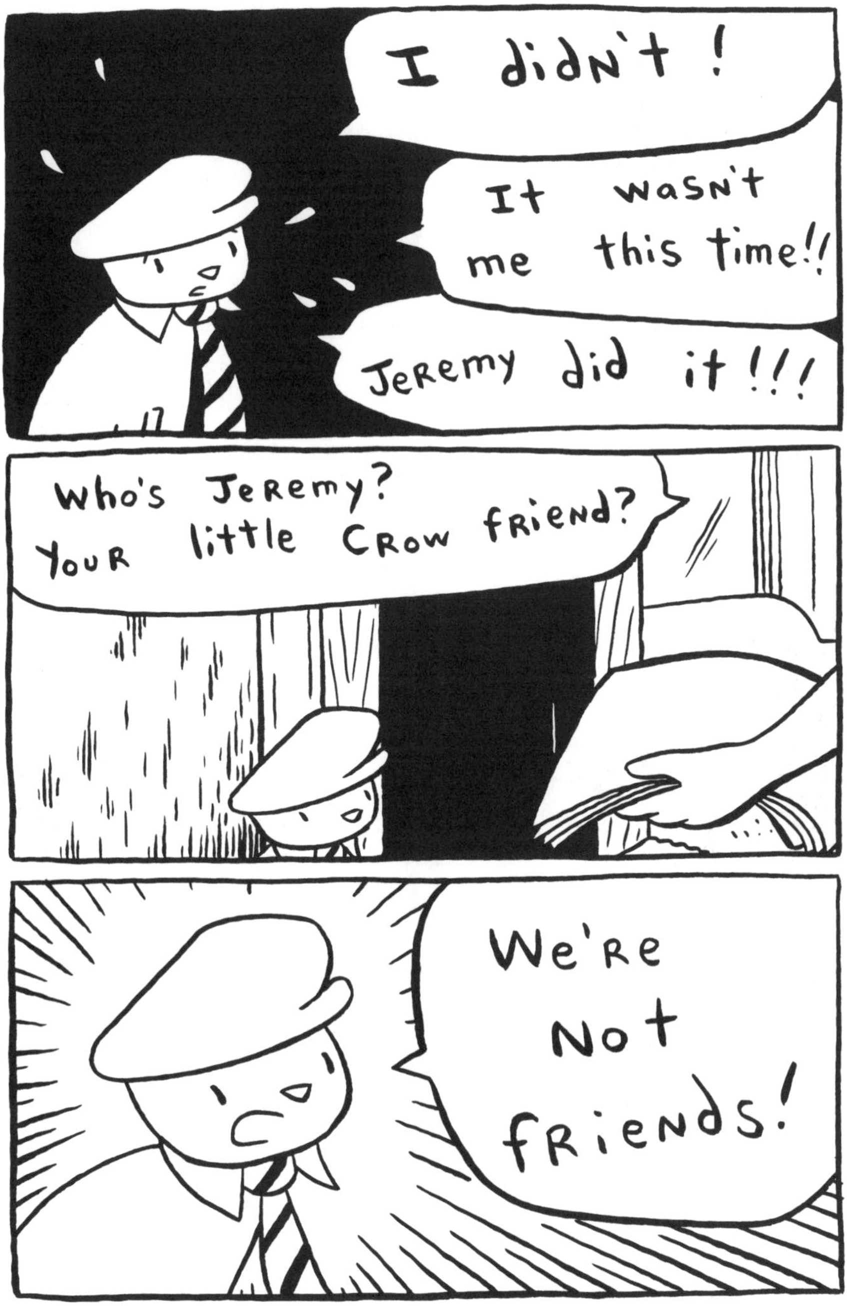
I didn't !
It wasn't me this time!!
Jeremy did it!!!
Who's Jeremy? Your little crow friend?
We're not friends!

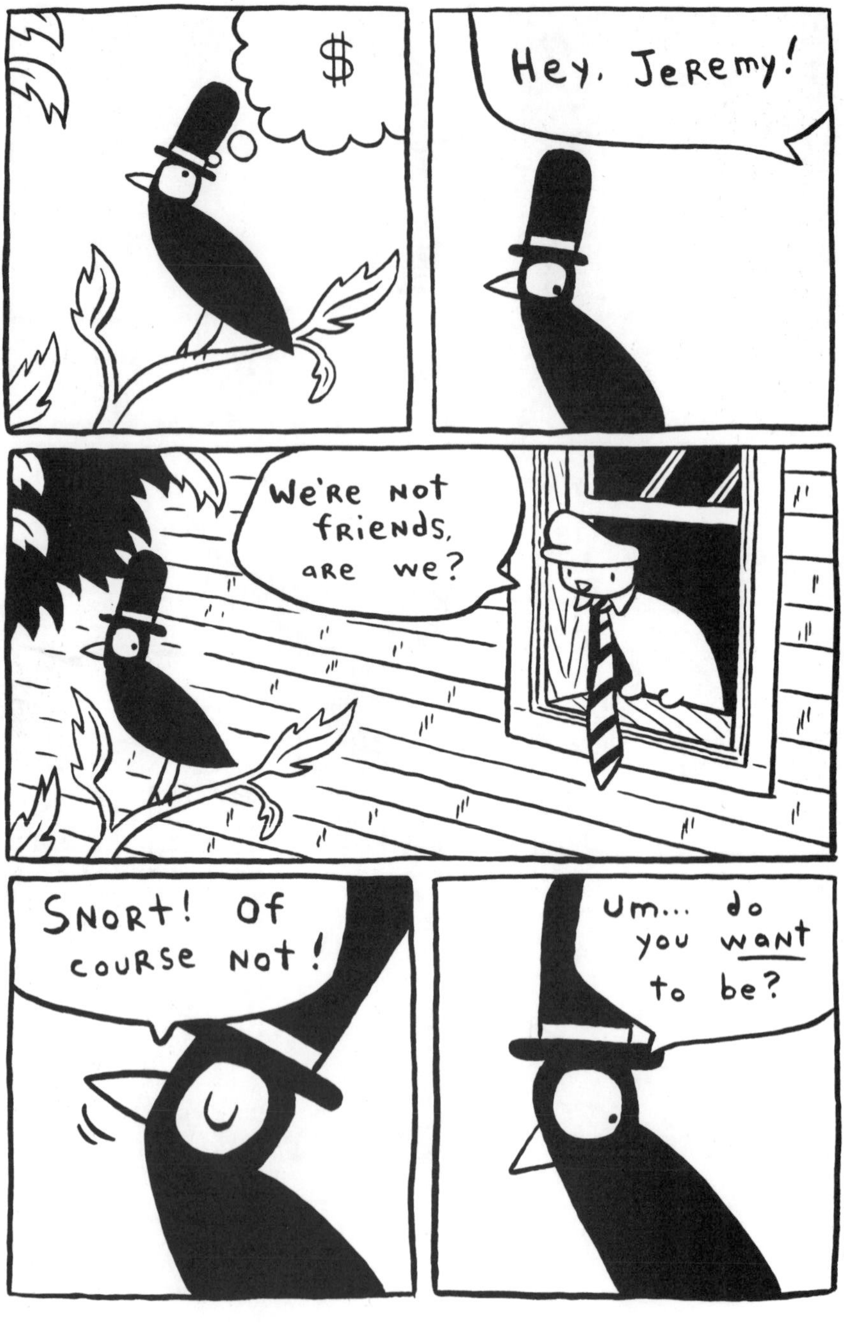
$
Hey, Jeremy!
We're not friends, are we?
Snort! Of course not!
Um... do you want to be?

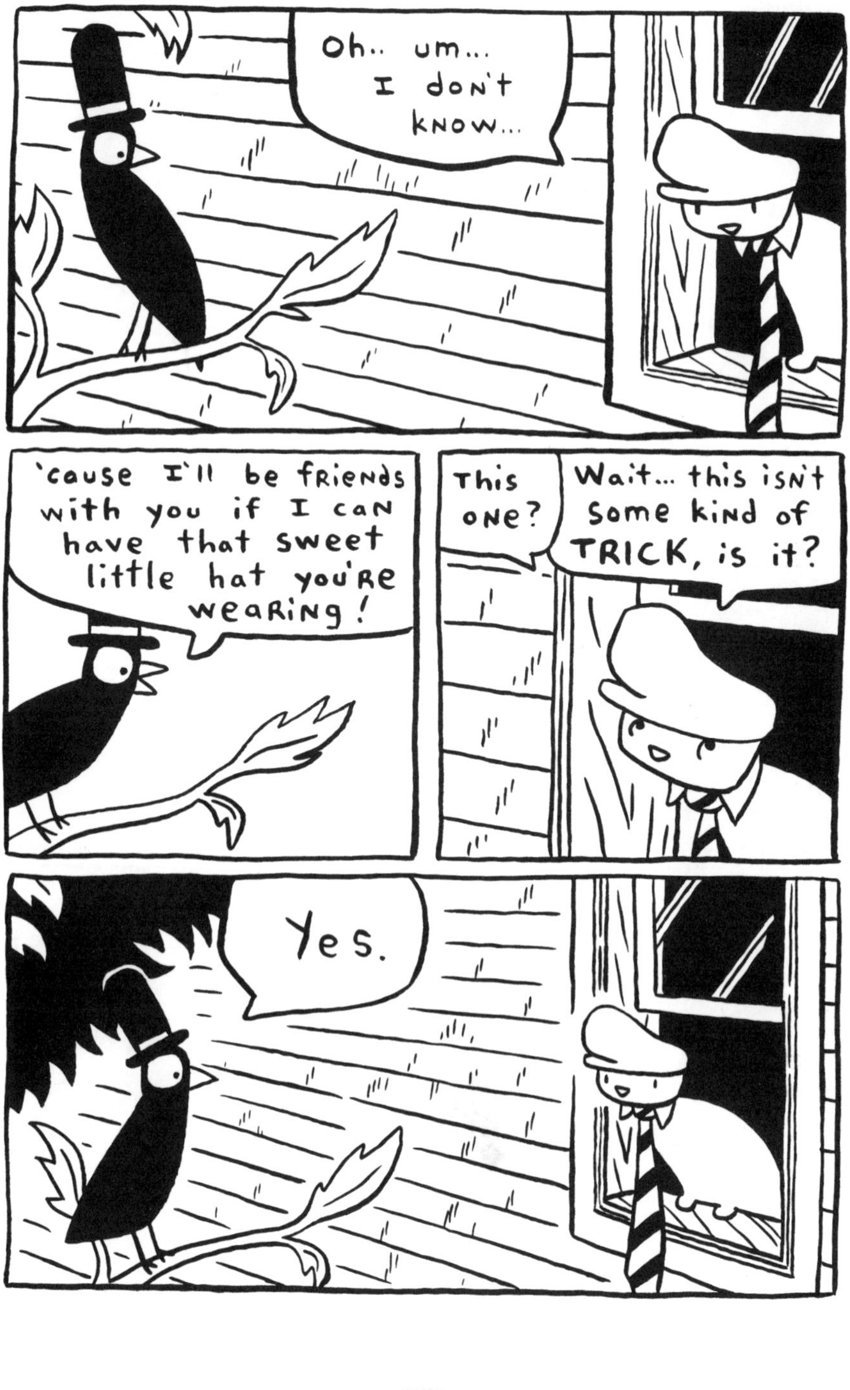
Oh.. um... I don't know...
'cause I'll be friends with you if I can have that sweet little hat you're wearing!
This one?
Wait... this isn't some kind of TRICK, is it?
Yes.

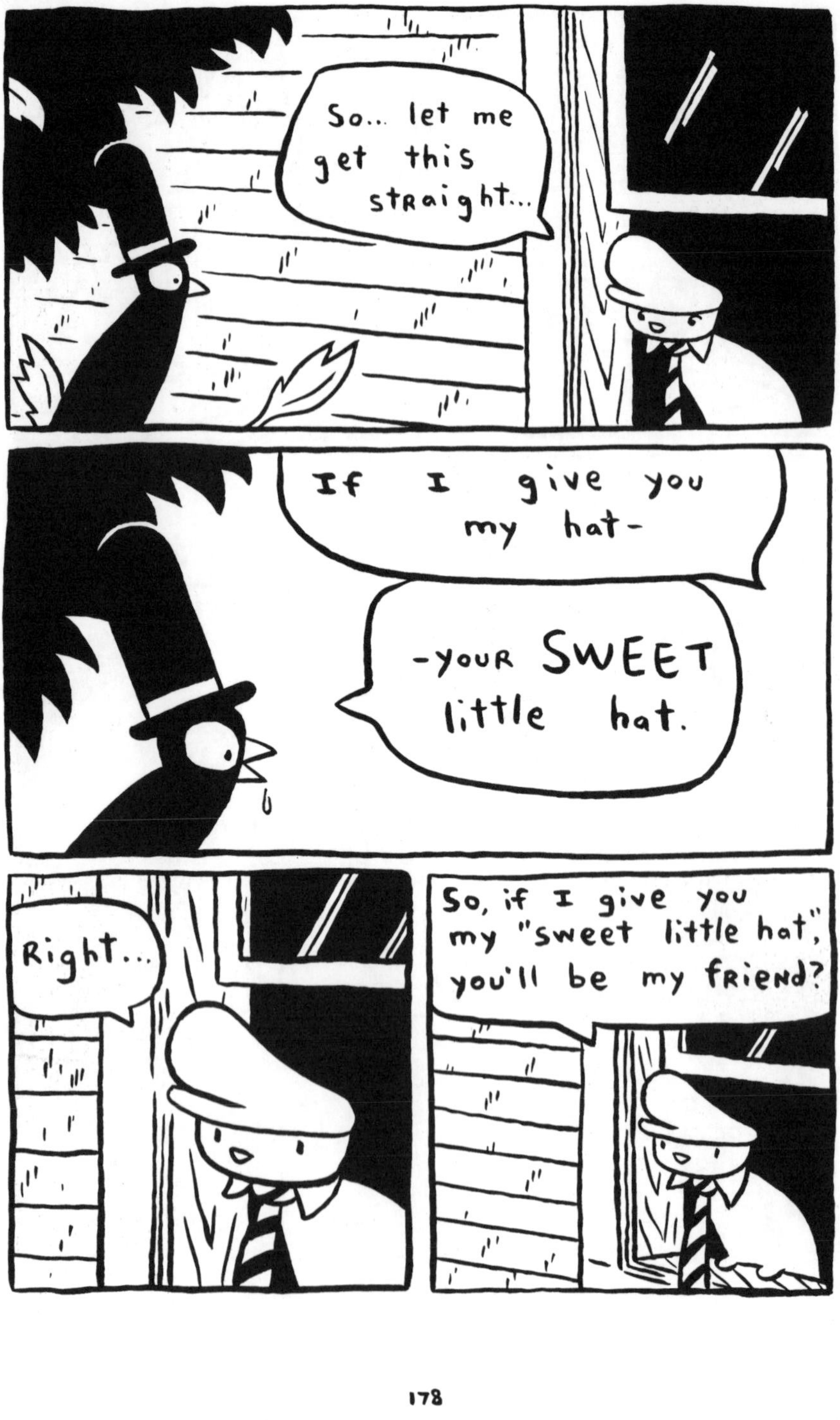

So... let me get this straight...
If I give you my hat-
-your SWEET little hat.
Right...
So, if I give you my "sweet little hat", you'll be my friend?

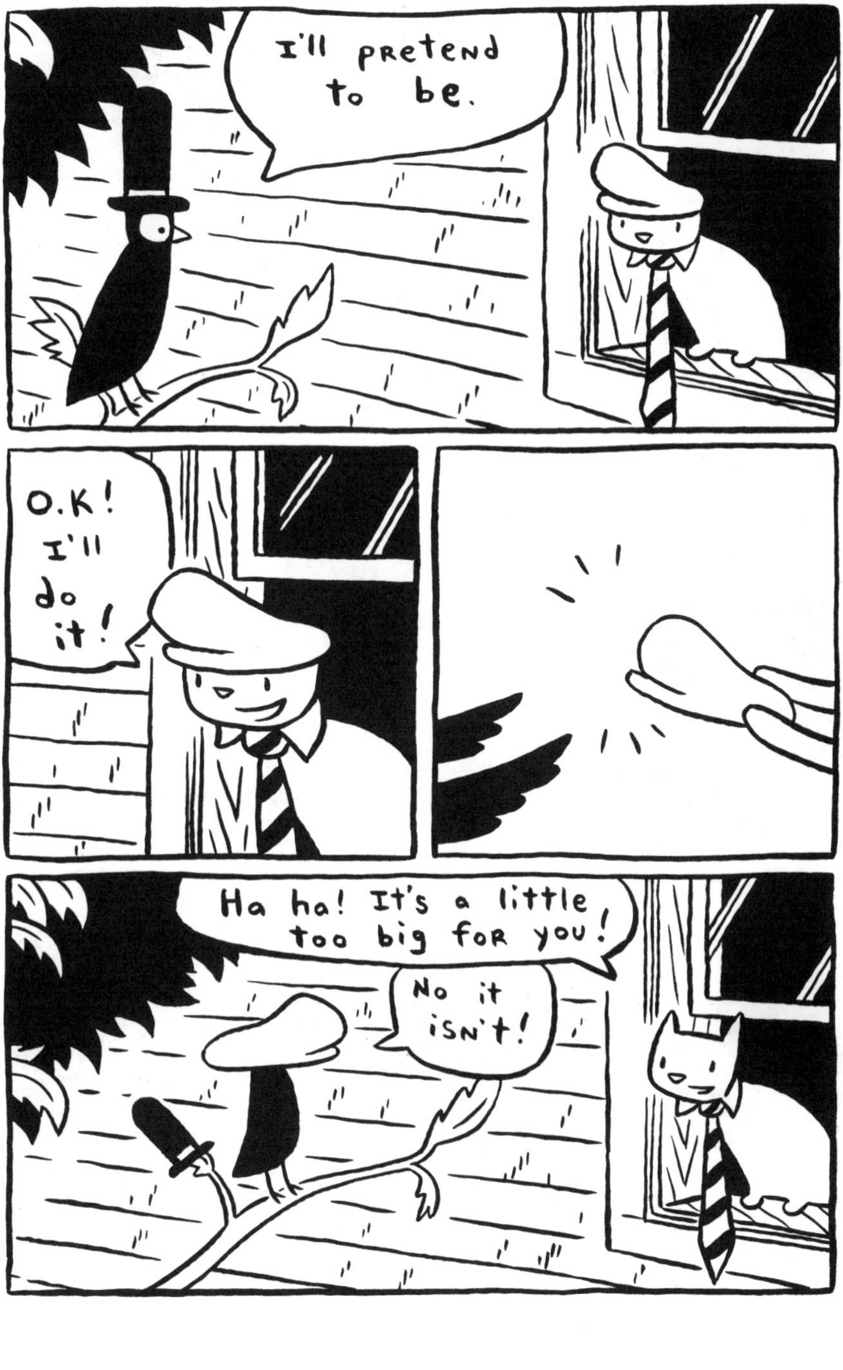
I'll pretend to be.
O.K! I'll do it!
Ha ha! It's a little too big for you!
No it isn't!

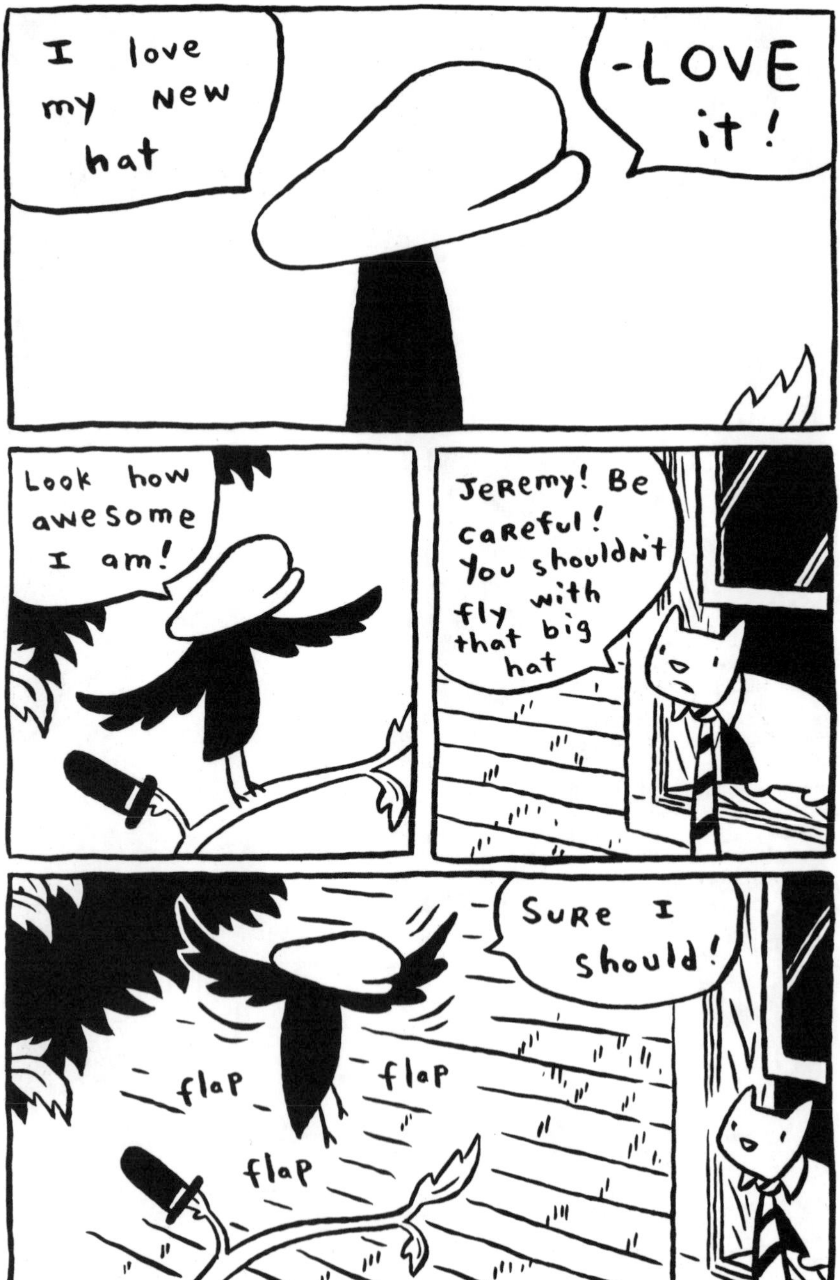
I love my new hat
-LOVE it!
Look how awesome I am!
Jeremy! Be careful! You shouldn't fly with that big hat
Sure I should!
flap
flap
flap

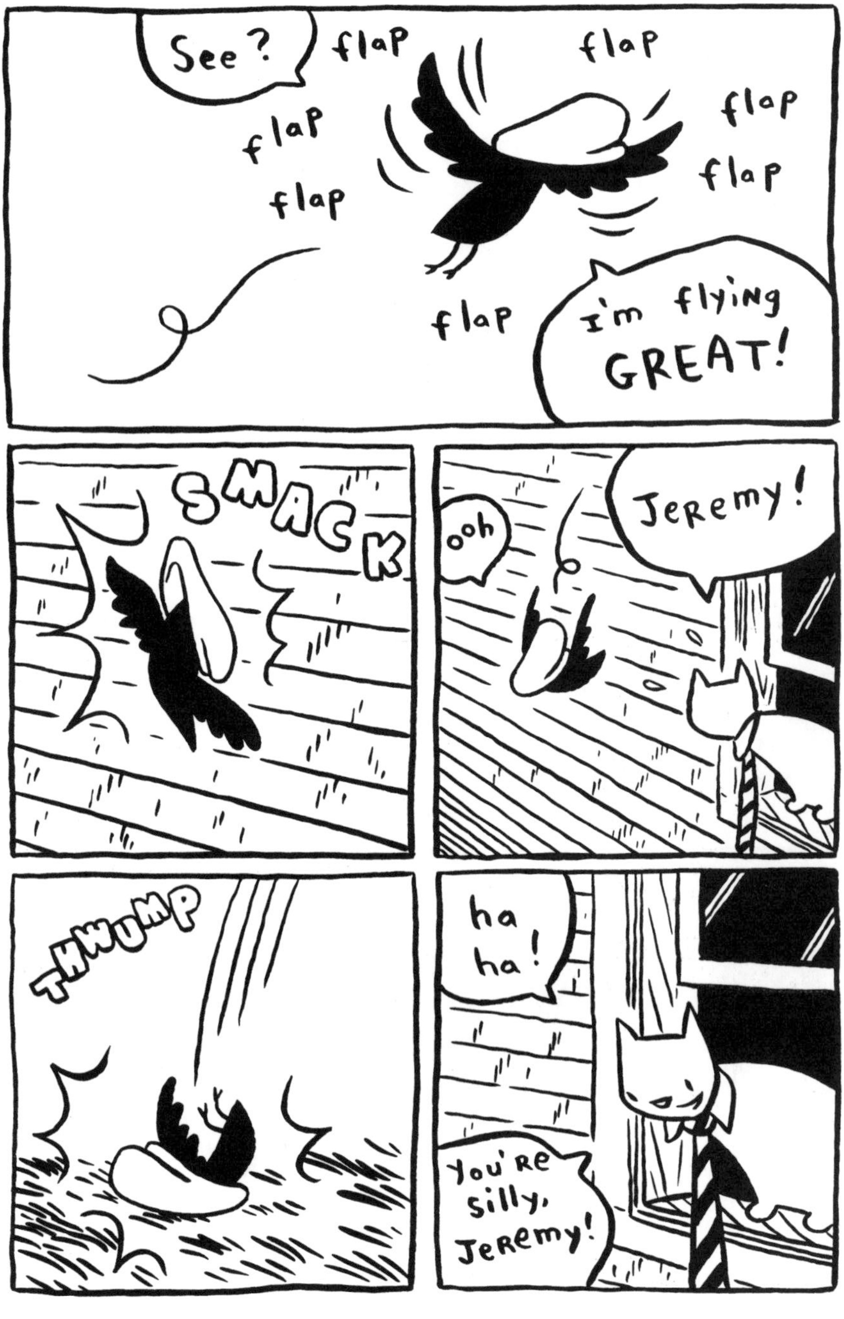

See?
flap
flap
flap
flap
flap
flap
flap
I'm flying GREAT!
SMACK
ooh
Jeremy!
THWUMP
ha ha!
You're silly, Jeremy!

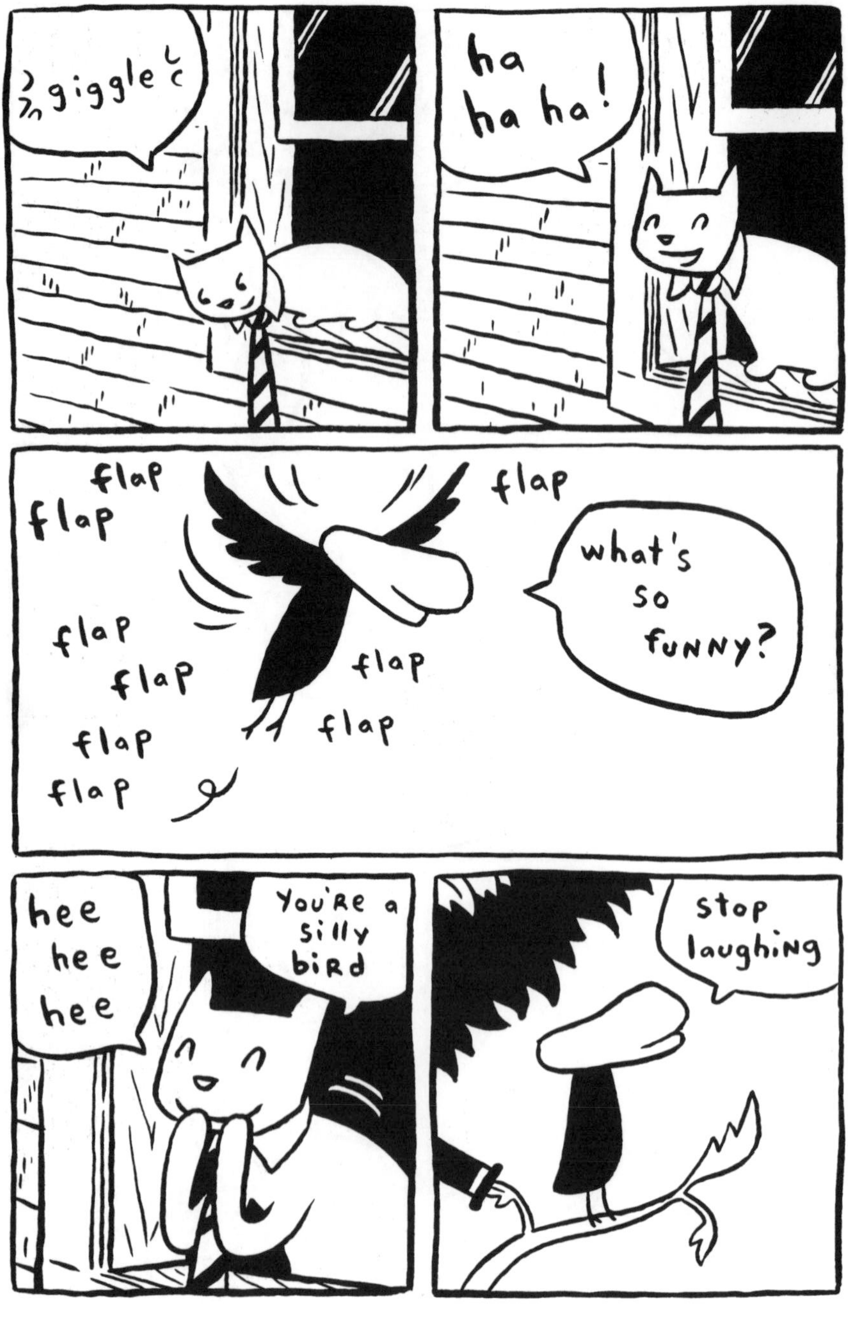
giggle
ha ha ha!
flap flap flap
what's so funny?
flap flap flap flap flap flap
hee hee hee
You're a silly bird
stop laughing

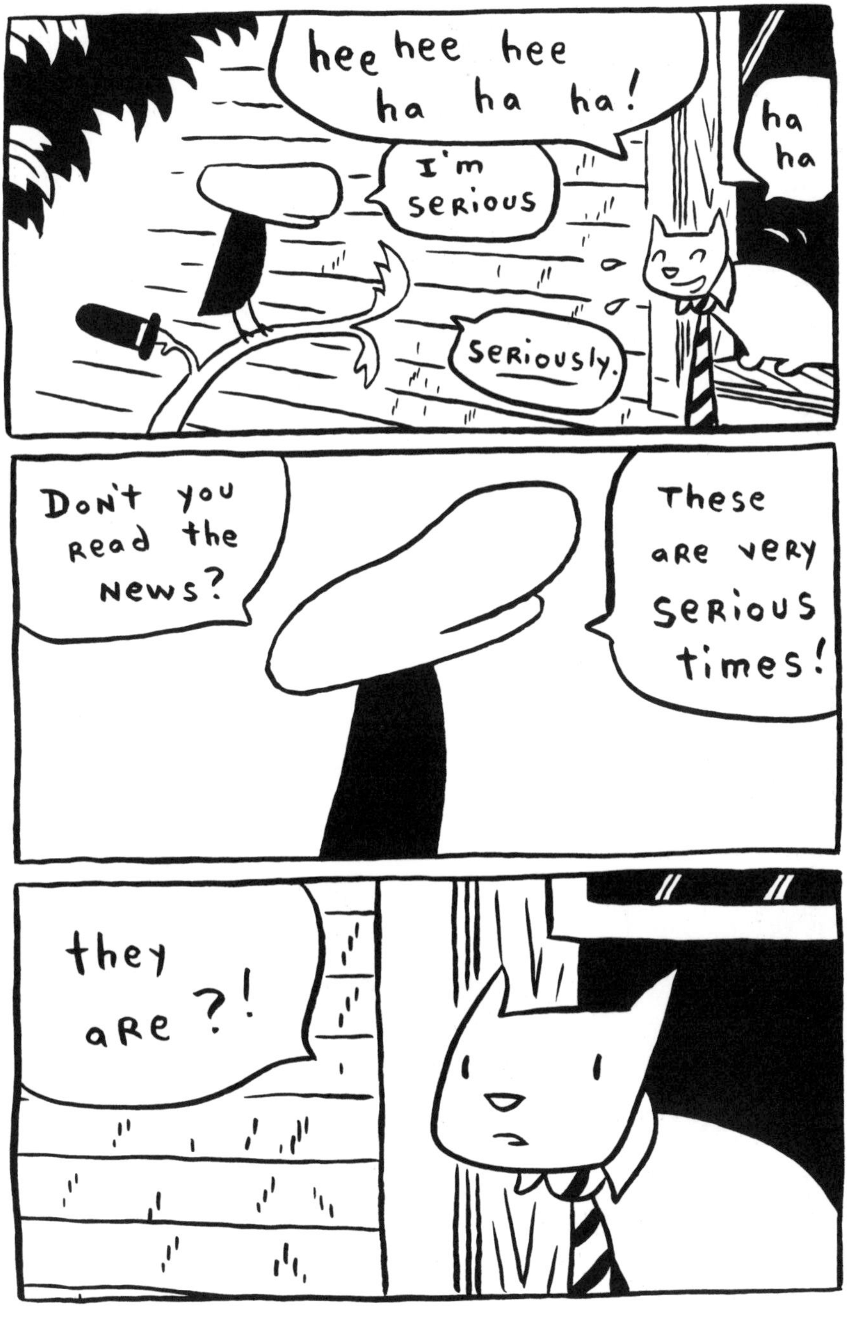
hee hee hee
ha ha ha!
ha ha
I'm serious
seriously.
Don't you read the news?
These are very serious times!
they are?!

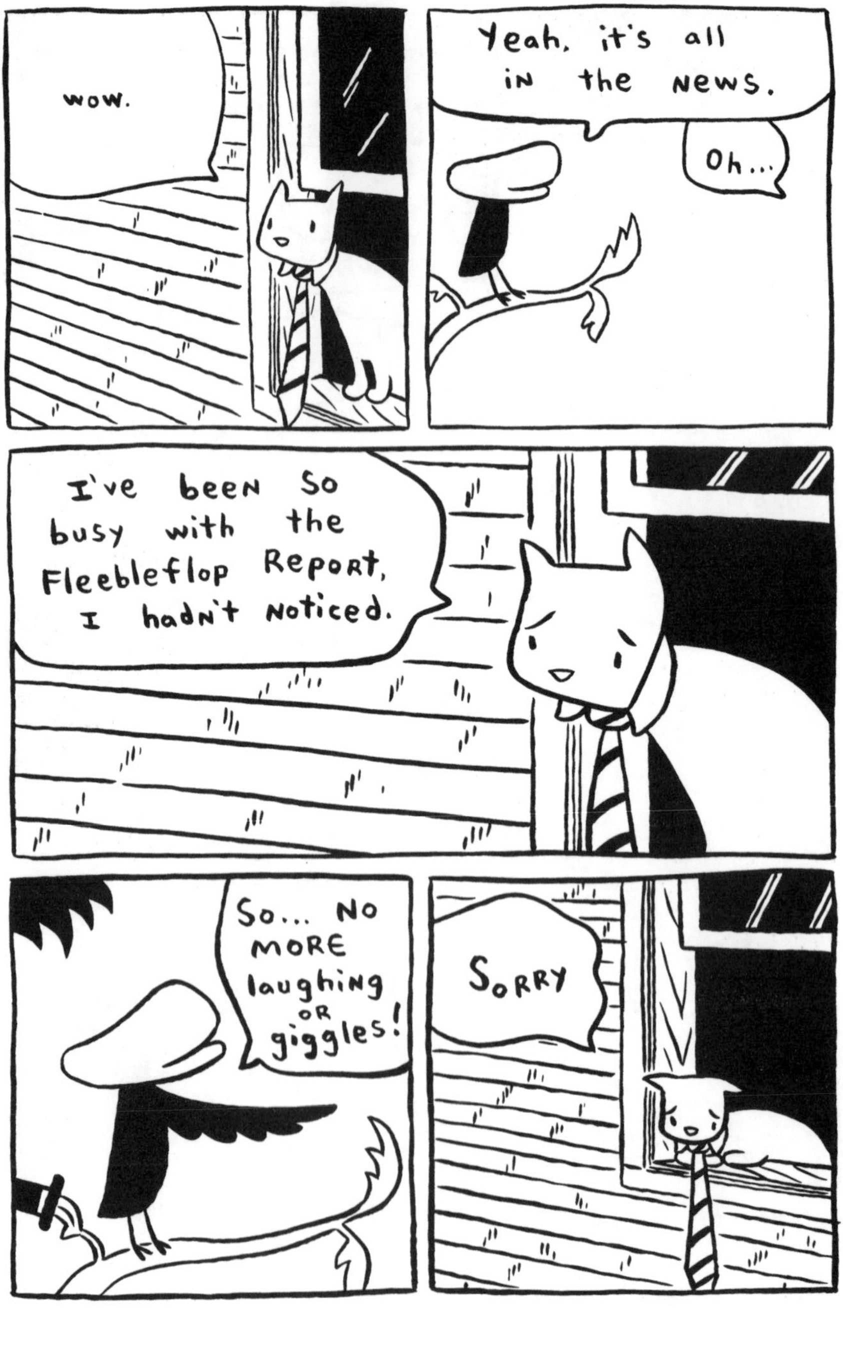
wow.
Yeah, it's all in the news.
Oh...
I've been so busy with the Fleebleflop Report, I hadn't noticed.
So... no more laughing or giggles!
Sorry

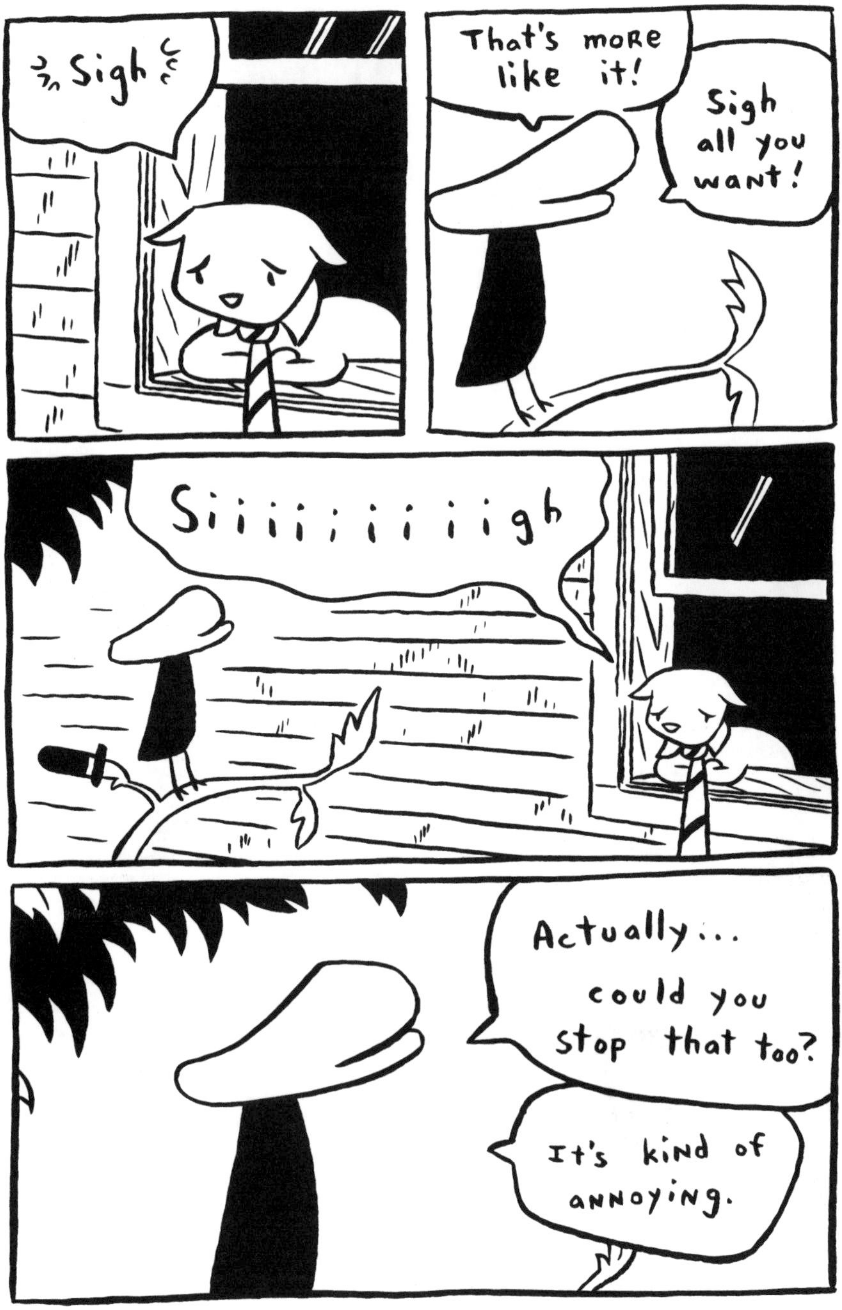
Sigh
That's more like it!
Sigh all you want!
Siiiiiiiigh
Actually... could you stop that too?
It's kind of annoying.

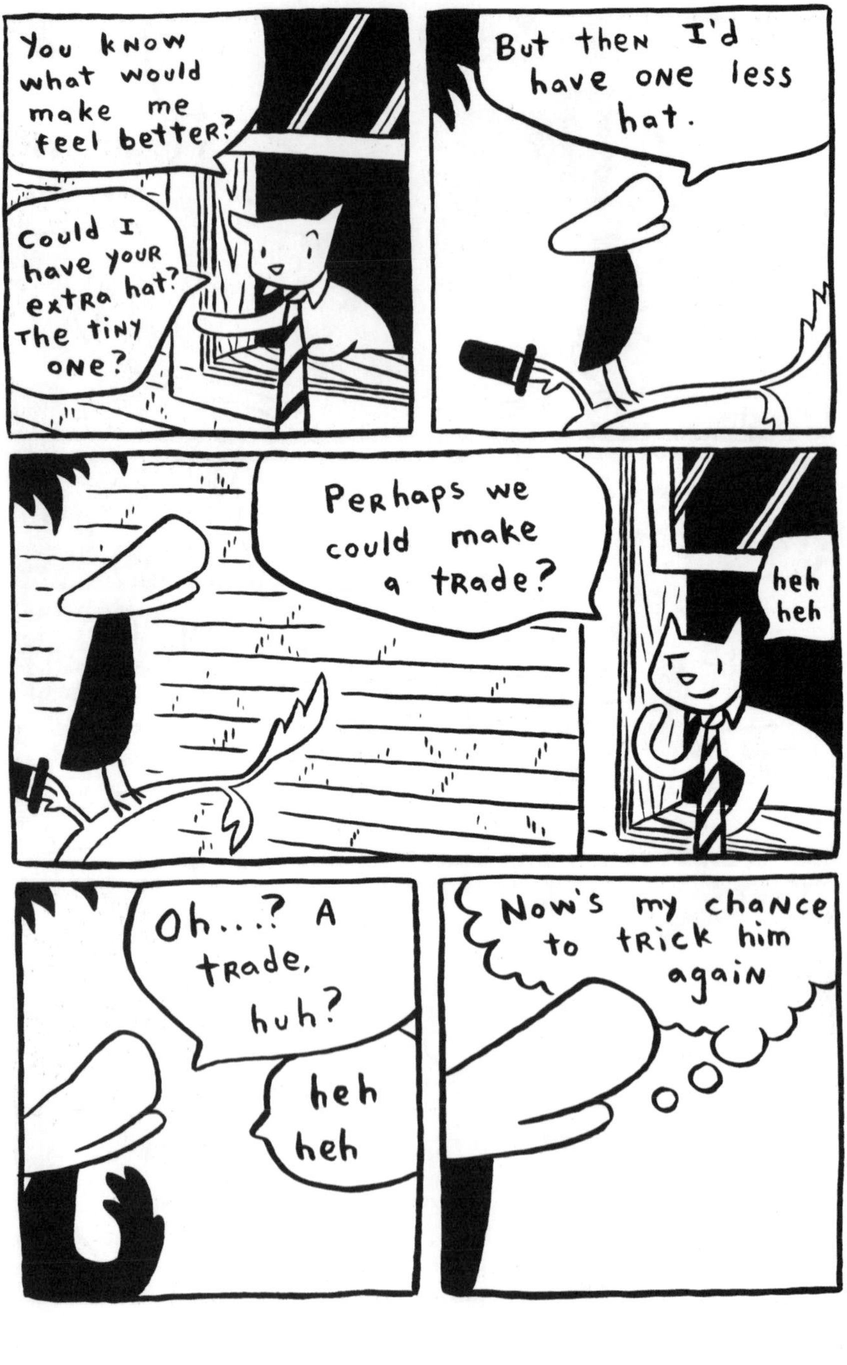
You know what would make me feel better?
Could I have your extra hat? The tiny one?
But then I'd have one less hat.
Perhaps we could make a trade?
heh heh
Oh...? A trade, huh?
heh heh
Now's my chance to trick him again

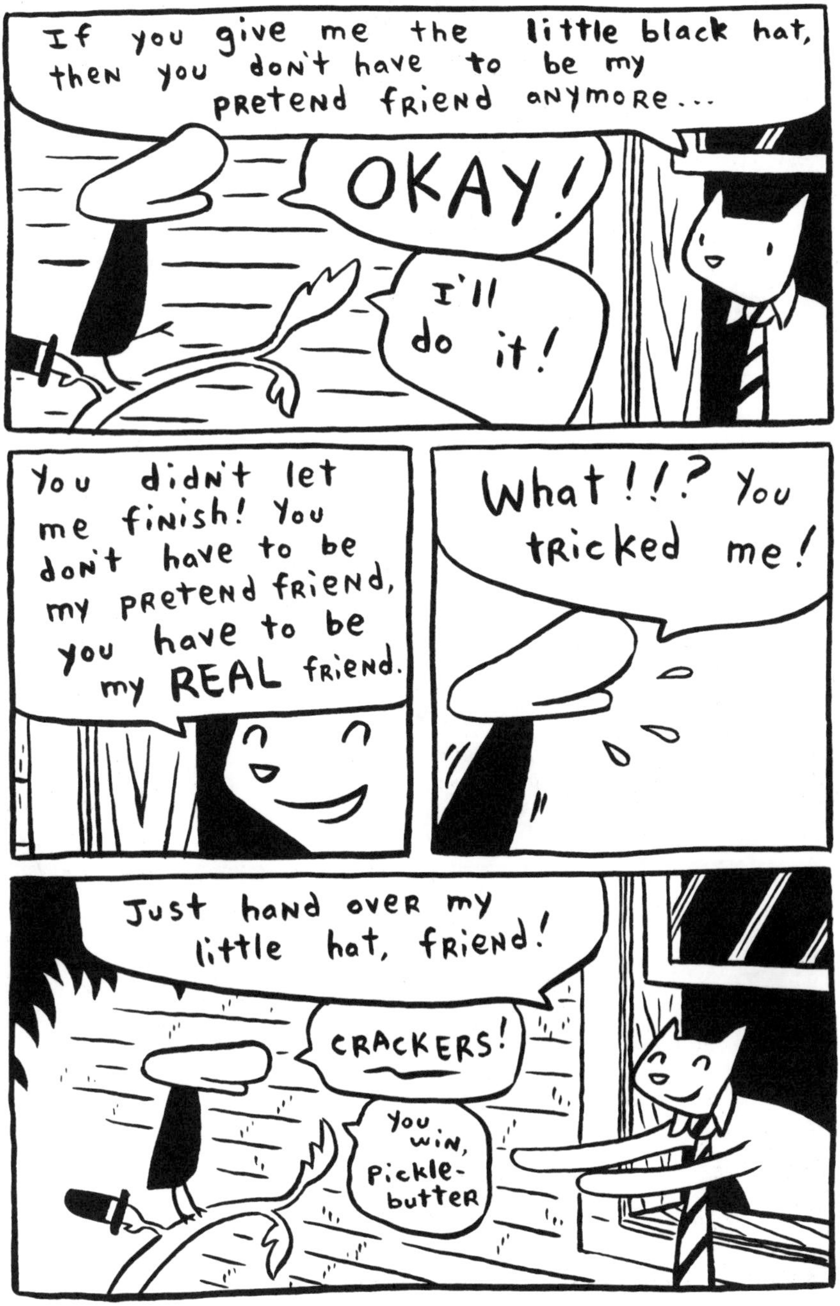
If you give me the little black hat, then you don't have to be my pretend friend anymore...
OKAY!
I'll do it!
You didn't let me finish! You don't have to be my pretend friend, you have to be my REAL friend.
What!!? You tricked me!
Just hand over my little hat, friend!
CRACKERS!
You win, Pickle-butter

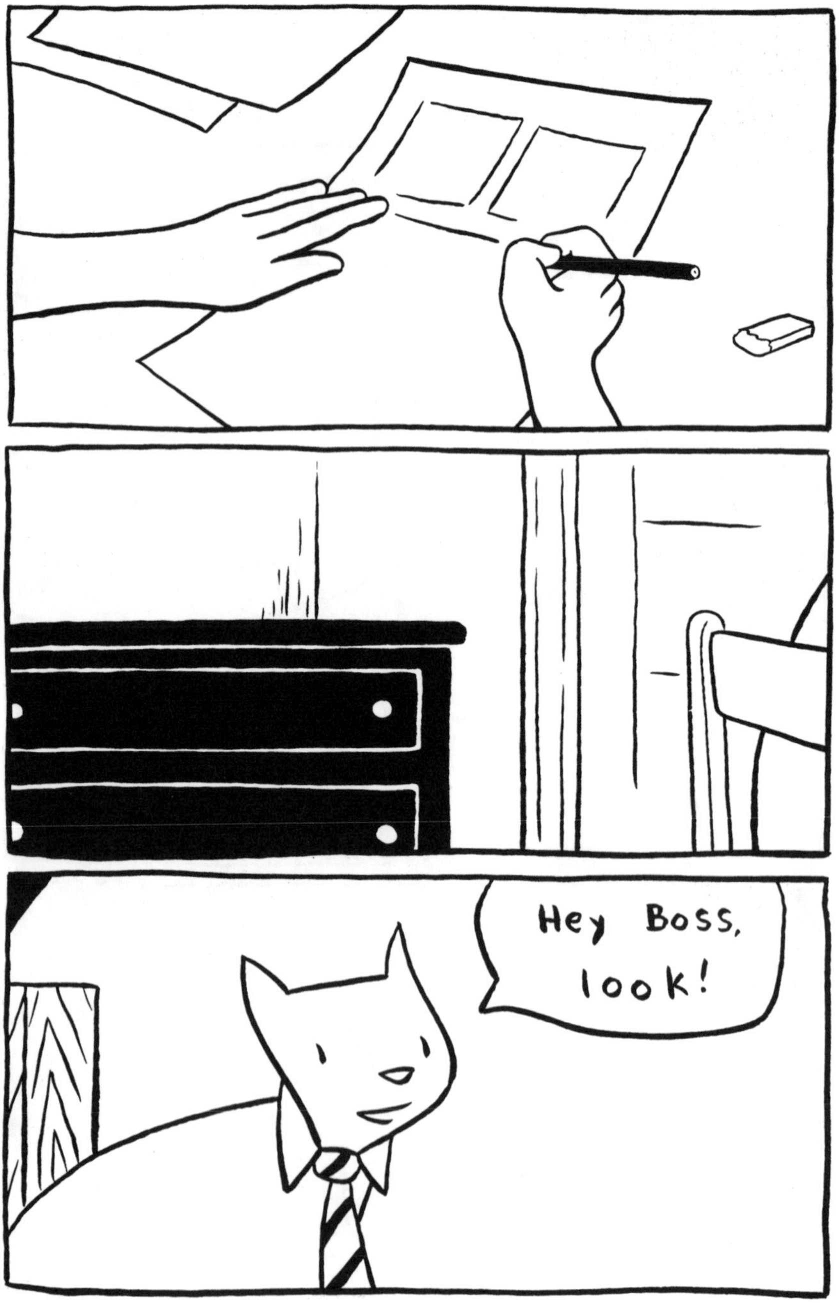
Hey Boss,
look!

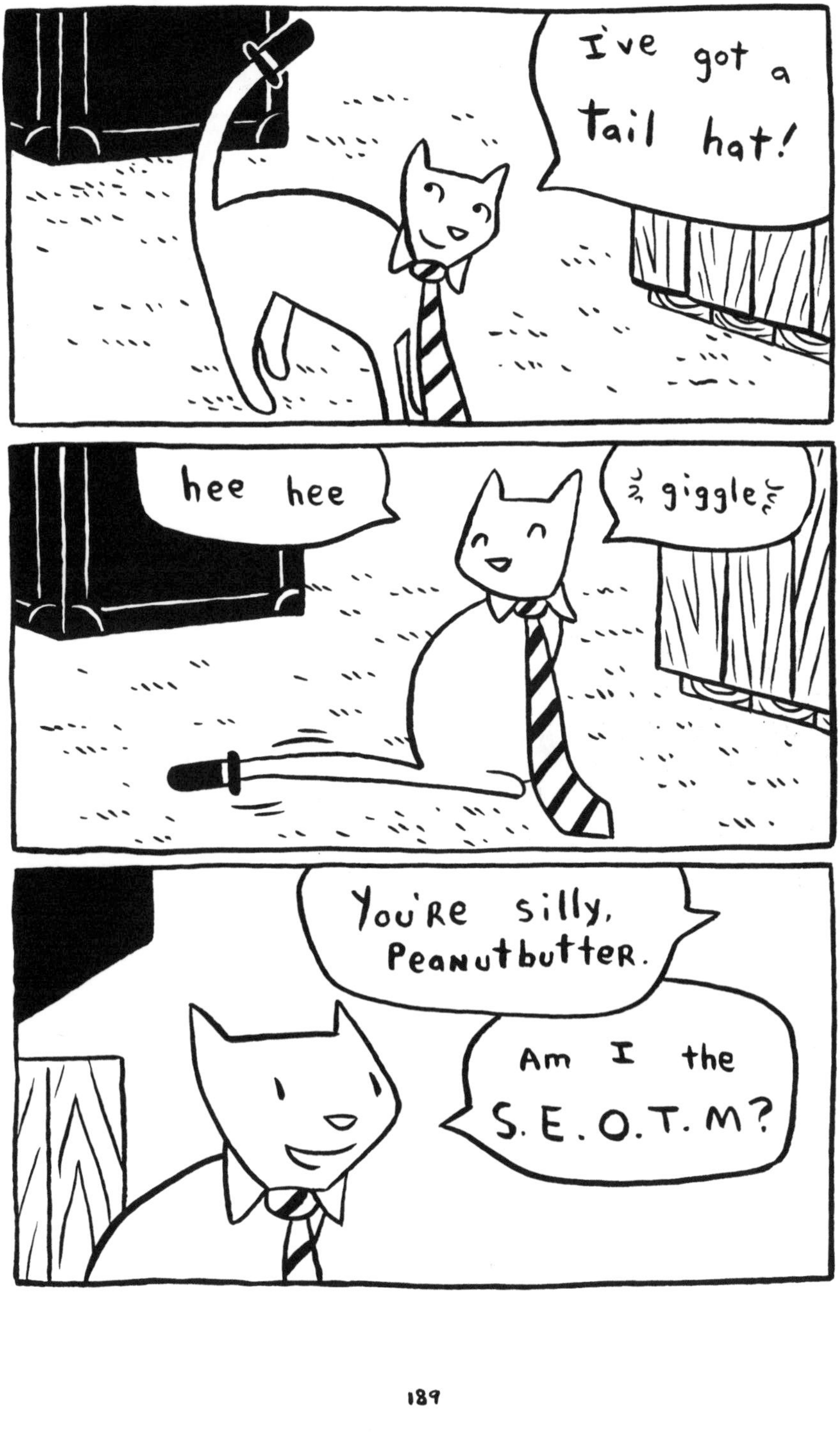
I've got a tail hat!
hee hee
giggle
You're silly, Peanutbutter.
Am I the S.E.O.T.M?

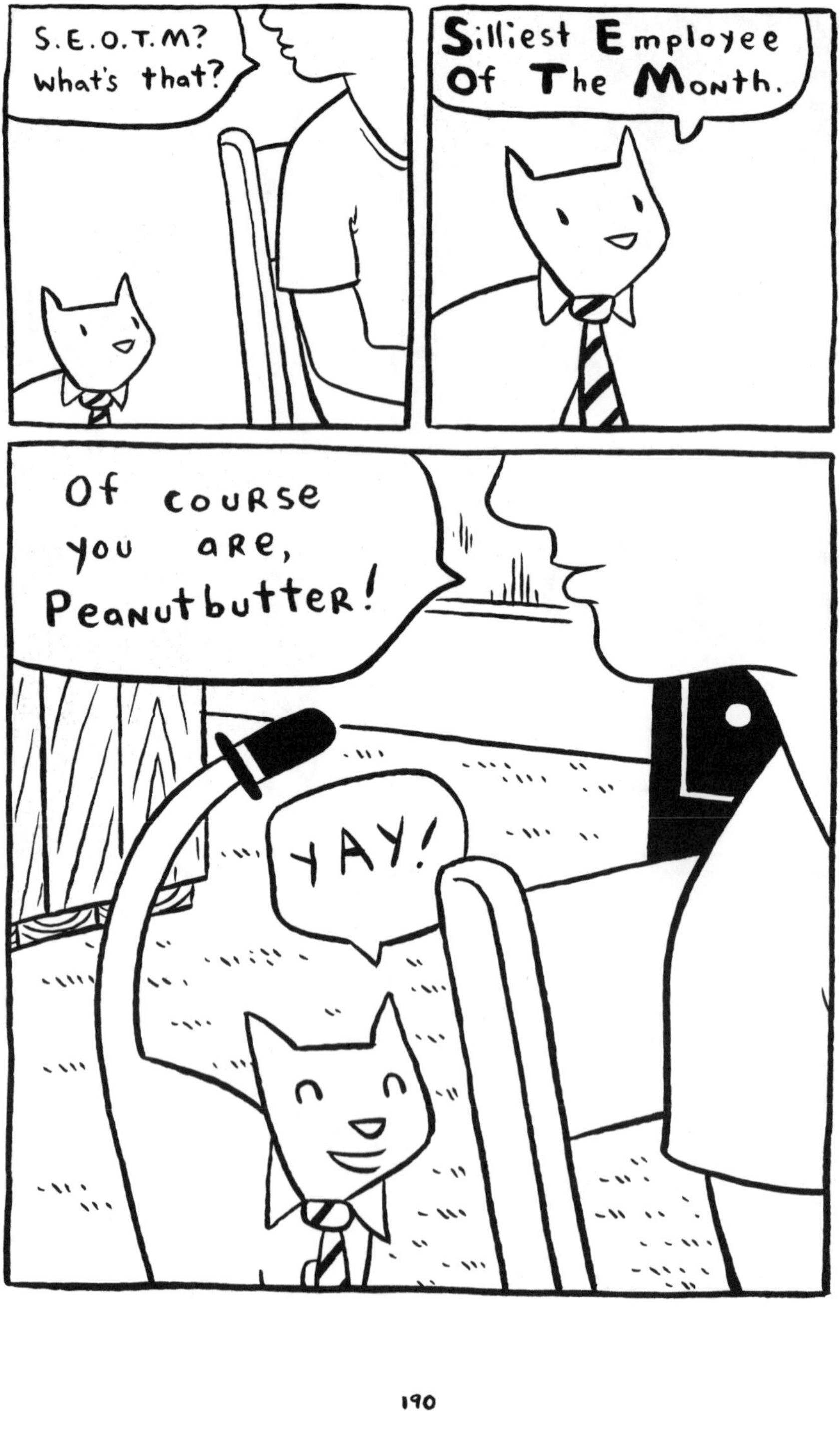
S.E.O.T.M? what's that?
Silliest Employee Of The Month.
Of course you are, Peanutbutter!
YAY!

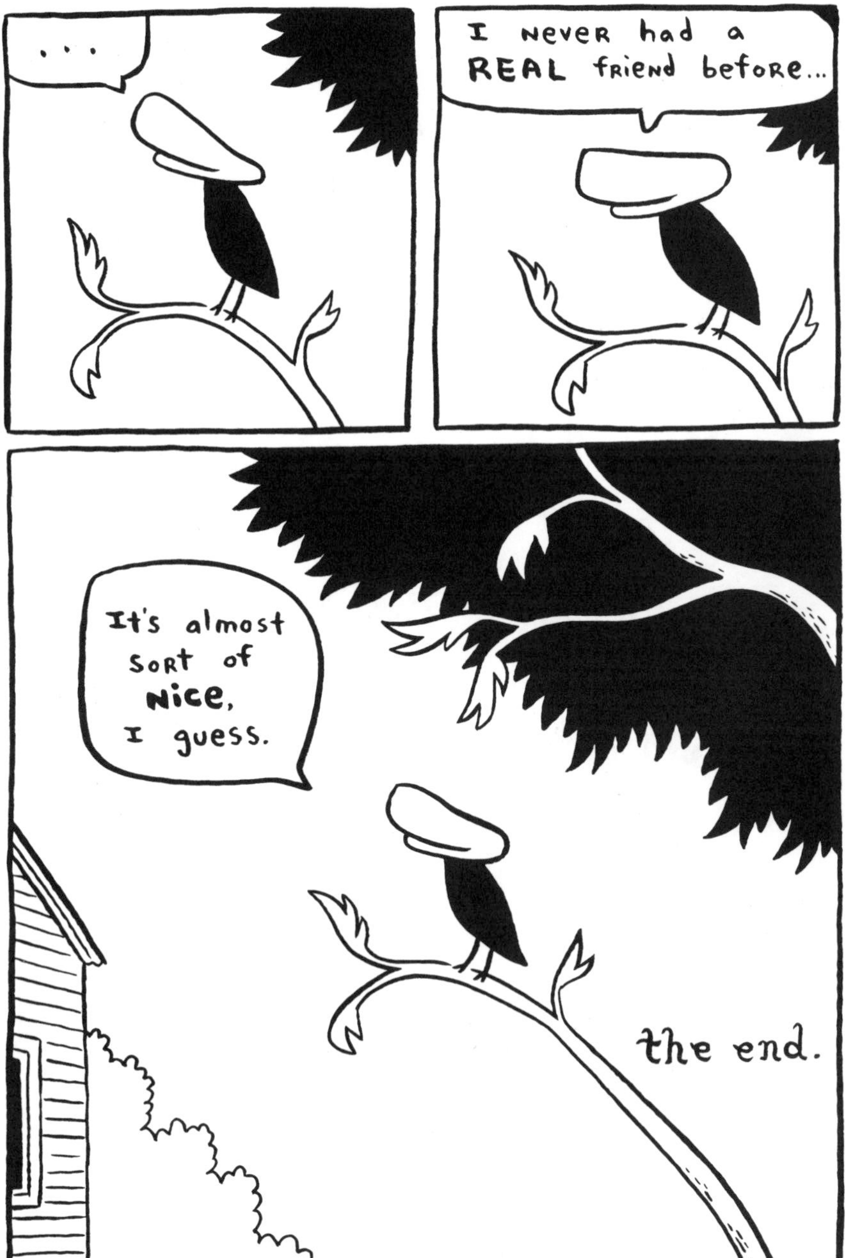
...
I never had a REAL friend before...
It's almost sort of NICE, I guess.
the end.

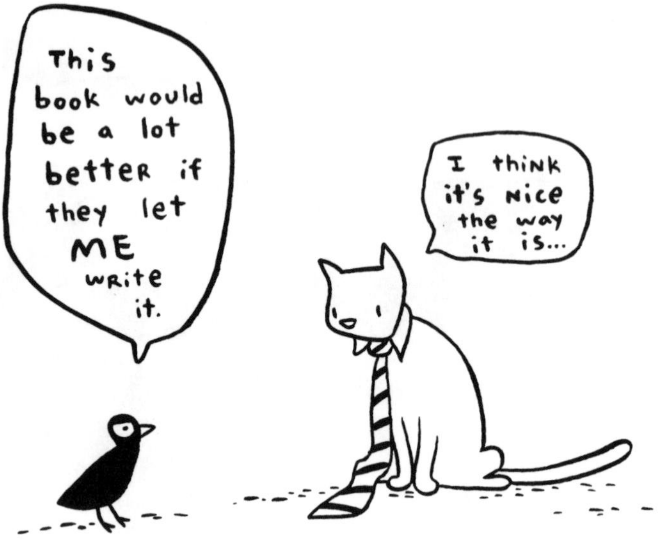
This book would be a lot better if they let ME write it.
I think it's nice the way it is...

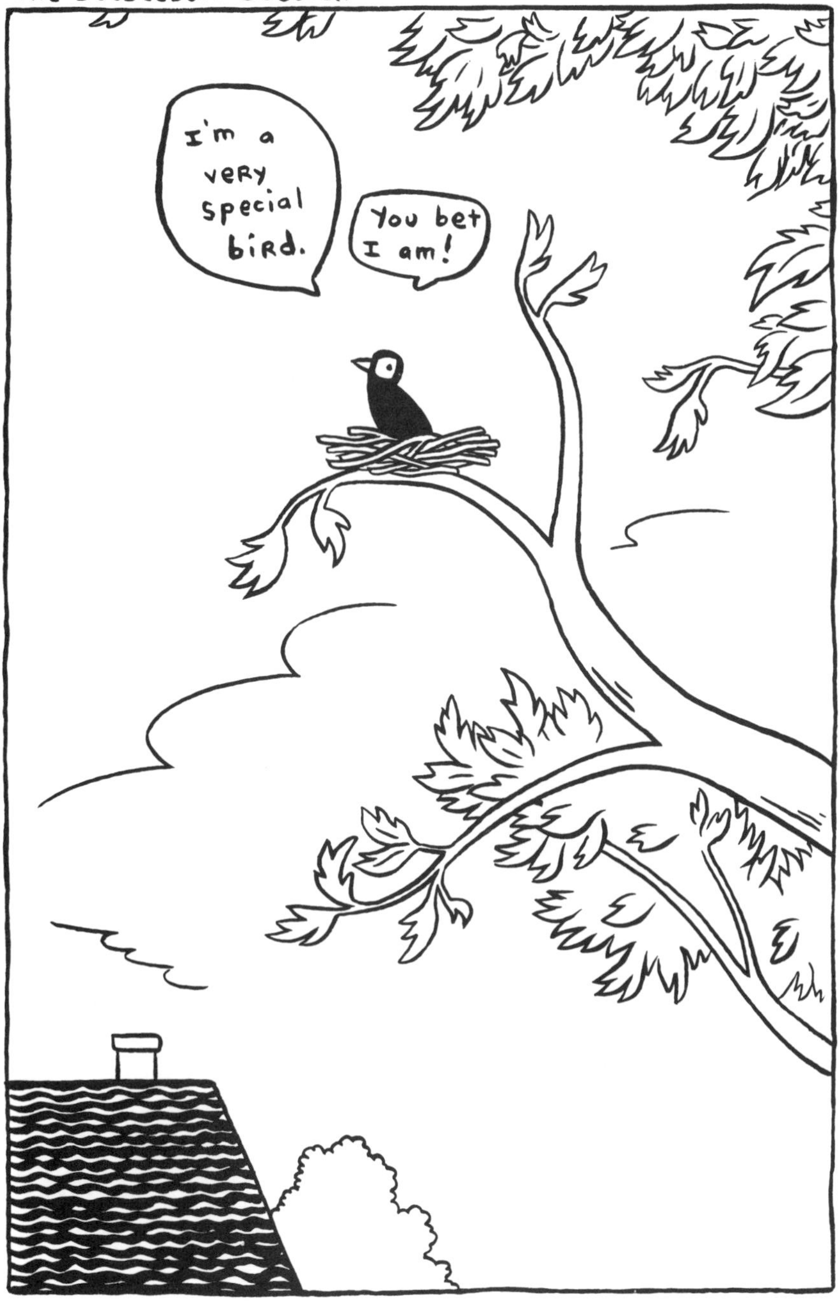
I'm a very special bird.
You bet I am!

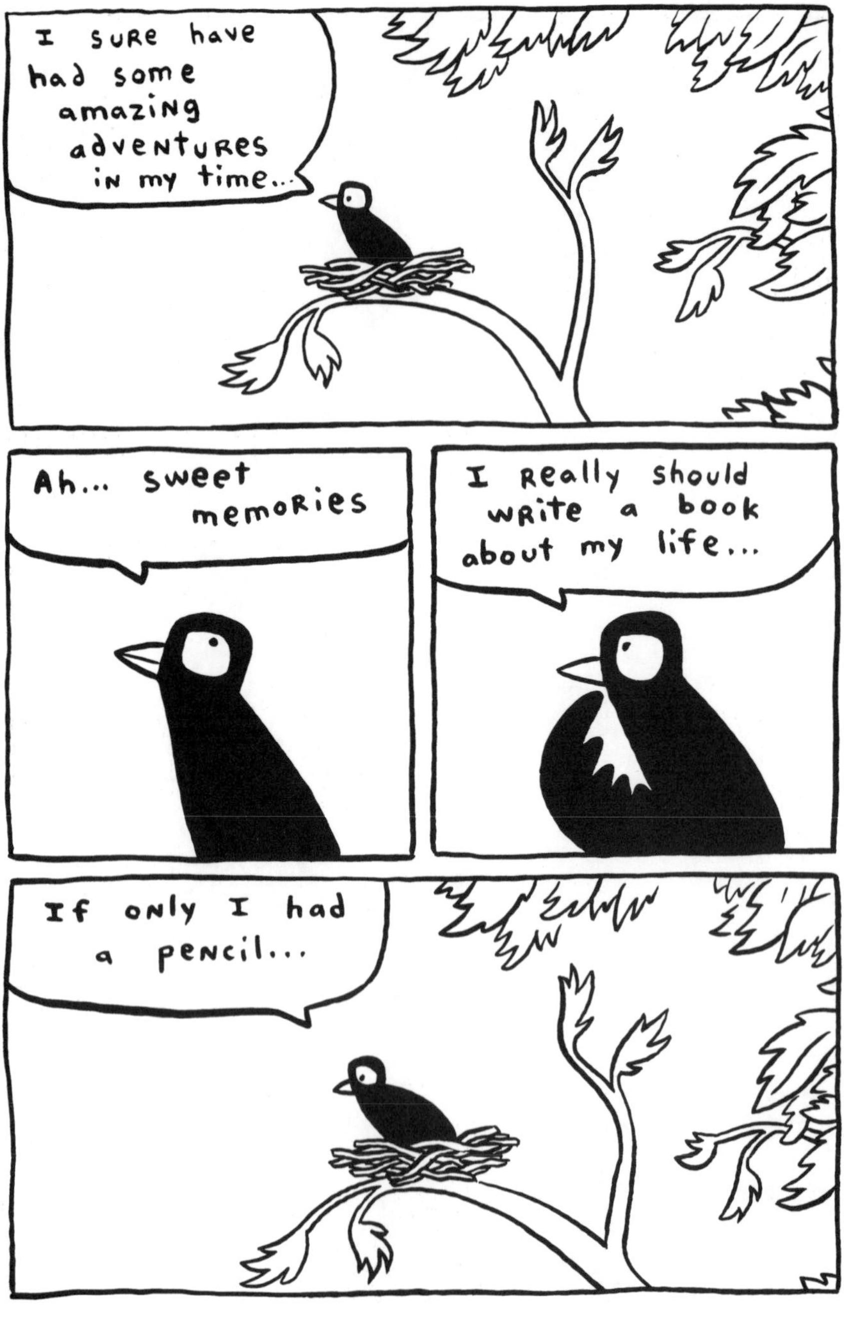
I sure have had some amazing adventures in my time...
Ah... sweet memories
I really should write a book about my life...
If only I had a pencil...

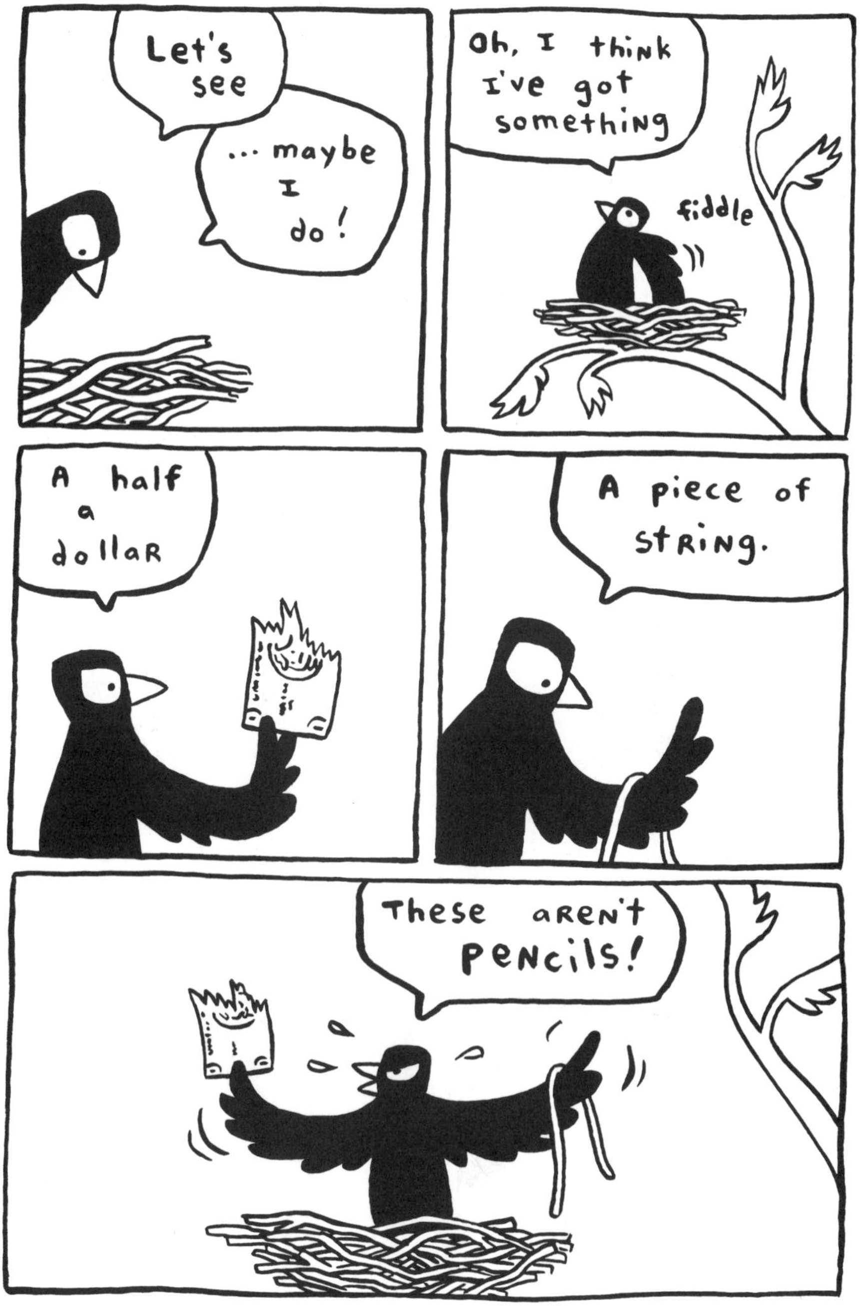
Let's see
... maybe I do!
Oh, I think I've got something
fiddle
A half a dollar
A piece of string.
These aren't pencils!

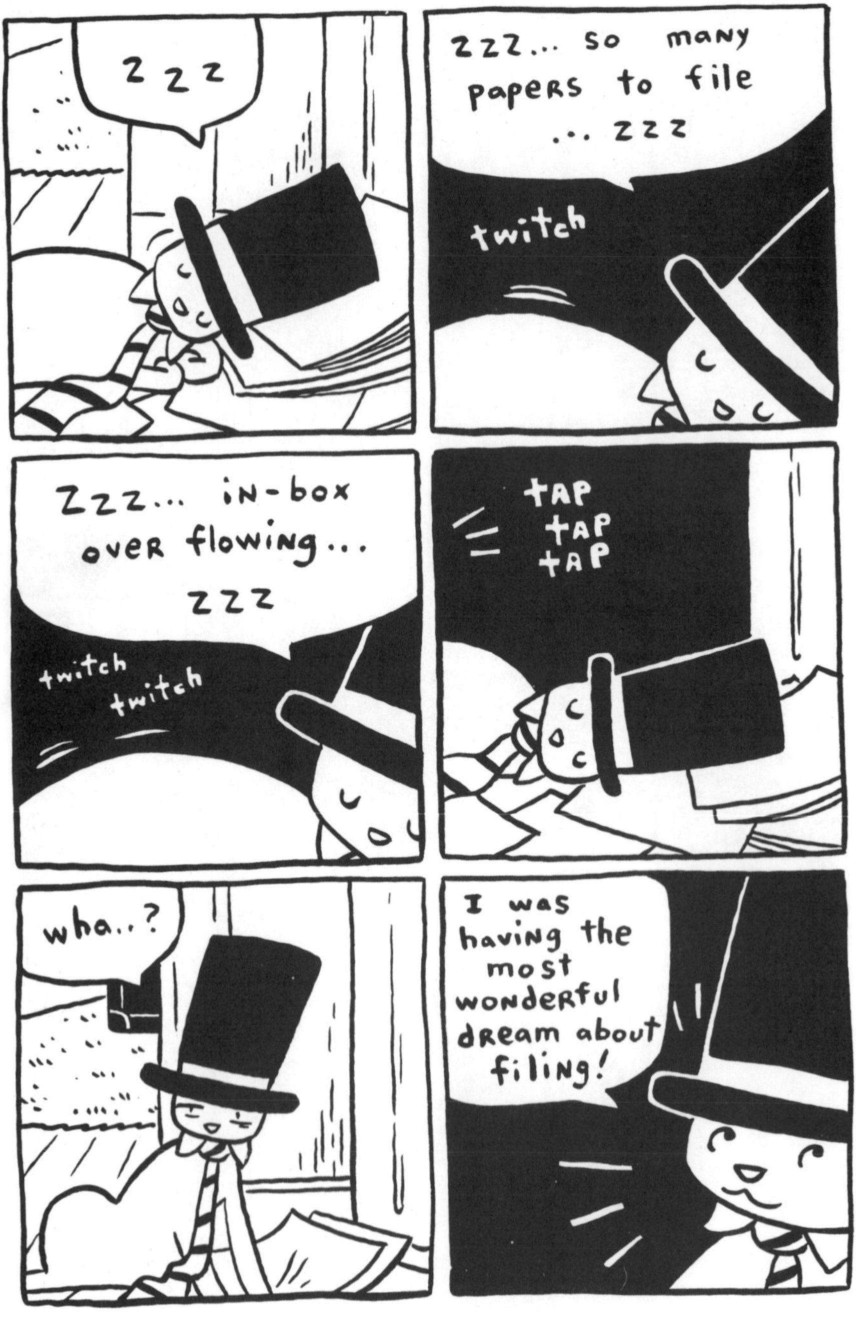
z z z
zzz... so many papers to file ... zzz
twitch
zzz... in-box over flowing... zzz
twitch twitch
tap tap tap
wha..?
I was having the most wonderful dream about filing!

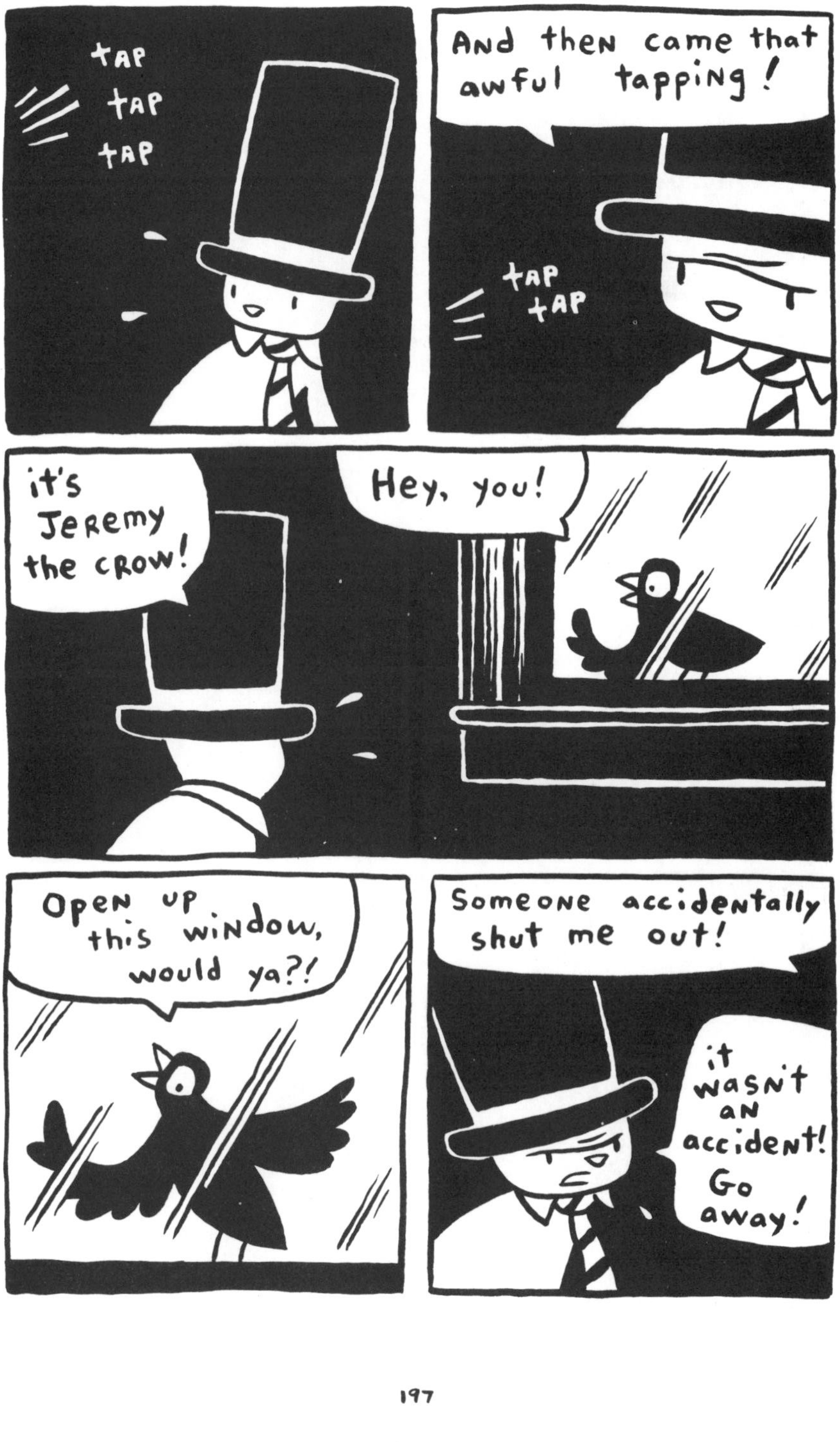
TAP
TAP
TAP
And then came that awful tapping!
TAP
TAP
it's Jeremy the crow!
Hey, you!
Open up this window, would ya?!
Someone accidentally shut me out!
it wasn't an accident! Go away!

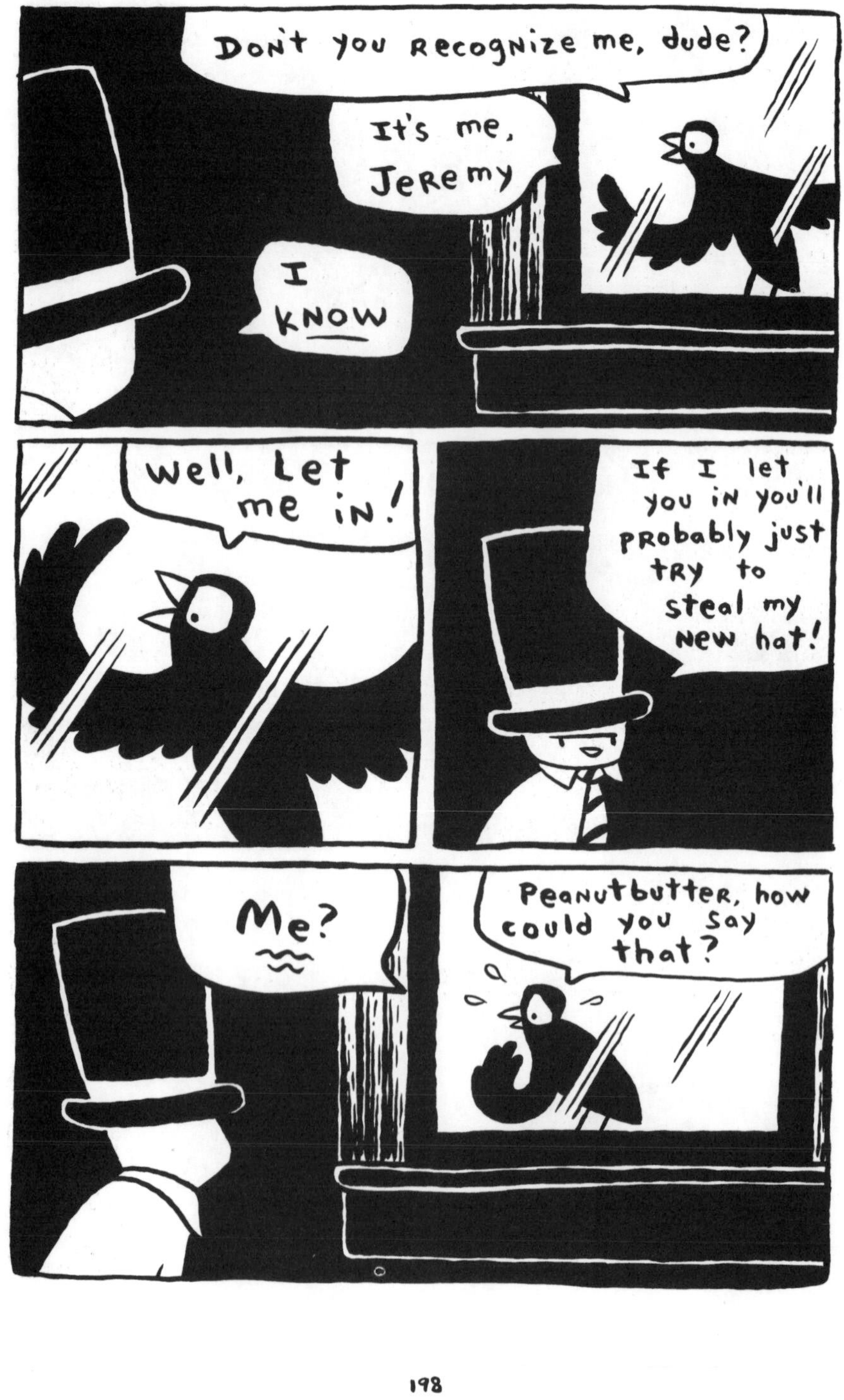

Don't you recognize me, dude?
It's me, Jeremy
I KNOW
Well, Let me in!
If I let you in you'll probably just try to steal my new hat!
Me?
Peanutbutter, how could you say that?

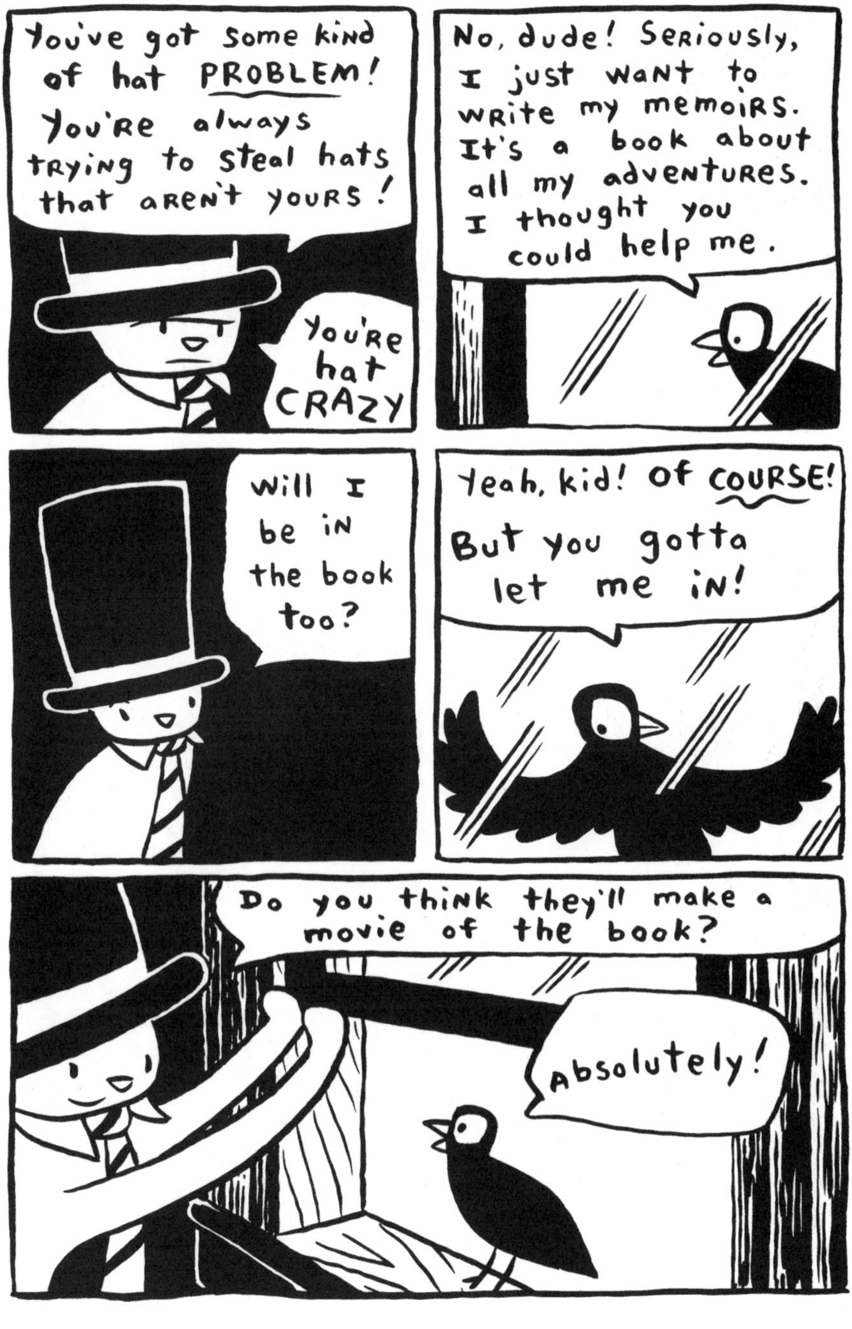
You've got some kind of hat PROBLEM! You're always trying to steal hats that aren't yours!
You're hat CRAZY
No, dude! Seriously, I just want to write my memoirs. It's a book about all my adventures. I thought you could help me.
Will I be in the book too?
Yeah, kid! Of COURSE! But you gotta let me in!
Do you think they'll make a movie of the book?
Absolutely!

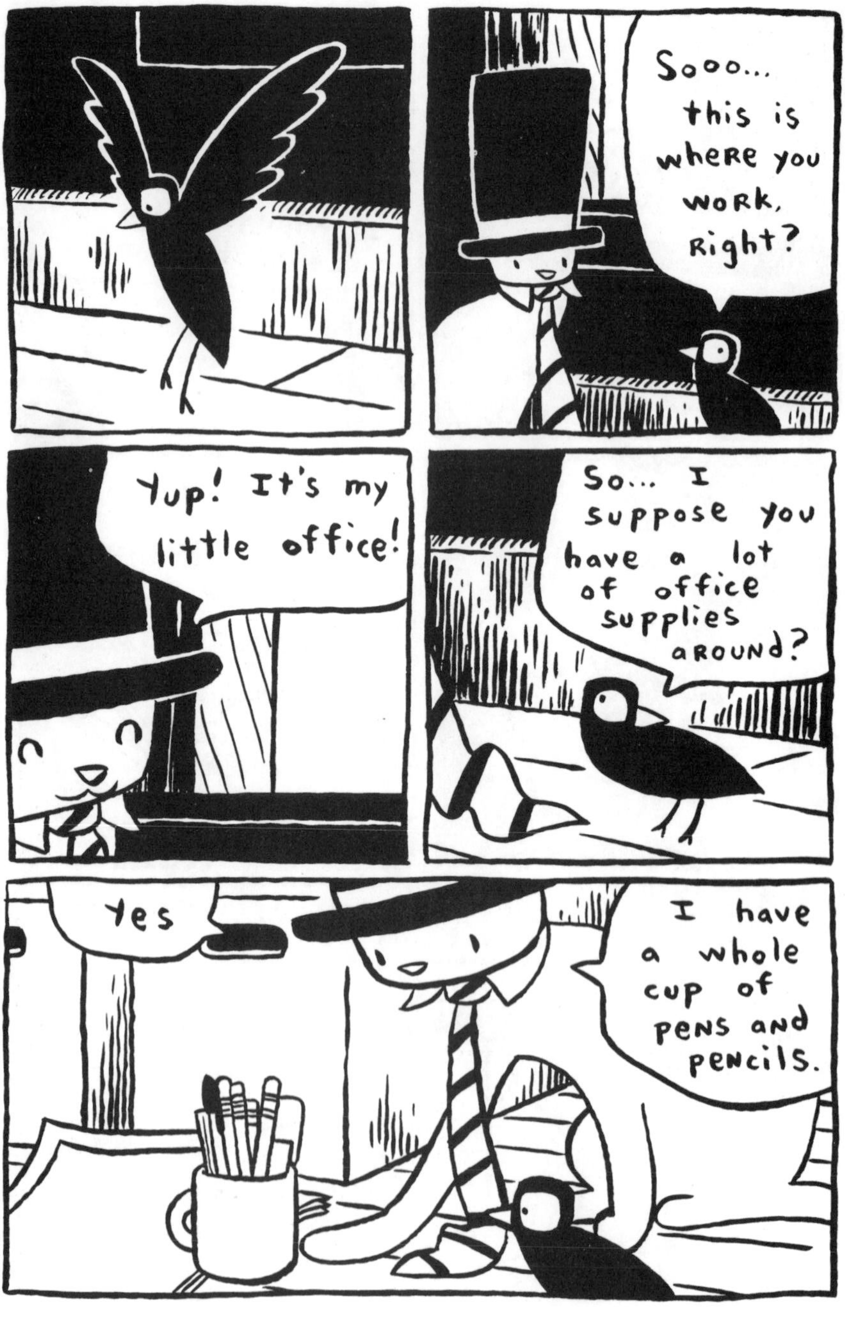

Sooo... this is where you work, Right?
Yup! It's my little office!
So... I suppose you have a lot of office supplies around?
Yes
I have a whole cup of pens and pencils.

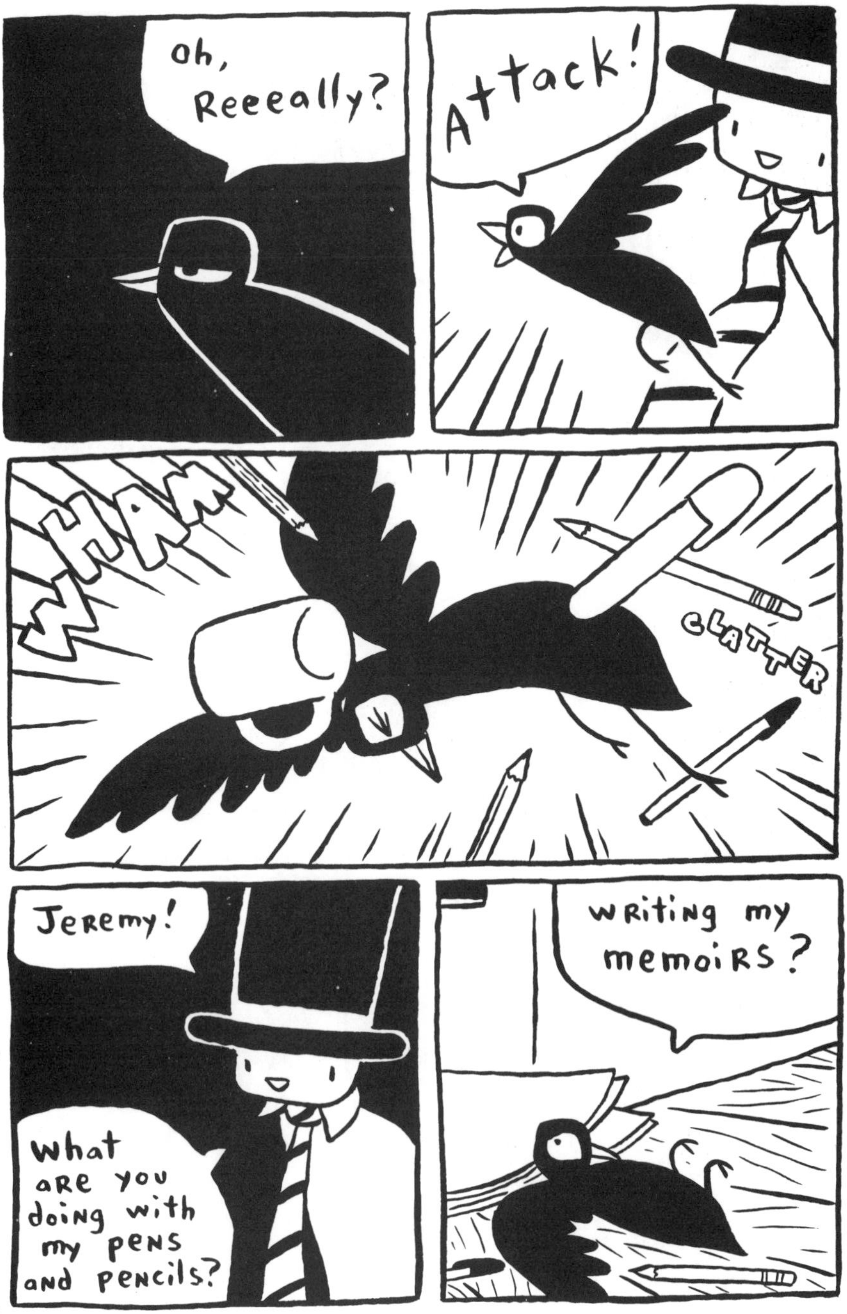
Oh,
Reeeally?
Attack!
WHAM
CLATTER
Jeremy!
What are you doing with my pens and pencils?
writing my memoirs?

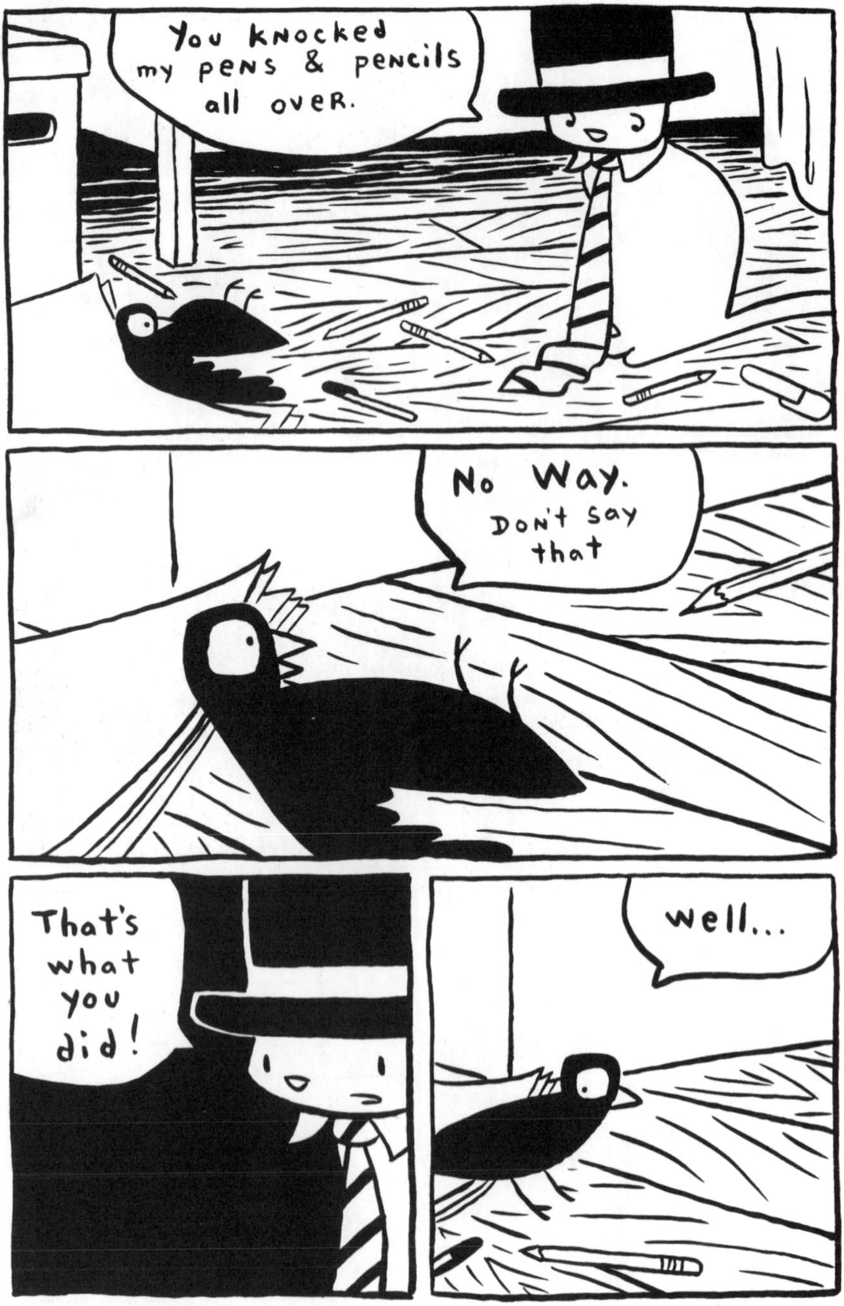
You knocked my pens & pencils all over.
No Way. Don't say that
That's what you did!
well...

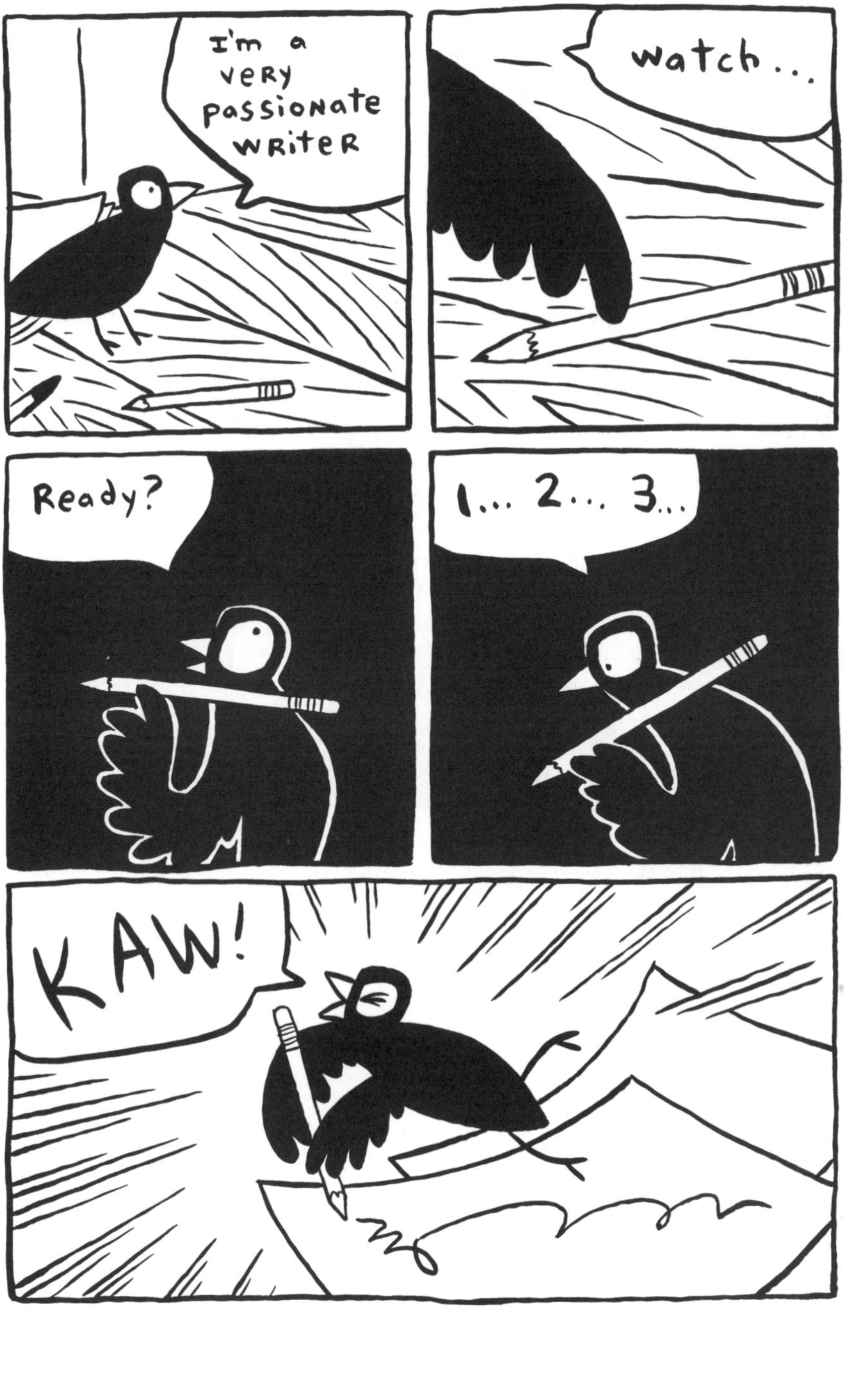
I'm a very passionate writer
watch...
Ready?
1... 2... 3...
KAW!

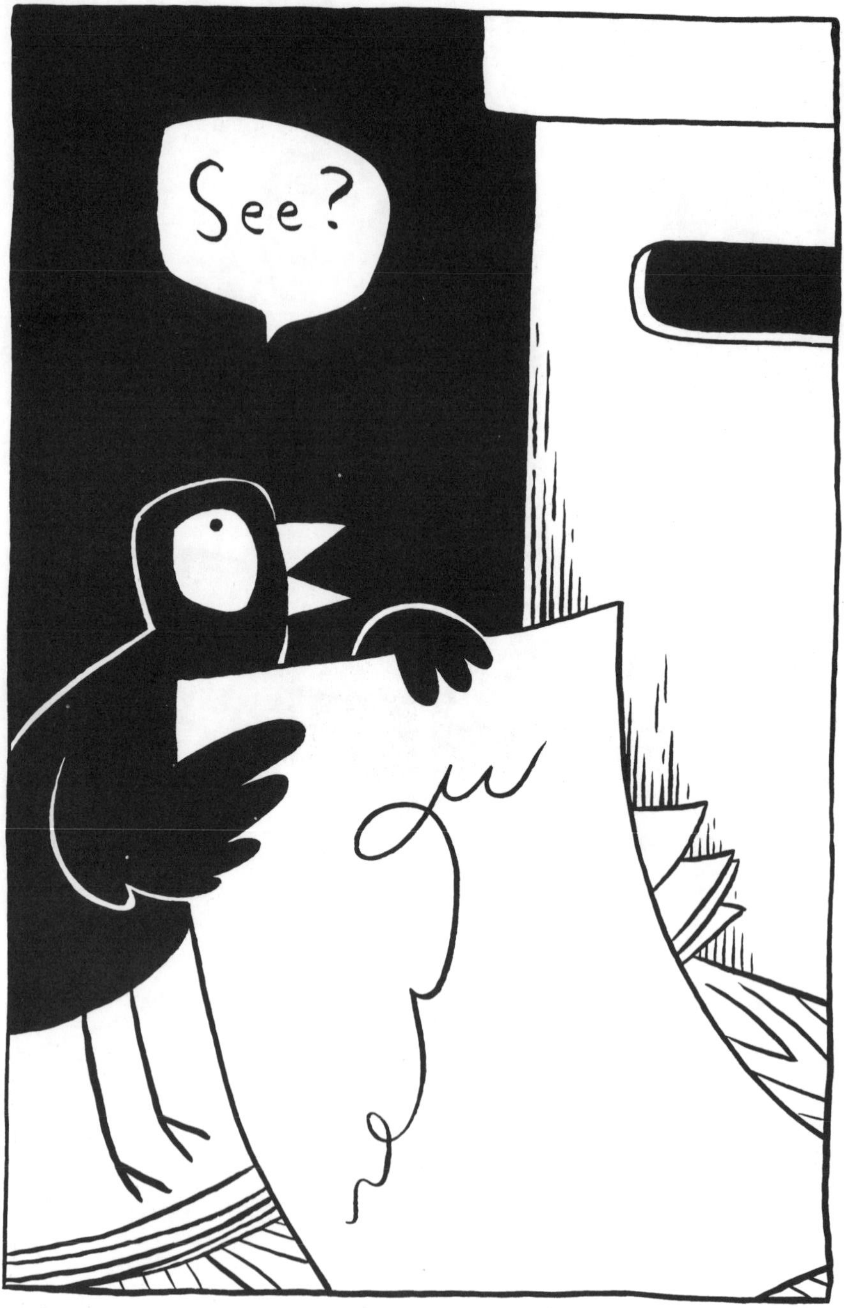
See?

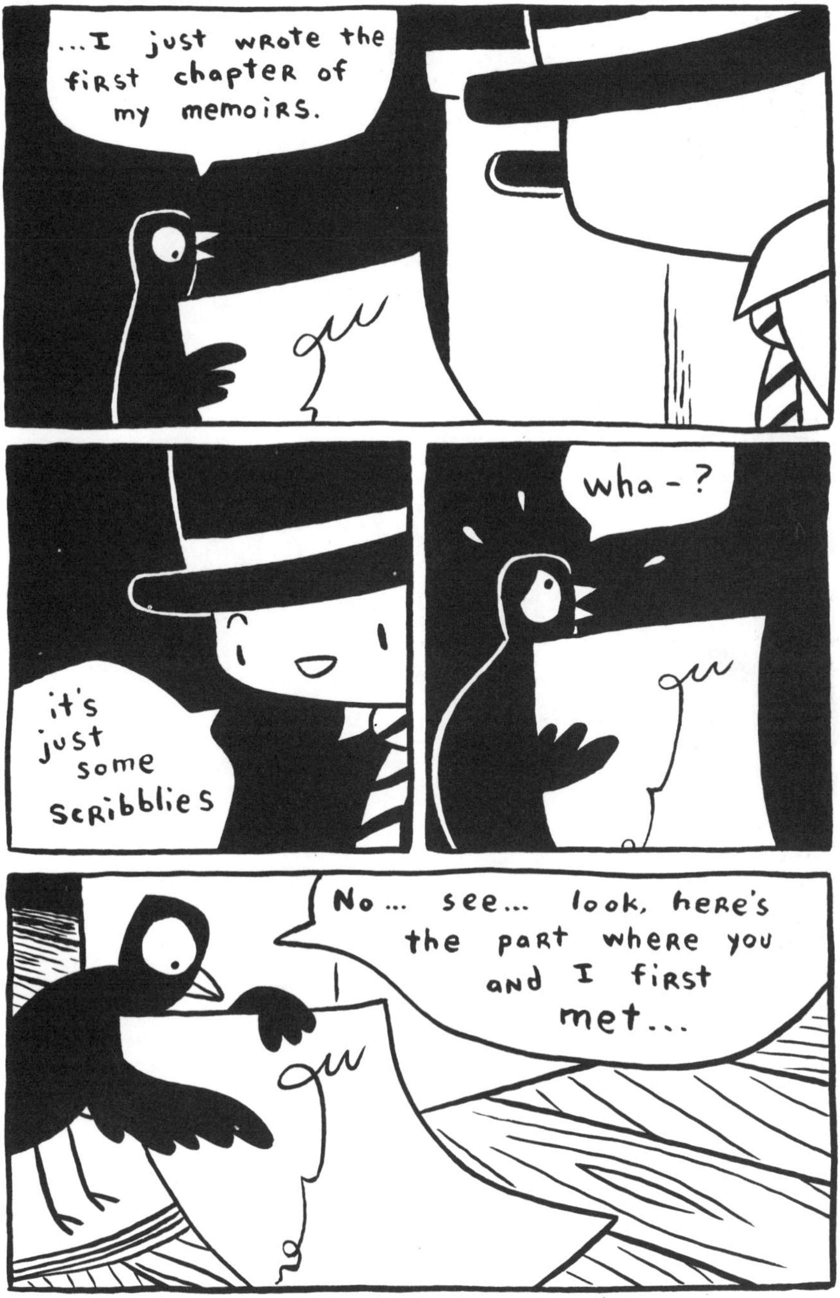
...I just wrote the first chapter of my memoirs.
it's just some scribblies
wha-?
No... see... look, here's the part where you and I first met...

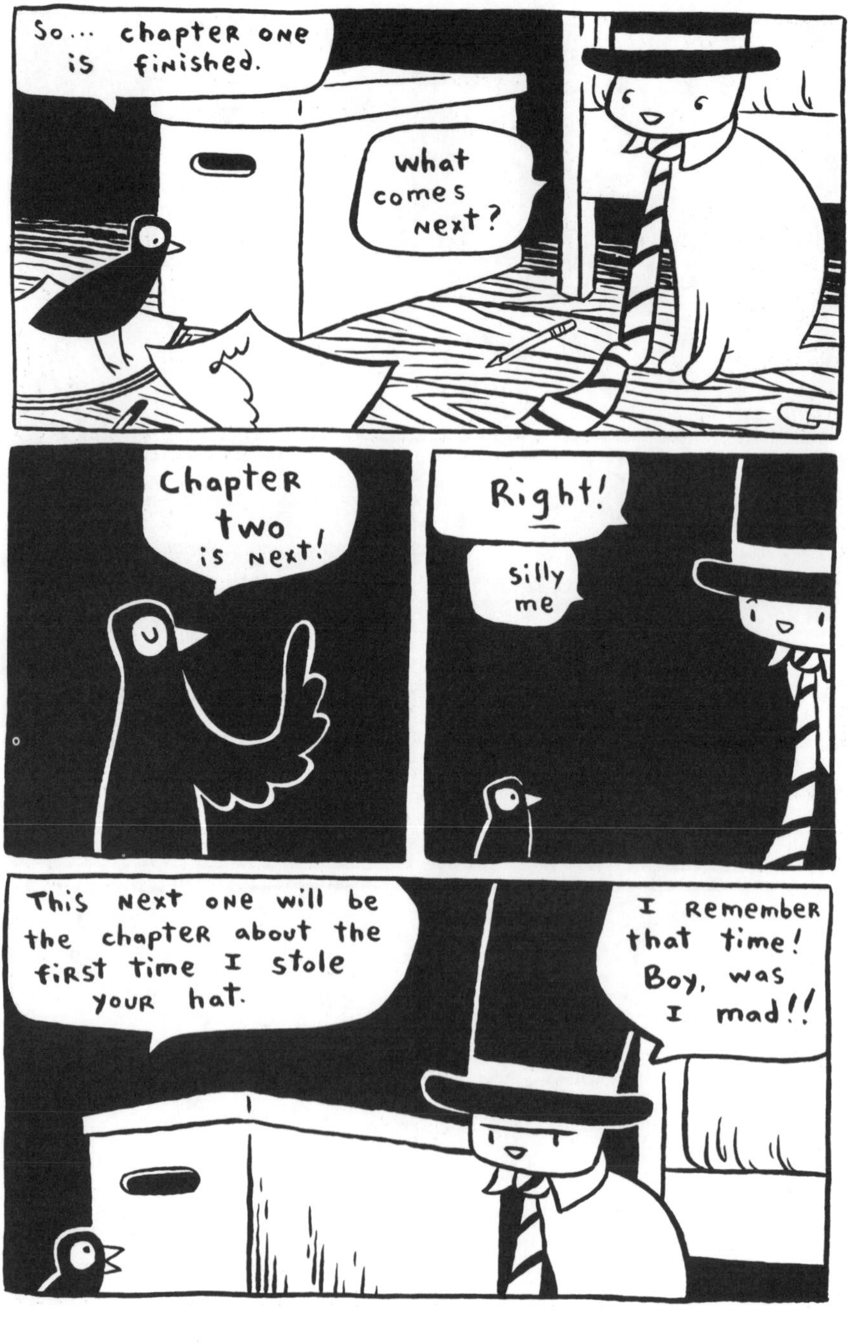
So... chapter one is finished.
what comes next?
Chapter two is next!
Right!
silly me
This next one will be the chapter about the first time I stole your hat.
I remember that time! Boy, was I mad!!

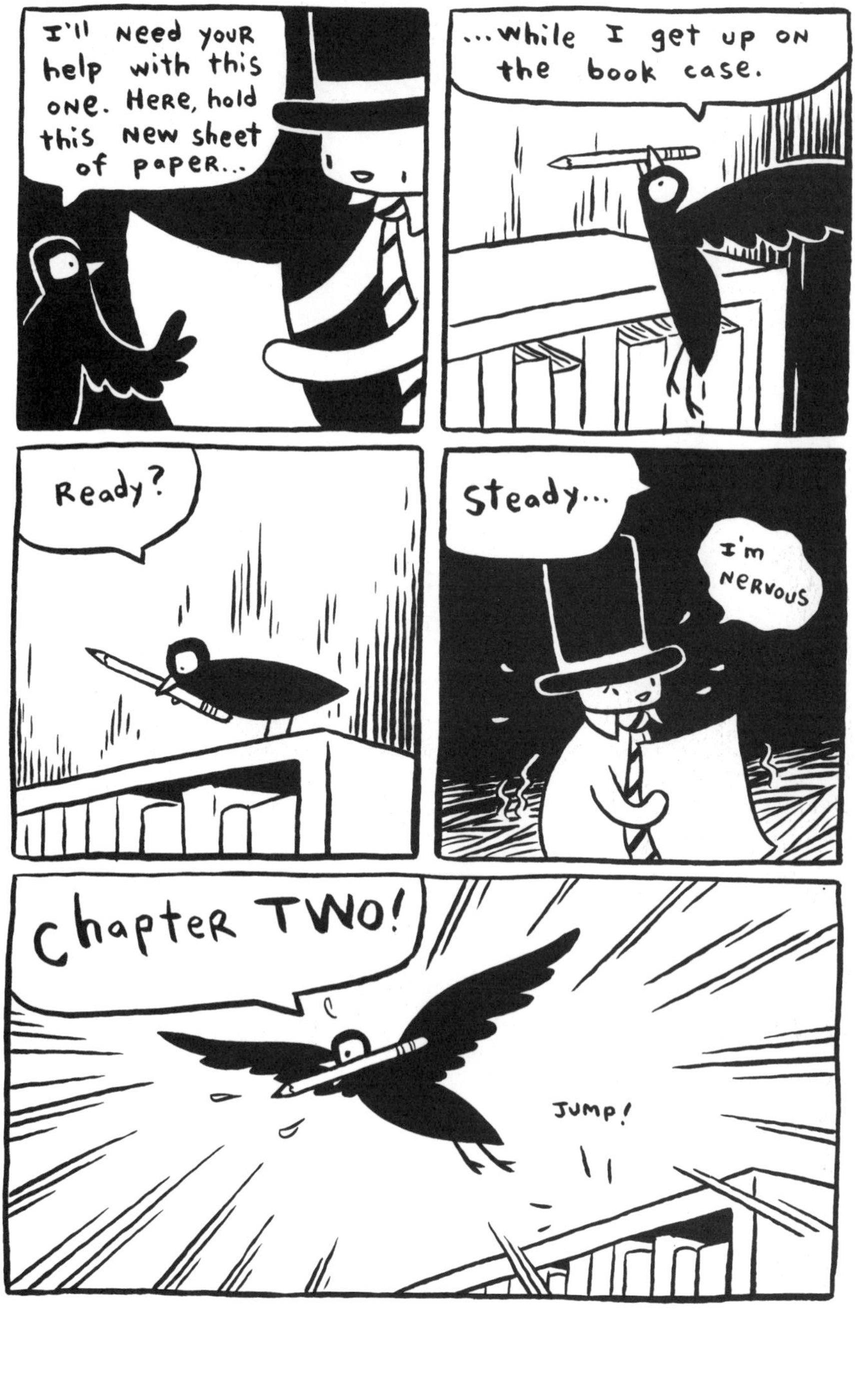
I'll need your help with this one. Here, hold this new sheet of paper...
...while I get up on the book case.
Ready?
Steady...
I'm nervous
Chapter TWO!
JUMP!

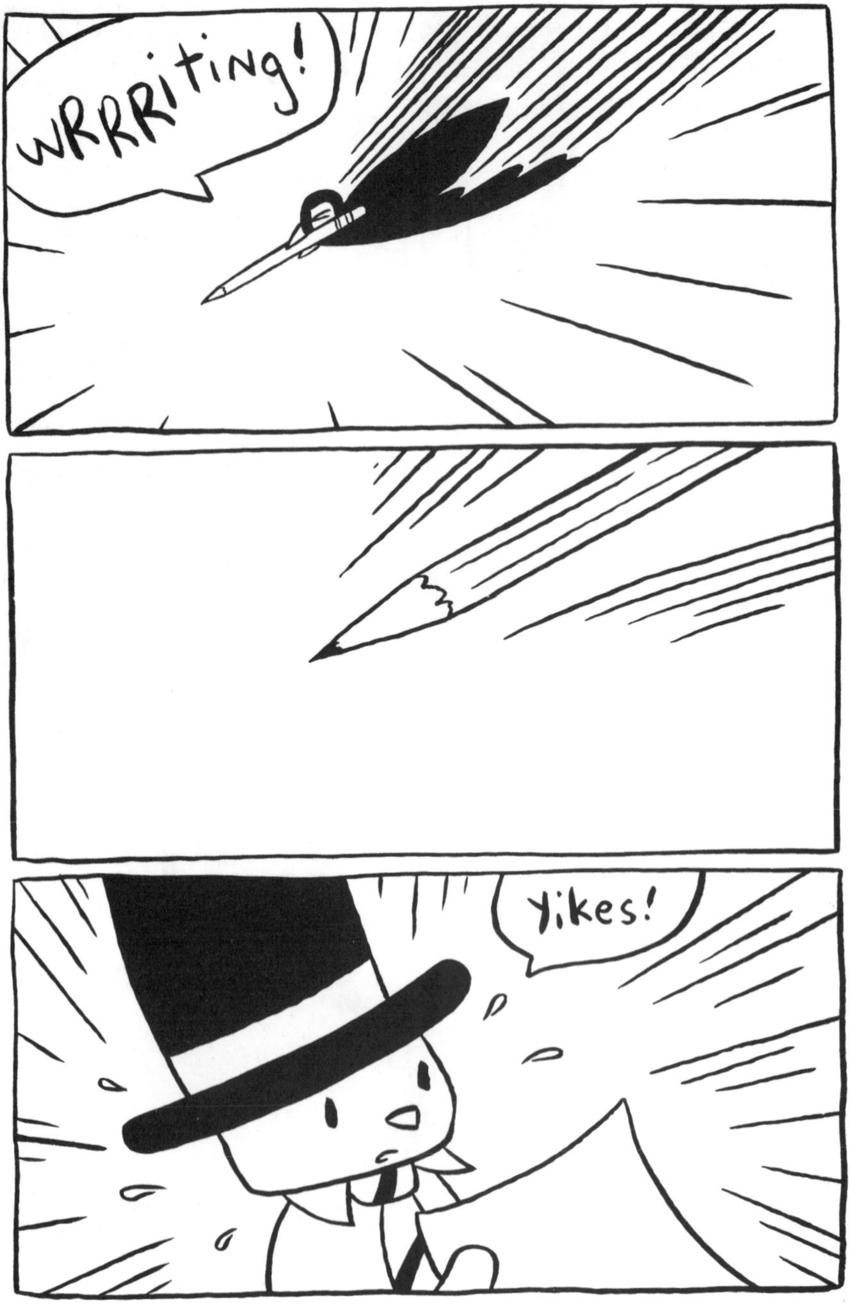
WRRRiting!
Yikes!

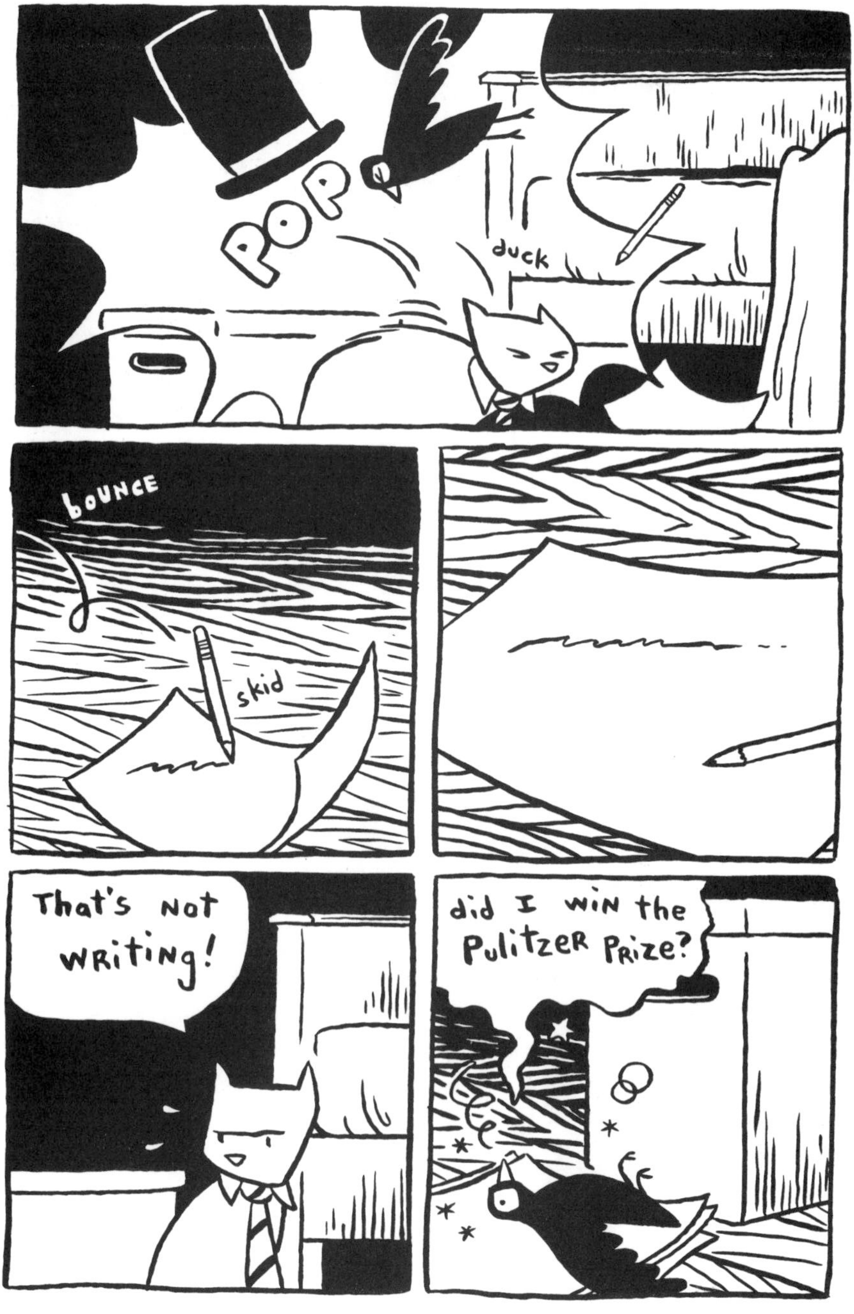

POP
duck
bounce
skid
That's not writing!
did I win the Pulitzer Prize?

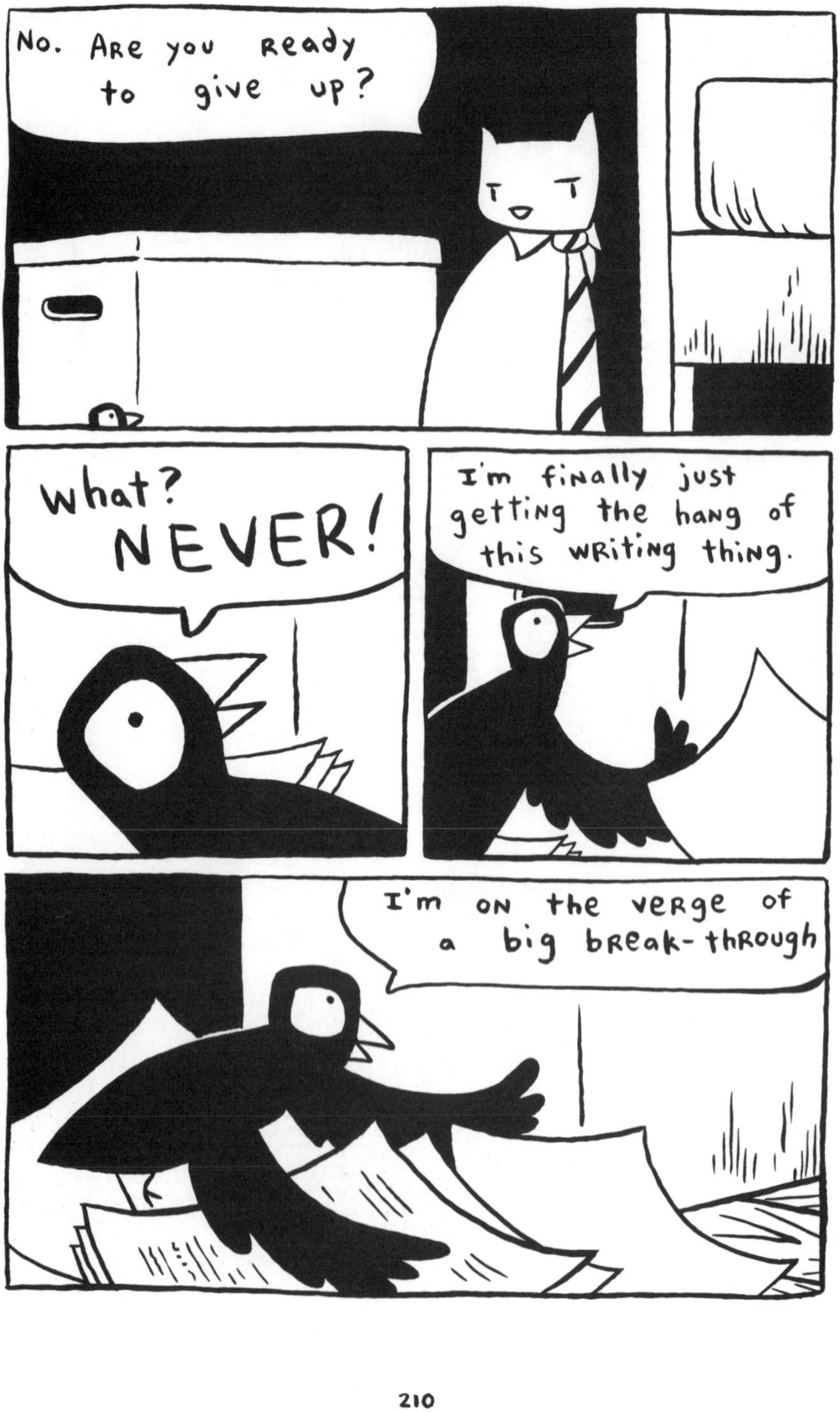
No. Are you ready to give up?
what? NEVER!
I'm finally just getting the hang of this writing thing.
I'm on the verge of a big break-through

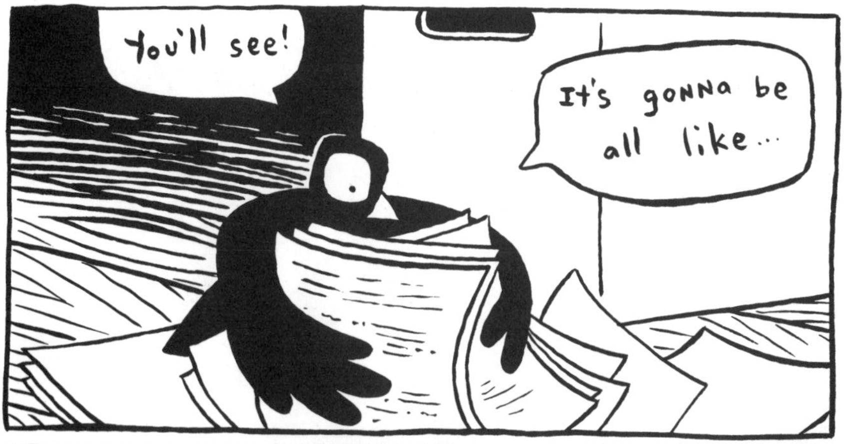
You'll see!
It's gonna be all like...

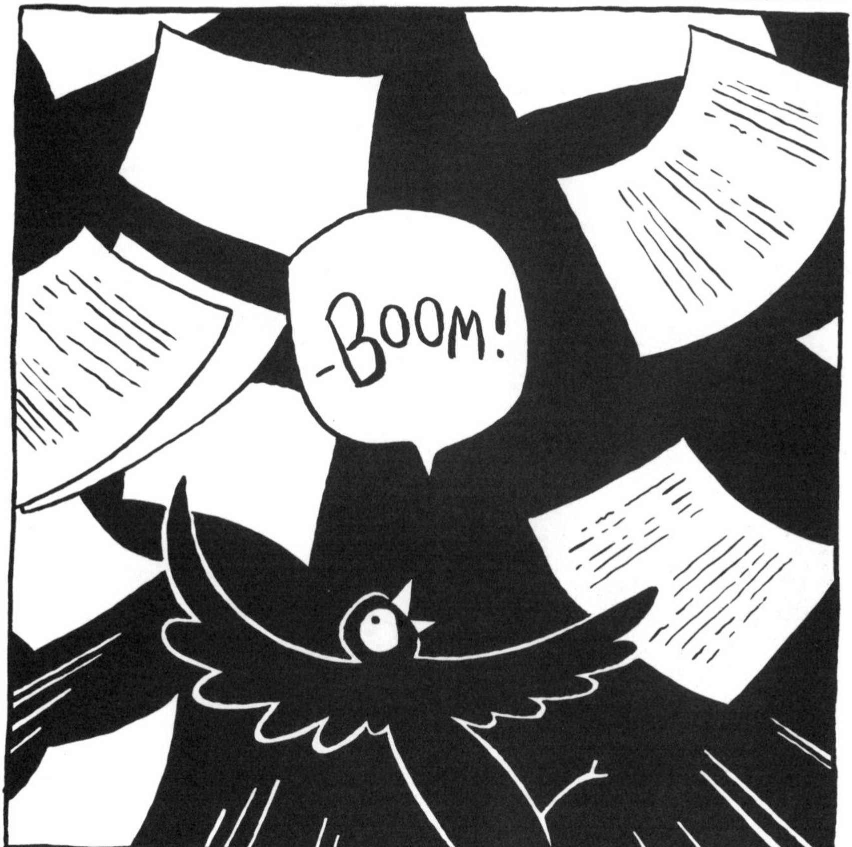
-BOOM!

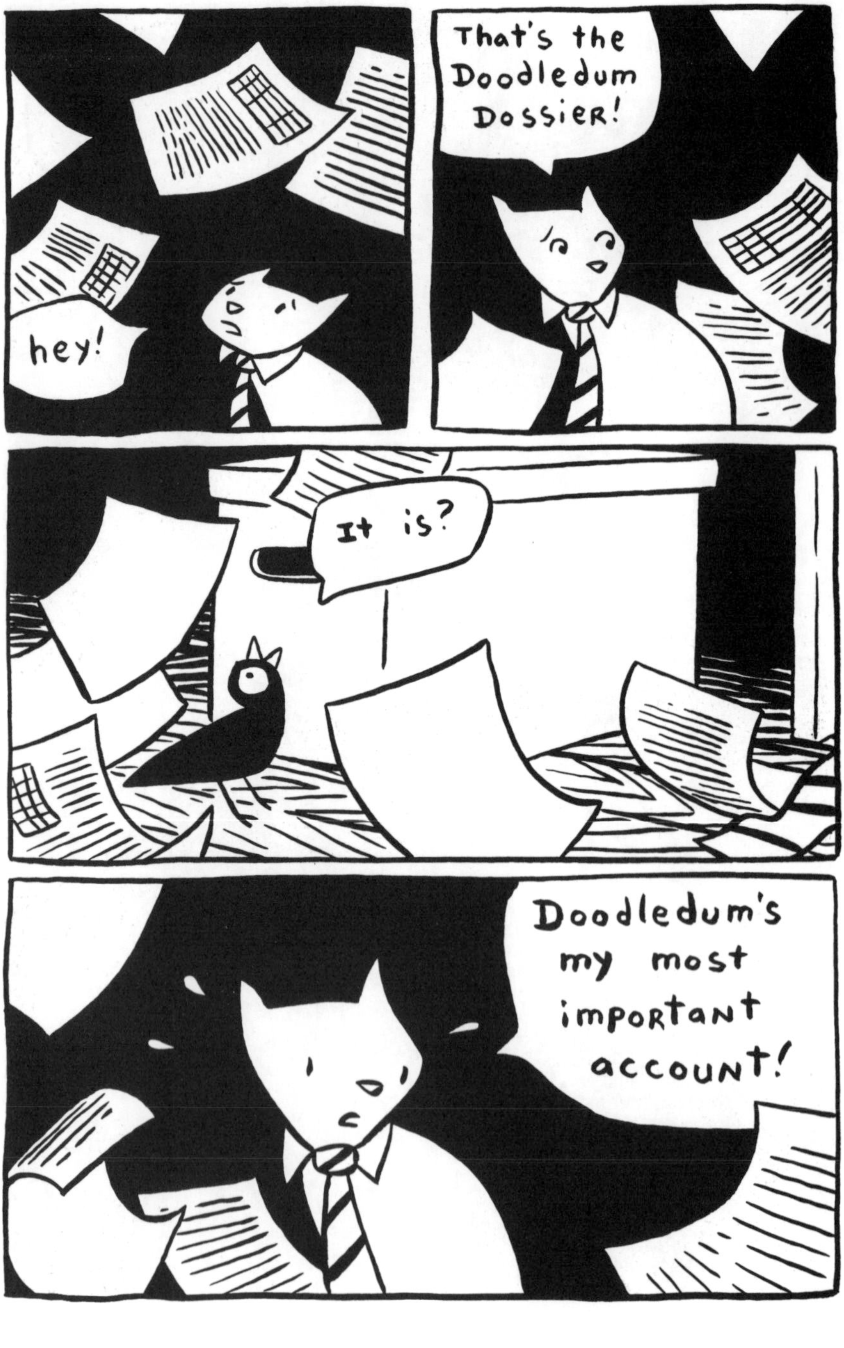
hey!
That's the Doodledum Dossier!
It is?
Doodledum's my most important account!

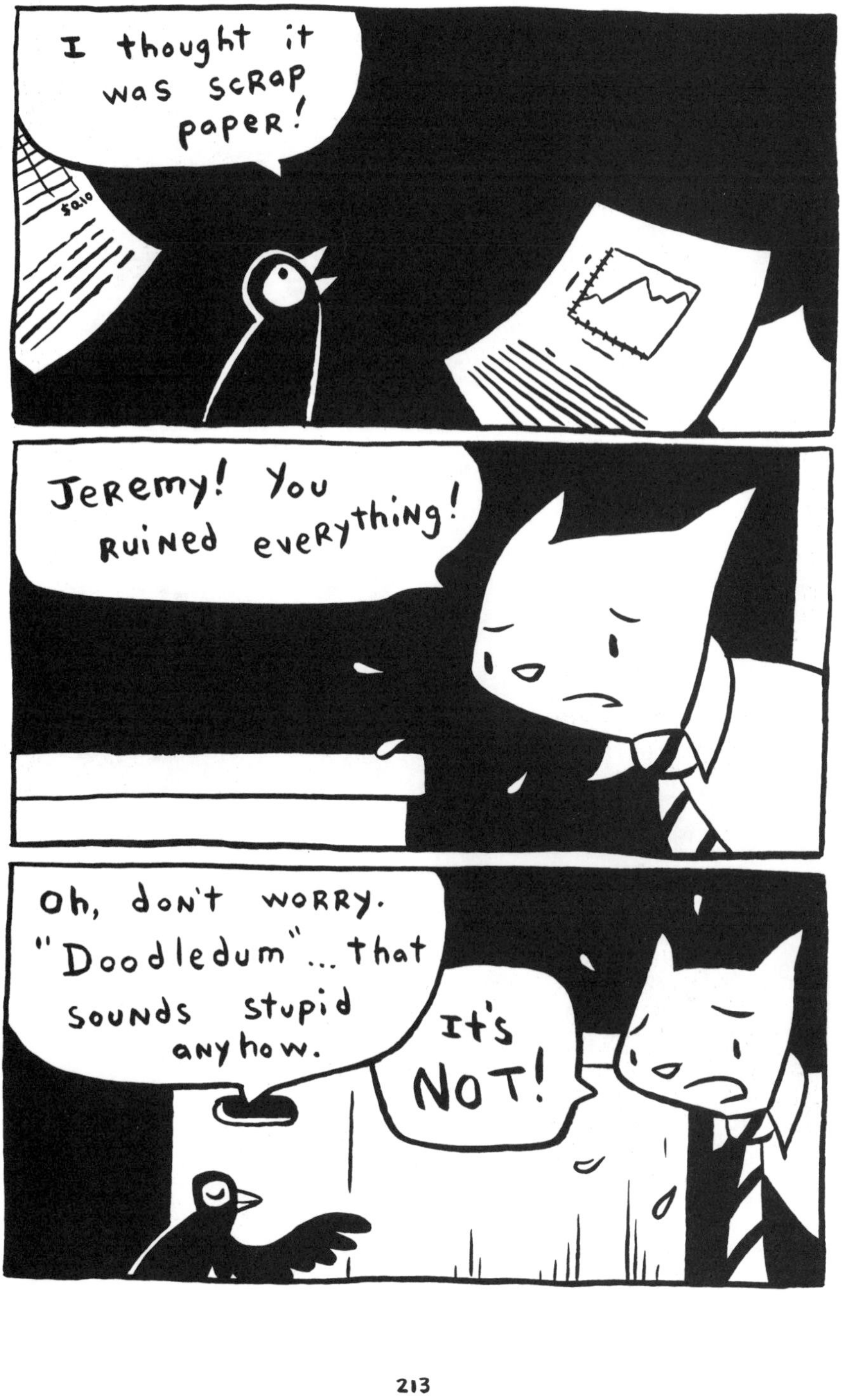
I thought it was scrap paper!
Jeremy! You ruined everything!
Oh, don't worry. "Doodledum"... that sounds stupid anyhow.
It's NOT!

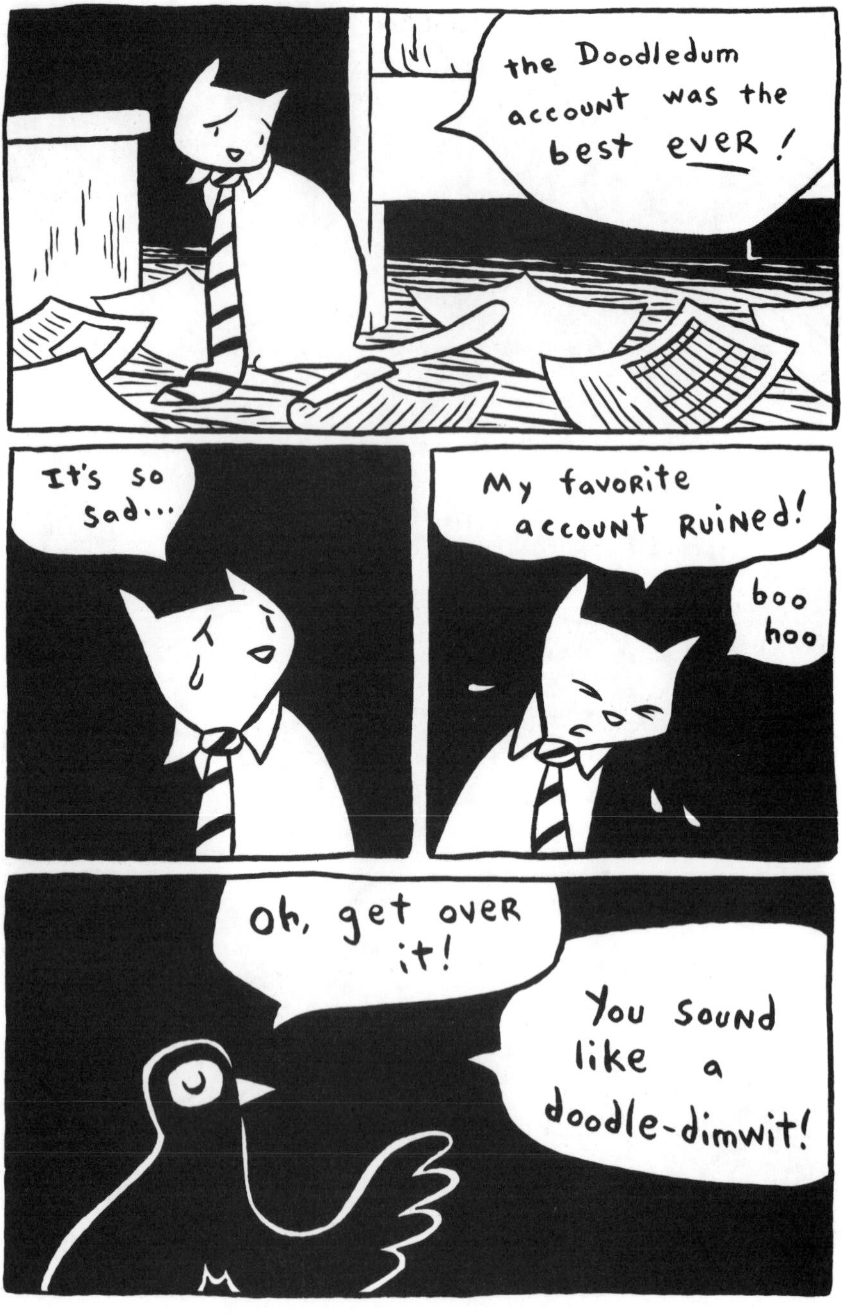
the Doodledum account was the best ever!
It's so sad...
My favorite account RUINed!
boo hoo
Oh, get over it!
You sound like a doodle-dimwit!

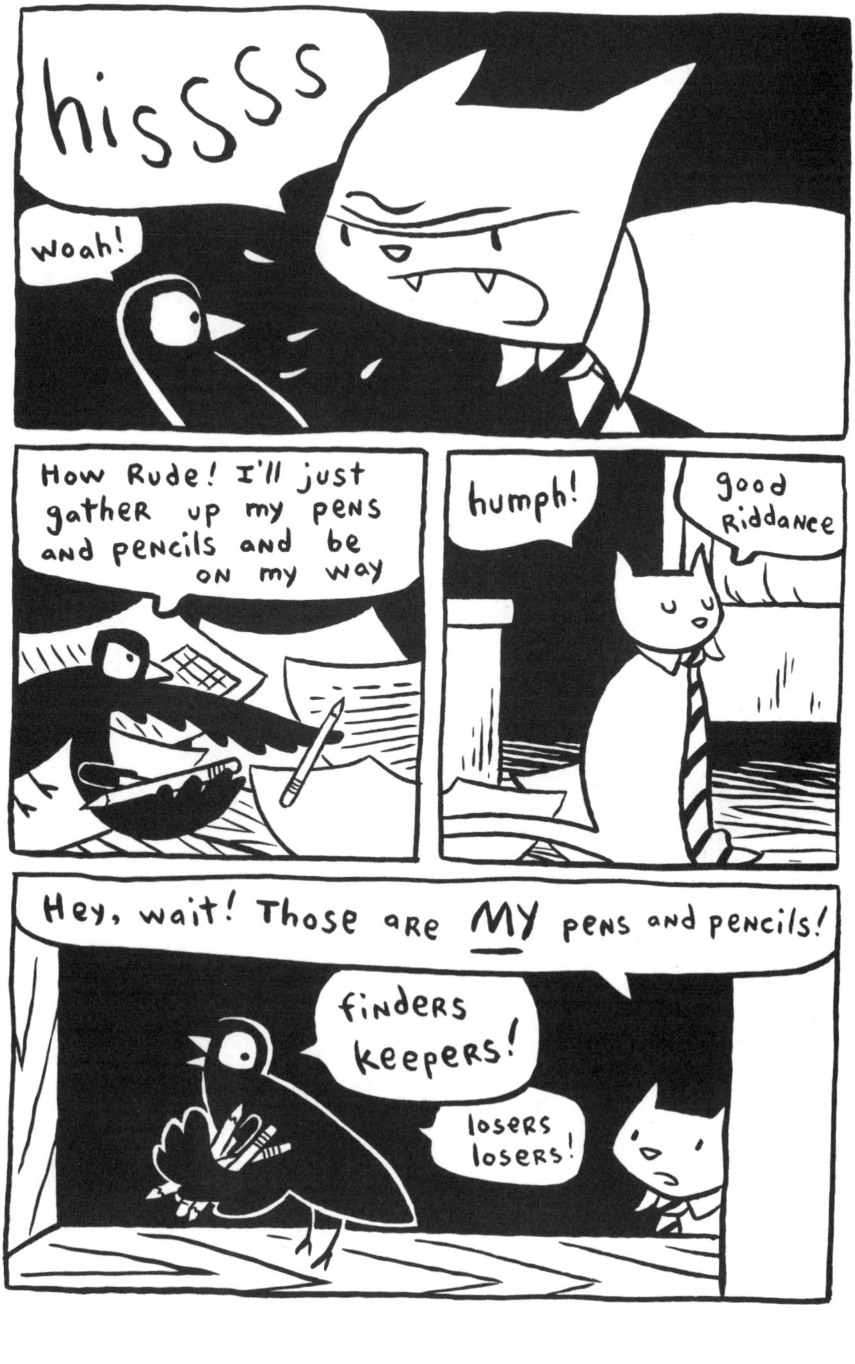
hisSSS
woah!
How Rude! I'll just gather up my pens and pencils and be on my way
humph!
good Riddance
Hey, wait! Those are MY pens and pencils!
finders keepers!
losers losers!

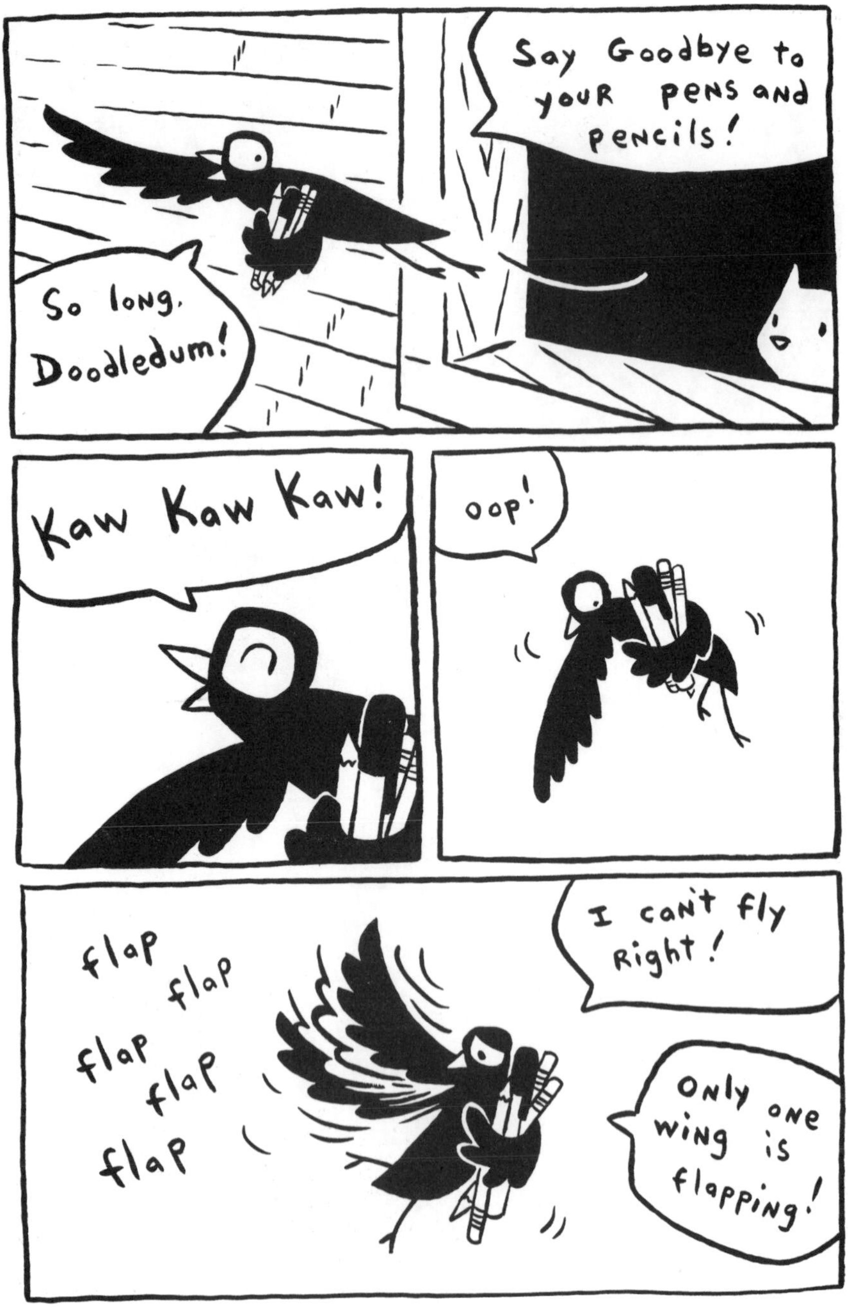
Say Goodbye to your pens and pencils!
So long, Doodledum!
Kaw Kaw Kaw!
oop!
flap flap flap flap flap
I can't fly Right!
Only one wing is flapping!

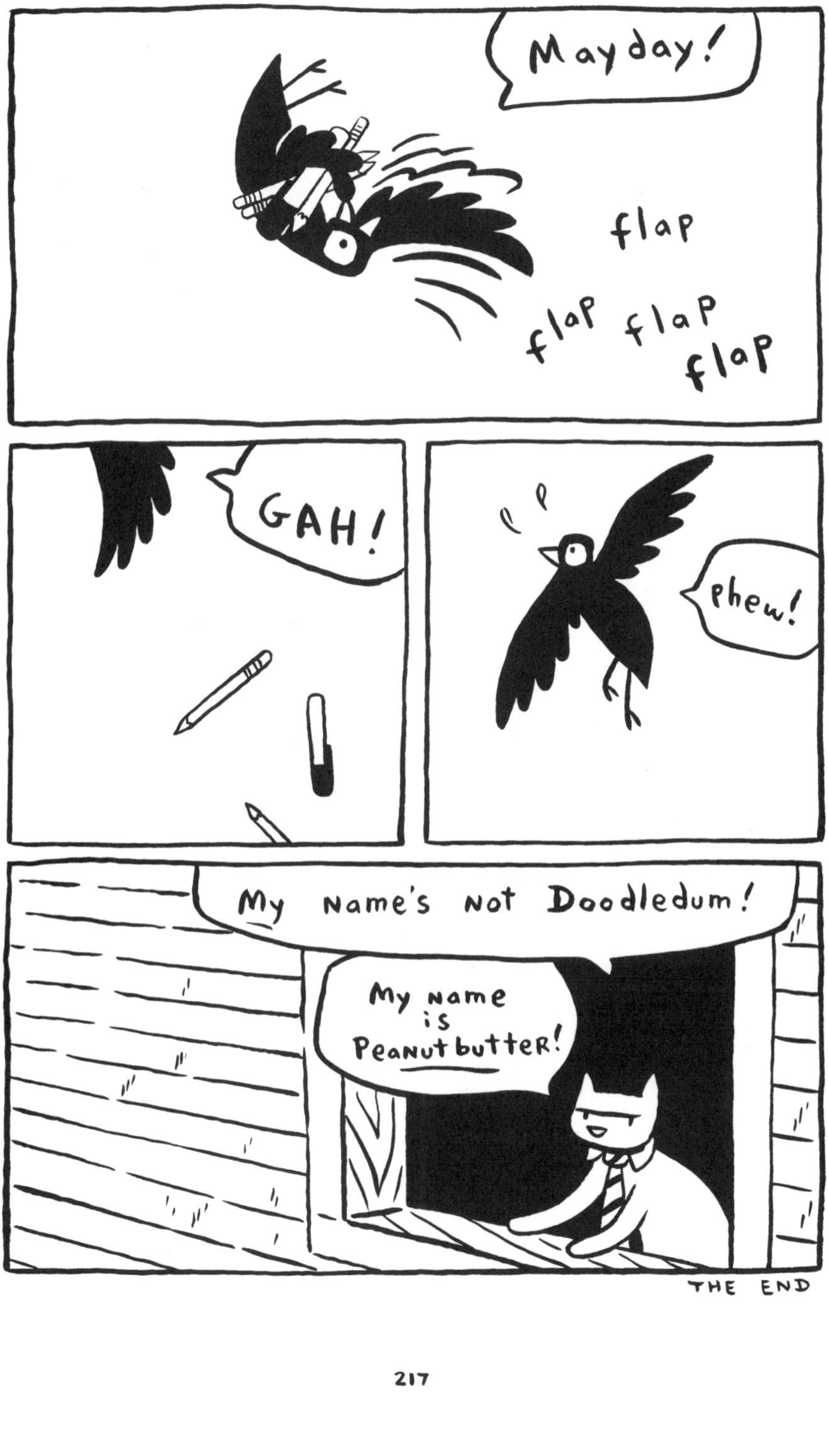
Mayday!
flap
flap flap
flap
GAH!
Phew!
My Name's Not Doodledum!
My name is Peanutbutter!
THE END

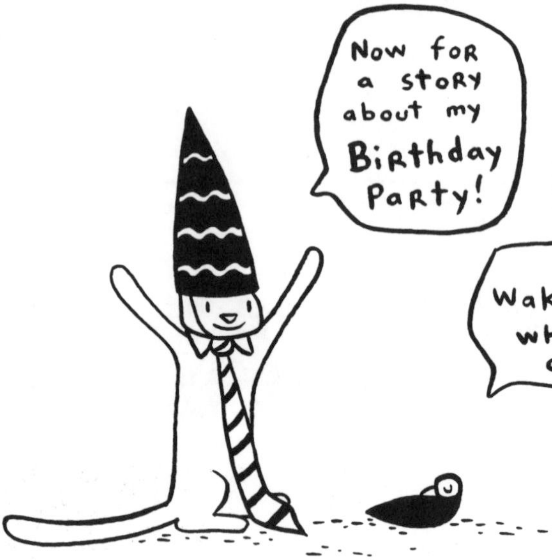
Now for a story about my Birthday Party!
Wake me when it's over.

THE BIRTHDAY PARTY

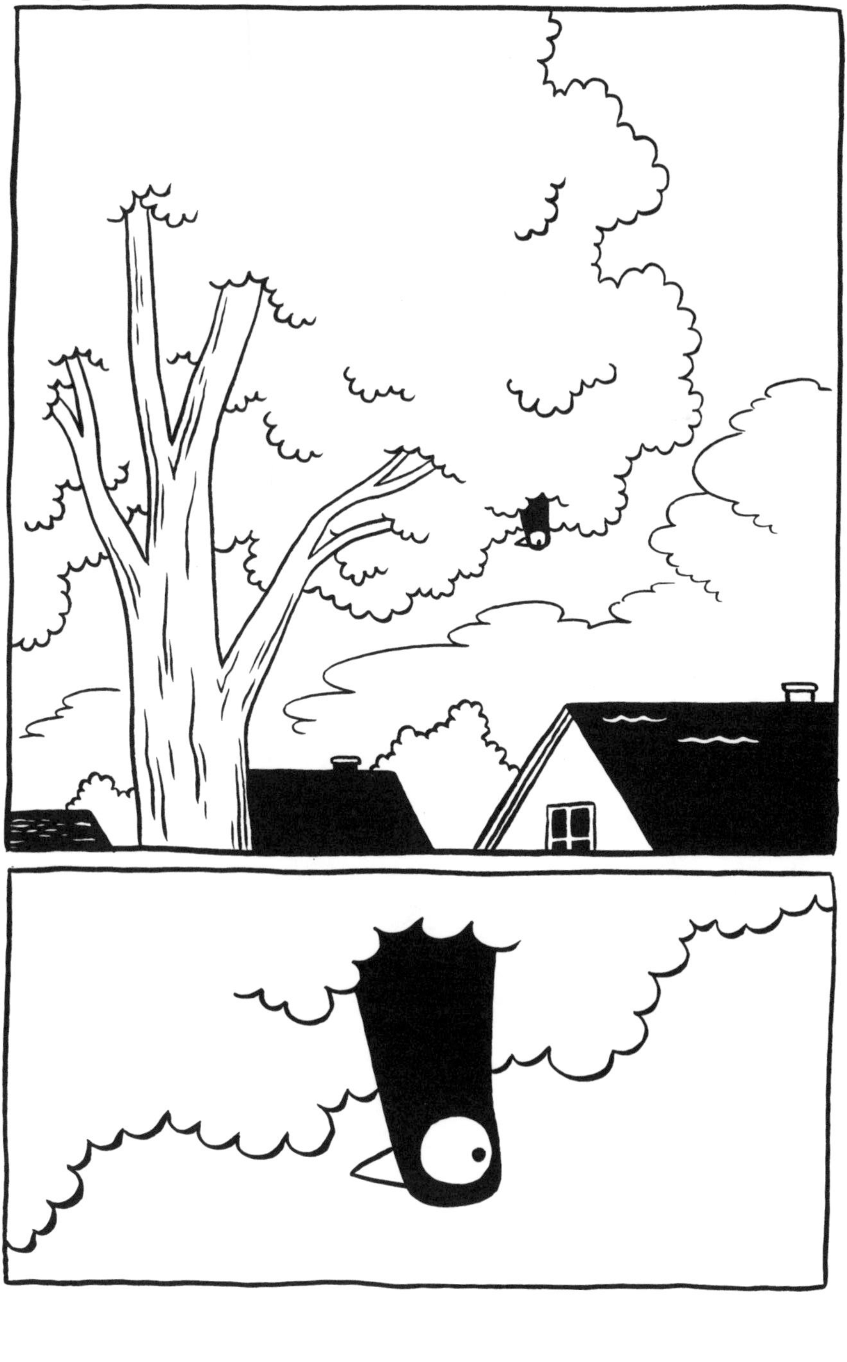

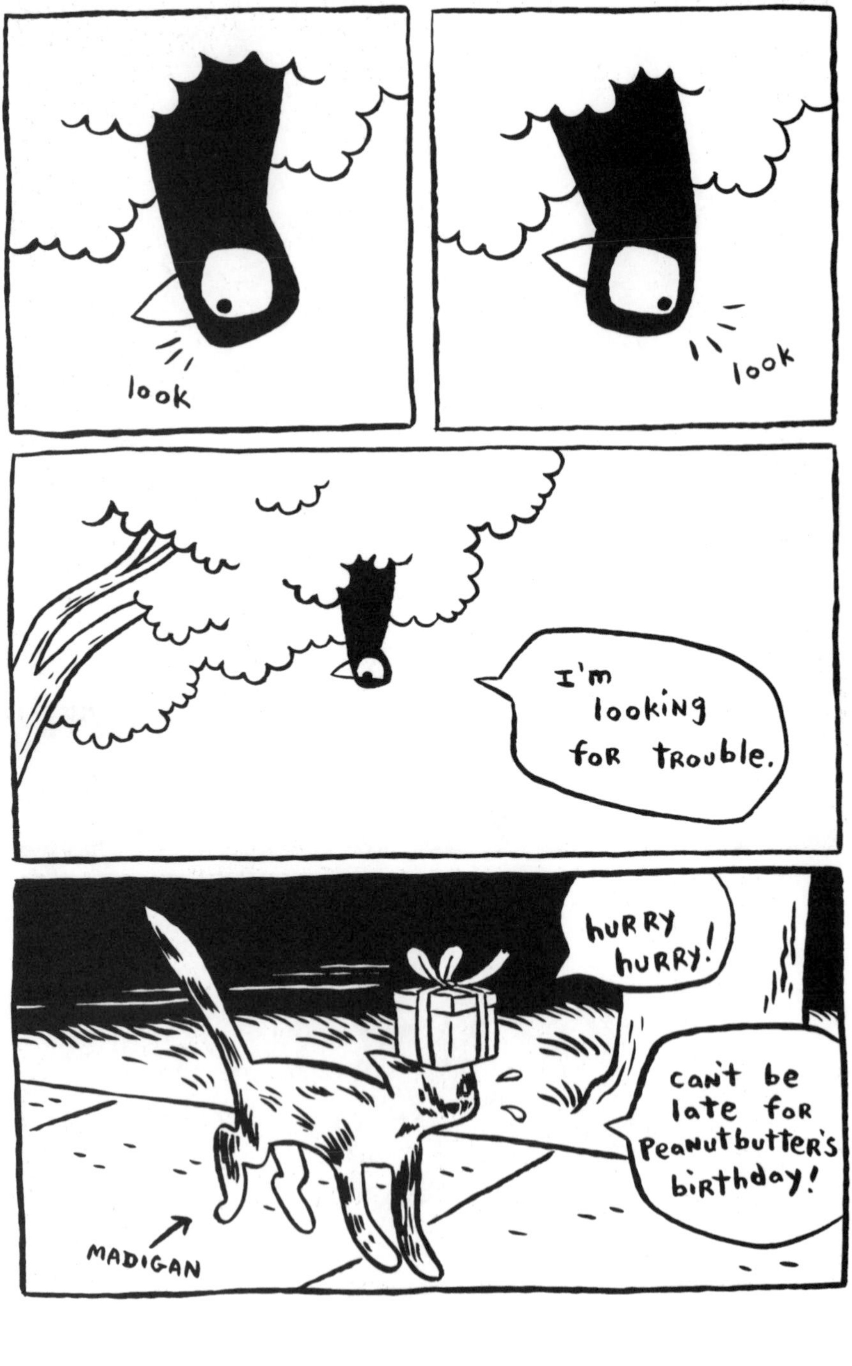
look
look
I'm looking for trouble.
hurry hurry!
can't be late for Peanutbutter's birthday!
MADIGAN

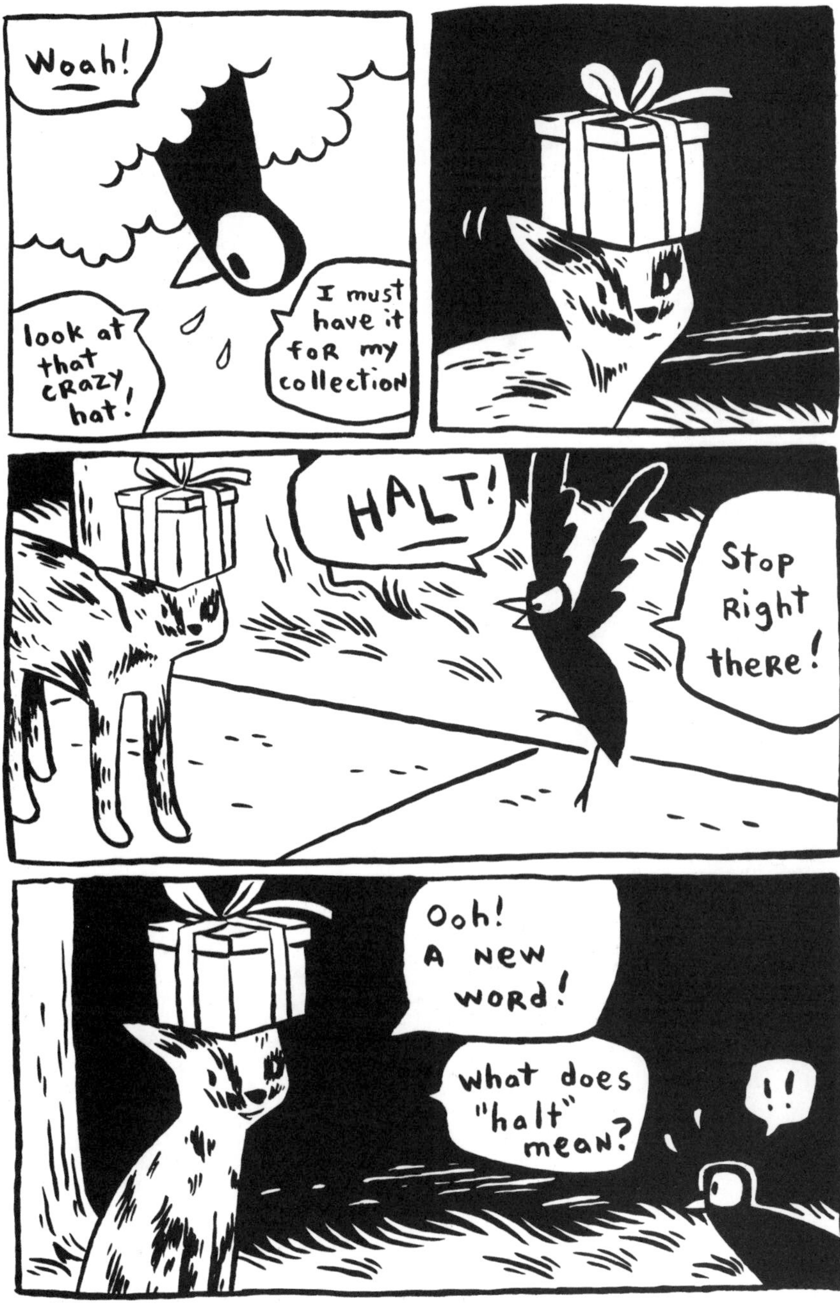
Woah!
look at that crazy hat!
I must have it for my collection
HALT!
Stop right there!
Ooh! A new word!
what does "halt" mean?
!!

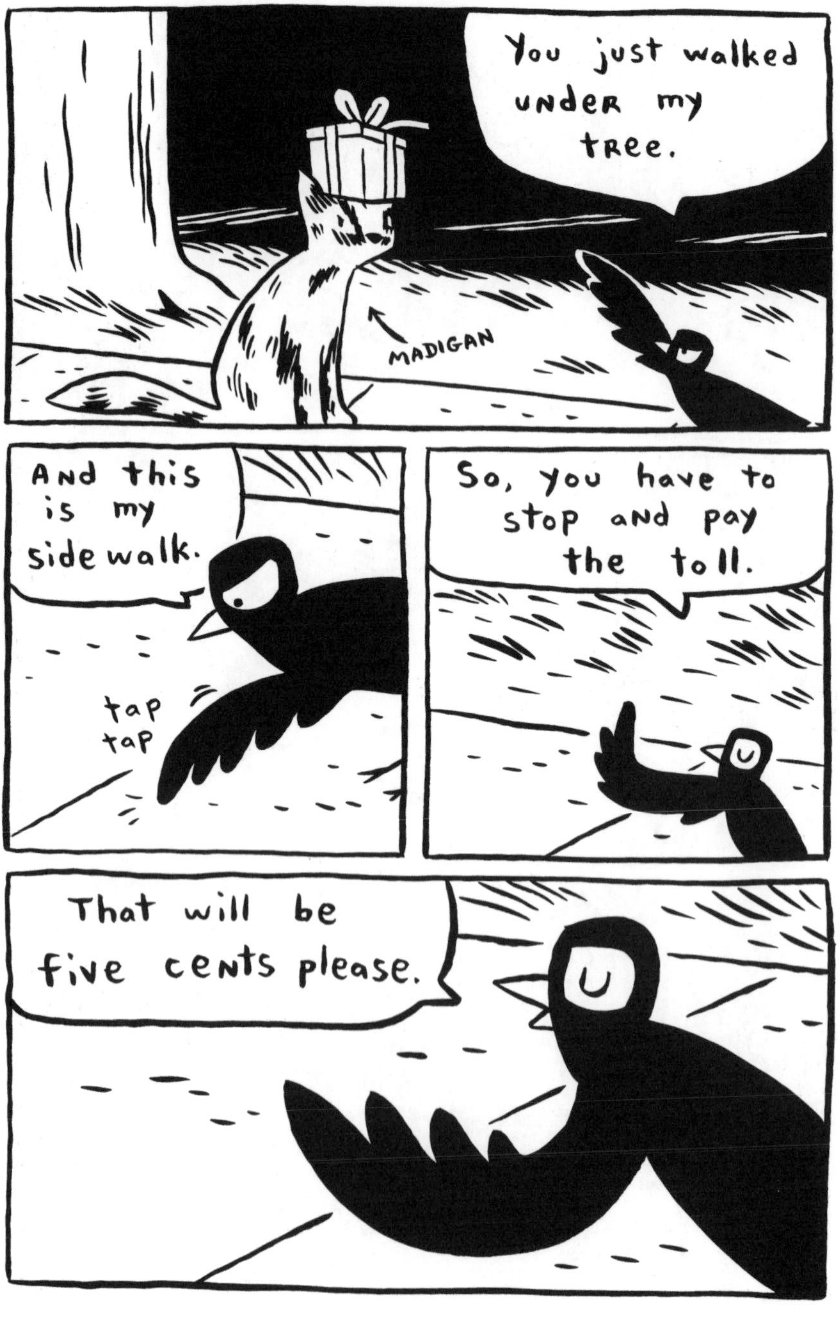
You just walked under my tree.
MADIGAN
And this is my sidewalk.
tap tap
So, you have to stop and pay the toll.
That will be five cents please.

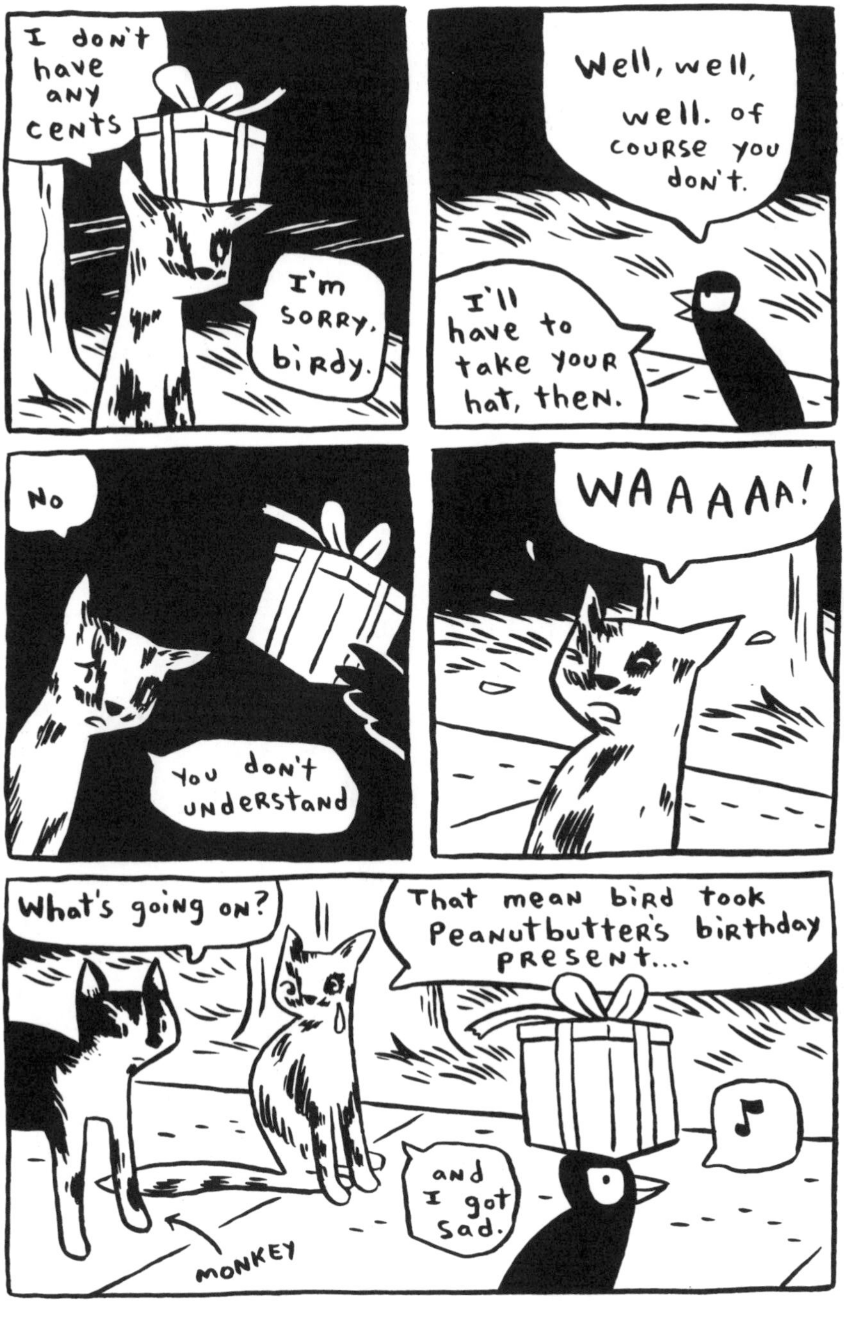
I don't have any cents
I'm sorry, birdy.
Well, well, well. of course you don't.
I'll have to take your hat, then.
No
You don't understand
WAAAAA!
What's going on?
That mean bird took Peanutbutter's birthday present....
♪
and I got sad.
MONKEY

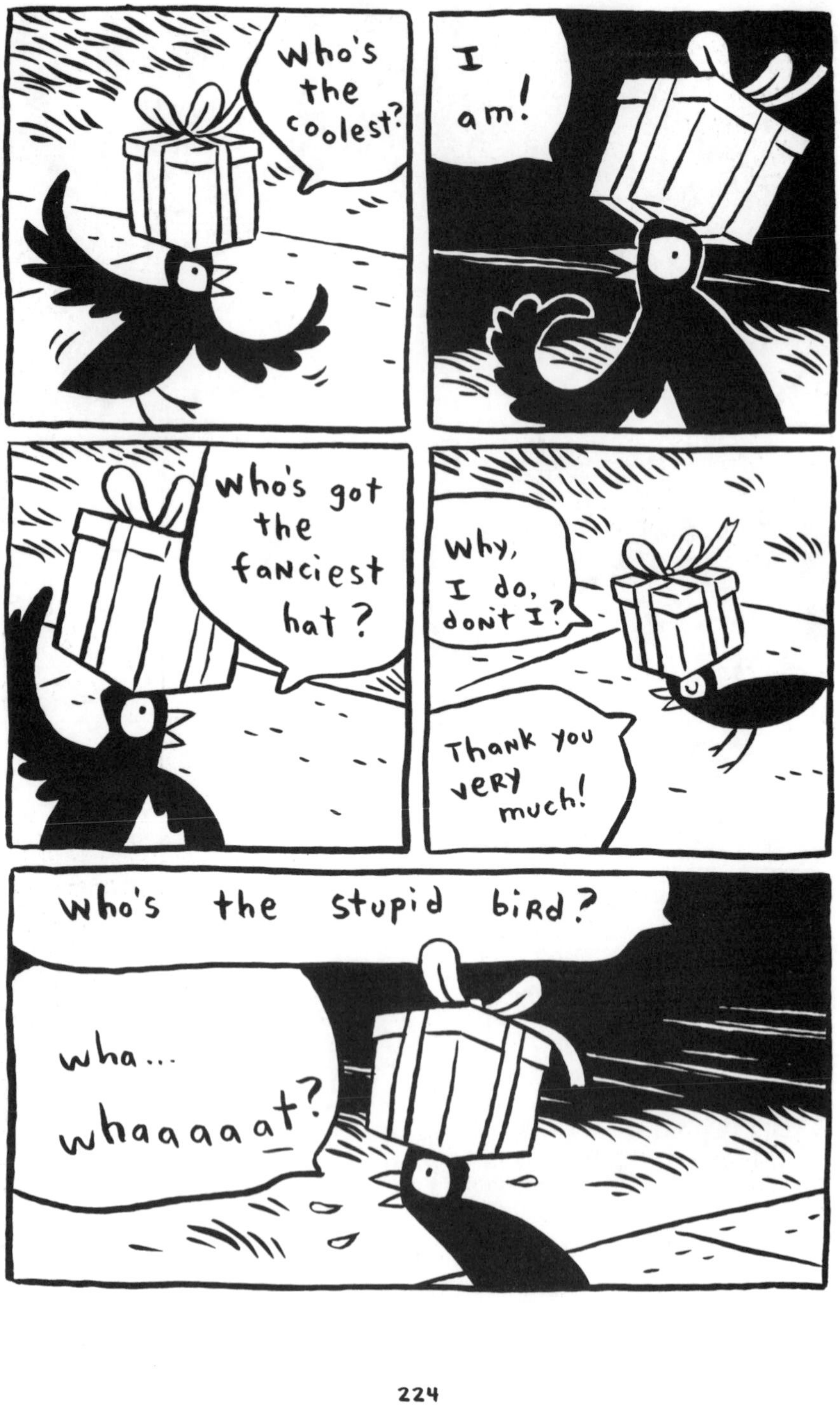
Who's the coolest?
I am!
Who's got the fanciest hat?
Why, I do, don't I?
Thank you very much!
Who's the stupid bird?
wha...
whaaaaat?

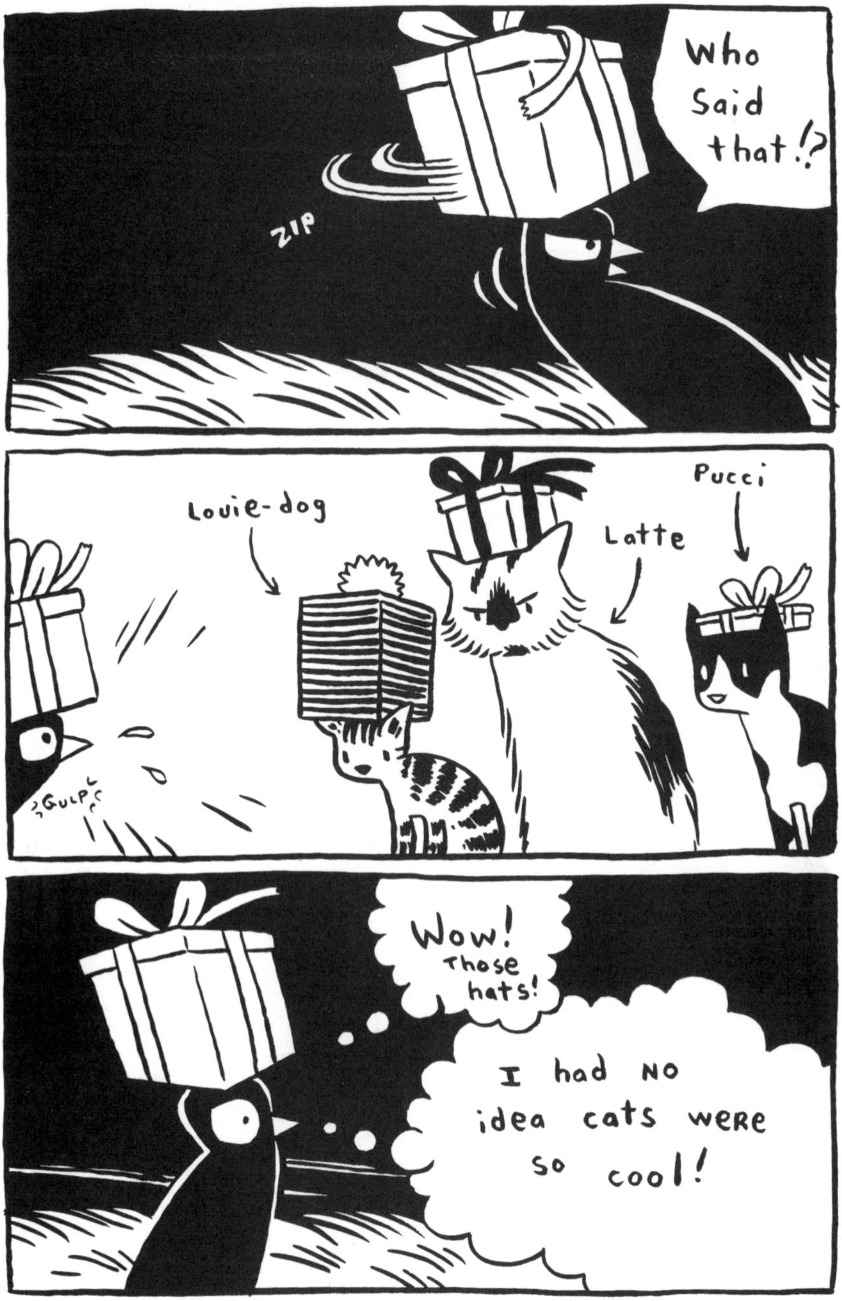

Who Said that!?
ZIP
GULP
Louie-dog
Latte
Pucci
Wow! Those hats!
I had NO idea cats were so cool!

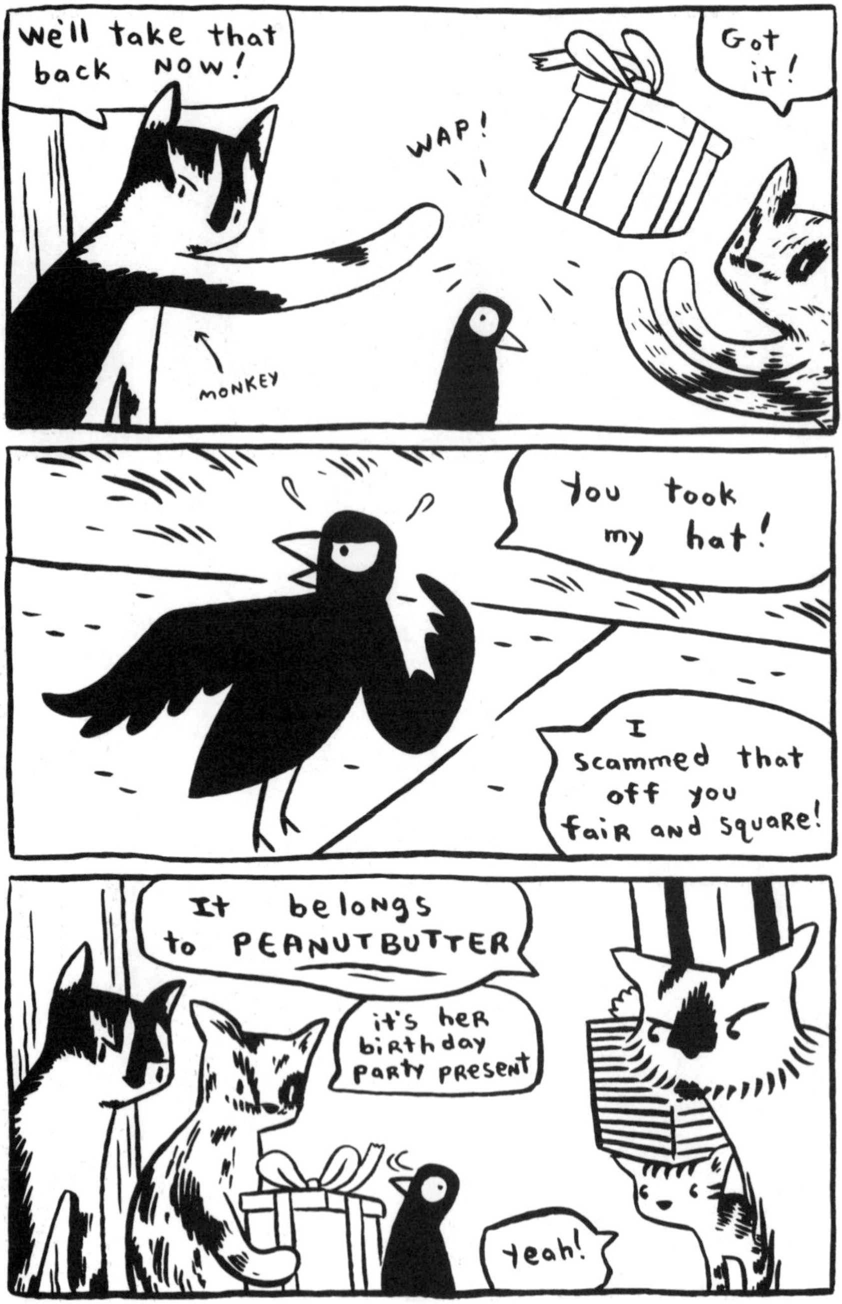
We'll take that back NOW!
WAP!
Got it!
MONKEY
You took my hat!
I scammed that off you fair and square!
It belongs to PEANUTBUTTER
it's her birthday party present
Yeah!

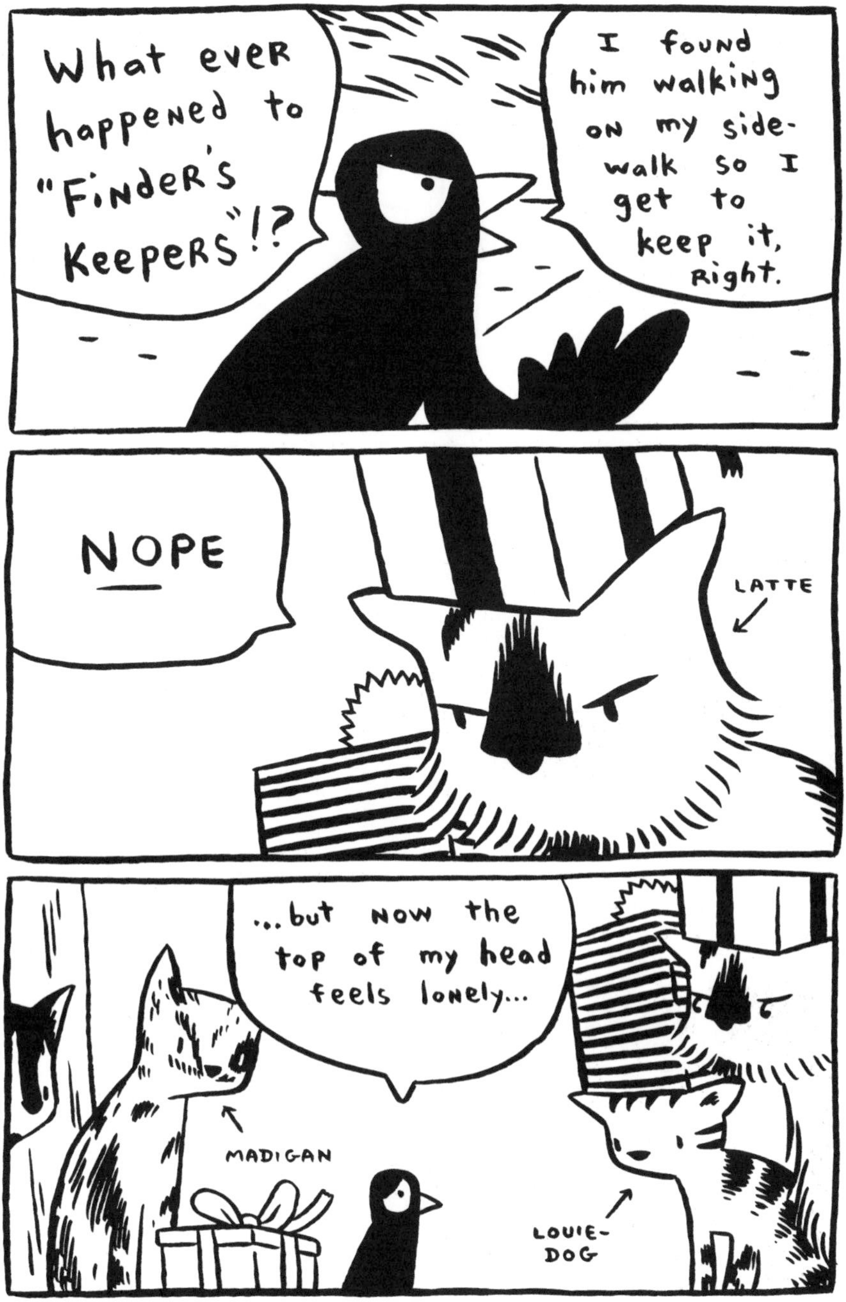
What ever happened to "Finder's Keepers"!?
I found him walking on my side-walk so I get to keep it, Right.
NOPE
LATTE
...but now the top of my head feels lonely...
MADIGAN
LOUIE-DOG

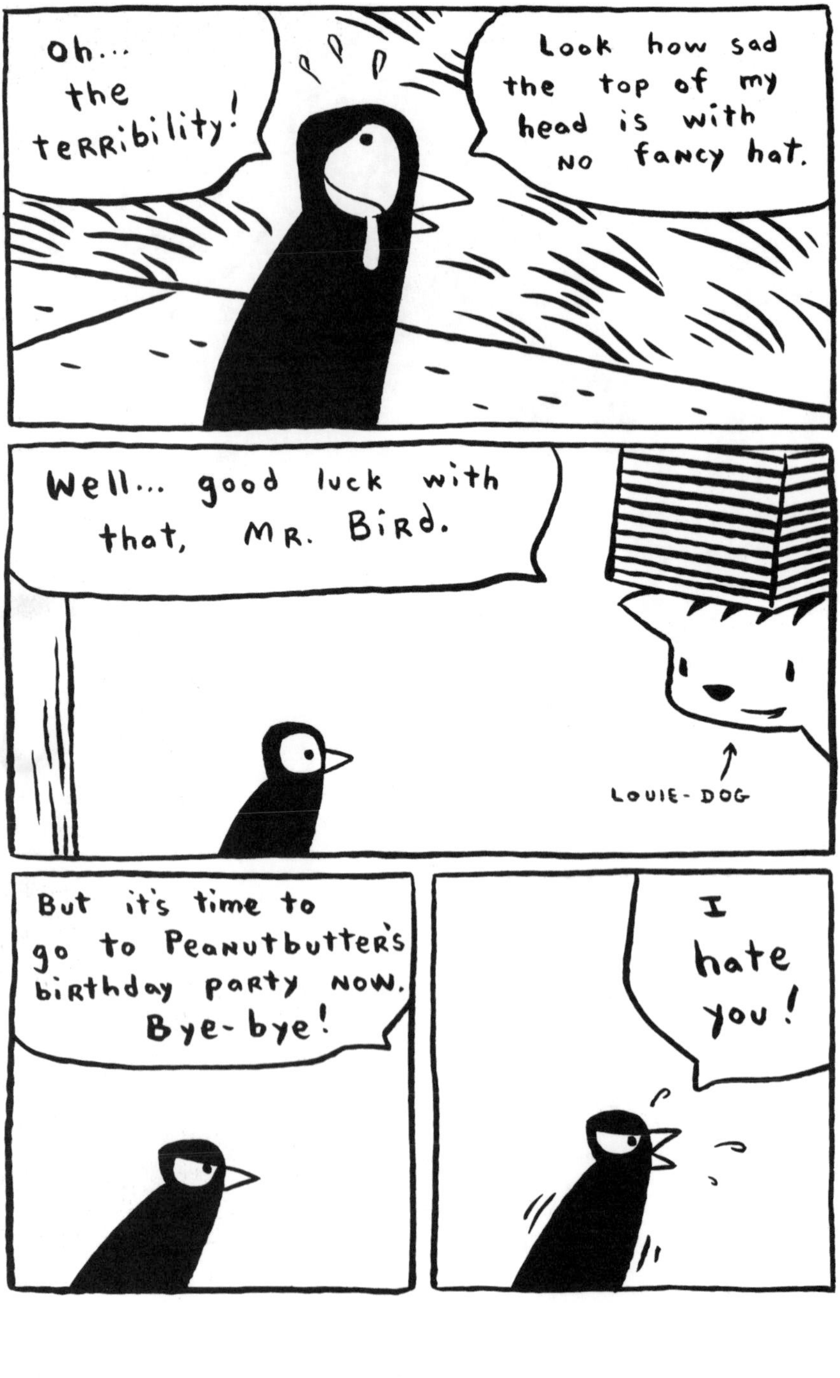
Oh... the terribility!
Look how sad the top of my head is with no fancy hat.
Well... good luck with that, Mr. Bird.
LOUIE-DOG
But it's time to go to Peanutbutter's birthday party now. Bye-bye!
I hate you!

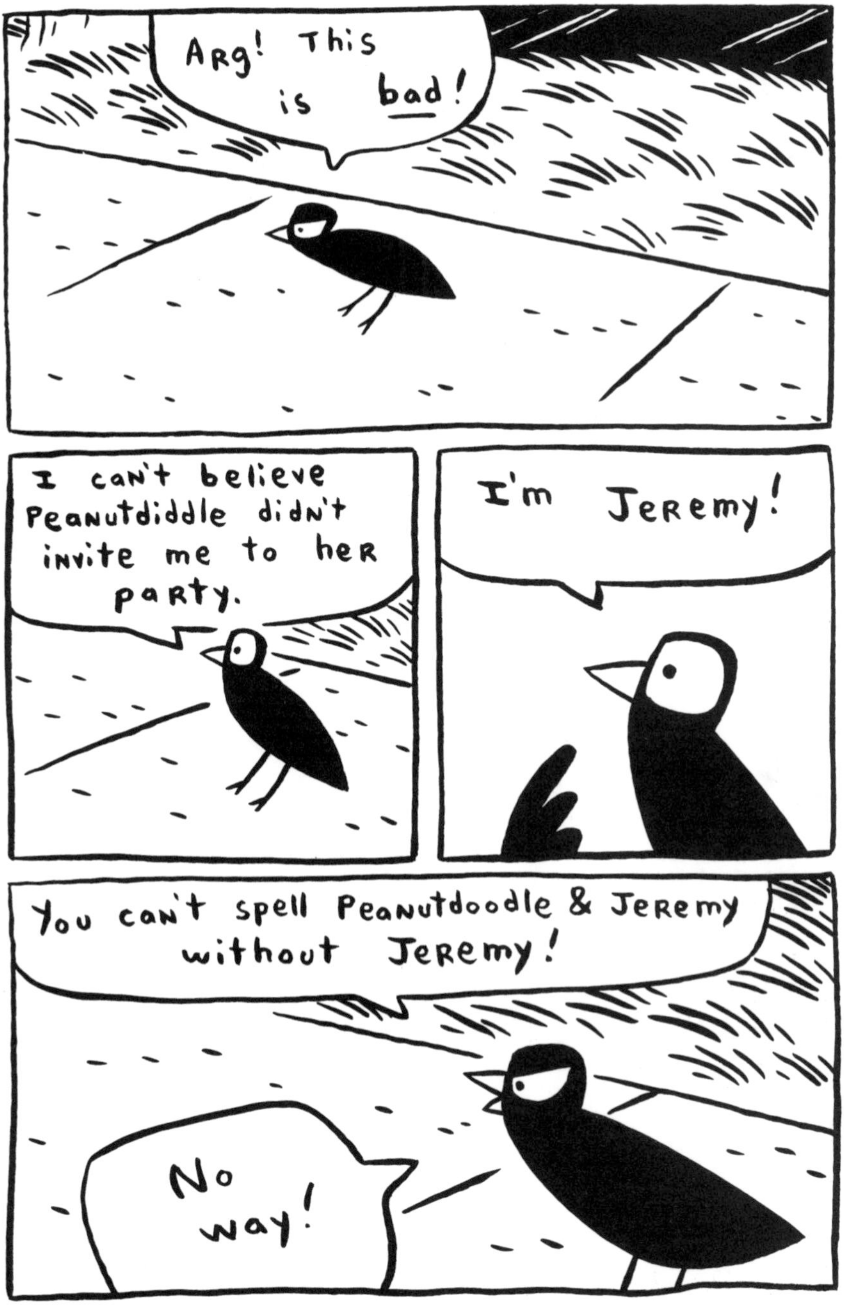
Arg! This is bad!
I can't believe Peanutdiddle didn't invite me to her party.
I'm Jeremy!
You can't spell Peanutdoodle & Jeremy without Jeremy!
No way!

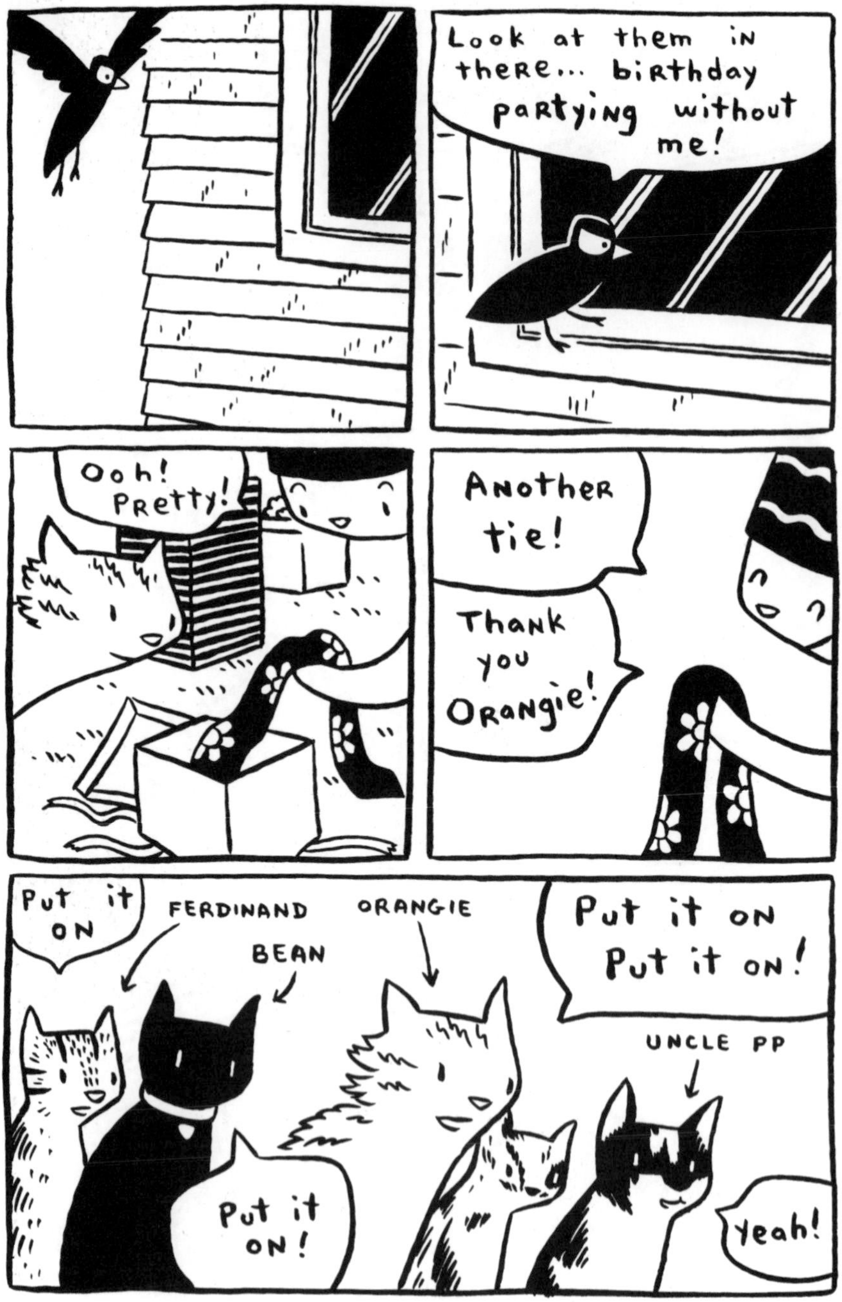
Look at them in there... birthday partying without me!
Ooh! Pretty!
Another tie!
Thank you Orangie!
Put it on
FERDINAND
BEAN
ORANGIE
Put it on Put it on!
UNCLE PP
Put it on!
Yeah!

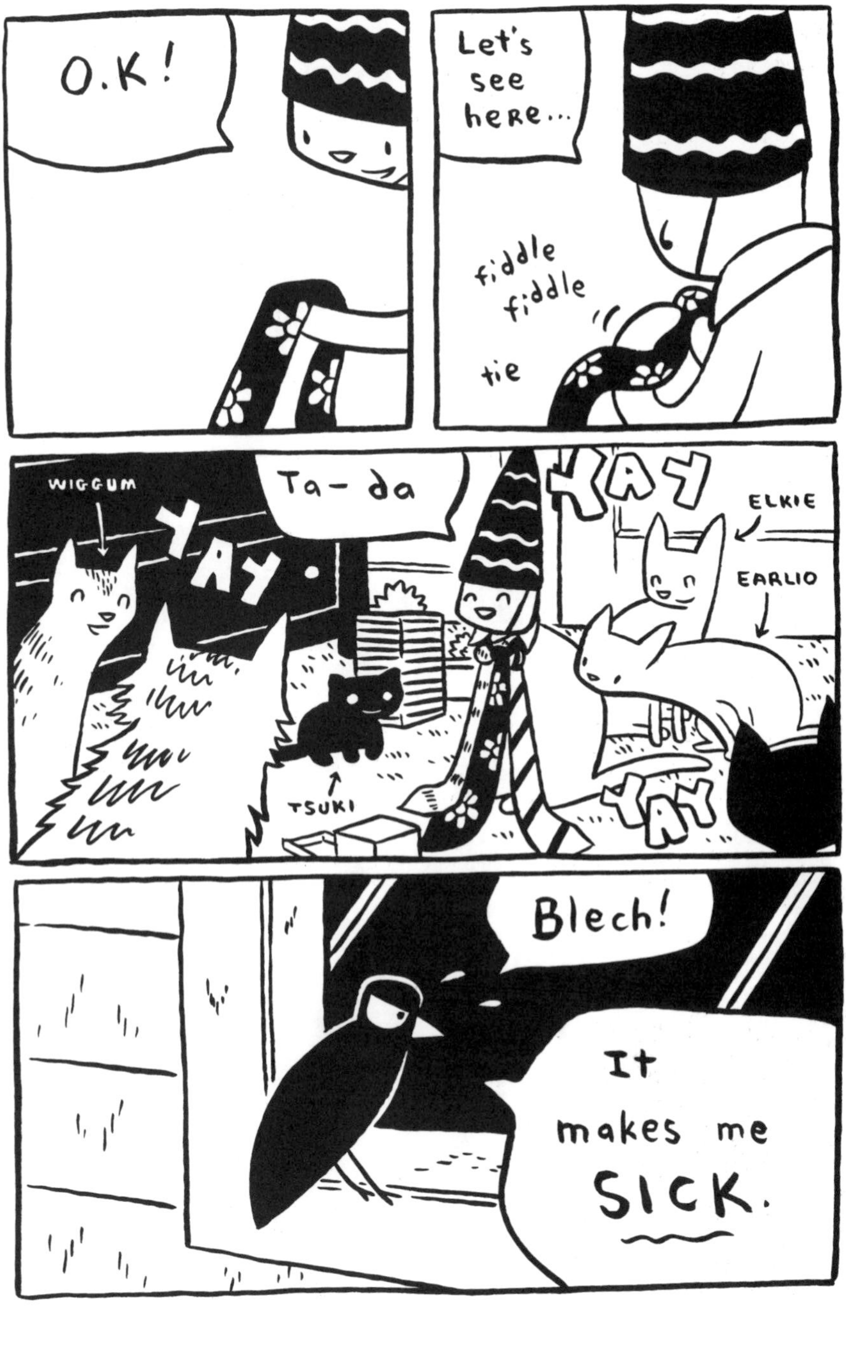
O.K!
Let's see here...
fiddle fiddle
tie
WIGGUM
Ta-da
YAY
YAY
ELKIE
EARLIO
TSUKI
YAY
Blech!
It makes me SICK.

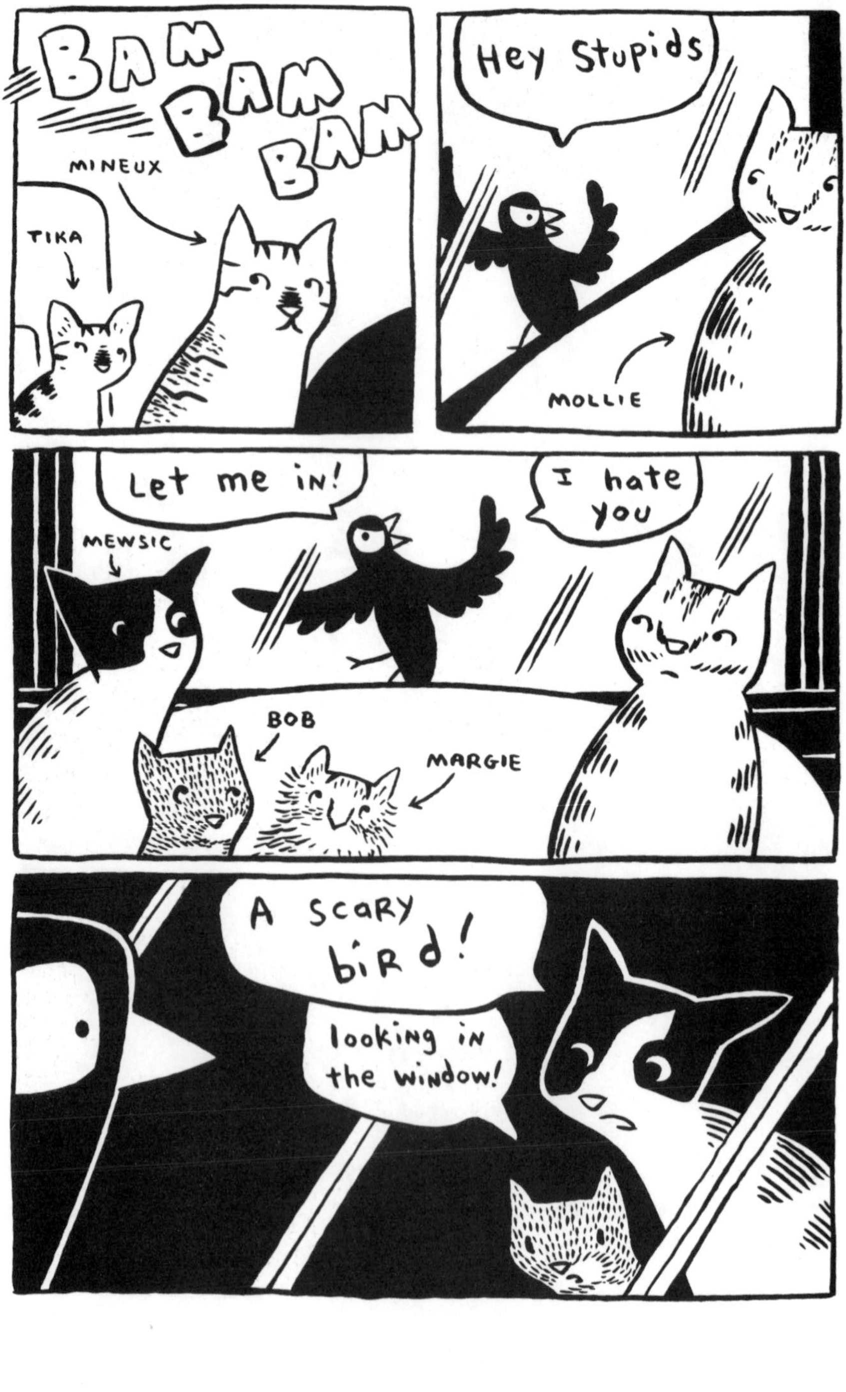
BAM BAM BAM
MINEUX
TIKA
Hey Stupids
MOLLIE
Let me in!
I hate you
MEWSIC
BOB
MARGIE
A scary bird!
looking in the window!

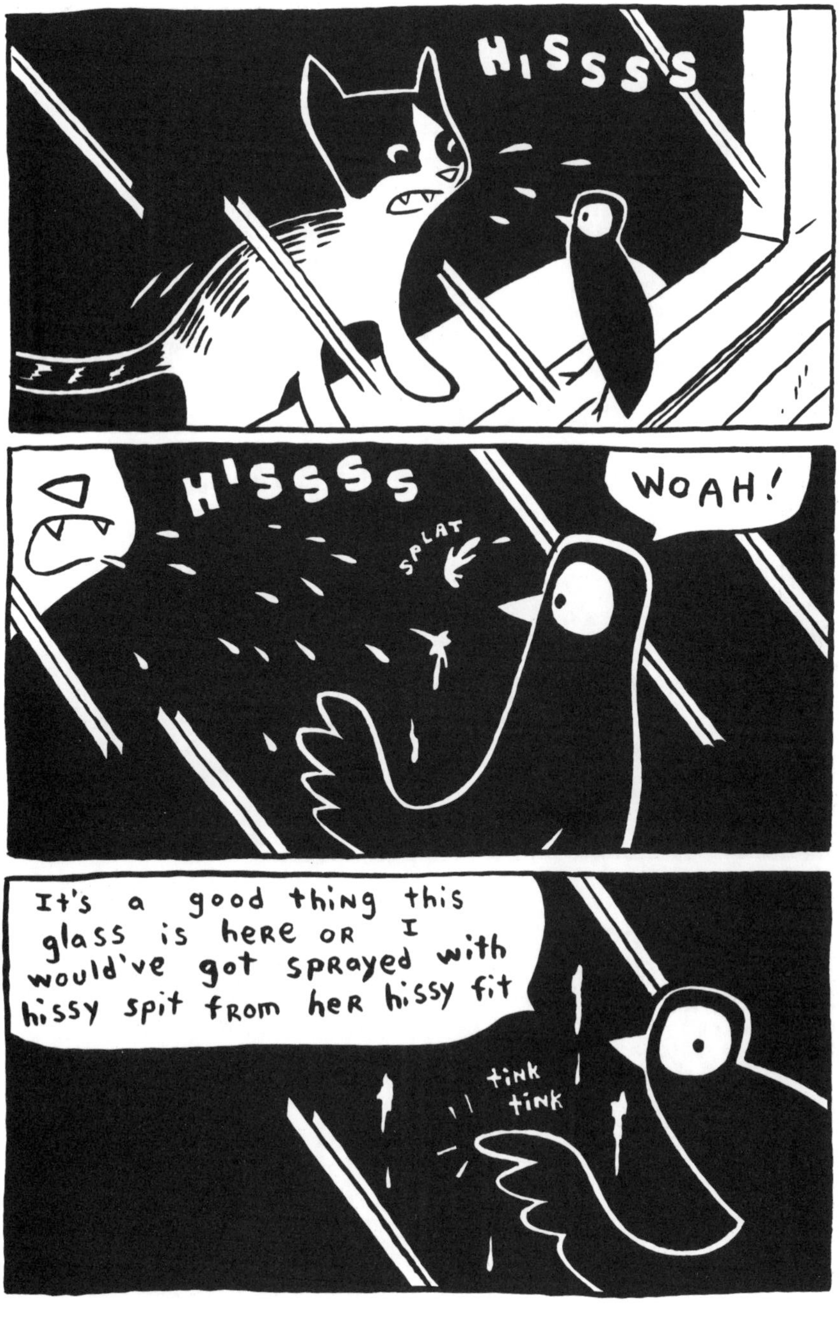
HISSSS
HISSSS
SPLAT
WOAH!
It's a good thing this glass is here or I would've got sprayed with hissy spit from her hissy fit
tink tink

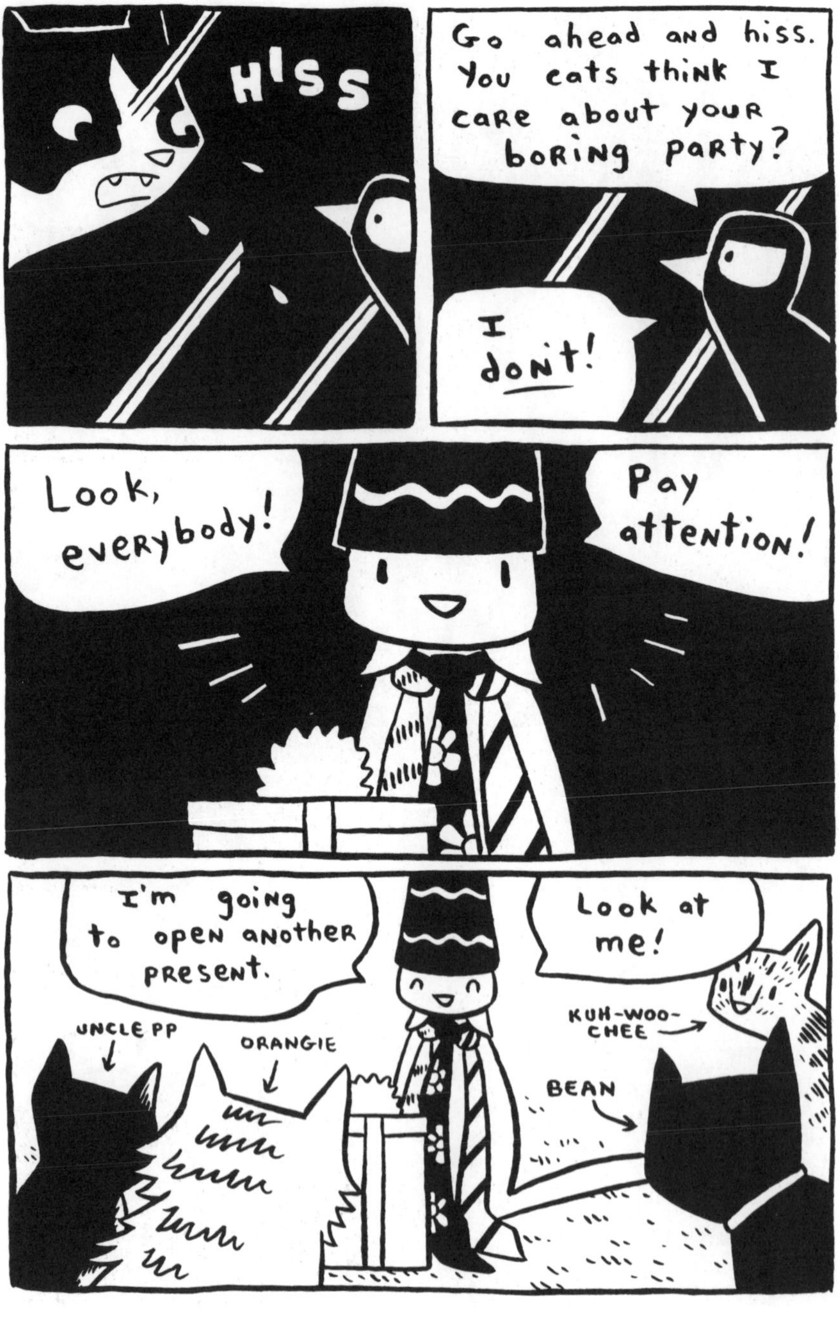
HISS
Go ahead and hiss. You cats think I care about your boring party?
I don't!
Look, everybody!
Pay attention!
I'm going to open another present.
Look at me!
UNCLE PP
ORANGIE
KUH-WOO-CHEE
BEAN

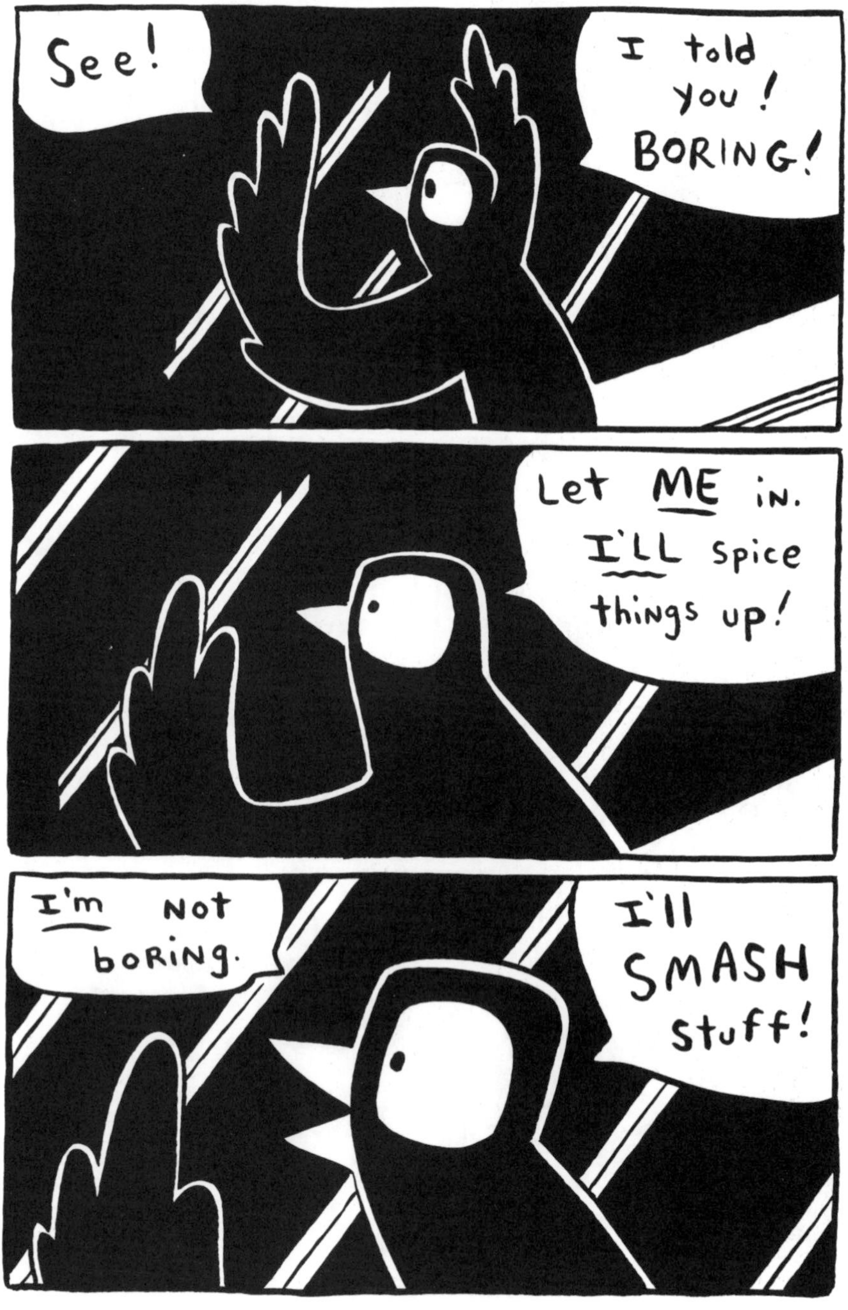
See!
I told you! BORING!
Let ME in. I'LL spice things up!
I'm not boring.
I'll SMASH stuff!

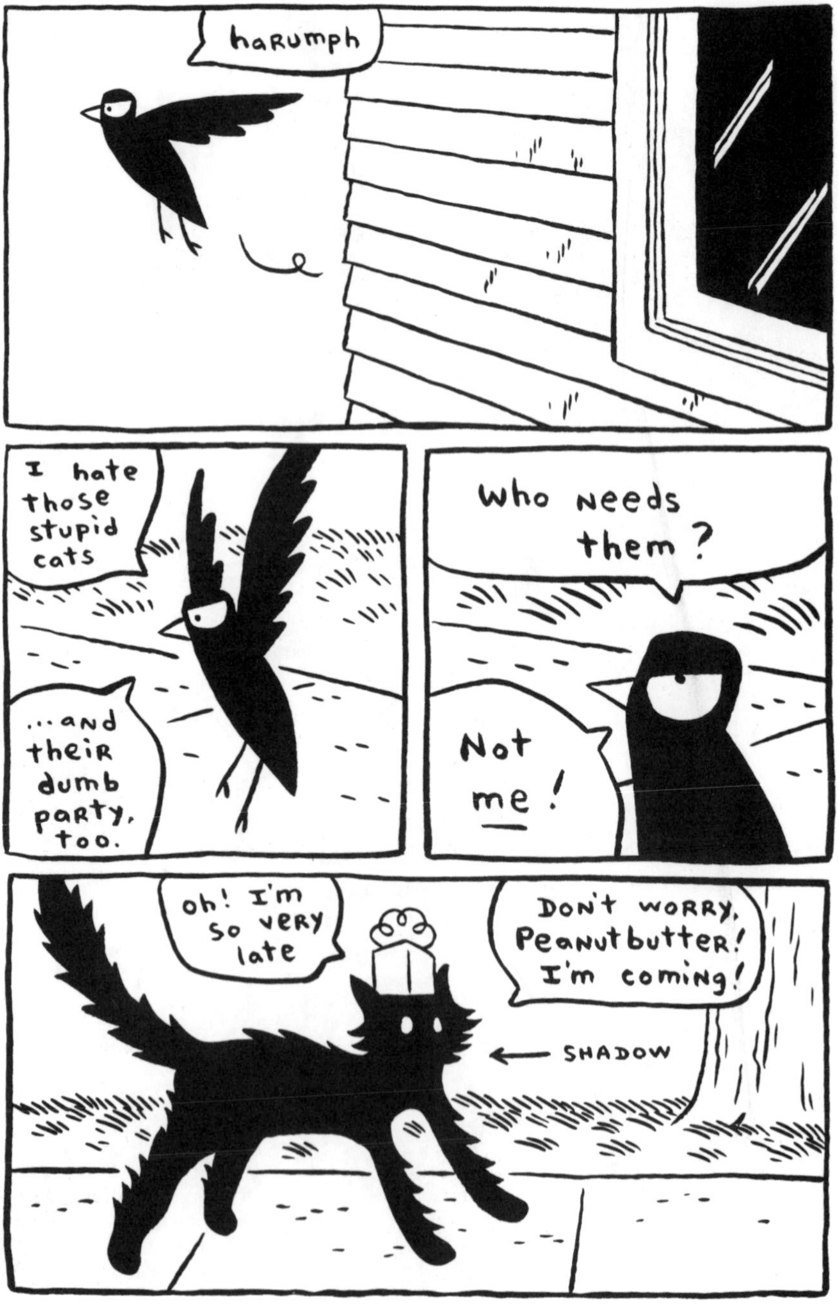
harumph
I hate those stupid cats
...and their dumb party, too.
Who needs them?
Not me!
oh! I'm so very late
Don't worry, Peanutbutter! I'm coming!
SHADOW

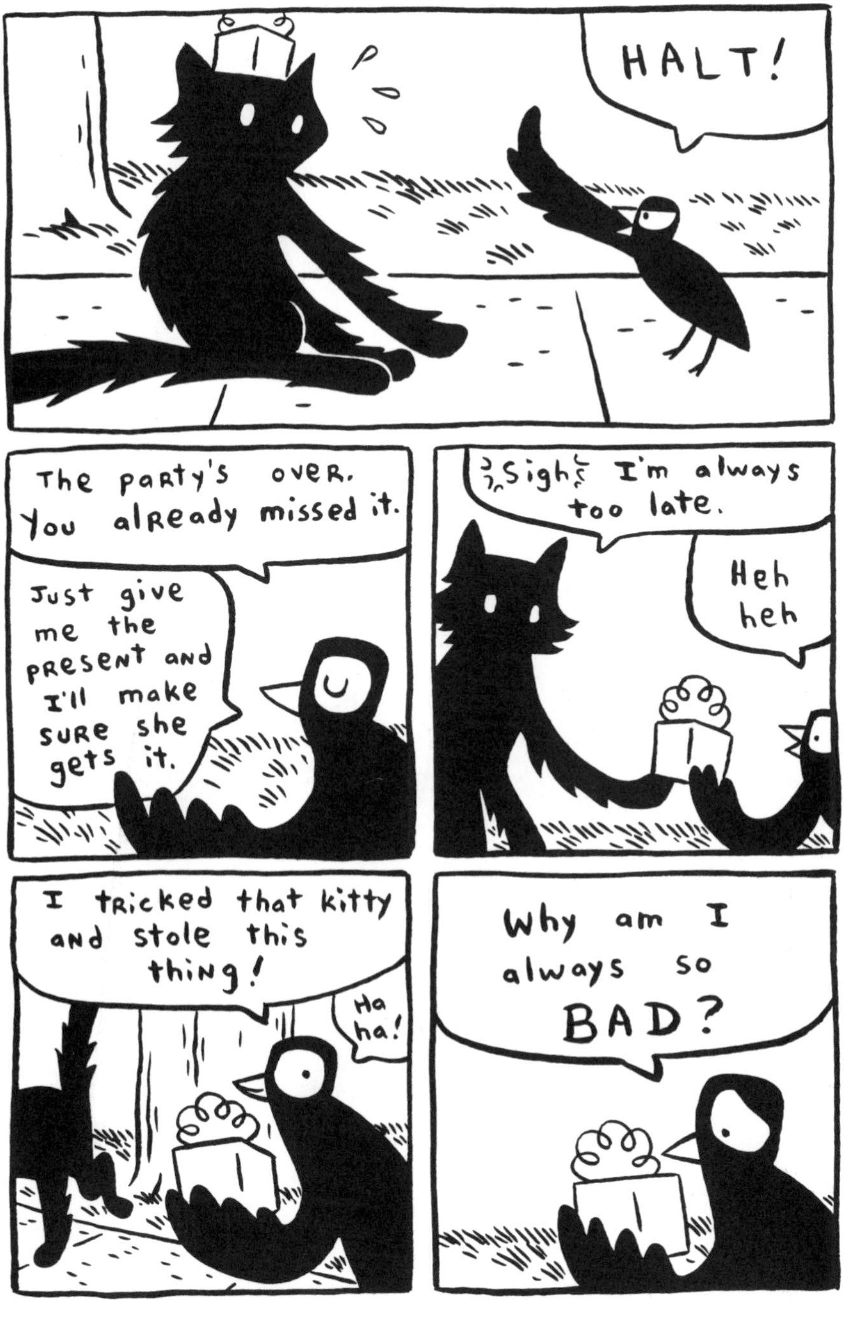
HALT!
The party's over. You already missed it.
Just give me the present and I'll make sure she gets it.
Sigh I'm always too late.
Heh heh
I tricked that kitty and stole this thing!
Ha ha!
Why am I always so BAD?

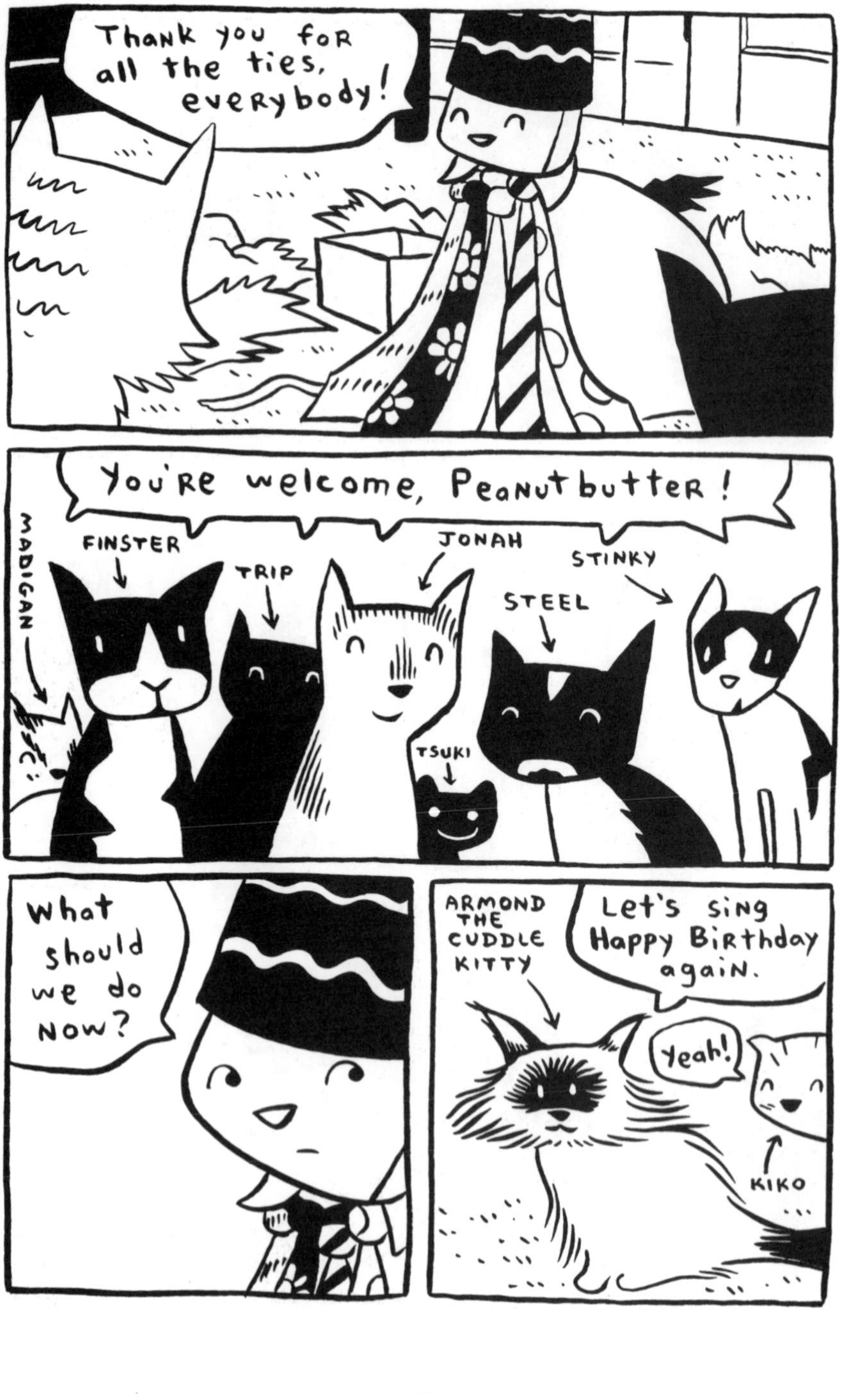
Thank you for all the ties, everybody!
You're welcome, Peanutbutter!
MADIGAN
FINSTER
TRIP
JONAH
STINKY
STEEL
TSUKI
What should we do now?
ARMOND THE CUDDLE KITTY
Let's sing Happy Birthday again.
Yeah!
KIKO

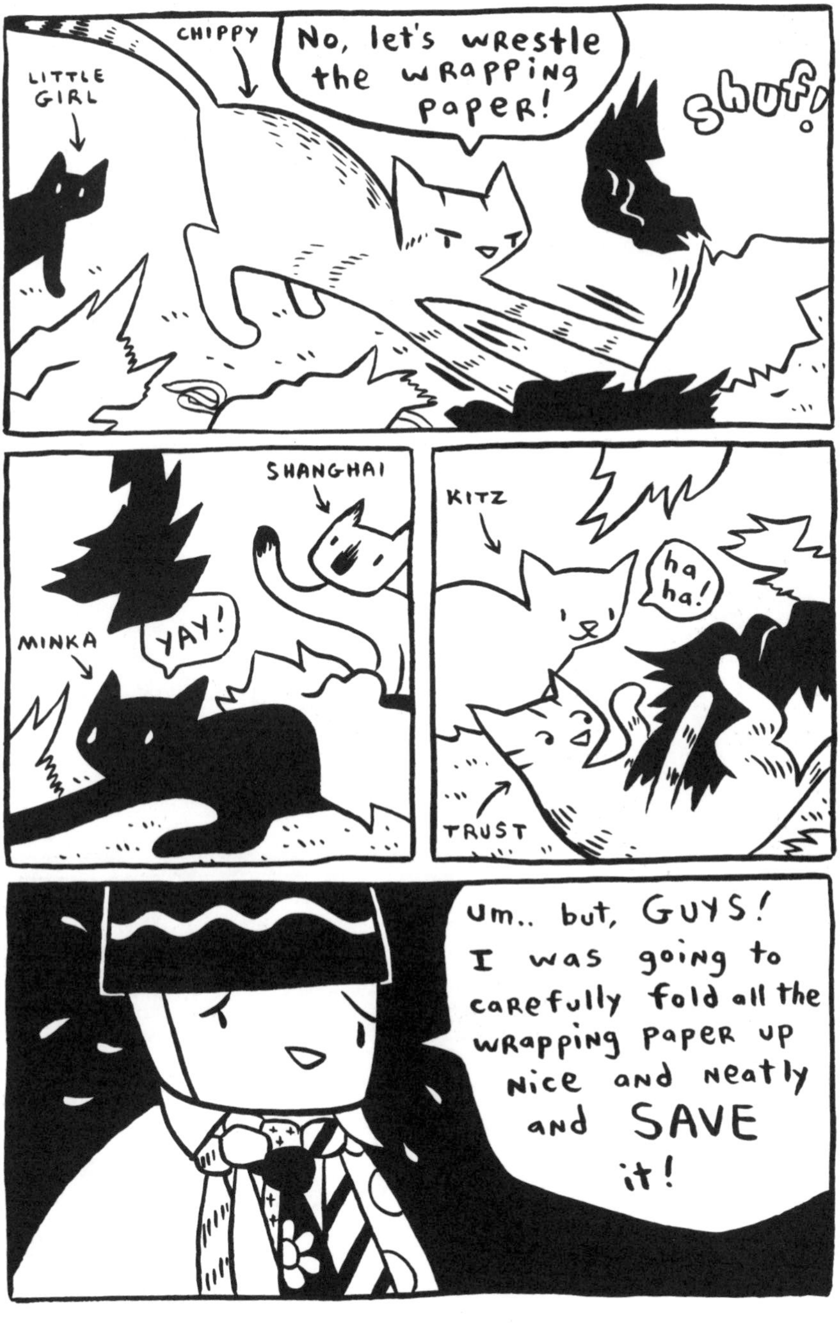
LITTLE GIRL
CHIPPY
No, let's wrestle the wrapping paper!
shuf!
SHANGHAI
MINKA
YAY!
KITZ
ha ha!
TRUST
um.. but, GUYS! I was going to carefully fold all the wrapping paper up nice and neatly and SAVE it!

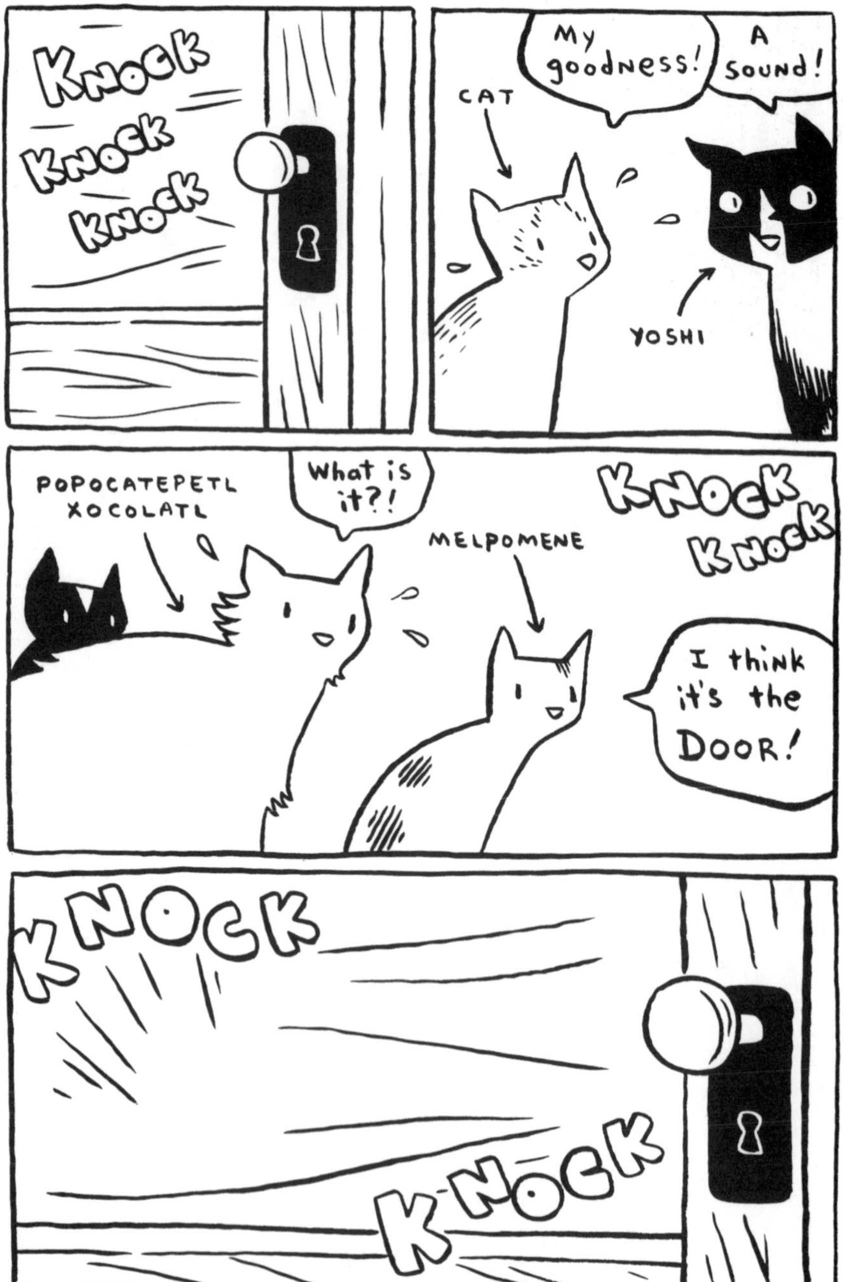
KNOCK
KNOCK
KNOCK
My goodness!
A sound!
CAT
YOSHI
POPOCATEPETL XOCOLATL
What is it?!
MELPOMENE
KNOCK
KNOCK
I think it's the DOOR!
KNOCK
KNOCK

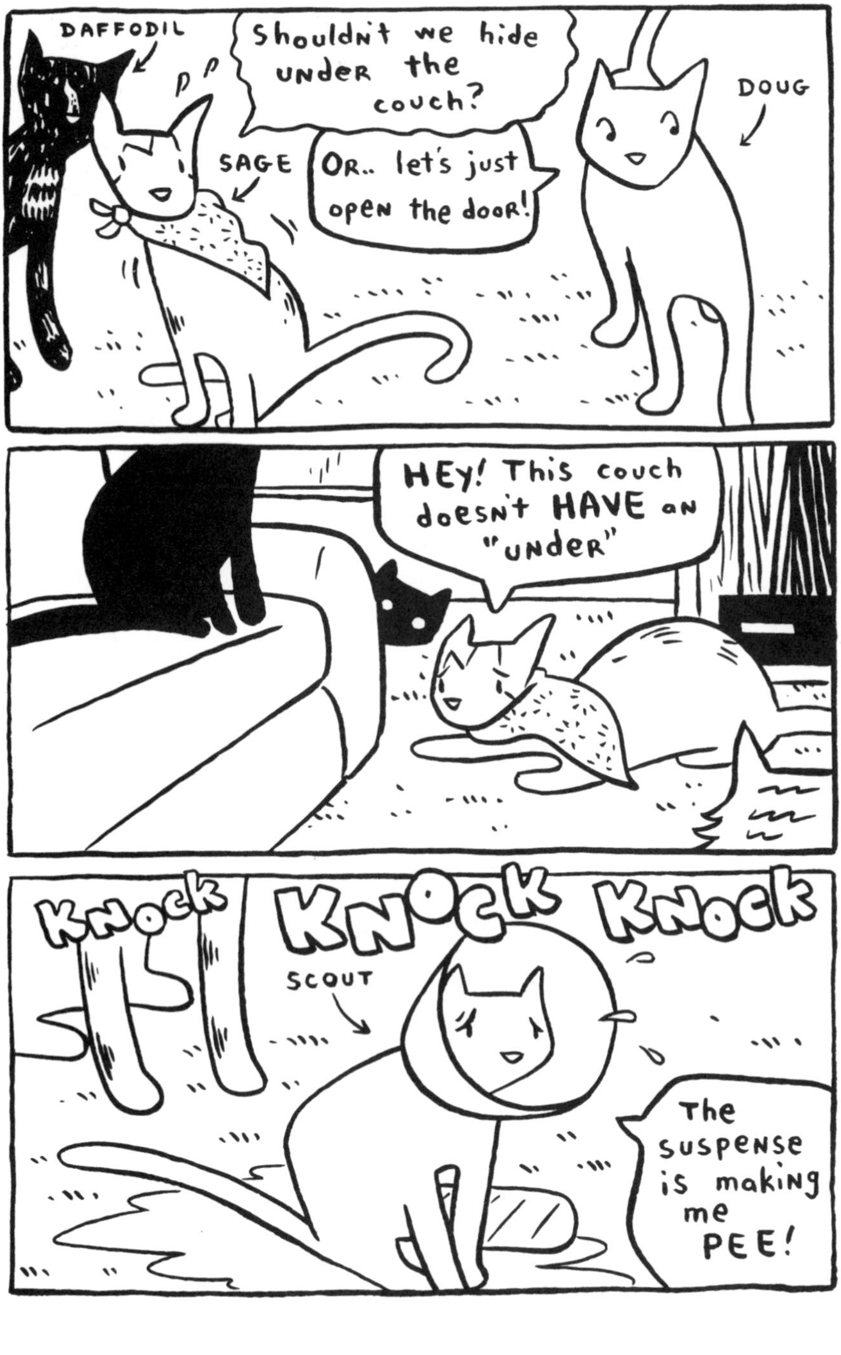
DAFFODIL
Shouldn't we hide under the couch?
DOUG
SAGE
OR.. let's just open the door!
HEY! This couch doesn't HAVE an "under"
KNOCK KNOCK KNOCK
SCOUT
The suspense is making me PEE!

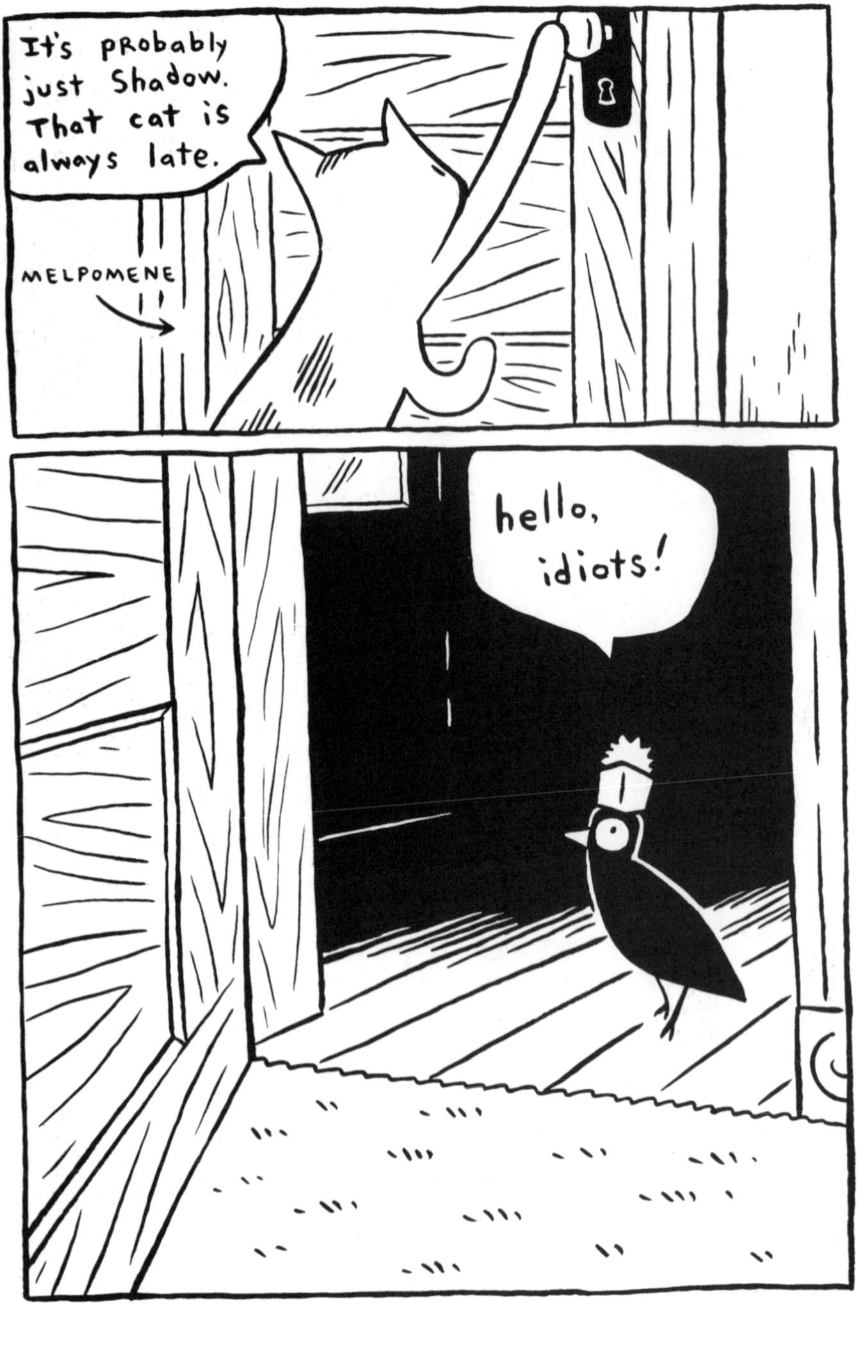
It's probably just Shadow. That cat is always late.
MELPOMENE
hello, idiots!

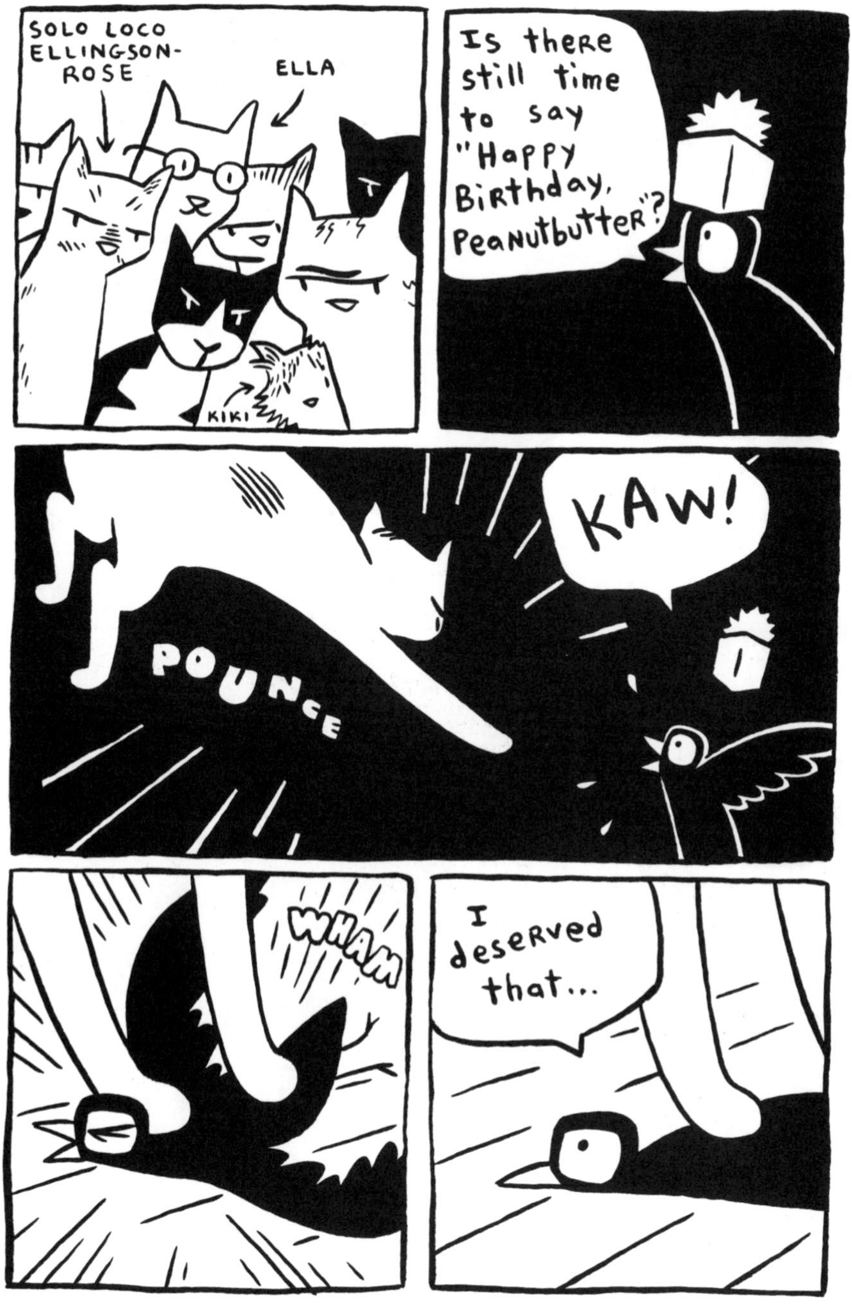

SOLO LOCO ELLINGSON-ROSE
ELLA
KIKI
Is there still time to say "Happy Birthday, Peanutbutter"?
KAW!
POUNCE
WHAM
I deserved that...

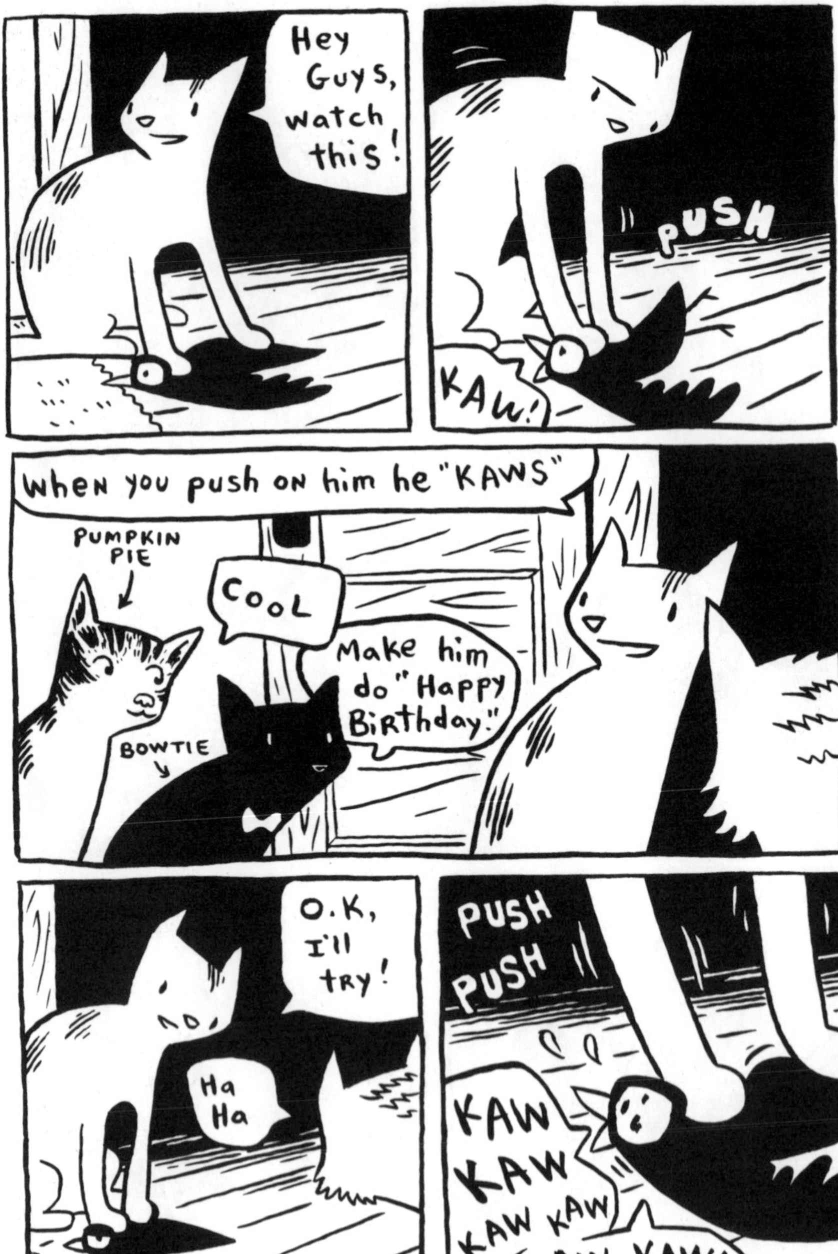
Hey Guys, watch this!
PUSH
KAW!
When you push on him he "KAWS"
PUMPKIN PIE
COOL
Make him do "Happy Birthday."
BOWTIE
O.K, I'll try!
Ha Ha
PUSH PUSH
KAW KAW KAW KAW KAW KAW!

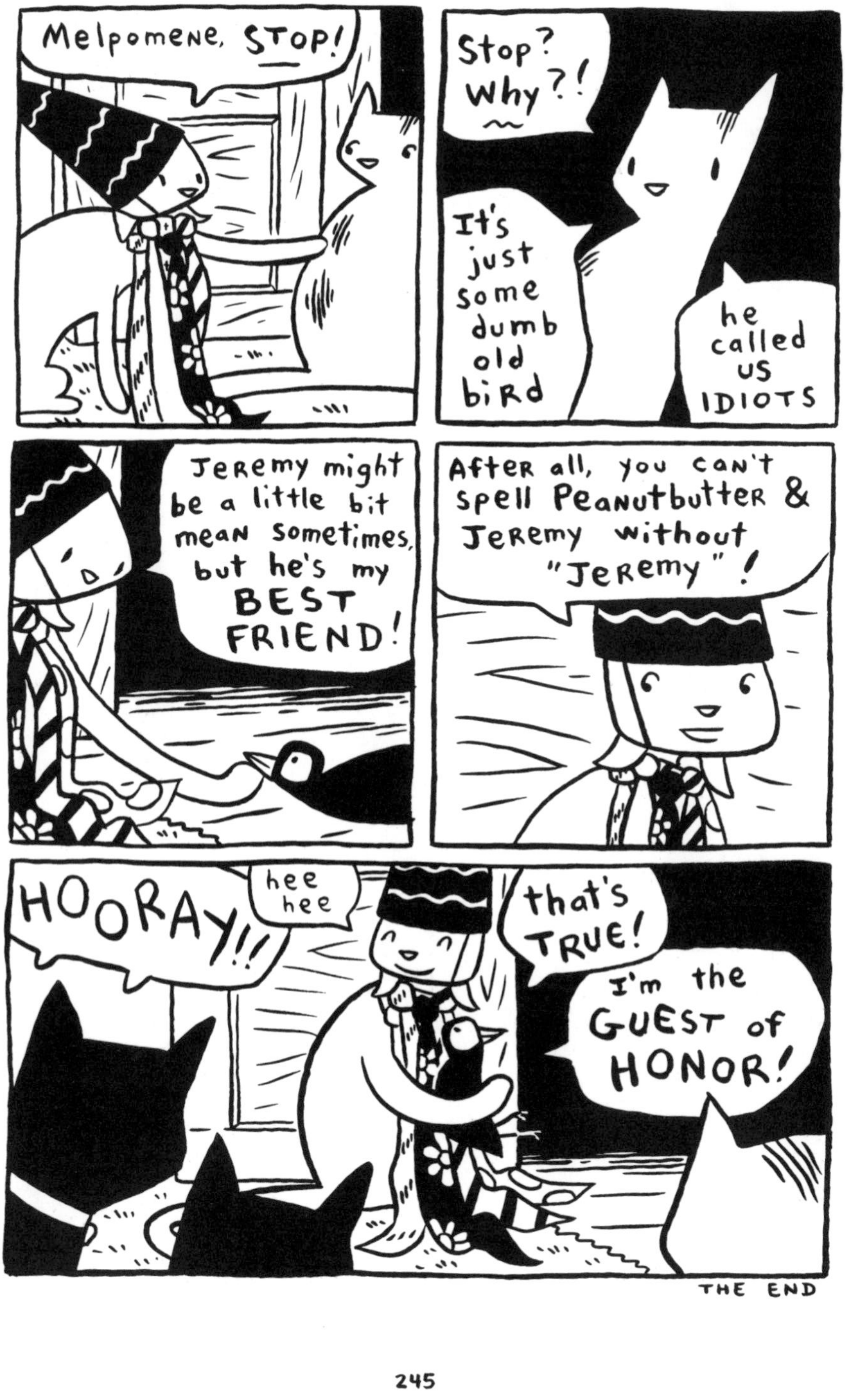
Melpomene, STOP!
Stop? Why?!
It's just some dumb old bird
he called us IDIOTS
Jeremy might be a little bit mean sometimes, but he's my BEST FRIEND!
After all, you can't spell Peanutbutter & Jeremy without "Jeremy"!
HOORAY!!
hee hee
that's TRUE!
I'm the GUEST of HONOR!

THE END

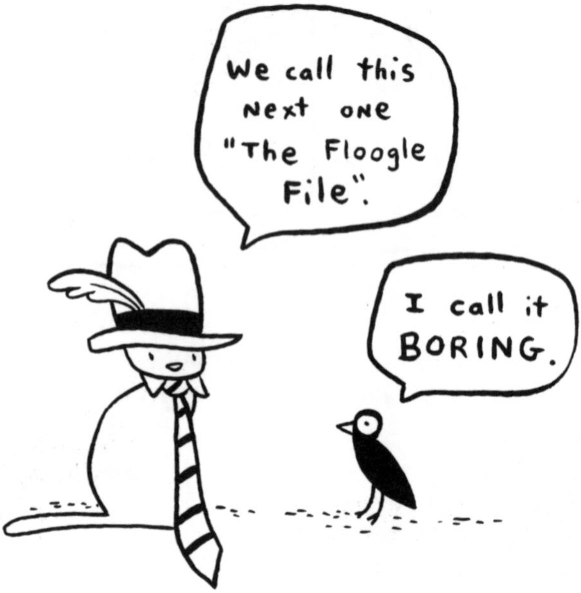
We call this next one "The Floogle File".
I call it BORING.

THE FLOOGLE FILE

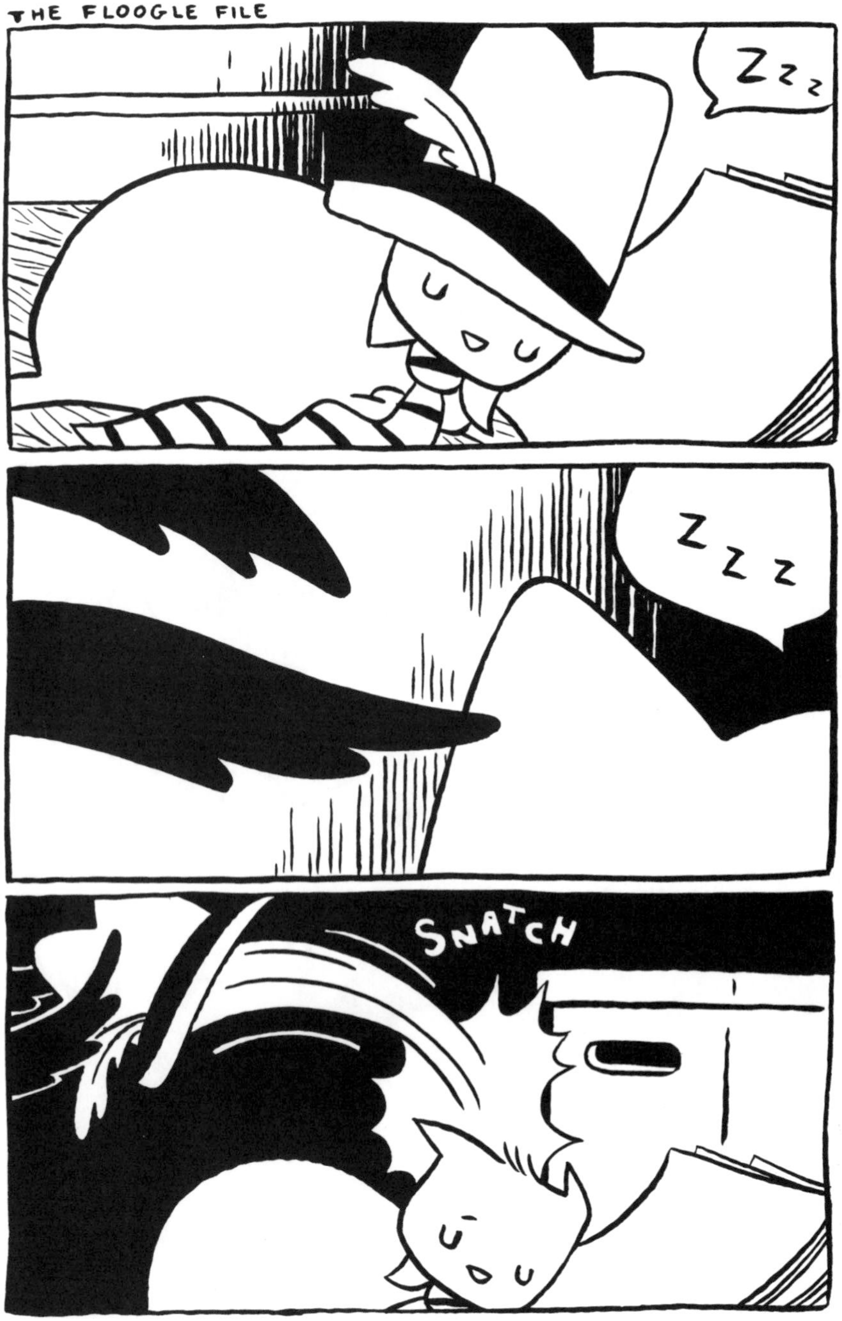
Zzz
Zzz
SNATCH

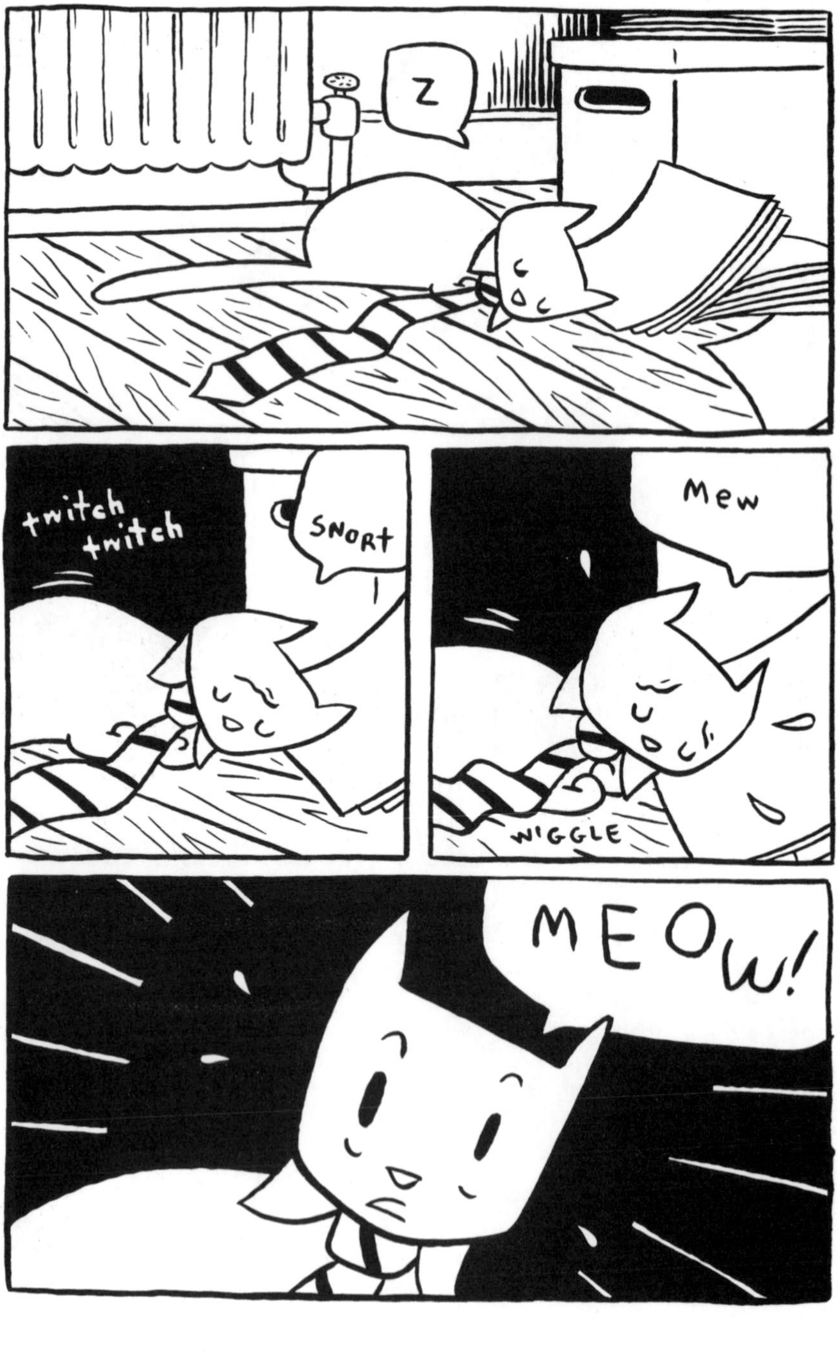
Z
twitch
twitch
SNORT
Mew
WIGGLE
MEOW!

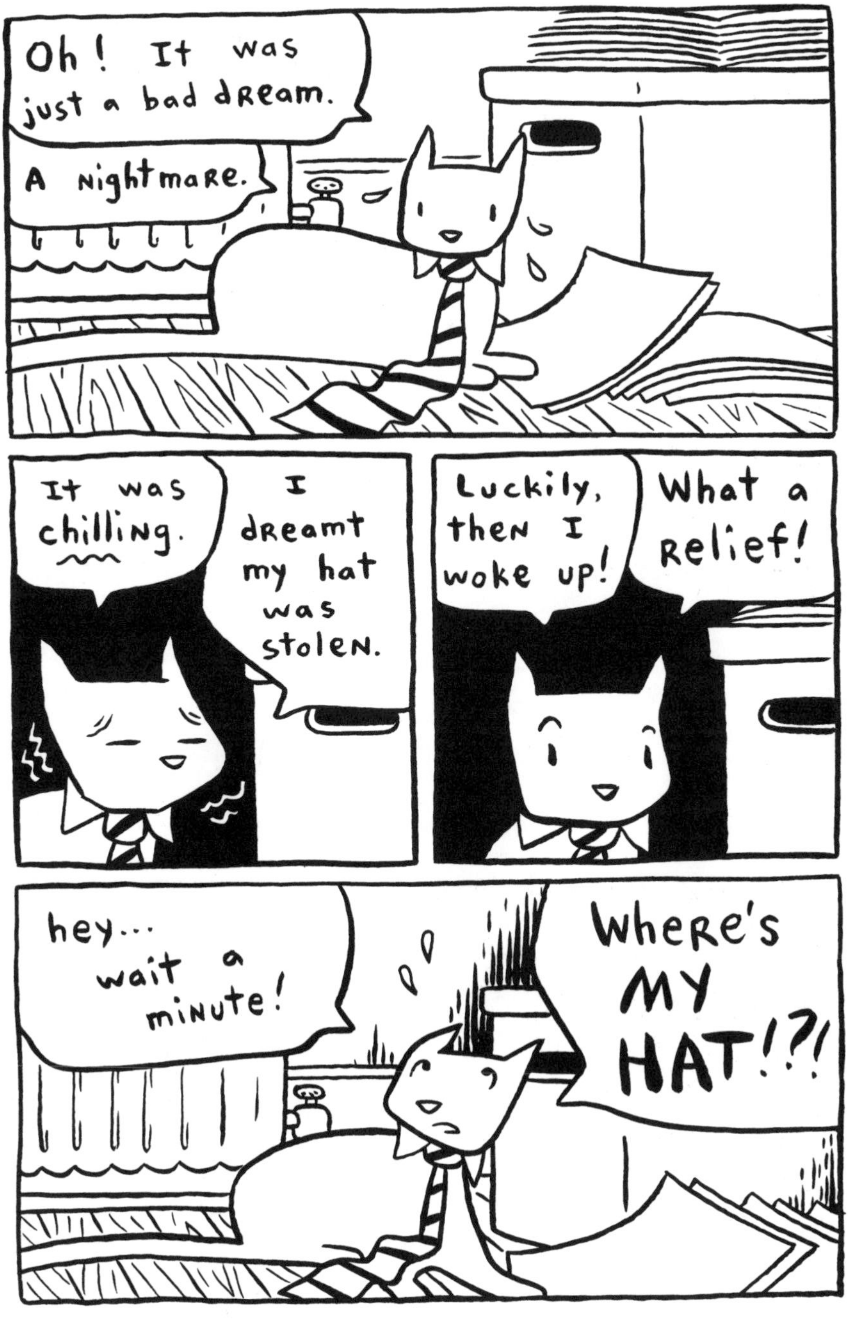
Oh! It was just a bad dream.
A nightmare.
It was chilling.
I dreamt my hat was stolen.
Luckily, then I woke up!
What a relief!
hey... wait a minute!
Where's MY HAT!?!

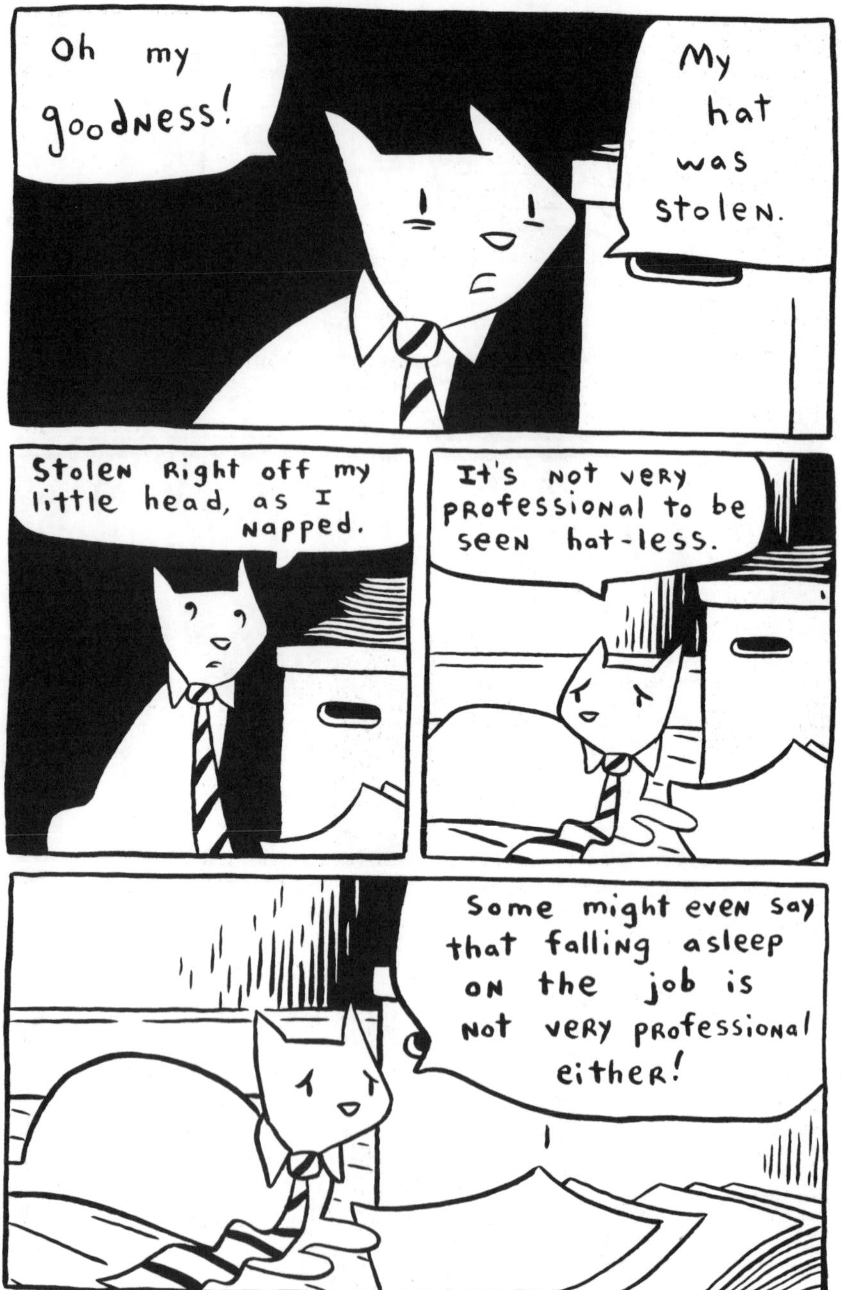
Oh my goodness!
My hat was stolen.
Stolen right off my little head, as I napped.
It's not very professional to be seen hat-less.
Some might even say that falling asleep on the job is not very professional either!

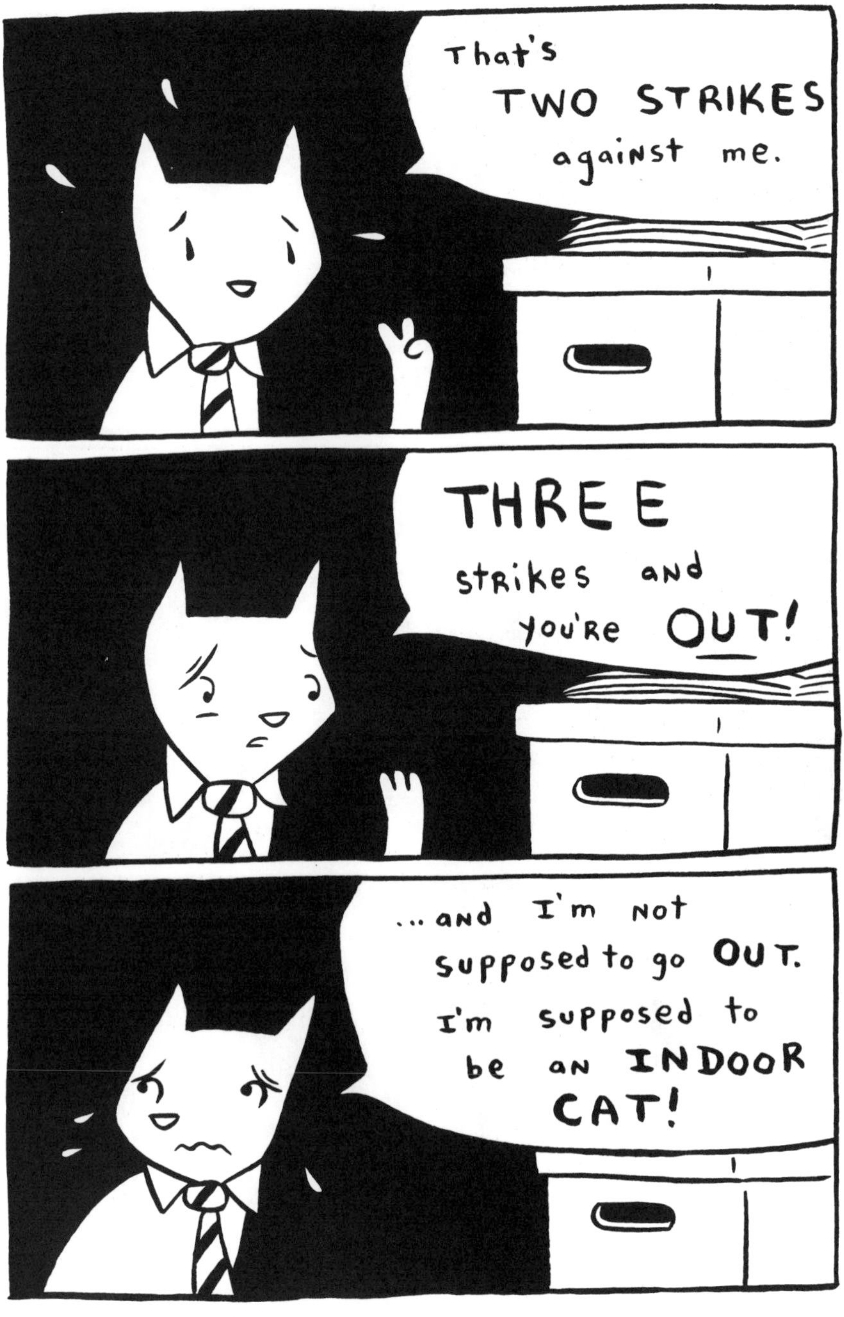
That's TWO STRIKES against me.
THREE strikes and you're OUT!
...and I'm not supposed to go OUT. I'm supposed to be an INDOOR CAT!

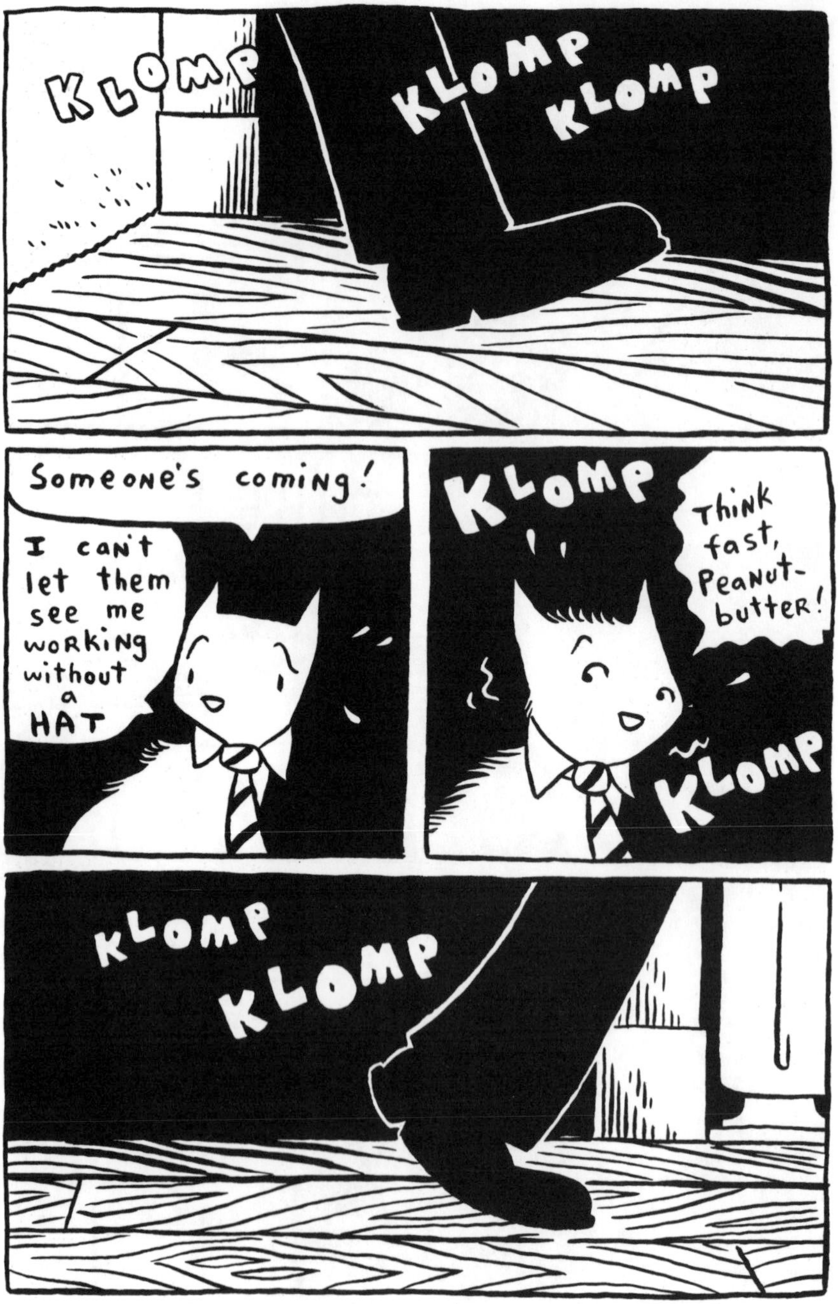
KLOMP
KLOMP
KLOMP
Someone's coming!
I can't let them see me working without a HAT
KLOMP
Think fast, Peanut-butter!
KLOMP
KLOMP
KLOMP

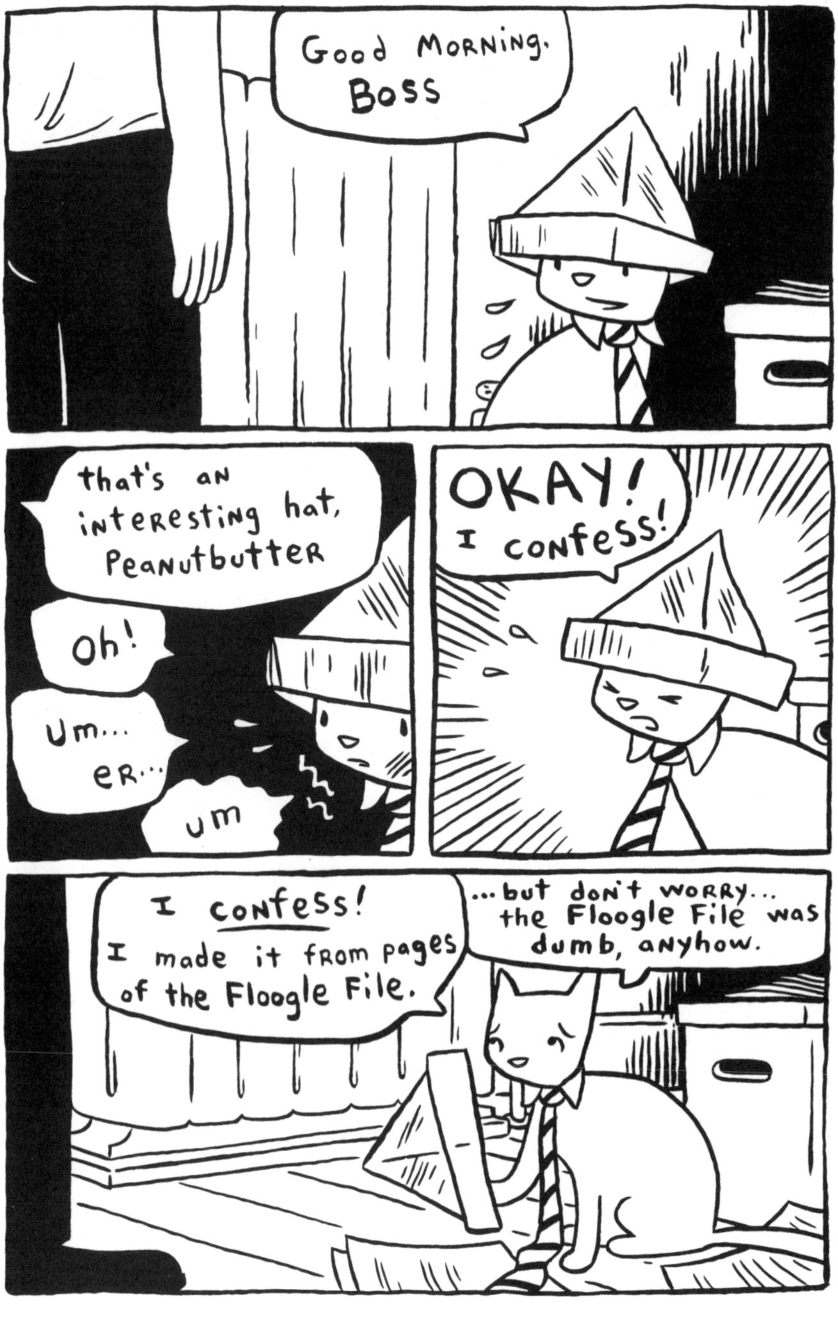
Good Morning, Boss
that's an interesting hat, Peanutbutter
Oh!
Um...
er...
um
OKAY! I confess!
I confess! I made it from pages of the Floogle File.
...but don't worry... the Floogle File was dumb, anyhow.

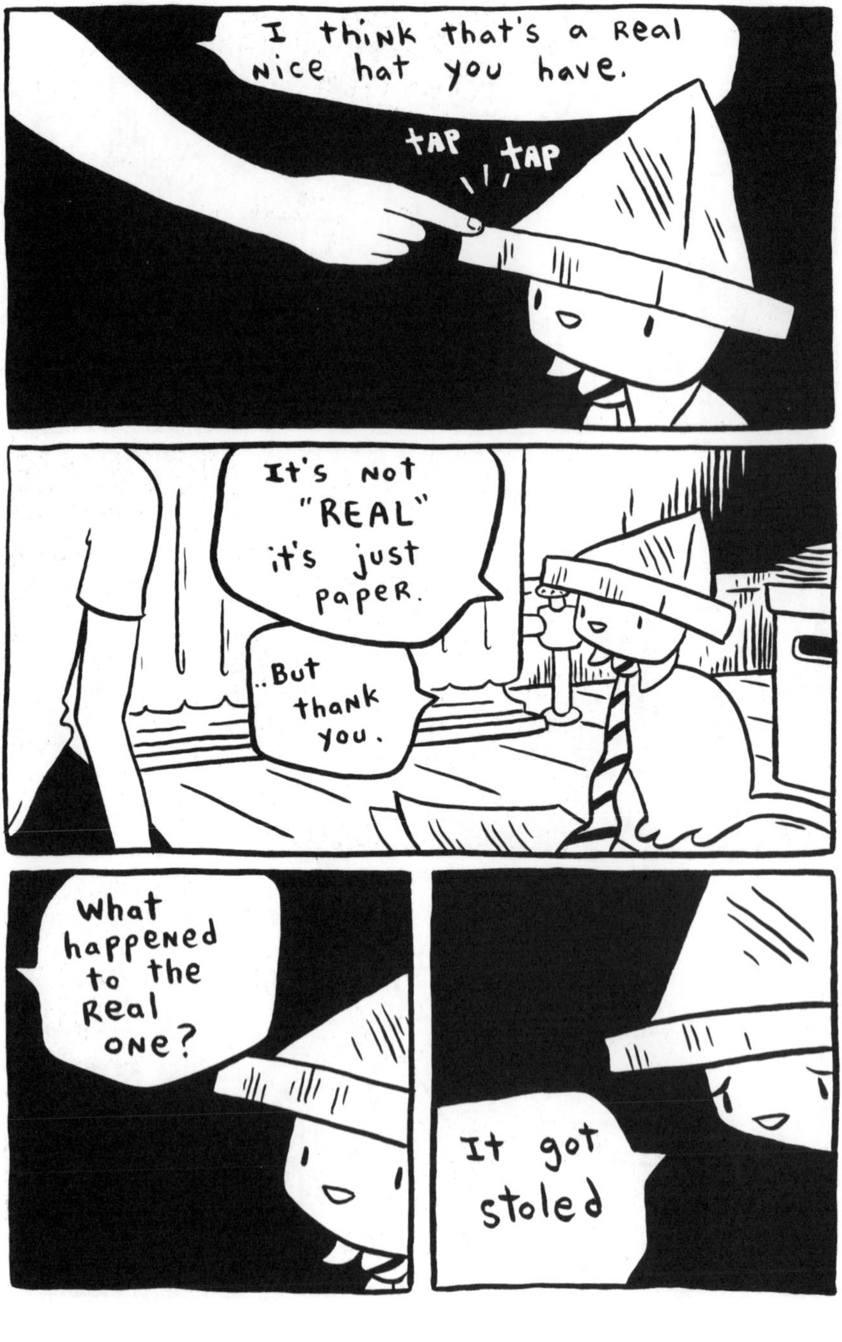
I think that's a real nice hat you have.
tap tap
It's not "REAL" it's just paper.
..But thank you.
What happened to the real one?
It got stoled

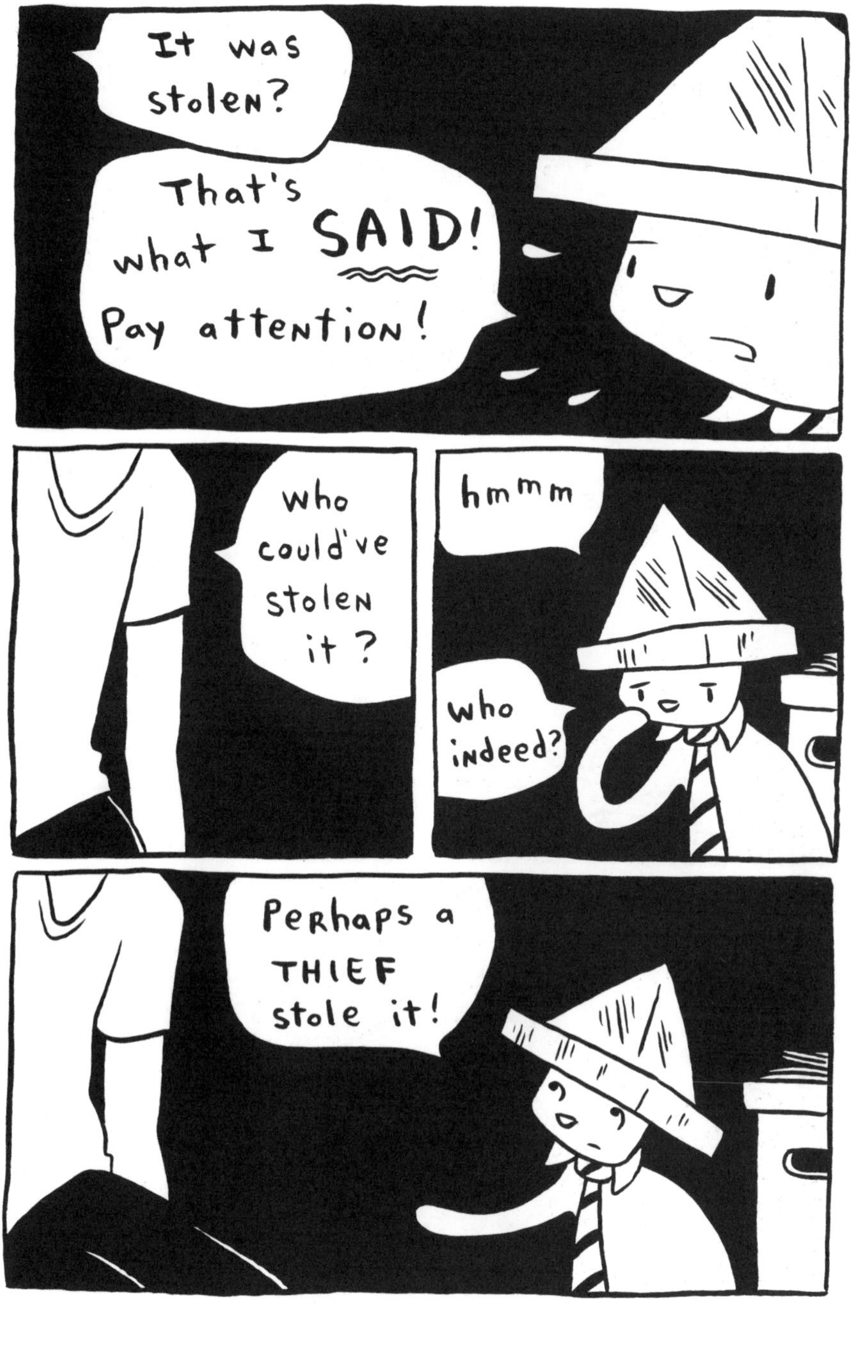
It was stolen?
That's what I SAID! Pay attention!
who could've stolen it?
hmmm
who indeed?
Perhaps a THIEF stole it!

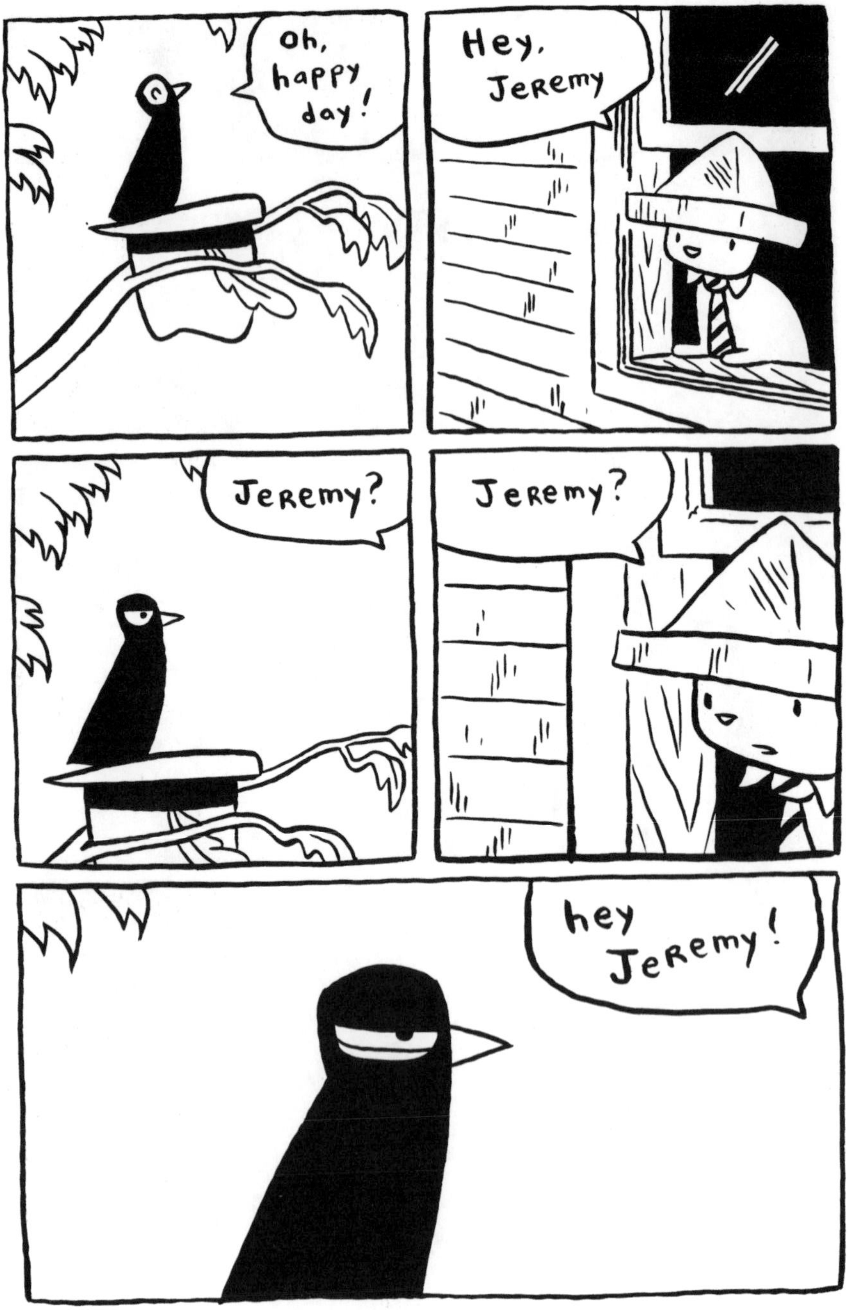
Oh, happy day!
Hey, Jeremy
Jeremy?
Jeremy?
hey Jeremy!

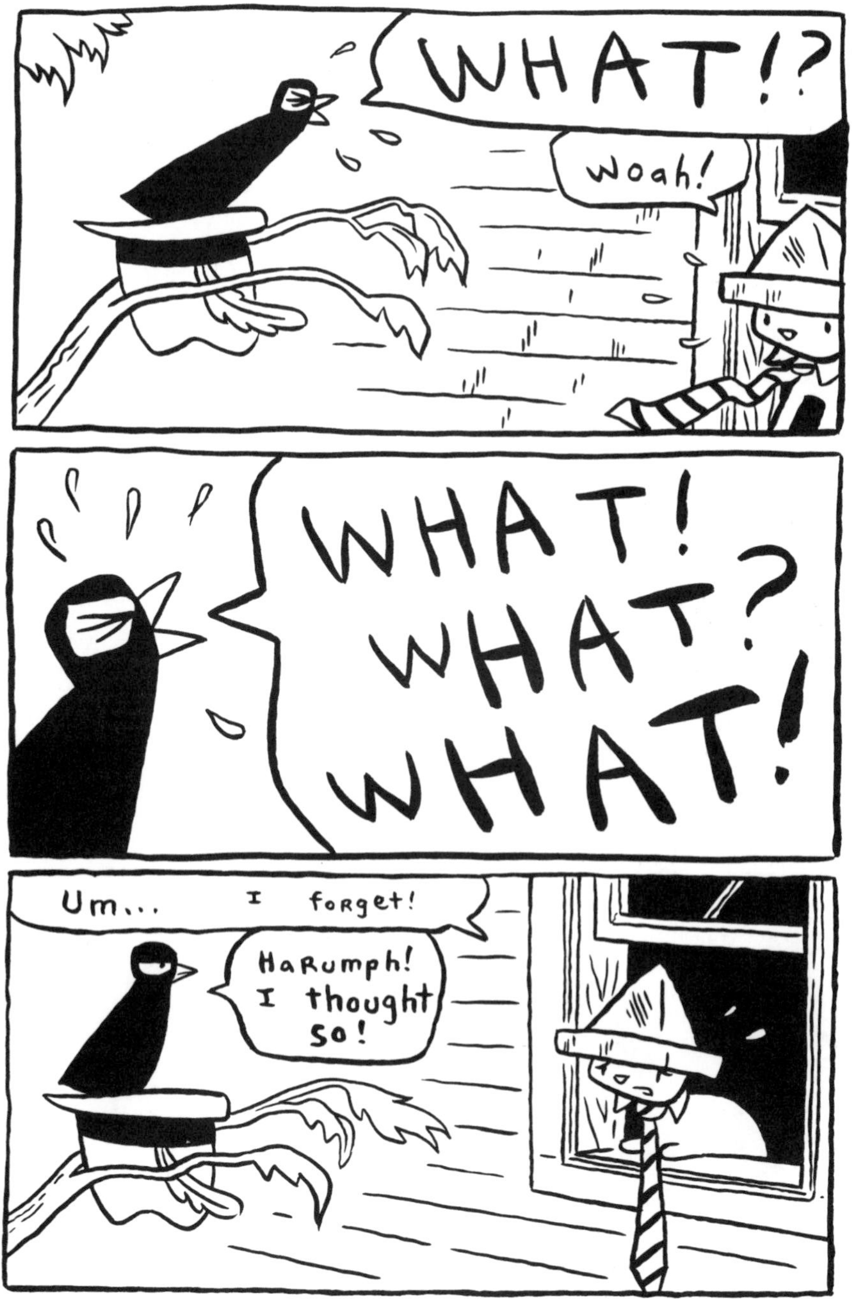
WHAT!?
woah!
WHAT! WHAT? WHAT!
Um... I forget!
HaRumph! I thought so!

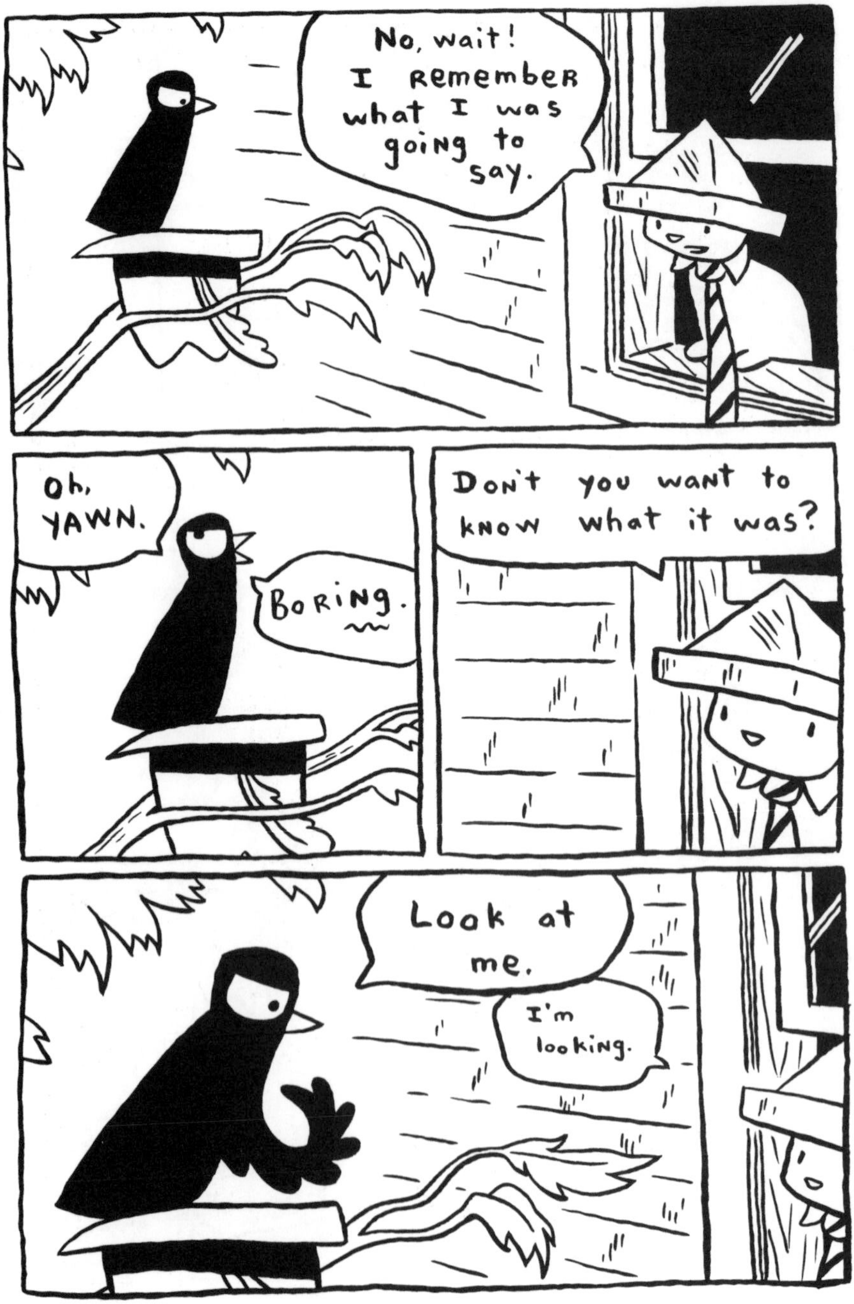
No, wait! I remember what I was going to say.
Oh, YAWN.
BORING.
Don't you want to know what it was?
Look at me.
I'm looking.

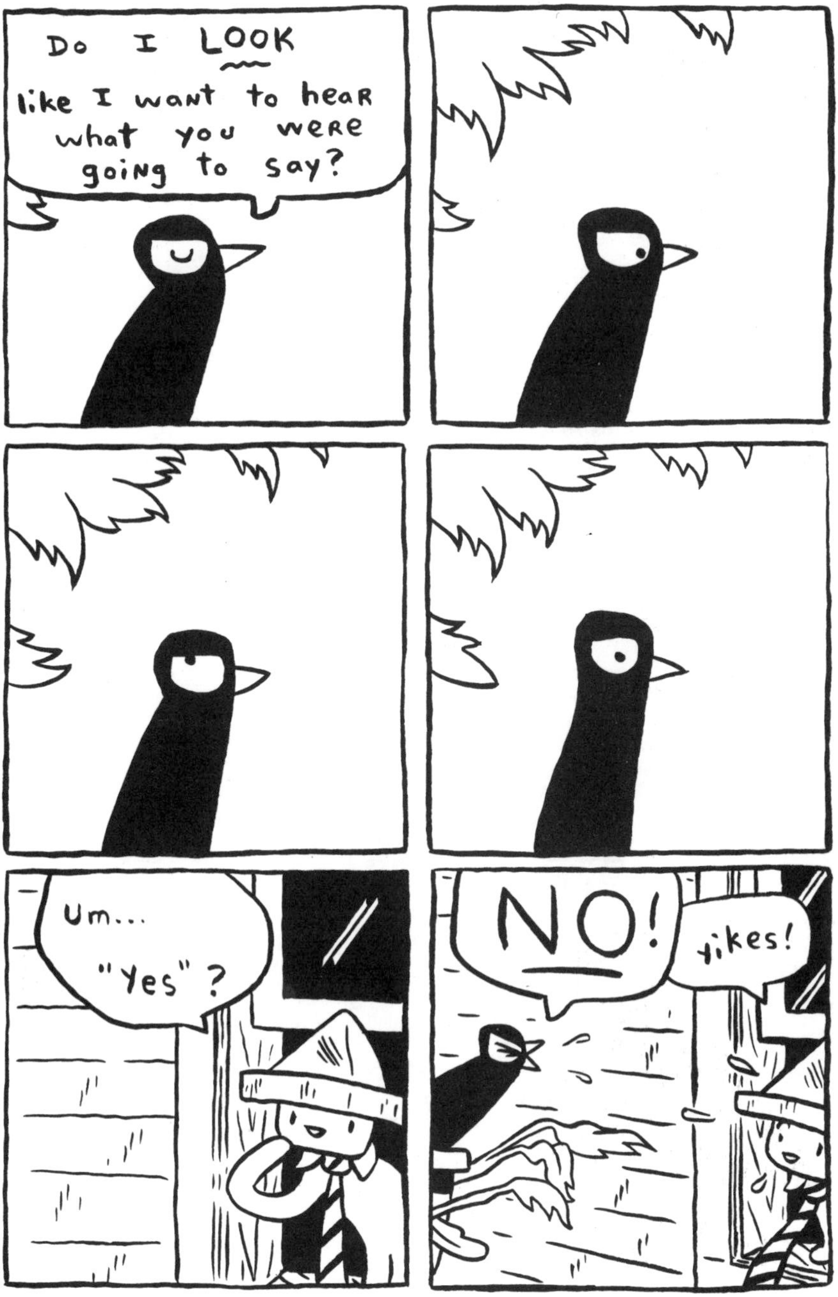
Do I LOOK like I want to hear what you were going to say?
Um... "Yes"?
NO!
yikes!

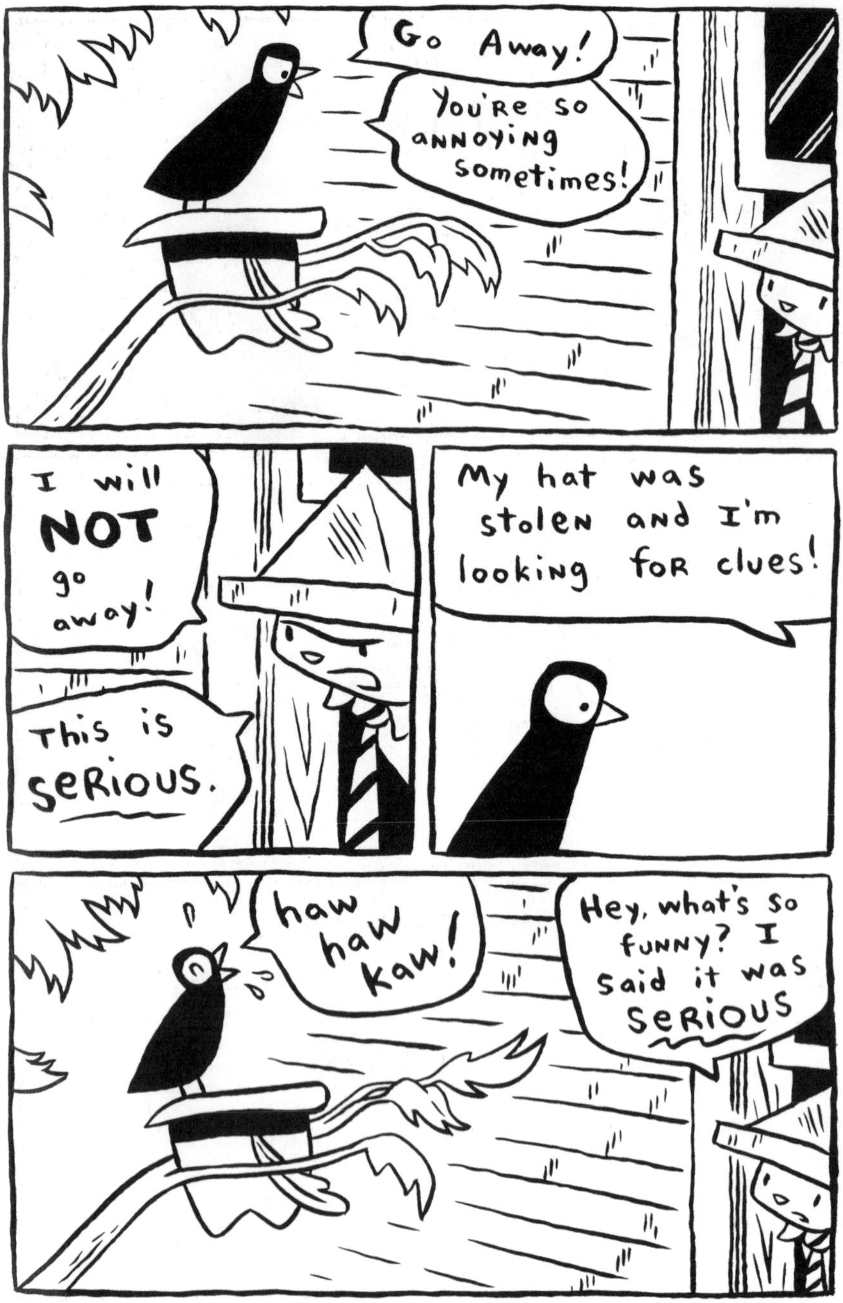
Go Away!
You're so annoying sometimes!
I will NOT go away!
This is SERIOUS.
My hat was stolen and I'm looking for clues!
haw haw kaw!
Hey, what's so funny? I said it was SERIOUS

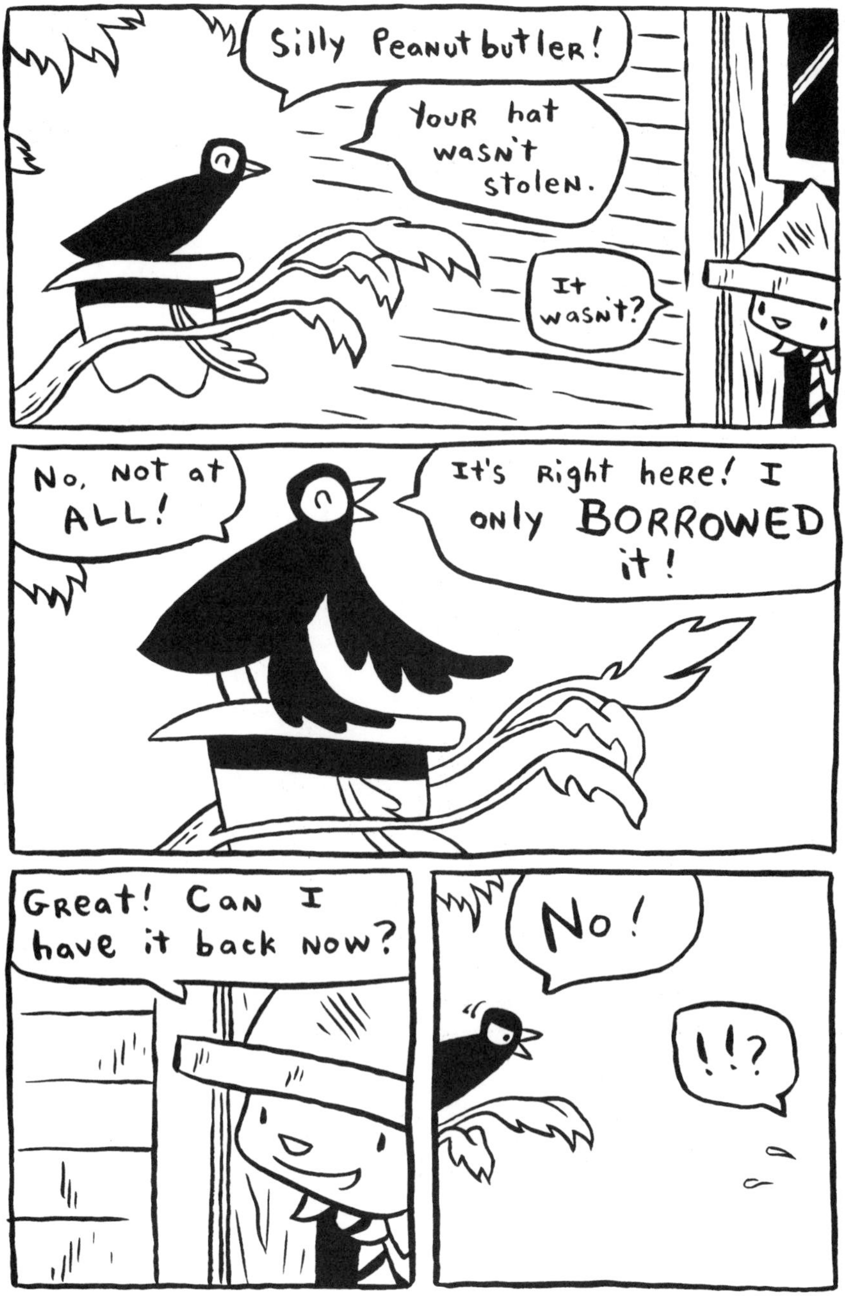
Silly Peanutbutler!
Your hat wasn't stolen.
It wasn't?
No, not at ALL!
It's right here! I only BORROWED it!
Great! Can I have it back now?
No!
!!?

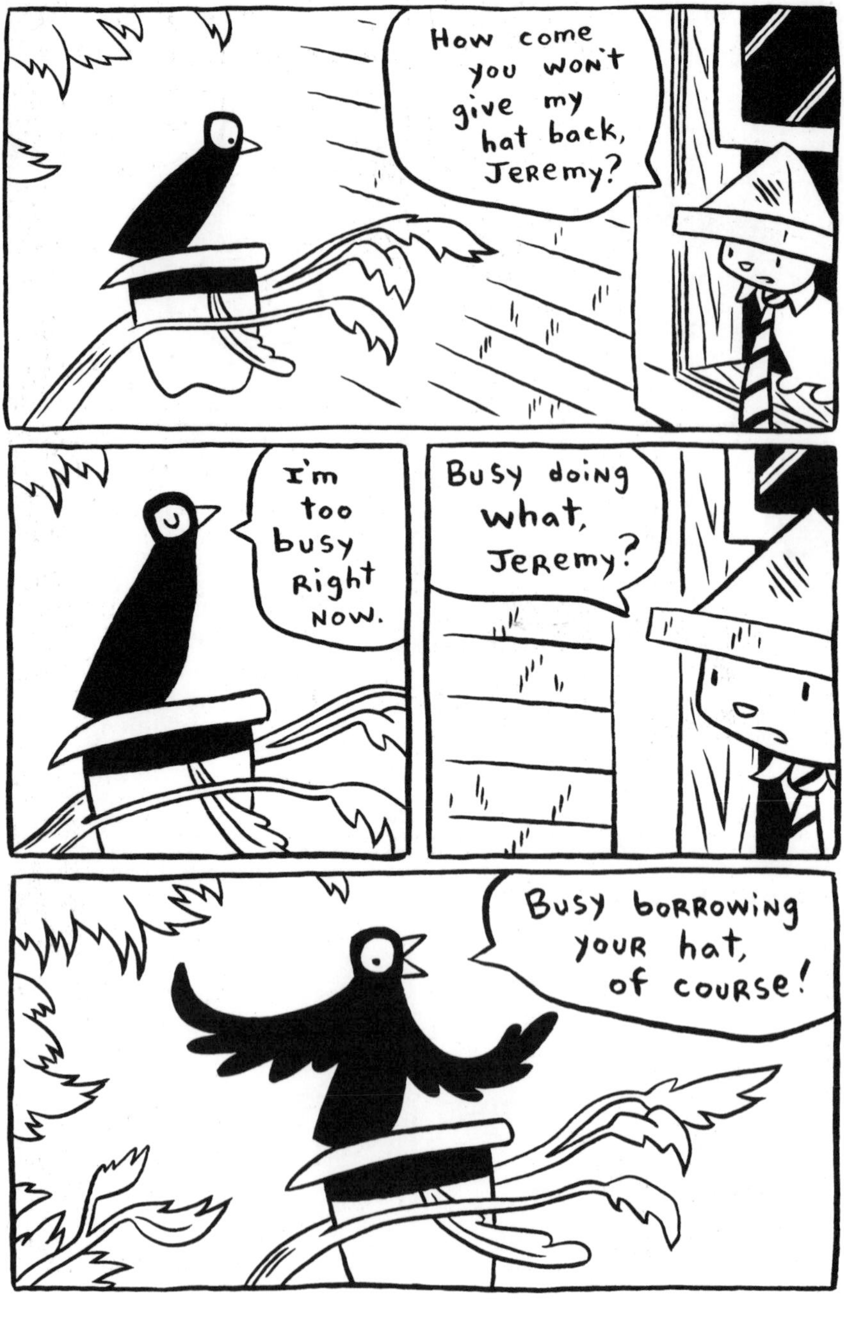
How come you won't give my hat back, Jeremy?
I'm too busy right now.
Busy doing what, Jeremy?
Busy borrowing your hat, of course!

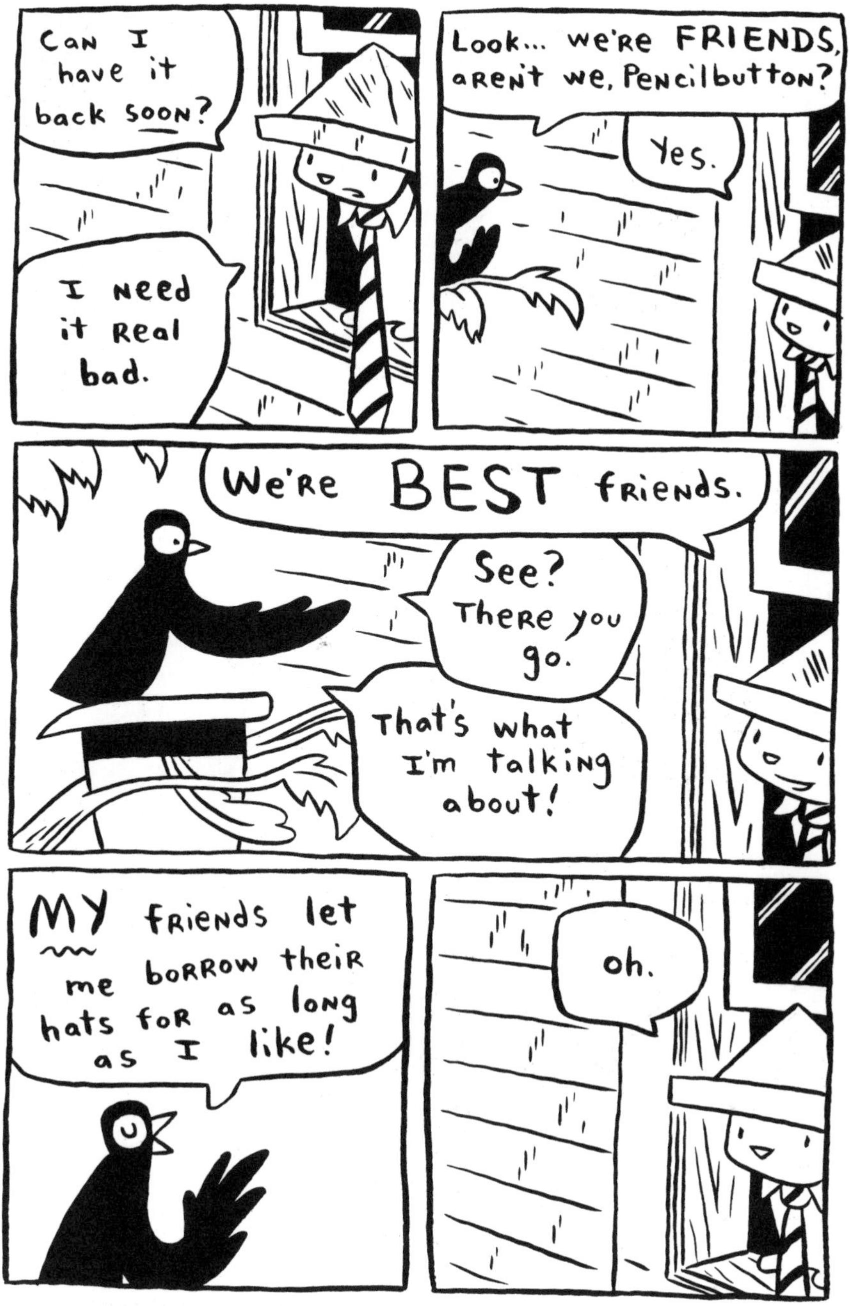
Can I have it back soon?
I need it real bad.
Look... we're FRIENDS, aren't we, Pencilbutton?
Yes.
We're BEST friends.
See? There you go.
That's what I'm talking about!
MY friends let me borrow their hats for as long as I like!
oh.

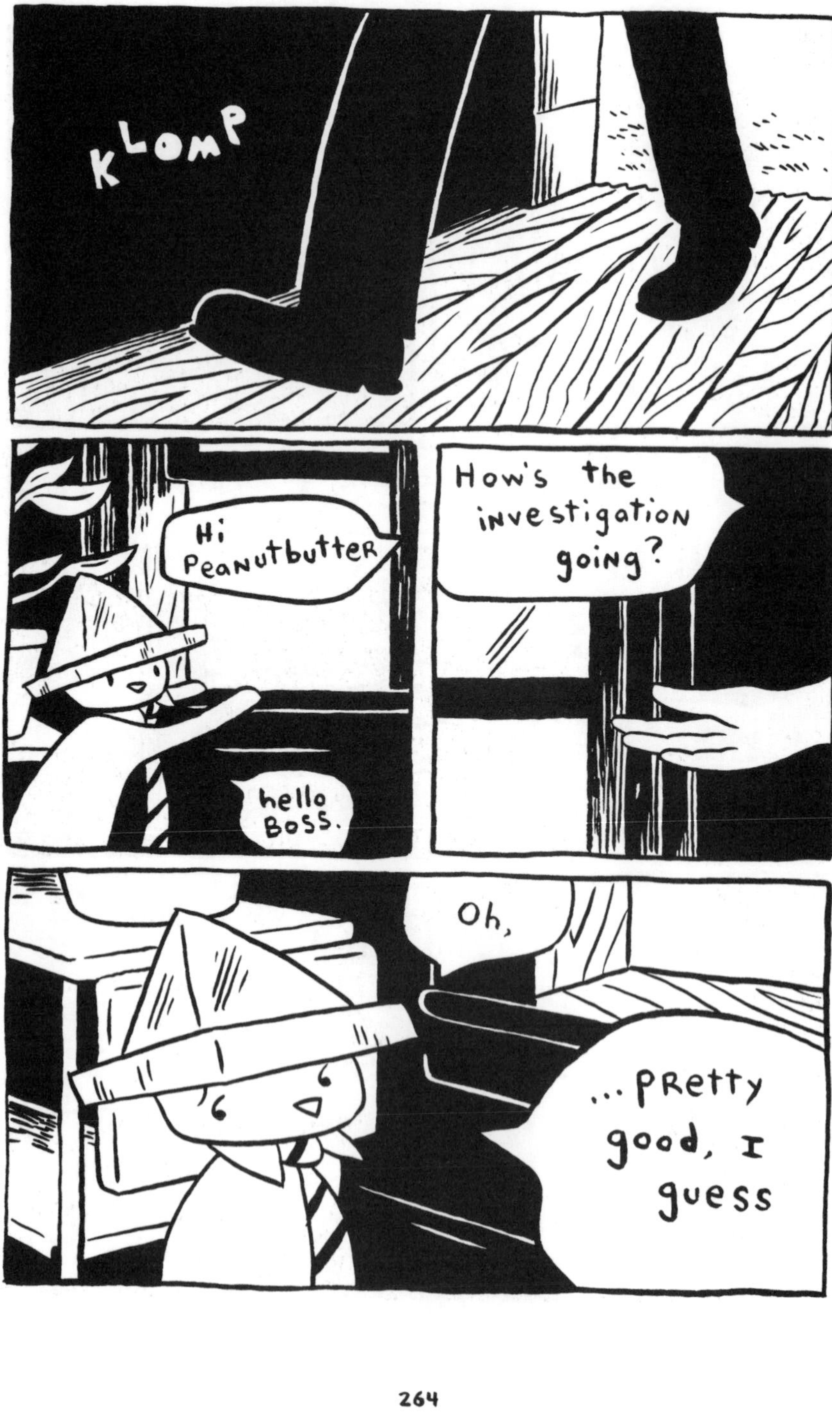
KLOMP
Hi Peanutbutter
hello BOSS.
How's the investigation going?
Oh,
...pretty good, I guess

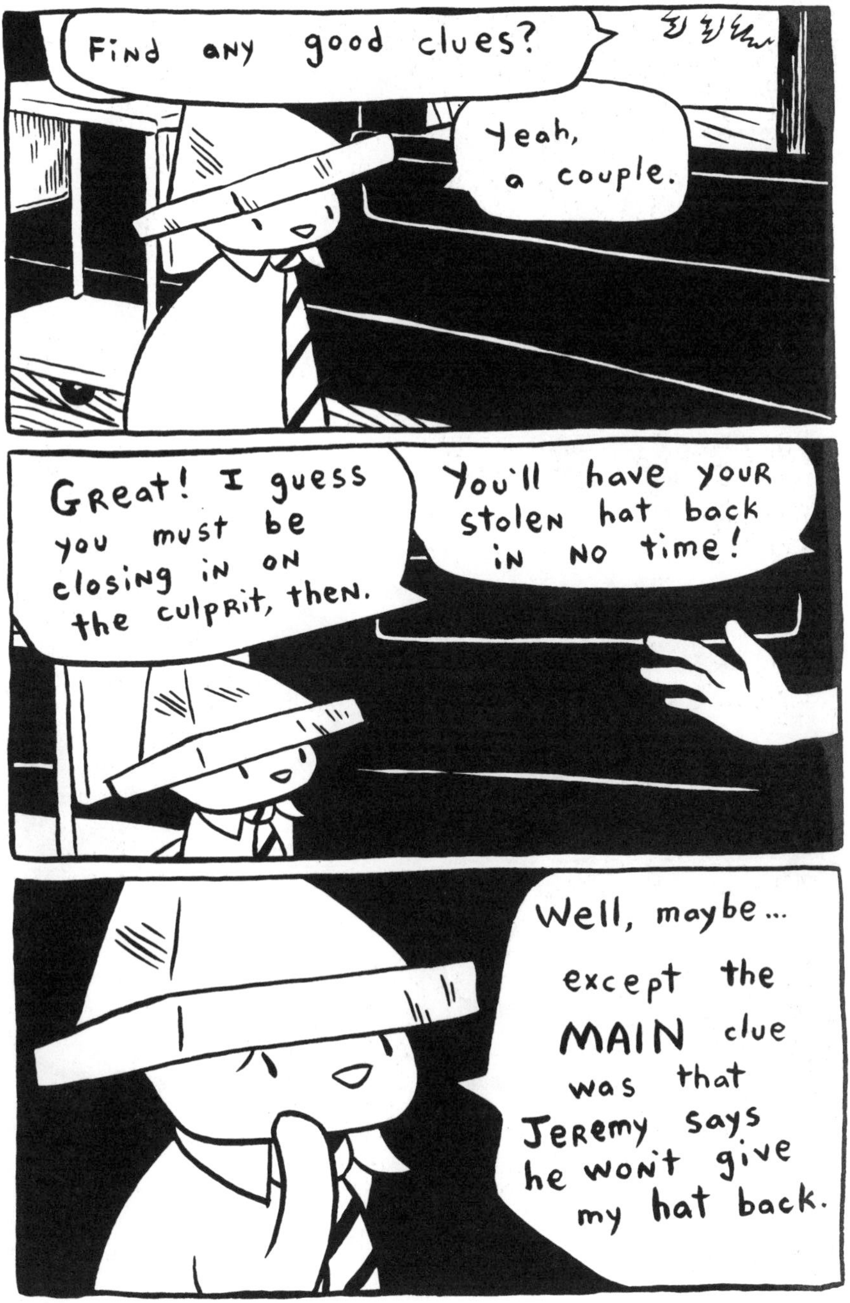
Find any good clues?
Yeah, a couple.
Great! I guess you must be closing in on the culprit, then.
You'll have your stolen hat back in no time!
Well, maybe... except the MAIN clue was that Jeremy says he won't give my hat back.

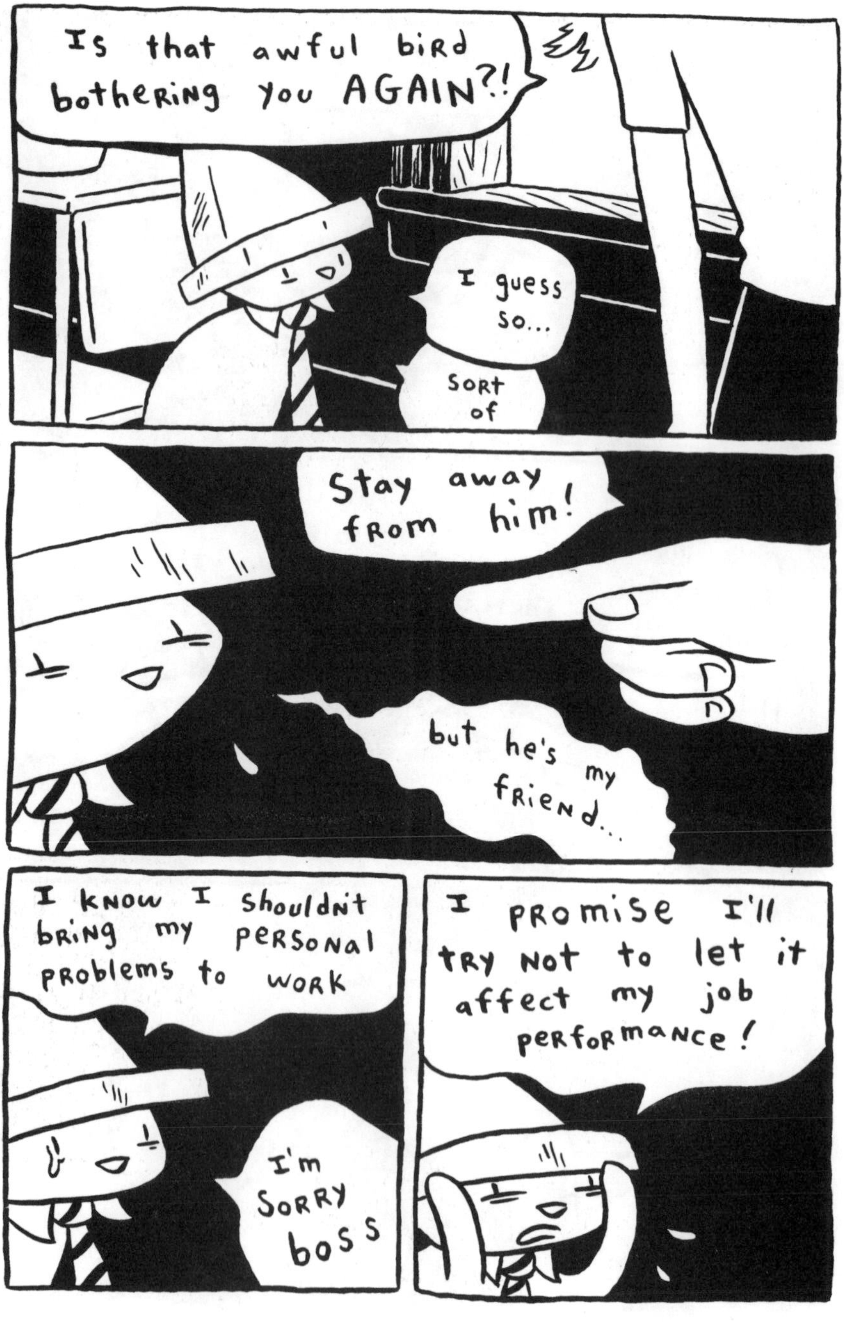
Is that awful bird bothering you AGAIN?!
I guess so...
sort of
Stay away from him!
but he's my friend...
I know I shouldn't bring my personal problems to work
I'm sorry boss
I promise I'll try not to let it affect my job performance!

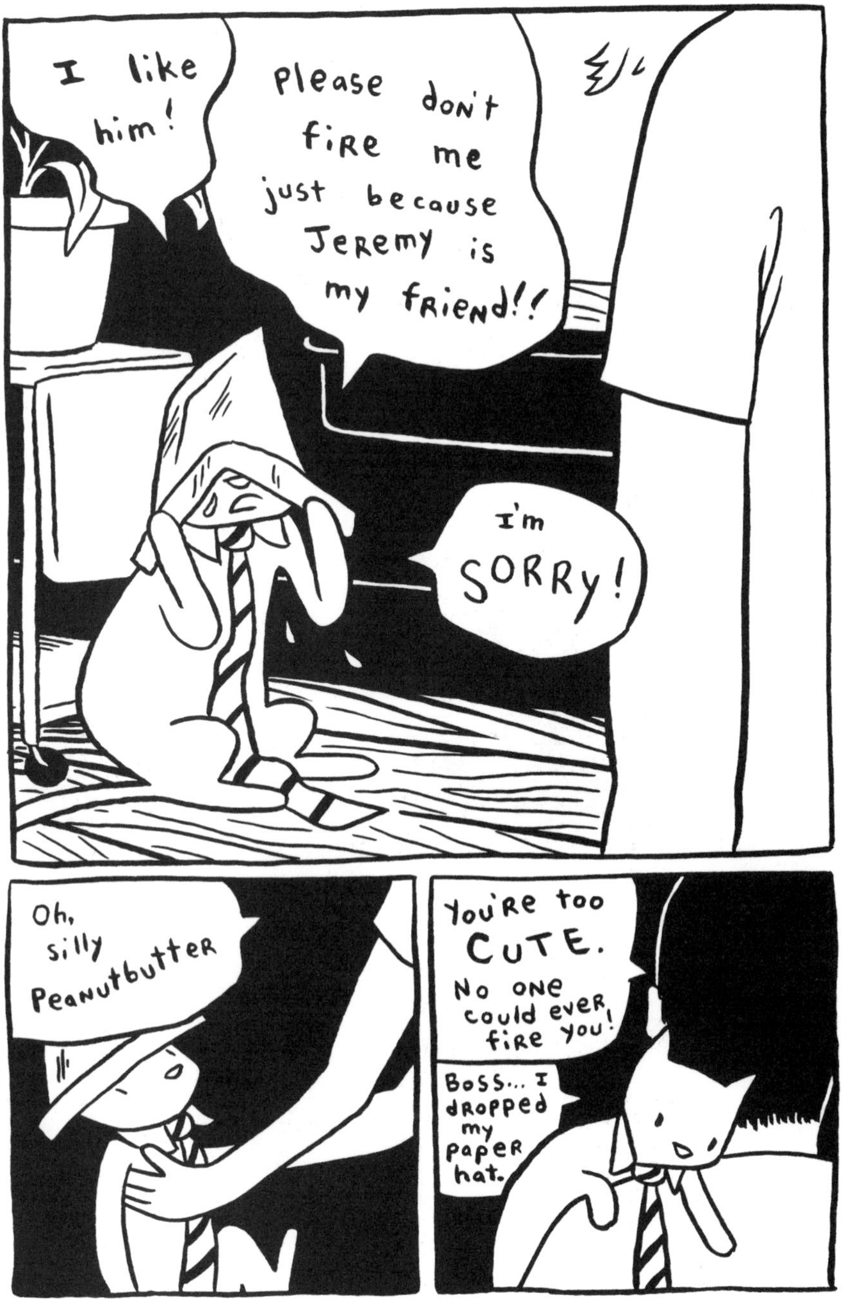
I like him!
Please don't fire me just because Jeremy is my friend!!
I'm SORRY!
Oh, silly Peanutbutter
You're too CUTE. No one could ever fire you!
Boss... I dropped my paper hat.

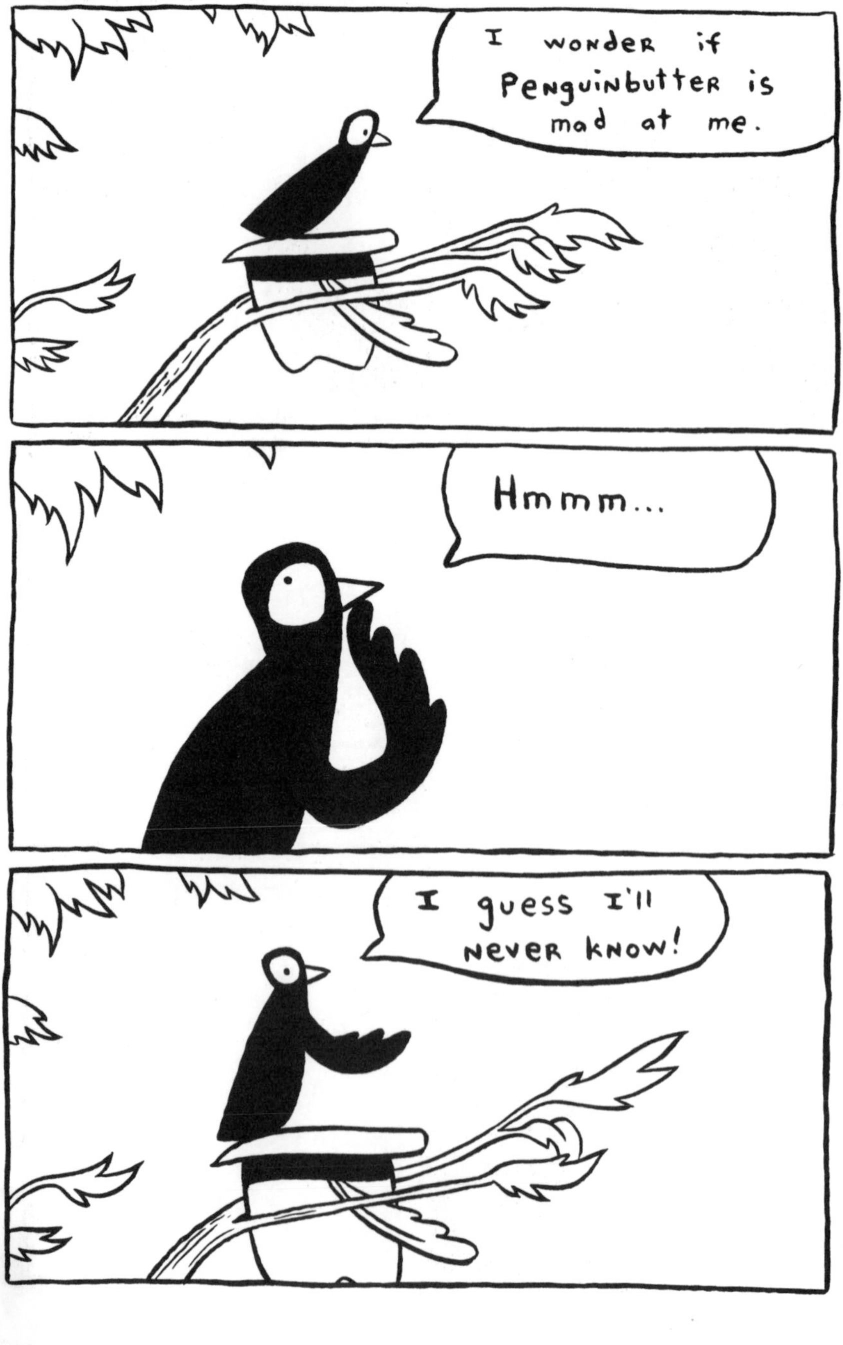
I wonder if Penguinbutter is mad at me.
Hmmm...
I guess I'll never know!

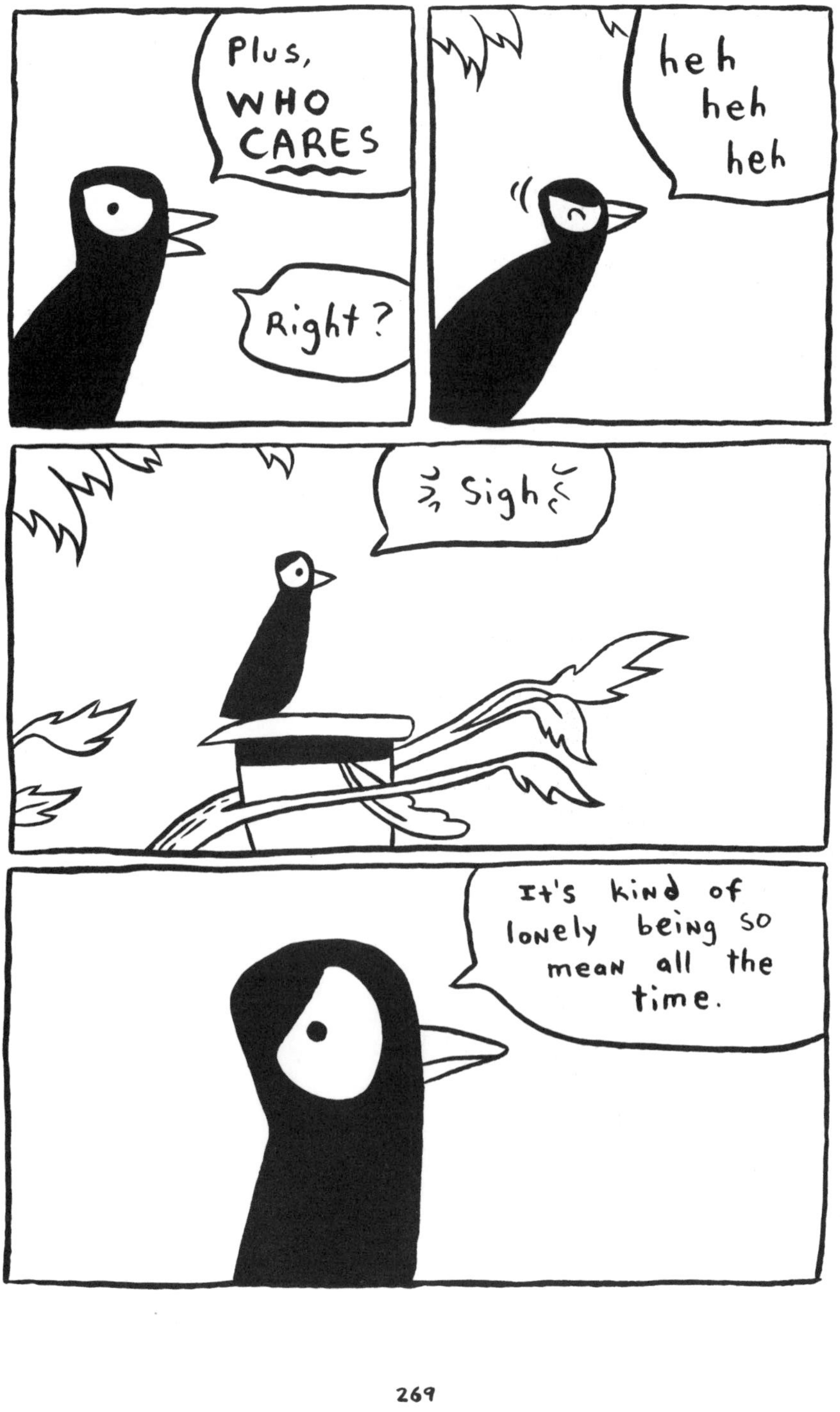
Plus, WHO CARES
Right?
heh heh heh
Sigh
It's kind of lonely being so mean all the time.

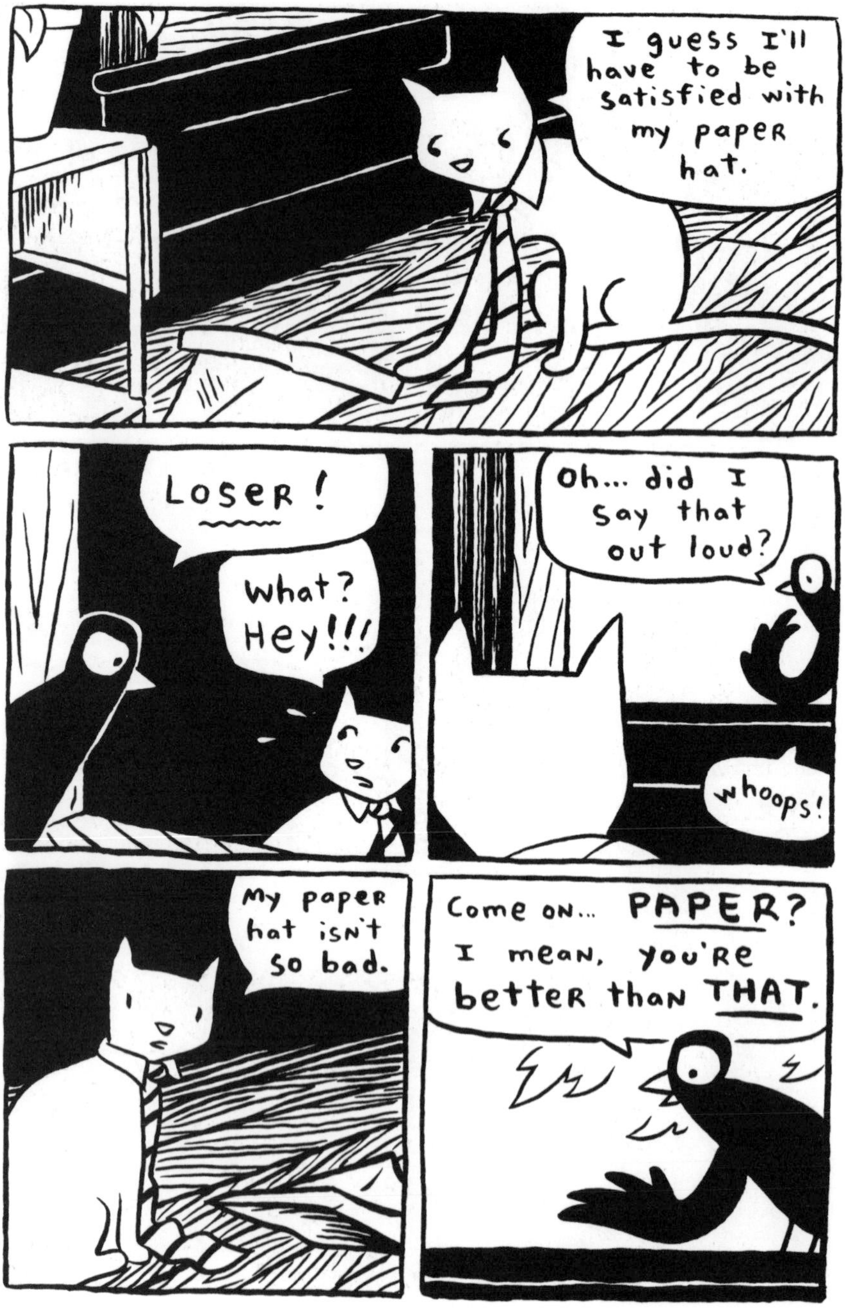
I guess I'll have to be satisfied with my paper hat.
LOSER!
What? Hey!!!
Oh... did I say that out loud?
whoops!
My paper hat isn't so bad.
Come on... PAPER? I mean, you're better than THAT.

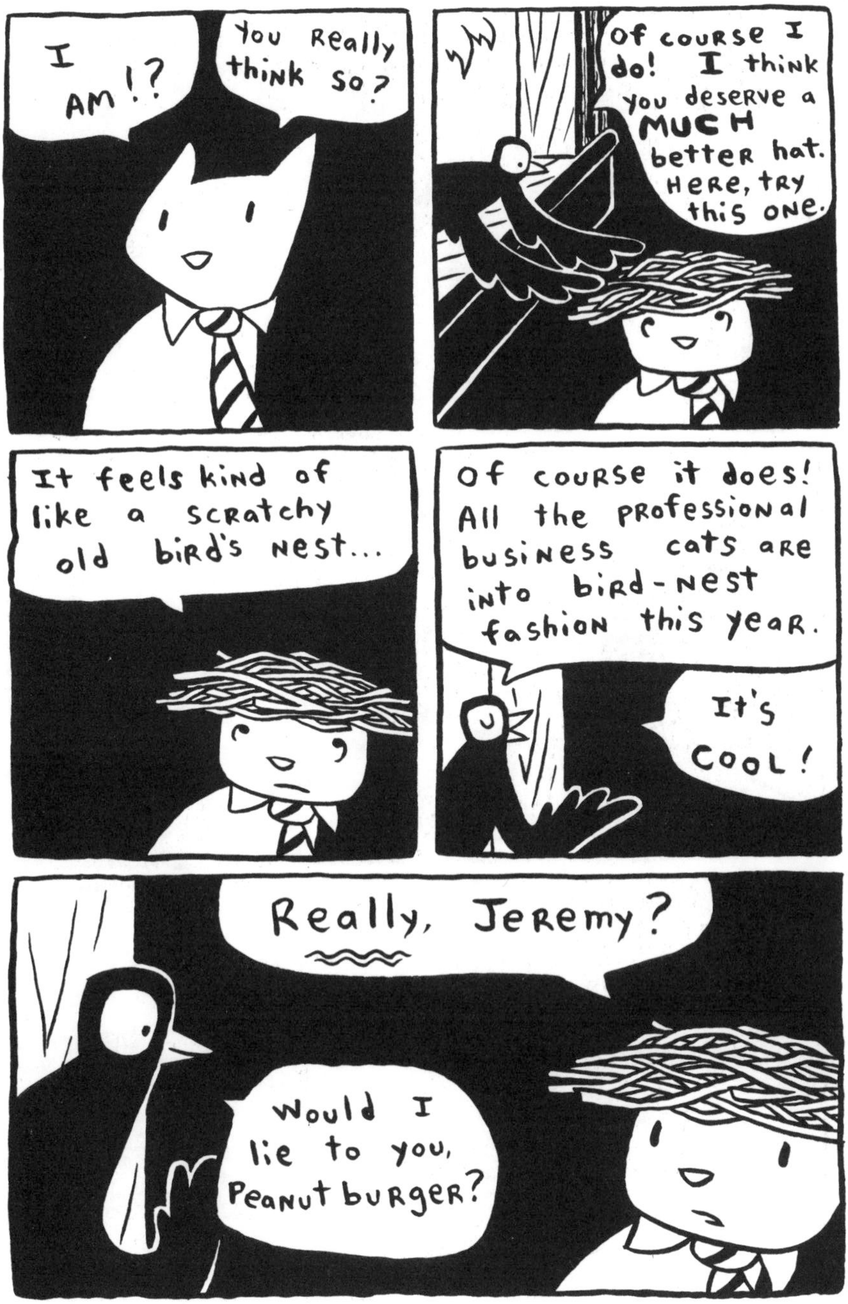
I AM!?
You Really think so?
Of course I do! I think you deserve a MUCH better hat. Here, try this one.
It feels kind of like a scratchy old bird's nest...
Of course it does! All the professional business cats are into bird-nest fashion this year.
It's cool!
Really, Jeremy?
Would I lie to you, Peanut burger?

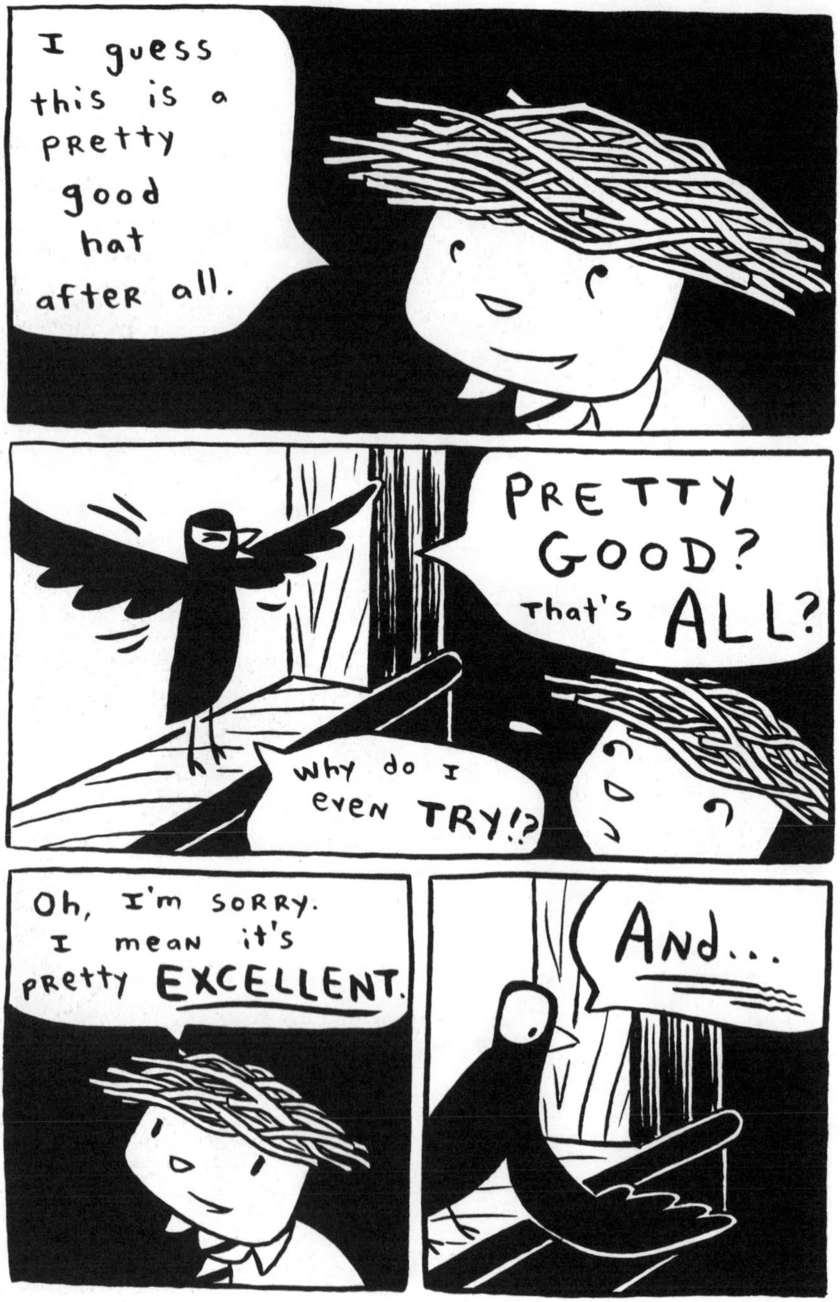
I guess this is a pretty good hat after all.
PRETTY GOOD? That's ALL?
Why do I even TRY!?
Oh, I'm SORRY. I mean it's pretty EXCELLENT.
And...

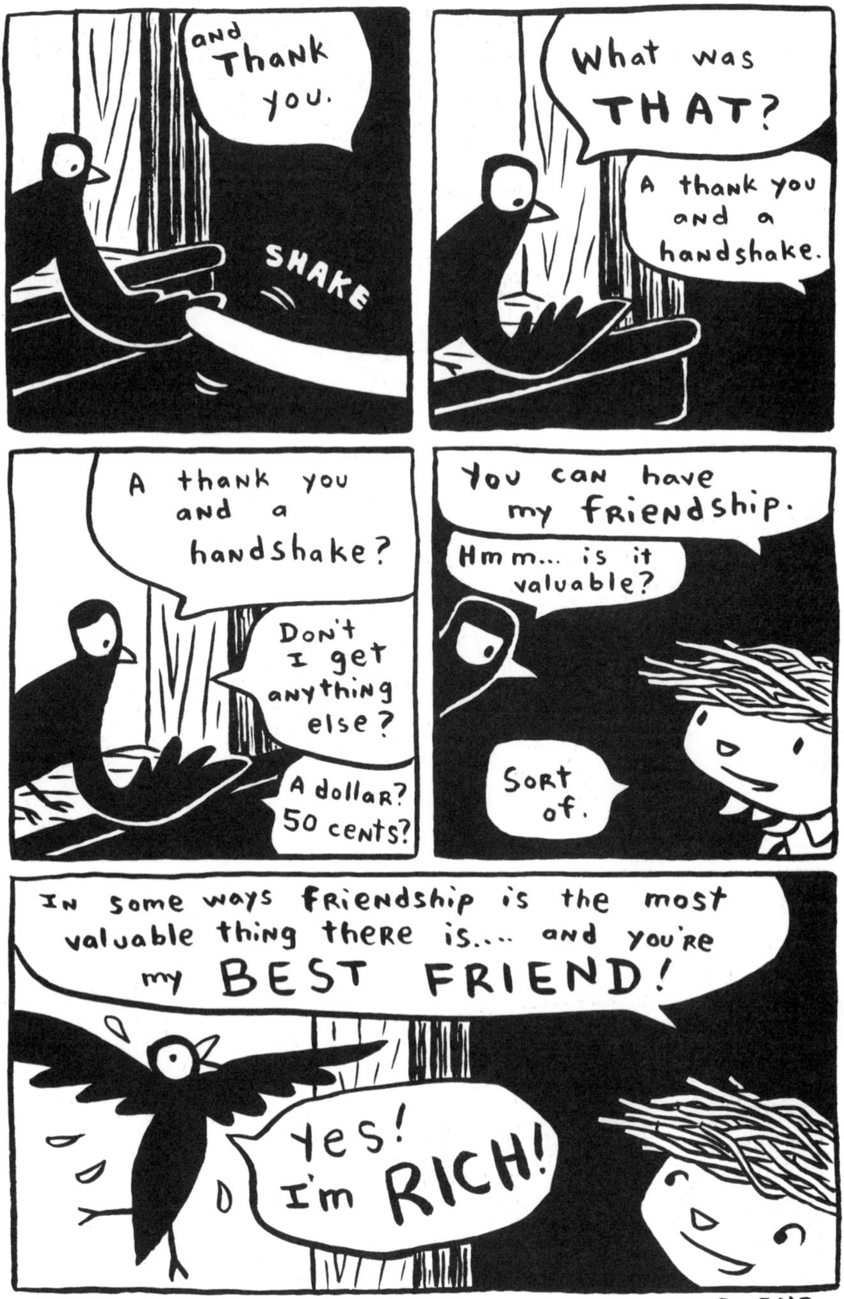
and Thank you.
SHAKE
What was THAT?
A thank you and a handshake.
A thank you and a handshake?
Don't I get anything else?
A dollar? 50 cents?
You can have my friendship.
Hmm... is it valuable?
Sort of.
In some ways friendship is the most valuable thing there is.... and you're my BEST FRIEND!
Yes! I'm RICH!

THE END

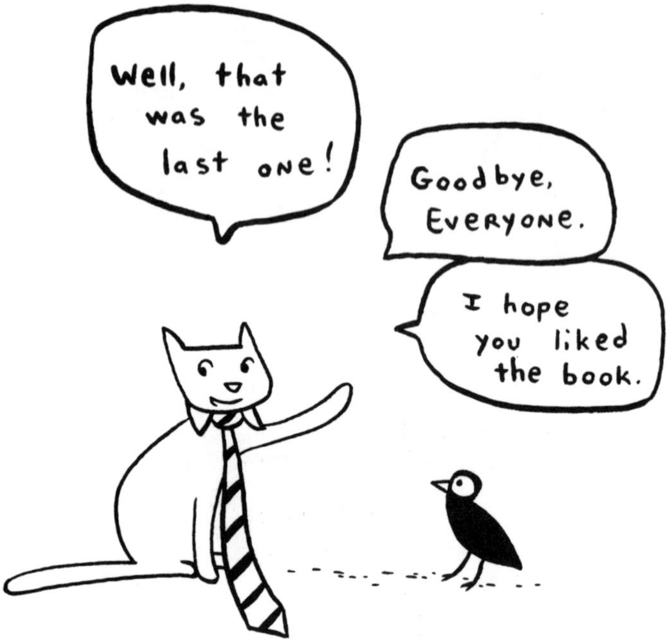
Well, that was the last one!
Goodbye, Everyone.
I hope you liked the book.

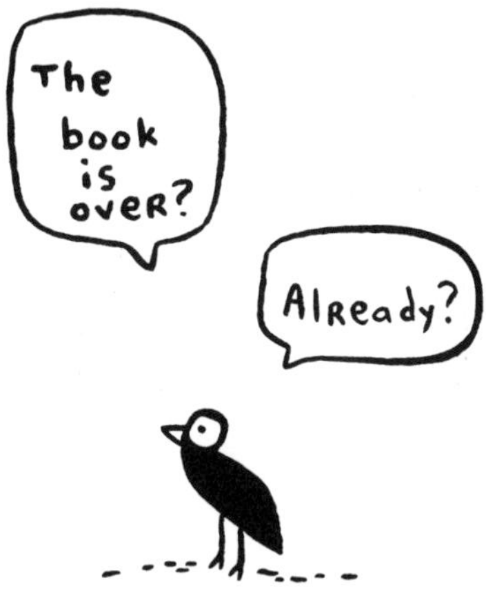
The book is over?
Already?

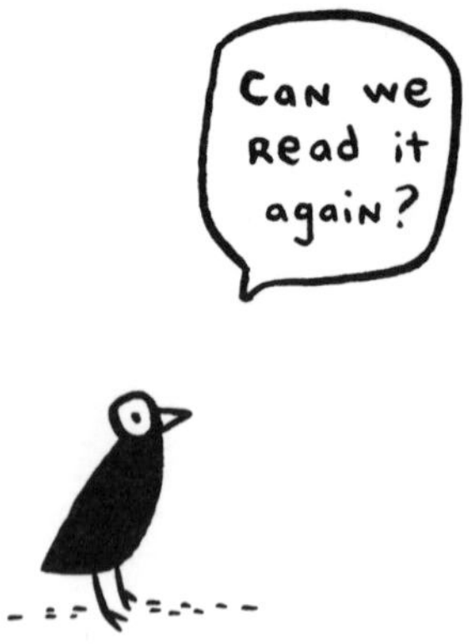
Can we read it again?

James Kochalka has drawn many many books.
Most of them are for boring grownups,
but here's a list that younger
—or young at heart— readers
might enjoy:

Vanilla Ghost
Highwater Books
This one's sold out! Sorry kids!

Monkey Vs. Robot
Top Shelf Productions

Monkey Vs. Robot and the Crystal of Power
Top Shelf Productions

Pinky and Stinky
Top Shelf Productions

Peanutbutter and Jeremy's BEST BOOK EVER
Alternative Comics
This is the book you're holding right now, silly!